A
Forthcoming
Wizard

Also by Jody Lynn Nye

An Unexpected Apprentice

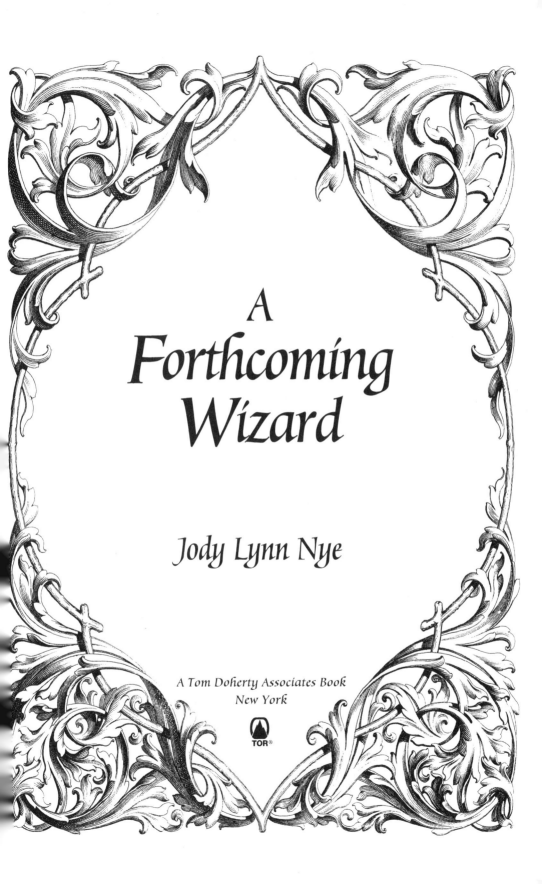

A
Forthcoming
Wizard

Jody Lynn Nye

A Tom Doherty Associates Book
New York

TOR®

A FORTHCOMING WIZARD

A Tor Book
Published by Tom Doherty Associates, LLC
175 Fifth Avenue
New York, NY 10010

www.tor-forge.com

Tor® is a registered trademark of Tom Doherty Associates, LLC.

Library of Congress Cataloging-in-Publication Data

Nye, Jody Lynn, 1957–
    A forthcoming wizard / Jody Lynn Nye.—1st ed.
        p. cm.
    "A Tom Doherty Associates book."
    ISBN-13: 978-0-7653-1434-5
    ISBN-10: 0-7653-1434-7
    I. Title.
    PS3564.Y415F67 2009
    813'.54—dc22

                                            2008046416

First Edition: April 2009

Printed in the United States of America

0 9 8 7 6 5 4 3 2 1

To the memory of my dear friend and editor,
Brian M. Thomsen,
without whom this book would not be.
Thanks for a lifetime of encouragement.

Acknowledgments

The author wishes to thank Tom Doherty, Patrick Nielsen Hayden, and Kristin Sevick for all their support and kindness on this project.

A
Forthcoming
Wizard

Chapter One

Knights! Form ranks," ordered the Abbess Sharhava. "We ride."
The imperious, pale-skinned woman in the light blue-and-white
habit ignored her pain as she sat erect on her mount's back. She
raised her bandaged right hand to the sky, then pointed down the trail. The
ancient and long-abandoned castle of the kingdom of Orontae lay behind
them. Ahead lay the ruins of a beautiful river valley.

Tildi Summerbee slumped on Rin's black-and-white-striped back. She
scarcely sensed the bump as the dark-skinned centaur shifted her hips and
began to walk, nor did she feel the cold wind whistling past them down the
mountain. The smallfolk girl did not look back over the file of riders at the
gaping wide doors of the once-grand entrance. The remains of stone giants
that had only hours before tried to kill them had vanished with Edynn.

Her entire attention was fixed upon the bundle in her lap, a bundle nearly
the size of herself. The Great Book was hers—no, not hers to keep, but hers
to protect and see secured against all harm.

Around her, the Knights of the Word, the so-called Scholardom, rode in a
square. They were not there to protect her so much as they intended to prevent her escape. Occasionally, they glanced at her sidelong, as though they
found it hard to believe that one such as she, who was no larger than a child
of their kind, with large brown eyes, and collar-length brown hair grown
shaggy and rough along the trail, could be considered a woman of power, to be
feared and guarded. And yet, she was. As a smallfolk girl growing up in the
Quarters, in the province of Ivirenn, she had known nothing of these solemn
men and women who wore armor under their blue-and-white habits, and
possessed both weapons and the skills to wield them. In the last few hours
she had spent in their company, she learned they were an ancient order whose
purpose was to possess and protect the Great Book, whereas she, an apprentice wizard at the beginning of her training, was the only living person in all
of Alada who could touch the substance of the book. Anyone else who tried
was burned horribly or killed.

The book was too real for them, more real than anything else in the world, for it *contained* the world. The runes drawn in gold upon its pure white pages described everything, living and nonliving, that existed, changing as they changed, vanishing as they ceased to be. The runes moved of their own accord, growing larger and smaller, though no one else seemed to notice the changes when she tried to draw attention to them.

Within the sphere of the book's influence, a radius of many yards, those same runes that described everyone and everything appeared upon that which they described. Tildi looked down upon her own rune, a complicated glyph that glowed upon her chest like a burning brand. It seemed right side up no matter from what angle she looked at it. She had become used to seeing it, but the wonder that it existed at all still sent a thrill up her spine. These runes were not mere labels; they truly described what they marked. If these runes were interfered with, they could change the shape of the thing or, terrifyingly, the person. At the rear of the file of riders, unarmed and under heavy guard, rode two soldiers who served King Halcot of Rabantae. Captain Teryn was all right, a fair-haired human woman of middle years, but Morag, her sergeant and contemporary in age, had been terribly deformed a few years before by the wizard Nemeth, he who lay dead in the castle behind them. Morag looked like a wild boar in human form, with an underthrust jaw and snaggled teeth, and thick, coarse black hair that never seemed to lie neatly no matter how long or short it was. He usually went with his head bent so no one could get a good look at his face. His hands were more difficult to conceal: thick paws with misshapen fingers. Everything he did seemed difficult. He persevered, though it surely cost him pain.

Tildi's life had been utterly changed. A few hours before, she was a wizard's apprentice, barely trained in the basics of her craft over the course of mere weeks by two masters. Now, though she possessed the most powerful object in the whole of the world of Alada, she was a prisoner in all but name. They had tied a rope around her waist. The other end of the cord was held firmly in the hand of the knight who rode at her right hand.

"As no one can safely touch you without sustaining injury," the abbess had said, sounding sweetly reasonable as two gigantic human males in armor had descended upon her, "we must have some means of saving you if you should fall or be carried off by some foe."

Tildi felt the rough sisal chafe at her skin through her clothes, but didn't dare to put it off. The Scholardom had seen her use magic to climb the air like a ladder. They were taking no chances that the object of their desire should take itself out of their reach in that fashion. She was not robust enough to take any of these gigantic humans on physically. *Later,* she promised the book. Later, she and her friends would find a way to free themselves and find a way to safety. More than anything, she wanted the book to be safe. Faintly, she felt that she should be frightened for herself, but her feelings were dimmed and removed from her as though they belonged to someone else.

"Let me pass!"

The wizardess Serafina pushed her way in between two of the knights. Her dark eyes flashed with anger. The knights regarded her with suspicion, but they did not challenge her. The abbess Sharhava must have instructed them not to interfere with any of Tildi's friends who wished to speak with her, so long as they did not try to remove her from the protective circle. The book must not be harmed.

Tildi glanced up at her. Her long dark hair was spread out over the shoulders of the moss-green cloak she wore over her white wizard's robe. She looked as neat as if she had just stepped out of a boudoir rather than in the aftermath of a few hours of a magicians' battle and many days hard travel. Tildi felt like a rag doll in comparison.

"Are you all right?" Serafina asked, her voice carefully even.

"I think so," Tildi said.

The young wizardess patted her upon the shoulder, then snatched her hand back. Tildi breathed in a hiss of sympathy. Serafina's golden skin reddened and puffed as if blistered by the brief contact. The wizardess touched the irritated digits with her other hand, and the color returned to normal.

"It's nothing to be concerned with," she assured the smallfolk girl.

"I don't want you hurt," Tildi said.

"Don't worry about me." Serafina said hastily. Their exchange had two meanings, as well Tildi knew. Tildi envied her easy skill of healing the body. Neither she nor Serafina had the means to heal their hearts. Serafina had lost her mother, Edynn, and had become the de facto head of their party—if one did not take into consideration the mistress of the company of armed scholars surrounding them. None of them had had the chance to work through the many changes and sorrows they had suffered in only a few hours. Tildi knew, as though she could read on a page, that the wizardess was angry, frightened, and overwhelmed. She regretted that she might be the cause of any of Serafina's pain, but she could not help it. Things were happening *to* her, rather than by her own effort. All of them were caught up in a fierce tide of fate. Who knew where it would cast them ashore?

"We must do something to balance the power flowing through you. Rin, are you in any discomfort?"

"I will bear it," the centaur said, shaking her head until the jeweled ribbons in her thick hair were a colorful blur. "Your spell gives me some protection, and I am acquiring a tolerance. Not as great as the little one, here, but enough. I am a Windmane, and we do not shrink from a challenge. I will carry Tildi and her new treasure as far and as long as she needs me."

Serafina turned her worried gaze back to the smallfolk girl. Tildi was aware of her scrutiny—indeed, she was aware of the world in a way that she never thought possible—but her awareness came with a sense of distance, as if she only lightly touched the surface of it. The book occupied too much of her mind at the moment. The voices coming from it enthralled her. She wanted to pay attention to what was going on around her, but they were so *interesting . . .*

"Hold fast, Tildi," Serafina said, laying a hand on her shoulder. The touch brought the smallfolk girl back from the inner world to which she was succumbing. "And do not do any magic. I am concerned you would have too much of a result, rather than too little. Do you understand me?"

Tildi pulled herself together enough to smile up at the young wizardess. "I won't."

Serafina nodded sharply and fell in alongside Rin.

Tildi felt grateful to her. The wound they both carried in their hearts at the loss of Serafina's mother, the great wizard Edynn, was so fresh that neither could speak of it yet. Tildi wanted to take the girl's hand and let her pour out her sorrow, but she dared not. Serafina might feel that her sympathy wasn't genuine, though it was. Edynn had been so kind to her, a runaway from her homeland, orphaned by the winged demons called thraiks. Serafina had carried the knowledge for years that the day would come when her mother was taken from her, and when the prophecy had come to pass Edynn had made her choice, and it had saved all their lives.

The threat of thraiks, however, still hung over them. The way that they had taken to reach the castle had been largely underground, but that road was closed off now for good. Tildi scanned the overcast skies. No shapes were silhouetted against the clouds, but they could appear at any moment. She feared them more than any other nightmare. They had killed the rest of her family. She was the only one left.

"Psst!" The voice belonged to Lakanta. The blond-braided trader clung to the back of her stout little horse in the file ahead of Tildi and Rin. As one of the imperious guards glanced down at her, the dwarf woman gave him a cheeky grin. He raised a hand as if he might deal her a blow, then turned hastily away. His expression of mixed horror and disgust made Tildi shiver. The knights hated her—indeed, all of them—for what they were. The abbess had assured her that they didn't, but she could read it in their runes. The book in her arms was the work of the great magicians of old, the Shining Ones, human beings who had brought into existence the sentient peoples known as dwarves, centaurs, merfolk, werewolves, bearkin, smallfolk, and perhaps more of whom she had not yet heard. Tildi shook her head. All her folk had believed for centuries that they had come about naturally, engendered by time and nature. The truth, which she had learned only a couple of months before, that only humans and elves were of normal origin, had been long forgotten. Perhaps the elders in the Quarters knew, but kept the terrible knowledge to themselves. They disapproved of all things magical. They would see Tildi as eternally disgraced for her participation in that anathema.

"I ask you again to turn back and postpone this journey," Serafina said, spurring her steed forward to confront the abbess. "Allow us to return to shelter until others of my order can come to augment us. Night comes soon. We are in danger. You did not hear the warning Nemeth gave us before he died. Others seek to possess the Great Book, others who have great power. I am not strong enough to protect a group of this size."

Sharhava did not rein back her horse. She leveled an authoritative eye upon the young woman. "I have told you, I have nothing more to say on this subject. We have agreed that the Scholardom will protect you upon your journey. The chapter house is much closer than any of your other safe havens. The sooner we reach it, the better. We must go quickly. The book and its guardian"—she aimed her gaze at Tildi—"must be protected."

"I tell you again," Serafina said, narrowly containing her fury, "you do not understand the book's powers. You will cause harm to yourselves, to everyone around you, if you do not take greater precautions than you are."

Sharhava did not seek to bridle her own anger.

"Do not lecture me! I know more of it than you do. Our order has studied ancient records and scraps of copies for millennia. The book is sacred to nature. We are ready to take on its stewardship . . . until it reaches its final destination."

Serafina's shoulders stiffened. She let her horse drop back, and was permitted to ride alongside Rin within the guarded circle. Even Tildi, feeling far away from emotion, knew that she was beaten for the moment.

"It sounds to me like you are just finding excuses for doing everything wrong," Lakanta said.

Sharhava rounded upon her, sea-blue eyes glowing.

"Silence!"

"You might as well ask my horse not to eat oats," the stocky merchant said, imperturbably. "I talk. It's something I do. When you are on the road as long and as often as I am, you exercise your voice, or it tends not to work when you get where you are going, and for a trader, that's as good as losing money. If I say what I think a bit more than you're comfortable hearing, then don't listen!"

Rin let out a snort of laughter. Sharhava's fair skin reddened.

"You forget yourself."

"No, highborn lady, it's you who's forgetting what just happened, not half a day ago. That boy back there"—Lakanta aimed her chin at Magpie, who was listening openly with every evidence of delight—"suffered a terrible hurt. That madman back there turned him into a monster—no offense to you, Morag—and little Tildi there turned him back again. Then you pop up through the floor like a mole burrowing into a greensward and say, just as boldly as you please, 'You risked your lives for that book, but give it to me anyhow.' The wonder is that you have the squeak to act so fearlessly about it when it bit you hard."

Only Lakanta was daring enough to speak openly of what had happened. Tildi saw astonishment written upon all of the knights, though none of her friends were surprised.

Nemeth had lain dead in the smoke-filled chamber only minutes when the knights forced their way in and surrounded them all.

Fire seared her memory. In her mind's eye, Tildi saw the flames again, the blazing ring that Nemeth had thrown up to protect himself from her and her companions. He had made lightning and handfuls of flame like blazing coals that he had flung at them. Tildi felt her skin sear as she dared to jump through the blaze to reach the book. She had wrapped her small self around it to protect it. Once she had touched it, all the pain was worthwhile. She could do wonders with it near her. On the stone floor, Magpie had lain, perverted in shape like poor Morag. Then the scholar-knights had burst into the chamber, demanding to know what was going on.

Tildi was still coming to terms with the wonders of the magic of which she was now capable. To her own astonishment and the awe of the others, she restored Magpie to his normal appearance from the freakish caricature of humanity into which the mad wizard had rendered him. Tildi still could not believe that he had retained that little scrap of parchment with his rune that she had drawn for him back in Master Wizard Olen's home months ago. It felt as if it had been years. She was relieved to be able to have helped him. Not only was he a kind man, but a very good-looking one, with his curious yellow-green eyes, his tawny skin, and his long dark hair streaked with russet and white. She was torn between wanting to look at the book and wanting to reassure herself that she had not made any mistakes, that Magpie was going to be all right.

Serafina left her to tend to the others who had sustained wounds in the fight, but returned immediately to her side when the abbess came to loom over her. Tildi had traveled with humans, and lived in Olen's company. All those people treated her with respect, even kindness. Sharhava was a different and most compelling figure. She seemed larger than all the other humans as she towered over Tildi. The smallfolk girl saw greed and excitement in her as well as anticipation of triumph. The combination was so overwhelming that she cowered. How could she, so small and frail, withstand her?

"The book!" Sharhava exclaimed, her voice trembling with emotion. "Give it to me, girl!"

Tildi closed her arms more tightly around the scroll. The voices coming from it whispered, almost drowning out all other noises. The room was cramped now, filled with enormous humans in blue and white, all looking down upon her with avid, hungry faces. She felt overwhelmed. Every word had the force of a stone thrown at her.

"Give me the book!" Sharhava had commanded, her voice rising to shrill tones.

Rin immediately leaped between the abbess and the smallfolk girl.

"Leave her be," the centaur said, flaring her nostrils.

Impatient of every wasted moment, Sharhava attempted to outmaneuver the centaur, but Rin had twice as many feet to put in her way. Sharhava glared over the striped back at Tildi. "Give it to me! Now! You have no right to touch it. It is sacred to nature!"

"It's an abomination," Rin said, calmly matching her movements until the abbess was red-faced with fury. "If that is the thing that you believe gives your kind sway over mine."

"That's not its purpose at all," Serafina said, trying to defuse the rising feelings. "Rin, the Great Book is an invention of the same people who formed the centaurs. It is but another tool of their devising. No one owns you but yourselves."

"As long as she understands it is no certificate of ownership," Rin snorted. "You may outnumber us, but that gives you no right to make demands."

The abbess looked from one to another as if amazed at their protests. "My order has sought this tome for thousands of years. You cannot expect us to wait a heartbeat more when it is before us!"

The Rabantavian soldiers flanked the centaur. Captain Teryn laid her hand upon her sword hilt, though she did not draw it. Morag held his polearm firmly in both hands.

"It was our mission to secure this book," Teryn said. "My orders are to escort it and these honorables to the proper place for its bestowal."

"Our sacred duty overtakes your mission!" Sharhava shrieked. She held up a hand. "Knights! To me!" The Scholardom became a wall of blue and white, surrounding Tildi. She bent over the book, as if to protect it from the sight.

"We have done battle," Rin said, snatching her whip from her saddlebag, to which she had just restored it. She wound it around and around her arm. The tassled end was still shiny with blood. "I still have fight in me. Have *you* enough strength left to withstand me?"

Sharhava let out a trill of laughter. "So few against so many of us?" she asked.

"I would test the mettle of a Windmane princess against a thousand of your kind!"

"And she doesn't stand alone," Lakanta said, ducking under Rin's front legs to face Sharhava, though she had to tilt her head far back to do it. Her blond braids were askew, her clothes were burned and torn, and soot stained her fair cheeks, but she bore a hefty rock in one hand. She beckoned with the other. "You'll come through me as well."

"Your challenge amuses me," Sharhava said, holding her head high.

"Stop all this!" Magpie said, moving in between them. He was still somewhat unsteady on his feet. His tunic and trousers, travel-worn, were torn and burned, and his tricolored hair remained askew. The small lady with blue-green eyes started toward him to offer her support, but was urged back to her place by a brief glare from the abbess. "You would harm them after coming to their aid?"

"It was for the sake of the Great Book that we came!" Sharhava's lieutenant Loisan exclaimed. "You cannot care for it as we can."

"You can't take it from Tildi," Magpie said. "She is the chosen representative of the Council of Elders led by Master Wizard Olen."

"Do not presume to dictate to me!"

"You cannot take the book," Lakanta said. "You forget that Tildi is not alone."

"You see that we outnumber you greatly," the abbess said, unimpressed. "You may kill or disable some of us, but we are seasoned warriors, trained over the centuries for the sole purpose of protecting that book." She pointed to the scroll in Tildi's lap. "Give it to us. It is ours by right."

Rin unrolled the whip at her side and tapped it speculatively in her palms. "It is only yours because you say it is yours. We say it is ours, under the authority of the council that sent us. Take it if you dare."

Sharhava glared at the Windmane, and signed to the knights. They all drew their swords and advanced upon the company.

"Be reasonable, Lady Sharhava," Magpie said. He sought to put a hand on her arm, but she threw it off.

"Do not touch me, you vagabond!"

The sudden movement made Magpie take a step backward. He staggered. The uniformed girl hurried to support him. Sharhava's eyes went wide with indignation. "Lar Inbecca! Come away from him. Rejoin your companions."

The girl started. "But, Aunt."

Sharhava's eyes blazed. "Are you sworn to me, or are you not? Do your vows mean nothing to you? Get in line!"

The young woman, whose pale skin and chestnut hair marked her as a close relative of the imperious abbess, shamefacedly let go of Magpie's hand.

She took her place in the ranks at the rear of the file. She was a princess, Tildi knew, but how she had come to be among the knights, she did not yet know. So much had gone on around her in the last hours. She had absorbed little but the wonder of holding the object of her search at last. It was dear to her.

"Please!" Serafina protested. Her voice sounded thin and hoarse. She pressed her way through the crowd to the center, confronting Magpie and the indignant Sharhava. "We have all been through so much. There is no need for fighting."

"No, there is not," the abbess said. "Our claim is clear. Our order was founded to take special care of this book once it was found. We are under no obligation to respect your so-called mission. You take more upon yourself than you should. You are too young to know a true calling."

"Ooh," Lakanta said. "She should not have attempted to tease *that* dog."

Serafina, tired as she was, straightened until her back was as erect as a poplar tree and fixed Sharhava with a baleful look.

"You want the book?" she asked. "Then, take it."

"No, Serafina!" Tildi protested.

Serafina pushed in between the two groups. "No! If you want it, Abbess, take it. Tildi, let her have it."

"But . . ."

"I am your teacher now. Listen to me."

Tildi gawked at her.

"Serafina!"

"Go on, child." There was a smoldering fire in her eyes. Tildi didn't understand the changes in her rune, but she did not choose to question it. "Give it to her."

The voices protested mightily, but Tildi lifted the Great Book in her hands and held it up. She could scarcely bear to watch it being taken away. In moments, it had become as dear to her as a friend. What would Master Olen say? What would Edynn have said?

The abbess, triumphant, lunged for the big scroll.

"At last, at last!" she crowed. "Brothers and sisters, behold! All these years . . . aaaggh!" She screamed and sprang backward. The scroll fell from her hands. Tildi dove for it.

The smell of burning flesh took them all by surprise. Tildi felt the acrid scent singe her nostrils as she gathered the book back into her lap. It had unwound partway and nearly bounced out of her hands. Miraculously, she had managed to save it before it touched the ground. She rerolled the long parchment and patted it back into place on the spindle, cooing to it to soothe it from the indignity. Only then did she look up at the others.

Sharhava had dropped to her knees. She held up her shaking hands and stared at them. In an instant they had burned to blackened claws. Her eyes were filled with tears as she glared at Serafina.

"You cast a spell upon it, sorceress!"

"Of course I have not," Serafina said. She handed her staff to Rin and knelt beside the abbess. She took Sharhava's left hand between hers and bathed it in a ball of cool light. "It is the book's nature that puts it out of the reach of ordinary beings."

Slowly, the hand returned to its ordinary color and shape. Serafina reached for the other one.

In that brief interval, Sharhava had recovered her dignity.

"Don't touch me, sorceress!" Sharhava thrust her away. "Take her!" Two knights grasped her by the arms and dragged her upright.

"Let me go!" Serafina protested. Four knights rushed to assist the abbess to stand.

"Take the book," the abbess ordered. A huge, burly man with a knobbly face like a rockfall stalked to Tildi and attempted to lift the scroll. He only touched the spindle with one hand, then jumped back as if a snake had bitten him.

"Black sorcery!" he exclaimed, holding his scorched and reddened hand up for the others to see. He tried again. Tildi had to admire his strength of will, though it was fruitless. He could never close his fingers around the parchment. His hand seemed to stop by itself an inch or more from its surface. The voices in her mind grew agitated every time he tried.

"You are hurting it!" Tildi protested.

"Never for the world!" the man said, but he withdrew at last. He shook his head at the abbess.

Trembling with rage and pain, Sharhava thrust her face at Serafina.

"You have put a spell on the Great Book," Sharhava hissed, her eyes full of hatred. "You dare!"

"No, this is the book's nature," Serafina said, pulling free of the knights' grasp. "It is more real than we are."

"Then how can *that child* hold it?" the abbess asked, almost accusingly.

Serafina knelt beside Tildi. "Her immunity is the result of a chain of events that no one among you would ever want to duplicate. Not I or any of my order can do what she does. Only she can return the book to its place of safety." She looked at Sharhava's still-blackened right hand. "Let me help you, Abbess. I can heal that as well."

"Do not touch me again!" Sharhava hissed. "I do not need aid from such as you."

The words were delivered like a whiplash of hatred. Serafina's face was still. "As you please. I only wish to ease your suffering. You see that the book has defenses. They extend to Tildi as well."

"Does it protect her from swords and spears?" Sharhava asked suddenly.

"Are you threatening her?" Magpie asked, aghast. "A child?"

Sharhava stilled. A moment passed and her face changed. "Of course I do not threaten her. I merely ask for clarification as to the limits of the power she bears. All our fears that the Great Book would fall into enemy hands are groundless. But to see a mere infant in possession of the most important tome of this or any age? How can this be?"

"She is not an infant," Serafina said. "She is a smallfolk. You see her feet?"

Tildi felt keenly embarrassed as everyone in the room looked at her feet, still bare and filthy with soot. She curled her legs up underneath the big scroll to hide them. It would have been a terrible breach of manners in the Quarters to have drawn attention to a person's physical appearance, especially a woman's.

The news of Tildi's race seemed to come as a terrible shock to the knights. Sharhava's face, too, had gone blank for a moment, and part of her rune seemed to manifest itself more strongly. She and her brethren did not like smallfolk, for whatever reason. Tildi was surprised and dismayed at the deep distaste that the knights manifested then sought to conceal. She knew, though. Her enhanced sight uncovered many secrets that she knew the owners wished to keep hidden.

"So, she is one of the toeless ones," Sharhava said, recovering magnificently. "My studies do not show them to possess unusual magical talents, especially ones as powerful as hers!"

"Her ability comes as the result of events I would hope can never be duplicated," Serafina explained. "She has made greater sacrifices than all . . . than most." Her voice trembled. Tildi put out a hand to touch her knee, then drew it hastily back when her fingertips left burn marks on the girl's gown.

"Then, she will bear the Great Book for us," the abbess said. "It will go back to our Scriptorium. Consider, Tildi," she said, kneeling down. "My order has sought this book for many long centuries. We would be grateful for the chance to study it. You will have a place of honor among us as the one who will make it possible to elicit the greatest good from the book. You shall have a title and quarters befitting your status." She reached to touch Tildi's shoulder, but withdrew the shaking black claw that was her right hand. "Help us preserve the treasure of the age!"

"It has to go to the south," Tildi said, trying to figure out what the difference in the rune meant. She was afraid of the woman. Sharhava made her think of some of the wives of the elders in her home village of Clearbeck, who tried to run one's life through sheer willpower, though their husbands were the ones in authority, not they. As a motherless girl, Tildi had withstood many like her over the years, but she was tired—so tired. "It is the only way to make it safe."

"That is what your masters have told you, chi—smallfolk," the abbess said, her blue-green eyes boring into Tildi's. "How far is it to your destination?"

"I . . . I do not know." Tildi looked up at Serafina for support. The wizardess held out her staff and a map appeared upon the air.

"Our destination lies a hundred miles from the north coast of Sheatovra," Serafina said. "I may not be more specific than that."

"Why not?" Sharhava said, beaming maternally upon them all. "We can be allies. Let us assist you, at least as far as the chapter house in Orontae. You have a long way to go. Your journey could take months."

"Months!" Serafina exclaimed.

Sharhava was quick to pick up on her dubious mien.

"Yes, of course. You are not used to the road, are you? Winter is coming. It will be slow going, and you will need to travel in stages. We are experts at foraging and making a camp secure against beasts and intruders at night. You can be safe in our hands."

Magpie frowned. "A moment ago you were ready to snatch the book out of their hands and leave them here. Why the sudden offer of aid?"

Sharhava turned her brilliant gaze upon him. "There is no need to mistrust me, my dear Eremilandur. You have said that there are powerful foes opposing this mission."

"You were among those foes," Magpie pointed out.

"But that was before we saw what powers the Great Book bestowed upon its favored ones," Sharhava said. "How can we speak against its Word? You shall travel to the south, with us as your guardians. We should go at once."

The young man's green-gold eyes were alight with wariness.

"I would prefer to await Olen and the rest of the council here," Serafina said. "I can summon him. He is watching for signs. It is too dangerous to travel openly. Nemeth spoke of voices . . ."

"Voices? What of that? He was mad; you said so yourself," the abbess said, interrupting her impatiently. "Was the man not dismissed from your father's service, Eremilandur? For incompetence during the war with Rabantae?"

"My father's reasons were an excuse," Magpie said hoarsely. Clearly he did not want to discuss what he had told Tildi. None of them looked back at the sad bundle on the floor, where Nemeth's body sprawled underneath Morag's discarded cloak. "Nemeth was a true seer. He said he heard voices, and I believe him."

"We should leave here as soon as we can. You will see how unsafe it is to remain here any longer. This place is unstable."

"How?" Magpie challenged her. "It has stood for a hundred centuries."

Sharhava shook her head, as if he were a foolish child.

"Not with stone giants pounding upon its walls, nor a malign lightning storm striking bolts upon it," she said, waving her good hand at the cracks in the high stone ceiling. "The monsters are dead, but the walls could collapse in upon us at any moment. The winds could return!"

"Now, that is a practical consideration," Lakanta said, eyeing the stonework with the air of an expert. "But for that, we can find a nice cave or a village to shelter in for a while until Olen comes."

"There are no villages nearby now," Sharhava said. "We saw only destruction on our way here."

"Nemeth's spell," Serafina said, looking pale. "He wiped them out. Can we return to the caverns?"

Lakanta looked shamefaced. "Well, now, I wouldn't count upon my kin for much. You know that we dwarves like our privacy."

"The dwarfhollows are closed to us now, are they not?" Rin asked gently.

"You know, I just can't ask them to let a lot of humans go tramping through," Lakanta said, her cheeks red. Tildi saw how deeply embarrassed she was not to be able to offer them the hospitality of her kin, but the words to offer comfort just wouldn't come. It seemed all the strength in her body went to holding the book in her lap.

"What would you have us do, Tildi?" Sharhava asked, ignoring the others.

The voice seemed to come from far away, interrupting the voices. Tildi looked up at her dreamily.

"Serafina is our leader. She will decide."

"But you are the one who carries the Great Book!"

Tildi shook her head.

"You are all weary. Let me take this burden for you," Sharhava said persuasively. "We will go now, before sunset, away from this place. We will make for our haven. There I can gather more of my knights. The Great Book shall have a mighty escort befitting its importance! Come, now!" She stood up. "We will make ready to ride at once. I will lead you to safety."

"Wait," Serafina said. "Not so soon. Give me a few hours. I must try to make contact with Master Olen. I must tell him . . ."

"If we wait too long, it will be nightfall," Sharhava said, overpowering her. "I cannot speak as to the safety of any of your party in this building overnight, let alone for an extended wait. We can be traveling toward Olen. That makes more sense, does it not? Come," she said persuasively, putting her good arm around Serafina's waist, "let me speak to you as I would to a daughter."

"Oh, come now!" Magpie exclaimed. "This is a transformation so thorough that a butterfly that had just finished turning from a grub would be impressed with you."

"Eremi, don't speak to my aunt that way!" Inbecca protested, but she did not look straight at him. Tildi could tell that she was torn between believing him or Sharhava. Tildi could tell by her rune that she was wavering. Magpie and Princess-Knight Inbecca were looking and not looking at each other. Tildi saw volumes of meaning in the runes that adorned them, then looked away, ashamed to be able to read their feelings so readily. Moments ago she had been blind to everyone's deepest thoughts. Now she could not help it. She longed for rest. None of this was really happening to her. Everything felt like it was happening in a distant haze.

In the Great Book, she found the story of a girl named Tildi, who was just like herself. But it was all so unbelievable! If she had read it at home, she would have put the book aside as a drunken tale.

Home. She felt pangs for lost home, loved ones, safety, comforts. But the book made up for a lot of her loss. She hugged it to herself. Over her head, the argument went on. Sharhava put her hand, her good hand, on Serafina's shoulder.

"You need time to think and to heal. Let those of us with more experience take a hand. We will make ready to go. The sooner we leave, the more distance we can put behind us before dark. As soon as I consider that we are in a safe place, you may contact Olen and tell him where to find us. Loisan!"

The gray-haired knight presented himself at her side. "Yes, my lady?"

"Gather up the horses. We leave within the hour."

"Yes, Abbess."

And that was that, Tildi realized. Serafina, coping with her own grief and the exhaustion from healing so many wounds, had been overwhelmed by the abbess. In fact, she agreed with the imperious woman many more times than Tildi would have thought she might if she were not so tired. The others were also too tired or disheartened to put up much of an argument in reply. Sharhava was triumphant. Tildi saw it in her rune. She knew Serafina could see it, too. Sharhava was a masterful woman.

Within less time than she would have believed, the horses were found and groomed, including Magpie's Tessera, Serafina's white mare, and Melune, Lakanta's obstreperous pony.

No food was to be found in the castle, nor would any of them have trusted it, but Nemeth's reconstruction of the ancient building appeared to have included the wellheads. A couple of volunteers from among Sharhava's force tested it and found the water not only good but sweet. They filled bottles and canteens, and washed off the dust and blood of battle.

The book spoke of all these things to Tildi, even when she could not see them. She found she could spin automatically to the page she wanted to see, though much of which she wished to know was on the few leaves surrounding the gaping wound where Nemeth had ripped pieces away. She touched the torn edges. It would take strength to tear the parchment. Although it was old, it was as sound as the day it had been made. Such a beautiful thing. She could not help but stroke it, even though the touch still sent fire racing through her fingertips. It did not burn as painfully as it had in the beginning.

She remained sitting on the floor where she had stopped after helping Magpie. The knights were careful to give her room. She sensed odd emotions from them, almost as if she could hear their thoughts. They were angry, in a way. She felt fierceness from them. They . . . hated her, or so it seemed, but why? She had never done any harm, and they were offering to help her accomplish her goal. She thought she understood all of it when she saw open envy on the face of one lanky young man. That was it: she could do what they could not. She couldn't do anything about that, nor could she help their feelings.

Her friends spoke to her now and again. She thought she replied to them, but so much seemed imaginary now that she was not certain if she had spoken or only thought about speaking.

With no duties and no responsibilities at hand, Serafina had settled in one of the big white thrones where she could see Tildi. Her rune was almost spinning. Tildi knew she had much to think about. So much had happened. So much.

Then it had been time to go. Tildi had seen the impatience in the knights' runes on the page of the Great Book. She did not need to look up to see how many of them stood around her, waiting for her to rise. She rolled the enormous scroll up and prepared to leave. Heat seemed to roll from her in waves. It was lessening every moment, but it still made the others step well back. They formed a double row that led to the hole in the floor.

She had looked down through it, and her heart quailed. The stone blocks had been a graceful staircase, then Nemeth's monstrous army lay scattered in heaps on the floor of the huge reception room far below. The knights had been pulling themselves up by means of rope ladders. Tildi did not like heights. If only the stairs were still there! Only a fragment of the uppermost end of the flight remained. Two stairs still clung together upon the section of the arch that had held them aloft. The rune, though slightly damaged, was largely intact. If that was how those parts were made, then it stood to reason that the other steps would have had similar if not identical runes.

At that moment Tildi had been certain she could see how the stairs ought to fit together all the way down. The voices coming from the book assured her that her vision was true. She put out a small hand.

"*Votaf,*" she said.

With a crash like a thousand bolts of lightning, the stones flew together. Tildi blinked. The stairs were complete. Well, nearly complete. Some pieces still lay in heaps on the floor below, but an entire flight did now stretch down from here to there. She gazed at it in astonishment, then looked at her hand. How had she done that? What did *votaf* mean? Where had the word come from? She had looked up to see Serafina studying her curiously. The knights were positively agog.

"Could you do that again?" Serafina asked.

"I don't know how I did it this time," Tildi admitted.

"It was well done, no matter how," Rin said, trotting down the flight ahead of them.

"Aye, I agree," Lakanta said, taking the tall steps sideways to accommodate her short legs. "I didn't like the idea of swinging down a rope like a spider, though I would have done it."

Tildi's legs were shorter yet, but somehow she managed to get down without falling or dropping the precious scroll.

In the courtyard the knights offered Tildi the choice of any mount she wished to ride, but the voices broke into loud whispers.

"Bearing her is *my* honor," Rin told the knights fiercely. She flared her nostrils, defying them to contradict her. They had appealed to Tildi.

"What is your decision?" Loisan asked, in his courtly way. Tildi felt nervous, but she managed to state her wish.

"I'd rather go with Rin."

That had prompted another huddled discussion among the knights. Tildi became fascinated with watching the runes in the book, until the circle broke.

"It shall be as you say," Loisan announced.

A stout man who by his bearing ranked lower than either Loisan or the abbess but higher than most of the others had come forward with an ancient leather satchel fastened with a gleaming buckle Tildi thought must have been of pure gold. He unfastened it and drew from it a cloth so white it almost hurt Tildi's eyes. She could tell the cloth was something special that the knights had carried with them for a very long time. The intricate embroidery looked to be of smallfolk design and the very highest level of workmanship. With Rin's permission he spread it over her back, then gestured politely to Tildi.

"May I assist you?"

"What is the cloth for?" she asked, a trifle suspiciously.

"It is to protect the book from soiling, honored one," he said.

"Oh."

She was impressed that they had thought to bring the cloth with them, since they'd been looking for the Great Book for centuries more than Olen and his council had. The two men knelt, as if they would lift her onto Rin's back.

"Better not," Tildi warned them. She started the flight chant.

"Stop!" Serafina interrupted her. "Until you have control of yourself, I had better do that." She continued with the chant. Tildi could see the lifting runes form underneath her feet and a similar spell appear on Rin's back. They were weaker than any she had seen Serafina create before. Distantly, the feeling part of her was worried about the young wizardess. She also had a faint hint of concern for herself.

Rin had let out one soft grunt when Tildi settled herself. It was the only complaint she had made or would make. Tildi was grateful to her, and vowed to make her presence as painless as possible.

"We are ready, then," Sharhava said. "We will go now."

I ask again, does she have some special powers that will preserve her life if you are beset?"

"No," Serafina said.

"Then she can die. So can all of you, and you shall, if you do not cooperate with us. She will bear the book for us. She will bring it, under our escort, to the chapter house of our order, or you can attempt to fight your way free of this place against all of us." She sketched a bow to Tildi. "You will have a high office with us, honorable, with all the things you will need to assist us in our studies. Since you are the only one who can handle it, we will protect you and the book forever. No one will harm you there. What do you say?"

Tildi looked at the others. She swallowed. She could not forfeit the lives of her friends to save the book. The only other answer would be to harm or kill all of the knights by changing their runes, and that she was unwilling to do. She looked to Serafina for guidance, but the young wizardess shook her head. Tildi swallowed.

"I . . . I am afraid we have no choice."

Sharhava beamed, as if they had reached an agreement willingly. "Good. We will depart. You will be content there, in your new home."

She pointed forward, and the party began to move once again.

"Why are you listening to her?" Lakanta demanded in a hiss. "Tildi! We can't stay in Orontae. We've got to get this thing to the south as soon as we can!"

"I know," Tildi said miserably. She couldn't explain. She could not believe that Sharhava could play her so cruelly. Why had she believed the woman at the start?

Tildi studied the abbess, who would no longer meet her eyes. Sharhava had the deepest control, and the deepest convictions of any of her followers.

When she and the knights were not concentrating upon the unwelcome guest in their midst, they seemed nice enough people. A few of them were unable to contain their joy at having the Great Book nearby. A young man with a long, thin face and very intense, dark blue eyes risked censure by riding up in between the stone wall and the lefthand file of guards to behold the bundle in Tildi's lap. He gave her a look of pure delight, before recalling that she was an unnatural creature who was not supposed to exist. His cheeks reddened. Tildi gave him a pleasant smile. He didn't seem like a bad man. One could grow up with a knowledge of the world that was completely wrong, yet be a genuinely good man or woman.

Serafina drew her mount back until she was riding in the protected circle with Tildi and Rin. Tildi could tell by her expression that the argument was not over, by any means, but they could do little at the moment. It was better to have an escort than not. None of them knew what other menaces Nemeth could have loosed in his quest for revenge.

Rin muttered to herself. "A Windmane does not take instruction from a two-foot. If I get the chance, I shall kill her."

"Save your efforts, my friend," Serafina said, though her eyes were aglow with the same ire as the centaur's. "The time is not yet. We do need protection, more than my magic or your strong arm can provide. Since we are forced to travel with them, they may as well guard us until another solution can be found."

"Can we send a message? Olen must be looking in on us, with his scrying ways."

Olen! Tildi's heart leaped within her for joy at the sound of her first master's name. If only he could rescue them.

"I will try to send him word," Serafina said. "He may already know. The face of the very world has been scarred. He must see. He must *know*. I hope that he can see us, too. We have other allies nearby as well."

"Who?" Tildi asked.

"Hush!" Serafina said as the guards turned their way.

"How silent it is!" Lakanta said, turning on her plump pony's saddle. "Not a bird, not a cricket, not a rustle anywhere."

Tildi listened. Except for the lonely whisper of the wind, not a sound but the jingle of harness and the clatter of shod hooves on the stone path reached her sensitive ears.

"Looks as though every living thing for miles got scared off by whatever spell your mother cast," the trader continued. Serafina stiffened, but the little trader didn't notice. She went blithely on. "On the good side, we shouldn't be seeing that Madcloud again!" She looked at Serafina speculatively. "Are you sure you cannot send these habited nuisances away the same as your mother did with the stone giants?"

"No!"

Tildi giggled to herself. Lakanta chattered on as if the knights couldn't hear a word she was saying, but they most certainly could. They rode as stiff-backed as Serafina. The trader pressed on.

"What about Tildi? She has all this power, now that she's got that big scroll, there."

The guards looked alarmed. Rin shook her head.

"Even if she could, friend, she does not have the control of a wizard," Rin said. "She is but an apprentice. I say this not to hurt your feelings, Tildi."

"It is only the truth," Tildi said. "I'm afraid of what would happen if I try."

"If it would rid us of these people, what harm could there be?"

"I had not known you to be so bloodthirsty!" Serafina said with a wry expression. "I chafe at this state of affairs, too. Wait."

Lakanta snorted. "Wait. As we trundle off to who knows where? And with no one tending my customers along my route—it'll take years to get them all content again, if my cousin doesn't steal my route before I can get back to them."

"If he has your winning ways, how could he but succeed?" Rin asked with a snort.

"*You* may go, if you wish," the abbess said suddenly, casting a glance back over her shoulder. "There is no reason for you—any of the rest of you, either—to remain. Only that one. We will escort her."

Lakanta folded her arms, gripping her reins in her round little fist. "We stay with Tildi, fine lady. And never you think I resent it. It's you and yours who give me the saddle sores."

The way Sharhava's spine stiffened, Tildi knew that the feeling was mutual.

"Lend me your assistance, Tildi. We need warding," Serafina said.

Tildi nodded and prepared to concentrate. One of her first lessons with Master Olen was to make wards. "For protection?"

"No. We require more than that. I wish that Captain Teryn had not been so impatient with her sword. Nemeth had much more to tell us."

"If he would!" Rin said with disbelief on her long face.

"He was in fear of his life," Serafina said, her face thoughtful. "He was terrified of more than our arrival. His quest for revenge was only part of the reason he had set himself in this citadel. It is a defensive location, and we are leaving it. I wish I could convince that stubborn woman that we face a much greater threat than we can defend against on our own."

"But the Shining Ones no longer exist," Rin protested. "How could they? They would be over ten thousand years old."

"What is that to ones who could harness all of existence in a single book?

You must not forget that they were in complete command of their magical abilities. We know so little about the advances they made in their studies." She tilted her head toward the Great Book. Tildi clutched it tighter. "We must study it later, Tildi, in hopes that perhaps we can identify the Shining One of whom Nemeth spoke, and locate him. In the meanwhile, let us try to shield ourselves from discovery, as Nemeth himself did."

Tildi nodded. The spell that concealed the wizard from them had been penetrated only because she bore with her a fragment of a copy of a leaf— not even a piece of the book itself. It had been enough.

She unrolled the pure white parchment scroll a short way, wincing again at the holes in the leaves. When they had discovered Nemeth, he had torn runes from the book and destroyed them. In turn, their destruction had triggered the cataclysmic damage she saw around her. Tildi's heart constricted at the ruin of the land as well as that of the book. How something so beautiful could be desecrated by one who had claimed to love it she didn't know. In time, she and Serafina would work out how they could keep the knights from using the book for their own deadly purposes. She hoped Olen and the others would come and help them before the caravan reached the Scriptorium of which Sharhava spoke. Tildi feared Magpie might be right about Sharhava's motivation, in spite of her protests that the knights were only there to provide escort. The knights would not tell her in which way the Scriptorium lay, possibly to keep them from making plans based upon the terrain through which they must pass.

Teryn and Morag openly disdained the knights, and Loisan in particular. The way Teryn's hand hovered over her empty scabbard told Tildi the guard captain wanted only an excuse to challenge their captors. Since the knights had not forbidden them to accompany Tildi, the guards had not revolted openly. Though she was certain that Teryn and Morag were trained to the uttermost of their talents, they could not succeed against forty armed men and women. Tildi could not give up hope that the guards would find some way to navigate a safe course for them that did not include the knights. She was certain that Teryn and Morag had more resources between them than a bit of paper or a couple of pieces of metal. Halcot said he believed in their cause. His chosen guards must have more means of defending her than the weapons that had been taken away. She hoped it would not be necessary to find out, unless the Great Book became imperiled. She had less concern for her own safety. The book required protection. It was precious.

"Tildi!" A spark of scarlet flame sprang up right in front of her nose. Tildi flinched, and recalled where she was and what she was meant to be doing.

"I am sorry, master," she said.

"Please pay attention," Serafina said. "I want this done before we are out of the shadow of the castle." She closed her thumb and forefinger, and the flame winked out. She held out her staff. Tildi had no wand, so she brought out her small dagger. "We must draw the runes. You know the enchantment. We face south, so we will begin with the ward for that direction. You will need every bit of concentration of which you are capable. I am too tired to create this spell without you, but I fear every moment we are not protected." She raised her arm.

Tildi let out a gasp. Suddenly a dagger was at the young woman's throat. Loisan had his arm around Serafina's shoulders, pulling her into his chest. It was his knife, and his hot amber eyes burned like coals.

"What do you think you are doing?" he asked.

"I am protecting us all," Serafina said. Her voice was constricted to a whisper. She nodded toward Inbecca, then winced as the sharp blade pressed into her neck. "She knows. She heard. The threat is not over."

"The words of the mad court magician?" Loisan said. "I have heard Lar Inbecca's recounting of what went on. I believe none of it. He was spinning a tale, trying to save his life. You will weave no enchantments. They serve no purpose in your journey."

"It will serve no purposes at all if the thraiks come for us," Serafina whispered indignantly. By that time, the entire file had come to a halt. Rin unlimbered the whip she carried in her saddlebags. She cracked it.

"Let her go!"

At the sharp sound and the cry, everyone turned to look.

"Lar Loisan, what is this?" the abbess demanded.

"She was attempting a spell," Loisan said, all traces of his courtly manner gone.

"To what purpose?" Sharhava demanded.

Serafina flicked her hand and Loisan lost his grip on her. He reached for her, but his hands never came within a span. She straightened, glaring at the knight as if daring him to touch her again. "To protect us! You continue to believe that there are no other powers interested in the Great Book, now that it is free and above the ground. You are wrong. Such blatant ignorance will cost lives."

"I care not if it costs all our lives, and yours, too!" Sharhava snapped, but she looked thoughtful. "If I permit you to draw the runes, will you swear by your heart's blood not to try and make contact with others who might steal the book away from us?"

Serafina looked scornful.

"I will make no promises under duress," she grated out, but with irreproachable dignity. "What value could you put by such an oath? Olen is already looking for us. He may find us without any effort on my part."

"It's more important that the thraiks will be looking for us," Tildi put in. "They are attracted to anything that has had contact with the book, even for a moment. It had a protection spell over it before, but it's broken now that Nemeth is dead."

The abbess was startled into looking down at the bandages around her right hand. She eyed Serafina.

"Very well, but my knights will watch you to make certain that wards are all you draw. We have power of our own. Lar Loisan!"

Loisan held out his dagger and whispered to it. To Tildi's surprise, a small rune in blue appeared upon it, almost concealing the golden rune of its existence. The new sign was the same blue as their tunics.

"You seem surprised," Sharhava said with a tiny smile quirking her lips. "We have not wasted all these centuries in contemplation alone. I look forward to supplementing our power with that of the Great Book. We shall make use of our time while we accompany you."

"This no longer sounds like a simple escort detail," Magpie said. "Do you forswear what you promised?"

"Of course not!" Sharhava said, looking insulted. "You cannot blame us for wanting to make the greatest use of this opportunity."

"But preventing Serafina from contacting other wizards—why?"

"You yourself pointed out that we have other enemies pursuing the Great Book. To create an enchantment to draw attention to our location for the benefit of Master Olen also pinpoints us to any other master wizard who wishes to obtain the marvel of the ages for himself! A spell is not the same as dispatching a page with a parchment to be placed directly in the palm of its recipient. We are not in a position of strength here, Eremilandur. Give me credit for that. I wish to keep the Great Book as secure as I possibly can. To do less would be to fail in my duty."

She looked sincere, but Magpie still looked doubtful.

Serafina looked uneasy. Tildi thought she could guess what the wizardess was thinking. How broad was the knights' magical knowledge? Could they distinguish between a ward and a defense spell, or were they bluffing in hope that the show of force would keep them in line?

"Very well," Serafina said. "We will continue, on condition that I can set up magical protection for us now."

"You will promise not to attempt a message spell until I give you the word that it is safe? I do this only for all of our sakes," Sharhava pressed.

The young wizardess nodded. Tildi felt even more energy slipping from her. "I will."

"Then you may proceed." The abbess nodded to Loisan, who pulled his horse away from them. Serafina neatened her cloak and held out her staff once more.

"Together, then, Tildi, and remember—control!"

Tildi nodded and held out the knife.

"Crotegh mai ni lio!"

Silver lines spread out from the tip of the wand and the point of the dagger and spread upon the sky to the south of them. To Tildi's surprise, even though she was trying to use as little power as possible, her lines outspread Serafina's, filling the quadrant of the sky with broad protective sigils. Serafina gave Tildi a nod, and they faced to the west, still writing as though they wielded giant pens. Tildi concentrated on making the correct runes for each direction. She was determined not to make a single mistake. The voices speaking to her from the Great Book were encouraging. Another whisper joined the low chorus: a high, singing note like the distant hum of bees. She had heard that sound before, but never so loudly: it was the noise made by the wards themselves. The power that flowed through her was as strong as a winter gale.

The knights watched with interest and not a little suspicion as Tildi and Serafina commanded the runes to broaden and spread out until each rune touched its neighbors, arched high to form a four-sided dome that closed over their heads. The lines thinned out to a mere glimmer, then vanished from sight.

"We should be invisible to malign forces," Serafina said. "And to all others who use remote sight."

The abbess turned to her lieutenant. "Lar Loisan?"

The rough man nodded and showed the blue rune. "No change. They speak true about what they did."

"Good. There will be no more magic from this moment forward, unless I give leave. Is that understood?"

Serafina hesitated, then nodded. Tildi followed suit. The knight drew away from them and sheathed his dagger. The abbess once again gave the word to ride.

"At last I feel protected," Serafina said. She gave Tildi and Rin a half smile.

Chapter Two

"ildi, the castle was the home of my many-times ancestors," Magpie said as the party rode down the overgrown, winding path that led south from the foot of the castle. "It has been abandoned for centuries. In fact, it was in ruins all of my life. Nemeth must have rebuilt it. I only wish that he had not chosen to use the stairs as warriors. I would like to have seen it in all the glory of its ancient majesty. My brothers and I used to play here when I was a boy. It was a few days' ride from our home, but sometimes we came up here to hunt. Plump orrens used to flock up here. Good eating. Have you ever tried any? They're a bird about this big, and just as big around." He held his hands about a foot apart. "My brother Ganidur always wondered how it was they could fly when they were so fat. I always thought it was because they were so foolish that they didn't know it was impossible."

Tildi laughed. She even saw a little smile dimple the cheek of the girl to Magpie's left.

"Quiet in the ranks!" one of the knights growled. The smile fled from Inbecca's face.

"I am not a member of your ranks," Magpie said amiably, regarding the knight with a smile. "I always find that a story or two makes a long journey more pleasant, don't you?" He looked as though he dared the other to force him to be quiet.

Tildi dragged herself out of the pleasant haze that the book provided to cushion her from the discomfort of the world. "Why did your people abandon it?"

"We began to trade more with our neighbors. It made sense to be closer to them. And work had begun upon the new temple." He looked guilty, and Lar Inbecca gave him a very perturbed look. If one could ascribe ordinary people's emotions upon human royalty, Tildi would have to say there was a story there, and one that was still stinging, by the look of it. She did not dare ask, though her curiosity was piqued. It felt as if she was listening to an interesting romantic tale told by a storyteller or reading in a book. The Great Book in her lap must contain many such stories.

As if in answer, the scroll wound a few turnings, from one spindle to the other. The book appeared to have power of its own. Tildi rolled it open a trifle, to behold the runes thereon. *Man; woman; horses; vows*, broken and kept; all intertwined together. There was no doubt, by the smaller markings that further described that man and that woman, that she was seeing the runes for Magpie and Lar Inbecca. Tildi blushed. The book could effortlessly reveal the innermost secrets of anyone's heart. As its keeper, Tildi would be privy to them. It was a good thing she was accustomed to keeping her own counsel!

Even Magpie fell silent as they reached the end of the stone road that led down the mountain from the castle and came to a steep cliff. Tildi had seen only a corner of the devastation caused by Nemeth's misuse of the book, but now she could see nothing before her but the scar in the earth's face. A giant hand had scooped up a living valley and taken it away, leaving layers of clay and rock exposed hundreds of yards below them. An irregular oval pool of murky water quivered at the bottom.

"So that's the depth a country goes to, eh?" Lakanta asked. "We should be thankful that the description of Orontae doesn't go all the way to the center of the world."

Her voice seemed to catch on an errant breeze that bounced it all over the hollowed-out landscape, dying away in faint echoes.

Serafina looked stricken, as did Rin. The knights showed no emotion as they guided the party to the east.

"How did he do this?" Loisan asked.

"With a word," Serafina replied. "A single word."

"*That* is the kind of power we want," Sharhava said eagerly. "Wizard, you will teach us!"

"To commit this terrible destruction?" Rin asked. "You humans!"

"No," the abbess said scornfully. "To rebuild. To make the world the way it must be. We will study the book and its effects, to see the most efficient way to restore the changes that the Shining Ones performed upon it. Thereafter we will seek out the abominations and restore them, when possible. To destroy," she said with a cold backward glance at the centaur, "when restoration is not within reason. However, we shall return this place to its natural state of beauty. I intend that it shall be done with a single word."

Tildi was struck dumb by the stunning arrogance of the woman and her company. Why, she would have to go all the way back to the visitor from the Eveningside Quarter who brought her own jam along to visit her son, declaring that no fruit in the Morningside could possibly be edible in comparison. After a time, the ladies of the town had stopped trying to please her. If she was the potential mother-in-law, small wonder her hapless son had trouble finding someone to marry. Her brothers had taken Tildi's name off the list of possibles as soon as they met the mother. Tildi's eldest brother Gosto had suggested poor Dray marry a hinny, who was the only female in town stubborn enough to stand up to her.

Tildi sighed at the memory. How she missed her brothers. She had scarcely thought of them in weeks. Her life would have been so very different if the thraiks had not carried them off. Her brother Teldo would most likely have been here in her place, at Serafina's side, and she would be at home cooking soup and baking bread and, she admitted wryly, wondering what it was like out in the big world. Well, now she knew. It was both frightening and amazing. Humans had turned out to be kinder and more complicated than she had dreamed. She had met elves and werewolves, bakers, brewers and housekeepers, and at bottom they were just like smallfolk.

She vowed that she would not go along with Sharhava's plans. True, they could manage the book without her. They could have prodded the scroll onto a blanket, and carried it between a pair of horses. They could, with care, manipulate the roll of parchment with long sticks to avoid touching it, and be able to see the beautiful runes within. But could they harness its power? Tildi hoped not.

The knights rode mostly in silence through the ruin of the valley. The pairs of riders murmured softly to each other. The loudest noise for miles, apart from the jingle of harness, was Lakanta talking loudly to herself. The trader woman was having trouble with her saddle and bridle.

"Teach me, it will, to let another living soul prepare my horse for me! They don't have a single idea where anything goes, and did they ask me? Not a chance! What do you think of that, Melune? Are there any lumps under your blanket? Did they put a stone there so you'll be rubbed raw? Terrible way they treat decent mounts, isn't it?" The little merchant went on talking to herself.

Though the sky was clear, Tildi had the feeling that a storm was brewing around her. The whispers coming from the book increased in intensity, like the sound of leaves stirring in the breeze. Yet the wind was still.

She turned the spindles, looking through the section on Orontae for a rune that described the part of the land through which they were riding. Even if what had been here before was gone, torn out and burned by Nemeth, what did exist now ought to be there. Her rudimentary knowledge of the ancient language, bolstered by weeks of drilling by Olen, gave her more insight into the words and compound phrases that the ornate glyphs indicated, yet she had not yet noticed one that meant 'deep, lifeless ravine.' The absence of the rune that *ought* to have been there might have had the same meaning.

This is the path I took to find you," Magpie explained, pointing to the southwest. "I guess that they followed me."

"Only one set of hoofprints heading northward," one of the young knights, Driel, said. "All others were facing south."

"I passed thousands of people fleeing from this place," the young man said sadly, unable to keep his eyes off the valley to their right. "My people."

He looked as if he could use a friendly pat for comfort, Tildi thought. Lar Inbecca seemed as though she ought to be the one to dispense it, but after the scolding from Sharhava, she never looked his way.

"It is not your fault," Rin said. "The madman made his own fate. In our land, he would have been driven away from the herd."

"That, I fear, is the reason why he became driven to do the unthinkable," Magpie said, his eyes unable to tear themselves away from the ruin of the valley. "My father drove him from court. He blamed him for our failures in the war with Rabantae. My father . . ." he added with difficulty, "is a man of extremes."

"And he is really a king?" Lakanta said with relish. "My goodness, I had no idea we were keeping such exalted company."

"Don't fear, I won't expect a bow every time you speak to me," Magpie said, planting a hand on his chest grandly. "In truth, my role as a troubadour has given me far greater pleasure and ease than I ever had as a prince."

"What is your family like?"

"My brother Ganidur is my dearest friend in the world. He's twice my size, and has always knocked me down when he thought my ideas were too foolish."

"He's not the heir, is he?" Lakanta asked. "Seems as though I heard a different name."

Magpie said tersely, "Benarelidur will be a good king, in the mold of my father, alas. But his wife, my sister-in-law, is a tempering influence. She is a gentle soul, and he lives for her."

"And are you married? This lass and you seem fond of each other."

"I . . . ask me later, friend," Magpie said, after a furious glance from Inbecca.

"Ah, well," Lakanta said, with more tact than he would have thought she was capable of mustering. "My brother lives for his little wife. She is a fine woman, but hardly says a word from sunup to sundown. Hair as orange as a tiger lily, if you can picture such a thing, and eyes bluer than the sky. She's the best weaver I have ever seen outside of the Quarters . . ."

The dwarf woman prattled happily on with her story, reeling off an impressive list of nephews and nieces that had blessed the union of the loving couple. Magpie's head sank into his shoulders. He didn't dare glance at the young woman beside him. Inbecca looked angry enough to burst into flames. It was all his fault, of course, including the fact that the Scholardom, against which Olen had warned them, was now in virtual possession of the Great Book.

Out of the corner of his eye he saw a flicker of light. The silver-gilt runes that decorated everything in sight should not have attracted his attention. He looked around for the source of it. His eyes widened, and he felt his heart pound with fear.

Good sir, you probably don't want to meddle with that."

Magpie's friendly voice had an edge of iron. Tildi glanced up from her studies. One of the guards at her right hand glared over his shoulder at the young man.

"Silence, ignorant one," the knight said. It was difficult for Tildi to guess his age, since human faces were so much heavier of bone than smallfolk, but she guessed he was young, perhaps in his twenties. He had thick blond eyebrows attached to bony ridges over a straight but broad nose and well-shaped, fleshy lips. "The blessing belongs to each of us. You have no right to tell me not to study what I choose."

"Study, yes," Magpie said. "Perhaps you don't know that each of us can see that you are trying to manipulate the rune on your body. You see it on your chest, but it's visible from every angle, to all of us. I saw that little fork at the top widen for a moment. You do not understand what you are meddling with."

"Mind your own business," the knight said. "This is part of our sacred cause."

"Now, now, Bertin, you ought to be trying to convert him, not offend him." Bertin's riding partner was an elderly man with nutcracker jaws. "We know it can be seen from all sides. That shows the truth with which the Mother and the Father have imbued us all. Thanks to the book, it cannot now be concealed. We are as we are."

"But he is trying to change it," Magpie insisted.

"*She* did it, you said, and you came to no harm." The young man tossed an obstinate chin toward Tildi.

Magpie nodded. "But she had a drawing of what my rune was like before it was changed. Did you write yours down somewhere lest you make a mistake?"

Bertin's face went red.

"Do not seek to tell me what I may and may not do!"

"Bertin, you didn't see what I saw," Inbecca said, her large eyes pleading with her fellow knight. "It would be best to study the runes now that we can see them before making any changes. The path counsels caution, does it not?"

"And you know the whole of the writings of guidance, having been of our membership for how long?" Bertin asked offensively. Tildi saw the boy's shoulders tighten up. No one liked to be called on bad behavior.

Inbecca raised her chin proudly. "I know common sense," she said. "How long has the Scholardom been trying to find the Great Book? You've never had it in your hands before. In fact, you haven't touched it at all. How well prepared are you?"

"Well enough!" Bertin exclaimed sulkily.

The older man sought to ease the sting of the rebuke. He patted the boy's arm.

"Lady Inbecca's right, boy. Give it time. The blessing is with us forever, now. What's another day, or another year, when we've waited ten thousand to have it in our hands?"

"Oh, I suppose, Auric," Bertin said at last, his fit of bad temper passing. Tildi knew it to be frustration, an emotion with which she was well acquainted.

"Good. Then pay no attention. We ought to be stopping soon. It's getting dark."

Auric was correct, to Tildi's surprise. Immersed in the book as she had been, she had paid little heed to her surroundings. The knights at the front and rear of the file sparked torches, but those only provided dim light. The wavering shadows they cast actually made the road under their feet harder to see.

Night was not all darkness, as it had been before. Even dusk was lit up by myriad little stars of the runes of the things within range of the book's influence. Night creatures zipping through the sky were invisible except for the pale gold glow of their name-sigil written upon them. She would never really get used to seeing the runes. She felt almost as if she—and her brother Teldo, too—had been deprived by their sheltered existence in the Quarters, missing out on the excitement of magic. She had attained magic since, far more than her share. She couldn't help but feel sad that Teldo had died too soon to have experienced it, too, though if he had lived she would never be out in the wide world, and she would never have touched the Great Book, a fact that would have diminished her happiness. Still, her brothers would have been alive, and that meant as much.

Tildi sat bolt upright, mortified. It should have meant *more*. She was horrified at herself that she equated possessing the book with the lives of her family. The voices coming from the scroll assured her that one could not be compared with the other. *Study,* they advised her. *Find contentment within these pages.*

She relaxed. Study would give her comfort. Obediently, she bent her head over the scroll, determined to dismiss such unworthy thoughts from her mind. Teldo would have taken this opportunity with both hands and a grateful heart. The least she could do was do the same, in his memory.

She had found her rune again, surrounded by a cluster of runes that looked familiar, on a corner of a page devoted to details of the country of Orontae.

A glimpse of rosy red light caught the corner of her eye. It was that boy again, she thought impatiently. If he had been a lad of the Quarters, she might have reached over and thumped his knuckles, as would any adult who noticed he was doing something that he should not.

"Sir Bertin," she said, hoping to distract him. "Do you know where we are? I hear a roaring ahead."

His fingers dropped from his chest in guilty haste. He looked as if he wanted to reply harshly to her, but she knew she was entitled to some courtesy to her face, as the bearer of the book.

"I know not what it is," he said at last. "I have never been here before."

"Do you come from far away?"

"Levrenn."

"Is your home a pleasant place?"

"Pleasant enough." He kept his answers as short as possible. Tildi knew he was uncomfortable speaking with her, and he wanted to return unobserved to his experimentation.

"Did you learn magic there?"

"We do not practice magic!" he burst out. "Magic is . . . magic is not for scholarship! You don't learn about the world, you just manipulate it."

"Ah, that's not what my masters have taught me," she said. "We must study everything very carefully. Magic is mostly scholarship."

"That's not true," he said.

He is so young, Tildi thought.

A white-sleeved arm went up at the front of the file.

"I smell fresh water," Rin said.

"What is the concern, Abbess?" Loisan called from the rear of the file.

"The path must have veered down toward the gorge and was cut off by Nemeth's spell," Sharhava said. "The road is gone. There is a waterfall ahead of us. We must backtrack to the last crossroads and find another way."

"The main road ran along the river," Magpie reminded them helpfully. "There are plenty of animal trails leading off, but not all of them are through routes. We have been very lucky to get so far on this one."

Loisan wheeled his horse and spurred until he passed the two Rabantavian soldiers and their guards. The others turned in place. Rin swiveled her flexible body until she was looking directly at Tildi, and eased her hooves in a tight circle until they were facing the rear. A couple of the knights near Tildi looked as though they envied her the maneuverability of her centaur mount. Their own horses were clearly nervous having to turn on such a narrow pathway, but there was no choice.

Loisan sent a rider with a torch out ahead of them to find an alternate route. The land to the side was mountainous, and any other path was likely to be treacherous and steep. Tildi didn't enjoy the idea of riding those ways in the dark. The ridge itself bore a huge, glimmering blue rune that loomed over them forbiddingly.

"Who is that?" Magpie asked her. "Old Man Mountain?"

"I don't know how to read its name yet," Tildi said.

"I am only teasing you," he said lightly. "I know a few songs about this part of the country. Shall I sing them to you? It would take our minds off the hazard of the journey."

Tildi looked at the knights around them, grim-faced. "Best not," she said. "But thank you. You have been so kind to me, and you a king's son."

"Smallfolk girl, I owe you my life and much more," Magpie said, serious for once. "Being a king's son is far less important to me than many other parts of my life." He cast a woeful glance at Inbecca, who was riding a few feet ahead of him, pointedly not looking back. "Perhaps you can tell me stories of *your* life. We know so little of the Quarters, really. Humans of my size are not encouraged to stay long. We sing our songs, vend our wares, and are invited to leave as soon as we possibly can."

Tildi laughed. "That is true. The elders don't want to be touched by *ideas,* you see. If you remained, you might get into *discussions.* Until Olen began to teach me, I didn't know that you could question a tutor. In Morningside Quarter, if you knew your lessons, you didn't get a smack on the hand or sent out of the schoolhouse to stand in the rain, but even questioning what my schoolmistress knew and how she knew it was asking to be expelled."

"Did you ever see anyone expelled?"

"Teldo," she said, smiling. "My brother. He was older by a year than I. We had dreams, you know. He was going to be a great wizard, and I would be his first apprentice. We never let anyone out of the family know our ambition, of course. My brother Gosto was the head of the family after my parents . . . died. Teldo was expelled for asking questions about history that were not in the history book. Gosto brought Teldo back in and made him apologize. The teacher let him rejoin the class, after a week outside to think over his sins."

"Mother and Father, I am glad that I had a tutor who let me talk!" Magpie exclaimed. "I'd have been out in the rain for years, the way I interrupted that poor man."

Tildi was charmed by how easy it was to converse with this young man. He was more than twice her size and of high birth, but he treated her as if she were his dearest friend whom he had known all his life.

A blaze of light rose up, along with a wild yell. Tildi forgot what she was going to say. She automatically clutched the book to her chest. Her guards clustered in close to her, protecting them both.

"Halt!" Sharhava shouted from behind them. "Go see what happened. Lar Romini might be in trouble."

Loisan snatched a torch from one of the riders at the rear of the file and touched spurs to his mount. Magpie kicked up his horse to follow, as did Serafina.

The lieutenant suddenly spun his horse sideways, blocking them. Serafina's normally placid horse reared. Magpie leaned out of his saddle. He grabbed the white horse's reins and held tight until it calmed down.

"Where do you think you are going?" Loisan demanded as Magpie sat upright and threw the reins back to Serafina.

"To assist," Magpie said urgently. "Think, man! I was brought up here, and this lady is a master wizard. If your man is in trouble, who can be of better help?"

Loisan scowled, but he was a reasonable man. He laid reins to his steed's neck. "Come, then, and hurry!"

Hot yellow flames licked the night sky, blotting out all runes but a wild red one that danced at the heart of the fire. It looked as though the entire road was ablaze. The horses danced, reluctant to get close to the conflagration. The riders dismounted, and went forward on foot. The fire baked

Magpie's face even from a distance. Sweat ran from under his hair and down his neck.

"Heaven's heart," Serafina exclaimed. "What happened here?"

"Romini, where are you?" Loisan shouted.

"Here, sir!" a voice called feebly. "I'm not hurt, but I'm stuck. The path is all spongy."

"It wasn't spongy when we rode over it," Loisan said. "Do you smell pitch?"

"It's all pitch," Magpie said, pointing to the burning road at their feet. "It looks like the entire trail is spread with it. An ember falling from Romini's torch must have set it ablaze."

"We're not alone? Someone followed us and laid a trap, knowing we would have to come back this way!" Loisan's beady eyes picked up the fire's fierce glow. He drew his sword and studied the wooded slopes for signs of impending ambush. "They will never take the book from us! I must tell the abbess!" He started back for his horse.

"No! How could anyone know we would ride this way?" Serafina asked impatiently. "Look down! Was the road *gold* before this?"

"What?" Both men looked where she pointed. Streaks of bright yellow showed in the path's surface. Magpie scrabbled up a handful of pebbles. He showed them to the other two.

"It *is* gold! I would have thought the dwarves in this country would have mined every scrap of precious ore centuries ago."

"It was not here centuries ago," Serafina said. "It has barely been minutes since that was created. Look at the runes."

"I cannot interpret them, lady," Magpie said. "I know some ancient signs, but these are too complex."

"I can read them somewhat," Loisan said, though uncertainly.

Serafina waved an impatient hand. "Let *me* translate. It says *resin* underneath the flames. It's not so far different from the ancient rune *soil*. This part under our feet is mixed up. The runes for gold and earth are interwoven with smaller runes for creeper and water. Don't you understand? No one is following us. It was a normal road until the book passed over it and unlocked the runes. *We* changed it by riding over it. Our horses' hooves altered the strokes. Romini is lucky to be alive. We might have noticed an abyss opening up underneath us, but not a change in surface unless it was so unusual we would perceive it without seeing it. Tildi is close to the rear of the line, so the changes might have been gradual. I do not know. All this requires study. I wish we had stayed at the castle until we knew more!"

"It was the abbess's will," Loisan said, though at that moment he looked as if he wished they had waited, too.

"Is that going to happen everywhere we go?" Magpie asked.

"It could," Serafina said, her brow furrowed. "Only Time and Nature know how Nemeth got all the way to Orontae from Sheatovra without making so many changes we could have tracked him by them. But perhaps it was because he was only one man, doing his best to stay away from anyone else. Once the influence passes, the runes are safe. As long as we ride close to Tildi, we trample the runes the book reveals."

"No wonder it was locked away!" Magpie exclaimed.

"Would that it still were," Serafina agreed. "None of this would have happened, but for Nemeth's theft."

"Can you pull loose, Romini?" Loisan called.

"It's sticky mud, sir, but it doesn't seem to be catching fire. I'm trying to dig out Burry's hooves."

"We'll get to you somehow, lad." He cast about him. "We're all trapped if it comes to that, until the fire goes out. We can't haul water up from the gorge to extinguish that blaze. It's too steep."

"Oh, that I can mend," Serafina said. She held up her open hand, then snapped it closed. "*Ano crettech tal!*"

The roar ceased as suddenly as closing a door. The flames sank like a mountebank falling through a trapdoor onstage, and vanished, leaving a simmering hot, shiny, black ribbon of road. Magpie had to wiggle a finger in his ear to make sure he had not gone deaf. It really had gone silent. He wiped his hot face.

No fool, Loisan had backed away from the altered portion of the trail with his torch, for fear of setting it afire again. They did not need it to see the knight, Romini, thirty or forty feet away from them, because he was lit by his own rune. He had a shovel in his hands. In the distance, the matter on the scoop looked like earth, until it started to ooze off in huge droplets.

"Can you do anything about that?" Loisan asked Serafina.

"I've never seen that rune before," she said after a moment's study. "It has only come about by chance, not design or nature. I hope it will not harm him."

Loisan watched the two of them, then appeared to make a decision. "Keep an eye on him, if you would, honorable. I must report to the abbess."

Serafina inclined her head. "I am grateful for your trust."

Loisan made a noise in his throat that said it was by necessity, not inclination, but he went alone, leaving them in the runelit darkness.

"What can we do?" Magpie asked.

"I wish my mother were here," Serafina said, staring at the shining black expanse of road. The sharp planes of her face were lit by runelight, a beguiling illumination. She was a pretty woman, though he had not taken the trouble to observe her before as a woman. She chewed upon a thumbnail. "I must think. Why would that woman not give us time to think?"

"She's impatient," Magpie said cheerfully, trying to lighten her mood. "She always has been. Haste runs in the family, I am sorry to say, for I otherwise love them with my entire heart, but Sharhava is an extreme example. Having secured her prize, I fear she saw nothing but success and long years of interfering in other people's affairs ahead."

"You should not be so disrespectful," the young man's voice broke in. Magpie looked up to see the knight leaning upon his shovel. The man's light-colored habit was marked with black stains, but his horse stood free upon the verge, cropping grass. "The lady Sharhava is honored among us. You should not speak of her for your amusement."

"I beg your pardon," Magpie said, sweeping him a bow. "I can't help myself. It's my nature. You scholar-knights believe in nature."

"As the superior species of Alada, it behooves us to cultivate courtesy to all," Romini said sternly.

"Well, he's told *you*," Serafina said, a little smile breaking the concentrated scowl.

Magpie would have been content to play the mountebank as long as possible to help lift Serafina's sorrow. She had taken over the leadership of the seekers without a moment to breathe, taking the responsibility placed upon her mother by Olen and the council onto her own slim shoulders. Kings and generals might have done worse than this young woman. Practical measures would be of more service than jokes at the moment. He looked up at the ridge, just visible against the star-flecked sky.

"I have lost most of my landmarks, but I think that there is a pleasant clearing not far away where we can rest for the night," Magpie said. "My brothers and friends often stopped here if our horses were too tired to make it all the way to the ruins. Hark, Romini, did you find a branching trail before you were mired?"

"No time, highness," the youth said.

"I will take a look. I shouldn't be long."

Magpie pulled himself up the bank with the help of a few handy saplings, and forced himself through the undergrowth. There was no point in trying to make sense of the runes. The very preponderance of the glowing golden sigils overwhelmed his brain, as though hundreds of people were shouting at him at once. Instead, he sought a void, a place where there were no runes, or just a few.

Only a few arm's lengths from the main trail, the trees thinned out so that he could walk easily. With his hands out, he sought a path wide enough for horses to pass.

*H*ow can the book cause a fire?" Sharhava asked. She glared at Tildi as though she were to blame.

"The wizard claims that its passage caused changes in the roadway. All it required was a spark, which Romini's torch provided," Loisan explained.

Sharhava digested the notion. "What a gift we have been given," she said, her eyes gleaming. "No foe could withstand us if we can change the substance of reality to thwart them. This invisible enemy that they say follows us will be vulnerable, he and all his minions!"

"Abbess, think what you are saying," Captain Teryn said. "Honorable men and women have died in great pain because of the misuse of the power. Look what happened to my colleague."

Morag cast his eyes down, not liking the gazes of the knights suddenly turned his way.

"And to Eremi," Inbecca added.

"We would only use it for the good of all," Sharhava said, waving away their protests.

Tildi was horrified. "I won't let you misuse the book!"

Sharhava turned a benevolent face upon her. "You cannot stop me. Enough discussion. We must find a way to continue. I wish to make camp as soon as possible."

Magpie came out of the darkness at a run.

"I have found another trail that runs more or less parallel to this one. It's very narrow. I am concerned about one part of the passage about fifty yards from here where it passes between the halves of a giant boulder that was split into two when it fell from the mountaintops ages ago. The space between them may or may not be wide enough for the horses, but that is the only impediment. The path is dry and solid thereafter. There is no other way, unless we backtrack all the way to the castle and divert to the west side of the river."

"No," Sharhava said. "I do not wish to encounter your father's forces coming northward."

"Forces?" Magpie inquired with a raised eyebrow. "What forces?"

"He and the king of Rabantae are aware of our quest. They may wish to take the book into their keeping. I claim the honor of escort for the Scholardom!"

Magpie shook his head. "My father doesn't believe in the book. As for King Halcot, his wish would be the same as mine, to take it and hide it away again!"

"That must not be allowed to occur, either, not now. We will continue. Lead us back. Loisan, you and Auric keep the Great Book to the rear of the party. If there are any more unmakings, let them be behind us."

"Yes, Abbess," the older knight said.

The stars were invisible among the branches, but Tildi could still discern them. "I am worried about you, little one," the princess of the Windmanes said over her shoulder. "You are withdrawing farther and farther from us every moment."

"I'm not!" Tildi protested.

"You are," Rin said. "I've spoken to you often, and you scarcely reply to me. I am afraid you are falling into the spell of the book."

Tildi took a deep breath as though she were surfacing from a pond. It did take an effort to bring her whole attention away from the leaf she was studying. She gave Rin an apologetic smile.

"It's just that it is so new and interesting. It is teaching me as we go. I will get used to it in time, I am certain."

"Keep your wits, then, so you can keep your head," Rin told her. "This is a tricky place. I would have been much happier if we had stopped before the sun set."

Tildi held on to Rin's mane with her free hand. How odd it was to know what kind of trees and shrubs were around her, and what birds roosted on the branches (though somewhat disturbed by the noisy passage of the riders) without being able to see them. She could *read* them, though true comprehension of all the details would take years, and that made her more aware of how many different things and beings were all around her all of the time. The sigils were repeated in the parchment under her hands. How clever the Makers of the book had been, to document every single thing in existence, and set it all down on paper. It was an undertaking she could never have conceived, comparable to naming every grain that her brothers might have harvested in their fields, and every other field in the Quarters.

Every grain is listed herein, a voice whispered to her. *See them, count them . . .*

No, Tildi said to herself, shaking her head firmly. *Not now, please.* She pulled her head up, concentrating on the living runes moving around her.

"Branch!" Rin called. Tildi bent over the book just in time as the bough came swinging her way. It swished overhead. They were past it before it swung back to its original position. She smelled the crisp scent of tree sap, moss, and the stony soil underfoot, and saw the floating names of each.

"Halt!" a man's voice called from up ahead.

Tildi peered at the bobbing runes that represented the riders. She had begun to recognize some of the runes. That sensible older man was beside her, holding the tether around her waist. He was her only guard at the moment. Magpie had been correct that the path offered little room. Tildi bobbed and lurched on Rin's back as the centaur sought the most secure footing.

"*Hiyin!*" Rin declared. "I have to step over a large stone here. I have just knocked my right knee into it. Be careful, all of you."

"The boy was right," a man's voice called from the front. "My horse won't fit in between these rocks, perhaps not even if I strip off her tack and lead her through."

"Can we push them apart?" Sharhava asked.

A pause, while two of the knight-sigils moved. Tildi could still see them beyond the symbol of the rock and creepers. It was as if all were made of black glass overlaid with fine silver etching. All that prevented her from seeing directly into the mountainside beyond was the preponderance of tiny symbols, each indicating a pebble, a plant, a leaf, a small creature, that carpeted the land with silver-gilt. The knight-symbols returned.

"No, my lady," a woman's voice replied. "The half on the left is braced against the mountainside. The second seems pretty well anchored. This stone has been here a long time. Vines are growing up the outer sides. I am slim, but can just barely squeeze around the edge. The cleft is clean, but narrow."

"We ought to be able to use our newfound gift to make way," the abbess said thoughtfully. "Mistress Serafina, how may we change this boulder's state? Can we render it into gravel?"

"It could be done," Serafina replied, studying the towering rune, an echo of the invisible ridge to their left. "I would require time to study the character of this rock, whether it serves a deeper purpose seated here . . ."

"Your talk is meaningless!" Sharhava interrupted her. "This is but a rock, a piece of stone, a lump of the solid earth, and it is in our way! Move it or dissolve it into dust, now!"

Serafina drew herself upward. "You do not understand magic, madam. Everything has its place in nature."

"But everything about it is written upon it," Loisan said. "Does that not tell you what you need to know?"

"That is but the thing itself," Serafina explained patiently. "It may anchor something below it. It might be the home of a being whose nature I cannot guess. I would rather not interfere than to destroy something that has purpose."

"This is why I have no patience with wizards," Sharhava exploded. "You mull over meaningless facts, and in the end you do nothing."

"They are not meaningless! You purposely misunderstand me."

"I . . . will move it, Abbess," a strained voice said.

Tildi felt the shorn hair at the nape of her neck stand up. She turned toward the knight who had spoken. He moved into the firelight and cast back his hood. It was the boy she had been watching most of the afternoon. His face was much the same as it had been, but the body had grown grotesque. His chest had swelled outward until it was twice as wide, with muscles like tree roots bulging from his collar. His arms jutted out, suspended from shoulders like a yoke of oxen, bursting free of his sleeves and the side of his surcoat. His unnaturally long legs fairly straddled his horse. The rune on his chest, stretched out and thickened compared with before, seemed to twist and heave against itself. Its natural shimmering hue was suffused with red and a hint of purple-blue.

"What have you done to yourself?" Tildi managed to choke out. Serafina looked as horrified as she felt. Rin let out a whinny of surprise.

"Do not chide me, unnatural creature!" the boy said, gritting to get the words out of his massive jaw. "I do not answer to you, only to the gods and the Scholardom."

"But *why?*" Tildi pleaded.

"I . . . serve my order," Bertin said simply. He raised his head, and the cords on his neck stood out. "I can move the stone, Abbess. It would be my privilege."

Sharhava's eyes gleamed.

"Lar Bertin, you may proceed."

He stepped backward over the horse's rump. Bertin handed off the reins to another knight. Unable to recognize its master, the animal danced in its panic as the huge hand passed its eyes. The other knights fell back silently, making way for him. Tildi saw the look of awe on their faces.

Morag, a few rows ahead of her, had dropped his eyes, unable to look at the misshapen figure. Tildi knew seeing Bertin so altered had to bring back terrible memories to the soldier. *She* could not look away. She was transfixed.

The other knights moved backward, making way. The two nearest the stone held up torches in both hands to give Bertin the most light. He hulked forward into the cleft. Tildi watched his rune flickering and changing color with each step. A human being was never meant to look that way.

He stepped in between the rock halves, braced his feet in the gap, and pressed his hands to either side. With an enormous effort, he began to push. A guttural noise escaped his throat as he put all his strength into the task. The halved rock could not possibly move, but unbelievably, it did begin to move. At first the delicate ferns growing on the top of the valley side of the stone began to tremble. Tildi stared, unsure whether she was imagining the shift, it was so slow, no more than the breadth of a wisp of grass at a time. The top of the boulder crept away from its twin.

"Aaah!" The young knight let out a gasp. His younger fellows leaped into the gap to help push. One of them pressed his back against the hillside rock and his feet against the other. Teryn and Morag sprang forward to assist. Sharhava did not call them back. Fraction by fraction, the gigantic boulder moved. A grumbling hiss erupted from underneath as the roots of centuries were torn asunder. The stone tilted back slightly, and the men and women behind it cried out in alarm, but they managed to push it outward again. Gradually, a little at a time, they got it to rock back and forth in its steadily widening socket.

"It's tipping!" Lakanta called out. "Beware! There it is—it's going!"

The youth threw himself against it with all his strength. The boulder heeled over, then crashed to earth on its side. The ground shook under its weight. Tildi heard the terrified squawking and footsteps of small animals fleeing from the disturbance.

A force of nature released, the stone began inexorably to roll downhill. It crushed the narrow saplings growing up beside it, which lurched over onto bigger trees and thicker growth. The stone ground them all into the dirt. The other knights retreated away from the spray of broken branches and scattered stones that it kicked up. The stone rumbled away, disappearing out of the torchlight, until its rune was lost among the myriad below. Tildi and the others listened to the crashing and thumping, until at last it came to rest and fell silent. She looked back up at the space where it had stood for so many centuries. It was clear of runes, except for flying motes of dirt. The way was open.

"Well done, Lar Bertin!" Sharhava shouted. "Honors to Lar Bertin!"

The others let out a rousing cheer. "Hail, Bertin! Hail, Bertin!"

The red face running with sweat that sat atop the hulking figure was still boyish, in a grotesque way. Its mouth stretched in a grin as he acknowledged the praise of his fellows. Then, almost exactly as the stone he had just moved had done, Bertin tilted gently over and fell onto his side.

The ground shook, not as deeply as it had under the stone, but enough to be felt. The knights rushed to Bertin's aid.

"Help him sit up!" a female knight ordered. "Help him breathe!"

"Let me pass!" Serafina cried, pushing through the crowd.

They made way for her. She put her staff on the ground and sat beside the stricken man. She tried to raise his head, but he was too heavy for her.

"Aid me," she appealed to the two men nearest her. They hoisted Bertin's enormous shoulder and supported his head. Serafina touched the big vein at the side of his neck, looked into his eyes, and felt his wrist. She shook her head and reached for her staff.

"What are you doing?" Loisan asked.

"I am trying to save his life!" Serafina said. "His body was never meant to be stretched this way. I must try and stop the vital forces from draining out of him." The jewel on top of the staff glowed pale green as she swept it over the distorted body beside her. The green light suffused Bertin's form and faded. She shook her head.

Mindful of Serafina's strictures against doing her own magic, Tildi very carefully hardened the air beside Rin and stepped down from the centaur's back, the book clutched to her chest. The rope around her waist tightened, making her fall back a pace. She glared back at Auric. Startled, he dismounted and fell into step beside her, careful not to pull on her tether. She knelt down beside Serafina. Auric squatted beside them. He put a hand on the boy's chest.

"Can I do anything to help?" Tildi asked.

Again, Serafina drew the gleaming staff up and down the young man's straining body. She had her lower lip caught between her teeth. The rune on Bertin's chest wavered, then snapped back into its deformed shape. "I fear there is nothing any of us can do," she said. "He is dying."

"No!" Sharhava said, looming beside them like a storm cloud. She fixed her gaze upon the wizardess as if by will alone she could change her words. "Help him."

Serafina bent over the young man, now gasping for every breath.

"Can you change back to your ordinary state?" she asked Bertin. "You made alterations, but I do not know what they are. Can you describe what you changed? Tildi might be able to restore your rune if you can tell us what you did."

"Did you write it down?" Tildi asked eagerly. The boy's lips puffed in and out, each breath an agony to him. He turned his bulging eyes toward the smallfolk.

"No . . . I . . . I thought . . . I would remember."

"Do you?" Tildi pleaded.

"No," Bertin gasped. "I can't . . . the rune was too complex. I only changed a little of it. I wanted to be strong!"

"You were, lad, you were," Auric assured him.

"You are the healer," Sharhava said, turning to Serafina. "Restore him."

Serafina rounded upon her, her temper spent at last. "I *cannot*. I can't begin to undo the damage his body is doing to itself. He exceeded the strength of his tissues by expanding them, and they are failing. Everything is failing, and he never troubled to sketch his rune so he could be put right again. I *warned* you. I warned *him*. Why will none of you listen to me?"

"Recriminations are pointless," the abbess said impassively. "Our ways are not your ways. What can you do?"

Serafina shook her head. "I can make him comfortable, that is all."

"How long?"

"Not long." Her tone this time was final.

Sharhava nodded. She knelt beside Bertin and touched his breast with her bandaged hand.

"You honor us, Lar Bertin," the abbess said. "What you did was an example to us all. You have proved we have no limits in what we may achieve. No living man has ever done what you have done."

The boy's eyes fixed upon her face hungrily, absorbing the words as though they were food and wine.

"I did it gladly for the Scholardom, Abbess," he whispered. "Pray to the gods for me."

"I shall." Sharhava clutched the symbol that hung around her neck. "We accept your brave sacrifice. Sleep well, Bertin. Your name will be remembered."

Bertin struggled a little while longer. His hands trembled as he tried to help himself up, but he fell back against his fellows' arms again and again. Tildi found it painful to watch. She pitied him, even though she knew he had done the damage to himself. Each breath grew more and more shallow. Bertin's face reddened as he struggled to draw in air. At last, his tortured body could do no more. He let out a pained gasp, and his eyes widened and fixed upon Sharhava's face. Lar Bertin lay still.

The abbess closed his eyes with her hand and rose. She addressed the rest of the knights, all of whom stood slack with shock. "Our brother has led the way in scholarship. Let us follow in his studies, and learn from both his success and his failure. His memory will be a beacon to us."

*I*n the shadow of the remaining half of the boulder, they buried the youth and pulled a cairn of stones over the grave. Tildi and her friends were not permitted to come close. The rites, Auric explained kindly, were private.

"I do not need to observe them," Rin said diffidently. "Tildi, do you need me?"

"I am all right," Tildi said. The sorrow she should have known still felt removed from her, as if it were on the other side of a thick wall. "I think Serafina needs us." She looked around. "Where is she?"

They all looked around, but the wizard was nowhere in sight. Tildi could not even discern her rune in the immediate vicinity.

Captain Teryn nodded toward the north, where the trees were thickest. "I saw her walk that way during the burial."

"She's gone off to be alone for a moment," Lakanta said. "Heaven knows we could all use a moment's privacy, if you ask me."

A soft chanting arose from the knights across the way. Tildi saw sorrow written upon them, but thought she could also detect hope.

Serafina returned to them after the knights had finished their grim task. Without a word, she mounted her white mare and fell in beside Rin and Tildi.

The path widened out upon Magpie's promised clearing within a hundred yards of the divided boulder. It was by then full dark, with enormous stars glimmering in the sky overhead. Sharhava called a halt. The knights immediately unsaddled their horses and gave them a rubdown. Once the animals had been given a long rein to forage for grass, the humans set about making camp. Tents were unrolled and erected, and rugs laid out inside for

a modicum of comfort on the cold, thin grass. A woman just older than Lar
Inbecca assembled a pyramid of logs and tinder inside a circle of rough
stones for a bonfire. She struck flint against steel, trying to generate a spark,
but the stones kept jumping out of her hands. Tildi suspected the cold of
the night had chilled them past feeling.

"I can light that for you," Tildi offered.

The knight gave her an eye-rolling look of dread. Tildi withdrew, feeling
stung. She sat on the cloth with the book in her arms for comfort.

"She does not understand," the Great Book whispered to her. "She cannot see reality."

It took the woman several tries to ignite the tinder with her flint and steel,
but she stuck at the task until she was rewarded with a spark. Perversely,
Tildi hoped it would go out. Soon a small blaze caught, and spread from one
to another of the dry logs until a fragrant and crackling fire filled the circle
of stones. Through the heat generated by the book, Tildi felt the edge of
the warmth as it spread throughout the clearing but she did not need it. She
watched the others relax as the cold was driven back. Their runes changed a
little, as did those of the plants around them. Everything flourished when it
was warm.

Three of the knights—Loisan, a stout, swarthy man, and a rangy woman
with very thin limbs and long fingers—appeared to be some kind of lieutenants to Sharhava, each responsible for a different part of the camp. The
rangy woman oversaw care of the horses and pack animals and their tack.
The stout man ordered his subordinates to unload heavy bundles from the
pack animals. By the shape of them, they contained cooking pots. Tildi also
saw food within the coverings of other pouches and skins. Idly, she imagined
what a convenient skill she now possessed, never again to have to look inside a canister or a crock to see how much of an ingredient remained. How
long, though, would it be until she was in a kitchen all her own once again,
with people to feed?

Loisan seemed to be in charge of securing the grounds. He wove in and
out of the trees at the edge of the oval clearing, his eyes moving all the time.
When two of the younger scholars had finished caring for their mounts, he
tapped them to begin a circuit of the encampment. They drew swords and
set off in opposite directions. Tildi was amused to see that they crossed in
exactly the same two places at the top and bottom of the circuit each time.
She wondered how long it had taken them to learn how to do that.

"They are completely mad," Lakanta said aloud, not caring if she was audible. A pair of guards had spread out a fine woolen rug of complex pattern
and vivid color for Tildi and the Great Book to rest upon. The cloth that had
been draped over Rin's back was folded up again in the ancient leather
pouch, no doubt awaiting the morning's departure. The guards stood over

Tildi, one of them holding on to her waist tether, but neither of them attempted to touch the scroll. They paid no attention to her companions, who made themselves comfortable on their own blankets and ground cloths around her. The other knights had withdrawn to the far side of the fire to cook their evening meal. "All this trouble, and they still don't know what they are doing."

"Do not underestimate them," Teryn said very quietly from her place beside Morag. "The Scholardom's reputation for competence is deep. They are prized as officers in every nation's army."

"Not in *mine*."

Teryn smiled a trifle. "I beg your pardon, Mistress Lakanta. In every *human* nation. I fought with them and against them in the war, five years ago. The general who commanded me was of their number."

"Is he here?" Lakanta asked, looking about. "Why will he not help us?"

"He died," Teryn said. "And he would not help us, even if he had lived. He was sincerely devoted to his cause, as these are. Never doubt that we are among enemies. I am sworn to defend you, Mistress Tildi."

"Not me," Tildi said. "The book, of course."

Teryn shook her head, her face grave. "My king charged me with your care, as did Mistress Edynn. It is your task to guard the book itself. You may count upon us remaining by your side, no matter what comes."

Tildi looked hopefully at the knights' version of journey rations. The contents of the pot that one of the men stirred over the fire smelled so good. She could not bring herself to protest. Damaged as he was, Morag had so few things in which he could take pride. Cooking, alas, was not one of them, but he was jealous of his task and allowed no one to help or supplant him. Even the outspoken Lakanta was too kind to comment upon the guard's ineptitude.

Morag kept his head bowed while he unloaded the much-mended pots and pans from their packhorse. He brought his cooking gear downwind and began to chop root vegetables, one of many gifts left for them by the dwarves whose halls they had traversed on the way to Orontae Castle.

"Those look like Rabantavian military gear. Served in the war, did he?" Auric asked, watching Morag's laborious gait.

"That is correct," Teryn said, glancing at Auric warily.

"Ah," Auric said. "I'm an old soldier myself." He raised his voice to call to Morag. "Brother, let me fetch water for you. Rachine said that there's a bit of a waterfall close by. It's on the steep side from here."

Morag nodded without looking up. The older knight took the heavy pot. He dropped the rope by Tildi's side.

"I'm trusting you, girl," he said to her. "Don't make me sorry."

Tildi nodded. She felt so forlorn at Bertin's death that she could hardly move.

"We must get away from these people," Lakanta said, unsaddling Melune with emphatic motions. The stout pony spat out its bit and began cropping at the thin grass. Lakanta poured oats into a nosebag and hooked it over Melune's muzzle. She looked up at the remaining sentry, a knight in her fifties with deep brown skin and dark, slanting eyes. "Why don't you go off and help your friend, eh? We won't be here by the time you get back."

The knight paid her no attention. Instead, she watched Morag with sympathy. Tildi was rather touched by their regard for his service as a soldier, though to be able to smell the knights' meal without being able to taste it was like hearing about a beautiful sunrise while one stood with one's face to the wall.

Teryn brought a bowl of food to her. Her eyes, edged by wrinkles drawn by time and care, made no apologies for the half-burned stew or the flat, half-burned, half-raw journey-bread, and expected none.

At least it was hot, Tildi reasoned to herself, finding her spoon and cup in the top of her rucksack. The homey carry-all was another reminder of her lost brothers. She found it comforting, as though they were with her. At the bottom of the bag she had hidden mementos of each one. Not for a moment did she think of bringing them out, not in the hostile company. It was bad enough she had to be there herself. Whatever construction the abbess put upon it, the knights blamed *her* for the death of their fellow.

"It will not be forever," Rin whispered, as though she could hear the smallfolk's thoughts.

Tildi nodded. The Great Book lying beside her added its whispers. The cool night breeze, warmer than it had been in the heights of the castle, whisked around the edges of the rug on which she sat, ruffled the edges of the fire. Its faint rune spread out upon it like a thin silver cloak. She fancied she saw more runes written on the back of the breeze, with interrogative strokes overlaid. Master Olen had taught her how to read those diagonal lines in some of the ancient texts. They were always meant to outline a question. Could a wind be curious? It played about her, then, to her relief, died down. She ate her swiftly cooling stew and mopped out the bowl with the chunk of scorched bread.

Lakanta vanished from the fireside and returned shortly with an earthenware jug full of water. She poured Tildi's cup full, then Rin's skin bottle.

"Drink up. There's plenty where that came from. Good water in these parts," she said to Magpie, who sat a quarter of the way around the fire on a stone.

"Thank you," he said gravely. "I made sure there were plenty of waterfalls along the way so we will have enough to drink."

"A good host. A pity you aren't the heir to the kingdom."

"It's too much responsibility for one such as I," Magpie replied. "I am far happier as I am, but thank you."

"Lar Vinim and Lar Mey, you are on first watch," Loisan said, appearing out of the darkness. Some of the others jumped, but not Tildi. She had seen his rune approaching. "Inbecca and Robi, second watch. Follet and Ecris, third. Lar Brouse, what do you need to prepare breakfast?"

The stout man looked up from the spit he was turning. "More water. A few more rabbits would help eke out the meal."

"I'll get them myself about dawn," Loisan said. "They're abed now. As the rest of you should be. We ride to the southwest tomorrow. My reckoning is three days' ride there, then three days more westward to the Scriptorium."

"Lar Loisan," Inbecca said. "The best path to the Scriptorium in Orontae is across the Arown and toward the southern mountain pass, just south of the capital. We could likely arrive in four days."

"We are not going directly there, Lar Inbecca," Sharhava said, stepping into the firelight. The cook's assistant set up a small table and chair and waved the abbess to be seated. The stout cook himself brought her her supper in a fine bowl with polished utensils and a gleaming white napkin. "I have another mission I wish to undertake before we settle into our studies."

"What mission is that?"

"You will find out in time, Lar Inbecca," the abbess said sternly. "You must learn not to question my orders. We have rules. You will read the first section tonight before you sleep, and you will not be late for the second watch. Mey," she said, looking at the tall, thin man who sat cross-legged on the ground with his bowl on his knees just out of the circle of the fire, "if she does not appear on time you will report to me at once."

"Yes, Abbess," he said, swallowing hastily.

"Aunt!" Inbecca protested.

"You will address me by my title, Lar Inbecca," Sharhava said. The girl's cheeks reddened, and not just from the heat of the bonfire. She opened her mouth to protest. Sharhava held up her bandaged hand imperiously. "No, you may not speak again. I will not hear you. Knights, when you have finished your meal, clean up, see to your horses, then take your rest. I wish to be on the way tomorrow before the sun touches the treetops."

"Yes, Abbess!" the others chorused.

Inbecca shot one embarrassed look at Magpie before leaving the fireside.

How could my own aunt humiliate me in front of the others? Inbecca thought furiously as she upended her saddlebag. The borrowed mare she rode only shifted when she had unfastened the pannier, but Tessera, Eremi's mare, scenting an old friend, let out a nicker of welcome. Inbecca smiled wryly and gave the piebald a quick stroke.

"You'd never do that," she said. The horse murmured into the girl's palm. Inbecca went back to her search.

The contents of the pannier, hastily packed, were largely items that she had borrowed from the other knights in Orontae. She longed for her fur cloak and her soft riding breeches, left behind in the guest chambers allotted to her in the castle. She had not expected to go on an extended cross-country chase lasting days and end up fighting stone giants in a downpour of colored rain. Nor had she conceived that she would wind up riding in a half-destroyed wilderness for days, sleeping on the cold ground and living on journey-rations, responding to barked orders and battling with unnatural monsters summoned up from paving stones. Whatever her mental picture had been of an intellectual escape by joining the Scholardom, this was worlds away.

How different things would be if she was at home in Levrenn. Inbecca thought of how she would be bathed and dressed for the day at home, by how many women. More would attire her for dinner in a fine gown prepared with care by seamstresses. Foot servants would have been waiting to open the doors for her, and pages scurried eagerly to escort her and do her bidding. If she needed an item she had left in her pannier, the grooms would express it their pleasure to retrieve it for her. Now she took care of her own horse's tack. She was too short to boost the heavy war saddle on without help, but she did the rest. Always, if she could not turn a stone out of a horse's frog there had been a groom to help. Now, she could have aid only if she asked. All the other knights were self-sufficient. She was most impressed with them. Sharhava's three favorite acolytes, who at court seemed like simpering fools, were as at home in the saddle and sleeping on stones as they were sitting at a reading table. They accepted without comment when it was their turn to scrub out the cooking vessels with sand or to mount sentry during the night. Inbecca had had to change her opinion of a lot of people. It was not too late for her to learn the value of others. She hoped such a revelation was to be within her aunt's lifetime.

She shook out the second habit, her only other suit of clothes. From it fell three sets of smallclothes, thick woolen stockings, a comb and a towel, plus two tightly wound scrolls. The one with blue-painted spindles was the object of her search, and her punishment. She had read the Scholar's Guide twice as a child, at Sharhava's urging, and a few times as an adult. Those last were when she had doubted her commitment as her mother's heir to the throne of Levrenn, as she now doubted her devotion to the Scholardom. Was she never to feel she really belonged anywhere in the wide world?

If she was to examine her wind-tossed emotions for more than a moment, she knew perfectly well when she had lost the rudder that steered her life. She had wanted to marry Eremilandur, third prince of Orontae, ever since they were children together. She wanted him more than anybody else or anything else in the entire world. As consort he would have lightened the burden of her future reign immeasurably with his sense of humor and his innate kindness. But having broken his betrothal vows in such a public fashion left her, she felt, with no choice but to withdraw. He did not want her, or so it appeared when he vanished from their engagement feast. It seemed that he had run off on a foolish chase, giving details to no one. In a fit of pique—she admitted it now—she had given her vow to her aunt, who had long sought to enlist her in the Scholardom. She, Inbecca, had sworn fealty to Sharhava right in front of her parents, Eremi's parents, and all of the royal families of the three noble kingdoms and the lesser realms, including King Halcot of Rabantae.

Of course, now she knew Eremi had had good reason—he was keeping a promise he had made to the wizard Olen. From what she had seen in the tower of the old castle, he probably *had* saved the world from destruction, by distracting Nemeth until Mistress Serafina and the others could take the Great Book away from him. How horrible it would have been if Eremi had ignored the signs. His big brother Ganidur had told the puzzled crowd at the feast that Eremi had seen the mountains moving. The only ones who really believed him were King Halcot and the knights. Inbecca was ashamed to admit that she had not. She had followed her aunt Sharhava to give Eremi a well-deserved piece of her mind, then nearly saw him die before her eyes. She still loved him with all her heart. The reasons that she had given her vow to the Scholardom were all wrong, but she *had* given it.

How could she possibly back away from her promise now?

She was not certain that she should. To what would she be returning? To public shame? To her mind Eremi had not apologized adequately for having run away from their joining ceremony. It was an affront to her, to the gods, to everything. She was a princess of Levrenn. She deserved better! Eremi had always been so careful of her dignity. Since they had learned what it really meant, he had shown respect for her rank and the difference between them, though it had not interfered with their friendship and the love that had grown between them. Inbecca felt forlorn. She was not accustomed to the sensation, and she didn't like it. Nor did she like being put in second place to any cause, however just. She drummed her fingers on the saddlebag, then snatched away her hand. Her father had always chided her about showing impatience. It did not suit the habits of a queen. She frowned. It would seem that she was no sooner to be a wife than a monarch. Eremi had to explain himself, then make amends in public, and in a serious fashion.

The two of them would have to have it out, but not yet. She was not ready to face him. It was painful even to ride beside him, having seen what she had seen, yet her pride smarted. He had disappeared many times in the last few years, without explanation or apology. He could do it again. Could she accept that her consort kept such secrets from her? She had forgiven him over and over again. Would this be one time too many?

What should I do? she wondered, clutching the small scroll in her hand. Where did her genuine loyalties lie? Would the gods condemn her for breaking one vow after another? Was she to blame for what happened? Should she have stayed in Orontae with all the guests in spite of the humiliation? It was her pride that drove her to kneel to her aunt. But she doubted her commitment to the cause. The Great Book was her aunt's passion, not hers. Though Inbecca believed in the sanctity of life, she had to make allowances for change. Was no one ever to breed a better hen or a faster horse, for fear of going against the plans of the Mother? Was no one to attempt to live longer and thwart the Father's creation of history? Yet, with a single promise, she had made the book her responsibility as well. It was an astonishing, amazing thing, too much for her to encompass in such a short time.

Rereading the Rules might help settle her mind, at least for the moment. Inbecca bundled the rest of her goods back into the saddlebag and went back to the firelight.

*T*he knights, all but the sentries and Tildi's guards, had gathered in a double circle around one of their number, a tall man with an austere, bony face. He opened a book and began to read from it in a low voice. The others murmured in unison at intervals. Magpie tried to read the title he could just see embossed in gold on the leather cover, but it was obscured by the silvery rune. That said *book.* He knew that symbol, at least. Nothing extraordinary there. Inexorably, his eye was drawn back to the one book within his vision that was extraordinary, down to the name it wore. The enormous scroll, set on the outspread blanket on the ground, shimmered with the rune *book*, but that pictogram was as ornate and intricate as a piece of lace that one of his mother's ladies might create. More so, probably.

Its protector was the most unlikely person possible, a smallfolk. Amused, he watched her trying to bed down in some semblance of privacy. The girl had dignity befitting a queen. If he didn't know smallfolk, he would have assumed she was a titled lady with a large estate and many servants. Probably she came from a tiny cottage, the only child of elderly parents who had passed away, leaving her adrift in their unforgiving society. In his fancy she had grown up surrounded by books and tutors, gravitating toward magic as the best outlet for her intelligence, curiosity, and undeniable courage. Lakanta would know the girl's story, Magpie thought, glancing at the dwarf woman, who was bustling around making herself comfortable. He hesitated to ask, since the girl's real history could not be as luxurious or as sheltered as he might have wished her to have had.

We put such importance on our little doings, he thought wryly. *None of it matters at all to the stars or the trees. Unless the Shining Ones meddled with them, too.*

He had to believe now that he saw what Tildi saw. The runes were an unmistakable sign he couldn't ignore. He felt a song starting to write itself. He felt deep pity for the young knight. What was his name, Bertin? He must get it right. If he was allowed to sing of these deeds, and he was by no means sure that he would ever do, the names of those who had sacrificed to restore the book to its hidden niche deserved to be remembered. In his heart he knew that it would be restored, no matter what the Scholardom thought. They wouldn't have things their own way forever.

Glints at the edge of his vision caught his attention: the eyes of someone looking at him. He didn't have to turn his head all the way to know it was Inbecca. He smiled at her. It gave him a warm feeling to know she was nearby.

She sat down about a quarter of the way around the big campfire, warily, as though she were a half-broken colt. The expression on her face was far from welcoming. Magpie dropped his head, ashamed.

I deserve that, he thought. *She has been through a great deal, and it is all my fault.*

But Inbecca's attention was not long claimed by him. When he looked up, she was studying Tildi. The smallfolk girl had settled herself, and was scrolling through the enormous parchment roll as though it were a bedtime book. She stopped now and again to admire a golden rune that seemed to glow with its own internal illumination in the twilight. Every so often, she would smile with wonder. After a time, she appeared to bid the book good night, rolled it up, and settled down to sleep with one hand on it.

"She is amazing," Inbecca said, surprising Magpie by speaking. "The book favors her."

"I am sorry about Bertin," Magpie said.

"I didn't know him," Inbecca said, not looking at him. "I admit, I scarcely paid attention to my aunt's attendants. They all seemed so interchangeable." She paused, then shook her head vehemently. "Silly boy! He died because he believed nothing bad could happen to him. I think we were all shocked. They wouldn't listen. But I am the only one who saw what happened to you. I know, and even I can't believe it. I told them, and they said I was blaspheming."

"They probably thought I had lured you up there as a joke. It's a shame that they arrived too late to see the whole matter unfold. Though it was not the greatest example of my diplomacy."

"Don't joke about it," she said severely. "You don't know what you looked like. Are you all right?"

"I am well," he assured her, rejoicing inwardly at her concern. "Tildi's handiwork undid not only the effects of Nemeth's spell, but all the months in between as well."

"All of it?" Inbecca asked, looking up at him through her eyelashes. He thought he detected a bit of impishness.

Could she be forgiving him?

"Only the physical effects," he said. "My thoughts are the same. My feelings are the same."

"Mine aren't," she said, her voice thickening. She sat up straighter and seemed to inhabit the blue-and-white costume more thoroughly. "The world has changed, Eremi. All at once, in a night. We rode out so fast that I haven't had time to think. But today, in the aftermath, I . . . it's hard to have you near me. If you only knew how angry I felt, sitting there in your father's court without you!"

He took her hand. She started to pull it away, then let it lie limply in his palm. He put his entire heart into his words, willing her to understand.

"You can see now why I had to go. I am sorry—a lifetime will not suffice to make it up to you, but that is all we have. Please, forgive me."

The hand tensed a little. She did not look up at him.

"Eremi, I don't know if I can."

The rustle of leaves attracted their attention. Magpie looked up to see the girl wizard, Serafina, shuffle into the firelight. Her usual self-possession had been replaced by distraction. Her cloak and her long black hair was disheveled, the jeweled pins that usually held the tresses hanging loose, and a tendril of leaves clung just above her ear. Without seeing them, she walked between them and the fire and settled with a thump on a large stone nearest the spot where Tildi and her guards sat. She stared into the flames, not seeming to see anything.

"Are you all right, honorable?" Magpie asked gently.

"Of course not!" she snapped, then tightened her lips. Tears formed in her large dark eyes. "I apologize, Your Highness. It has been a most . . . eventful day."

Letting go of Inbecca's hand, he rose and knelt beside Serafina. He took both her hands in his. He fixed his eyes on hers. "I doubt any of the Scholardom will have thought to say it to you, but we respect and honor the sacrifice your mother made to save all our lives. I will never let her name be forgotten. I'm composing a song about her. I hope you will allow me to play it for you when it is finished."

"She would have liked that." The tears spilled down the girl's golden cheeks. She suddenly looked very young. She wet her lips with her tongue tip and shook her head. "All these years I have known that I must lose her. I braced myself against the day. And now that it has happened, I don't know what to do. I was never ready. I am not ready now. Yet I must assume her responsibilities."

She was not asking for help, only for understanding. Magpie nodded.

"Tell us about Edynn. I met her first in Olen's study. I had heard of her, of course, but she retired from the world before I was born."

"She chose to have her family then," Serafina said with a small smile. "She had had too much of war. She wanted to see things burgeon and grow. The lords for whom she had done service gave her a fine estate in the hills of Ivirenn. It had wonderful gardens, most of them planted by my mother. A stream flowed north through the land from a source in the Quarters, I believe. My father was a local magistrate, with no talent in the mystic arts, but a kind and loving man. I did not know him long; he died when I was a child. My brothers are much older than I. They chose not to study magic. Mother did not mind. I believed that she was glad I did. She encouraged us to follow our hearts. She was . . ." She halted, searching for words.

"She seemed wise and kind," Inbecca said. She came over to sit on Serafina's other side and put her arm over the girl's shoulders.

"More than that," Serafina said emphatically, pulling back from the ministrations. However kindly meant, she still had her dignity. "She was a great teacher. I had other masters when I began to study, but she could put a task before me that I would understand all the better for her guidance. I learned more from her than from anyone else."

"I think," Magpie said, "that I will remember the twinkle in her eyes."

Serafina looked at him solemnly. "She admired you, Prince. She kept your secret where we traveled. She said you did important work. I thought you a clown."

"Don't put too much importance into my small tasks," he said hastily, with a glance at Inbecca. "She was the one who was doing the real work of the world. I was only a messenger."

"That's not true!" Inbecca said. "If you hadn't stood up to Nemeth, who knows what he might have done! You persuaded him to stop his destruction."

"In my capacity as clown," Magpie said with a warm smile for Serafina. She seemed embarrassed to have admitted her feelings. "You were in control of the situation, much more than I could have been. If I served in any way, it was to allow you room to exercise your talents. I am sure your mother would have been very proud of you."

Serafina stared into the fire. "I hope so," she said quietly.

"Depend upon it, she was," Magpie assured her, squeezing her hands tightly. "She put you in charge. She trusted you, no one more. In that moment of crisis, it was you in whom she put her faith. When that castle door closed, I feared we would be finished, but thanks to both of you . . ."

Serafina could hold back no longer. The tears fell down her face like a rivulet streaming down a granite cliff face. She wept silently, blinking long black lashes like wet silk strands.

"Ah, now, now, now," Magpie said, reaching into his belt pouch. He brought out a linen cloth and dabbed her cheeks. It was clean. "Don't make me break into song now. Think how many people I would wake up!"

"You . . . I know you do not mean to be frivolous," Serafina said, taking the cloth and drying her face carefully. "I have not lived much in the world, I know. People make light of issues they ought to treat seriously."

"It is like the face of the sun, Mistress Serafina. We find them hard to look upon directly, so we find oblique ways to deal with them. We know we can't ignore them," Magpie assured her solemnly. "My admiration for you and your mother is as great as the sun. If I can serve in any way, you have but to ask."

Inbecca watched Magpie focus his yellow-green eyes intently upon the girl's. His gaze was full of understanding, caring, and deep sympathy. His regard was so worshipful that Inbecca felt jealousy well up from the center of her soul and overflow in a black wave. She knew she shouldn't be upset or angry. He was just being kind because she was grieving for her mother. That was all, wasn't it?

You have no claim on him any longer, her inner voice told her. *You have another calling now.*

Inbecca rose suddenly. When Magpie glanced up at her questioningly, she raised the small scroll in her hand.

"I must study," she said, and left the two of them alone by the fire.

Chapter Three

The dark-winged creatures swirled around the high ceiling of the enormous, windowless stone chamber. They were agitated and fearful, wheeling to stay out of the gaze of the angry man on the floor. Though he was small for a human, wizened and white-haired, he showed no lessening of strength as old ones usually did, making them easy, tasty prey. If anything, they were his playthings, and they feared him. They would never think of swooping down upon him and rending him into gobbets of flesh. Their instinct told them the mere taste of his blood would poison them. It didn't matter that his limbs were thin, or his spindly neck looked as if it could be snapped with a quick flick of the wing. Experience had taught them that trying to kill him resulted in death. Their death. He was like no other species they knew over the face of Alada. Their slick, green-black skin was nothing like his, furrowed as it was into myriad tiny wrinkles, like the trunk of an ancient tree. If his face had had any color at all, it had leached away long ago, leaving it the sickly hue of a mushroom that had never seen sunlight. In contrast, his irises contained every shade of the rainbow. Those eyes had a force of their own. Once pinned by the gaze, whatever he was looking at lost the will to move. To fall into that gaze was to risk death. They moved, hoping to keep ahead of it.

"How could you have missed your goal?" he demanded, following their frenzied flight with amusement and irritation. "You had the strongest possible spoor to follow, and what have you to show me? A corpse. A much abused, scorched body." He gestured at the sad heap on the floor. It stank of decay and ashes. He shook his head. "So that is my namesake Nemeth. Thanks to his gift I was able to see the world as I have not in countless years." He surveyed it and sighed. "I feel as if I have lost my only friend, even if I could only speak to him when he let his guard down. He is the only human mind I have come to know in many, many years. He kept out from my reach a very long time, and out from yours, too. I must know how. How I regret I cannot ask him."

The thraiks shrieked a protest.

"No, children, no," he said, waving a hand at them. "I know you are not to blame for his death. That responsibility lies elsewhere."

Wrinkling his nose in distaste, he pointed a finger at the body and drew a sign on the air. The corpse shrank in upon itself slightly and turned paler. The clothes crumpled together, the fabric gathering closer to the cold flesh. Knemet nodded. Now the body would last until he could study it further.

The book—where was it? Only a short time ago, Nemeth had possessed it. Somehow he had discovered its hiding place. Knemet himself had given up hope of ever finding it. It had been hedged around with spells until it was entirely invisible to divination, physical searches, or intuition. The ones who had taken it from him had done their work so well that he had wasted hundreds of years searching for it.

He set the thraiks a geas to find the Compendium. They knew its magical scent, and how it transferred to anyone or anything that touched it. They were to bring back those people and things for Knemet to examine. Yet none of their discoveries ever led to the book itself. Minor wizards had been permitted to make copies, each of which possessed a touch of the original's magic that allowed the copies to change to reflect the world around them changing. In the early years his hopes were raised falsely countless times, as the thraiks brought home pieces of scrolls and bemused scholars who were terrified to be torn away from their studies by the black-winged beasts. The book itself was nowhere to be found.

Life had become too long. It was a terrible thing for a scholar to admit, but all subjects that he had once found fascinating had palled. Every exercise of his mind or his powers felt as if he had done it before, over and over, and the result would be no different in the thousandth trial as it had in the fifth or fifteenth. In the end, he had returned to one of his private places of study and made it comfortable enough to sustain him without requiring him to venture forth for his minor needs.

The thraiks still served him. They brought him food, and news if he asked for it, which was seldom. He languished in this underground fastness, waiting for the death that would not come. Knemet felt as if he had grown dust and cobwebs inside his skull.

Then, after untold years had passed, a tickle of magic that he thought never to feel again had come to him. It was unmistakably the Compendium. It still existed! Where? Where?

He felt it. The book was in the south. Knemet was outraged. He had searched Sheatovra for years! The Compendium must have been concealed there while Knemet was weakened and almost blind to magic. Whoever had unearthed it must have been aware that the Compendium was a prize beyond all prizes, and concealed himself immediately. All the thraiks had found were traces of his passage, intermittent exercises of creative power that could only have been accomplished by one of the Makers, and Knemet was certain the bearer was not one of his old fellows, or one who possessed the book.

Knemet had sought without luck to track him. The wizard had warded himself with spells, of course, but his gift as a true-seer left his mind open to the unseen world, a tiny keyhole that Knemet had exploited, insinuating himself into Nemeth's consciousness. He could not see where Nemeth was going. When the book had been taken from him, all those years ago, he felt the same. To hunger for, not the blood, but the humiliation and abasement of others was a sensation he knew well. His friends and enemies alike were all dead. To obtain the book was his only remaining goal. To his surprise, the next time he managed to see into Nemeth's mind, he discovered that he had returned to Niombra. The book was safely in his hands. Where he went from there, Knemet did not know until he felt the book reappear in the distant north.

He had felt it the moment Nemeth's spell of concealment had been broken. For a short, glorious time, Knemet had sensed the book's beauty. He could see the rune in his mind's eye. It lay far to the north. It was surrounded by a crowd of beings, their runes too unimportant to distinguish. At the moment of its revealing, Knemet had called every thraik from all points around Alada to hurry to that place. They had gone, but only half had returned to him, and those had returned empty-handed. Knemet could not contain his fury. Someone had wrested the book from Nemeth, killed him, and destroyed numerous thraiks, then disappeared into another enveloping spell. Knemet could not see the conqueror. He had only the impressions that the unfortunate wizard had had, and those were confusing. Males, females, tall, small, dark-skinned, light-skinned, were all jumbled together in his thoughts. It had often been difficult to tell Nemeth's dreams from visions or what he actually saw with his eyes. How disorienting it must have been to live his life. Knemet would have felt sorry for him, if he was not so desperate to find the treasure that his prey had carried until so recently. The thraiks could have obtained it for him! They should have! Knemet could have torn himself apart from the frustration that he felt at his failure. So close! So close!

Suddenly he put a hand upward toward one of the thraiks and squeezed his hand in the air. The thraik fell toward him, shrieking out its helplessness. The man caught it before it struck the ground and held it so it hovered in midair. He looked deep into its eyes, which were the color of dried blood, except for a golden pattern like a piece of intricately braided thread glowing in the centers. This he studied, nodding to himself.

"You still have the right rune for your seeking. But you were too slow, my pet." He raised a finger and touched it to the rune in the thraik's chest. He touched a line, which adhered to the fingertip. Studying it carefully, he caused it to spread apart, leaving a gap between the edges. That gap filled with intricate threads as fine as capillaries. The thraik gasped, then fetched in a deep breath. Knemet nodded. "You feel it, don't you? That greater speed you will have for all time. Show me now." It flew at him.

Knemet grinned as he watched, small teeth crowded in his shrunken jaws, looking as helpless as a rabbit. He let the thraik get within a foot of him, then threw up a barrier. The beast saw the floating gray rune too late, and slammed into it. It fell to the ground, landing in a heap at Knemet's feet.

"Fool," Knemet said, almost fondly. He poked it with a foot. The thraik groaned, pulling itself up onto all fours. Its wings wavered feebly. "I made you. I can unmake you. Go. Enjoy your gift, but try that not again."

"Yes, Creator," it breathed. It gathered itself and sprang into the air. The others, which had hovered out of reach to avoid being dragged into any punishment their fellow might suffer, were drawn into the chase once again. They tried their best to catch up, but the altered thraik twisted and soared, threading in between them without effort. It led them in an intricate pattern, laughing at them for failing to lay a talon upon it.

Soon all the thraiks came to hover near Knemet, timidly twisting their long necks. Each was eager to have that new speed for itself, but they still recoiled away from his touch. He captured each one briefly and recast the rune to the new shape. Now that he had made the change to his satisfaction once, it was easy to draw over and over again. Faster, smarter, more enduring— all those traits were desirable in his hounds. They had but one task. Now they could do it better.

It was not the first time he had changed them. The thraiks' purpose had

once fulfilled a more general need. In the days of experimentation, when he
and his colleagues—not yet enemies—had been playing with the stuff of reality, nothing seemed beyond their abilities, no end beyond them.

Knemet put his hand on his heart, feeling it pound at the thought of that
phrase. A merciful end. How he longed for one. He had enjoyed deathless-
ness while he had had a fresh topic to study, one that excited his intellect
and curiosity. Like the rest of the Makers, Knemet had had the leisure to
watch his creatures grow, breed, adapt, and, sadly, die, but they continued in
a natural fashion, finding a niche for themselves in the greater world of Alada. To have some of the scoffers say that all the beings that should ever or
were ever to exist already did was a gauntlet thrown down at the Shining
Ones' feet. The critics came around, though. It was a rare king or rich merchant who did not fall in love with the winsome pegasus or admire the courageous gryphon. They clamored for a unique creature of their own. For the
right price, a few of the Shining Ones undertook to combine animals that
were only found together in a coat of arms, never in nature.

However absurd the requests, the practice brought in both funds needed
to continue their studies and the respect of the most influential people in
the land, leaving the Makers free to work on the combinations they really
wanted to try: mixing humankind with other species. At first they kept these
great workings a secret, swearing the volunteers to utter secrecy with terrible
oaths and spells, but it soon became difficult to conceal them. The Makers
quickly discovered they could not keep centaurs contained on the grounds
of their estate. The human-horse hybrid was one of the greatest successes
that the Shining Ones enjoyed. The Windmanes, as the new people called
themselves, had the curiosity of the human coupled with the restlessness of
the horse. The lords east of the Arown had given the fascinating creatures
many hectares of open grasslands that were of no use to their own subjects.
Within a surprisingly short time, the Windmanes had established a culture of
their own in the new home that they called Balierenn. They loved adornments, but cared for little else in the way of possessions. The merfolk were
much the same. Calester scoffed at the females as being vain, until the Makers had time to observe the males, who would go so far as to kill or maim another of their number for the handsomest coral or most beautiful pearls. The
werewolves were the same, as violent and excitable on land as the merfolk
were beneath the sea.

The shapes alone were not the most intriguing facet for the Makers; it
was how the new-made beasts *lived*. Seeing the character of the species develop, their tastes and fears, their likes and dislikes, come into play as if they
had been born at the dawn of time, was a heady liquor to the Makers. The
Windmanes had a strong tradition of justice and spent much time discussing
the rights and privileges of centaur-kind. Merfolk were born thieves. They

considered any object that touched the sea to belong to them. They loved to cause mischief among land-born seafarers, who learned that bribery usually bought safe passage. The werefolk were skittish, owing to the instability of their forms. The Makers could not spend enough time wondering over the marvels of the new races.

Reluctant even to consider departing before their fascinating experimentation was finished, the Makers had all extended their lifetimes to a hitherto unnatural degree. They spent the better part of three hundred years at first in close proximity, then spread out across the face of Alada, but still keeping in contact to share their discoveries. At first they were proud of their longevity. It was yet one more piece of proof that though they were commoners in rank, they defied Father Time's bony hand, but kings and queens must still bow. He had lived long enough to have buried all of his critics and enemies. Or had he?

Knemet did not know if any of the other Makers had followed him into infinitely long life. By the time he had made that breakthrough, few of them were speaking to one another. Success made them cocky and arrogant. Little disagreements became major arguments. Making the Compendium had been the greatest mistake, Knemet knew that now. It provided a focus for those arguments. Every one of them wanted it exclusively. Knemet could not stand to be apart from it for long. It had been his idea in the first place, his hand that drew most of the initial runes and who cast the spell that gave it the ability to gather new ones and change the old to reflect reality. The thought still filled him with rage: how dared they try to limit his access to the Compendium!

Knemet admitted that he was the one who discovered how the rune could change the object, from afar, from anywhere, as easily as the object changed the rune. By accident, the Shining Ones had formed a perfect microcosm. Knemet could not resist playing with the notion. He was successful beyond his wildest hopes. With the collusion of wizards at remote locales, he tried altering places and beings he could only see through the book's pages.

Calester and Boma were horrified by his action. Calester wrested the Compendium from him. Knemet protested. Did he think that the rest of them were any different than he?

Apparently, they did. When he was not present, they used the book to change some of his marvelous beings back to their old shapes. Their patrons, they explained, were frightened by the new creatures. The intellectual discourse they had previously enjoyed was replaced by shouted arguments, and more. Knemet felt a tickle of power just in time to ward himself against an attack. He barely saw the rune before it disappeared, so he was uncertain who had waged it. What could he have done, with no evidence to point a finger? That was, until the next attack came. That time he was on his guard.

He saw the rune before it descended upon him, and fought it off. He saw the telltales, and was horrified to see that it had been constructed by those very three he had accused in the beginning. It was meant to tame his mind. If he had not stopped it, he would have retained his intelligence, but not his full will. He demanded a meeting of the Makers.

The three perpetrators were defiant. No one would give in. Knemet saw his foes as fearful, underhanded, and greedy. They saw him as power-mad and uncontrollable. It was clear to them all that the fellowship of magic they had enjoyed for so long was broken. Knemet was sorry, but he saw no choice. He retreated with the Compendium to a safe place a hundred miles from their college to continue his studies.

By then the others had come to understand the book's importance, and were reluctant to leave it in his hands. Deelin and Calester came to reason with him that the Compendium ought to be put out of reach, to avoid accidents or, he was rather more certain, deliberate misuse. He no longer trusted the others to make that judgment, since he was well aware that they believed he was the one who would misuse it. He refused to allow it to be taken away. Deelin and Calester withdrew. Knemet knew it was not the end of the argument, but even he was surprised at the ferocity of the attack on him when it came. The war, for war it was, continued for years. He could barely think of that last magical battle. He was no longer whole, and would never again be so, but he still retained the Compendium.

When his power had been so drained he could barely draw breath without risking death, he went to ground, hiding in humble places among some of his own creatures, including the gentle mimburti. Four of the other Makers joined forces to hunt him down. They wrenched the book from him, but spared his life. He had fled on a fast ship to another continent, seeking a haven in which to heal his wounds and muse upon revenge. He hid his trail so none of the others could pursue him. Evidently his efforts had been sufficient. He had never seen his fellows again, nor the Compendium.

Now and again he missed the other Shining Ones. He could not have conceived of a more exciting time to study magic than those years he spent in the company of equals possessed of such intriguing and inquiring minds, the equal or near equal to his own. Every day, every moment, every second, something new came to light to be discussed and exclaimed over, then examined with an eye toward betterment. In collaboration, he and one or more of his colleagues came up with new beings, new plants, or combinations of both. They were solving the great mysteries, in a way that no human mage had ever been able in recorded history or before.

Through the bleak years that followed his defeat and exile to the island-ringed continent of Oscora, he often thought of them. The few times he saw something new, he would turn as if to pass on an insight to his colleagues, only to find they were not there. It was like being dead, but without peace.

Nor had he realized how much power they had all devolved to the Compendium. They had grown lazy, relying upon it to describe things for them, instead of seeking out runes and processes for themselves. Once it disappeared, Knemet found himself blind to so much that lay apart from him. He could no longer watch flies land on a beached fish in Tledecra, nor a gleaming sunset paint a glacier in northern Niombra in scarlets and oranges, as he had when he had been able to unroll the big scroll to the correct leaf. Worst of all, he could not see any of his precious creations. All was lost to him. He had sunk into depression, scarcely moving except to renew his body's vitality, though he cared little. Seeing through Nemeth's eyes had given him an opportunity as he had not had in centuries. He could not and would not return to the blindness he had suffered. He wanted the Compendium back!

His thraiks had flourished in his absence. They had evolved from the way he had made them, inevitable, perhaps, over the course of thousands of years. He had created them by combining the best traits of humans with silent hunters like bats and swallows. They possessed a sleeker line than he had designed. They looked better. He had furnished them with at least four more back-curving spines on the tops of their wings to cut the air, but over so many years traits that did not make for the fastest and the strongest dropped away. They had also, he observed, grown four more teeth.

Thraiks were a necessary evil, he had argued to his fellow Shining Ones millennia ago. If they made creatures that were a danger to the rest of the world or to themselves, they must dispose of them. In response to this need he had created the ultimate tracker. They could follow a spoor of the most minuscule quantity. Most importantly, they were absolutely obedient to him.

He no longer cared about the greater good. All he wished for was an end. Without the Compendium, he was powerless to undo his own endlessness. He needed its power to unlock his rune. Thanks to the concealment spell cast first by Nemeth and afterward by his successor, the thraiks were unable to follow it directly. All they could do was trace the last places where its changes had been seen. Witnesses, especially those who bore the trace of having been touched by the book's power, could tell him more.

Knemet turned his attention to the latest such, a pathetic example of what humanity had evolved into over these many millennia. This latest find of the thraiks was a riverman, perhaps thirty years of age, who made a marginal living fishing and tending to boats.

Knemet wrinkled his nose. He could have guessed at the man's profession without looking at him. The peat-colored rags that clothed the short and stocky body stank of fish, and terror. Knemet had no room for sympathy with the man's fear. The mark of the Compendium was on him. It glowed faintly, but those with eyes to see or noses to smell, like the thraiks, could detect it. With a gentle nudge of magic, he pulled the man's head around and stared down into his muddy gray eyes with his multicolored ones.

"You have had time to gather your wits," Knemet said. "I seek a book, look you. Its pages are pure white with runes of gold. It stands this high." He gestured from the ground with his hand. The man followed the movement as if the hand were a snake that might strike at him. "A book. A tome containing words and images. You can't deny you were near it! Tell me what you know!"

"Nothin', oh, nothin', terrible master," the man gasped out. "Don' know what yer excellence wants o' the sorrowfulness o' me. I see no books, not from one year to another. Harbormaster, he might have one—but I never seen it. My wife, my sons—do they live, master?"

Knemet looked up impatiently at the thraiks, who scattered at his impatience. "Have you killed?"

Only taken, master, the lead thraik assured him, with terror in its eyes. Knemet saw they were telling the truth. It was in their runes. They were too frightened to lie. Knemet returned to his subject.

"I know not where they be, but that they may live," Knemet said. "Now, the book! It passed by you at some time. What will you tell me? Did you observe anything of the weird upon a day?"

"Weird . . ." A chord seemed to have been struck at last in the man's excuse for a mind. His muddy eyes brightened. "Ah, master, that was it! The fish pie m' wife made for feastday—sparkled with gold, it did!"

"With gold? Like this?"

Knemet held up a finger and drew a rune upon the air. He made the sign for a pie. No way to tell what kind of fish or other hideous river denizen that this man and his family dined upon. Obediently, the pie came into being, hot and fragrant and as perfect as the sigil that occupied its center.

"S-s-sorcery," the man stammered. He goggled at Knemet, his round chin quivering.

"Magic," Knemet corrected him, with a lift of his narrow shoulders. "What care I? Call it what you will. Did you see this? What feastday was it? How long ago?"

But he had surpassed the riverman's capacity for accepting the strange. Trembling, the man collapsed to his side and curled into a ball. He lay, muttering to himself and picking at his clothes.

Knemet groaned. No more intelligence could be gleaned from this one. He raised a hand and beckoned. The thraiks withdrew to the highest point of the room and hovered.

Nearer the ground the mossy walls shivered as though they were curtains stirred by the wind. Heavy rectangular blocks of the shaggy greenery pulled away and shambled toward Knemet. The liches surrounded him, waiting for his orders. Unlike the thraiks, these plant-men were uncurious, utterly obedient, and patient.

"Take him down," he told them. "Feed him . . . feed him that." He pointed to the fish pie, now cooling. Its rune had faded as its newness passed. The liches shuffled away and took up the riverman, hefting him up like pallbearers carrying a coffin. The man struggled to his side and appealed to Knemet. His eyes were wide with fear.

"No! Master, let me go, let me go! M'wife, m'sons!"

Knemet waved the protest away. The liches trudged slowly out of the room. They would take the man to one of the dark rows of cells carved out of the living rock below the chamber. He requested that the man be fed and cared for, but Knemet could not afford to let him go. The riverman's shrieks receded down the echoing corridors.

He looked up at the thraiks, who scattered to the highest corners of the chamber.

"Where found you that creature?" he asked the thraiks.

"On the banks of the Arown," one replied.

"I could guess that! Where?"

"The western bank."

Knemet nodded. The book must come south. It was a long way from Oron Castle, but it must pass by his fastness to return to Sheatovra.

"Where?" he asked.

The thraik hesitated. "Near Tillerton."

"What?" Knemet shrieked. "They could not come so near in this short a time. Even a master wizard cannot cross a continent in days! You fools!"

The thraiks swirled about the ceiling, terrified.

"Go," he commanded them. "Go back to Orontae. Find more trace. The bearer might be shielded by a concealment spell, but he cannot cover the trail once he passes. Find it! Follow it, and bring him, or anyone else who has seen him, to me. I cannot wait forever. Go!"

The air split, revealing a gash of blackness against the gray stone ceiling, and the thraiks fled into it. When it closed again, Knemet was alone except for his memories.

orning did not dawn so much as glow. So much fog filled the clearing where the party rested that Tildi woke in a silver haze. She looked around her curiously. Ghostly figures in the mist, the knights in their white-and-blue, passed around her silently, going about their tasks. They were as unreal as the dreams that had filled her night. Tildi tried to recall those phantasms. She had seen swirling figures like thraiks but brightly colored, not green-black like the winged menace that had killed her family. Green, silver, red, blue, white . . .

"Well," Lakanta said, breaking the spell. The dwarf woman sat up and clapped her hands. "It's a mime play! Do we guess from their charades what we are going to do next?"

"Breakfast, then back on the trail," announced one of the knights standing beside Tildi's rug. Tildi jumped. This man had dark eyebrows almost meeting over a thick nose. He had not been there when she went to sleep. The knights had managed to change shifts without waking her. However restless her dreams had been, she had slept soundly. He held out a hand. "May I offer assistance?"

"You must not touch her," Serafina said. "By my art I still see the power rolling off her in waves. You will do yourself harm."

The man let out a snort, but he moved no closer. "Very well, honorable."

"I want to wash," Tildi said, then added pointedly, "by myself. Where is the waterfall?"

The man pointed. "I will accompany you."

"I won't bathe with a man looking on!" Tildi said, aghast. The man regarded her with a puzzled expression.

"Don't you know about smallfolk?" Magpie asked. "They are famously modest, especially the women."

"Never met one before," the knight admitted. "She dresses like a boy."

"Well, take it from one who has traveled in the Quarters. Skirts don't make the lady. Would you invade your abbess's privacy like that?"

The man didn't say "heaven prevent such a thing!" but he might as well have. He left Tildi's tether in the hand of his companion, a middle-aged man who was trying hard not to laugh at the first man's discomfiture. In a moment, a young woman with a severe, square face came out of the swiftly thinning mist.

"I will go with you," she told Tildi. She took the tether and nodded toward the trees.

Tildi nodded. She had no choice. She gathered things from her rucksack and followed the towering young woman into the mist.

Around her, the party of humans was preparing for the day. If it was not for the enormous difference in scale, it could have been a group of smallfolk on an autumn picnic.

She glanced back over her shoulder at the book. It lay as if it slept. She chided herself, assigning the characteristics of a living creature to it, but it almost seemed to be. Her dreams had been full of voices as well as fluttering wings.

"There it is," the knight said, gesturing through the undergrowth. A thin stream flowed in a narrow bed almost at their feet, a miniature river complete with tiny moss-covered rocks pretending to be boulders, against which the water bumped and curled. "I'll be right here. Don't try to go anywhere."

Following the small rivulet upstream, she pushed her way inward and found herself among lush ferns surmounted by a cloud of water droplets, gray in the faint light. No sun would touch this part of the slope until almost high noon. It was cool, but not unpleasant. The promised waterfall, narrower than her hand, splashed down over brown, slick rocks. Tildi saw its rune projected like a rainbow upon the mist.

This, too, bore the marks of a query. How interesting. Did wind and water share characteristics she had only associated in the past with living beings? Did all of existence share certain traits, like a curiosity about its surroundings? Perhaps contact with the Great Book, the real thing, not her scrap of a leaf, had made her more perceptive. The thought delighted her. Every day would bring fresh revelations. She would know the world in the way that the Makers had. *To the best of my ability, of course,* she thought hastily, shamed by her assumptions. *I don't believe for a moment that I am the equal of such masterful wizards.* Yet, on only the second day in its company, she was reading rainbows. Master Olen would be so surprised, and gratified. He was the only one who had believed in the overarching powers of the book. How dearly she wished he could see it. She wished she could see him. But that was not to be, at least for the moment. The knights were forcing her and the others toward their order's home. They intended that the book should be theirs. Couldn't they . . . couldn't they see just how wrong a notion that was?

You must flee these people, a whisper said in her ear. *You must be free to make your way to me.*

"Who are you?" Tildi asked.

No answer. She looked around. It had not sounded like the voices in the book. After all, why would she need to come to it? She was already there. Perhaps it missed her. She was only a few yards away.

"Is someone near you?" the knight asked, from beyond the fernbrake.

"No," Tildi replied. She made her toilette in the ice-cold water and hastily dressed. Gathering up her brush and other goods, she plunged out of the undergrowth. The young woman had drawn her sword. She looked over Tildi's head and pushed aside some of the plants to see. She shook her head.

"Best be on our way," the knight said.

Show me the page for the land through which we are now riding," Serafina said.

Obediently, Tildi rolled the Great Book upon her lap, seeking the correct leaf. The book seemed to spin of its own accord. She liked the feel of the pages. It tingled less underneath her hands that day, and Rin complained less of the burning sensation Tildi had given off during the first few hours. In fact, the big scroll felt almost weightless now, and cool as any parchment might be on a breezy autumn morning. Once the mist had cleared, the sky had turned a heartbreakingly beautiful, clear blue. The leaves on the trees around them were just tipped with red and orange, and the heavy moist air was a delight to breathe. Tildi had never felt so . . . alive.

"Pay attention!" Serafina exclaimed, her voice breaking into Tildi's thoughts. "I hope you were not such a trial to Master Olen."

"No, master," Tildi said apologetically. She found the place in the book and laid her fingertip underneath the complex rune that described the party riding on the woodland path. "Here it is."

"Good," Serafina said. "Now, let's analyze the strokes."

The young wizard was doing her best to behave as though there was nothing strange at all about their surroundings, going on with Tildi's lessons as her mother had asked her to do. If this had been a day of no consequence in the Quarters, Tildi would have been cleaning up from making breakfast for five to three dozen people and contemplating how much washing needed to be done before she could steal a little time for herself, to read a book, do a little embroidery, or work on her magic lessons with Teldo. Well, perhaps this day was not entirely out of the ordinary. Serafina tapped the page with the end of her wand.

"Can you separate out the runes for each person?"

"Yes," Tildi said. That was the easiest part. The complex pictogram moved as she watched it. The horses drew closer and farther away from the central group. She, Serafina, and one guard rode at the tail of the queue.

"Without looking up, draw Master Auric."

"What?" That scholar spun in his saddle and glared at them. "You're not changing me, wizards."

"It's an exercise," Serafina said patiently. "I want Tildi to see if she can distinguish individual symbols. It will have no effect upon you."

"See it doesn't," Auric said. With one last glare at them, he turned forward again.

"Go on, Tildi."

Tildi nodded, keeping her eyes averted from the figures ahead. The way the characters were arranged was not necessarily the manner in which the riders were lined up on the pathway. She made a guess that her rune was nearly in the center of the group because she was carrying the book with her, and Sharhava was beside her, as the most important person to the greatest number of the others. Such a hierarchy should, in her opinion, have placed Magpie and Inbecca close by, but instead the rune nearest was that of poor Morag. Perhaps the knights were thinking about him after Bertin's terrifying death the night before. Of all their small group, he was the one the knights treated with the greatest kindness. Serafina was easy to pick out, as was Lakanta, but Teryn nearly blended in with the rest of the knights. Tildi had a hunch that the female rune she was studying belonged to that of the Rabantavian captain, but she didn't dare look up to check. That upright character to the left, an older male by the markings, with an air of kindness about it must be Auric. Tildi raised her finger and began to draw upon the air in thin gray lines that hovered beside her.

She had made only a few strokes when Serafina commanded, "That's well enough. Let it fade."

Tildi waved her hand, and the lines vanished.

"How can you do that?" the guard holding Tildi's leash asked.

"Practicing runes," Serafina said. "Common practice in magical studies."

"Show me," he said. It was partway between a request and a command, but his eyes were wistful, not demanding. Serafina shook her head.

"I am not your order's teacher. I have no wish to incur your mistress's further disapproval."

"Oh. Aye." The guard withdrew his horse a hoof's width. Tildi thought he was sulking. She had no time to wait and see whether her speculations were correct, for her attention was brought sharply back to Serafina who *was* her teacher.

"Draw Teryn."

Again Tildi picked out the rune on the page and hoped for the best. She reproduced the most distinctive characteristics before Serafina bid her stop.

"Very good!" she said.

Tildi thought she noticed some interesting facts about the closemouthed captain in the few lines she had drawn before they dislimned on the cool, moist air. The blond woman had sustained a terrible injury to one leg—her right, Tildi believed, by the way the stroke ran—but it had healed long ago. She ought to be limping, but her iron control forbade the display of any weakness. Tildi smiled at the captain's back. She and Morag rode near the front of the line now, ahead of three knights who stayed behind them with spears leveled at their backs. Escape would be impossible. *Or would it?* Tildi wondered.

Now that she had had a decent night's sleep, her head was beginning to clear. Why should they be prisoners? The Scholardom couldn't keep them, if she altered a rune or two to prevent their pursuit. The knights numbered nearly forty, but between the book and Serafina's own magic, surely they had sufficient power to allow them to be free. She glanced at Serafina. The wizardess looked quickly away, refusing to meet her eyes. Tildi felt a niggle of frustration. Master Olen was counting upon them to take the book to Sheatovra and secure it once again in its hiding place.

If Serafina had had any of her wits about her, she might have been able to prevent the knights rounding them up like sheep—Tildi looked with resentment at the rope around her waist—and making them set out on a hard road after a long day's battle.

The book must not reach the Scriptorium, that she knew. The moment that it was locked up in that place, wherever it was, departure with it in hand would be a good deal more difficult.

She, Tildi Summerbee, was not going to let some snippity uppity woman like the Abbess Sharhava upset the plans that had been set in motion by people with more foresight than she had, however noble she was and whatever she and her followers believed. Without Serafina's assistance, however, the chances of escape were likely to be nil. Tildi had to find out what the wizardess was thinking, but it was not easy. Serafina kept avoiding Tildi's attempts to have private speech with her.

"Do you not think that this matter is one for *wizards alone?*" Tildi asked pointedly, drawing as far from her guard as she could. She gave the young woman a hopeful look and a tilt of her head, hoping not to look too obvious.

"They can listen to us," Serafina said imperturbably. Her long, beautiful face was grave and her eyes sorrowful. Tildi felt her heart go out to the girl. She must still be in the shock of having lost her mother. Tildi felt ashamed for pressing her, but she was anxious to be away from Sharhava's disapproval. "Without the necessary talent and experience, it would be no more use than an audience watching a musician learning to play."

Tildi gave the guard a sideways glance. He looked scornful at the last statement, obviously thinking that anything a half-educated smallfolk could do, he could, too. Thankfully, he seemed to have missed the deeper meaning.

"I'm uncomfortable having them watching me," Tildi said with another meaningful look. "I don't want to make unnecessary mistakes."

"You have performed difficult tasks in company before this," Serafina said impatiently. "If I must admit it, I respected you when you stood up before the council to assist Master Olen. Mother guessed, of course, that you were a very new apprentice. If you can find a voice before wizards and kings, then practicing conjurations in the company of scholars should cause you no embarrassment whatsoever. If you make mistakes, you will learn something from them. Please stop wasting time."

"But I want to discuss the appropriate uses of this new magic. I am concerned that I might not be able to manage this much . . . power. What if . . . what if it became necessary to wield it?"

Serafina sighed. Her eyes looked sad.

"There is a great risk anytime you consider making use of it," she said. "I would employ any other means before you would rely upon the book, because there is a chance of unmaking or changing to anyone who alters the runes. Wherever it goes, the runes are as delicate as a rising cake. One wrong touch, and a living creature could collapse and die, entirely by accident. Recall what Master Olen's friend from the south told us. I would rather have an unfortunate incident come to pass by my inaction than destroy an innocent being. It behooves you to think most carefully than most would about the outcome of any action you might perform."

Tildi looked guiltily over her shoulder. The road's surface had been churned up by their passage, but not as greatly as it had been the night before. The solution to have her nearest the rear and to spread out the party over a distance farther from the book's influence had minimized the random changes wrought by so many feet.

Serafina followed her eyes.

"That will be a good practice for today. There are places where the runes have been unmade. Let us try to restore them as we go." She spurred her horse away toward the front of the queue, leaving Tildi in the care of her single guard. Over the chinking of tack and the thudding of hooves on stones and earth, Tildi heard Sharhava's unmistakable voice raised in some querulous complaint. Serafina dropped back again a few moments later. She nodded worriedly at Tildi.

"Here is the word for this entire road." With the tip of her wand, the wizardess sketched a word upon the air between them, then drew the wand outward to make the symbol larger. "It will change in small details over the course of the day. Your object is to change it back to this state whenever it does. It may result in a surprise, if an animal is digging in it. You will cause the hole to fill up over and over again." Tildi giggled at the thought, and Serafina smiled like a girl of her own age. "I want you to concentrate upon it for an hour. I will keep track of the time. All you must do is remake the rune."

Tildi checked the long, thin symbol as Serafina had scribed it against its counterpart in the book. It would have taken her three times as long to have written it as accurately as her teacher.

It was already altering. A slight curling at the top right looked like the symbol for water. It must be raining ahead. Hastily she drew her knife and smoothed down the edge. The rune returned to its original shape. Tildi was pleased with herself, then she thought about the possible consequences. She gave Serafina a worried look.

"Did I stop the rain?" she asked.

"Perhaps," Serafina said. "We will see if we reach that area before the hour is up."

Tildi had to keep an eye on the top right of her subject rune, for the rain in the image persisted a long while. In the meantime, she corrected several strange anomalies that popped up, some again and again.

"We are causing those," Serafina observed. "It cannot be helped. Just keep at it. It's good practice for you."

"Can't we just hide the rune or obscure it, so nothing can change it?" Tildi said, closing a fissure in the surface with a pinch of her fingers. The lines obeyed her so well that soon she felt as though she was working on a piece of her own embroidery.

"No. We can't change them to be invulnerable against the influence of the book. Such was the magic of its creators. Its preponderance of power unlocks all runes."

"Can't we remove or destroy them from the things?"

"To destroy them is to destroy what they describe, what they brought into being. They will fade over time. Once we have passed, the ability to alter them will fade. Only adepts such as you and I will be able to see them thereafter."

"There must be a way to make them different," Tildi said stubbornly as she changed a stretch of road back to dirt from mud. Tildi scribbled on the rune in haste. The gooey substance coarsened to soil. Tildi was pleased. "I think there *must* be a way to alter the book itself."

"It might be possible, but you must not, not without deep consideration," Serafina said firmly.

"Wouldn't it be useful, though?" Tildi asked. She spotted a twisted stroke that at the moment was out of their sight, and corrected it as they rounded a long bend. She had the satisfaction of seeing masses of thorns dissolve into air, leaving a clear way for them to ride. "You could protect a person or a place, perhaps a whole region, by making sure nothing happened to its rune."

"You have not had a chance to read much history of the wizard wars in the distant past," Serafina said. She tilted her head toward the group of riders around them. "These here know far more than you do. They have studied the stories of the Makers. Much of what you suggest was tried, and in some cases was accomplished successfully, but not always. Terrible stories abound as to the mistakes they made. There are perils involved in any facet of change. We lack the expertise of those who first unlocked the runes. Their deep knowledge is lost to us. We do not try anything as daring as they did— we are not so reckless. These knights are at the extreme of wishing to return things to the way they were before the first day of that knowledge, but they are not alone at all. The power of the book makes it possible again, and in that lies more peril than that of the mere physical."

She leaned over and spoke in a low, urgent voice. "Don't you understand, there is *nothing* you cannot make if you know the rune for it? Unimaginable wealth, thousands of servants, islands, volcanoes, the perfect body that will live a million years in perfect health! I dare not use it, for fear of awakening a greed in myself that I can't stifle."

Tildi was horrified. "Neither would I, except I would try to keep harm from coming to those I am near. How do I know that people aren't changing because of being close to the Great Book?"

"You don't," Serafina said. "That is why it is necessary to keep an eye on one's rune. If it begins to change, change it back. There is no harm in that. But other alterations—you don't know what havoc you can wreak if you begin to play with reality as though it were a toy."

"I would use it," Rin said. "I feel as that poor boy last night did. To use it to make myself healthier and stronger would be my goal. I have no need of those other things."

Serafina shook her head. "But others would feel that they did. The greatest wizards of the ages would be tempted—I am tempted—but I will not succumb. The book must write itself. We can only copy from it or study it. We must not change the book itself. If unscrupulous people knew that it existed, we would be fighting much more dangerous foes than our current escorts. I intend to stay by you, in hopes that between us we may prevent the ones around us from giving in to their misguided doctrine of correcting what they see as the Creators' mistakes." With a final significant glance at Tildi and Rin, she sat upright in her saddle.

Tildi rolled the scroll back and forth. It hovered a few inches above her lap. It had been so easy to make it levitate. When Teldo had been trying to teach her magic, she had despaired of ever managing such a difficult enchantment. Now it was one of the least spells that she was capable of. She would have been proud to show him her accomplishments. Teldo would have adored the Great Book. It was everything that they had longed for in their studies. The entire world rested here, all the land and sea, and all the beasts and beings who lived thereupon, on one long roll of shimmering whiteness like a landscape of cloud. Such beauty caught at her throat and made her sigh with pleasure.

She came once again to the leaf from which Nemeth had torn pieces and burned them. The missing places in the pure white page wrenched her heart.

"How sad to leave it damaged like this," she said. She drew one finger up and along the torn edges. From them she could feel a jangling as of upset nerves.

Serafina smiled. "The book has endured millennia. There are powerful spells binding it. Either it will heal itself in time, or not. We can but wait to find out."

"Perhaps Master Olen knows how to fix it," Tildi said.

The knight riding beside Tildi cleared his throat.

Oh, yes. He was reminding them that the book was the property of the Scholardom now, and no wizard was going to interfere with their precious treasure.

We'll see about that, Tildi thought, though she didn't let her feelings show in her eyes.

When the sun had reached its highest point, Loisan raised a fist. The party jingled to a halt. The almoner began preparing lunch. Teryn trotted over to Serafina and Tildi. Her gaze hovered between them, not certain which one to address.

"We are short on supplies," she said very casually. "We expected to go back by way of one of the villages on the west of the river. I seem to recall that there is a town not far ahead. We should reach it by twilight."

A town! Tildi felt her heart leap within her chest. The Scholardom could hardly parade her through the streets with a rope around her waist. There would be questions if they appeared to be escorting prisoners. Magpie— Prince Eremi, as she must try to think of him—would have authority there.

"Serve us what you can," Serafina said, her voice even. "We will find a way to replenish our stores as soon as possible."

Chapter Five

ildi ate her meager lunch of scorched bread and hard cheese without complaint.

Rin knelt down beside her. "Apple?" she asked, offering a wrin-kled sphere. "They are a little past their best, but sweet. There are many in the trees, above the horses' reach."

"Thank you," Tildi said. The apple was the size of a melon in her small palms. She turned it over until she could find a place narrow enough to take a bite. The crunchy flesh was sweet and juicy enough to fill her parched and dusty-tasting mouth with liquid. "Do you know this part of the land? I know we are north of your homeland. I just don't know how far."

"I have been here before," the centaur said, chewing an apple meditatively. She gestured with the core to the south and east. "Some of it is disputed land between Orontae and the plains of Balierenn. Once in a while hot weather drives the Windmanes north to the cooler borderlands. We have few permanent buildings, so we can move as we please. Other times, the humans come south to gather grasses and roots. Over the course of a year, our peoples see little of one another. It has worked out this way for centuries. There are wastelands that neither of us claim to the east, full of stinging desert creatures and few wells. It is good country to run in, but useful for little else. I look forward to introducing you to my people one day."

"Soon, I hope," Tildi said pointedly.

"We're not going there," the guard said, interrupting them.

"Your pardon," Tildi said, putting on her most imperious go-to-Meeting expression, "but we weren't addressing you."

The guard withdrew to the end of Tildi's tether. Rin laughed, her long throat rippling.

"Little one, unless you want to make the rest of the trip in chains, you will stop showing your eagerness to run. Everyone knows we are approaching a town. Do you think they will let you have an opportunity?"

Tildi felt her face go scarlet. "But why are you being so patient with them?"

"They outnumber us," Rin said simply. "We are weary. We have been through much, and little has been decided beyond the end of the day's journey ahead of us. We will end up harming one another, and there is no reason for it. Life is not over. The book will reach its destination, just not yet. Be calmer. None of us are content, but we must protect you."

"I can take care of myself," Tildi said, feeling very foolish.

"But you cannot take care of us," Rin said. "Be patient yourself. It will be all right in the end, I promise you."

Beyond the trees, a team of oxen pulling a broad wooden cart appeared at the edge of the field. Men and women wearing gartered trousers and loose-sleeved tunics, just as if they were smallfolk about to conduct a harvest. They climbed out and began to pull up root vegetables.

The harvesters shouted to one another, laughing. A tall, strongly built woman in a brown dress with a honey-colored apron and head kerchief laughed over her shoulder and started walking toward the row nearest the concealed knights. Tildi stared in amazement. She was coming toward them! Hope surged in her heart. This woman was a fellow farmer. She would understand Tildi's plight.

"Move," the guard ordered at once, tugging on Tildi's waist rope. "Into the bushes. The rest of you, follow us."

"I will not!" Tildi said indignantly. Impulsively she sprang to her feet. "Help!" she screamed, waving her arms to attract the attention of the woman in brown. "Save us!"

Unceremoniously, the knight threw the rope around her, pinioning her around the arms, and lifted her off the ground. He clapped a hand over her mouth.

"Silence!" he hissed.

Tildi fumed, wishing the man would shrivel up and die like a slug with salt poured on it. She kicked and struggled against him.

At the end of the field, the humans looked around for the source of the unfamiliar noise. Tildi scratched at her captor's arms, but the rope restricted her reach. She scented burning flesh, as if Morag had scorched yet another joint of meat. She realized the smell was coming from under her nose. She twisted her head, wanting to get away from the stench. She caught a glimpse of the knight's face contorted with pain. It was he! His skin was burning from contact with hers, but he didn't let go. He staggered backward across the road.

Twigs tore at her hair and face as he dragged her into the far hedge, out of sight of the field hands. She kept kicking, but it was no use. She was as weak as a kitten compared with a human. He forced his way underneath a hazel copse and dropped to his haunches on the bare soil next to the roots of the arching switches. He nodded in the direction of the field. Tildi could still see a tiny patch of blue sky, but she was surrounded by shadow. His voice murmured in her ear like a hot breeze.

"If you keep struggling, I will order my brethren out there now, and they will kill every single person in that field. Do you understand me?"

Tildi gawked at him, horrified. Slowly, she nodded. He winced. The pain in his hand must have been excruciating.

"I'll move my hand, now. You let out another caterwaul, and the blood of those farmers will be on you. Do you understand?"

"Yes," she whispered, chastened. Freedom had seemed so close!

"Do you have her, Lar Findor?" Abbess Sharhava asked.

"Yes, Abbess," Findor said. Tildi clambered to her feet. He thrust a finger into her face. "Stay there, curse you!"

Tildi was so shocked at the sight of his black-scorched finger that she stopped and sat down.

"Get the others," Sharhava said over her shoulder to the knights behind her. They rushed away.

Two more of the scholars shoved into the small shelter and thrust Serafina down beside Tildi. The wizardess gathered her up like a child. Lakanta and the others were forced in behind her. Teryn and Morag were bound with ropes.

"Are you all right?" Serafina asked.

"Yes," Tildi said. "I am so sorry. It's my fault. I . . . I had to try."

"The book," Sharhava demanded, pushing aside the branches and glaring down at them. "Where is it, Findor?"

"She must have dropped it," the knight said. "I had to get her away from there, Abbess. The peasants were coming to see who shouted."

"You were right to do so, but the Great Book must not lie unguarded. Where?"

Findor gestured in the direction from which they had come. Sharhava parted the bushes to look. The road lay empty. Sharhava hissed orders. The knights fanned out to search.

"How could it be gone?" Findor asked. "I never saw it fall. It wasn't there. Where did you put it?" His hand started toward Tildi's shoulder, but it was shaking in pain. Angrily, he pulled it back.

"I was holding on to the book until you grabbed me," Tildi said indignantly. "*You* made me drop it!"

"The Great Book is worth your life!" he snarled. Tildi retreated as far as she could from the angry human.

"You are hurt," Serafina said, looking at Findor's hands. "Let me help you."

"I don't trust your spells," Lar Findor said, batting her away.

"Can you ride with both hands burned? Let me help! We will do you no harm. I swear it by my honor. You have no reason to doubt me."

Findor hesitated, but he looked at Morag. The dark-haired man nodded dumbly. Findor held out his hands and turned them over. Tildi gasped. The flesh of the palms was black, and the white bones that connected to the fingers were exposed and yellowed.

Serafina closed her eyes and put her hands over his. Tildi watched as the man's rune changed very slightly, two thin, tight scribbles near the center widening out to graceful strokes. When Serafina moved back, his hands were restored. Tildi noticed that they were beautiful in shape. She was glad that they had not been maimed forever.

"That's better," Findor said, his voice hoarse. "My gratitude, honorable." Serafina nodded gravely to him. He didn't look at Tildi.

"Why would I take it?" Magpie's voice asked indignantly, from outside the shelter. Tildi peered through the curtain of thin branches. The tall, imperious abbess confronted Magpie, almost eye to eye with him.

"Because you are a mischief-maker," Sharhava said impatiently. "Did you?"

"No. I have been near Lady Inbecca all this time. She can vouch for me, if she needs to."

"*Lar* Inbecca?"

"Yes, Abbess," the young woman whispered. "He has done nothing. He has not touched the book. How can he? It would destroy any of us, except the smallfolk girl."

Sharhava was in no mood to apologize. She turned to her lieutenants.

"It is still nearby. The runes are strong upon us yet. We must find it before anyone else does! All of you, seek!"

A trio of knights attempted to herd Rin away from the road. The centaur reared and kicked at them with her front hooves.

"Hands off me! I am a princess of the Windmanes!"

"Go farther from the road!" the stout almoner demanded, stepping up to her with hands on his hips.

"I do not take orders from you, nor your mistress," Rin said, her deep green eyes flashing. The blood was high in her dark cheeks.

"Please come with me, highness," Magpie said, stepping in between Rin and her tormentors. He bowed deeply and stretched up a hand for hers. "They do not wish to attract the attention of the field hands."

Rin was somewhat mollified by his polite tone. "They should ask, not offer violence."

"So they should," Magpie said. "It is clear that their studies do not include advanced manners. Will you keep me company during this pause in our journey?"

Rin snorted. "Very well, then." She placed her fingers in Magpie's and aimed a glare over her shoulder at the knights. Magpie led her away from the copse. Tildi felt forlorn, having them out of reach.

The humans fanned out among the trees, their eyes intent upon the ground, going over the path that Findor had taken when he carried Tildi away from the road, and moving outward.

"They aren't going," the voice of a male knight whispered, almost beside her. Tildi could not see him through the thicket. "Curse those people to nonexistence! We cannot have them interfering with us."

Another speaker, a little nearer, let out a long sigh. "Keep an eye on them. They have seen the runes. If they become too inquisitive we must deal with them. We cannot have rumors fly." The cold way in which the second voice spoke chilled Tildi's heart. They did not care about the lives of others. She huddled in a miserable bundle beside Serafina, determined not to cause any further offense whatsoever.

The searching went on for what seemed an endless time.

At last, the Scholardom congregated beside Tildi's hazelwood prison to confer.

"Report," Sharhava demanded, though she kept her voice low.

"We have not found it, Abbess," Brouse said, his frown creasing his doughy face.

"The book cannot have disappeared into the air, Abbess," Loisan said. "It must be here."

"Perhaps the Mother and Father have called it home," said the sturdy female ostler.

"Impossible. One of the cursed wizards must have put a spell on it," Sharhava said. She pushed aside the curtain of switches. "It must be you," she spat at Tildi. "You want us to be stopped. I tell you this is the way to your death. You will not deter or delay us. Where is the Great Book?"

"I don't know!" Tildi protested.

"Keep your voice down!" one of the knights hissed. Tildi subsided, huddling close to Serafina's thin side. "You magicked it away somewhere we cannot find it, but none of us leaves this spot until it is found."

"It has not been 'magicked away,'" Serafina said impatiently. "The runes are still upon everyone and everything, are they not? You have observed that—in fact, that is the main point of your complaint. If the book was gone, they would be gone, too. I will assist you to look for it." She rose, unfastening her cloak clasp. "Tildi, remain here. No one will harm you."

"Don't leave me," Tildi asked. Serafina knelt and tucked the rose-colored cape around her. Her dark eyes looked deeply into Tildi's brown ones.

"Wait. It will be all right. I promise you. Stay here."

"I'll help, too," Lakanta offered.

"No!" the almoner said, pointing. Reluctantly, the dwarf woman settled down again. "You stay here. Just her."

"It will be all right," Serafina assured them all. She slipped out silently behind the knight.

Tildi fretted in her absence. What if it had gone to ground of its own accord? What if it did not want to be by her any longer?

"Did you make it invisible?" Lakanta asked curiously. "I'd dearly love to be invisible sometimes. It'd be a wonder to hear what people were saying if they didn't know you were there."

"Why, do you want to know what a nuisance they all think you are?" asked the knight guarding the copse. "Silence, or it'll go worse for you."

"I'm not impressed with your threats," Lakanta said. "I haven't been out on the road all these years without knowing how to take care of myself. And my friends," she said with a wink for Tildi. The two Rabantavian guards said nothing. Teryn ignored her bonds with dignity. Morag stared at the ground. "Pay them no mind, Tildi. They don't know what to do, and they don't like looking foolish."

The smallfolk girl appreciated the cheerful encouragement, but she was worried. The book was a sacred trust to Olen. How could she have been so careless?

A hum of voices swirled about Tildi as the wind rose. Dust blew through the finger-thick stems. Tildi squeezed her eyes shut and huddled deeper into the borrowed cloak. The garment was much too warm for the day, but she appreciated the comfort. How kind Serafina was. She shifted her feet. Her oversized boots struck an obstruction. She lifted the edge of the cloak.

A bar of shimmering white all but lit up the inside of the copse. Tildi gasped. The book was there! It rested beside her hip like a faithful dog. She snatched it up and held it to her. The voices inside it thrummed with pleasure.

"Why, it's back again," the almoner said in a low voice. "She must have been carrying it inside that cloak."

"She wasn't," Findor said. "It hasn't been here all this time."

"Then, how did it get here? Walk?"

They all looked at Tildi. She shook her head, unable to believe the wonder of it. The knights gathered around to gaze at it. Sharhava frowned at Tildi, but Tildi was too delighted to have her treasure back in her arms that the abbess's anger rolled off her like raindrops on a roof.

"Where was it, and how did it return to her?" the abbess demanded.

"A mystery we won't solve," Loisan said dismissively. "The Great Book is found. Let us be on our way."

"Very well," Sharhava said. "Make preparations." Loisan nodded and turned away. The others followed him. Tildi sprang up, the book hugged tightly to her, and followed her nemesis out into the clearing.

"Please don't hurt those people," Tildi begged. "I was impulsive. Don't punish them for my mistake."

"Harm human beings?" Sharhava asked. "Why would you think we would harm them?"

"Lar Lindor said if I wasn't quiet he would order the rest of you to kill them."

Sharhava gave her a superior smile. She leaned down, her gaze almost a leer, and spoke in a very low voice, too low for the others to hear. "You are gullible. We would never think of harming a natural human, child." She brought her face so close to Tildi that the smallfolk girl could feel the warmth of her skin and dropped her voice to a whisper. "But I will tell you this: if you try again to run away or steal the book from us, we will go directly to your homeland and dispatch as many smallfolk as we possibly can. Your kind does not belong in the world. They will be the first ones to be transformed back into whatever they had been made by the Mother and Father before the so-called Shining Ones began to meddle."

Tildi was mortified. She sputtered.

"You can't do that!"

"You cannot stop us," Sharhava said, rocking back on her heels. "What changes we can wreak, with you or without you, we will do. Prove your worth, and perhaps we will spare your folk for a time. How long you stave off their doom depends upon how cooperative you are with our cause."

With that, she rose and stalked away. Tildi felt angry tears on her cheeks. A horrid woman! The worst she had ever met!

She clutched the book to her. *Where have you been?* she thought at it.

Feeling exhausted with worry, she returned to sit beside Serafina. The young wizardess looked down at her with curiosity written large in her eyes.

"How did the book come to you?" Serafina asked.

"I don't know," Tildi said, smoothing the open page with her hand. "I didn't summon it."

"Perhaps not consciously," the wizardess said. She patted the ground beside her. "Put it here, and go to the other side, next to Lakanta."

Very reluctantly, Tildi put the book on the ground. She hated to be without it, even for a moment, even for an experiment, but she obeyed. She crawled toward the other end of the small enclosure. Behind her, Serafina let out a chuckle.

"Look behind you," she said.

Tildi glanced over her shoulder. The book was hovering at her shoulder, about two feet off the ground.

"It is obedient," Serafina said. Tildi gave her a sharp look wondering if the wizardess could possibly have heard what Sharhava had said to her.

Serafina smiled as Tildi reached out and gathered the book to her like a beloved child.

"It seems it does not wish to be separated from you, either. That gives me food for thought. I must consider what that may mean for us all."

"The farmers are gone," Lar Vinim said, sticking her head into their shelter. "Make haste. We depart now."

Chapter Six

Nemet was angry. He had reached out through every means available to him—plants, animals, even stones—but he could not touch the new owner of the Compendium. More than once, he thought he had touched another magically oriented mind, but every contact was tenuous. He thought he had felt an echo of thoughts about the Compendium once, a few days following Nemeth's death, but the touch was as nebulous as a spiderweb. If he had found that wizard, the guardian spell around him prevented any definite means for Knemet to identify him or his whereabouts.

The thraiks had been frustrated. This new wizard seemed to be everywhere at once. The thraiks saw runes all along the full length of the road to the east of the great river, no portion of it seeming to be stronger than any other. As to the source, they had no indication that was any use to him.

The most recent brought to him by the thraiks was a sad specimen of humanity, a peasant with a thick-jowled face and rough black hair that must have been cut with the same scythe he used on the crops. Knemet had had to draw a rune to rid him of vermin, for the man's skin crawled with them. It was almost certainly, Knemet thought with a touch of humor, the first time in his life he didn't have lice.

"Why this one?" Knemet asked the hunter who had brought the man to him. "He is from the west side of the Arown."

Touched, the thraik indicated.

"The book itself, its bearer, or a copy?" Knemet demanded. He spun to confront the man, who shrank into the corner. "What did you see, man? What made my thraiks bring you here? What did you see?"

The man seemed confused. "A mir'cle, 's all." Uneasily, the man looked up at the thraiks who hovered high above him. The leader flicked his tongue at him. He shuddered. Knemet cleared his throat noisily. "I seen those things o'erhead, lordship."

"They won't harm you, not if you speak to the point!"

"Yes, lordship. What can I tell ye? I'm but a humble man, lordship. Not worth bein' carried off, no."

"What kind of miracle was it? Did you see a book? A scroll, as long as this?" Knemet held out his arms to indicate the dimensions of the Compendium. "What was this miracle? Tell me! I want to know what you saw!"

The man looked up at him shyly. "Shining, 'twas."

Knemet leaned close to him, the multicolored irises of his eyes focused upon his subject. "Tell me what you saw."

Unlike so many of the witnesses discovered by the thraiks, this man was eager to talk his "mir'cle." He held out his clasped hands.

"A month and a day it was we had it," he told Knemet. "Bright as the sun. Gold, though I never seen gold. I mean, gold like the merchants talk about. They never bring us none but bronze. They say it's brighter. A twisty thing like a word, 'twas. Most beautiful thing any o' us ever known. We still talk o' it, betimes. Came and went and came again."

"Yes, yes," Knemet said impatiently. "Gold, for a month and a day?" That was impossible. The runes always faded after the influence wore off. "Where did you see it?"

"Our village tree. Middle o' t'green. Walnut tree, 'tis. Call oursel's the same. Stands to reason, don't it?"

"I decline to dispute your founders' logic," Knemet said dryly. "When came this miracle?"

"Two moons gone, 'twas. One day t' tree started shinin'. We was all struck awed by it. Sometimes when we was close by, we had twisty markin's on us, too. Headman said 'twas a blessin'. Gave sacrifices, as is proper. Tree accepted 'em and all. I gave it t' best of my crops, and m'wife her best cookin'. We didn't spare nothin', lordship."

"I trust you did not," Knemet said. He wanted detail, but he saw he must distill it from this man drop by drop. "Did you see anything unusual in the tree? Anyone in its branches?"

"Nay, sir! We'd a seen a man. Just a tree, when all's been and all. At the center of Walnut Tree these four centuries, it has."

"A venerable tree, you say?"

"Aye, venerable. 'Tis a good word, lordship." The man tried it out on his tongue. "Must tell t'headman that, when I go back, sir. Hope 'tis soon." He twisted his big, calloused hands together and regarded Knemet with hope. "Crops must come in, lordship."

"But the miracle departed, did it not?" Knemet said, leading him back to the matter of importance.

"Aye. T' end of everything when it went. Our hearts broke, d'ye see? Like the sun goin' away. But, ye see, 'twasn't t' end of it all, at all," the man insisted, meeting Knemet's eyes earnestly. "Not too long a'ter, the mir'cle come back."

"It came back? When was that?"

The man had the dates at the tips of his calloused fingers. "A moon and five days agone, lordship. Three wizardesses come to us with sojjers t' protect 'em. Not that we'd a-hurt them. They's powerful ladies, lordship."

Knemet raised an eyebrow. "Three?"

"Aye, m'lordship. Come from the south, they did. One was a woman-horse."

"A centaur?"

"Aye, lord. That's what they's called, I hear. I never seen one like it. Like an honest woman, but half a horse. Girl on her back was a bitty slip of a thing. The light seemed a-shinin' off her, it was. Same as the dark-haired wench in white, might'a been an elf maiden, glowin' like the moon. I seen an elf wench once in the woods. Vanished all quiet like she was made o' water. The third was a stout lass with long braids o' bright gold. All as clean as if they was new-made."

Knemet fingered his lip. A centaur wizard? Was such a thing possible? He had been away so long. Standards may have become lax in training, or this was a prodigy too profound to ignore. He must study the notion. "But you say this was after the miracle left you? Why did it come back?"

The man shook his head, his eyes earnest. "Dunno, lordship. I tell y' true, that's what we know!"

"One of them was carrying a book," Knemet said. "Which of the three had it?"

"N'er saw a book, lordship," the man said. "The girl had a bit o' parchment w' sommat scrawled on it, a picture or two. We thought about it all later. Must've been a blessin' of some other kind. They's mir'cles of many shapes, is there not?"

Knemet nodded, careful not to show his triumph. Nemeth had been careless, leaving pieces of the book behind him, then. But it might just be a page from a copy. His thraiks had been fooled over and over, bringing him putative witnesses who had had the bad luck to come into contact with one of these sad imitations. But even a bad copy had its connection to life itself. It could be that the wizardesses this plowman described were following the golden thread between the copy and the original. They sought its power. Well, who was to wonder at that? But had they been the ones who had taken it from Nemeth in Orontae?

"I will cast my net wider, then," he said thoughtfully. "I had not thought to look for more than one mage, now had I?"

"What, lordship?" the man asked.

Knemet looked up in surprise. His musings had made him forget about his visitor. He made a sign. "Take him down."

"Wha'?" the man said, as the liches surrounded him. "My lordship, I tol' ye all I know about the mir'cle. Do not punish me!"

But Knemet was already pondering the threat of a triumvirate of power. "With it in their hands, could they withstand my influence?"

It would seem so. Three was traditionally known as a number of great strength. Yet, three minds that could be steered, instead of only one. If he could trouble just a single one of them and create strife among the three, they might break the spell that concealed their precise whereabouts from him. Then the thraiks could strike. The Compendium would be once again in his hands.

Yes, Knemet thought, ignoring the wails fading away down the stone passage, *divide and conquer. Three . . .*

*T*ildi felt every jar as Rin negotiated the rocky road ahead of them. She could scarcely bear Magpie's backward glances of sympathy. She was so mad she was shaking. She hated Sharhava with all her heart. To threaten her people like that took an absolute disregard for living creatures. She had not really believed until that moment how the knights viewed nonhumans.

Escape must be made, as soon as possible, for all their sakes. Somehow. But, oh, how? Her people would suffer if she did leave. She was torn between the welfare of all smallfolk and fulfilling her promise to Olen. As dearly as she loved it, the Great Book needed to be hidden away. The Makers struck her as impossibly irresponsible for having set it loose in the first place. What could they have been thinking?

What could she do about the knights? She could not let them lock her away and keep the book for themselves. It was too dangerous. Some of them had dangerous burns to prove it, and one of them was dead. If that wasn't warning enough, what could be? She must take it far away, as soon as possible. The Quarters would suffer. That would be horrible. Tildi couldn't have that on her conscience, but she was left with few choices.

Tildi felt a thought tickle at the back of her mind. What if . . . what if she changed the knights. Just a little, just so they would stop wanting to undo the Makers' magic. What if she studied them all very carefully, and made the tiniest alteration. She could make them *like* smallfolk. It would be a minor difference. They would be angry that Tildi had gone away, but they would stop short of taking out their frustration on her people.

Tildi nearly moaned with frustration. Oh, but that wouldn't help the centaurs or any of the other people who had been made different by the Shining Ones! Anyone could see the disgust in their eyes when they looked at Rin or Lakanta. They even treated Serafina with disdain because she was a wizard. Protecting the smallfolk wouldn't mean that the other races would go unscathed. All things must be kept in balance, Serafina had said. If Tildi changed the knights' minds about one thing, the balance of anger might tip over in a different direction, and she would be responsible for harm to other innocent beings. Serafina was right again. To alter anything was almost impossible. That left her stewing in her own roiling, boiling thoughts, day after day after endless, bumpy day.

If only Olen had been with them. He would have had no trouble straightening things out and setting them all in motion once again.

Tildi laid a protective hand on the book, which floated sedately beside her.

Don't worry, the voices said. *We are with you.*

What are they?" Magpie asked, peering through the trees in wonder.

The Scholardom had ridden another three days to the southeast, keeping their right hands to the river, and being careful, even when seeking supplies, to avoid any more entanglements with other people. Magpie had chafed at the enforced isolation, but he knew his duty was to protect Tildi and the book, and by extension the others who accompanied her. And Inbecca, of course, though she showed little need or wish for his care. She rode by his side, responding occasionally to his conversational sallies but refusing to engage with him. She was still angry or hurt, or both. Magpie accepted that he owed it to her to offer his back to her verbal lash, should she choose to take out her frustration upon him, but she had been so contained, so distant. At the moment, he was pleased to see that she was as curious as he was.

The autumn noonday sun beat down upon their backs, but their shortened shadows were invisible to the objects of his study.

"They don't have a name," said Braithen, a middle-aged man with a sardonic face. "They cannot speak. They can only make the grunting noises you hear them making."

To Magpie's ear the noises sounded more like singing than grunting. The beasts, for so he felt he should call any creature with such a pelt of hair, greatly resembled mimburti, the small, almost manlike animals who occupied much of the southern end of the continent of Oscora, halfway around the world. He had seen them while accompanying his father on a diplomatic visit to a sister queen who ruled in that part. Mimburti had sharp faces, whereas these had almost humanlike, softer visages, with intelligent eyes. He had been charmed by the mimburti, as he was by these beings now. If he squinted and ignored their outward appearance, he could pretend he was watching the daily activity of a small human village. He could tell right away which were nurturers, which were hunters, and which of the largest males was the leader. Females and smaller males picked through piles of spiny seed pods, the fruit of one of the evergreen tree species of the area, breaking them open and gleaning the shiny red seeds. Some they ate, but most they put into a pile in the center, obviously a supply to be used in common. Another group sorted heaps of black seeds that came from long, gray, oval pods, but ate none of them. Magpie wondered why.

"What are those?" he asked Rin.

The centaur shook her long mane. "I do not know. They grow only here, in this small patch of land. These hairy people do not allow visitors to pluck from the bushes where they grow. They are very protective of their territory. If any of the Windmanes have tried the black beans, I never heard of it. The red beans are tasty, but more of a confection than nourishment. They make Windmanes giddy."

"They are to be pitied," a woman named Vreia said. "They are more lost than other beings that we have known of. We of the Scholardom have watched them for centuries, waiting until we can aid them."

"Aid them?" Magpie asked. "What for? They seem happy."

"They are," Rin said, stamping a hoof. "They are the most harmless of creatures. We Windmanes pay little attention to them. They never attack us. They hardly seem to know that we are here. In fact, they seldom leave their small hunting grounds. Their territory is no more than three runs by two. A good thing that the area is very fertile, and gives them good forage and hunting."

"One might even say that it was designed for them," Lakanta said with a sharp nod. "I've seen them before on my travels once in a while peeking through the trees. This is not far off my usual trade route. They seem very much at home here. They are very protective of that cave of theirs, though no one else of sense would ever want to live here."

"That is precisely the point," Sharhava said. "These are not natural beings. Our annals show that they did not exist in ancient days. Their image is not among the many inscribed upon the walls of the Universities or the Bestiaries, or the Caves of the Beginning of Time. The wizards you name the Shining Ones made them."

"Why?" Magpie asked. "Do you have any idea what was their purpose?"

"For the same reason the Creators made so many other beings," Loisan growled. "Because they were curious. Because they wanted to. It is unconscionable to meddle with the Mother's designs."

"Hmph!" Rin said. She stamped a hoof. "I find that the Creators did good work."

The knights paid no attention to her comment.

"They are not normal," Vreia said. "Look how they play with sticks, for no purpose."

A group of smaller, slimmer beasts were indeed sitting around a pile of sticks, but not purposelessly. They used their quick hands to sort through the heap, which was constantly being added to by other workers, for so Magpie might name them, in search of the straightest twigs with a hook or crotchet on the end. When they had selected a stick for shape, they snapped or chewed it to length, approximately the distance from the sole of one of their leathery feet to the hair-covered knee, then peeled off the bark until the smooth, pale wood was exposed. A heap of these sharp, hooked sticks lay to one side. When one was finished, it was added to the pile. When the pile reached a certain height, one of the workers gathered it up and brought it to the leader, who sat by himself underneath a tree. He inspected each stick, discarding a few but keeping the others in neat rows.

"They seem very normal to me," Tildi said, venturing an opinion. Magpie grinned at her. She had been so frightened since she had tried to get help from that group of field hands. The knights' rough treatment had put a lid on her practical and outgoing personality. He hated to see her stifled by Sharhava and her ilk.

"To themselves, I am sure that they are," he said. Tildi gave him a wavery smile.

"You have not seen as many of their errors as we have," Auric said, not unkindly. He, too, seemed now to have spent enough time with Tildi to see through the horror of "anathema," though a knight would almost certainly have gone into exile rather than admit it. "We have found suffering beings in out-of-the-way places, clinging to marginal existence, and all because not enough thought went into their makeup. Yet they continue to live and to breed. It is wrong. They must not suffer further."

"Suffer?" Lakanta asked. "They don't appear to be suffering."

"You cannot see it as we have. To be mutilated as these creatures have been must weigh heavily upon their souls. At last, we are able to remedy this wrong." He bestowed a paternal smile upon Tildi.

Magpie's heart thumped in his chest.

"What are you going to do?"

"Correct the problem. The Creators no doubt realized what a terrible mistake they had made by inflicting change upon so many beings. Yet, they were as mortal as we. They had not time to restore their natural shape to all the things they had changed before Father Time claimed them."

"Are you certain?" Magpie asked. "The Shining Ones seem to have gone to a great deal of trouble to make this habitation everything that these lovely beasts need to exist independently forever."

"I won't argue with you," Sharhava said. "If you think they are so harmless, watch now!"

From the mouth of the cave, two of the beasts came running. They fell down before the leader and launched into a litany of grunting and moaning. The chief rose to his feet and let out a loud cry. The remaining adults dropped what they were doing. Most of them followed the chief's ululations to the big tree. A few of the others, mostly smaller females, gathered up the children and made them take hold of a long vine that had been tied in a circle.

"What are they doing? Is it a ritual?" Lakanta asked.

"They are afraid of the creatures in the cave," Vreia said. "I studied them for two years during my postulancy. Watch and see."

The beasts were mustering together now. No sign of the placid, peaceful mien they had shown. They were wild-eyed, showing sharpened teeth. The fur at the back of their necks stood out in a ridge. They grabbed up the hooked sticks and thrust them into the air, hooting like a pipe organ out of tune. The smaller adults clustered around them, trilling encouragement. The chief, stick hoisted on high, pushed his way through them and led them toward the cave.

He had not quite reached it when something boiled out of it like a pot overflowing. Green tendrils, like those of a plant crossed with a sea monster, rolled across the ground, flicking and curling back upon themselves. Magpie wondered what kind of a land monster had boneless, muscular limbs like that. They clustered together like a school of eels, undulating in a hypnotic pattern. It made them look like one huge monster.

"Horrible!" Tildi exclaimed. "What are they?"

"A cave snake of some kind," Vreia said. "Fairly harmless, or so we believe."

"It is not a cave snake," Serafina said, her brow furrowed. "Look at the rune it bears! It is connected to the earth in some way. These are roots feeling upward from the core of Alada."

"Impossible!" Vreia said. "They are just some kind of animal. The hairy ones are afraid of them."

"I have never seen their like in all my life," Teryn said hoarsely. Beside her, Morag nodded agreement. He was slack-jawed with astonishment.

Vreia pointed. "Watch. They are fearsome hunters."

The beasts did not let the cave snakes progress farther than a few yards. They leaped upon the tendrils and began stabbing at them with the sticks. The tendril-monsters fought fiercely back, throwing loops around the bodies or necks of the beasts, hoping to strangle their opponents. Undeterred, the beasts went to one another's defense, tearing with their teeth or blunt claws until their fellows dropped free and lay on the ground panting. As soon as they got their breath back they continued to stab, getting covered with green goo. When one of the hairy beasts got a stick hooked firmly into the heart of a thick pseudopod, it yanked upward. A red vein or tendon surfaced through the mass of fibrous tissue. The beast leaned over and chewed on it. Wine-red liquid spouted up around its face. Magpie recoiled at the sight, imagining how horrible it must taste. Inbecca, beside him, was as green as the tendrils. The coiling snake dropped limply to the ground. The beast let out a howl of triumph and leaped upon another pseudopod.

Sticks and teeth were not their only weapons. Three of the older beasts stood behind the fighters. Each time another cluster of tendrils started out of the cave and attempted to spread out to the sides, evading the small army, they raised their hands and pointed their palms at them. The clusters recoiled. Magpie felt his jaw drop. They were using magic! They were able to herd the monsters in the direction they wished them to move. These were not ordinary animals, as the Scholardom kept insisting, not when they could use spells.

"We should aid them," he said, starting to rise.

"They can manage," Vreia said.

"Stay where you are, Prince," Loisan said. "I'll not hesitate to bind you or any of your friends if you interfere. You are an observer only."

Quelling his impatience, Magpie crouched in his place.

As abruptly as it had begun, the battle ended. The few moving tendrils snapped and swayed to get away from the beasts. Sensing victory, the chief stood up and let out his musical "hoot hoot."

The others let go of their prey and jumped back. The tendrils withdrew hastily into the cave mouth, dragging the lank limbs behind. The beasts howled and danced, celebrating. The older ones turned their power upon the recoiling pseudopods, hastening them away. Some of the beasts ran after the limbs, threatening them with their sticks, or even throwing their weapons after them. In a moment, the monster had retreated so far into the cave that Magpie could no longer see it at all. The beasts bumped shoulders and elbows, grinning and hooting happily. The smaller females ran to the heaps of fruit and brought it to the combatants. Hungrily, the warriors bit into the yellow rinds, revealing brilliant pink, juicy flesh. They ate and drank and called to one another across the glade. If they had been human, this would have been the time for swapping tales of their prowess and bravery and, no doubt, a few lies. The beast wizards tottered carefully to fallen logs or large stones and settled down upon them with the weariness of elders who had exhausted their strength. The young females brought them fruit with an attitude of respect. The chief received the most plentiful offerings of fruit and red seeds, which he shared with fighters whom Magpie had observed defeating the most of the enemy. He felt glad for them all. They had been valiant.

"What heroes!" he said to Inbecca. "By Time and Nature, I am glad we came to see these people. They are amazing. I shall sing of them from one end of the land to the other."

Sharhava gathered herself up and addressed her knights.

"Brothers and sisters, the time is now! We strike while they are too tired to fight us."

"Fight?" Magpie echoed, springing to his feet. "You must not harm these beings. They deserve to be left alone."

"We intend to do what is best for them, Prince," Sharhava said placidly. "It will not harm them at all. It will make them normal." She nodded past him. Magpie felt strong hands take his arms and a knife tip touch the side of his neck. By the sounds of breath on the back of his head, there were two guards holding him. "You will stay out of the way. I do not wish your interference. Lar Inbecca! Your duty."

"Inbecca, you can't participate in this," Magpie said urgently. He held out his hand to her. The knife blade poked a little farther into his flesh. He let it drop. "Inbecca!"

She met his eyes for a moment, then bowed her head and walked away from him hastily.

"I must obey," she said.

"Inbecca!"

She didn't look up, but her shoulders slumped beneath her habit. Magpie leaned forward to go after her, but the knife tip changed position, pricking a spot just over his collarbone. He clenched his hands in frustration.

The other knights spread out among the furry beings. The beasts showed no fear of them at all. They were openly curious, patting an arm or a leg as one of the humans walked by them. The server females even offered them fruit. The knights regarded them coolly. Magpie decided they were observing the beasts, but not in a way that a naturalist would.

His blood chilled in his veins. They were looking for weaknesses.

He leaned over to Serafina, who sat nearby, watching both knights and natives with an air of curiosity.

"I believe they mean mischief," he said. "Don't let anything happen."

"What do you fear?" Serafina asked.

"Slaughter," Magpie said. He felt for the knife in his belt, wishing that the knights had not taken away his sword. The men flanking him said nothing, either to confirm or deny.

Children followed the knights as they walked between them. They tried to get the human's attention, smiling and performing antics. Magpie smiled at them, but when the children tried to approach, his guards thrust them back roughly.

"Stop that!" he said. "They don't deserve your ill treatment."

The children didn't take offense from the guards' shoves. Instead, they turned their regard upon Tildi. The sight of the smallfolk girl made them break out in musical trills and coos. Tildi smiled shyly at them. The little ones, encouraged by a friendly face, hurried to meet her, but her guardians moved toward them threateningly. The children scattered, laughing, unafraid of the armored men. They regrouped behind Rin, whom they appeared to regard as a safe ally. Centaurs must have been a familiar sight, as their land was not far away.

Shortly, Sharhava called the knights together. "Have you made your study?"

"Aye," the group said. Inbecca's hesitant tone came a beat behind the others.

"Are they more human or animal?"

"Animal."

"Animal."

"Human," said Follet. The others looked at him. He shrugged. "That is my analysis, Abbess."

"Lar Inbecca?"

Magpie bent his eye upon her, as if he could sway her by pure thought to spare the beasts from whatever the knights had in mind. She didn't look at him.

"I . . . I don't really know. They seem intelligent, though they don't speak."

Sharhava frowned at her. "The rest of you?"

"Animal," the others agreed.

"Then we are agreed. I also say animal, therefore we shall work in concert. Together, now. Concentrate. These creatures will be returned to their blessed state in nature. Let us pray, brethren."

The knights held up their hands and touched them palm to palm with the ones who stood nearest to them, arm over arm with their fellows, until they formed an intricate knot of humans with Sharhava at the center. They closed their eyes and began to intone softly. Beside Magpie, the guards, too, began to chant. He listened but he could not distinguish what they were saying.

"Can they do anything?" Magpie demanded of Serafina, who sat a few paces away. "They haven't got any magic of their own."

"I . . . yes, it is possible. They have studied the wherefore for centuries. Now they have the means to execute their will. You don't believe they mean to use the book's power . . . ?"

"Yes!" Magpie said. That was it. The beasts *were* people. They weren't animals, not in the sense of a deer or a dog. If they lacked a language, they still had culture and intelligence. Whatever Sharhava had in mind, he knew it would be the end of their existence.

The worst came true before he had had a chance to imagine it. Before his eyes, he saw the runes upon the beasts' bodies begin to change. Lines were being erased as if they were being scraped from parchment with a knife blade. Behind the golden runes, the beasts' bodies were twisting and altering. Soon, their history would be wrenched away from them, like a book the adults deigned too difficult for them to handle.

Magpie leaped up. His startled guards made a grab for him, but he darted back and forth, eluding them light-footed. Their armor kept them from being able to move as swiftly as he. Magpie ducked between them, leaving them clutching each other instead. All he could think of was stopping the power at the source. He ran for Tildi.

The smallfolk girl was watching the knights with fear in her big brown eyes. Magpie dodged in between her two watchers and picked her up, snatching the tether out of the hands of the larger man. She weighed less than a child. With her in his arms, he fled toward the road. The horses were there. He could cut one loose and be on his way south. To Olen. Yes, he must take her to Olen.

"No!" Tildi cried. "Take me back! Please. They will destroy my home! They want to hurt my people."

"Call the book to you," he pleaded. "Don't let them harm *these* people. I will help you, I swear it. Stop them."

"I don't know what to do," Tildi said.

"You are a wizard," Magpie said desperately. He felt the heat of her skin sear his, but he did not slacken his run. "Stop what they are doing! Please, Tildi. Counter their spell!"

The smallfolk girl put her hands on his, unaware of the pain she caused him. "I don't know any counterspells. I haven't learned that much yet. Please, have pity."

He didn't reply. All he could see in his mind's eye was the confused looks on the faces of the beasts.

He must get the book far enough away that it no longer cast the runes on the beasts, so Sharhava's plan would be foiled. How far must he go? How far? He put his hand over Tildi's head to shield her from the branches that swung toward his face. They raked his cheeks. Runes glowing in the trees taunted him. How would he know when he was far enough away?

"Do what you can," he said. "I will help you protect the smallfolk, in any way I can, I promise, only stop them!"

"I can't stop them," Tildi said. The great scroll flew beside them like a hunting hound. "It is already too late. I *heard* it happen. Take me back. The Quarters are in danger!"

Crashing noises behind him told Magpie that the knights had recovered from their surprise and were in pursuit. The noises drew closer. Something lashed the side of his leg. He hissed at the pain. Suddenly his ankles slapped together. He tried to save himself, but he couldn't. He fell flat on his chest among rough-skinned roots and creepers. Tildi went flying out of his arms toward an immense tree trunk. Magpie scrambled to his knees, hoping to save her.

It was too late, but not for the reason he feared. Tildi had not crashed into the tree. She hovered several feet in the air, the book in her arms. She had saved herself by magic. The guards clustered around both of them, swords pointed at their heads. Tildi waited obediently until the larger knight took her waist leash and followed his curt nod, walking on nothing between the big men.

"Are you hurt?" she asked Magpie as she passed. He lay stretched on the ground panting, like a deer shot by hunters. He smiled at her, though his ribs ached.

"I am all right. Are you?"

Tildi cast a fearful look at her captors. "Please don't tell anyone what I said."

"I won't."

The knight tugged her lead, and she turned away.

He couldn't move his legs. He rolled onto his side, and saw that lengths of rope weighted with round stones had tied themselves around them. They had used a hunting snare. Two knights, Braithen and Vreia, stared down at him, stony-faced.

"How appropriate," he said dryly. "Would anyone care to help me up?"

Braithen knelt beside him and yanked his legs into the air. He unwound the whiplike weapon from around Magpie's shins and tucked it into a pouch on his belt.

"Get up, Your Highness," he said.

Reluctantly, Magpie climbed to his feet. The knight tied a rope around his elbows, securing it behind him so he couldn't move his upper arms, then led him toward the clearing. Magpie's heart was full of dread.

Chapter Seven

The children still danced about the knights surrounding Sharhava, but they had changed. The first thing Magpie noticed was their eyes. They seemed less bright, less intelligent. The knights let down their hands, breaking the knot of humanity that had forged the spell. The sudden movement startled the children. One of them let out a scream of terror, and fled from the clearing. His shouts alarmed his friends, who backed away from the strangers, eyes wide with horror. When they reached a safe distance out of reach of the knights they started shouting in shrill voices.

"It is finished," Sharhava said, raising her voice over the din. "The human element has been removed from their rune. It did not belong. They are returned to their proper state."

The adult beasts rose from their repose. Their fur seemed to have coarsened, and their faces had become sharper, less human. His heart aching with pity, Magpie saw the difference in the runes. Where once they had been complex and cleanly drawn, the sigils that remained were simpler, almost blurred, like inexpert writing by a child. The children went running to their parents. The elders gathered them up and followed the frantic pointing. Though they had accepted the knights' appearance before, the adults now seemed confused by the sight of smooth-skinned, uniformed beings in their clearing. They put the children behind them and growled fiercely at the threatening strangers, but the children had lost their understanding of safety. They kept dashing between the knights and their parents, trying to make sense of the visitors. They were all alarmed and confused. Magpie felt so sorry for them.

"Isn't there anything we can do to help?" he asked, appealing to Tildi. "I know the names in the book look like the ones they have now. Aren't there any more of them somewhere that the spell didn't touch you can look at, to repair the harm?"

The scroll spun from spindle to spindle at Tildi's touch, but she shook her head sadly. "All of them in the world are here," she said.

Magpie evaded the attempts of his guards to pull him back to his place. He threw himself down on his knees beside the smallfolk girl.

"Change them back, Tildi. You know how."

"I haven't got the rune for them," Tildi said forlornly.

"But it was in the book. It was on their backs. You saw it!"

"I can't remember it," she said. "It changed before their bodies did. I told you, I heard it happen. The voices told me."

"This is awful," Lakanta said, watching the beasts with pity in her wide blue eyes. "They are acting as though they are drunk."

"They are disoriented," Serafina said. "As you would be, if half your history was torn away from you in a twinkling."

"An excellent outcome, brothers and sisters," Sharhava said, surveying the beasts in the clearing. "I admit it was a spur-of-the-moment decision to come here, but I could not resist the opportunity to see the result of our work face-to-face. With the book we shall now be able to do our work at a distance. It won't be necessary to travel to where the abominations are to be found. Locating the page upon which they are described will be enough. The long waiting is over. Alada shall be cleansed of the mistakes imposed upon it by the so-called Creators. See how well these are adapting to normalcy?"

Magpie was aghast. Sharhava could not have been more mistaken. Any semblance to normalcy was fast vanishing in the clearing. Magpie felt as though he were watching a boatload of dear friends sailing downriver toward a raging waterfall. The adult beasts circled around the knights, trying to scare the intruders from their home with bared claws and teeth. A few of the biggest ones grabbed sticks off the ground, still stained with scarlet and green ichor, and brandished them. In response, the knights merely drew their swords halfway. The slick sound of steel grating on metal or wood alarmed the beasts. Some retreated, snatching up their children and fleeing to the edge of the forest. Some of the males, the leader among them, stood firm. They looked pitiful and weak compared with just a few minutes before. Magpie's heart ached for them. He had seen men struck in the head, in battle or as the result of an accident. Some became childish in their behavior. Many of those realized that they had lost something vital, but they could not call it back to them.

To their credit, not all the knights were complacent about their deed. Loisan had the decency to look shaken. His normally rosy face had faded to gray.

"We should depart from here, mistress," Loisan said. "Our task is complete. We have no further business here."

"In a while, brother," Sharhava said. She seemed well pleased. She made her way into the heart of the clearing and sat down upon the humped root under the leader's tree and placed her hands, both good and bad, upon her knees. Magpie longed to remove the smug expression from her face. "I would find it satisfying to observe them for a time."

Her lieutenant knew better than to argue. He bowed his head. "As you will, Abbess."

Sharhava made herself comfortable, leaning back against the tree, into the worn spot in the bark that marked the spot where the leader had reposed, no doubt for years.

The leader found this invasion of his territory unacceptable. He breasted up to Sharhava, hooting and shrieking fiercely and waving his hands. His message was clear: she should vacate his seat. She glared back, not moving a hair. The leader backed up a pace. He picked up a pointed stick from the ground and hefted it. He charged.

"Guards!"

Sharhava's bodyguard rushed in, meeting the black-furred male with a grid of crossed steel yards before he would have touched the abbess. The leader windmilled to a halt. He shook the stick at them and at Sharhava. She stared at him, imperturbably.

The leader had had enough. Nostrils flaring with anger, he raised his hands as the elders had done during the battle against the cave monster and pressed his palms toward Sharhava.

Nothing happened, certainly not what the leader was expecting. He tried again, throwing his whole body into the effort. Sharhava remained unaffected. The leader stared at his palms, horror on his face. His magic was gone. His body sagged. He rallied, remembering that he still had a weapon: his stick. He raised it on high, calling a challenge to Sharhava. The quartet of knights hunched toward him. He struck at them. They turned the flats of their blades upon him, driving him back with blows to the limbs and chest. He did not want to retreat, but he had no choice. The knights pressed him inexorably. Magpie could tell they didn't intend to hurt him, but the more he threw himself at them, the more bruises and cuts he got.

"Stop it, old fellow." The largest of the guards took him on directly. The leader snarled a wordless reply. The guard kept his calm. "You'll not get to our abbess through me."

The leader kept trying to sidestep him to get back to his seat, but he was outflanked with every move. He dodged from side to side. The guards kept step with him. At last, the big man took his sword in both hands like a quarterstaff, and shoved. The beast went staggering back.

He was beaten.

This opportunity was what some of the younger males seemed to have been waiting for for some time. Their chief had been proven powerless. A handful of them started urging one another forward, cuffing each other half playfully, half seriously. In a moment, a clear winner had emerged among the young males. This fellow, a healthy specimen half a head taller than the others, breasted up to the leader. Throwing his head back, he let out a long wail.

The leader seemed startled by the challenge. He held up the stick, still in his right hand, as if to say, "Remember who I am?" Unimpressed, the youngster fleered his upper lip and flexed his arms. Finished with verbal warnings, the leader snarled and jumped at him. The youngster fell over backward with a yelp with the leader on top of him.

The pair rolled over and over across the clearing. The others jumped out of the way, their cries egging the fighters on. The young one clamped his teeth into the leader's hand that held the stick. His face contorted, the leader struggled, but he finally had to drop the stick. The young male let out a screech of triumph as he flipped out of the leader's grasp and, with a complicated move that would have been the pride of an Orontavian wrestler, scissored his legs up and over. He ended up sitting on the leader's back, pounding the elder's face into the dirt. He accepted the acclaim of the crowd, kicking the leader in the head whenever the elder tried to raise it. Magpie felt sorry for the older male.

"A dynasty changes," Rin said. "The strongest leads."

"Why did you unmake them?" Magpie asked Sharhava, who appeared to be enjoying the spectacle. "Do you call this a responsible use of power? They had a hierarchy that worked well for them."

"I cannot expect you to understand our cause. These beasts were changed horribly. They needed to return to their normal state. Their king was old. He would have been superseded in the natural way of things. Soon they will remember the way things were before the meddling wizards interfered with them, and adapt."

"This is not a recent alteration. It goes back millennia. Look at them," he said. "You have destroyed them."

Sharhava regarded him steadily. "Nonsense. This is the way they were meant to be. You cannot let sentiment fool you into thinking otherwise. They would be grateful to us, if they had the capacity for logical thought. Now they can live the lives they were always meant to have. Nothing important will change. If their king has been replaced by a younger beast, it was his time, nothing more than that."

The leader picked himself off the ground. He was not going to let his office slip away from him unchallenged. As the youth accepted the accolade of his peers and the worship of some of the fruit-pickers, the leader gathered himself, then leaped at the young male from behind. The two of them went down together. The others crowded in upon them, shouting. They clawed and hit at whatever they could reach. Magpie could no longer see the original combatants, but the two factions, that of the old chief and that of the new, started to draw blood from each other.

The melee was short and brutal. Without their magic, the elders could not withstand the strength of the young. One by one, they were kicked to the side of the clearing. They huddled together, trembling, covered in blood and wounds. The crowd of youths went on beating the old leader. He struggled to get up. He went from shouts of outrage to cries of pain and, finally, whimpers. The youths stopped and backed away, leaving the young leader looking down at the body of the old. He turned the limp form over with his foot. The male on the ground was dead or unconscious. The youth suffered only a moment of shame or regret. He raised his hand to the sky and hooted.

The call was echoed by a gang of children who had retreated from the fray to the mouth of the cave. They ran out, their eyes wide, and threw themselves at the feet of the new leader. That could mean, Magpie thought with horror, only one thing.

"The snakes are back," Lakanta said.

They were. The terrifying green serpents erupted from the cave mouth in greater numbers than in the previous attack. The crowd of beasts gathered in a circle around the new leader, wailing, appealing to him for leadership. The young male stared at the roiling mass of tendrils. One of the others tugged at his arm. It was an urgent plea for action. The youth hooted wildly at his fellows. They began picking up sticks, turning them over without seeming to know what to do with them. He ran at them angrily and slapped them. Magpie realized he did not know what to do. The beasts were without leadership, without intelligence, and without magic.

"They are doomed," he said.

"They must learn to cope with their surroundings," Sharhava said. "They have been sustained artificially all this time. The Mother and the Father are surely less offended by this state of being. The beasts will find a way to survive."

"The beasts?" Magpie said, aghast. "Do you think only the beasts are in danger from the snakes?"

At last he had gotten their attention. The entire Scholardom turned to look at him.

"What do you mean?" Vreia demanded.

"What will happen when the beasts can no longer hold back those tentacles? What did Serafina call them, the roots of the earth? They're strong enough to strangle a man. Once they are let loose, what will they do? They strive to kill anything that moves. Obviously the beasts are not the only ones who lack logic and foresight!" He rounded on Sharhava. "You caused this, and many more might die because of it!"

A heavy blow from behind knocked Magpie to his knees. Magpie clutched his ringing head and looked up. Loisan loomed above him, his sword drawn.

"Show more respect to the abbess," the big man growled. But he looked uncomfortable at Magpie's words. So did some of the other knights.

None of their aching consciences helped the situation at hand.

In disarray, the beasts mounted an indifferent defense against their ancient enemy. The snakelike creature cast loops around two of the small females and squeezed.

As Magpie watched agape, the leading end of the snake opened up like a funnel and engulfed the smallest beast. The green maw closed over the red-furred legs. The feet kicked for a short time. They stilled shortly before they, too, were swallowed up. He glanced at the knights. A few let momentary regret move across their faces, but he could tell they did not particularly care what became of a lesser species.

Unhampered by the beasts' spells, the snakes fanned outward, seeking other prey. The smallest snakes must have been the vanguard, for the newest to emerge from the cave were even larger than the first. They rolled on past the thrashing army of beasts and made for Sharhava. She rose to her feet, her eyes wide with alarm.

"Abbess, behind me!" Loisan bellowed. He rushed to interpose himself between his mistress and the questing monsters. The bodyguard formed around him, swords drawn. "Knights, on defense!"

No question now whether or not to involve themselves.

Sharhava's bodyguard fended off the advances of the two huge snakes. Loisan parried against the coil of the first one, then chopped his blade down hard. Ichor ran from the cut, and the beast shrank back from him for a moment. The lieutenant called for help, and four knights came to his aid. Inbecca was among them. Together, they managed to sever a couple of yards of tendril, which continued to writhe and twist on the ground while the rest of the creature withdrew. The second snake, as if sensing the defeat of its companion, responded furiously. It grasped Brouse in its toils and squeezed him until the stout almoner's face was as red as a cherry.

"Abbess, you should withdraw," Loisan called hoarsely over his shoulder.

"No, I will not retreat!" Sharhava said. She drew her own sword and marched into the fray. As little as Magpie liked her, she was the aunt of his beloved and he respected her courage. He drew his belt knife and ran into the clearing to help. Two of the knights wrestled the end of the monster away from Brouse's neck. Magpie plunged his knife into the writhing tube. The others sliced into the body of the second monster until they were all spattered with green fluid, and the slashed remains lay motionless upon the ground. Magpie backed away from it.

"It's no easy task to slay these," he panted.

"Ware enemy!" Rin shouted from behind them. "Prince, your ankle!"

There was a flash of black and white as Rin leaped over the bushes and dived into the midst of the action. Magpie looked down. A gigantic vine was stalking his foot as a terrier pursued a rat. He danced away from it. Rin galloped in and pushed him aside.

"Now, menace, feel the wrath of a Windmane!" she cried. She reared up and brought her front hooves down upon the gigantic tendril. It shrank from the blow, and retreated as soon as she lifted herself up again for another blow. Comprehending that these were not easy targets, it reared up on half its length and reached for a trio of beasts. Rin cantered after it, wheeled, and began to kick at it with her back hooves. The beasts cowered from her at first, but when they realized she was helping them, they hooted their war cries and leaped on the monster. The tendril could not withstand the combined onslaught and tried to creep away. Rin let out a bloodthirsty laugh and galloped along its length. She leaped into the air and came down with all four hooves sinking into the crisp flesh. Red fluid scattered everywhere. The beasts followed her, shrieking, and dug into the tendril with their weapons.

"You're not going to have all the fun on your own," Lakanta exclaimed. She picked up a sturdy fallen branch and waded in after the centaur. With a brief glance at their captors, Captain Teryn and Morag hurried to join in the fight.

"We must drive them all back again," Serafina called. "They cannot be allowed to stray from this clearing! Drive them back!"

A trio of enormous cave snakes appeared, bowling over the crowds of beasts and humans in their way. Magpie tripped backward in haste to avoid being knocked askew by the leading coil.

They curled to either side to allow for the passage of the biggest monster yet. As though it knew there was something special about her, it bore down upon Tildi. The smallfolk girl stood transfixed, staring at the huge creature as it rushed toward her. The maw opened.

"Flee! Flee!" Magpie shouted.

The guards seized Tildi's arms and backpedaled, but he knew it was futile. No human could outrun the sinuous tendrils. The king of the monsters reared up, preparing to swallow the girl whole. The knights drew their swords and struck at the funnel-like mouth. It recoiled in pain, but snapped back. Dripping ichor, it moved to engulf Tildi. She screamed.

An insubstantial gray sheet interposed itself between Tildi and her fate. The wide mouth struck it and rebounded, like a bird striking a window. It struck again, but its head came no nearer than a yard. A thin-limbed rune hung in the air between them. It looked too fragile to withstand such an attacker, but it held. Tildi seemed to recover her wits at that moment, and her hands began to move. She put out a forefinger and drew marks on the air in thin black lines. The monster retreated farther.

Only then did Magpie remember Serafina, standing silent at the side of the clearing. He turned to see her pulling an invisible mass between her hands. Her face was like that of a stone statue, flawless and emotionless. She spread out an invisible sheet and pushed it from her, as if launching a sail into the wind.

The beasts continued to fight for their lives. Some had fallen. Their relicts had no time to mourn them, lest they become the next to die. The smaller adults picked up the children and ran out of the clearing. Others tried to pull the wounded out of the way of the questing tendrils.

A thinner, more insubstantial veil joined the first one. Together, the shields spread out throughout the glade. Where they extended, the snakes' progress halted as though a wall were thrown up. Some of the serpents attempted to climb it, but their bodies found no purchase. The veils drove them back over the blood-soaked ground, inexorably forcing them toward the mouth of the cave. The snakes struggled against the translucent shields, but ended up rolling and squirming over one another and their victims as they were driven along. The beasts, now harried by both seen and unseen enemies, grew hysterical with fear. They raged against whatever they could reach, biting and scratching.

"The hairy people are caught in it," Tildi said, her small face straining with the effort to concentrate.

"Surround them," Serafina said simply. "Build a wall around each. Draw them through. The wards will hold."

Tildi nodded and began to make small designs in the air. As she completed one, it floated away from her to join the wall she had created, melted into it, then separated from it in a different shape: a cylinder. Each of those glided over the torn ground. As it touched a beast, it popped like a soap bubble, then re-formed with the besieged one within it. The beasts all cried in terror, and started beating their fists upon their insubstantial prisons. The snakes, robbed of their prey, threw themselves at the faint cocoons. They could not get through. The denial frustrated them into frenzied attacks. With open maws, they launched their whole lengths at their prey. The beasts threw themselves against the far wall in panic. Yet they were not as unintelligent as the knights believed them. Some quickly came to understand that while they could not get out, their foes could not get in. Magpie fancied he could see glee erupt on more than one hairy face. They waited for whatever providential miracle had occurred to finish working its will upon them. The rest were terrified, cowering at the bottom of the spell-cast cylinders. Magpie ignored the protests of the knights standing by him and went for his pipe, tucked in his right-hand saddlebag. He played soft but sprightly melodies, hoping to calm the fearful ones.

"Put them to the side," Serafina instructed Tildi, working her hands as though she were folding a cloth. "I intend to wall these snakes up within the cave with a warding. They do not belong here on the surface, but I am wary of destroying them."

Tildi nodded. Magpie admired the way the girl took to the task at hand with no more fuss than if she had been told to cook supper for a hundred guests. One by one she rescued beasts and set them close to him. Parents looked for their children. When they saw they were safe, they became more aware of their own surroundings, and became at peace with them. They were far more trusting than a human would be under similar circumstances, Magpie thought, most likely because nothing in their environment had ever harmed them but the snakes. Everyone else they had ever encountered had been benign or friendly.

He played a lively dance tune with his fingertips. The beasts caught on to the melody very quickly and started singing along. Magpie took only a moment to wonder at their facility with music, because his eyes were still fixed upon the spectacle at the cave.

"That's the last," Tildi said.

"Well done," Serafina said to Tildi, scowling. Her eyes were fixed upon a distant point. "I see this will be more difficult than I thought. Do you have strength to spare me?"

Tildi thought for a moment, then gave a surprised nod. She smoothed down her mussed tunic with her palms and folded her hands together neatly. "I am not tired at all, master."

"Good. Aid me. We must build a permanent warding here, one that will seal this being in its cave, but deep within. The beasts use it as a shelter against bad weather. We must not deprive them of that."

"No, I can see that," Tildi said, frowning thoughtfully. "What an uncomfortable neighbor to have while one is hiding from a thunderstorm!"

"It is one we all have," Serafina said. "Somehow the roots of the earth have reared up in this place. Only the vigilance of this one species has kept it from creeping out upon the surface, where it was never meant to be."

"Roots of the earth?"

"Read from it," Serafina said, indicating the enormous rune that overlay the impatient tendrils. "It is one creature, and it is joined to the heart of our world. No, don't let your concentration lapse! There will be plenty of time later. We will weave a net. Air and water must still move freely, as must the smaller creatures of earth, but the roots may not leave the underground anymore. They learn by devouring, and they have no sense of the harm they do. They are blindly curious, that is all." She moved her hands, and multicolored light left the tip of her wand to join with the gray sheet. "Do you see what I have done?"

"Not really . . . Oh!" Tildi's face wore the pleased expression of discovery. "I do see."

I wish I did, Magpie thought. He sat as the knights did, fascinated but uncomprehending. He felt wisps of will moving around him like a breeze through curtains at night. They were less like physical touches and more like thoughts made tangible. Except for the council meeting at Silvertree, he had never been able to witness great magical working. The court wizard in his father's court in Mimalda had been poor Nemeth, a puissant seer but nearly lacking in wonder-working ability. Magpie was able to enjoy the sensations as he would the legerdemain of a stage conjurer, but the scholars around him looked jealous. He did see now that there was just one rune upon the mass of tendrils. In the melee, he had not noticed. Nor had anyone else, he fancied. He had more respect than ever for Serafina's skills and powers of observation.

Tildi held out her knife, and a concentration of color, a captive rainbow, flowed from the tip to augment Serafina's power. All at once the veil looked less impenetrable. Magpie knew at once that it was permeable to air. He didn't know how he knew, but he would have bet the last coin in his pouch that it was true. With hand and wand, Serafina directed the flow. It captured the errant tendrils—roots—and gathered them almost tenderly within the sac of power.

"Now, back!"

The tips of the pseudopods flailed against their prison, but the delicate curtain drew them inexorably into the cave. Soon, Serafina nodded. She drew a final silver rune upon the air. It flew into the cave. A flash of light burst out, illuminating the mossy stone walls, then died to darkness. Magpie found he had been holding his breath. He let it out.

The boldest of the hairy beasts broke away from their huddled group and went to examine the wizards' handiwork. They crept into the cave with exaggerated wariness, like mountebanks. Their hooting echoed off the cave walls and they came racing out to share the good news with their fellows. The merriment lasted for a while, then the able-bodied beasts became solemn. Under the guidance of the eldest males, the crowd gathered together at one side of the clearing with some of the hooked and pointed sticks and began to bury their dead. The knights watched the activity curiously.

"Animals do not inter or mourn," Vreia observed. For the first time she sounded uncertain. "Did we miss some human characteristics that ought to have been excised?"

"Oh, you!" Lakanta exclaimed. "Let be! Have you not done enough harm?"

Serafina folded her hands and bowed her head. "We are finished. Seal off the power."

"As you say, master," Tildi said. She closed her hands around the hilt of her knife, trying to copy the gesture of her teacher. Magpie felt a kind of release, like an arrow loosed from a bow. The task was done. The air around him returned to normal. No tension, no sense of urgency or purpose remained. The completion also set the knights free.

"That was . . . unnecessary," Sharhava said, her voice sounding oddly far away. She cleared her throat. "Further use of magic was not required."

"It was not unnecessary," Magpie said. "I believe that Tildi and Serafina have saved our lives—all of our lives. What about your action? It robbed these poor people of their wisdom and their own skills."

"They are not people!" The abbess's cheeks turned scarlet. "We did what we had to to restore the balance of life on Alada. Do you question the wisdom of ten thousand years of our study?"

"I will not argue against your *beliefs*. You have done what you wish to those poor beasts," Magpie said. "But you would have left them defenseless against a fearsome enemy. How is that responsible use of power? How is that restoring balance?"

Sharhava held her chin out defiantly. "These creatures were not blessed by the Mother and Father with human intelligence or magical ability."

"Do you believe you equal the judgment of the Mother and Father yourself?" Magpie asked. "These creatures have existed the way they were for thousands of years, without either Nature or Time cursing them."

"The Mother and the Father placed us here as stewards of their gifts. They do not punish or reward directly. We set fate in motion according to our actions. We spent those centuries studying ancient texts, so we could be certain, if—*when* the opportunity came, to correct the mistakes by those you call the Makers," Sharhava said. Her words were too emphatic. Magpie could tell she was shaken, but refusing to back down. "We will continue our studies, now that their tool is in our hands." She turned her gaze to Tildi, who quailed.

"It is foolish to meddle with what you don't understand," Serafina said firmly. "You say that you have studied the book, but not what the book describes! You think rewriting is the only cure—but you don't see the greater picture. And now, you have done unimaginable harm. My specialty is not barricades. For that you need Olen or Komorosh, or one of the southern wizards. I hope that I can get a message to someone. You must let me send a message."

"No!" Sharhava exclaimed. "You will not communicate outside. No one must know . . . what happened here."

"But they will," Rin said. "They cannot help it. The Windmanes will know very soon."

Sharhava had no stomach for further argument. She rounded upon Serafina.

"*You* put us all in danger meddling with a native force."

"The roots?" Serafina asked, stunned. "How did I endanger *you*?"

Sharhava waved her good hand in Tildi's direction. "You allowed that untrained creature to pierce your wards over and over again, and to close the spell at the end. She is no master. You should not have trusted her."

Tildi gaped at the abbess, but Serafina waved at her to remain silent.

"Because of the book she has far more power than I have," Serafina said. "I needed her help to accomplish all of our aims without harming any living being. It was more than my skills could encompass. It gives her nearly the ability of a Creator. When she is fully trained, she will be formidable."

"Well," Sharhava said, swallowing. "There will be no possibility of that in the Scriptorium! No sinful wizardry will be performed within its grounds. All will be done according to the rule of the order! Remember my words, girl!" She shook a finger at Tildi, who lowered her head meekly. Serafina regarded them both and clamped her lips shut. "The evil of your kind must not manifest itself. I forbid it!"

"Evil!" Serafina said, mortified. "She is a child, and a courageous one. You wrong her."

Sharhava was diffident. "She comes of a race of unnatural origin. In time, once we have achieved control of the book, we will reward her for her service by returning her to the state from which her ancestors came."

"What a ridiculous notion," Magpie said, but he was shocked. She could do it. She had just demonstrated that she was capable of upsetting the lives of a people just as old as the smallfolk. Tildi had told him that Sharhava had threatened them. In the frenzy of the moment he hadn't believed her. Perhaps he should have. "They have intelligence, their own customs and culture, their own language!"

Sharhava frowned. "We will make them human again, or render them the species they once were. Then they may carry on with their lives. Nothing will be lost." But she sounded less than sure of herself. "We have much to do before that time comes. Our order will restore all the ills that were done to the world by the Makers."

"We'll see about that," Lakanta said cheerfully. "You don't control the book yet. With luck, you never will."

Sharhava ignored her magnificently. She addressed Loisan and Auric.

"We must make ready to go. Our work here is done, and overdone. There was no need to pen up the cave monsters, but it is done."

"You do not understand what they just did," Magpie exclaimed.

She waved a dismissive hand.

"I know that a natural creature has been restored, but yet another has been interfered with using sorcery. If I had the time . . ." Her voice trailed off. "It is not our business. I will mark it in the annals to correct once we have undone more important infractions against nature."

"That isn't fair, Abbess! She did heroically."

It was no use. Sharhava was not listening. She marched away, her officers in her wake.

Magpie turned back to Tildi. "I can see I will have to add another verse to my song, this time about your puissance in the high arts."

"Aye," Rin agreed. "Where those fool knights meddled, she stepped in. We would have been prey next."

"You are the equal of every legend I have ever heard sung," Lakanta said, patting her on the knee. Tildi recoiled, fearing for her friend's safety, but Lakanta lifted her palm to show she was still invulnerable to burns. "When this lad sings his tale across the world, you'll get the praise you deserve— Oh, sorry, highness, I keep forgetting you are not a bard."

"I have been one for many years, good merchant," Magpie said gravely. "But I have never been a hero. I hope my words will be worthy of the deed Tildi has done." He glanced through the trees toward the beasts. Their culture was remaking itself as they watched. The weaker ones had gathered up small gifts of berries and sticks to present to the new chief. "Poor creatures."

The girl smiled modestly. "I wouldn't have known what to do without Serafina. She is a fine teacher."

"So she is," Magpie said. "She was a rock for the rest of us to cling to. I must tell her so." He looked around for the young wizardess.

Serafina had gone to see to her horse. He found her leaning against the white mare's side, shaking as her hands fumbled within a saddlebag. He put an arm around her and held the bag steady. She drew from it a fine cloth packet smelling strongly of herbs.

"Tea?"

"A restorative," Serafina said. She did not look directly at him. Her cheeks were damp and her eyes suspiciously bright. "I fear we all need it at the moment."

"Allow me," Magpie said. "You rest here. I think you need a moment's privacy."

He brought the packet and a jug of water to Tildi, who had returned to her rug. She sat surrounded at a polite distance by knights. Her tether had been lengthened to two lengths of rope instead of one, a mark of fear or respect. "I think our hosts won't wait for a fire to be made and water boiled, but your teacher needs a cup of tea. Can you . . . ?"

The girl's eyes widened with amused interest, but she took the packet from him. The jug removed itself from his grasp and hovered in midair.

"A fine idea," she said. "Would you like some, too?"

"Not I, but there are others who surely would." He watched the earthenware pot hover. A flame appeared at the bottom, also unsupported. It was green. The knights were fascinated, too, but they kept their faces void of emotion. "You are getting amazingly good at that."

"It is easy," Tildi said, surprised at admitting it out loud. "There is so much power around that it seems almost a shame not to use it. I mean, this is a very unimportant purpose, but it doesn't seem to mind. I . . . I have to admit that I enjoy it. Magic is not approved of in the Quarters, you know."

"I did know. I have visited your homeland many times."

Tildi looked apprehensively over his shoulder. Magpie turned to see the abbess, who was giving vigorous directions with her good hand.

"Don't worry. She can't hear us."

"I fear her," Tildi said in a very low voice. "I fear them all."

"Oh, you don't have to worry about all of them," Magpie said. "I think Auric's getting to be quite an admirer of yours. Loisan seems to have some sense. And Lady Inbecca . . ." His voice trailed off, unable to complete the accolade. She had gone along with the abbess's orders without a murmur of dissent. To have stripped the humanity from those poor creatures, after ten thousand years of intelligence, was a crime. He was angry with her, and was ashamed for the feeling. He needed to puzzle out his thoughts, and he mustn't drag Tildi into his private turmoil. He smiled at her. "Don't fear them all. Human beings are fallible. I wish they could be more like smallfolk, who are never wrong."

Tildi dimpled. "I see you have been to at least one evening Meeting. If you have listened to the elders, you know they have all the answers to every question, right or wrong."

He patted her on the hand. "I will bring cups."

Chapter Eight

harhava's order that she not cause offense left Tildi very much alone with her thoughts over the following days. They turned more to the Quarters all the time since Sharhava had made her threat. So much had been stripped away from Tildi that the thoughts of her now-lost home struck harder than they would have months ago.

Tildi stole a glance at her teacher. She had often noticed the young wizardess weeping when Serafina thought no one else could see. Tildi had done her best to give Serafina her best attention and tender what kindness she could offer. She knew Magpie had also sought to ease her loneliness, amusing her with tales and songs. Lakanta, in her rough, hearty way, had probably done more for the wizardess than any other by voicing outrageous threats against their captors. It let some of the pressure lift from their own thoughts of escape and revenge. In spite of her fears for her people, Tildi would never stop trying to turn her path southward, toward far-off Sheatovra, and that mysterious mountain fastness where the book belonged.

She did not fool herself into thinking such a task was without peril and hardship. Duty kept Tildi's spirits up during the most difficult hours. She had made a promise to Olen, and she had never let a promise go unfulfilled unless it was impossible to keep. She did not count such things as promising her eldest brother Gosto never to whisper or giggle in Meeting when she was eight years old, for what child could remember to keep such a vow? Any oath she had taken once she reached maturity, though, she kept. She counted upon the native stubbornness with which she had been born to see her through this present ordeal and on to the goal of her journey, however she must accomplish it. Her reward would be rich: to rejoin Olen in his living home of Silvertree, and resume her studies of magic with him in that peaceful and nurturing environment. Not that she scorned Serafina's teaching, but the wizardess had only assumed her as a student at the urging of her mother. Tildi knew Serafina had resented the task, and meant to lift it from her as soon as she possibly could, but Tildi had much to learn from the wizardess in the meantime.

Power was a strange feeling. She had never had any before. The knights knew more of the old words than Serafina did, but lacked comprehension of their function or how their variations worked. To them, what was written was an absolute, instead of a living language as the wizards used it. To keep her mind active, Tildi kept on with her spells, making fire, making objects float, and rebuilding the road as the hooves of the horses unmade it. She could not help that some of the knights, Auric especially, observed what she was doing, and began to put some of it to use, such as helping to move heavy logs for the evening campfire. She feared what Sharhava would do with the talent once she got used to having it.

To have more power than anyone in history save for the Shining Ones who had actually created the book was a daunting responsibility. Serafina's warning of the corrupting influence of unlimited power made Tildi think a dozen times before attempting even the smallest spell. It had taken her a moment to allow herself to make fire to boil water for Serafina's tea, and even more for each act of power since that day. The abbess might be ready to march in and change anything she wanted, but if she could only feel what

Tildi did, the sense of the world Tildi received through the book, she might hesitate even to threaten. Tildi hoped so, anyhow. If it weren't for Sharhava's insane desire to remake the world from the way it was, Tildi would have welcomed the knights as an escort to the south. They were doughty fighters, that she had seen while in old Oron Castle, and they were unmoved by riches or personal power. Listening to tales in Olen's household and along the way in Edynn's company, she had learned far more about the ways of the world than she had ever known in quiet little Morningside Quarter. She was learning to make practical and dispassionate choices far beyond her simple beginnings. If only she didn't have to, but who else was there to do it?

She felt tears prick at her eyes.

"What's the matter, little one?"

The troubadour prince's murmur interrupted her thoughts. He had brought his mare up beside Rin. The parts of her tack that might jingle had been tied up in scraps of cloth and braided grass to respect the order of silence. Tildi looked up into his curious yellow-green eyes, so startling in the deep tones of his face.

"She has been sad," Rin said in a low voice, turning her flexible body to face them while still trotting forward. "I have noticed it. Perhaps you can cheer her up."

"Anything," Magpie said, bending down over his saddlebow. He fixed a meaningful look on her. "What may I do to help?"

"I wish you could," Tildi said ruefully. "I wish anyone could."

"I'm often told I'm good at giving advice. Let me try."

"Well . . ." She looked past him at the nearest knight, who was trying to look as though he wasn't straining to hear. With a will, she drove all thoughts of the poor beasts from her mind. She could not risk sounding discontented. Anything that might cause the abbess to wish to punish her for misbehavior was to be avoided. Tildi met Magpie's eyes, and gave him a nod. His quick intelligence picked up at once on its significance. Magpie's wry smile told her he, too, had noticed the knight's scrutiny. She relaxed. "Tell me where I am. I ought to be enjoying this journey. I never went farther than fifty miles from the place I was born. This is so different than the Quarters. It's . . . frustrating. I can see by the book that there is a great waterfall just a couple of miles that way, and I cannot go and see it for myself."

Magpie waved an arm. "It's as dainty as you are."

"You are so much like my brother," she said, blushing.

"Which one?" he asked.

"Oh, Pierin. He was very charming, you know. He always had four or five girls following after him like ducklings."

"You're a harsh one," Magpie said with a wry grin. "If he was like me, then they couldn't help themselves, could they? What about a tune?" He held up a rough-carved pipe. "I made this last evening. It's not pretty, but it is well tuned."

"Play, Prince," Rin said, swiveling her tall ears upright. "There's little to interest me on a straight road when I cannot run."

Magpie twinkled at her. "I know an excellent song about racing that I learned from the merfolk. You'll have to imagine the words, because I can't sing and play at the same time. How I wish I hadn't left my jitar behind!"

"You were thinking of something else," Lakanta reminded him, urging her fat pony, Melune, to Tessera's side.

"So I was," he said gravely. "Attend the minstrel, if you please." He put the pipe to his lips.

A stream of liquid sound trilled from the instrument, and a matching burst of gold threads filled the page beneath Tildi's fingertips. She was delighted. She had no idea that music would have an image at all.

Magpie helped lighten the long days on the road, and Tildi was grateful to him. He reminded her not only of Pierin, but of all of her brothers rolled into one. He appeared to be such a clown, but his feelings and his intelligence ran deeper than anyone knew. He missed little, with his poet's eye, and he had a kindly heart.

He was upset with Inbecca, whom he saw as having assisted the knights in their terrible work.

Inbecca was upset with herself, too. Tildi watched her following Magpie with her eyes filled with the deepest longing. Tildi had never been in love, but her brother Pierin had always been enamored of this girl or that, and she knew all the signs. Unlike his puppy crushes that lasted only weeks at a time, this was true.

In fact, she knew much more about Inbecca and Magpie and all of the others. The truth was there in their runes. She could read people like stories. Surely anyone who had that knowledge could pick up the surface facts, but because the book talked to her she had insights into her companions' emotions and thoughts. The way the ideographs moved and changed told her so much. A part of her was mortified at the invasion of their privacy. Another part felt removed from the turmoil, observing rather than empathizing. The warm cocoon that the book wrapped around her gave her that perspective, but separated her from feelings that she normally would have had.

From that inner knowledge she saw the frustration of her friends and companions. They suffered many different feelings, too. Rin was eager to be off, to run south to her people and race across the plains. Tildi found the rune in the Great Book and was delighted by the extent of the Windmanes' realm. Yet Rin was earnest in her refusal to leave Tildi to the mercies of the knights. The part of Tildi that felt loved her for her loyalty. Lakanta had disposed of her responsibilities and was prepared to stay by her until the end. She had protectively motherly—no—auntly feelings toward Tildi. Serafina was in turmoil, and Tildi purposely refused to concentrate further upon her. Her teacher deserved to work through her sorrow without a voyeur, however well meaning, following every nuance. The voices kept urging her to read more, but she turned her attention to her surroundings.

Tildi glanced up from the scroll to see the abbess's eyes fixed upon her with an angry scowl between them. Tildi felt her heart jump in surprise. Sharhava had been watching her. What had she seen? Had Tildi done anything to make her suspicious? Could she read her rune the way Tildi could read others? She dropped her eyes to the book. Sharhava's sigil seemed to glow with anger, even in her written image.

Tildi regretted horribly the ability that Sharhava and the others possessed with the book in their reach. If she had the courage, she would escape. Sharhava had changed over the last days, becoming more surly and snappish. Tildi feared the abbess's chancy temper would get the better of her. After the situation with the beasts, she was striking out—her rune showed it—because of a hollow place within her. Tildi didn't know enough about the woman to understand what was troubling her. It was difficult enough just to stay out of her way.

She and the others must get free of the Scholardom. She could not allow the knights to harm other creatures the way they had the poor beasts. Yet she could not let Sharhava invade the Quarters. Tildi felt more trapped than ever before. She felt that she could not go on indefinitely in that fashion. *Something* must be done. Perhaps Olen would find them.

What is it that you lack?" Sharhava asked Brouse, the almoner, once the knights' morning meal had been served at their latest campsite on the fourth day. "We are near to Rainbownham."

"Every kind of supply is running short," Brouse said, rocking back on his heels on the thin grass. The stout man had lost some inches since they had set out from Oron Castle. His round cheeks were slowly receding to reveal high, molded cheekbones. "We need flour, meat, and salt, at the very least. Wine. Oil. Butter. Tubers, potatoes, turnips and such, would keep well in the food packs, and provide sustaining meals for us all. My staff can pick greens for a while more, but few young shoots are sprouting. It's fair and away autumn, Abbess. We need everything."

"We'll need more money than we have to make it comfortably to the Scriptorium," Loisan said, consulting with Rachine, who kept the communal purse. "We had not counted on such a long journey, truth be told, not without being able to come and go freely within towns and villages."

"Well, then, you need an expert to help stretch the coins as far as possible,"

Lakanta said, bustling up to the almoner. With him balanced on his heels, he was eye to eye with her. "I couldn't help but overhear, since you always speak as though none of us can understand you. You fine ladies and gentlemen are used to having servants go out and bargain with the farmers and traders in the market, but out here on the road they know you must accept the price they name, or travel miles in another direction. I know all the merchants and farmers along these roads. I'll know who's holding back on the freshest produce and the soundest goods. It's my profession, after all. You may as well let me do the deals for you. Send me."

"No," Sharhava said, looking alarmed. "We do not need your help."

"But we also need food," Lakanta pointed out. "Do I trust you to buy for us?"

"You will," Sharhava said. She turned a cold eye upon Tildi, who cringed. "I do not wish Scholardom business discussed in the marketplace." She gestured to her knights. "Take her back with the others."

"Are you accusing me of gossip?" Lakanta sputtered as two burly men in blue and white habits lifted her by the arms. "You'll get nothing but rotten potatoes and spoiled meat, if you aren't wise to all the tricks. What is wrong in your head that you can't see that?" She continued her protest while they carried her back to her pony and deposited her on the ground beside it. She picked herself up and brushed gravel and grass off the back of her skirts. "Ugh! I do hate stubborn people."

When Brouse and his crew returned in the afternoon, their horses laden with sacks, the dwarf woman could hardly help herself.

"I told you so!" she crowed as she turned over scrawny roots and wilted vegetables. She held up a clutch of greens, thin roots dangling, in one hand, and a limp brown knob in the other. "Oh, for the love of stone, look at these carrots! If these had been children you would have said they were too young to go out without their mam! Except these potatoes could be their grandparents, so old they are. And spoiled oats! Give these to your horses, and you'll have a month of colic with them. I would bet every hair on my head that you bought that lot from a skinny man with a thin beard and eyebrows like the peak of a roof, eh? Made it sound like he'd give you a better price than anyone in Rainbownham? Aha! You did! You were cheated raw. Do you still have your boots? It'd be a wonder if you do."

The knights blushed scarlet. Tildi could tell that it was on the tip of their tongues to ask if she could do better, and every one of them knew she could. Shamefacedly, one of Brouse's aides brought a couple of the sacks to Morag. The soldier with the misshapen face accepted them without saying a word and retired to the far end of the campsite to prepare dinner. For once, Tildi thought wryly, she would not be able to blame the bad taste of the meal on his cooking.

"I'm coming with you the next time," Lakanta declared, pounding her forefinger into her other palm. "You all claim to be scholars, and a lot of books I am sure you've read, but you don't know a thing about your fellow humans."

"We've news as well, Abbess," Lar Mey said. His cheeks were red with shame.

"Tell me," said Sharhava.

Tales of the cataclysm have spread widely," the young knight said with a sideways glance at Magpie. "Rumor is mixed freely with the stories of eye-witnesses. Most of the displaced survivors did not stop until they reached Mimalda. The king is distraught."

"My father? Why?" Magpie asked, shouldering into the circle of knights.

Mey turned to him and met his gaze seriously.

"Highness, it is known that you departed your betrothal secretly. Word spread as soon as it occurred. Rumor had it that you fled into the north, for what reason it was not really known."

Magpie's face went dusky red, and he slewed a glance sideways toward Inbecca. "I should have realized it was an irresistible topic for gossip."

"Aye." The knight turned to the abbess. "The groom disappeared. That would be important news at any time. Thereafter, we departed to follow him, with the bride in train. That brought more talk. Within days, the terrible destruction of the land took place in the shadow of the ruined castle. Many people and cattle were swallowed up. Whole farms—whole villages—vanished. We have not been seen since that day. I must report we were greeted with shock once we let it be known who we were. We are all believed to be dead. I assured them that we were not dead," he said dryly. "Word will get back to your father, highness, and to your royal mother, Lar Inbecca. They will be greatly relieved."

Inbecca held her head proudly, though her face was bright pink with shame. "I thank you."

"I should go back to my father and explain," Magpie said, ruffling his tri-colored hair with an agitated hand. "He will be displeased, but that is nothing new."

"I am certain that he will rejoice that you still live," Rin said. Magpie offered her a grateful look.

The abbess waved an impatient hand to silence them.

"You did not speak of our business," Sharhava said.

"No, Abbess," Mey said, looking displeased that she would even consider him to have a loose tongue. "They knew nothing of these." He gestured toward Tildi and her friends. "Our secrets are safe."

"Did any of the villagers follow you?"

"Several wished to, Abbess, to make certain that the prince and princess were indeed alive," Mey said. "We led them on a roundabout path through the woods until they all turned back. I swear to you none came as far as the edge of the book's influence."

"Well done," Sharhava said. Mey held himself up proudly. The abbess turned to Serafina. "It seems your devotion is to be repaid. You wished to accompany the smallfolk. I had said the rest of you *may* leave at any time. I now insist that you all come as far as the Scriptorium. Once the Great Book is installed behind our walls, then you may depart, if you choose. Until then, you will remain in our charge. Anyone who attempts to flee will be killed."

"What?" Rin said. "You threaten a princess of the Windmanes?"

"You do not dictate my movements," Serafina said furiously. "How dare you try to command a wizard of the council?" Sharhava snorted.

"You had every opportunity to depart. Now it would jeopardize our plans." She made a sharp gesture with her good hand, and two knights spurred in to flank Serafina. More surrounded the other members of Tildi's party. Each of the scholars carried a bloom of blue power in the hand not holding his or her reins. Tildi regarded it with horror. The rune upon it was not unlike her spell of green demon-fire. It promised pain and destruction. "It is only for a few days more. Then you are free to go. All but her." She threw her ruined hand toward Tildi, who felt the gesture like a slap in the face. "She will stay at our pleasure."

"You cannot confine us." Serafina stiffened her back. "Our duty is to return the book to its original resting place."

"I care nothing for your duty. Our mandate is centuries older than yours."

"You will regret this, Abbess."

"I doubt it," Sharhava snapped. "Let me clarify the position. You won't be allowed to have the book from this day on. After we reach the Scriptorium, I care not where you go. You may tell your precious council it will not see the book again. It belongs of right to the Knights of the Word."

Serafina didn't reply, but her eyes flared with anger and indignation. Tildi could tell that she was containing her temper with difficulty. The abbess, unconcerned, turned back and signaled to the knights to go about their business.

"And me?" Magpie asked, his voice suddenly cold and still. "Do you include me in your threat?"

Sharhava swiveled her head to regard him. "You are of the blood royal. It would be a dire breach of the concord of kings to harm you. Bear in mind, won't you, that I hold the power of life and death over all my knights. *All* of them?"

Magpie was shocked. He saw the feeling echoed on the faces of some of the senior knights, especially Loisan.

"Even you wouldn't stoop to such means," Magpie said. "You are not thinking clearly if you believe that justice will not follow you. Inbecca is in no danger from you."

"So you believe!"

"Abbess!" Loisan said, horrified. "You are not yourself!"

"Pah," Magpie said, hardly believing what he had heard. A contrary impulse made him dare to defy her just to see what would happen. He pointed toward where Tessera was tethered. "I'll start riding now. Either you strike me down now, or you strike Inbecca. One of us will survive, that I promise you. Then what will your sister the queen say to you?"

Even Sharhava seemed to realize she had gone too far. Her fair face grew red, and she began to shake. "How can you say I would ever harm my own niece? You would hurt her if you departed. It would be your doing. Yours!"

Brouse came to put a hand on her shoulder. She threw it off. They exchanged looks, and the wild expression melted from her face.

"Then, I stay," Magpie said.

"Indeed you will," Sharhava said. She clapped her hands together, wounded and whole, and closed her eyes briefly. Her lips moved silently, mouthing unfamiliar words. A spark of red formed between her palms. She spread out her hands, and the spark grew to a sphere. Magpie felt the air crackle. A shock of force struck him in the chest like a gust of wind and passed through him as though he were no more substantial than cloth. The redness kept spreading and thinning out until the land and sky around them bore a faint reddish tint. He frowned, wondering if he was imagining it. Sharhava looked around her with satisfaction. "Do not go beyond the pickets without an escort."

"What have you done?" Serafina asked, horrified.

"Enforcing my order," Sharhava said. "You understand now, don't you? The force that was centered upon you is now centered on me. I control the borders of safety. You will obey my orders now."

"You misuse the power," Serafina said. "How can you . . . do you understand what you have done?"

"I dare," Sharhava replied simply. "If you had the conviction of your beliefs, you would have protected what you had. It is mine now, and I do what I must. You will all remain."

Magpie stared from one to the other. "What *has* she done?"

"Come, go, stay, come, go, stay," Lakanta chided her. "You can't make up your mind, can you? Well, wild horses couldn't drag me from Tildi's side, no matter what dire plans you have. I wouldn't want to be anywhere else at all."

"Nor I," Rin said.

"As you please," Sharhava said, as though the outburst had never occurred. "The matter is settled now. Loisan, send out the scouts. We will have our meal, then move as soon as the way ahead is clear. In case the townsfolk do pick up Mey's trail, I wish to be away from here. We will travel for a couple of hours after dark. This is a good road."

The lieutenant seemed happy to go elsewhere. He bowed.

"Yes, Abbess."

Her senior officers gathered around her and escorted her away up the road, away from Magpie and the others. Inbecca stood bolt upright among her fellow knights, a stricken look on her face. Magpie started toward her, to stand by her side, but Inbecca's eyes flashed blue-green fire up at him, and he halted. He knew better than to approach her with that look on her face. She had been hurt to the depths of her being by Sharhava's callousness. One by one, the people in whom she had put her trust had betrayed her. Magpie felt guilty. He went back to the other side of the encampment, but kept her in view in case she needed him. He thought it was unlikely.

Serafina walked frantically up and back, her two guards keeping pace with her, half a body length away on either side. The senior, a stern woman with a broken nose, looked impatiently at Magpie, but made room for him beside the wizardess, obviously considering him of little concern.

"What has Sharhava done?" Magpie asked in a low voice, falling into step with Serafina.

"It's monstrous," she said, coming to an abrupt halt. "She's . . . I never guessed the Scholardom would be prepared to use the Great Book's power so readily. You are aware of the wards Tildi and I cast about us, to prevent anyone from finding us by magical seeking?"

"I am."

"She . . ." Serafina was nearly sputtering, "she tied a spell of her own to the wards—a fire spell. It will scorch anyone to the bones who passes it. Birds and animals will have the sense they were made with to avoid touching it, but humans, dwarves, and smallfolk won't! I cannot remove it without destroying the warding, leaving us vulnerable to thraiks and other menaces. Oh, I should have insisted we go long before this!" She wrung her long hands together.

"You couldn't," Magpie murmured, not without sympathy or disagreement. He caught the flailing hands and held them against his chest, forcing her to look up at him. "You were tired, in shock. You weren't ready."

"Now I am," she said with an angry glance in the abbess's direction. "And I cannot. The warding is under my control, but the burning sphere is under hers. To dispel them both would stretch my abilities to the limit. My mother would have known what to do. I don't. I am not a second Edynn."

"No one expects that of you," Magpie said soothingly.

"Let us eat, then," Lakanta said. "As long as we're not going anywhere at the moment, it makes no sense to try and puzzle this out on an empty stom-

ach. Not that I think we'll get either satisfaction or nourishment out of anything the Scholardom provides for us."

*T*ildi's heart sank with the sun. She huddled on her rug with the book beside
her. The limits of her world at that moment were marked out by six handfuls
of blue fire. No one would be looking for them now. They believed she and
the book had been destroyed by Nemeth. That could not be true, could it?
Master Olen would *know*. Wouldn't he? He would see them in one of his
crystals, or with the aid of one of his scrying spells.

Yet the party was shielded against being seen by a magic search. Had the
spell thwarted Olen's ability to find them? Now they were openly prisoners,
held behind that hot wall. "I dare," Sharhava had said. Tildi could have
echoed Olen's lesson, that all wizardry involves risks. In the abbess's mind
the price of failure outweighed the potential death of innocent beings. Serafina said no animal would cross the invisible line. Tildi missed the sound of
the birds' evening song. Those cheery notes had helped to raise her spirits
during the hard miles they had ridden over the last many days. What few
trills she could hear were as distant as thoughts of home.

She toyed with her plate of scorched bread and undercooked meat.
Thoughts of the poor beast-men kept coming back to her, as they had every
night since it had happened. She had never seen such a terrible thing done
deliberately in all her life. They must get away from Sharhava and her evil
plans, but could she dare to count the cost in the lives of her kinsmen?

In spite of the increased guard around them, her companions were muttering together about how to defy Sharhava's will. Rin especially was angry
about the forced confinement.

"I would have stayed in any case, but it was my choice. My brother will
visit vengeance upon them."

"Forget about those windbags," Lakanta said cheerfully. "We'll leave
when we're good and ready to. It's been convenient having them around,
but I don't like their way of doing business, and I'm not about to let them
take my livelihood for granted. Keep your eyes ready, and whoosh!" She
mimed a bird taking off to the skies.

"No, we can't," Tildi said. She glanced over her shoulder at the abbess,
who had her head bent in prayer over her meal. "Don't make her angry,
please."

"Why and wherefore?" Rin asked. "She's just a human."

"Hush!" Serafina hissed, leaning over to them. She shot a significant
glance at their guards. "Do not make them take more dire action."

"And just what can they do to me they haven't done?" Lakanta asked.
"Not that I don't prize your company, or that I don't believe in our task. I do
not like my comings and goings constricted, either. Why would I have left

the caverns of my people to the open road if I wanted someone to stop me moving about as I choose? Let's go now, Tildi," she said encouragingly.

"I . . . uh . . . it's growing dark."

"What of that? I have lived in caverns most of my life, and you can make all the light you choose. Let's defy these people and let them choke upon our dust."

Tildi could hardly say a word one way or another to that. They were so badly outnumbered that except by using the power of the book itself, they stood no chance of getting away. Lakanta continued to try to get her involved in the conversation. Two things prevented that: the number of guards who surrounded her like an enormous picket fence, and her own fears. She could think of no good alternative.

"Please," Serafina said, and for the imperious young woman it sounded like begging. "We will speak later, I promise." Her eyes were full of meaning. Tildi's hopes rose. Serafina did take the threat to heart. She would find a way to take them south, without jeopardizing the people of the Quarters. They would find an opportunity to speak privately.

"Oh, all right," Lakanta said, throwing up her hands. "Morag, what have you got for me? Can I have a morsel of stew that's merely overdone, instead of over-overdone?"

Tildi was so distracted that she wasn't even seeing runes correctly. It looked to her that one of the women halfway up the camp was wearing hers backward. That was impossible. Runes always looked right way around no matter what angle one was seeing them.

The Scholardom finished their meager dinner, which for once smelled almost as bad as Morag's cooking, then Sharhava summoned the group to her. All but the guards near Tildi formed a tight knot at the abbess's feet. Tildi could guess as to its subject: the gossip in Rainbownham about the survivors of the terrible cataclysm that included a prince and a princess. She had wished desperately that some of those curious-minded townsfolk would have found their way to where she sat before they set out again, but they could not now come within the bounds of the wards. Now she hoped that the knights had hidden their tracks well.

"Bring me the Third Book of Guidance," Sharhava said. One of the young men went running back to the packs stacked near the tethered horses and removed a foot-long scroll wrapped in crimson brocade.

The knights bowed their heads as Sharhava wound through the book to find the page she wanted. She pointed to a page and began to read aloud. Tildi strained to hear the words. She was curious about their rituals. The knights refused to discuss the structure of their order with her, as a member of a race named anathema. In spite of the open insult, she could not help but be interested in what they were doing. Olen would have told her it was natural to want to investigate cultures she had never seen before. The book helped her. The voices within it repeated what Sharhava was saying.

"*Toklevi camroh sati enlevi . . .*"

To Tildi's annoyance, the chant was in the ancient tongue. Most of the words were unfamiliar to her. She recognized a phrase here and there. It must have been the retelling of a story of how the Scholardom came to be founded, since the words she knew spoke of relaxation and freedom from fear. Knowledge would bring them a measure of comfort.

She was not comfortable. She felt as though she was at a party where everyone was snubbing her. The six knights around her cloth kept her friends at a distance. They didn't speak with her, and every so often one would get up and exchange places with one of the knights attending the reading. The constant movement was just another discomfort she must endure, until Serafina or one of the others could figure out how to free her from this place.

The book, unable to teach her to translate, still provided company. She perused the signs she did know. One symbol was very like one Olen had set her to learn that stood for a family of mint plants. It was undoubtedly related. When she laid her finger upon the sign, she found herself seeing the leaves of the plant. It looked like all of the others. But, wait, apple mint had hairy leaves, and peppermint was serrated like a carving knife. She knew this one, had rubbed the dry leaves grown in her garden into powder with her own hands. She forced her mind to concentrate, trying to decide what it was. Soft music from Magpie's pipe coupled with Sharhava's murmured litany added to the intellectual puzzle put her into a state of ease. In spite of herself, she began to relax.

She caught a trill of laughter from her friends.

Something was wrong with her companions. Sharhava's threat seemed to have made no impression on them. They laughed and joked together as though they were out for a country ramble.

". . . And that's when he tipped up the bottle and found I had drunk the last of the ale!" Lakanta concluded triumphantly, tossing the last crust of bread into the bonfire. She dusted her hands together and glanced past the crouching human at the edge of the embroidered cloth. "Tildi, that's one of my best stories. Not a single chuckle? Smallfolk are hard audiences!"

"I think it was a good story," Rin said encouragingly. She sat on the coarse grass with her long, thin legs curled under her.

Tildi looked up at her friends and tried to smile. "I am so sorry. I wasn't listening."

"Don't worry. We will be on our way soon to the south," Lakanta said. "I pay no attention to that woman's bluster. We have all the power between us. The sooner you realize that, Tildi, the better off you would be."

"That's not true." Tildi suffered a terrible mental picture of the smallfolk falling under the blades of the knights. The most fearsome weapon anyone had was a shotgun or crossbow for dispatching the wolves or foxes that threatened the henhouse. She could scarcely bring herself to picture their slaughter by steel or, worse, what had befallen the hairy beast-people. She felt tears starting in her eyes. "We have no power. She has it."

Lakanta stepped over past the nearest guard to sit beside her and tapped her knee.

"Don't ever think that way, Tildi. Often the biggest bluster conceals the hollowest chest."

Tildi looked at her in horror. Lakanta grinned.

"Oh, it is true! You are used to bowing to authority. I'm not. We dwarves are always arguing among ourselves. That way we know who is right, because we have discussed it in so many different ways."

"I have heard that you never get anything done because of all the arguing," Rin said, pursing her long lips.

"Oh, no!" Lakanta said. "If it is all taking too long, we go ahead and do what we think we should. In the long run, *someone* is right."

A chuckle forced its way out of Tildi. She felt better for having something to laugh at. She looked around for the others.

Morag and Teryn had joined the Scholardom for a cup of ale and serious discussion. The knights had accepted the two guards as fellows in service to a higher cause, even if it was not their own. Magpie was among them with his pipe. Tildi enjoyed his music and his endless good humor. His gift was true. He was also unafraid to ask the questions that no one else dared voice.

I had never heard of the earth having roots before," Magpie said casually as he bent his head over the pipe, embellishing the design he had carved in the raw wood. He often found that taking his eyes off those with whom he was speaking made them feel they weren't giving him information he shouldn't have. The ploy had served him well in his role as a spy during the war between his nation and Rabantae. Fortunately, none of the knights knew of that. He had never told Inbecca, but even if he had, she was unlikely to have passed along information to her aunt, no matter how angry she was with him.

"Do not believe the wizard," Thyre said dismissively, glancing at where Serafina sat by herself on the edge of the firelight. "That was some kind of cave plant, probably invented by the Makers."

"Aye," Pedros said. After several days he still seemed heady on the liquor of power. He seemed so young, for all he appeared to have the same number of years as Magpie himself. Magpie suspected he was a little drunk, having indulged in too much ale to make up for their meager dinner. "Another of their inventions that shouldn't have been. We caged it up for good, didn't we? I'm eager to confront the next abomination they made, and snuff it out or pen it up. There's nothing we can't do now, is there? The world's been waiting for us, and we are ready!"

"Easy, now," Loisan said. His mug was still mostly full, but Magpie had seen him dilute the strong ale in it with juice. His head was clearer than the young man's. "Pride is a slippery slope, boy."

"Yes, Lar Loisan," Pedros said.

"That was a fine song," Loisan said, turning his gaze to Magpie. "You'll have to favor us with another tune when we stop for the night."

In other words, go away and leave us be, Magpie thought. He rose and bowed to the circle around the fire.

"Excuse me," he said. "I thank you for your company."

The knights murmured courtesies. Magpie felt Inbecca's eyes on him, but he didn't want to single her out, not when her aunt was watching. As dearly as he longed to sit by her, it was best to remove himself. He went to sit beside Serafina.

She glanced up only for a moment when his shadow fell across her knees.

"They only believe in their own will," she said. "Olen warned us not to let the book fall into their hands. We failed. I failed. We cannot stop the Scholardom now."

"No," Magpie said. He took her hand in his. It was long and narrow, but it felt strong, much like his own. Their skills at magic- and music-making must not be that different. "We can't. No, that's wrong," he said, shaking his head. He still disliked his aunt-in-law elect, but he felt strangely reluctant to defy her. He glanced toward the fire, where Inbecca sat, pointedly not looking at him. It displeased her that he didn't get along with a relative whom she prized, though often enough in the past both of them had joked about Sharhava's imperious nature and her devotion, which at that time seemed like a quaint superstition. He felt as if Sharhava had come into her own here, on this wild trail. The control of the book must be hers. He sensed that impulsion. Olen's claim was too new. He had not studied it as they had.

"I miss my mother," Serafina said, turning her gaze away. "I was not ready to be on my own. You may think that odd, a grown woman unused to finding her own way."

"Not at all," Magpie said, giving her hand a light squeeze. "I am not as close to my mother as you, but she continues to guide me though I have been a man for years, with many an adventure to sing of."

"Now we must follow in the path of others," Serafina said. A fine line formed between her thin, dark brows. "Mother would say it was wrong, but it is not. I feel it is not."

"I feel the same," Magpie said. "At least we all have one another's company."

Serafina turned her head to look into his yellow-amber eyes with her dark ones. "That is the one comfort I can take." She smiled at him.

He felt his heart warm to her. It was good to speak to a woman who did not shower him with an endless rain of disapproval for a change. He held up the pipe.

"May I play for you? Would that give you comfort?"

"Comfort, perhaps not," Serafina said. "That must come in its own time." He bowed his head, crestfallen. "But pleasure, certainly."

"Ah," Magpie said. "Music's other gift."

He took the half-carved pipe and began to play.

"Thraiks!"

*T*ildi jumped up, scanning the sky, her heart pounding with dread. Yes, there they were. High in the purpling sky were three sigils that she would never mistake.

"What thraiks?" Brouse asked, on his feet at her side. He drew his sword.

"I saw them in the book," Tildi said. "They just appeared. Look!"

She pointed up. The black-winged monsters were so high up that they were indistinguishable from the bats who circled in the thermals of the campfire searching for twilight-flying insects except for their runes.

Brouse looked. By then, half the encampment had come running.

"Are you certain, Tildi?" Rin asked. She was on alert, whip in hand.

"There are three of them," Tildi said. "They are trying to find me. And the book."

The centaur set her mouth grimly. "I will protect you. No monster will get past me."

"Or me," Lakanta said. Silently, Teryn and Morag made their way to Tildi's side. The knights had taken away their weapons, but Tildi felt better having them nearby.

"I see nothing," Brouse said, squinting into the gloom.

"What do you fear?" Sharhava demanded, advancing upon Tildi with a scowl that made her as formidable as the circling demons. "The wards will protect you! If there is any foe in the skies, it will be destroyed. You have never been as safe as now!"

"Perhaps we had better move away from here," Loisan said. "If we take the road we will be under the trees. If there are thraiks abroad they will lose sight of us."

"There are none," Sharhava said. "Look up. Those are bats. You come from a farm, girl," she chided Tildi scornfully. "You must have seen them before. Nothing else. Now, to horse. I want to gain some distance before we sleep this night. Your stations, Scholardom. Douse that fire!"

"Nothing in the sky but birds," the almoner, Brouse, said with a scornful chuckle. "Don't seek to make us fear the invisible."

"No!" Tildi said. She looked up again, but the thraiks' sigils were gone. "They were there!"

"Come with me, Tildi," Rin said, beckoning to the girl. She aimed her chin at the retreating knights. "I believe you, even if they don't."

Obediently, Tildi solidified the air under her feet and gained her seat on the centaur's back.

"We also believe you, honored one," Captain Teryn said. With a nod, she sent Morag running. In a few minutes, he returned with their horses saddled and bridled, including Lakanta's Melune. He held the stirrup as his superior officer swung herself up.

"Well, that I call courtesy, Master Morag," Lakanta said. "Almost makes me forgive you. . . ."

A high, thin scream that Tildi knew she would hear in her nightmares for the rest of her life echoed through the glade, and ended on a descending moan. Rin reared and danced nervously.

"What was that?" she demanded.

Over the acrid smell of doused embers, Tildi scented the aroma of roasting meat. Sharhava, a shadow distinguished only by her rune, halted.

"Guards, arm! Go see what that was. Take care not to penetrate the wards."

Two of the knight-runes jogged away from her, growing smaller by the moment until they were the size of the bats who still played overhead. Tildi squinted. What kind of terror was that?

In a moment, the men came running back.

"It was a stag, Abbess," Romini said, his normally ruddy face pale. "It must have touched the wards. There is . . . not much left of it."

"Proceed with caution, then," Loisan instructed them all. "Send scouts ahead to make certain no humans are in our way. That's a double reason to make sure we meet no one."

Tildi could not stop shivering as the group made its cautious way out of the glen. Her scanty dinner had left her hungry, but she felt as though she would never eat again.

"That poor stag!" she said to Serafina, who was walking her mare beside Rin. "Sharhava made a killing spell out of our protection!"

"On the good side, it will kill thraiks, too," Serafina said encouragingly.

"How can you not care?" Tildi asked, shocked.

Serafina frowned, as though her thoughts had been called back from far away.

"I do care," she said. "It should not have died, but it was an accident."

"Are you saying that because we made the wards in the first place?"

"No, of course not! Tildi, I won't have that disrespectful tone from you."

Tildi leaned close to her, heedless of the tug her guard gave her on her waist tether.

"I want to go away from here," she said. "That will break their spell, and there will be no deaths. We can remake it as soon as we're free."

"We can't go," Serafina said. Again, she looked puzzled, but the expression passed as swiftly as it had come. "Not yet, but soon. It will all be fine, Tildi. You should listen to me."

"I do, master," Tildi said patiently. "But you are listening to the abbess. You never do that."

Serafina frowned again and moved away from her. Tildi looked after her in dismay.

"Patience, Tildi," Rin said. "She is having a very hard time."

Tildi sat back, outraged to her very center. They were all to blame for that harmless animal meeting such a horrible doom. It had a speedy death, but it died in such pain that eddies of its suffering were written upon the air. She had never seen anything like that before, not even when the beast-men were killed fighting the earth-roots. It must be the addition of strong magic that caused the agony to echo on after the stag was dead.

She sat on the centaur's back, feeling as though she was to blame. She hardly cared what happened to her any longer. How could Serafina take her magic being perverted without even a trace of the fury she showed earlier?

A cry of annoyance rang back from the file ahead.

"One of you wizards, pay heed! The road is all mush up here."

Dutifully, Tildi began rewriting the road.

Chapter Nine

hree runes writ themselves upon the dark sky. More thraiks. Tildi sat bolt upright.

"What is it, smallfolk?" asked Vreia, who was on guard at the north edge of her sleeping cloth.

"Thraiks," she said. "They could be the same ones who were looking for us earlier."

Vreia looked up. "I see nothing. You must stop worrying about such things. The abbess has set a magical guard upon us that they cannot penetrate, even if they were there."

"But they are there," Tildi insisted.

"Please go back to sleep. Morning comes all too soon." The woman rearranged the skirts of her habit and shifted on the hard ground. "My fellows and I will protect you if anything does come. Now, please, no more alarms."

Tildi shivered as she lay down. Thraiks flew often, circling and circling overhead, even in daylight. She supposed that she ought to be grateful to Sharhava for once: if they tried to penetrate the wards this time, they would be destroyed.

She watched them circle for a while. In spite of the double wards, they must have sensed something. When they grew frustrated they disappeared through a black gash in the sky, a featureless stroke in the midst of the stars, its own rune darkness upon darkness.

They always returned, day after day, even though she was the only one who noticed them most of the time. The unknown enemy was tireless in his pursuit. The spell of protection must never falter even for a moment, or the winged beasts would be upon her.

The knights kept telling her that there was nothing to worry about, but she knew they were wrong about that, too. Just because they couldn't see it didn't mean it wasn't there, just like the thraiks. She was getting a bit annoyed with people doubting her word. Such a thing would never have happened in the Quarters, where she was known to be truthful.

Under Sharhava's new order, the contingent of six guards who watched her awake also hovered around her at night. Two of them were awake during each watch of the night, no matter what the hour. It was unnerving for her to wake up to the sight of firelight glittering off eyeballs fixed upon her. The book, when it was not in her arms, lay upon a cloth on the ground. The knights had a wealth of them. This, like the others, was no ordinary ground sheet, but pure silk as thick as her little finger and embroidered with runes in gold, red, and blue. She suspected that it might have been made to suit the purpose, but how could the Scholardom ever know that they would need it? From what Tildi understood, the knights had left the castle of Magpie's parents in a rush to pursue him. Did they carry around with them at all times the paraphernalia necessary to care for the Great Book, should they just happen upon it? To every event they attended? She could just imagine seeing them in the marketplace, basket on one arm and bag of impedimenta on the other. In spite of her annoyance, the thought still amused her. Of course, no one would dare make fun of them. As a group they had no sense of humor. Tildi had begun to see a warming in a few of the knights who guarded her the most frequently, Auric especially. Sharhava remained obdurate. She treated Tildi with care but no friendliness.

Her reasons for disliking Tildi she made clear. No matter how much magic they had gained through proximity to the book they still could not take the book away from her, because it seemed that no matter how far away from it she was, all she had to do was call for it, and it was by her side. She had an affinity for it that not even Serafina could explain. Even though she had told them the story of the fragment of parchment and her early life, Sharhava just could not bring herself to believe that Tildi's immunity had come to her "so easily!"

How well named her kind was. She had never felt as small as she did at that moment. The entire world was too big for her to handle. A chattel-marriage to that oaf Bardol that the elders had proposed for her would almost have been welcome. Almost. Tildi smiled ruefully at the night sky and turned over on her side. She was weary, that was her trouble. With rest, perhaps optimism would return, and she could think her way out of her troubles. The Great Book, like a faithful dog looking for a pat, rolled over and insinuated itself under her hand as if to reassure her. With the smooth, cool surface under her fingers, Tildi sought sleep.

Tildi fought for air in her dreams. The world had turned into water, drowning her, pulling her down into a maelstrom of spinning runes in darkness. She struggled to climb to the top of the water, but it bound her arms in wrappings of gray silk. She was pulled downward, too deep to save herself. Her lungs were bursting, exploding for lack of air.

Her eyes flew open. To her relief, the water had not been real. A single, floating golden rune in otherwise total darkness hovered before her eyes. She sought to gasp in a breath, but something warm was covering her mouth though not her nose.

"Easy, now," a whisper beseeched her. "Fear not. Breathe. Be silent."

She clawed at the hand. The other, much larger than her small ones, captured her wrists and pinioned them together.

One of the knights was trying to kill her! Wards! She must make wards! How did they go again? Without hands she must draw with her mind. A shaky line began to take shape. It was erased almost as soon as she had made it. Terrified, she started again, much larger. The silver-gilt line faded like smoke. She tried to make a noise, to call for help. Her captor was not burning at her touch. Why was she not burning?

"Stop!" the voice whispered in her ear. "I am not harming you. Do you know me? No, it would seem not."

Tildi gawked at the rune. It was the backward one that she had seen a few days before.

"Please do not cry out. They are all sleeping. I am a friend. I do not harm you. You will see. I will move my hand. Only, be silent. Will you?"

Tildi nodded. Her nightmare receded, and she relaxed. The warm weight moved away from her face. She sat up.

The bonfire had reduced to a glow of red embers. In the cloudy night sky she could see the runes of the stars better than the twinkling lights themselves, so the people around her were no more than their sigils, rising and falling gently as they breathed. Even the guards around her slept.

"Come," the voice whispered. A hand took hers. Tildi stood up. She felt the book rise from the cloth beside her. "Yes, bring that, too, if you wish. Step off the ground so you won't make noise."

Tildi obeyed. Thinking the floating spell as hard as she could, she left the unyielding surface of pebble-strewn clay soil for the air. The hand guided her away. Tildi felt the tether that was always around her waist tug loose from the grasp of an unseen knight. He or she did not wake up. Tildi gathered the cord and looped it up over her shoulder. She stepped over the cordon and followed the backward rune.

She and her mysterious escort glided into the woods. Tildi read the many beeches, oaks, and walnuts, both saplings and mature trees. Until a twig or two brushed her hair, they had no reality to her. The presence guided her around the bulky rune of a large stone and down a shallow slope to a flat place carpeted with the tiny symbols for grass and clover. Beyond, the muffled roar of water told her they were close to the river.

"Tal," the voice said. Tildi saw the rune just before a warm golden flame flickered into existence. An oval face with golden skin and large, dark eyes looked at her. The woman to whom they belonged could have been Serafina's sister, but she was not human. Tildi recognized her at once.

"Irithe!" she burst out joyously. She threw her arms around the elf's neck and embraced her.

"Hush!" Irithe said. She patted Tildi's shoulder. The smallfolk girl let go, embarrassed. The elf had never been effusive in any emotions. "Well, my old companion, I am glad to see you as well. It has been many a long mile since we walked together out of The Groaning Board at Rushet, has it not?"

"Oh, yes! What are you doing here?" Tildi asked, remembering to drop her voice to a mere whisper.

"Ah, well, each of us has our secrets. Have you revealed all of your secrets?"

Tildi shook her head. "I don't know if any of them are worth anything to anyone."

"They are. A friend of yours sought me out since I saw you last. He says that since you learn from everyone, you should know that you may continue to learn even when you are not with your teachers."

"Olen!" Tildi exclaimed. "He sent you?"

"He did," Irithe said. "He was concerned for your well-being."

"Olen!" Tildi felt a rush of affection and longing for the old wizard, followed by the deepest relief. "Thank Mother Nature! Is he all right? Does he know we are alive?"

Irithe's austere face allowed a slight smile to curl the corners of her mouth. "He is well. Of your life, he said his spells were uncertain, but his heart said yes. He needed someone who was adept at tracking and who knew you. Therefore, he sent me."

"How did he find you? I told him about you, but he said he didn't know you."

"He did not know me before. Now he does. He sent messages to many of the elvenholts asking for me by name. I knew of the council meeting. Like my brothers and sisters of the forest, I knew of the changes in the wake of the book's passage. I have been more than three weeks seeking you once he set me on your trail. This is what he sent you in pursuit of?" She looked at the Great Book, hovering like an ivory pillar in the gold of the witchlight.

"Yes," Tildi said, feeling as proud of the book as she would have of a prize calf. Irithe leaned close to see. She ran a hand around it but did not touch it. She sat back and regarded Tildi.

"It has a scent like yours when I first met you, but much stronger. It is ancient magic. I was surprised to sense it in a smallfolk, but it was not natural to you, was it?"

"No. It was . . . well, I am sure that Olen told you everything."

Irithe showed her little smile again. "I do not need to know everything. He asked me to find you and bring you to him. I have, and I will."

"Where?" Tildi asked eagerly. "Is he close by?"

"No. He waits for us on the banks of the Arown. It is many days' walk even if we take the sky road. We can make several miles' distance if we depart now."

"Oh, I'll be so glad to see him! I have so much to tell him *and* show him!" Tildi took in a deep breath. "But I can't go."

"Why not?" Irithe frowned at her.

"The knights," Tildi said desperately. "Their leader, the abbess, said that I have to bring the Great Book to their Scriptorium. If I tried to leave, they would march on the Quarters and slay everyone. I have no family left, but I fear for my people's lives. She also said that any of my friends who tried to get away would be killed, too. They could all have gone free, but they stayed with me, and now they don't act as they did before. I feel responsible."

Irithe frowned. A small line etched itself between the finely drawn brows.

"Olen said there were obstacles, but these are not insurmountable. I warned you before not to give all your trust, but will you trust me on this?"

"Of course," Tildi said, surprised.

"Then prepare your friends. I will make certain that you have an opportunity to go with me, and your enemies will not follow. Be ready!"

*I*rithe doused the golden light with a gesture and took Tildi's hand. She escorted Tildi back to her place on the mat, then glided silently from the glade. Tildi followed her rune into the forest, but lost it. The elf was the best woodswoman she had ever known. A glamor seemed to lift from Tildi's surroundings, a faint rune fading away. No doubt Irithe had laid a charm of calming on the glen to keep the knights from rousing, as she did to avoid being harmed by Tildi's touch.

She was going to see Olen again! Tildi found it difficult to go back to sleep, knowing he was waiting for her. How Irithe was to extract them from their unwanted escort she had no idea, but the elf was resourceful. She must be ready.

Purely out of defiance Tildi began to think of outrageous plans that would trap the knights like flies in jam. The image of Sharhava floundering in raspberry goo made her giggle. One of the guards at her side sat up at once and felt for the fallen cord. Tildi felt it tug at her waist.

"What is it?" he demanded. "I heard a noise."

"It was nothing," Tildi said. "I am sorry. A thought struck me funny."

"Aye? Well, go to sleep. Dawn comes too soon."

Tildi settled down, her hand on the book.

Chapter Ten

old tight," Rin said. "This is a steep slope."

Tildi felt her stomach lurch at the endless downward path before them. In an effort to prevent anyone going downhill from catching a foot and tumbling for miles, someone had cut steps into the stony soil, but they had eroded from years or centuries of rain into angled, knee-deep troughs crisscrossed with tree roots and stubborn weeds. She clutched the centaur's thick, wiry mane. Every step Rin took jarred her forward until she was resting against Rin's back.

"My apologies," Tildi said, trying to scoot backward and failing.

"No matter," Rin said. "You do not hurt me. I am accustomed to it."

Tildi grimaced and peeked around Rin to see if the guards nearby had heard her, but they were concerned with the feet of their own mounts and were paying little attention to her, except to see that she was safe. As time had gone by, Tildi had become less harmful to the touch, though not much less. She feared that soon the guards would be able to seize her, or think they could. She recalled what had happened to poor King Halcot when he had touched her fragment of a copied leaf at the council at Silvertree. His hand was burned black, as Sharhava's still was. And that sad corpse they had found on the road outside of Walnut Tree, whom Edynn thought must have run afoul of Nemeth. Tildi didn't want to harm anyone, but if the book's magic should leap to her defense there was nothing she could do. It had been four days since Irithe had come to her. She found it difficult to wait for rescue. What could take so long?

The book itself floated serenely along beside her like a swan sailing on a pond. Tildi gave it a loving glance. She had come to rely upon it as a trusted guide. It had opened itself to a complicated jumble of runes illuminated with green and blue. The names were unfamiliar, but the page unmistakably described the land through which they were now riding. Even with her inexperienced eye she could pick out high stone bluffs surmounted by weathered caves on either side of a mighty river, still the Oros. She wasn't certain what the signs in between those banks meant.

"What is this place?" she asked. Magpie usually answered those questions, but he and Serafina rode today in the center of the pack ahead of her, absorbed in each other. Shamelessly, Tildi spied upon their runes. Magpie's radiated hurt feelings, interest, and confusion. Serafina's had confusion, too, but also warming as one did when flattering attention is paid. Tildi was glad of that, though a little cross with Magpie. He had a young lady who was interested in him, to whom he was betrothed, and there was no confusion whatsoever in her rune. Inbecca gave him nasty glances, which he didn't notice. Hurt added spikes to her name-sign. It had been days since Tildi had noticed Inbecca and Magpie speaking alone to each other. Had one romance broken off only to give way to another?

"We are riding toward the Delta Bridge," Auric explained kindly, answering the question she had asked out loud. He was immediately behind her. Because of the narrowness of the path, they could only ride single file. "Our order's nearest home is set between the two tributaries at the south corner of where Orontae and Levrenn touch Melenatae. This bridge is to the north of our destination. Our mother house is in Levrenn, but there are many other chapters as well."

Tildi followed his description in the Great Book. At her eager touch, the scroll obediently turned until it opened upon a page of small runes arrayed according to their geographical location. It was better than a map, because Tildi could see every detail in these, much more than in line-pictures of countries, rivers, and mountains. The features seemed to be as large as life, even though at the same time she could cover each with the tip of her thumb. What wonder-workers the Shining Ones had been! She pointed to the river, its sinuous perfection interrupted by matter-of-fact, practical sigils: the bridges.

He looked over her shoulder, leaning as close as he dared. "Aye, that's it. It'll be tricky crossing that bridge."

"We must do it in the dead of night," said Rachine from behind him. She shook her head. "It's the only bridge for sixty miles in either direction. Unless we want to ford over. It might be shallow enough at the moment, with the Oros down to a trickle."

"The abbess won't allow it," Loisan said, dropping back. "Mud's too deep and dangerous, even now. Water might endanger the book. We cannot have that."

"Not to mention how little I care for trotting withers deep in mud," Rin said, tossing her head.

A *harrumph* from Loisan told them how little he cared about the centaur's discomfort, but he did not say so aloud. He slowed his pace and kept an eye on the sky.

The whole party had been watching the sky with trepidation since early morning.

"I do not like the black clouds," Rachine said, looking up at the sky. Tildi followed her gaze. The sky was darkening ominously in the west. If she had been at home, everyone would be moving the animals inside. "They are coming this way. How long until we reach the bridge?"

"A few miles. We still cannot cross in daylight," Auric said. "We will have to find a place to halt where we cannot be detected."

"We *must* make for it."

"Not yet! The abbess will not permit it. Vreia has not yet returned. That means other travelers are still within range. We do not wish them harm."

"Can't we risk it?" Rachine asked. "There are caves to shelter in on the other side. I smell rain. I believe that we are in for a terrible storm. It is nearly upon us."

"It is all as Mother Nature sends," Romini said blandly.

But, natural or not, the woman's prediction came true. The sky tore open like a full waterskin, and rain roared down upon them.

"The book!" Sharhava called back, her hood plastered to her head. "Save it!"

"It is safe," Tildi said placidly, tipping a hand toward the scroll. She hadn't known how to build a ward to protect her from rain before, but the voices seemed to know what she needed before she needed it, and whispered words in her ears, words that for once she knew. The rune covered her, the book, and Rin like an awning. No drop of water touched her.

"That's a blessing," Auric said, blinking water out of his eyes.

All the horses slipped on the beaten-clay road. Tildi could not see them well through the rain, but she saw their silver-gilt sigils twisting suddenly or dropping several feet. She heard an annoyed yell as one of the knights was tipped out of his saddle and cascaded downslope through the mud. He picked himself up, swearing. Droplets of liquid mire, each marked with its own symbol, flew off him.

Rin kept her balance, but only by holding her arms out to steady herself when the path sloped precipitously downhill toward a curve.

"It's a pity you cannot shield the way before us from water as well," Rin said. "Only fools would not have hesitated when they saw the skies."

"I do not dare," Tildi said. "I wish I could, but I might make things worse."

"They cannot be worse." Rin picked her hooves up carefully. "I am carrying pounds of mud with every step."

Rain roared down upon them, growing more intense the farther they descended. Whoever was ahead of the party that the abbess was trying to avoid must have been moving at the speed of a crippled ox. The sound of the cataract all but drowned out the knights shouting to one another.

"We might as well be in another world," Rin said, eyeing the silver wall. "I cannot see anything ahead of us. Can you lengthen the shield a little so I can judge my footing?"

"I don't really know how I did it," Tildi admitted. "The voices told me what to do."

"Never mind, then. I will hoof it gingerly and hope that nothing . . . who are you?" Rin danced as a hooded figure slipped into the dry circle. The centaur's hand flew to the whip hanging from her waist. The newcomer pointed a long finger at her, and Rin stopped in mid-movement. The centaur's eyes flashed fury. "How dare you bespell me? Name yourself!"

In answer, the figure threw back its hood to reveal long dark hair framing a golden-skinned face and two large, dark eyes.

"Irithe!" Tildi exclaimed. She leaned over to clasp the elf's hands.

"You know this person?" Rin asked.

"She is a friend. What are you doing here?"

"I have little time," the elf said, stepping lightly beside them down the muddy slope as if it was a fine spring day. "The moment is coming. Trust in what you can actually feel. Keep your friends close if you can. Do not fly. You must stay upon the ground. They must be able to hear you approach."

"Who are they?" Tildi asked.

The elf's hand flew to her lips. "Hush! You will see. The knights must not cross the river. Go south. My allies will find you. They will identify themselves. Trust them as you trust me—with reservations." Irithe gave her quick smile, and Tildi echoed it.

"I trust you. What do they look like?"

"You will know they are not friends to your enemies," Irithe said tersely. "Move slower now. You are missed. The weather has made them nervous. It will continue to do so. I do not know when we will meet again, meadow child, but we shall. You have my word."

"I will be glad to see you anytime at all," Tildi said.

Irithe gave her a quick smile. "You open your heart so swiftly. Farewell, then, for now."

She pulled her hood over her head and backed away from Tildi. At once she was swallowed up in the roaring silver curtain. At that same moment, the rope pulled taut around her waist.

"There you are!" Loisan shouted hoarsely as he broke through the rain, hauling himself closer hand over hand on her tether. His horse snorted and gasped, out of breath at struggling with the weather. "The abbess said we must risk the bridge. We cannot find shelter here. It is not far." He backed away, and was instantly swallowed up by the deluge.

"Who was that elf?" Rin asked.

"Her name is Irithe," Tildi said, feeling hope flood her like the warmth from a fire. "She is a friend I met on the road north to take lessons with Olen."

"What did she mean by her allies?"

Tildi hesitated. She didn't know whether her friends' unnatural complacency extended to revealing confidences to the enemy, but time was short. "She is going to try and help us get away from the knights. She said she can help. I don't know what will happen, but . . . don't be frightened at whatever comes."

"A Windmane, frightened?" Rin demanded, sounding affronted, but she snorted to show it was a joke. "If your friend will free us of these pests, then I am all for it."

Within a few yards the weather began to change again. The silver wall softened and began to churn into clouds of fog. The roaring lessened, then ceased. Tildi saw the rune of the spell over her head break apart. It must have been meant specifically to cope with rain. The rolling mist brushed Rin's flanks and washed around Tildi, surrounding them in a moist cocoon.

"This is what she meant by help?" Rin demanded, putting her hands out before her. "I cannot see the ground at all now."

"Hush!" Tildi said. "The others can hear you now."

"Do I care if we are about to be set free?"

"Rin!"

"Oh, very well—listen! What is that?"

Tildi felt her ears perk at the low growling ahead of them. She huddled tightly against Rin's back and pulled her knife from its sheath. The book huddled to her other side, providing her with a shield.

Howls erupted all around them. Tildi felt her blood turn chill.

Rin reached for the whip that Irithe had prevented her from drawing. She unwound its length partway and looped it over her other hand. Suddenly three figures, man-sized but not man-shaped, appeared out of the mist beside them as if surfacing in a pail of milk. Their faces had long snouts with black noses and tall, triangular ears. Their dark brown lips were pulled back to show sharp fangs. Tildi let out a scream. The newcomers snarled at Tildi and Rin, then vanished again as swiftly as they had appeared. Tildi heard one of the knights give a wild yell.

"Werewolves!" Rin exclaimed. "Yes, there was a full moon last night. The Pearl was at her height."

"Knights!" came Loisan's voice, echoing down the muddy slope. "Ware enemy!"

Rin turned one way and another. More werewolves bounded past them, heading downslope. They carried no weapons that Tildi could see except for coils of rope, but she wondered if they needed any, with their sharp teeth and claws. One male bounded into Rin's path, making her rear in alarm. He scanned them with hot yellow eyes, which stopped in surprise when they lit on Tildi. Before either of them could move, he was gone again. A loud ulu-lation made chills go up Tildi's spine.

"How did they get through the wards?" Rachine yelled.

"The spell is broken," Loisan said. "Treachery! Where is that wizard?"

"Serafina!" Tildi shouted. The knight was correct: she could no longer feel the wards around them. Someone had undone the protection. Thraiks could see them! Had something happened to Serafina? She scanned the for-est of runes for the wizardess's sign. Everyone was moving so quickly.

"Look behind you!" Mey's voice shouted.

"Where?" Braithen shouted back. "How can you see . . . aagh!" Tildi heard the snick of a weapon being drawn and the grunt of effort from Braithen's throat.

"Lightning strike you, monster!"

Tildi saw the flash of light and read the rune of lightning as Mey came to his brother knight's rescue. The Scholardom's study to employ the book's magic as an offensive weapon had borne fruit. Tildi cringed. To her relief the werewolf rune was thrown backward but not destroyed. Another word had interposed itself between them.

"Why do you not die?" Mey shrieked.

More snarls came, followed by a cry of pain. Horses shrieked in fear. Rin danced at the noise. More steeds, both before and behind them, echoed the scream. The cries of humans mingled with them as werewolf teeth and claws must have found their marks. Jingling tack and the thud of hooves on the slope added to the cacophony. Tildi cowered. She had never been in the midst of battle before.

"Olen said they were allies," Tildi said, frightened. "Why are they attack-ing us?"

"We must have killed one of their number with Sharhava's spell," Rin said grimly.

"Get us away, Rin!" she pleaded.

"I'll carry you safely," Rin said, gathering herself. "Guards, let go!" She pulled forward. Tildi felt her tether drop loose.

"Smallfolk, where are you?" Auric called. He had been on the other end of the quirt.

Tildi took a big breath to shout, but something clapped over her mouth. She gasped as she saw a huge male wearing leather gauntlets hold her tightly. He was clad in a dark green tunic over sable fur.

Rin twisted to see what had touched her side. "Let her go!" she shouted. She reared, trying to dislodge the werewolf. Her hooves skidded on the slope. Rin snapped the whip at him, but he dodged it.

"Not you," he said. His blazing eyes bored into Tildi's. "Get down. Run! Run! Go now!"

Before she could wind the whip up for a second blow, he disappeared into the fog with the speed of thought. Rin twisted to face her.

"You heard him. I don't intend to wait for a second invitation."

"But what about our other friends?" Tildi asked.

"They'll have to fend for themselves," Rin said grimly. "They're well capable of it, I vow." Without another word, she launched herself down the incline. Tildi could hardly stand the terrifying scenes that came and went as swiftly as she could blink. Around them, shapes surfaced in and out of the mist, knights and werewolves rolling over and over together. The humans flailed at their hairy attackers with mace and knife. The lycanthropes gnawed at mailed shoulders and necks. Red blood poured over the blue-and-white-clad breast of a knight lying on his back. He was dead. Tildi couldn't recognize his face, so contorted was it with fear and pain. Two werewolves lay not far from him, huddles of fur on the clay-smeared earth.

"I'll get you across the river," Rin promised. Her hooves thudded on the slippery ground. A woman screamed just a few feet from them.

"No! Not the bridge!" Tildi listened. She swung off Rin's back and used her hovering charm to let herself lightly to the ground.

"What are you doing?" Rin twisted around and reached for her. "You could be killed!"

Tildi eluded the Windmane's grasp.

"Irithe told me not to leave the ground. She wanted me to run south. Which way is that?"

Rin threw up her head and sniffed the air. "The water is that way," she said, pointing to their right. "Straight ahead."

"Hurry," Tildi said.

A werewolf somersaulted out of the mist, followed by a knight wielding a war hammer. It was Pedros. He blinked at Tildi.

"Smallfolk, run! Save the book! Get to the abbess! She's back there. No, you don't!" he shouted as the werewolf leaped back, landing on his chest, rope in one hairy hand. Pedros rained down blows of the hammer on the lycanthrope's back. "The Scholardom!" he yelled.

Tildi's eyes were blinded by tears as she dashed away. The two were lost in the swirling white, but she heard their grunts and cries of pain as they scored against each other. She wanted to launch herself into the air, to get away from the fighting, but she remembered Irithe's warning not to leave the ground. She threw an arm over the book and ran, heedless of the twigs scoring her skin and slapping her in the chest.

Another terrifying tableau met her eyes as she slipped sideways to avoid a thornbush. Romini lay on the ground on his face as a werewolf tied his legs together. Tildi retreated and ran around the other side of the bush. Her heavy boots made her clumsy. She bounced and bounded down the hill. Shapes loomed up at her, coarse shapes with many fingers reaching for her face. She threw up a hand to protect herself. To her amazement, green fire bloomed on her hand. She hurled it at the shape. Just before it touched, she saw that it was a bare tree. For a moment, the demon fire drove back the fog, showing her that the beclawed foe was nothing more than a dead tree.

Too late, she groaned. The green flames consumed the twisted, naked branches in a twinkling.

"*Never* do that again!" she shrieked aloud. What if it had been a living being? What if it had been one of the troubled tree-men cared for by the elves of Penbrake? She would have done murder! "Serafina! Where are you?"

No answer from her master.

"Serafina!" More howling and screaming resounded down the hill toward her. Tildi realized with horror that she was alone. She stopped and shouted at the mist. "Rin? Where are you?"

A bellow that could have been Rin's came down to her, followed by a chorus of sharp howls. Tildi was too terrified to do anything but break into a run again.

Had the werewolves taken everyone? Was she alone now?

"To me, knights!" A shape in white and blue fell into her path, measuring its length on the stony ground. It was the almoner Brouse, sword drawn. His lips were drawn back from his teeth, which were gritted in concentration. When he saw her, his mouth dropped open.

"Smallfolk! Thank the Mother and Father." He scrambled up. "Come with me! I will guard you!" He held out a hand to her.

Tildi was ashamed to feel how grateful she was to be near one of the knights when all she had wanted to do for weeks was to get away from them, but there was no time to think about that. She didn't want to be alone in the confusion. She ran to his side and huddled beside the split skirts of his habit that were splashed with mud and blood. The book stayed with her, pressing against her like a friendly cat.

"They are inhuman beasts," Brouse said, turning his head from side to side, listening. "Stay close to me, please. We must find our way across the bridge. The others will join us if they can, but we must get to the Scriptorium. We will be safe there. It is not far beyond the river. Hurry!"

A howl drowned out his last words. It was so close that it felt as though the werewolf were right beside them. She clapped her hands to her ears, trying to block out the angry noise.

"Follow me," Brouse ordered. He produced a handful of blue fire, both for protection and illumination, and set off downhill at a run.

Tildi ran through the thick whiteness, now becoming gray as the sun went down and the full moon rose. She kept low behind Brouse's bulky, pale shape. It ducked and bobbed. She followed it, feeling as she had in the first days when she first had the book, removed from all things, all sensation. None of what was happening to her seemed to be real. She had become numb to the number of twigs that had pummeled her, the stones that slipped under her feet, the tops of the boots slapping against her shins, the harsh cries battering her ears. She had no idea which way south was. If the fog held, she would elude Brouse once they reached the river but before he could get her onto the bridge.

Where were the horses? Where was Rin? Was she certain the werewolves were the allies that Irithe had spoken of, or was the peace between humans and their kin broken for some offense that had happened while she was in the north? Would the werewolves treat her as they did the humans? Did they see her as an ally against the knights, or would they see her as a collaborator?

Suddenly the towering shape before her collapsed.

"Oof!" Brouse grunted. Unable to stop herself, Tildi ran into his legs and tripped to the ground. She felt around her for the book. It was safe. It hovered over her head. Another shape, long and thin, was in the air above her as well: a rope. Someone had slung it between two trees, to catch anyone who got this far. She and Brouse scrambled up. Suddenly they were surrounded by a press of bodies, five huge werewolves in long tunics. Too swiftly for Brouse to respond, they knocked him off his feet again and began to loop cords around his limbs.

"Save yourself," he gritted. Tildi backed away, the book following her.

Something light touched her on the back of the neck, and she screamed. She tried to leap away, but hairy claws each greater than the size of her head, bigger than she had remembered from Olen's council, larger than she had ever dreamed, clapped her between them. All the air was knocked out of her lungs. She gasped aloud.

"Smallfolk!" Brouse shouted. They must have gagged him, because he spoke no more.

Tildi struggled in the strong grasp. The green fire came to her hand as she prepared to defend herself to the death.

One big paw clapped down on top of it, and it went out. Tildi gaped up at her captor.

"Not necessary, little sister," he said in a voice deeper than the bowels of the earth. "I am a friend. Irithe told me not to let you reveal all your secrets. Now, come!"

The paws lifted her off the ground and wrapped her up in one massive arm. Long black fur blotted out her sight of the fog.

Chapter Eleven

he fog hid all but vague shapes. Magpie whirled on his heel, sword drawn. It felt as if they were all drowning in grayness. It was unnatural. He couldn't see more than an arm's length ahead of him. If the rain had been bad for visibility, this was ten times worse. How had the weather changed so swiftly? He had been knocked off his mare several yards back, and he couldn't see her in all the haze.

"Tessera!" he shouted.

Her answering whinny sounded more like a scream than a reply. He called again, hoping he could figure out where she was.

The cries and shouting of the knights at bay seemed at once adjacent and far away from him. Two figures, one dark and one light, wrestled together a couple of yards downslope. He dashed down to help, and lost his footing. By the time he tumbled into the place where he had seen them, the opponents were gone. All that remained was churned-up wet earth with boot prints and long footmarks with pinpricks before the toes to indicate sharp claws. He knew that cast of footprint!

Another shape hurtled past him, hurrying downhill, this time close enough for him to see the long snout and thick fur pelt. His guess was confirmed. They *were* werewolves. What were they doing here so far from their home in the south, or any of the trading ports along the river?

A long snout emerged from the heavy fog close to his face. Magpie leaped backward and slashed with his sword. The werewolf ducked underneath the blade and came up within his guard. *Father, but they were fast!* It snapped a loop of rope off its belt and flexed it in both hands. The two of them moved around one another. Magpie thrust his sword at it. The werewolf dodged in and tried to catch his sword hand in its rope. Magpie countered by advancing into its guard. He threw all his weight into its chest. It toppled off balance and tried to sidestep. He swept a leg underneath its feet. Surprised, it fell backward. As he dove for it, it rolled away from him and escaped into the enveloping mist.

He had not succeeded in striking it. Why had it fled? What were they doing here? Had they mistaken the party for someone else?

He heard the sound of grunting and scuffling near him. For a moment, the fog parted enough for him to see two large lycanthropes hustling a long-legged knight down the slope. The man was bound tightly with dark-colored ropes, and a rag was stuffed in his mouth. Magpie bounded after them, but the ground was too wet for him to move fast. He slid and came down hard on one knee. The fog closed again, leaving him unable to determine any direction except downhill. He picked himself up and wiped the mud from his palms onto his already sodden trousers.

The rising moon lit the fog with an eerie radiance, making it even harder to see. The sounds of battle were everywhere. Something was different, he realized, something odd. He looked down at his chest. Then it struck him: there were no runes. The silvery words he'd become accustomed to seeing day after day were gone. That could be for only one reason.

"Tildi!" he shouted. Where was the girl? The book followed her like a hound. Where she went, it went. Had these raiders carried her off?

There was a cry of answer, but such a stentorian bellow couldn't have come from the smallfolk girl's throat.

"Let me go, you monsters!"

Magpie whirled. Another knight, the woman he knew as Vreia, stumbled into view. One of her wrists was caught fast in a loop of rope, but she was striking out with the mace in her other hand. A band of werewolves scrambled to surround her, avoiding the random blows.

"Prince, aid me!" she cried.

As soon as they saw him, two of the werewolves dragged their prey back into the fog, and the rest came after him. Magpie backed away, sword raised in a position of guard. He came up against a thornbush. It was as good as having an ally watching his back. The werewolves feinted, ropes at the ready.

A gust of wind from downhill swept a curtain of fog into their midst. Magpie blinked at the cloudy whiteness, trying to keep his foes in sight. They slunk in and out of sight, so the few looked like an entire host. He turned from side to side.

"Wait!" he cried. "We are friends." He switched to their language, a harsh guttural plaint. "I have traded with you many times in peace."

"Who is that?" a voice called back in the same language.

"Pay no attention," a second voice shouted. Magpie recognized it as female. "Get all the humans!"

"But I mean you no harm!"

Hands thrust through the thornbush at his back and seized him around the neck and waist. Magpie tried to twist away. His natural impulse to recoil from the twigs hitting his face caused him to close his eyes. The moment was just long enough for the others to swarm him. Several hairy arms pushed his upward. He gasped as something sharp pressed into his wrist. He felt his sword fall from a suddenly nerveless hand. Loops of rope seemed to be everywhere. He kicked and writhed, determined not to let them take him.

"Do not move, or it will be worse for you," a hairy face growled at him.

In no time he was unable to move, even if he wanted to. The werewolves had him trussed up like a pig for the spit with knots that would not slip. He fought to keep them from thrusting a wad of linen into his mouth, but one put a sharp thumbnail into the joint of his jaw. It opened just enough for them to wrench his mouth open. While he tried to spit out the gag, they tied another piece of cloth around it to keep him from doing so. Thankfully the linen was clean. It tasted of nothing but fresh dye. Another cloth was tied around his eyes.

With amazing strength, two slightly built lycanthropes hoisted him to their shoulders and carried him downhill. His head rested upon the hairy shoulder of one of his bearers, so it was jogged roughly with every pace. He felt cloth underneath his cheek, not fur. Perhaps, he mused, he could loosen his blindfold by rubbing it against the shoulder of the werewolf's tunic at each bump. He tried nudging the cloth upward the next time he was jostled. Within a few steps, he could see perfectly under the edge of the blindfold. His captors were so intent upon their footing that they didn't notice.

Turning away from the river, they pushed through the thin switches of young willows to emerge in a natural hollow. At the foot of a tree about the same thickness as Magpie's thigh, they dumped him to the ground, then hauled him up into a sitting position. Once he was firmly bound by his upper arms to the tree trunk, they untied his ankles and left him.

"Prince Troubadour!" came an urgent whisper. Magpie twisted his neck, trying to see around the bole of the tree.

It was Lakanta. The blond-braided trader had been tied to a stump of rock that protruded at an angle from the hilly ground. She had not been blindfolded. He wiggled the knot in the cloth against the bark at his back until the rest of the linen sash fell off, but he could not shift the gag at all. She raised her eyebrows at him.

"Well, now, seems I'll have to talk for the both of us. No trouble for me. Are you all right?"

He nodded.

"Have you seen any of the others? Do you know what became of Tildi and Rin?"

He shook his head.

"My apologies. I'll try and keep to one question at a time—What was that?"

A loud howl resounded from high up the bluff. They both turned to look in that direction, though they couldn't see more than a few yards in the fog.

"Well, well, this is a turn-up," Lakanta said in a heavy whisper. "They haven't done this to me since they drank some flux medicine I sold them, and it made things worse. How was I to know werewolves can't tolerate poppy? I've never known them to take hostages, but they do take offense at the least little things that I've seen. I wonder what is the matter with them this time?"

The silver mist roiled and tumbled. From it emerged a pack of eight or so young wolflings, led by a gray-coated, tall-eared female in a flowing robe that had a slit from the waist down at the back to accommodate her thick tail. She pointed at them, and two adolescent males crawled forward on hands and feet. They sniffed Magpie up and down. He tried to assume an amiable posture, as best one could while bound and gagged. They left him, and investigated Lakanta. One of them turned to the robed female and let out a noise that was a combination of snort and sneeze.

The female approached her. "Stone-woman."

"Moon-howler," Lakanta replied courteously. "I was just passing through here. My name is Lakanta. No family name, no, thank you, if you don't mind. I'm a trader."

"Private talk," the leader, the female Magpie had heard before, snarled in hushed tones. "Keep your voice low. I am Patha Yelia. I've heard of a dwarf that trades among humans, but I thought it was a man."

"My husband," Lakanta said promptly. "He's dead or disappeared. I pray it's the latter, but who knows? He always . . ."

"Less chatter!" Patha snarled, putting a paw over the dwarf woman's mouth. "I would as soon kill these blue-and-white monsters for the fear they put into my people. What are you doing with these humans? Briefly!" She let her paw up.

"Some of them are friends of mine," Lakanta said. "Not all of them, if I must tell the truth."

Patha nodded. "It's as we were told." She snarled an order to the young ones. One produced a long, thin knife and slit the cord holding Lakanta to the finger of rock. The dwarf woman stood up and stretched her back. "Choose your friends and go. I will take you among the others. Wait, I must appear to treat you as a prisoner." She produced a rope. Lakanta held out her wrists. Patha bound them.

"Is there a little one here?" Lakanta asked. "A smallfolk girl. She's the most important. I am concerned about her safety."

"Gone," Patha said shortly.

"Gone!" Magpie exclaimed. The gag squelched his outburst into a wordless groan. The others turned to look at him.

"He's my friend, too," Lakanta said. "That's why I talk so freely in front of him, though the skies know I talk freely in front of anyone."

Patha nodded over Magpie's head. "Cut him loose."

A black-pelted werewolf leaped over the great stone. He knelt at Magpie's side and slashed the knots holding his wrists bound. Magpie rubbed his hands and pulled the gag off. The black-furred werewolf took it from him and stuffed it into a pouch slung over his shoulder, then clipped the rest of his bonds.

"I'm a friend," Magpie said, climbing to his feet and making a bow to Patha. "I know many of your people. I have traveled a good deal in Sheatovra, near Bosska and Parouna. I'm a troubadour." He stopped, feeling his cheeks burning. "I mean, I travel as a troubadour. I have bought and sold among your people. I bought silver from Jenada Chorich."

"I have heard you sing, then," Patha said, showing her teeth in a friendly grimace. "I come from Parouna."

"Why have you taken us prisoner?" Magpie asked.

"You have too many questions. Come. I am to let your friends go free. Tell me who among these you trust. We are to keep the others. Make haste. The fog will not last forever."

"Well, glory to the skies!" Lakanta said. "Come along, then."

Magpie crept along behind Lakanta and Patha, staying in the fraying fringes of the thick mist. The members of the Scholardom had all been tied to individual trees, far enough apart that they couldn't see one another. Most of them were blindfolded and gagged. Few, if any, were wounded. Magpie suspected that those who showed bruises or torn habits had been too difficult to take down without a fight.

Sharhava looked the most miserable. She had been tied up at the greatest remove from the others. Her scabbard was empty, and her hood had been thrown back on her shoulders. Her hair lay scattered and tangled around her face. Her hands had not been bound.

"This one," Lakanta whispered, pointing to Teryn, whom they found bound upright with each wrist tied to young trees five feet apart. She bore the signs of a good fight. A smear of blood had dried in a crust under her nose.

"Fierce one," Patha said, removing the cloth from her eyes first. "I am an ally."

Teryn nodded, and Patha untied the gag.

"Teryn, sworn to Halcot of Rabantae," the captain said stoutly.

"Forget your taciturnity for once," Lakanta said. "They are friends."

The guard captain looked past the werewolf to the trader, astonished. "I beg your pardon, then. Where is my soldier?"

"Morag," Lakanta said. "Black hair, big bony face. Same livery, of course."

Patha smelled Teryn's outstretched sleeve briefly, and nodded to the left. "This way."

The royal guard sat huddled against his tree, only looking up blindly when Teryn spoke to him. The young werewolves sprang to free him. Whatever Morag thought of his situation, Magpie could not tell by his expression. He obeyed his captain's order to deport himself calmly and with courtesy.

"Where are our weapons?" Teryn asked, keeping her voice to a murmur. "Our horses?"

"You will be given them when you leave us," Patha said.

Teryn nodded. "I acknowledge prudence."

Rin had been hobbled by all four legs and her hands had been tied behind her back, and was spitting mad by the time she was freed.

"I am a Windmane," she said, aiming a kick at the young female who cut the last tether on her back hooves. "You just wait until you try to visit our lands again. My royal brother will show you what it means to treat us roughly."

"They are allies," Magpie said soothingly.

"I know! Tildi told me. That doesn't excuse it."

"Silence," Patha ordered them. "You are not inaudible."

"My apologies," Magpie said.

"There's another friend I haven't seen," Lakanta said. "A woman in white with a green cloak." With a curt nod, Patha turned to glide away into the mist.

Serafina sat in a small cave, under guard by two young females wearing glowing amulets. Her hands were not bound, nor was she blindfolded. She tried to rise when she saw Patha, her eyes blazing above her gag, but the werewolves had hobbles on her ankles. A sharp tug made her stumble and sit down again. She glared at the females. Magpie and Teryn hurried to release her.

"I have been here for hours," she spat. "I do not kill without reason. I have waited all this time for an explanation, but these two would say nothing except they wished me no harm, and I had no urge to race around in the dark."

"My apologies on your isolation," Patha said. "We meant to sort out the humans as soon as we could, but we would trust only one who was not of the blue-and-white haters of all things not human."

"I am a *wizard*," Serafina said. "I am a member of the council, not a Knight of the Word."

"Grolin?" Patha turned to her second-in-command.

"She was the first one we took," the black male said with a shrug. "She was not armed. We didn't see her staff. She threw magic on three of my pride and broke their amulets before we took it away. They are still asleep on the ground. The blue-and-white ones were also throwing magic. It was an honest mistake."

"The paralysis will wear off soon," Serafina said. "They will not suffer any lasting effects." She scanned the group clustered around the small enclosure. "Where is Tildi?"

"I don't know," Rin said, suddenly anxious. "She is not with you? We tried to get away from all the hurly-burly, and I lost track of her. She said these people were friends."

"How did she know?" Serafina asked. "She has little knowledge of scrying."

"She's no more of a seer than I am," Rin said. "We had a visitor in the rain."

"I was that visitor," a voice said. Out of the mists, a slender woman appeared. Magpie thought that except for the newcomer's tall, elegant ears she and Serafina could be sisters, with their golden skins and large, lustrous dark eyes. She exchanged a cheek rub with Patha. She turned to the companions. "Tildi is safe. I will bring you to her. Come quickly."

"What will become of these others?" Magpie asked.

"We will keep them, as we agreed with our woods-cousin Irithe here," Patha said. "They will be safe, if not happy. How comfortable they remain depends upon whether they can accept the inevitable. My young ones are *very* proficient at knot-tying. The angry ones will not escape, now that their illicit magic is removed from them."

"That is all I can ask," the elf said, exchanging another cheek rub. "You have repaid your debt to me, and more beside."

"The balance is maintained," Patha said with a twitch of her left ear. "I do not keep a tally scratch by scratch. I leave that to my bookkeepers. Go now. The more talk, the greater the chance the knights will hear us."

"Wait," Magpie said as the werewolf female turned to go. "My lady Patha, there is one more I would have you free. A good friend."

"A half friend," Irithe corrected him. "I have been watching you for some days. I can tell who has been well disposed to Tildi, even if you did not tell me. The young female with sea-green eyes."

Patha bared her teeth. "I know the one. She is one of the blue-and-white-clad who believe we are monsters."

"It would take too long to tell, but she doesn't believe the way they do,"

Magpie said. He dropped to one knee before the werewolf chieftess and lifted his chin to show his throat. "Please."

Patha gave him a summing look. Her almond-shaped eyes regarded him with sympathy. "She is your love?"

"Mine, forever," Magpie said, "but whether I am still hers, I do not know."

"Come, then," Patha said.

The werewolf chieftess backtracked along the river path for a goodly distance, but stopped before walking uphill. She scanned the group behind her. "There are too many of you now, and you make too much noise."

"I will guide the prince," said Irithe.

"We will wait here," Serafina said at once. "Your Highness, go alone."

Magpie nodded. "Thank you. We will return as soon as we may."

You are taking a risk," Irithe whispered as she led him easily through the roiling bands of fog. "Her loyalties are divided, between you and the severe woman with the wounded hand. She might choose to betray you."

"I know Inbecca," Magpie said. He managed to sound confident, but in his heart he dreaded putting the choice to her.

Inbecca had not been blindfolded, but sat calmly watching the group of werewolves approach. Her studiously placid demeanor only broke when she saw Magpie among them. Just for a moment, hope lit her face, but she schooled herself back into expressionlessness. His heart swelled with pride for her. She was a queen to her marrow.

He crouched down beside her and removed the cloth from her mouth. "Are you all right?"

"I am. I was worried about you. Have you seen my aunt?"

Magpie hesitated. "She is being cared for." Inbecca must have noticed his ambivalent expression, but she only accepted his words. He nodded toward Irithe. "This is a friend. She has come to set Tildi free and help her take the book back where it belongs."

Inbecca's eyes flashed.

"She was the cause of the attack? We could all have been killed!"

"None of you were in deliberate danger," Irithe whispered. "If there were any deaths, it was accidental. You fought back with ferocity. It was not easy to capture you."

"Why capture us at all? Why not whisk Tildi away?"

Irithe smiled slowly. "You surprise me, Princess."

"And me," Magpie said.

"I have been thinking of this for some time," Inbecca admitted. "It seemed the obvious thing to do. It is good that it happened due to an outside agency. My aunt would never have let Tildi depart. It is well said that putting a scepter into a hand can corrupt the mind, if the mind has not been schooled in humility first—and that is no guarantee of wise governance. The book has been too much of a temptation. I would have it out of reach of . . . some people. I do not know why another attempt was made before."

"There were mitigating factors," Magpie said. He was hesitant to accuse Sharhava on Tildi's fearful words after the transformation of the beasts, though he was sure the smallfolk girl had no reason to lie. But Inbecca accepted his reasoning with a mere nod.

"I'm not surprised," Inbecca said dolefully. "I was not privy to the councils. My aunt mistrusts me. Perhaps she has reason."

"We must leave as soon as possible," Magpie said. "You are not part of your aunt's mad plans. Come away with us."

Inbecca frowned at him. "You know I can't do that."

"Why not?"

"Would you have me so easily forsworn? I am a member of the order now, whether or not I like my aunt's methods. I took a solemn oath."

Magpie felt ice in his belly.

"It is as I told you," Irithe said.

"Then, tie me up again, too," Magpie said resolutely, sitting down on the wet ground and placing his back against the tree. "I will stay. I will not leave Inbecca alone with these people. I would love to see the end of this tale— Mother and Father know I couldn't help but write a song about it—but my loyalty is to Inbecca, first and foremost. I have sworn it."

"No, Eremi," Inbecca said, tears starting in her eyes. "I released you when I took this vow. I have searched my soul to know what would happen if there was ever a parting of the ways, and we have come to it. You must go. I will stay here."

He gazed at her in dismay. "What of our love?"

"It still exists," Inbecca said. "It must only change its course. We have different duties, you and I."

"Don't you love me anymore?" he asked ruefully.

"More than life itself," Inbecca said with a smile that was only for him. "I didn't know what that meant before. It was always something that poets said. Now I know how precious it is. I would still make the choice. Go."

"And leave you here?" Magpie asked. His voice had thickened, making it hard to get words out.

"I am not alone." Her cheek creased in an irresistible dimple. "I still have my aunt. Eremi, someone with sense needs to stay with her. We will be all right. I know why you must do this. I only hope I will bear my captivity with as much grace as Tildi did hers. I have admired her greatly over these last many days." She swallowed hard, and Magpie knew how difficult it was for her. "Tell her . . . tell her I wish her well in the hard task she has ahead, and that if we ever meet again I hope she will allow me to call her friend."

"I know she would be honored." He bowed to her.

"The honor shall be mine," Inbecca said gravely, inclining her head with royal gravity.

Irithe cut the bonds holding her to the tree. "You stay out of loyalty," she said. "There is no need for other bonds."

"I thank you," Inbecca said. She turned to the elf. "Will you excuse us for a moment?"

Irithe's mouth rose in the corner for one brief smile. "Gladly." She rose and disappeared silently into the haze.

Inbecca grabbed Magpie by the front of his tunic and pulled him to her for a last kiss. He wrapped his arms around her muddy habit and put all the love he had into that embrace. After an eternity and not nearly long enough, Inbecca drew back. She smiled at him tenderly.

"Hurry and go. I want the others to think I am as upset as they are that you have fled. My aunt will be very angry that the runes are gone. But I must say it will be a relief not to fear that a passing butterfly will accidentally give me another nose."

Magpie leaned in for just one more kiss. "Farewell, my love. I will think of you every moment."

Inbecca dimpled. "Not every moment. I hope you will be looking after Tildi! Hurry!"

She sat back against the tree and tried once again to look like a dejected prisoner.

Irithe beckoned to him. Magpie crept after her. Within a couple of yards, the fog swallowed up the last glimpse he had of his love. He was running away from her yet again, but he could assuage his conscience slightly. This time he was not departing without saying goodbye. He had her permission and her blessing. She would not be embarrassed again in his absence. What cost, what cost would *he* pay for leaving her behind? He hoped she would be safe.

Magpie emerged into the moonlit cloud where his companions waited impatiently.

"Ooh! You startled a year's growth out of me," Lakanta said, putting a hand over a supposedly pounding heart. "Oh. You're alone. Where's the young lady?"

Serafina turned from the edge of the towpath, her chin in her hand. She swept him with an analytical eye, ending with intense scrutiny of his face.

"So she is not coming," she said.

"No," Magpie said, forcing himself to accept the inevitable. Inbecca had chosen duty over her own happiness. He would probably have done the same in her place. In fact, he had done so. "I agree with her reasoning. She is more noble than I."

"Do not deride yourself," Serafina said tersely. "We each must make our choice." She turned to Irithe. "I have been patient, but I must know. Where is Tildi? My mother put her into my care. The council trusted me, and I have failed them. She was not to leave my sight for a minute."

"She is safe and among friends," the elf woman said. "You will see her soon. We must travel this way." Irithe turned so that the gurgle of the river was on her right and began walking. Serafina hurried to stay alongside her.

"What friends? Where are they?"

"You will see. We will be with them shortly."

"I know 'shortly' doesn't mean the same to you that it does to me," Lakanta said, opening her stride widely to keep up behind the two tall women. "How long is *your* 'shortly'?"

Irithe regarded her with amusement. "Perhaps two hours' walk."

"Ah. That kind of shortly," Lakanta said, stamping her feet well into her shoes. "Well, are we walking there? I lost everything I had up that hill, including my horse."

"That is arranged."

Ahead, the fog parted to reveal Patha and a pack of the young werewolves.

"I believe that these belong to you," she said.

Magpie heard the tick-tock of shod hooves on the pebbles before he saw the horses they were leading. Tessera must have caught his scent, because she threw back her head and nickered. He hurried to her and took the reins from the white-muzzled oldster leading her. The mare rammed her head against his chest, and he fondled her ears.

"Good girl."

"A fine horse," the old groom said, a gleam in his eyes. "Strong and fit. You'll have many a good long year yet with her."

"I hope so," Magpie said. He noted with gratitude that Tessera had been well curried. His tack had been cleaned and repaired, including a handspan's length of his reins that he had noted before would need to be replaced sooner or later. "She's cleaner than I am. You have cared well for her."

The yellow eyes flashed. "And you'd think that I'd not?"

"I'd have expected nothing less," Magpie said with a bow.

"Fed her, too. Likes sweet feed and oats, doesn't she?"

"Too much than is good for her."

The oldster let out a bark that sounded like a laugh.

Two more werewolves appeared. Each of them was loaded down with packs and gear that looked far too heavy for such slight creatures to carry. Patha grinned her sharp-toothed smile at Magpie's surprise.

"We are stronger than we look, in both shapes. It is useful for traders not to have to rely upon loaders or beasts more than we need to."

The pair dumped the bags into a heap on the path, then came to sniff each of the travelers intently. The smaller one, a female with a brown pelt, went back to the pile and returned with Magpie's saddlebags, sword, and flute.

"These smell like you," she said. "I didn't find anything else on the hillside. Is anything missing?"

"No, thank you for your courtesy," he said, buckling on the scabbard. He threw the bags over Tessera's back and fastened them in place behind the saddle. "There, old girl. Good as new."

And indeed they were. In the time Magpie had fallen off his horse, gotten into a fight or two, and been carried down and tied to a tree, the werewolves had retrieved and wiped all the mud off his property. It all looked nearly as fresh as it had when he left his father's castle weeks before.

The other horses had undoubtedly met werewolves before, because none of them danced away skittishly from their temporary caretakers despite the strong smell of musk in their fur. Serafina's white mare shone like silver. Even Melune's rough coat gleamed like polished wood.

The larger bearer, whose pelt was pale gray, brought swords and shields to the Rabantavian guards along with their personal belongings and Morag's cooking gear.

"These were in the pack animals' panniers belonging to those humans, but when we scented your trace, we brought them out. We saw the royal crest." The young male grinned. "My grandsire engraved the royal seal itself for your king on his coronation."

"Werewolf metalwork is known throughout the world," Teryn said gravely.

"And these things belong to the little one," Patha said, extending a small knapsack. "Such a curious collection of goods to carry on such a journey. So many things, and each with a different scent."

"They carry memories for her," Rin said. She took it and placed it in the saddlebags that had been returned to her. "She will be glad to have these back. I know how precious it is to have mementos of those who are no longer with us."

"Aye, that's true," Lakanta said.

Serafina counted the horses. "One of our beasts is missing," she said.

"No, there isn't," the little trader said, frowning. "One for each of us to ride who needs to ride, and the one to carry the heavy bags."

"My mother's mare!" Serafina said. "I want her with me. Mistress Patha, the other white mare and her saddle, if you please."

"It'll be trouble," Lakanta warned. "She'll need someone to guide her all the time. It was one thing when she was running with all the other beasts of burden, excuse the reference, but she'll be largely on her own now. She'd be better off staying behind."

Serafina looked at her coldly. "Did you not just agree that it was normal to want to have mementos of those lost?"

"But you can't tuck a horse away in a pouch!"

The wizardess refused to be reasoned with. "I will not leave my mother's steed here with the knights. She's been with us since she was a foal. She has trusted my family to care for her all these years. My mare is her daughter."

Patha put an end to the argument by sending one of her assistants running. A few moments later, he reappeared, leading the white mare. Serafina took the reins.

"Let me, sister," Rin said. "We can speak to each other. I will guide her."

"Very well. We must go." Serafina bowed in her saddle to Patha. "I thank you for your aid. It will not be forgotten."

Irithe nodded, and began trotting southward along the towpath. The companions kicked up their steeds.

Magpie waited until they had ridden a few miles before he nudged Tessera up so she was neck and neck with Serafina's horse.

"This obduracy is not like you, honored one."

Serafina cringed slightly at the title.

"I apologize. I have taken out my temper on those who do not deserve it." She glanced back over her shoulder and let out an irritated breath. "That woman put a *spell* on me. On me! A member of the council! I cannot believe I rode complacently in her train, against my better judgment, letting her corrupt my runes, which were there to protect her as well as us. And then, to cloud my mind, so I would not undo her foul magic, was overstepping any bounds. She will pay for this indignity, I promise you that."

"She is paying, I assure you," Magpie said, seeing Sharhava tied to the tree. "She is suffering. The runes have faded. Her dream has left her."

Serafina was too high-minded to rejoice aloud. Her lips thinned at another thought. "The runes have faded, but the wards are also gone! That means Tildi is not protected, either."

"She is safe," Irithe called back.

"How can she be? Do you know what you have done, breaking the spell open?"

Irithe stopped and waited for them to catch up with her. She looked up into Serafina's face. Magpie was struck again at how alike they were, but observed the wisdom in the elf's that Serafina had yet to earn.

"I know. She was revealed for a short time, but it was a sacrifice that needed to be made, to accomplish your rescue. Would you still be in the Scholardom's power?"

Serafina looked mortified. "No. Of course not. But she is out of my care."

"She is with those who can guard her against peril from the skies. I am taking you to her. You do not need to trust for long. You will have proof. Now, let us not waste more time."

"I am sorry," Serafina said, humbled. "I do not mean to be ungrateful."

Irithe regarded her with a kind expression that made Magpie think of Edynn. "When you have the leisure to be grateful, you may be, if it will give you comfort. Now, let us go while the moon is high."

Behind them, howls rose to greet the silver disk. The mist was lifting.

Chapter Twelve

Inbecca couldn't help but cringe when the big, gray-furred female appeared beside her without a rustle of warning. The almond-shaped eyes, glowing yellow in the moonlight, seemed amused by her discomfiture. Thank the Mother that these were civilized beings, not the barbarian cannibals that some of the fireside stories made them out to be.

"Come," the werewolf whispered to her, extending a long, black-padded paw to help her up. "We must gather your fellows. We will return to our camp for what remains of the night."

"Are they . . . ?" Inbecca asked.

"Well away."

Without another word, the female whisked around and glided away. Inbecca followed her more slowly in the monochrome twilight. It was less foggy than it had been but the ground was still sodden from the rain. Sticky mud clung to her borrowed boots and hung in big flakes all over her robes. The smell of wet wool, leather, and linen, coupled with the stink she had acquired during a long day's ride, made her eyes water.

When she saw her fellow knights, she realized that she was much better off than any of them. Many bore the signs of the battle.

The chieftess took her by the shoulder and led her to a place along the rope.

"Hold tight," she said. "You will all be safe, I swear it." She brought a short length of cord from a pouch and looped it loosely around Inbecca's wrists. She tied it with a slipknot, such as one might use to fasten a child's shoe. Inbecca could have undone it with her teeth in a twinkling.

None of the others were being granted the courtesy of a cursory bond. In truth, Inbecca would have trusted none of her fellows to behave calmly. Some shouted angrily at the werewolves who came near them, even the ones who bandaged their injuries. Lar Vreia struggled and kicked out at her captors with one leg. The other, by the unnatural angle at which it lay on the ground, looked to be broken or sprained. Two females tried to set it, but Inbecca could see she was too frightened to allow them to help.

"Stop fighting!" a large male snarled at her. "You'll make it worse."

"Let her be!" Lar Romini shouted as he was half dragged to the cable. The young man's tunic had been slashed, leaving glints of his mail shirt exposed. His gag hung around his neck. By the redness of his lower face, he had managed to loosen it himself and scrape off the first layer of skin as well. It took five of the werefolk to force him over and hold him near one of the trees while two more secured his hands. Inbecca observed wryly that if the lycanthropes didn't care whether or not they hurt their captives it would have taken fewer of their number to manage them.

Romini twisted suddenly. He wrenched one hand free. A bloom of blue light appeared on his palm, but it was hazy and translucent, not the lambency that had surprised and terrified Inbecca a few days before. He thrust it into the chest of the werewolf holding his other hand. A sound like a snapping branch erupted, and the male fell backward a yard. He sat on the ground looking dazed. One of the female healers left Vrcia to examine him. Romini looked astonished, but undoubtedly because the werewolf hadn't died.

He kicked away from his captors and dashed for the edge of the clearing, hoping to disappear in the thinning mist. His bid for freedom was short-lived. Before he could take more than four steps, half a dozen werewolves jumped on him and bound him tightly with his hands behind his back and a hobble on his ankles that gave him a pace of about half a yard. He was tethered to the big cable by a stout cord around his waist.

"Has anyone seen my aunt?" Inbecca asked as Loisan was pressed forward at claw-point and tied in place. The big man shook his head.

"No, Lar," he said. "I have seen none of you others until this moment. I pray she lives."

"I am sure she does."

Loisan glanced at the werewolves as they secured another knight behind them. "We've got to find a way out of this. Wait until we outnumber them. I've counted sixteen so far. How many do you reckon them?"

"I . . . I don't know." Inbecca looked about her. Too many strange furred people, moving about so swiftly, to be counted. *Gather your wits*, she admonished herself. How often had she had to learn all the delegates of a party visiting Levrenn to honor her mother? To address one by the wrong name was a terrible social error. *That female has a tunic that gleamed red in the returning moonlight. That one, who also wears red, has lighter fur and wider set eyes. The two males behind them were good friends or brothers, the way* they roughhoused together. The one with black fur was missing half of the lower right canine. The gray one, the elder or wiser, stooped a little around the shoulders.

Shortly, her court training allowed her to identify all of the werewolves visible in the clearing.

"Fifteen," she said.

"We have the advantage two to one," Loisan said. "They assemble us to a purpose. When we are all together, we must move!"

Inbecca was distracted from Loisan's words at that moment as her aunt was helped into the clearing. All the knights stopped struggling or moving to watch her. Sharhava walked stooped over like an ancient, shuffling her feet on the ground. Her escorts treated her with care, almost tenderly, and attached her to the long cable by a rope looped around her good hand.

"Abbess!" Loisan exclaimed. Sharhava raised her head. Even at a distance, Inbecca could see her eyes glittering with hatred. Sharhava nodded sharply at her lieutenant. Meaning had passed between them.

"Pass the word," he said over his shoulder to Lar Vreia. "As soon as they try to move us, we strike." She nodded. "Pass the word!" he told Inbecca.

What choice did she have? She whispered his instructions to Lar Colruba, who had just been added to the chain ahead of her. The woman nodded and leaned forward to whisper to the next knight.

"Lar Inbecca!" A more insistent voice intruded into the muttering.

Inbecca looked around. Loisan leaned toward her, his eyes intent.

"Your bonds! Your bonds have slipped!" he whispered. "Free me! Quickly, now!"

Inbecca looked down at her hands. Patha's knot must have fallen apart. She looked at Loisan, who urged her forward with his chin.

"Hurry, Lar Inbecca, before they notice!"

Inbecca dithered. If she aided the knights' freedom, they might manage to overpower the werewolves and hie after Eremi and Tildi again. Yet she must not be seen as a traitor to the Scholardom.

"Hurry!"

The urgent voice jerked her into action. She edged backward very slowly, hoping that Patha and her people weren't so busy with the last of the knights that they would not notice what she was doing. She longed to be caught. Keeping one hand on the cable, she felt behind her with the other.

Loisan's voice guided her. "Up a bit. Over to your right."

Suddenly her cold fingertips touched his warm hand. "There you go, now. If you work the bit of rope you can just feel there toward you, it'll come loose, and I can get a hand free. There you go, now."

The werewolves' ropes were dry and good, so it was easy to get her fingertip under the loop to which Loisan directed her. She strained to undo the knot. She could feel the man twitching impatiently for her to finish. She clawed at the strand, pulling it out like a shoelace, all the while keeping her face as still as she could.

"There, now," Loisan said. He bent down swiftly and pulled a thin dagger no longer than his finger out of the side of his boot. He slit the rope holding his other hand in place. Without hesitation, he turned and cut Vreia loose. She started on the bonds of the knight behind her. Then there were two more free, then four, then eight.

"What goes on here?" Patha asked, suddenly deducing that mischief was afoot.

Instead of answering, the knights turned and prepared what magic they had left and flung it at the werewolves.

With no time for the strike to be coordinated, some of the furred beings were struck by three or four puffs of magic, some not at all. Those who were hit went flying backward, wailing their distress. The others leaped toward their attackers, claws out. Loisan and Romini took the two ends of the heavy cable and ran toward the werewolves with it, as if hoping to round them up like sheep.

Patha snarled out a command in their tongue. The four werewolves upon whom the knights were bearing down leaped straight in the air, making Inbecca gasp with wonder. They came down on the other side of the line. Without hesitation, they thrust their way through the rest of the knights like a ball striking ninepins. Those who remained standing vanished into the trees opposite as if they had dissolved. The knights halted and went on guard, gazing around them warily, holding the rope before them like a shield.

"Stand aware," Sharhava ordered. "They are canny beasts."

Inbecca wanted to cry out that they were not beasts at all, but it wasn't the time to argue.

"We can't just wait for them to strike again," Rachine said. Her hair was as wild as her eyes. "We're powerless!"

"We are not," Sharhava said. "We still have magic." She held out her hand. A tiny blaze like that of a candle flame danced on her palm. Her face pinched as she concentrated, trying to get it to grow. Inbecca pitied her aunt.

"The runes are gone, Abbess!" Ecris said. "What shall we do?"

"We need our gear and horses. Then we will pursue the book. It cannot be hidden from us, you know that. Do not fear! We will bring it again into our care, and punish those who have separated us from it!"

"I'll find our weapons," Loisan said, the voice of reason injecting a note of calm that quelled the rising panic. "You five, with me. They came from that way. It must be where they are keeping our goods." He pointed with the small knife. The knights he indicated followed him.

A howl erupted at the opposite end of the clearing. Loisan spun, the tiny knife in his hand. The others assumed a fighting posture. More howls sprang up at different points around the circle.

Inbecca felt her heart begin to pound with fear. Perhaps she was wrong about the werewolves. Their intentions might not be friendly, now that the elf who had engaged their aid had gone. Why had she not fled with Eremi, as he pleaded with her to do? She could die here! She stooped to find a stick or a stone, anything she could use as a weapon. The knights prepared themselves to fight.

As quickly as snuffing a candle, the moon went out.

The knights all began to shout orders at one another, with Sharhava booming to be heard above all. Plunged into darkness, Inbecca didn't know where to turn. A heavy body careened into her. She staggered, hands out. Her palms were scraped by the rough bark of trees. She felt her way up the bole, trying to regain her feet.

All around her, the howls continued, coupled with the shouts of her fellow knights. She felt bodies fall by her, heard the scuffle of battle. A long wail arose close to her ear, making her heart pound with terror.

"Do not let the demon spell confuse you!" Sharhava said. "Strike! Strike!"

Blue energy, like the afterimage of firelight, flared in Inbecca's eyes. The howls coupled with cries of surprise, but no wails of pain or death. Without the book, the magic the Scholardom had enjoyed for weeks had dwindled to a mere squib, a wet firework. Instead, Inbecca saw glints of yellow eyes glowing of their own light.

"How could that girl rob us of our power?" Sharhava shrieked. "She will pay! She knew the cost of my vengeance, and I will make her pay!"

Inbecca had no time to wonder what her aunt meant. Hard hands covered with wiry hair caught her and thrust her hands roughly behind her back. Ropes wound around her body from shoulders to thighs, then a sharp push sent her to the ground again. Without her hands to save her, she fell hard.

Other bodies joined hers. Swiftly, the entire Scholardom was recaptured and secured more firmly than before.

To Inbecca's surprise, all of the knights were tied together, in a bundle like twigs for the fire. Inbecca stood on tiptoes to find her aunt. Sharhava was two rows away from her at the front, glaring at their chief captor.

Patha surveyed them with disdain in her golden eyes. "It will be easier if you cooperate, but no matter. Follow me, then. I am sure you are as tired and hungry as we. There is food to eat and water to wash with at our destination. Come along."

She thought it would be tricky to maneuver the mass of humanity down-slope to the moonlit towpath, but the werewolves managed to keep the group together and upright. Her fellows were too angry or exhausted to do more than try to stay on their feet, so the swearing and vowing of vengeance was kept to a minimum. Inbecca had to trust what she could feel with the toes of her boots, since while she was on the move she could see nothing but her neighbors.

After what seemed like hours, Patha called a halt. The pressure on Inbecca's rib cage lessened as the ropes holding them all together were untied. The knights staggered away from one another, and were led instantly to the base of individual trees, where they were secured with the same care as before. Inbecca pleaded with the two gray-furred individuals who came to claim her.

"Please put me near my aunt," she begged. "She will need me."

The two nodded at each other. "It will be as you ask," they said.

*I*nbecca sat calmly as the werewolves tied bonds around her upper arms, but left her hands free. Sharhava was less than five feet from her, secured in the same fashion. The abbess held herself taut, like a bowstring, refusing to look at anyone else. To be captured twice in one night must have taken a toll on her aunt's notorious pride.

They were in a campsite, laid out by practiced travelers. Unlike the last. Once the knights were secure, Patha's people disappeared into the array of colorful marquee tents pitched at the edge of the clearing. Around them, a new contingent of werewolves went about their business, as if unaware that they had a coterie of angry humans in their presence. There were no young but, Inbecca realized, it was long past midnight. Children, even lycanthropes, were almost certainly in bed. Or did they stay up nights when in their wolf-skins?

A young female with brown-gray fur who might be close to Inbecca's own age noticed her scrutiny and smiled at her. She approached her, squatting down to eye level with her, and placed a bowl on her lap. It was half full of water, the warmth of which was welcome to Inbecca's cold fingers. The girl added a small cloth and a chunk of soap.

"Thank you," Inbecca said. "I would be glad to wash."

"Are you hungry?" the girl asked. "We have good food. Meat? Cheese? Soup? What is your pleasure?"

"Anything," Inbecca said, relieved. "But, please, take care of my aunt, first."

"I will eat nothing prepared by monsters," Sharhava said, pitching her voice to carry.

"That is absurd, Aunt," Inbecca said. She smiled at her server. "If you please, I would be grateful for anything hot to drink. The night is chilly."

"Autumn is here, is it not?" the girl said. "We have cider." She whisked away.

"Lar Inbecca, I will not have you consorting with the enemy!" Inbecca turned to Sharhava, but the abbess was still staring intently into the heart of the fire. Inbecca frowned.

"I am not consorting. I am being practical, Aunt. A starving mind is a desperate one. If you choose to see it as a weapon, then eat what they have and use it as a means to feed your strategy."

The sea-blue eyes turned to her for a moment. "If you are mocking me . . ."

"I am not mocking you, Aunt," Inbecca said with a sigh. "They are not mistreating us. They have offered us food, which any decent people would do . . ."

"These are not people!"

Inbecca had a terrifying flash of memory, of the hairy beast-men in the north, reduced to animal intelligence by an act of will.

"Yes, they are people," she said calmly. "Levrenn has traded with the werewolves for millennia. My bride's gift from Eremi came from them."

"I have never approved of consorting with the lesser beings," Sharhava said.

"I know you haven't, Aunt, but they are a fact of life. Some of them have been loyal friends to Levrenn."

"Hmpph! Friendship of convenience. How could anything they do be true?"

Inbecca tried not to show her impatience or her embarrassment.

"How are our horses?" Inbecca asked her hostess when the girl returned with a bowl of soup and a plate on which bite-sized morsels of meat and cheese had been laid, alongside thick slices of buttered bread. Her ears were twisted at a curious angle, which Inbecca knew to be the equivalent of an embarrassed flush in humans. She could not have helped but hear what Sharhava had been saying. No one in the camp could.

"I will find out for you," the girl said, grateful for an excuse to glide away.

Washbowls and food were being brought to all the other knights that Inbecca could see on her side of the fire. It seemed that there were many more werewolves here than just the few who had captured them above the bridgehead. Now the knights were truly outnumbered. Loisan might think of escape from here, but it would be more difficult.

She glanced at her fellow humans. This was her place, now. She was a member of the Scholardom.

She would have given anything to abandon her oath there and then, but she knew she had done the right thing, even if she had decided in haste. Eremi had given her the choice—several choices, in fact. There had been no time for careful deliberation.

Twice in the same season she acted on impulse. Her mother would shake her head in disbelief to see her careful daughter behave so recklessly. She was doing the right thing by keeping an eye on the knights.

And at last, she now believed in the cause. The book *must* be protected and kept aloof from society, perhaps only in the hands of those who would use it well. She was all the more certain that her aunt was one of those in whose hands it should not be. As a guardian of the Great Book, it was Inbecca's responsibility to keep Sharhava away from ever coming close to it again. If that meant an undefined term of captivity, so be it. Tildi was away and safe, and Eremi with her.

How hard it was to think that these fierce creatures were the same ones who had made that delicate silver piece he had given her. She had known few werewolves, and none well. The ones who visited her mother's court did not mix much with the humans. She often heard them fighting among themselves, as they were there in their encampment. She could hear but not see several on the other side of the fire from her who were engaged in a squabble. A few of her fellow knights cringed at the rising snarls and howls, but Inbecca knew the argument would be over as swiftly as it had begun.

They were good cooks, though. She supped the warm broth from the bowl, then spooned up a piece of fragrant white root vegetable. As her hunger was sated, she began to feel drowsy. She fought against it, needing to stay awake for her aunt's sake.

With the prisoners—for that was what they had been, in spite of her aunt's high-minded words—gone, the knights' care went to the abbess and to herself. Many of them were Levrenn-born and knew her as the crown princess. Former crown princess. Inbecca regretted having taken the oath at all now. Who would take her place on the She-Tiger's Throne? One of her younger sisters or female cousins, most likely. Who had the greatest tact? Her mother would look for diplomacy before any other characteristic. Tact and patience were vital in such a thicket of thorns as a royal court.

Impatience was how she had gotten herself into this situation—impatience and hurt pride.

Patha came out of her tent, wearing a clean gown of soft slate-blue. Her fur was clean and fluffed out, giving her the look of a well-groomed hunting dog. Inbecca hastily set the thought aside as though afraid the werewolf would have been able to see it in her eyes. The large female crouched before Sharhava.

"You should not waste food," Patha said. "It is an insult to those who hunted and farmed it."

"I would rather swallow poison," Sharhava spat.

"And I would feed you poison if you so chose," Patha said, her voice a low growl. "But I have given my word to those whom I respect to keep you safe and well. And I shall."

"You will loose these ropes at once," Sharhava demanded. "Free me and my knights!"

"No. If you will not eat, you will be hungry. My people will not bring you food again until you ask. And ask nicely. We extend respect to you. We expect it in return. It is only civilized."

"Civilized! What could you know of civilization?" Sharhava asked. "Do you know who I am?"

Patha spat into the dust. "Yes. You are a killer. You murdered two of my men. Two men with children! Two friends whom I will miss greatly."

"You speak of murder as though you are innocent of it," Sharhava rejoined. "*You* killed Lar Driel."

Patha's hard expression softened for a moment. Her lower jaw hung loose, which Inbecca recognized as a sign of shame. "It was not intentional. We are traders, not fighters, so we do not possess the subtleties of defense that you must be trained in. Our task was to capture you, and capture you we have. Do not fear. We will bury him decently and sing him peace."

"Do not . . ." Sharhava's voice trembled with the hatred that boiled in her. She was so red in the face that Inbecca feared for her heart. "Do not keen your unnatural noises for the loss of a true knight and scholar. Do not dare!"

Patha inclined her head. "As you wish. He will be buried with care, then, and without song. You may give what rites to him you choose when we let you go. Until then, you must trust us that we give him all honor."

"No! We will bury him! You will let us free, immediately!"

"No. That would defeat all purpose."

"Do you know I am the sister of the queen of Levrenn?" Sharhava pointed at Inbecca. "This is her daughter. She is the heir to the She-Tiger's Throne!"

Patha bowed to her. "My honor."

"The honor is mine," Inbecca said sincerely. "I am truly sorry for your loss."

"As I am for yours. I would that this acquaintance was under other circumstances."

"As do I." Inbecca felt strange, making all the correct civilized responses while tied to a tree.

Sharhava would not let civilized discourse deter her from her complaint.

"You cannot keep us here forever," she insisted.

The werewolf shrugged her shoulders. "We do not need to keep you forever, or so is my hope. Would you knowingly loose the instrument of your own destruction? We will remain your caretakers only until your object is out of reach and you realize that your further intentions are futile. Then time will tell when you may leave."

"Intentions? What intentions?" Inbecca asked.

Sharhava was scornful. "To get the Great Book back, of course. To take it to the Scriptorium where it belongs. That is all."

"There is more," the werewolf said. Her yellow eyes narrowed. "You have not told all to your sister-daughter."

"Told me what, Aunt?" Inbecca asked, alarmed.

At her question, Sharhava looked uncomfortable. She shifted against the tree bole. She gave Inbecca a stern glance. "There is no more. She knows what her duty requires her to know."

Patha's eyes blazed. She shoved her muzzle toward the abbess's face. "You lie. The light of truth is not upon you, even if I did not already know."

"Tell me," Inbecca said.

"No! It is all lies," Sharhava insisted, drawing herself up. "You will not listen to her, Lar Inbecca. Such are my orders, and you will obey them!"

Patha's gleaming eyes bored into Sharhava's. "I have heard the truth from one who will not lie. The little one feared for the well-being of her fellow smallfolk, should *she* not obey you. And I, seeing your response to our intervention, would also fear for our people, should you regain the treasure you lost. I have heard what I need to about this Great Book, and I have no need to see it for myself. I can tell that it is not a fit thing for you to have."

Sharhava struggled against the bonds holding her, her face red with fury. "Of course you fear! What weed does not fear being plucked out? When we have the book back in our hands, you will be wiped out. I will see to it that every one of your kind is returned to base animals."

"Aunt!"

"Abbess!" Loisan added his outrage from partway around the campfire. Sharhava ignored them, so intent was she on her tirade.

"You dare not interfere with our plans. You, who are scarcely human!"

Patha gathered herself and leaped, landing inches from Sharhava with her leathery nose nearly touching Sharhava's bruised one. The abbess recoiled. Patha's eyes gleamed fiercely.

"And whose doing is that? I would kill the one who made us what we are, but we will live on when those who believe as you do are dust and bones," she snarled. "You will stay here, and stop complaining! Otherwise, your misery will be doubled and doubled again!"

Sharhava's face went pale in the firelight. She closed her lips and tightened them until they were a thin line. Patha stood up and, turning her back, scratched dust toward the abbess with a scornful foot.

A shout went up a quarter of the way around the circle. Inbecca heard sounds of a struggle. Suddenly Auric scrambled over the corner of the fire, narrowly avoiding the roasting jacks. He leaped onto the corner of the logs and bounded toward the woods. The traders were caught by surprise. Howling, a handful of the young males gave chase. Auric, in spite of his age, was tough as whipcord. He kept ahead of his pursuers for a few yards before their superior stride helped them catch him. The whole band bounded forward and brought him down. Together, they brought the struggling man back into the firelit circle and forced him back to his post.

"Let me go!" he bellowed.

"Tie him tighter," the large, black-furred male shouted, coming out of his tent.

"Don't be so rough on him!" Brouse called. "He is an old man."

"He was not injured," a pale brown werewolf said. "We are giving him good care."

"Check the others," Patha commanded. "We do not want any of them escaping. It is not safe to be abroad this late."

The commotion gave Inbecca the chance she wanted to speak in decent privacy. Oblivious to the attempted escape, Sharhava had resumed staring at the fire. Her face was concentrated, and she muttered to herself.

"What did she mean, you were going to attack the Quarters?" Inbecca whispered. "Aunt Sharhava! You couldn't possibly be thinking of such an atrocity."

Sharhava turned furious eyes upon her.

"No one should have been able to get through the protection spell. It had to be treachery. Treachery! It was that freak child. She had it all planned. She escaped while we are humiliated. She will pay!"

"Pay?" Inbecca asked. "She is gone, and good riddance to her."

"But her people are not. She knew what the penalty would be—all I required from her was to bring the book to the Scriptorium, where it would be safe. *She* would have been safe. Now it is gone. She will have to live with their fate on her conscience!"

"What about your conscience?" Inbecca asked dismayed. "How can you even think of attacking a harmless people."

"You forget yourself, Lar Inbecca. My conscience is clean." But the haunted look on her face told Inbecca she had uncomfortable memories. Inbecca pressed against her bonds, moving as close to her aunt as she could. "In any case, once we have the book again, I will cause the smallfolk to cease to be. They will return to their proper state, the way they were before the so-called Makers. The same goes for these shape-changers. They will be humans again, or animals. I know which I would prefer."

Inbecca was terrified by the feral look in her eyes.

"Shouldn't you leave them alone? Look at the harm you caused one species by changing them."

"They laid hands upon us. That shall not go unavenged."

Inbecca was horrified. "Is that what the Scholardom truly is for? You always sounded so high-minded when you spoke of the Great Book. When I was a child and you wanted to convince me to follow you then, you told me that your cause was to find the book so you could safeguard it, and nothing more. I believe in that cause. It should be safeguarded. How can you reconcile revenge with your goal?"

"You can't possibly understand," Sharhava said, batting away Inbecca's words as though they were so many gnats. Her face twisted with pain. Inbecca didn't know if it was from the memory of the beast-creatures or her burned hand.

"Of course I can understand," she said urgently. "But don't you? What you propose is a deliberate act of revenge. Will you only be satisfied when there is nothing left on Alada but humans and animals?"

"Do we not deserve our dignity?"

"Of course, but as our host pointed out, we need to give it as well."

"That would be as senseless as giving weapons to a child," Sharhava said. "They wouldn't know what to do with it. Once we are freed from here, you will be on penalty duty, Lar Inbecca, for questioning my orders and my judgment."

Inbecca leaned back, exasperated, and stared at the Pearl. How pointless it was to argue with someone who would not look beyond the end of her own nose. How right Eremi had been about her. Perhaps she should get a little sleep. She glanced around her for the young girl who had been kind enough to serve her. Maybe she could persuade her to bind her in a different position so she could lie down, though at the moment she was weary enough to sleep standing up in a snowstorm.

A black shadow passed over the flawless white surface of the moon. *Not another storm*, Inbecca thought with a low groan. Her habit had dried in the front where she faced the fire, but the rest was still soggy, and her mail shirt was rucked up against her back in a crease.

No, the shape was much too sharp for a storm cloud, nor any other kind of cloud, and it moved much too swiftly. It was joined by another shape, then another. Something that large could only mean one thing. She sat bolt upright and felt the ropes cut into her arms.

"Thraiks. Aunt, there are thraiks in the sky."

"What of it?" Sharhava said miserably, slumped in her place. "The book is gone, so they will have to seek the smallfolk elsewhere."

"Of course, you are right," Inbecca said. She looked up. Soon the winged monsters would pass. She hoped they were heading in the opposite direction to Tildi's.

A harsh cry, muffled by distance, surprised her. The three shapes wheeled against the disk of the moon, then appeared to grow larger.

"What are they doing?" she cried.

She was not the only one to have observed the movement in the skies. The black-furred male sent up a howl of warning.

"Thraiks! Thraiks are coming!"

Many of the werewolves hurried into their tents and emerged holding spears. They resembled the ones used in Levrenn for boar-hunting, with a crosspiece not far from the tip, to keep the impaled prey from pushing itself farther along the shaft in its frenzy to get to the hunter.

"What do they want?" one of the young ones asked an elder. For answer, he only got a shake of the head. The knights began to throw themselves against their bonds.

"Let us loose," Loisan demanded hoarsely. The male hesitated. "Hurry! We would defend ourselves. Would you deny us that?"

The male took a knife out of his belt and flung it. It landed point down in the dirt beside Loisan. The burly lieutenant lost no time in cutting himself free. He sprang up and hurried to Lar Romini. Romini pulled a skewer out of the fire to use as a makeshift sword. As his fellow scholars were unbound, they went for whatever they could find for weapons, their eyes constantly returning to the descending fiends.

Inbecca strained frantically against her bonds, but these were no courtesy knots. The dark wings swirled down toward them, blotting out the moon. The three thraiks screamed, tearing the air with the sound. Inbecca cowered down. She had never seen them so near before. No wonder Tildi was terrified of them. The werewolves and the growing pack of freed knights went on guard.

The winged beasts had dark, greasy scales that picked up the firelight. Their featherless wings were like those of bats, but horrible, with claws like scythes at the end of each joint. Their long tails whipped around their legs as they dropped to mere yards over the campsite. The leader, bigger than the other two, let out another horrifying shriek. He dropped like an eagle, talons first, toward Sharhava. The abbess was agape with terror.

"Aunt!" Inbecca screamed.

Almost before the word left her lips, a form flew past her like a ball shot from a cannon. The black-furred male sprang in between Sharhava and the descending thraik. He set the haft of the spear against his chest and snarled a challenge.

The thraik arrested its stoop and fluttered upward, surprised. It took little time to rethink its attack. Hissing, it wheeled around, wings spread, looking for an opening. The male tracked it with the point of the spear. By this time the slower-moving humans had joined in the defense. Loisan, clutching a burning branch, brandished it at the enemy.

"Come here, foul creature, I dare you!" he bellowed.

He was knocked sprawling from behind. The other two thraiks descended upon the crowd of defenders. They lashed out with spread talons. Loisan picked himself up and retrieved his torch. He thrust it into the face of the thraik behind him. Brouse, hurrying to his side, smashed upward with a piece of wood as thick as his arm, knocking away the spread talons of the attacker. It shrieked and closed its jaws on his forearm. Brouse let out a yell of pain. The wood went flying. More knights came to Loisan's aid. The werewolves moved in to aid the knights, battering at the creature with their spears until it lifted clear. Lar Pedros fell back, clutching his eyes. Blood streamed from under his hands. Lar Rachine put an arm around him and guided him away from the fray. The thraiks revolved like whirlwinds, tearing and clawing. A werewolf male dropped his spear and fell, his chest spouting blood. His fellows clambered over his body to get to his assailant. They plunged their weapons into the legs and tail of the beast. Lar Romini pushed in beside them, flailing the iron bar at the creature's side. It screamed in agony and anger, and snapped at them. Dark ichor rolled down and dripped off its claws. The ground was rendered slippery under the defenders' feet. They drove the pair of hovering thraiks back. The flying monsters were fast, but their speed was matched by the werewolves. The humans' faces turned red with effort as they kept pace with their temporary allies, striking out with whatever came to hand. The two thraiks bobbed up and down, irritatingly just out of reach, screaming their defiance at the knights. Some of the bigger werewolves sprang into the air with their powerful legs. The large black-furred male managed to pierce the foot of the beast that had attacked Brouse.

"Good hit!" the almoner growled. The thraiks keened with pain and dropped slightly in the sky. The humans and werewolves leaped at it, hoping to drag it down and finish it off. Its companion swooped above them, slashing at heads and arms. The defenders were forced to duck, giving the wounded thraik a chance to retreat farther away in the clearing. The humans followed, shouting hoarsely to one another. The werewolves swarmed behind them.

The leader, however, had not forgotten his intended prey. As soon as the others had drawn most of the fighters away, it wheeled around and dropped down before Sharhava. It wrapped one set of talons around her body and pulled.

"Knights! Knights, to me!" she shouted.

Sharhava punched at its bulging eyes and prominent nostrils, trying to strike vulnerable points. The thraik's snakelike neck whipped back and forth as it tore at her bonds with its fangs.

Without hesitation, the rest of the defenders abandoned their battle with the other two. They rushed back, slashing and hitting at the thraik. It had chewed through the ropes holding her. Drawing her close to its body, it spread its great wings and gathered its haunches. Inbecca gasped. It must not be allowed to take off with her!

"Help!" Inbecca called.

Four of the werewolves including Patha and the serving girl bounded the short distance back to Sharhava and beat at the thraik leader's back and wings. It twisted its ugly head on its long neck over its shoulder and snapped at them. Patha howled an order. Her people spread out and glided in from several directions, making the thraik leader have to snake its head about constantly. The knights filled in the circle, beating at the creature even as its underlings tore at the knights at the rear.

"Let her go, beast!" Loisan demanded, trying to force himself in under the creature's greasy arms to save his abbess. It kicked him backward into the arms of a dozen other knights.

Sharhava fought like a wild cat, striking with every limb, including her wounded hand, trying to break free of the thraik's grip. It held tight to her. Its flexible spine allowed it to keep her close to its chest while kicking and biting at the defenders. Inbecca clawed at her own ropes, vainly trying to free herself. She might be the thraik's next victim.

It raised its head over the heads of the others, and she could see its mud-brown eyes. It seemed to have runes for pupils, gold ones like those that had until lately been written on everything and everyone within the book's range. Inbecca felt a thrill of fear, not for herself, but for her aunt. The rumors were true: the flying monsters only sought people who had made contact with the Great Book. Sharhava had touched it. The thraik must think she had it. Inbecca was in no danger, but she feared for her aunt.

"Strike it! Kill it!" Lar Follet shouted.

Sharhava shoved her feet hard against the ground, bringing her head up underneath the chin of her captor. Its head snapped back in surprise. She wrapped her arms around its throat and tried to bear the long neck down to the ground with her.

"Now, scholars! Strike!"

Together, a host of humans and werewolves surged in upon the thraik leader. It writhed and twisted, throwing them off. As many as were flung away, twice that number came in again. They scored upon its flesh. The weapons came away drenched in dark ichor. To her relief, Inbecca saw two werewolves, their tunics torn, drag Sharhava out of the melee. They pulled her arms over their shoulders and started to help her across the campground.

The leader sprang free of its attackers with a powerful leap and hung hovering over the crowd. It screamed defiance at them. With a hard flap of its wings, it pursued Sharhava and her rescuers. It landed on the defenders, one foot on each back, and seized Sharhava in its arms.

The werewolves sprang up in a heartbeat. The larger of the two wrapped itself around Sharhava's waist and pulled. The smaller one seized her spear off the ground where it had fallen and plunged it to its hilt into the thraik's side, pinning the sail of its wing. The creature let out an ear-tearing ululation that echoed over the clearing and tossed its head in pain. Its muddy eyes seemed to clear for a moment, and the ugly head darted for the girl's throat. She dodged it. The thraik lifted its head and prepared to strike again.

She tugged at the spear, but it was stuck between the creature's ribs. She would have to rely upon her own gifts. She grabbed for the creature's flailing wing tip and plunged her fangs into it. The thraik howled. It bent and sank its own teeth into the back of her neck. Inbecca was grateful she could no longer see the girl's face as the werewolf sank limply to her knees and fell on the ground.

By that moment all the other defenders had surrounded the leader. They struck and stabbed at it with all their strength. It fought back, but it was weakening. The girl's spear had done its job. The thraik was dying. The rune left its eyes, leaving them dull. Lar Auric brought a long tent pole down on its head. It collapsed beside its last victim. The ground shook under its weight.

The last thraik let out a panicked cry and sprang into the sky. A black gash seemed to open up beside the moon, and the winged monster disappeared into it. Inbecca let out the breath she had been holding.

The knights hastily pulled Sharhava free of the monster's dead embrace. She allowed them to set her on her feet, but waved away any other help.

"Let me go, please," Inbecca begged. "Let me go to my aunt."

Patha herself came to cut the bonds holding her in place. Inbecca ran to Sharhava's side.

The abbess showed no expression of fear or pain, but when Inbecca put her arms around her, she found her aunt was quivering.

"Come and sit down," she pleaded, guiding her to the logs surrounding the fire. "Water, someone."

Lar Rachine ran to the water butts and filled a bowl. She brought it to the abbess. Sharhava nodded her thanks and took a drink, holding the bowl unsteadily between her hands. Even the good one was trembling. Inbecca pulled her small cloth from inside her habit, dampened a corner, and cleaned the dirt and ichor from her aunt's face. Anxiously, she searched the stiff countenance. Sharhava stared away from her, seemingly at nothing.

"No scratches, thank the Mother," Inbecca said. "Are you injured anywhere?"

"No," Sharhava said, but her voice was hoarse. "See to the others. Go."

Against her better judgment, Inbecca left her sitting alone next to the fire and went to help. Werewolf healers had already begun to tend to the injured, of which there were many, of both races. Inbecca, having no training in healing herself, held a bowl as Dunnusk, a werewolf male with russet-brown fur, pressed cotton lint into Lar Mey's shoulder to stanch the blood seeping from a gash made by a thraik's rear claw. The healer glanced under the pad to make sure the flow had stopped, then swabbed the gash clean. The young man had his teeth clenched, whether from pain or discomfort at being treated by a werewolf Inbecca could not guess.

"I will try to heal this all at once, but it is deep. I fear it will leave a scar," Dunnusk said with a yellow eye fixed on Mey. The young man nodded, still not speaking. "Very well."

The neat and orderly camp had become a field hospital. Inbecca lost track of how many people, both human and lycanthrope, passed under the healer's hands. Most of them were saved by the skilled use of magic and medicine, but a couple were beyond his help. She followed him from patient to patient. Colruba, the Scholardom's healer, had her hands full taking care of minor injuries. Their captors supplied her with salve and bandages. The Pearl had sunk to the treetops, so lanterns had to be sent for. The place smelled of blood, fear, lamp oil, and the greasy stink of the thraik corpses. No one wanted to touch them yet, so they lay where they had fallen. Inbecca couldn't help but look back at them over and over again. She had heard of thraik attacks, including the one that had befallen Tildi's kinsmen, but had never seen one. Please the Mother and Father, she never would again.

She found herself sitting alone. Dunnusk and a male helped up his latest patient, a dark-furred female heavy with kits, who had been smacked in the side of the head by a thraik's tail, and escorted her to a tent on the far side of the encampment. She had no open wounds, but her speech was garbled. Inbecca found herself sitting alone, too tired to think for herself. She looked up when a shadow fell across her. Patha looked down on her, a grim expression on her face.

"Will you help to bear the dead?" she asked. "Our lost one was about your age. We would honor her with her peers before taking her to be buried."

"I will," Inbecca said, rising.

She fell in behind Patha. Three young werewolves joined them. Patha led them to the thraik corpses, and kicked aside one of the greasy paws that had fallen across the werewolf girl.

"There she is. Please bring her to the circle."

Inbecca and the others carefully turned the girl's body over. Inbecca let out a low moan of despair. She recognized the girl who had served her and her aunt only an hour earlier. She looked up at Patha.

"You have my deepest sympathies," she said. "Those monsters! But she fought so bravely. I never knew her name."

"Then will you mourn with us?" Patha asked.

"Gladly."

They placed the girl's body gently on a blanket and folded her arms across her chest.

Once the living were tended to, the knights were herded together again and held under guard by a few of the largest werewolves. The guards held hunting spears on them, but it was unlikely anyone had the strength left to cause trouble or attempt to escape in the cold early hours. Dawn could not be far away, Inbecca realized.

A few of them gave her suspicious glances as she helped carry the girl's body to the edge of the newly stoked bonfire. She schooled her face into a diplomatic expression: a courteous smile to show camaraderie on her lips, and a furrowed brow for concern. Neither was untrue. How could she not feel compassion for someone so young who had given her life so selflessly.

"Raluftin was her name," Patha said as her people gathered. "Twenty-two years of age. A fine, honest girl, always willing and helpful. My children will miss her. Wadu will miss her, as I believe the two of them were coming to an arrangement."

A pale silver youth across the circle from Inbecca nodded miserably, not raising his eyes.

"We sing you rest, Raluftin," Patha said. She drew her nose upward to the sky, and began to keen. It was not like the war howls Inbecca had heard from them before, rather an ineffably sad sound. Wadu joined in, followed by a brown-furred couple she guessed might have been the girl's parents. The rest raised their noses in turn. Their ritual was so different from the measured and somber funeral rituals of Levrenn. Some humans might have said that a crafted elegy might have been a more fitting memorial to the lost, but Inbecca couldn't stanch the tears rolling down her face. She found it hard to choke out much of a sound, but she looked up at the sky and added her wail of mourning.

Low-pitched chanting was added to the full-throated musical cries, a rhythmic drumroll under the hornlike ululations. Inbecca looked around in surprise to see that several of the knights, led by her aunt, were reciting the Scholardom's death rites. The werewolves didn't miss a note. A few, touched and encouraged by the humans' participation, redoubled their howls, until the trees rang.

Gradually the sorrowful noise fell away, leaving the glen silent. Patha nodded to Wadu and the other young people. Inbecca bent with them to lift her corner of the blanket. Wadu and his friend who carried the feet led the way into the forest, uphill from the river, until they came to a small clearing.

The burial did not take long. A few threads of silver light struck the trees around them, but it was not enough to let her see more than moving shadows. Werewolves saw much better in the dark than humans. Inbecca waited until the sounds stopped and someone touched her on the arm. She followed them back to camp.

She heard the voices long before she reached the firelight. An argument had broken out, not between the werewolves this time, but among the Scholardom. Sharhava and Romini were at the center of it. The others, by force of their confinement by the werewolf guards, had no choice but to observe, but they clearly did not want to be a part of the dressing down underway. Inbecca could not blame them.

"Lar, would you be relieved of your vows?" Sharhava asked, glaring at the young man.

"No, of course not, Abbess," he said. "But . . ."

"No excuses. You are under my orders, or you are not. Make your choice! Will you be a guardian of the Great Book, or find another profession, where you can defy your master at will?"

"Abbess!"

"Well?" Sharhava demanded, taking another step toward Romini. Involuntarily, he took a pace backward. He stopped when his back touched one of his companions.

"I will obey," Romini said sulkily.

"Good. Then apologize to the chieftess."

With ill grace, Romini turned to Patha, whom Inbecca had not seen standing outside the crowd of scholars.

"I apologize," he said, though the words seemed to be chipped from stone. "I regret not mourning for your dead."

Patha bowed slightly. "I accept your apology. It was not necessary," she said to Sharhava.

The abbess bowed back. Her cheeks were red, and it was not merely from the heat of the fire.

"It was. I would surely not be alive if that girl—Raluftin was her name?—had not thrown herself at that thraik. All of you," she said, gathering the assembled werewolves with her gaze, "came forward without hesitation when we were beset. You bought our lives back from the monsters, and not without cost to you. I am grateful. You have my respect. If our positions had been reversed I would not have done the same for you."

"I know," Patha said. "But you were helpless, and any decent person would come to your defense. She who gives birth and He who makes the stars to turn know that all we have done is what any creature of charity would do. You require protection now?"

Involuntarily, Sharhava glanced at the sky. "Yes. The warding spell which one of our . . . which one traveling with us had cast is gone. We are not wizards, and without the Great Book we cannot remake the wards. Those creatures will certainly come back. It will be difficult to resist them, but we will fight."

"Grolius!" Patha called. The black-furred werewolf detached himself from the watchers and slipped away. He returned in a moment with a dark wooden box and held it open for his chieftess. Patha plunged her hand into the velvet-lined casket and produced a fistful of wooden charms.

"We are merchants, so we carry many things our customers require. We are like you in that most of us do not have a talent for magic, but we respect it highly. These amulets and magical trinkets are made by the Yelia family's own magician, a male who lives a city away from my home, and whose things we carry for sale. You saw that the beasts ignored us entirely. We have enough charms of protection, such as those we wear, for all of you. We offer them as a gift. They will fool the monsters into thinking no one is here. We have used these for years. I guarantee they will work."

"We cannot accept it," Sharhava said.

"You refuse our gift?" Patha snapped, dropping the charms back into the box. Her eyes blazed with anger. "Are you a fool? Didn't you see the harm that came to you and yours? Would you denigrate the sacrifice you say you honored?"

"No!" Sharhava said, her jaw set. "We will *pay* you for these things. You have already saved my life. That I can never repay. You will not be made out of pocket for your goods."

Patha was still a bit sulky. "They are a gift or they are nothing," she said. "Take them or don't. Decide now! The night is almost gone."

Inbecca felt more shame than she had before. The sacrifices that the werewolves were willing to make for those who wished them ill showed the Scholardom in a bad light. She knew, as Sharhava did, that to turn back a gift was an insult to the giver, but she suspected that the abbess had already been pushed to the edge of her mind's comfort to know that a race she saw as inferior had behaved in a more noble fashion than she could or would have.

Head high, Inbecca stepped forward. "I accept on behalf of my noble aunt, Patha," she said. "Thank you. We will be glad to have the protection. The smallfolk girl who was with us told us how fearsome the thraiks were. We didn't know how terrible they were until now. Since we cannot protect ourselves, we will be pleased to have aid from those who can provide it."

Patha's harsh expression softened as she turned to Inbecca. She gestured to the one holding the box to step forward. "Take, then. Yours shall be first choice. We have chains and strings of every kind, depending on what will be comfortable for you to wear."

Inbecca didn't look carefully in the box, but took the first charm on the top, a small piece of carved stone the size of a lesser silver coin. "Thank you, gracious Patha."

The werewolf chieftess waved away her courtesy with an impatient hand.

"It is only practical. We do not wish the winged monsters to descend upon us again."

To this, Inbecca said nothing. Though her back ached with exhaustion she held her regal posture in tribute to her hosts.

"Quackery," one of the knights sniffed.

Inbecca didn't wait for her aunt to discipline him. She turned and gave him the kind of glare she reserved for courtiers who made a rude remark in her mother's court. The knight caught it, and his expression changed to one of shame. She turned her back on him and chose an amulet for her aunt. It appeared to be made of cherrywood, with a slate-colored vein running through the smooth russet wood. The looped and complicated carving on it soothed the eye without confusing it. Sharhava took it in her good hand. All the command seemed to drain from her. It was up to Loisan and Brouse to line the others up to take a charm from the box and thank the donors. Once they had all donned their amulets, Patha raised her voice to be heard by them all.

"You will all be well cared for," Patha announced. "But you will stay with us until we are allowed to set you free. I hope you will not make things more difficult for us than need be. My people will see to it that you will have comfortable places to sleep. Let us make better use of what remains of the night than we have."

She nodded to Grolius, who put a gentle paw on the abbess's arm. Sharhava allowed him to guide her away. Others took charge of the remaining knights. Romini's eyes were bright as though he might weep with frustration as his escort steered him around the sinking bonfire.

"Come now," Patha said, taking Inbecca by the hand. Her long, strong fingers felt as comforting as a nursemaid's, in spite of the wiry hair laid along the backs. "You shall sleep here in my tent for what is left of the night."

The werewolf helped Inbecca pull off the creased and stained habit, the mail shirt and padded tunic, and the by-now unspeakable shift and drawers she wore underneath. Patha rummaged through a very neat bronze-bound wooden chest and found a clean chemise that she pulled over Inbecca's head.

"Lie down," the werewolf said, turning back a handsome woven blanket. The golden eyes glinted at her. "You have been of great help this night, in spite of being a princess and a human. Good night."

Inbecca murmured something she hoped sounded polite, and turned her face into the scented pillow. Her drowsy mind incorporated the sky-splitting howls that arose outside the tent into her dreams.

iamond-bright, it came into his mind and lit it like a summertime meadow. The Compendium! He saw the pure white scroll as if it were there before him. Knemet sprang up from his sleepless rest in his carved stone chair and began to pace the floor. Once again the book's protections had fallen. He could see its rune through the walls of his prison. Its hyperreality shone like a beacon, illuminating those mortal things around it. He knew exactly in what direction it lay, in the ancient realm of Mele-natae, not far short of its northern border with Orontae. The book was hundreds of miles closer to him than before—how considerate of its keepers to bring it toward him. Convenient, and not before time! His hands ached to hold it. He reached for it, feeling its warmth across the miles. *This time I will have it,* he vowed.

"My children, hurry!" he shouted to the thraiks.

The black shadows swirled down from their niches near the high, domed ceiling, shrieking.

"Where, master, where?" the creatures cried. They swooped around him, eager to please.

Knemet spread out his hands upon the air. He made the shape of the land appear as the book caused it to reflect in his mind's eye. He didn't recall if he had ever visited that place, but after so many years the world was no more real than a page in the Compendium. The book and its keepers were near a river, on a bluff above a bridge. He could just see the posts and the first span. Yes, a bridge was there in his day. It had been many times renewed, he was sure; this form was not familiar to him. Yet he could describe it. Not only did he show them, but he drew a rune that gave the thraiks the location in a form they could understand.

"You cannot fail to find this in your first try," he admonished them, putting as much detail into the word-picture as possible. But as he scribed its golden lines he became suspicious. It was too easy and too vulnerable a location, high and with little natural protection. After so many miles and so many days of caution, why would the bearers reveal themselves now?

"They may be taunting us," he warned them. "They want to draw us out. If it is a trap, return to me at once! I will not let them make sport of me! Hurry! The light is fading! Make no mistakes this time!"

The winged hunters had not waited for a second admonition. They sailed up to the ceiling and disappeared through the blackness that rent the air.

Knemet could not be still while he waited. Nervous energy propelled him to stride aimlessly around the great chamber. He had not had so good a chance to regain the Compendium in thousands of years. Unlike the last few times that it had reappeared, it was not being concealed again as swiftly as before. Why? Were the keepers dead or injured? Accidents did happen, even to the most careful of magicians. This time the thraiks must be successful!

He paced the ground in frustration. How narrow the walls of his stronghold felt when he knew the book was so far away. Night was falling, but the thraiks could see the runes that the Compendium cast upon everything in its aegis. All they had to do was aim for the center of that circle. What was taking them so long?

Knemet felt the moments passing, each one an agony. Why must he live through more of them? They mounted hundreds upon hundreds, dogging him, taunting him. He could not sleep. He could not rest. The Compendium still lay in the open. It was moving again. Yes, it was coming southeast, and speedily! Did the thraiks have it? But, no, he did not see their runes coupled with its glowing sigil. The strange wizards must still have it. He was desperate for it, desperate for the freedom it held for him. He railed at the thraiks, though they could not hear him in the midst of Melenatae.

"Come to me!" he cried, holding out his hands to the distant book. It did not appear, and he was not surprised. It had never obeyed any of the Makers, not the way their other creations had. It must be obtained by physical hands. Otherwise he would not need those of his thraiks. His frustration threw him back into an energetic walk. The thraiks must return soon.

The rush of air overhead drew his attention. The thraiks had returned, but fluttered in a nervous and confused knot near the ceiling. They did not descend to deliver his long-awaited prize. He already knew that they had been unsuccessful, but he was shocked at how few of them had returned.

"What happened?" he asked, staring at them. "I sent six of you. Why are there only three?"

The thraiks gibbered all at once. Out of the nonsense, Knemet gleaned the kernel of what had happened. An overwhelming number of humans—intelligent, trained humans—had attacked the thraiks on sight. He must push them aside to take back the book. It should never have been out of his hands for so long.

He turned his mind toward the place where he had last divined its presence. He was not surprised to discover that it was hidden once again. Knemet crushed his fist into his palm, and a shock wave sent the thraiks squawking and blew a crater a yard wide in the stone floor. With a wave of his hand at its rune, he repaired the hole. He couldn't stand it. To have the book keep turning up like a rabbit popping out of one of many holes was frustrating. What was the goal of the new keepers of the book? Nemeth's goal of the destruction of Orontae had been in the late wizard's mind since the moment he had touched it. All of his efforts to hear the thoughts of the three wizardesses had been unfruitful. Neither the human, the dwarf or the girl child was vulnerable within the concealing spell.

Knemet lashed out against the walls in his fury, sending shards of rock flying.

What good was he as a wizard and a Maker if he could not solve his own problems? He had been too tentative in his approach so far. He must bend his intelligence and his will to the task. He needed a species that was more effective in searching out the book than the thraiks. While they had the strength and the speed, they lacked the numbers, and they were too easily fooled by shield charms. They were too flighty for perseverance. Knemet needed a new species. Yes, that was it! A new being whose sole task it was to spy out the Compendium, no matter what magic stood in its way.

The energy that had propelled his feet now concentrated in his hands. He felt his palms tingle with anticipation. It had been a very long time since he had created new beings. Such a thing was not lightly undertaken, even in the days of his youth, when everything and anything seemed possible. It was the challenge that pressed him to his greatest efforts—the challenge, and the chance to prove those wrong who said he would fail.

With all his will, he cudgeled his thoughts of the past, both glad and angry, out of the way. His mind must be clear to create.

Knemet threw himself into his chair and propped his chin on his knuckles. His rainbow eyes stared out into the center of the room at nothing. The primeval nothing, whom the religious said was only Time and Nature waiting to separate into their eternal forms and begin the act of creation. Symbolically, he found it satisfying to start as they had.

Removing his wand from his sleeve, he drew a few lines on the air to describe movement. An arching line pleased his eye. He pictured his new animal, longer than it was tall, dancing nimbly, running across the landscape, diving into burrows or water with equal ease, like a fish or an otter. Large eyes. It must be able to see the book's rune at a distance. A shield spell kept those with second sight or a scrying crystal from seeing what was behind it, but it was impractical to maintain for a long journey. The Compendium was therefore visible. He would pair excellent vision with an innate sense of the book's rune. It had not changed since it was made.

Knemet sketched more details on the glowing framework. A keen nose wouldn't be needed. The ability to sense magic came from a place in the brain behind the eyes and nose. That point of focus he would make most sensitive after the eyes. The creature must be just intelligent enough to send a sign to the thraiks when it had absolutely found the book—and unstoppable. He drew more signs upon the air, fleshing out the complete animal, halting just before they became real. Would this beast be able to sustain itself on its search, finding wholesome food and water? Would it have the sense to avoid danger or unnecessary encounters? It must have an instinct for self-preservation, or the search would end soon after the creature left his hands. It had been so long since he made a live beast. He needed examples to form the proper runes.

"I need you," he called to the huddled shapes. "I am not angry. I must have examples to make proper runes."

Reluctantly, a few of the larger thraiks swirled downward and hovered as far from him as they could go.

"Seek for me natural animals," he instructed them. "Find me snakes, eels, fish. Find me otters and weasels. I need both land and water creatures. Bring them to me alive, mind you! If you wish to eat some of them, do it out of my sight. Now, go!"

He could sense their relief as they ascended to the heights before vanishing. As swiftly, he forgot them and went back to his designs.

Knemet was interested as he had not been in centuries—in millennia. There was such satisfaction in research and experimentation. After four unsuccessful attempts, he made the correct mystic passes to bring his sketches to a kind of semi-life. A few didn't move well. They would find survival difficult if he rendered them into flesh. They were poor designs, unworthy of him. He flicked a finger at the wrong shapes. They popped like bubbles. He was left with few of his sketches.

The thraiks did not keep him waiting. With glad shrieks, they soared through the gash in the air and sailed down to make their offerings to him. Knemet shook his head at the pair of gasping salmon the largest thraik clutched. He pointed a finger and the two fish were enclosed in a floating cube of water. They swam in rapid circles, no doubt puzzled in their tiny brains as to what had just happened to them.

"Well done," he said. "Where is the rest?"

The other thraiks pushed at one another, each seeking to be next to hand over their prey. A river otter bit and scratched fiercely at its captor. Knemet could see the thraik's short temper was about to let loose. He laughed.

"Drop it," he said. The thraik let it go, and it bounded around the room, looking for a way back to its littoral home. "Later," he promised it.

The eel was nearly dead, its slime-covered body gouged and scratched, no doubt in the effort to hold on to it. The thraik that had captured it looked ashamed. Knemet shook his head. There was nothing to be done for it. He examined its sinuous muscles and sleek sides. He could do something with those traits, but the face was too narrow, the eyes too small, to be of use in his plan. He took notes in glowing glyphs, then threw a hand toward the eel.

"Dispose of that for me," he said.

The thraik didn't hesitate. It opened its jaws wide and dropped the creature inside. Knemet gestured dismissal, and it took off for its perch. The Maker gloated over the rest of his specimens. He had not seen such snakes in centuries. He especially admired the brilliant red snake with the black ring just behind its head. Those did not hunt in underground caverns like his. Such beautiful skins they had, and the sacs of poison behind their long, curved fangs were undeniably deadly. He admired them and set them free to wind across the floor.

The mongoose and weasels, brought from opposite ends of the continent, immediately went on the hunt for their old enemies as soon as he had examined and released them. The lizard was one he had not seen before. He watched it camouflage itself by changing hue depending upon what it was near, and immediately suspected it had been created by one of his colleagues of old. He let it run free, and enjoyed the play of color upon its scaled hide. It could not run away from this chamber, and he would always be able to locate it by its rune. It scented the snakes and ran up the wall. Knemet had to separate them all with magical wardings. When his job was done, he might let natural selection have its way, but in the meanwhile, each of these animals provided him with invaluable templates.

Like an artist, he built up a picture one characteristic at a time. Should it be armored? No, such protection would weigh it down. What Knemet wanted was speed. He drew several arching lines and added those traits he wished to incorporate. Limbs or no limbs? Two of his ideas were worth bringing to semi-life. The iridescent shapes were as different as could be. One beast was capable of swimming, but not for long. The Compendium might be found on water as easily as on land. He put that one aside, and concentrated upon the second shape. He turned its rune around and around in midair. It wriggled, in tribute to its snake heritage, the primary shape upon which he had based it. It was bursting with strong, bandlike muscles. He would have liked to make use of the strong otter limbs, but they might be injured or torn off. He did not wish it so easily crippled. The toughness of its belly would substitute for legs. He made it narrow, so it could cut knifelike through underbrush.

The silvery, thin creature could swim, but not as swiftly as he would like. He let the tip of his wand quiver slightly, and minute fins appeared at either side just behind the head. It would be a swift swimmer. It could move rapidly over land, and into the smallest cracks in stone, burrow through sand or soil like a drill with the sharp, hard nose like a turtle's beak. It would eat what it could catch. The digestive system was like that of the weasel and eel. One could scavenge more successfully than hunt most times. It would excrete efficiently, to rid itself of waste. Gender was not important. This chimera was meant for a single task, not to breed. Defense—it needed little, for all it had to do was find his quarry for him—but Mother Nature had made many fierce beasts of her own. He gave it poison; let it be a rapid toxin that paralyzed. He did not wish to kill if he didn't have to. He altered the swirling rune that circulated inside the sacs within either side of the upper jaw. Fangs as sturdy as the red snake's would dispense the poison if needed.

Then, the moment of creation. Knemet held his breath. The sleek little beast existed only as a complex rune, a charcoal sketch before the painting. He reached out to it and touched it with the tip of his wand. The image stilled, frozen as if in crystal. He began to follow each line and stroke of the rune with the tip of his wand. Bones and muscle came into reality in the heart of the rune. Skin covered with nearly invisible silver scales covered them. The fins, beak, and fangs he traced with loving care. Lastly, the eyes, saucerlike and out of proportion to the narrow skull, he redrew in gleaming gold. Inside the word, the beast came into being. Knemet gestured to it, and it rotated in air. Nodding, he caused the rune to shrink into the animal. It had its own reality now. As soon as the strokes of the rune touched the beast's side, it took a shuddering breath and began to race in a circle, chasing its own tail. Knemet laughed with joy. He had done it!

"It must have a name," he said. He had not named a creature in centuries, either. He tilted his head to one side to contemplate it. It was long, slender, and silver like a knife. It moved with the grace of a breeze. It was deadly, and it was inexorable. *Kotyr*, he thought. He tried the name on his tongue.

"Kotyr." The chimera stopped its endless chase. The big, round eye on the left side of its head stared at him. "That will do. You are the first of your race, kotyr." It seemed unmoved by the honor.

First it was, but not the last. Now that he had the template, Knemet drew one after another, then brought them into being in the tens, then the hundreds. They came to life wriggling and active. They ignored the natural animals, but sniffed one another curiously, sensing the image of the book's rune in one another's minds. Soon, the floor of the great chamber was a seething, glinting carpet of kotyrs. Tired but pleased, Knemet lowered his wand and turned to see them all. He tilted his head back to address the thraiks.

"What do you think?" he asked.

"Hmmph!" the senior thraik grunted.

"You do not think much of them?" Knemet asked, raising an eyebrow. "Well, these will lead you to your quarry. Pay heed when they call to you. Kotyrs! Let me hear your voices!"

The kotyrs responded with a shrill cry that could have shattered crystal. The thraiks let out a protest in reply. Knemet smiled.

"Go now!" he commanded the kotyrs. He opened the spell that sealed the chamber. The kotyrs slipped into crevices between the stones as though they were drops of water sinking into sand. He was pleased. Theirs was the signal that the thraiks would follow. Anywhere upon land or sea that the Compendium went, they could follow, with the thraiks close behind them.

"Away, my last and least creation!" he cried. "Find my treasure for me."

The kotyrs shrieked their eagerness. Soon they were all gone.

Suddenly weary, Knemet hunched back to his great chair.

"In the meantime, let us see nature unbound." He whisked a hand, and the barriers between the specimen animals fell.

Chapter Fourteen

ildi tried to stay awake as she was carried along, but wrapped as she was in darkness, she could see nothing. The thick fur pelt of the one carrying her was so warm and the musk scent so comforting that she felt her eyelids drifting closed again and again. This was the rescuer that Irithe had promised, of that she was now certain. She trusted him, and not just because the elf had said she could. Something about his rune just exuded honesty.

The rune itself was a curious one. She had not seen its like before. Tildi wished she could look it up in the book and see where its kind belonged on the face of Alada, but the book itself was out of her reach. She could see the book's rune bobbing along beside her and her gigantic escort. If she hadn't been wrapped up so close she could have stretched out an arm to touch it. Since she couldn't, and she knew both of them were safe, she let herself drift off.

The next thing she knew, she had stopped moving. Fragrant, musky fur still surrounded her, but it was not the arms of the one who had saved her. She stretched out her hands and explored the darkness. Her head had been pillowed on her own folded cloak, but that was the only thing she recognized. She lay in a small enclosure like the inside of an egg, lined and padded with combings of fur like hanks of sheared sheep's wool. The book's rune was close by. Tildi reached out automatically to touch it. It was upright against the curved wall. The familiar voices greeted her in their ancient tongue when her fingers made contact with the smooth parchment. All was well.

No, not well, she realized, sitting upright. Her head touched the top of her shelter. The wardings that she and Serafina had built to hide them and the book from searchers—they had been broken! The rune that should have been over all of them on the slope had gone. Tildi remembered feeling vulnerable as she ran through the thick fog. A protective rune, a different one, had been established overhead, to protect her and the book. But where was Serafina? And where was Rin?

Beyond the fur-lined wall were dozens of runes. None of them were familiar. She felt shy about approaching strangers, but she must know where she was, and what had become of her friends.

The rounded opening of the egg was low to the ground. It was necessary to creep out on hands and knees. When Tildi stuck her nose out of the shelter, a cold wind almost nipped it off. Reluctant to leave the comforting warmth behind, she wriggled the rest of the way out and wrapped herself in her cloak. The book followed her. Despite the fact that her muscles were sore and her ankles were bruised from running, she pulled herself forward into the wind. It occurred to her how odd it was to feel cold. She had not noticed the weather for weeks, thanks to the book's influence. Yet it seemed unchanged. All of the other elements of its presence seemed to be in place. The feeling of power that thrilled through her was unabated, and golden runes were written upon everything. The enormous trees around her reminded her of Silvertree, Master Wizard Olen's home. Their runes incorporated a sense of wisdom and serenity, such as the giant tree possessed. They had the air of having been there since the earth was made. She laid a hand on one as though to ask it for permission to pass. The bark, formed in enormous scales each as large as a platter, felt smooth and welcoming.

She tiptoed over the needle-strewn ground toward the yellow firelight that illuminated the circle of thick trees as if they were the ribs of a horn lantern. Low voices murmured together, rising and falling like music. The speakers were visible only as large shadows, spangled with runes, which fell upon the thick bushes that surrounded the fire. As she approached, the voices stopped. She felt at her belt for her knife. With shock, she realized that the sheath was empty. The knife had surely fallen from her hand when she was running away from the fighting. Her pack had been in Rin's saddlebags. She had nothing now but the clothes on her back and the boots on her feet. Ah, but the book was there. It nudged up against her as if to offer comfort.

She touched it and felt contentment thrumming through it like a heartbeat, she thought. Yes. It was not the only heartbeat here. A humming seemed to resound in the very ground she walked on. She must find her friends. They could find an explanation for the noise.

She had only taken a couple of steps before an enormous shape loomed over her. Tildi gasped. She looked up to see a broad furred face. It was not a werewolf, but an upright animal half again the size and easily twice the breadth, with a blunter muzzle, round ears, brown-black fur, and small, gentle, light brown eyes. Colored beads had been woven into its fur: at the sides of its face, in patterns on the massive chest, and in a fringe on the upper arms below the shoulders.

"We heard you stirring," it said in a voice so deep it seemed to add to the humming.

"How? I was trying not to make any noise," Tildi said. Her voice sounded like a bird's peeping in her ears, in contrast to the big beast's deep bass.

The red-brown lips drew back and showed a set of fanged teeth that were the equal and better of any werewolf's.

"You make your own rhythm in the pulse of the earth," it said. It put out an enormous paw, held palm out, to her. Thick, dark fur sprouted in between wrinkled, black leather pads that marked his fingers. Her hand was smaller than the oval pad at the base of his thumb. Timidly, she reached up but recoiled before touching it. He closed the distance, and she felt the warmth of his skin against hers.

"Do not fear contact with us, little one."

"I might hurt you," Tildi said. "You don't know . . . I have a power in me. It burns flesh."

The big beast grinned, his white fangs glinting. "Not now. We heard the disharmony in your part of the eternal rhythm and sang while you slept until you belonged again to the earth. You will no longer harm anyone unless you mean to do so. I cannot speak to your treasure," he added, nodding solemnly toward the book. "It will defend itself as it will. It is too ancient for us. But you are as you were."

Tildi sagged. "What a relief!" she exclaimed. "You don't know what a worry that's been to me. Oh, manners! I'm Tildi Summerbee."

"I know your name. I knew it before I brought you here. I am Jorjevo. You are welcome among the bearkin. Komorosh told us about you. You met him at Olen's council. He is one of us."

"Komorosh?" Tildi thought back hard, and came up with the image of a taciturn man with hollow cheeks who huddled in a huge fur cloak. He never seemed to be warm, though the council chamber had been cozy. "I thought he was human. Oh, but you change, don't you?"

Jorjevo smiled, his kind eyes patient. "No, we remain as you see us. Whereas the werewolves are ruled by the moons, we are as constant as the land. Komorosh took the shape of a human by enchantment so he could relate to humans. Our Makers, the ones who created our shape as well as yours, and the book that you guard, left only a few traits of our human forebears inside us—intelligence, manual skills, and speech. We are more patient and sensitive than the hairless ones, less subject to the elements. That comes from our bear ancestors. We feel we belong more to the forests, to the direct creations of Mother Nature. We could not live in cities or towns, as you do."

"Then you knew you were . . . were made up by the Makers," Tildi said, feeling her words were inadequate for the concept. "We smallfolk didn't know, or if any of us did, they never let on to the rest of us. You have no idea what a disgrace they would consider it to be! As far as our schoolmasters are concerned, we sprang into being on the first day."

Jorjevo smiled with delight. "How very funny not to want to know the rolls of ancestors. We keep records going back more than a hundred and fifteen centuries. Alas, many of our grandparents before the change were poor archivists. Annals before that are spotty, but since then we have been most careful."

"I would love to see your archives," Tildi said. "I can only name my grandfathers back about eight generations."

"It would be our pleasure. In return, our archivists would like to see your treasure," Jorjevo said, indicating the book floating along beside her. "They are fascinated by the runes they wear."

"Oh, be careful!" Tildi exclaimed, suddenly alarmed. She had a vision of curious bearkin distorting like reflections in a pool. "They must not try and change them—the most horrible things happen if you do."

"We know," Jorjevo assured her gravely. "Komorosh had plenty of time to warn us since your departure from the council. We will be careful. Come and sit by the fire with us. We await your friends."

Tildi was appalled that she had let her mind wander from her companions' safety. "Are they all right?" she asked.

"Strife has been abroad tonight, but not on the road along which I brought you," he said. "Come. The others want to meet you."

He reached down to her. Tildi put her hand in his huge paw and wrapped her fingers around one finger, as though she were a toddler walking with her father. How wonderful it was to make contact with another living being, and not be afraid that she would burn it to death!

*T*here!" Serafina exclaimed, pointing ahead. "Runes! We have found her."

Magpie was almost asleep over Tessera's neck, but the excitement in the wizardess's voice brought him out of his daze. He had grown used to the dim, charcoal-gray landscape that he only saw in detail out of the corner of his eyes, as if the features picked out faintly by the stars and the full moon receding somewhere to his right kept slipping furtively away from him. Ahead, the path, the trees, and, however improbable it was and had been, the sky were wildly decorated with gold-tinted squiggles, curlicues, and dashes. He breathed a deep sigh of relief.

"You did not trust me," Irithe said wryly, dropping back so she ran between Rin and Serafina's horse. "No matter."

"Don't you ever get tired?" Lakanta asked, letting out a huge yawn. Her mare snorted and shook her head.

"I will rest when I stop," the elf said. She took the bridle of Serafina's mare and jogged to a halt. She looked up at them, her eyes dark pools in her pale face. "They already know you are coming. I must go now. You will be safe from this point onward. I wish you well. I hope we wayfarers will meet again. Tell Tildi to think of the new stories she will have to tell at The Groaning Board."

Magpie grinned. "I will tell her. Thank you for your assistance. You have done us great service."

"You won't guide us the rest of the way?" Serafina asked peevishly.

Irithe tilted her head. "Do you really need me to? You'd have to be blind not to find your way from here."

Magpie saw Serafina's face turn sour and spoke up hastily before she could say something.

"We will be fine," he said. "I have been on this road before. Good wayfaring to you. I hope we do meet again."

"And I," Serafina said with a shamefaced glance at him. He knew she did not intend to lose her temper. "You have my gratitude for your skilled guidance. If ever I can repay the kindness, you have but to ask."

"And I," Rin added. "A Windmane does not forget such obligations."

"This favor was for another," Irithe said, shaking her head. "But I will keep your offers in mind. Goodbye."

She backed away from them a few paces, and vanished into the darkness like smoke dissipating in the wind. Though his eyes were used to the night, Magpie blinked several times.

"When I think of all the instances in which such an exit would have been useful . . ." Lakanta said, letting out a whistle. "Sometimes I don't think they're completely solid, elves."

Rin danced suddenly, lifting her hooves rapidly. "The ground is shaking. I do not like it."

"Humming," Serafina said, putting out her hand as if feeling the air. "I feel it, too, like a tuning fork, or a harpstring plucked and left to ring."

Teryn and Morag drew their swords. Teryn nodded to her soldier, who trotted to the rear of the group. She looked around uneasily, not knowing from which direction to guard.

"What is it?" Magpie said, feeling the vibrations in his hands and his teeth.

"Well, well," Lakanta said with a chuckle. "I'd no idea we were so far south."

"You know what this is?" Serafina asked.

Lakanta laid her reins on Melune's neck. "Nothing to do but wait and be patient," she said.

"For what?"

"For us."

The deep voice seemed to come from the depths of the earth. It did not jar with the low vibration filling the air, but sounded in harmony with it. Magpie's head snapped around on his neck to see the speaker, and found the group was surrounded by tree trunks. Not trees, he realized, as he peered at the huge, almost cylindrical shapes, but creatures, big, furry creatures. He picked out features in the faint light, especially rounded ears on the massive heads, shoulders like mountains, and eyes that regarded them solemnly from either side of a wide muzzle like a hound's. They remained silent, massive, and forbidding. To Magpie it felt as if they had grown there from the bedrock, and had always been there, like stones.

"Are we intruding?" Serafina asked as her mare danced nervously.

"I'd say not," Lakanta replied. "I've found over the years that there's no one home when they don't want to see you. This is where the elf led us, no mistake. Greetings to you! I'm Lakanta. My goodness, how long's it been?"

"Since springtime," the deep voice said. One of the gigantic shapes stepped forward. Serafina held forth her staff, and green light lit the blunt muzzle and showed the small eyes to be a gentle brown. "I greet you. I heard your song."

"Happy to sing it, Jorjevo," Lakanta said, grinning. She swung down off Melune's back and went to throw her arms around the beast. Her short arms made it less than a third around his shaggy frame. Magpie could now see that the speaker was one of the bearkin. If werewolves were rare in Orontae, bearkin were almost a lost legend. He grinned. "You haven't got a smallfolk who ought to be with us, do you?"

"She has been pacing with impatience to see you," Jorjevo said. "How fast these little ones move!"

"We would see her, if it is not an imposition," Rin said.

"How can I prevent her?" Jorjevo said, his small eyes twinkling.

A commotion erupted from behind the circle of thick-furred legs. A small hand pushed through and caught the light.

"Oh, let me by!" Tildi's voice came, full of frustration.

Magpie swung down at the sound, so relieved that his knees wobbled under him, and he stood waiting on the stony roadway as the smallfolk girl emerged between a pair of bearkin like a vixen threading its way through tree trunks. She made straight for Rin, and hugged her about the forelegs. Serafina gasped, and held out a hand of warning. Magpie held his breath, realizing that he was waiting for the smell of burning flesh. It did not come.

"I am glad you are safe, little one," the centaur said, leaning down and kissing her on the top of the head. She stroked the smallfolk's soft brown hair. "I was concerned when we became separated."

"I know," Tildi said apologetically. "I couldn't find you, but I couldn't see where to run back to. I hate fog at night! Oh, I am so happy to see all of you! Jorjevo said they could feel you were close by. Come back where it is warm. There's soup and tea and—and I am so glad you are safe!"

Lakanta enveloped the girl in a sound embrace, then held her out at arm's length. "Well, you are looking fine. We were worried to pieces, I must tell you, with you disappearing like that. Not a rune in sight, and here they are all over again!"

Tildi beamed at her. "I feel wonderful. I . . . I feel as though I have been set free. I can't tell you how good that is. I vow that if I ever have a dog again, I will let him run free all the time. How I hated that leash. I am so glad we are together again."

The smallfolk girl took Magpie's hand shyly in both of hers and squeezed it, before climbing the air to saddle-height and throwing her arms around Serafina's waist.

"I am long overdue to show you proper sympathy, master," she said, dropping her voice to a murmur that Magpie could barely discern. "I am sorry for your loss. I am sorry for both of us. I can't ever repay the debt I owe Edynn, or you, but I hope you will be assured I will try. What is wrong?" Serafina had stiffened in her embrace. Tildi let her go, looking guilty. Serafina examined her own shoulders, then took Tildi's hands and turned them over to see the palms.

"You . . . you don't carry the power any longer?" Serafina asked with concern. "You're cool again. Is the book lost? We saw the runes. I thought it was here."

"Oh, no! It is here, master, I promise you!" Tildi beckoned in the direction of the rune-studded forest. A pale shape swooped over the heads of the bearkin around them, and came to hover beside her. "See? But don't touch it. It still doesn't want anyone else to touch it."

"But what did you do?" Serafina asked.

"It wasn't my doing," Tildi said with a glance over her shoulder at their gigantic hosts. "They did it."

"The fire in her hands was an imbalance waiting to be corrected," boomed a smaller and lighter boned bearkin beside Jorjevo. "We listen to the pulse of the earth here. The Great Book is so powerful that we could hear the blockage of power like rapids in a river hammering against a weir, trying to break free. It disturbed us, even at a great distance. We are glad to have set it on its course again."

"What caused the imbalance? And how did you correct it?" Serafina asked, as though she still could not believe it.

"Peace!" Jorjevo laughed, his deep voice rumbling. "Why stand here where it is cold and damp? Come to the fire and ask your questions, my daughter."

Tildi dashed down to help her enormous hosts lead the way. Magpie had never seen the reserved little smallfolk so uninhibited. She nearly sang every word she spoke, and her steps were just a twitch away from dancing. Her joy was infectious. Tired as he was, Magpie was ready to join in. He could well understand her relief. They were away from the onerous presence of the Scholardom. He for one was glad to be out from under the eye of his aunt-in-law elect. Should everyone survive to see the Great Book put back in its place and return alive to the north, he would never again be able to trust Sharhava for any reason at all. She had been showing signs of a dangerous insanity that had grown since the book came into their hands—or, rather, into Tildi's. He hoped that the werewolves could handle her. They weren't easy to get to know, and they had chancy tempers, but Sharhava could match anyone for acrimony. He respected Inbecca's choice to stay with her aunt. Perhaps she could persuade her aunt to reason, but he doubted it. He'd known them both all his life.

He missed Inbecca. The ride from Oron Castle to the bridgehead was the longest uninterrupted period they had spent in each other's company in their lives. He'd loved being near her all that time, though half of it she was angry with him. The other half, when she had permitted him to think she knew he was alive, and even liked it a little, had made it worthwhile. Ah, but the very end, when he had left her in the company of the werewolves, that had been the sweetest moment of all. When he had seen her for the last time for who knew how long, though her face was tanned and polished by the wind, and her hair was all down over her shoulders and wet through, and she had not a trace of the heavy court makeup applied, she was more beautiful than any woman who ever trod the royal carpet. She loved him. She said so. It boded well for compatibility in their future marriage—if such a thing was even possible now that Inbecca had taken the Scholardom's vow. He sighed. He kept berating himself for having pushed her into it from keeping too many secrets.

He was not the only one to have the Scholardom on his mind. Serafina had ridden most of the way from the werewolves' encampment to the bearkin's homeland without speaking, though she had occasionally let out a snort of disgust. She could not let go of the notion that Sharhava had manipulated her, not once, but at least three times: when she had persuaded her that only with the Scholardom's escort could they reach the book's hiding place, when Sharhava had perverted the protection spell that had concealed them from thraiks and other spies, and when she had clouded their minds to the thought of escape. Serafina's dignity had to have been sorely bruised. Then, for her to lose sight of Tildi had to be the final blow that brought down the hewn tree. All was well, now. Almost all.

Tessera was restless under his legs. He dismounted and tied her reins to a clump of brush beside Serafina's mare.

"Poor girl, you ought to have been resting hours ago. So should I." He patted Tessera on the nose.

"Give her this." The voice at his shoulder should have made him jump, but it was so soothing that he smiled as he turned to the speaker. The lighter-boned bearkin held out to him a small bundle tied up in rough cloth. Magpie smelled the sweet scent of flowers on it. "Crystallized honey. We enjoy them as sweetmeats. It is something we have in common with the plains people, both horse and centaur." He offered some to Serafina as well.

"Thank you," she said. The white mare lipped the golden crystals delicately. For the first time, Serafina smiled. The expression made her narrow face breathtakingly pretty in the soft light.

"I am Danevo," the bearkin said. "Be welcome here. I hope you can find some peace."

Magpie gave him a wry smile. "I think your people's ability to read minds is more disconcerting to my kind than your size."

Danevo showed his impressive set of teeth. "We do not read minds. We listen to the sounds of the earth. You will see. Go. All of you. Join the others."

"Come!" Jorjevo roared as the companions came into the firelight.

Magpie was reminded of a castle courtyard. Lanterns brimming with light hung from stout tree branches in an irregular clearing.

Rin settled near the roaring campfire with her legs curled under her like a great cat. Tildi sat with her back in the curve of Rin's body, talking intently in a low voice, holding the book in one arm as one might hold a cat. Such an odd couple they were, Magpie thought, the smallfolk and the centaur, but he realized how close they had become over the months that they had been together on the road. Rin's strength and good humor had been a bulwark to Tildi. When the smallfolk girl was in danger of letting the Scholardom's prejudice beat her spirit down, Rin was always ready to defend her, until she regained her natural sense of independence. They had become good friends, something that would be worth the telling in the smallfolks' frequent town meetings, though the princess of the Windmanes might be thought of as an exotic monster rather than a friend. For Rin herself, the friendship was an odd one as well. A centaur wasn't likely to make a bosom-friend out of a stranger, but they found common ground in their pride of home. And who could resist an open ear for one's most exciting stories? Tildi sat agape, listening to even the most outlandish tales with enjoyment, if not belief. Magpie was wondering himself how he would get along without such an audience as Tildi once their task was at an end.

Ah, but that was selfish. One day this mission would be over, and they must all go their separate ways. Alone. He felt a trifle sorry for himself. Inbecca was in the custody of the werewolves, suffering who knew what, all for the sake of the greater good. The least he could do was stop his foolish self-pity in its tracks. It wasn't like him. He must be very tired.

Serafina could not seem to settle down. She kept frowning at Tildi nervously, going over a dozen times an hour to touch her arm.

"Are you well?" she asked. "You aren't catching a chill here?"

"I am well, master," Tildi said, for the twelfth or thirteenth time. "I am as I was before. That is, except for the book." She reached up to caress its surface, as if it had been a child's face.

"The hell-heat is gone," Rin assured Serafina. "The pain had been lessening slightly since the first day, but it is gone entirely. The little one has no more fire in her but her spirit."

A piercing cry in the distance made them all sit up in alarm. The Great Book took off from Tildi's grasp like a startled bird and hovered protectively above her.

"What is that? We must be miles away from the werewolves by now."

"I hear it, too," Serafina said, settling herself down on a fold of her cape. The wizardess looked immaculate once again. She had taken the time to bespell her garments clean again. "It sounds like their voices."

"But we must be miles away from them by now," Tildi said, alarmed. "The bearkin walked for hours before we came here!"

"Their voices carry, my child," Jorjevo boomed, his eyes twinkling in the firelight. "You are away from them now, but they are not your foe. Those who would thwart you are gone from your sight forever. Can you take comfort in that?"

"Their voices terrify me," Tildi said.

"It is only in the way they call to one another," Jorjevo said. "Since you can't help paying attention, listen to the music in their cries." Tildi gave him a doubtful look. "There is poetry in their speech, if you allow yourself to hear it."

Magpie grinned at the notion. "Come on, you've heard singers that bad in your day, haven't you?"

"Well, I admit that I have," Tildi said with a nervous glance up at him. "Not you, of course."

"Thank you for your reassurance," Magpie said with a laugh.

"Is all well, then?" Serafina asked.

"Stay by us," Tildi said, putting a hand out for the wizardess. With a glance back at him, Serafina hesitated, then sat down.

"Of course, if you need me."

Magpie was a trifle disappointed. He had hoped to have Serafina be with him for a time.

"Come, friend," a huge, dark gray bearkin said, embracing him soundly in limbs like fur-covered bolster pillows. It draped one arm fondly over his shoulder and led him to sloping stones set around the fire that he saw served the big folk for backrests. "Sit with me. Do you drink beer?"

"Willingly," Magpie said. "Though I may not be awake long enough to enjoy it."

"Come, then, and we'll sing with the others until you are ready to rest. I am Chviaga."

"Eremilandur," Magpie said, "but call me what you like."

"We have heard of you, prince of Orontae. Name yourself as you choose."

"We called him Magpie, after the bird, Chviaga," Lakanta called, "but it turns out he's a bird of a different plumage." She grinned up at them. "How I'll just travel by myself in years to come when I've grown used to such distinguished company, I don't know."

"Then, so shall we," Chviaga said. "It sounds more like your true self than the many syllables."

How odd, Magpie thought, that like him they were all thinking of the end of the journey they had yet to make. Chviaga dragged him down with a hearty hand.

"Beer for the traveler!" he boomed.

Lakanta had made herself at home at once, slapping bearkin on the sides and calling them by name. She seemed to know everyone, Magpie thought. At the sound of her voice, a handful of the smaller beings galloped toward her—children, he realized, though they were easily his size. They towered over Lakanta, but she treated them as if they were knee-high to her small stature. She tweaked their ears and laughed at their antics. When they clamored for presents, she felt in her pouch and produced sweets and handfuls of colored beads.

"Scatter, now!" she cried. Laughing, they tumbled over one another to catch the treats.

She must be a popular visitor. A female, with a very young cub at her heels, lumbered over to hand Lakanta a gigantic rounded beaker foaming with beer. Lakanta accepted it, but not before giving the female a hearty hug and scratching the cub between its little round ears. They settled down together with a bunch of the others for a natter.

The two Rabantavian guards did not look as comfortable as the trader. All three sat stiff-backed among their hosts. The guards, Magpie thought with a grin, were unaccustomed to being treated as guests. They had removed their armor and hoods, but not their wary manner. They regarded refreshments offered them with open suspicion, which luckily did not offend the bearkin at all.

For the first time, Magpie got an unobstructed view of both their faces. Captain Teryn was quite a pretty woman. Her wide, molded cheekbones would be envied by any lass, her neck was slender and long, and her hair, still severely braided for the trail, must have been honey-gold when she was young. Morag's appearance shook him. The misshapen bones of his face Magpie was familiar with from weeks together on the trail, but the deformity carried on to the skull itself. It had dents and bulges like a potato. His neck and wrists seemed to have too many joints to them. His coarse black hair escaped from its queue in shocklike tufts. Magpie felt horribly sorry for him. He knew Tildi could not rebuild his rune for lack of an original model to work from. From his expression Morag looked as though he would like to hunch down and conceal his face, but his training required him to be upright and ready to defend at a word. He was the picture of courage, Magpie thought. It was one thing to be brave in battle, but to live with the scars forevermore afterward took inner strength. He deserved a ballad to be written about him, though it would mortify him to hear it.

One very large bearkin, Magpie couldn't tell at the distance whether it was a male or a female, took a fancy to Morag, and sat with its arm around him, singing a song in its subterranean voice, crushing him to its breast every time it emphasized a syllable. To Magpie's surprise, and no doubt that of the human guard, the limitless goodwill began to warm through Morag's glum exterior. His rigid back began to relax. The bearkin ruffled his hair, fed him a sip of beer from its own mug, and launched into another song. Morag glanced at Teryn in apprehension. In turn, the captain looked to Serafina for instructions. The young wizardess seemed not to know what to do, but she was loath to offend their hosts. She shrugged. Teryn passed the gesture to her soldier, who gave a shy grin to the bearkin. The big furry creature embraced him again.

"Sing with me, friend!" it cried.

It enunciated the words to its song carefully line by line. Morag repeated them slowly. To Magpie's delight, they started singing together, the soldier's raspy voice underscoring the musical boom of the bearkin like the roll of a drum beneath horns. Tentatively, Teryn joined in. At odds to her stern face and upright carriage, she had a sweet, lilting voice, adding a flute to the orchestra. Shyly, Morag tilted his craggy face toward her, and the corners of her mouth lifted in a gentle smile. Morag returned it. His smile lifted his countenance and made it handsome and noble. Suddenly he became aware that others were looking at him, and the rare moment passed. Teryn's face went stern, and she glared around warily.

She loves him, Magpie thought in wonder. *Bless the Mother and Father, there's someone for everyone.*

"Do you know a song or two?" Chviaga asked Magpie, interrupting his thoughts.

"I do," Magpie said emphatically, though he was sorry to miss what might come next between Teryn and Morag. "Do you know 'The Boatman and the Lock-keeper's Daughter'?"

Magpie thought he would find it difficult to tell his hosts apart, but it was not. The youngsters, of whom there were many, were always coming over from their games at the perimeter of the fire circle for a cuddle. Magpie often found himself face-to-face with juveniles who were almost his size. Except for infants in the arms of massive mothers, Tildi was the smallest being present.

She seemed to have made herself right at home without hesitation. He had always known she was exceptional among smallfolk.

As night waned and the fire burned down, conversation still continued in low, musical rumbles. Magpie found himself unable to stay awake. Hoisted gently under the arm by a massive hairy limb and assisted to walk in between trees by Tirteva, a friendly soul who was younger than Jorjevo but older than the young ones who played among themselves at the perimeter of the firelight. Found himself on a staircase that spiraled downward. The walls smelled like a healthy garden after a rain, and the steps, though squared off, did not ring like stone. After he had completely lost his sense of direction, he and his guide emerged into a vast room. It was like a great hall, but beehive-shaped. Another bonfire like the one below burned at the center of the room, banked by rounded rocks that his eye told him were just the right shape and size. Everything in the round room had pleasing proportions that were restful to his spirit just to look at. More of the bearkin sat at this fire. He wondered where the smoke went to, since the air in the chamber, though fragrant with the scent of the burning hardwoods, was clean.

Like spokes on a wheel, corridors led off the beehive chamber. Magpie followed his guide along one past leather or woven curtains that served the bearkin for doors. Each of the curtains was beautiful and unique in its pattern of beads, paint, quillwork, or embroidery. He could not guess how far each of the passageways extended, but his guide stopped at the eighth room on the left and held aside the exquisite blue-painted curtain.

"This shall be yours for the time you are with us, Master Eremilandur," Tirteva said. He had Magpie's saddlebag over his other arm. He set it on the ground beside a pile of furs that was obviously meant for a bed. They were too far underground for windows, but a hole in the packed-earth ceiling brought a refreshingly cool breeze inside. "If you have need of anything, it is yours for the asking. Good night to you, and welcome."

"Thank you for the hospitality," Magpie said. He sat down on the bed to take off his boots and sank halfway into the cozy heap. His thoughts could not help themselves: they turned to Inbecca, and hoped that he would justify the sacrifices she had made for all of them. If he could no longer hope to be her husband, he would be as true a friend as he could be. He would make certain Tildi reached her goal. The book must be put out of the way of ordinary people, and as soon as possible.

For Inbecca's sake, he would do whatever it took to accomplish that goal. No matter how unpleasant the trek that lay ahead of him, he thought as he pounded a depression in the soft bedding to fit his body, she had the more distasteful task. She, who had sacrificed all her future for a cause she hadn't known existed until she had seen the Great Book for herself and the havoc it could wreak.

"I hope I'm as strong as you, my love," he whispered.

*F*aces flew at Tildi, shouting demands at her. Sometimes they wore the blue-and-white habit of the Scholardom; sometimes they were bareheaded. The one that frightened her the most was the man with eyes like rainbows. He darted at her, shrieking in an unknown tongue, then his face pushed out and became a werewolf's snout. They all sounded angry, and the anger was contagious. Tildi found herself shouting back. She felt as if she would explode with the fury within her. She had to protect the book from its enemies. Everyone wanted it. Everyone wanted her to make something change into something else. In her mind, human beings twisted and mutated until they were trees, sheep, giant fish, or anything but what they were. And once they had changed, they were unhappy. They all shouted at her. Their hollow, haunted eyes were fixed on her. Instead of feeling compassion, she was angry.

"Stay away from me!" she shouted. "You have what you want! You don't like it, but you chose it! Let me be!"

"Tildi! Stop!" A sharp rap on the back of her hand interrupted her. "Open your eyes! Now!"

She obeyed. Serafina sat on the puffy bed beside her. In her hand was her staff. The green jewel at the end glowed, casting the girl's sharp cheekbones into relief.

"Look what you have done," the wizardess said sternly. "What were you dreaming?"

Tildi gawked at the chamber. It ought to have been dark except for the few runes of the plain walls, floor, and handsome door cloth, but it was filled with glowing words. Knobs and other freakish excrescences that had not been there when she fell asleep protruded from the walls. The floor had erupted in layers like a broken pastry. Over their heads, the book flew around the room like a frightened bat.

"I don't know!" Tildi said, watching in bewilderment.

"Then just make it stop," Serafina ordered. "The disturbance is spreading throughout the settlement. A cluster of roots just flew up through the center of the bonfire above. It was alive, and in great distress. Jorjevo and the others are trying to bring it under control and comfort it."

"Stop it? How?" Tildi held out her arms, and the book flew to them. She held it to her, and the voices clamored at her all at once. They sounded like her nightmare.

"You are in control of it. Whether you know it or not, you are changing runes in your sleep. Why now? What has happened? Tell me! What was the last thing you remembered before you went to sleep."

Tildi felt lost and miserable. Her first impulse was to snap at Serafina. She was shocked at herself.

"I . . . I hardly know. I was happy then. This is the first time that I have really been able to rest since I have had the book. I thought about Edynn. I miss her dearly. I wanted to grieve for her, but I was so tired."

"We all were," Serafina said reassuringly. "Thank you for your care."

"I've been frightened all of the time since then." Tildi allowed her memories to unroll like the scroll itself, trying to recall her thoughts. "I didn't mean it to, but my fear started to turn to anger. I couldn't help myself. I am so *angry* that I could just go back and kill them!" Serafina put her hand down on Tildi's fists. The book wriggled like a live thing. The walls moaned, and more protrusions appeared as the runes altered. "It's not like me, but I have never lived like this in all my life. They threatened me, and I couldn't do anything back!"

Serafina tightened her grip and forced Tildi to look into her eyes.

"Stop, Tildi. Stop. You'll do us all harm. Take a deep breath, now. Obey me! I am your friend."

Tildi stared into the wizardess's eyes. At first their darkness fed the hot temper she felt rising, but gradually the steady gaze doused the flames in her soul. From pools of night, they seemed to become like the peat-colored meres that lay at the edge of the deep forests of her home. She almost heard the soughing of the wind as it played in the trees. The tension in her shoulders loosened. Tears began to drip down her cheeks. Serafina gathered her close. Tildi was grateful for the strong embrace. The dreams receded to a bad feeling at the edge of her mind.

"I am so sorry to cause trouble," Tildi said miserably.

"You have been through so much, it would be unnatural if you didn't react in some way. The book amplifies your desires. You wished destruction, and the runes began to change as you willed them."

"Did I kill those roots?" Tildi asked. "I didn't mean to bring it to life."

"No one expects you to command your thoughts even in your sleep, Tildi," Serafina said, a tiny smile on her face. "It isn't your fault."

"May we enter?" a deep voice asked from behind the door cloth.

"Come in," Serafina said. "She is all right now."

The comfortable room seemed suddenly tiny as four of the massive bear-kin crowded in. Magpie and Rin, looking child-sized in comparison, came behind them.

"Are you well, little one?" Rin asked, curling up on her knees beside Tildi's bed. "We heard so much noise, and things began to happen."

"That's a mild way of putting it," Magpie said. "It was worthy of the greatest theatricals of the finest troupes in the world—I don't criticize you, Tildi. I only wish I could have made such impressive effects when I was a troubadour! And you did it in your dreams."

He meant to make her laugh, but she felt more foolish than before. Tildi looked at them helplessly. "Won't I be able to sleep ever again?" she asked.

Jorjevo sat down upon his massive haunches, but his broad snout was still so high up that Tildi had to tilt her head back to meet his eyes.

"Sleep is not your enemy, child. You have been ill-treated, and with so much pain in your soul, it is little wonder that you crave to release it. We bearkin were able to calm the pulses of the earth somewhat, though we could not undo everything that you did. You must be ready to go on, not keep looking back. Time will heal those wounds, but it will continue unless you let go of that which troubles you. Tomorrow—hmm, it is nearly tomorrow already!—we shall help you. I have already sent for the wisest of my kin." He gave Serafina a summing look. "You and your friends can make use of the chance to heal."

"What will you do?" Serafina asked.

"We will gather together for a dance. To involve the entire body makes the spirit follow along until it can fly free on its own. The ritual will bring her peace. For now," Jorjevo said, turning to Tildi, "I can help you to rest for what remains of this night. Will you trust me?"

Tildi saw no guile in the warm, syrup-colored eyes. "I trust you."

"Good. Lie back, then." She obeyed, and he laid the top pads of two of his enormous fingers on her eyelids. "Until tomorrow, child."

Chapter Fifteen

here was something about the bearkin, Tildi thought, snuggled be-tween two cubs twice her size the next day in the great stone circle, that made it impossible to be gloomy for long. Not that they talked one's ear off; in fact, they were silent as often as they spoke. If you didn't feel like talking, it was just as comfortable to sit near them. When at last you decided to get up and do something else, you felt as though you'd just had a good conversation, even though none of you might have said more than "pass the wine." It was restful. No one had any expectations of her, and no one showed disapproval for anything she did or said.

Tildi had rested well, and rose feeling happier than she had since the morning before her brothers had been killed. She could not be completely content or at peace, though. She was aware of the undercurrent of anger that had so surprised her the night before, and so were her hosts. She saw the rage worked into her own rune like a thread in complex embroidery, and wondered why it had not been visible before, or why she had not sensed it. Most likely, as Serafina suggested, she was so busy being afraid that there hadn't been room for other emotions. There was no sign of the unfortunate root creature that she had summoned accidentally into life.

Everyone seemed to know about her nightmares. They made sure she was never alone. Serafina did not hover over her, for which Tildi was grateful, though she kept an eye on her from wherever she was. Tildi often felt eyes on her. All of her friends were keeping a protective watch. She was glad they couldn't see her thoughts. How many miles had they traveled to reach this spot? Who knew how badly damaged the road was behind them, or if she had accidentally left any animals deformed in her wake? She located a rune she called *forest* in the book, and sought to keep it intact, though her current company made it difficult to concentrate.

Her companions, Vidavo and Ohtakiva, were very young children, the equivalent of perhaps five or six years to smallfolk. They liked to rest their big heads on her shoulder, when they talked to her, which made her fold over like a pillow, but they were friendly and warm. Ohtakiva, a precocious female, had a terrible sweet tooth, and kept nibbling honey crystals from a bag made of preserved leaves that she kept on a cord around her neck. She was always careful to share, though Tildi had a suspicion, confirmed by the baby bearkin's rune, that she would have enjoyed eating them all herself.

"Wouldn't you like another?" she asked, offering yet another glistening golden shard. The visible sign on it only made it look more appealing.

"No, thank you for your generosity," Tildi said. "I've had plenty, and I'm full of breakfast. Why don't you eat them for me?"

Ohtakiva grinned, showing rounded baby teeth. "You don't have to do that," she said, giggling, her voice deeper than the biggest man in Clearbeck. "I like honey, but I like to share."

Vidavo paid little attention to social niceties, and snagged the sweetmeat out of his friend's paw. He crunched it, looking smugly satisfied.

"I'll eat them for you, Tildi!" he said.

All about the clearing, more and more bearkin kept appearing in between the rustling greenery, embracing those who were already there, and waving to others who were still approaching. The space seemed to fill in with furry bodies. Tildi thought she would be crushed, but they always seemed to leave a little room for her and the book. The rune she was protecting kept altering slightly. She had to keep redrawing it in her mind to prevent accidents.

"Look at that!" Ohtakiva exclaimed, pointing. Tildi looked up in alarm. Had she missed a line of the intricate pictogram? "That's great-grandsire's sister's daughter Neva. I bet she brought me some more dried fish. She says they are to help my coat grow sleek. I don't like dried fish. They are smelly, not sweet."

"My relatives used to bring us nourishing foods we didn't like," Tildi said with a smile for the memory. "My father's aunt liked to make us a big pot of shin soup in the winter."

"How many of you are there?" Ohtakiva asked.

"We were five, but I'm the only one left," Tildi said, keeping the smile intact. Vidavo, with the frankness of children, pushed his companion with a heavy paw.

"She doesn't want to talk about it. Don't ask."

The girl looked abashed, holding her paws over her square snout and peeping out between her fingers. "I am sorry, Tildi."

"There's nothing to be sorry about," Tildi assured her, patting her between her furry ears.

Tildi became aware of a humming that seemed to come from deep underground, and the more bearkin who arrived the more intense it grew. She thought that she had heard such a sound the night before, but it was less a tune than a sensation. Booming, humming, pounding like the sound of a big drum, all seemed to come from the earth itself. Her whole chest thrummed with the power of it. It wasn't frightening, but it did overwhelm her to the point where she couldn't sit still any longer. Her two young companions seemed to catch the excitement. They rose to their feet and started to rock from foot to foot. They pulled Tildi up, and she fell into their rhythm. It felt natural and right, as though it were her own heartbeat she heard. A rune came into being at the heart of the clearing, thirty feet above the circle of chair-stones, and grew as the intensity of the rumbling grew. Power was building here. Tildi felt awe for her hosts and their easy acceptance of magic.

"Come, now, children," Jorjevo said, appearing before them. He held out his giant paw to Tildi. In his other hand he had her knapsack.

"What is that for?" Tildi asked, closing her fingers around a single pad.

"For the shedding of the past," he said. "Come, smallfolk. Dance with me!"

He led her on an intricate path through the swirling, bounding group. Among so many towering beasts, Tildi quickly lost sight of her two small companions. She kept the book close to her side, fearing one of the others might touch it by accident in such a crowd.

Unlike feasts in the Quarters, there was no formal beginning to the dance. It just began once there were enough bearkin present. She felt magic building. The very air hummed. She was enwrapped by the sensation. Jorjevo looked back at her and smiled.

Though the pace of dancing was not rapid, her legs were so much shorter than Jorjevo's that she had to take three to each one of his. She found herself flushed and out of breath before they had passed before the tallest chairstone three times.

"I can't keep up," she panted. Her piping voice was lost in the chanting and humming, but Jorjevo had heard it.

"You are trying too hard," he said, looking back at her. "Let yourself follow the pulse. Hear it. Let your feet follow it. You are working against yourself."

"How?" Tildi asked.

"Like this—ta thum ta thum thum. Ta thum. Ta thum thum. Simple. Come on!" He turned in a slow circle.

Tildi tried to emulate his footsteps, but her hand slipped from the bearkin's pad. He took one more pace and vanished into a sea of fur. "Wait for me!"

She chanted the spell that made the air solid beneath her feet, and climbed high enough to see the faces. There were too many, and they looked so similar. Was that Jorjevo, a quarter turn away from her, bowing to pass under the joined hands of two honey-colored females? Or was that him, cavorting in the center of a ring of eight at the heart of the clearing? It was all so confusing. If she kept on dancing, could she catch up with him?

As soon as she left the ground, she noticed that the complex rhythm lost its focus. She lost her step and became confused. The pattern of cascading steps taken by each dancer in turn seemed random. She didn't know where to put her feet. The huge bearkin began to bump into her, rumbling apologies but carrying on with the dance. The voices in the book, immediately on guard for her well-being, began to mutter. She saw the rune above their heads start to twist and change.

"Stop it!" she ordered the voices. They sounded confused, but the unnatural winding of the rune's strokes halted. She was responsible, but she had no idea how to make it the way it was before. She hoped no one would be harmed because of the change. The voices began to protest in her mind. Tildi grabbed the book and held tightly to it. She crouched in a ball in midair with the book on her lap and squeezed her eyes shut. She must find a safe place. More bearkin cannoned into her, scooting her through the air like a stone on ice.

"Hold on, little one!" Rin's voice said. She felt hands catch her around her rib cage. She opened her eyes to see the centaur's wry grin as she set the smallfolk girl on her back. "They are all so big, they forget the rest of us cannot withstand their love-taps!" Her hooves cavorted to the beat. Tildi realized the moment she touched Rin's back, the music made sense again. She crumpled with relief. The voices stopped their clamoring. "They can charge through trees and rocks for days, but the rest of us must stop."

"Now, don't say that," Lakanta chided her, whirling and capering beside the centaur with surprising ease. Her cheeks glowed a becoming pink. "Some of us can keep up just fine. I've never taken part in this particular festival before, but I've never sat down before they did."

"Where is Serafina?" Tildi asked.

Rin craned her neck and peered through the crowd. "There!" She pointed. Tildi stood up and held on to Rin's mane to see. The wizardess gripped the hand of the black-furred female leading her, and Magpie held tight to her trailing hand. Serafina looked solemn, concentrating hard on cutting the right figures, but the prince beamed with delight. If he made a mistake, he didn't let it bother him. Tildi tried not to let it bother her that the two of them seemed content together.

"Are you ready?" Jorjevo asked, coming up behind them. He took Rin and Lakanta by the hands and led them in a delightful step, a dip, hop, and half turn to the side, then back the other way.

"When does the ritual begin?" Tildi asked, clinging tight to Rin's mane.

"It has already begun. You might say it never ends. We pay heed to the eternal song, that of the great Lovers who formed this world between Them, and Their joy in Their creation. Their hearts beat with a single purpose, but we hear many different tempos from all the different children They made. We join together in a dance to become more open to the oneness of Their union."

"It sounds . . . it sounds like our festival meetings," Tildi said, relieved to find common ground. "We hear the lessons in which Father Time instructed Mother Nature to make all the parts of Alada."

Jorjevo's eyes twinkled. "Smallfolk, it would be unwise for a lover to instruct and not assist in such a great undertaking. But take comfort in that which is familiar to you." He regarded them all kindly. "All of you have those things that tie you to your sorrow. Bring them into the dance. I already have yours, Tildi." From the pouch, he took a handful of small items. Tildi recognized the mementos she had kept of her brothers: Gosto's handkerchief, Pierin's knife, Marco's flute, and Teldo's scrap of parchment that was a copy of a leaf in the Great Book.

"I haven't looked at those in weeks," she said. "I'm ashamed to say I had almost forgotten I was carrying them."

"Don't be," Jorjevo said. "Your brothers would be honored by your devotion. I am sure they have never been far from your thoughts."

"They aren't," Tildi said solemnly.

"What sorrows would you shed?" the bearkin asked her friends.

"Well," Lakanta said slowly, "I do have the last letter my husband sent me."

Rin said, her chin out in defiance, "I am sorry for those poor beasts we left behind us. I regret those who died because of mad wizards and greedy kings."

"We know of whom you speak," the bearkin said. "We felt the pulse through the earth's skin change around them when the monstrosity that the orind had guarded was freed. We were aware of them. A not-so-successful experiment, roots, roots of clay, roots of the earth itself that were creeping out, curious, and strangling everything they touched. Surface dwellers must beware of digging too deeply."

"But you live underground, too. Aren't you afraid of the roots?" Tildi asked.

"So do our stone-brothers," Jorjevo said, indicating Lakanta. "But none of us have burrowed down to where those originate, down in the hidden places. Truly, the roots are content as they are, and should never have been allowed a doorway to the upper world. But they did not thrive well in light. They were better off underground, where their reaching out harmed nothing. Everything belowground has a tough skin, devoid of color. The creatures are attracted to bright lights, bright colors. They cannot help themselves. They are not evil, but they are out of place. The orind kept them from roaming."

"The orind?" Rin asked.

"That was the name of the beasts of whom you speak. They were simple beings, until they were changed."

"By the Shining Ones?" Tildi asked.

"Yes, as they called themselves. They had many names, all brimming with arrogance," Jorjevo said, without rancor. "We record their actions, but what is done is done. They are out of the world now."

"I hate them," Rin said. "I do not regret that my people were brought into being, but they had no right to make one species eternal captives because it happened to be convenient to look after a mistake they made. I would kill them, if any still live."

They do, or at least one does, Tildi thought, but she didn't want to say it aloud.

"You shouldn't look forward to killing," Lakanta said.

Rin looked at her in surprise. "How can you say that, when the Makers' work robbed you of your husband? You and Tildi have more reason than any of us to call for their blood."

Tildi was shocked that Rin would speak so freely. Lakanta wasn't offended, but her blue eyes were solemn. "It is because I have had time to think, and mourn. Hate gets in the way. I don't want my memories of him tainted. We were too happy together."

"You have a warrior's spirit, Windmane," Jorjevo said. "Would you let go your anger? It weighs down your heart. You may defend the helpless all the better for its lightness."

Rin nodded, her thick hair bobbing. "Then, I will."

"Then we begin." Jorjevo tilted back his head and let out a bellow to the skies. His people echoed it, and the sound formed a wall around them. "Join us, sisters!"

Rin opened her arms and screamed out a defiant challenge to the unseen. Lakanta laughed.

"That's telling them, Princess," she said. "Eternal Ones, I love you!"

Feeling a trifle silly, Tildi looked up. The spherical golden rune against the disk of blue sky stared down unblinkingly at her like a gigantic eye. What should she say?

"I still obey," she called, thinking of the elders and what they expected of females.

"Does that give you peace?" Jorjevo asked gently.

"It ought to," Tildi said. Suddenly she felt like weeping. "If I tell the truth, I was not so obedient to the strictures as I should have been. I practiced magic. I thought myself a match for any one of my brothers. I was a stranger in my own homeland, and I never knew it until I lost them."

"Then let me add one more item to your sacrifice," Jorjevo said. From the heart of her knapsack he produced the white cap she had worn all her life, and the long braid folded up within it that she had cut off on the night her brothers died. "Turn your back on that which restrains you. The Mother and the Father will always love you, as we do."

"But what will I do with them?" she asked.

"Ho-ah!" Jorjevo cried.

"Ho-ah!" the bearkin responded.

As if in answer, the glowing sigil descended from its height. The bearkin pushed back from the center of the clearing to make room. When the globe of light touched the ground, it burst into golden flames that flared up as high as the treetops. Tildi recoiled, throwing up her hand to protect her eyes.

"Give your sorrow to the flames," Jorjevo said. "Throw them into the fire. Get rid of that which holds you back from reaching your heart's desire."

She clutched her brothers' possessions to her heart. "I can't do that," she said, horrified. "This is all I have left of them."

The bearkin's eyes were kind but insistent. "You have your memories, and you will have them still when the physical objects are gone. You will lose nothing but your grief. Come with me. Will you trust me?"

Tildi hesitated for a moment. "I will."

Jorjevo lifted her off Rin's back and carried her through the swaying bodies to the innermost ring of dancers. She stepped down from his arms, holding the few things tightly. She wasn't given time to think. The bearkin already near the scorching blaze took her by the shoulders and led her around in a circle.

"Wait, we are going anti-sunwise," she protested.

"We are unmaking sorrow," the female nearest her explained. "Let it go. You do not need it."

Am I ready to let go of my memories? Tildi wondered. She thought back to the day the thraiks had attacked her family in the meadow over Daybreak Farm. She pushed away the painful sight of her brothers disappearing one by one into the black gash in the sky. Her mind refused to let that vision go. Instead, it added the terrible day, ten years before, when her parents had been carried off by the terrible beasts as well. Then, suddenly, her mind was in Oron Castle, at the north end of Orontae, seeing the doors close behind Edynn for the last time. The image of the white-haired wizardess gave her a kind and affectionate glance, then was lost from view forever.

Tildi thrust her hands away, as if she could drive the memories from her heart. To her horror, she also let go of the trinkets: the cloth, the knife, the flute, and the strip of parchment, her cap and braid. They tumbled into the fire, which flared up greedily and engulfed them.

"No!" she cried, leaping after them.

"Yes," her escort insisted, holding her back effortlessly. She held the protesting smallfolk by the shoulders. "Be rid of them. Remember the good. Let your strength come from those times."

She tried to move back through the line, to the spot where she had flung her treasures into the fire. Perhaps she could rake them out. Oh, but what would be left? A lump of metal from the knife? But she was too small and weak to resist the tide of dancers who swept her before them.

She saw then that Serafina had come into the ring. The wizardess held a white saddlebag in her arms. Tildi saw that there were tears standing in her big, dark eyes. She flung the pouch as far into the licking flames as she could. The fire leaped high where it fell. Serafina bowed her head, and was swept into the dance and out of Tildi's sight.

Why would she destroy her own property? Tildi wondered. Then she realized that it must contain Edynn's things. Her heart ached for Serafina. She wished that the young wizardess would find some comfort in the ritual. Serafina turned away hastily, not wanting anyone to see her weep. Yet Tildi watched something rise from the heart-stroke of her rune, like a drop of dew rolling along a blade of grass, and vanish.

Magpie came forward with his hands cupped together. Tildi guessed what was within them belonged to Lady Inbecca. He thrust his hands toward the flames and opened them. No object fell from them, but a rune appeared and hung briefly before it faded away. Tildi could read that one, for it had changed little since its ancient days: *regret*. She gave him a sympathetic smile. He returned it, but his eyes were ineffably sad.

"My turn," Lakanta said. She clapped Tildi on the shoulder as she pushed by. From her belt pouch, she took a much-folded parchment. Her round cheeks were pink. At Tildi's puzzled glance, she explained, "It's the last letter I ever received from my husband. If I'd known it was to be the last . . . well, then." She swallowed hard and gave Tildi a brave smile. "Got to let it go." She opened it, scanned over the lines within it, then thrust it from her. The flames rose up in a gush, making all standing nearby fall back from the heat. "It's done," she said, her voice thick. Tildi reached out to squeeze her hand. Lakanta gave her a grateful smile. She pulled Tildi along as the rhythm sped up, and they did a gavotte.

"Ah, they always could dance in the Quarters," the dwarf woman cried.

The bearkin nearest her bent to take Tildi's other hand. As soon as they touched, Tildi was able to hear even more clearly the pulsing rhythm that drove her feet. It made her happy and sad at the same time: sad with a deep and inexplicable longing for things she would never know and things she had lost yet happy to be alive. The music passed through every fiber of her body, driving her to dance. The book followed her. The voices inside it sounded glad as well. Lakanta let go of her hand, to make way for one of the smaller bearkin, who gave way to Morag, who let his singing companion take her for a wild reel that made her laugh out loud. She did feel lighter, knowing that the terrible moment was only the end of the happy life she had had with her brothers. She knew the good things about them, which she couldn't wait to share. She had stories of Gosto and some of his yarns, and Pierin's conquests, Marco's music, and Teldo's fascination with magic. She and the others exchanged tales as they danced.

"So Olen was not your first teacher," Serafina said as they stepped gaily in a circle with Magpie and Jorjevo. She seemed more at peace than she had been, ever. The small frown line between her eyes faded, and Tildi was struck again by how pretty she was when she wasn't looking severe. She beamed at Magpie, who held her other hand. "It was Teldo."

"He learned, and he taught me," Tildi said. "He would have made a good wizard if he had lived."

"You carry on his legacy," Serafina said. "We live, so they are not forgotten."

"What have you cast off?" Magpie asked the towering bearkin.

"Frustration," Jorjevo said with a laugh. "I am too impatient for my people. I must give up my hastily begun projects and finish only that which is important. When I think of an idea, I wish to pursue it. When I cannot, it irks me and disturbs the harmony of our life. You could not hear it before, but my loves were complaining that I was upsetting the balance."

"I would never have thought of you as rash," Magpie said, grinning.

"Nevertheless, sometimes my will to act speedily comes of use," the bearkin replied. "If it were not for my jumps, it might have been a long time before we agreed to intercede when Irithe called upon us. Forgive me. I speak in pride."

"Oh, no!" Tildi said. "I can't tell you how glad I am you did it."

Jorjevo looked pleased. "So I am vindicated. That gladdens my heart, Tildi. We also thank you for the gift you have brought us."

"I haven't given you any gifts," Tildi said, alarmed. She wondered if she had neglected some facet of the bearkin's traditions. Jorjevo pointed to the silver-gilt rune on his chest.

"Indeed you have. We are delighted to see our true names. We also find joy in seeing our song made manifest." He pointed to the rune at the heart of the bonfire. "All of these things please us. You have given us much more than we have given you."

These must be the happiest people in Alada, Tildi thought.

Not far away, Teryn and Morag danced together, looking happy. Tildi did not know what sorrows Morag and Teryn had given to the fire. The guards had gone to the center of the circle together very late in the ceremony, after most of the bearkin had taken their turns. Teryn had emptied out a small bag tied at the neck. The flames leaped up to greet whatever fell out of it. To Tildi's astonishment, Morag had surrendered his sword. Teryn had put her arm around him and drawn him back out of her sight. Tildi was glad to see them now. She observed the tendrils that connected their runes, even here, not on the page of the book that followed her, and was glad for them. As the music changed tempo to a softer, slower dance, Tildi sank into a heap with a bunch of the small bearkin behind her. They all fell on her like pillows toppling out of a cupboard. She was buried beneath them like a furry avalanche but she couldn't stop laughing. She felt so good inside, the best she could ever recall. The children helped her up, holding her close, rubbing their noses with hers. It was wet and cool, and she giggled.

"What a funny way to kiss," she said, and offered her nose to the others. They were all giggling. Big ones clustered about to pick up the children and Tildi and joined the embrace. Tildi offered her small nose, and had it tickled by the stiff whiskers around Danevo's snout. She was passed from hand to hand, as each of the big bearkin wanted to share their joy with their guest. The sun sank in the sky, until the light around them was red and golden. Everyone was still singing and laughing. The book floated along behind her. She guessed that it was taking notes. The voices from it sounded as happy as she felt. She had been handed all the way around the circle many times. Wine as sweet as nectar was offered to her by a pale golden-furred maiden. The jar was too big for her, but dozens of bearkin helped steady it so she could drink. Trays of food came along afterward. The cooks had thought of her: on every platter there were pies and cakes and dried meats cut to a size she could consume. Everything tasted so good. The wine and the food gave her more energy to dance, and the dance made her hungry and thirsty again. When the sun had long set, she sat by the fire with her new friends, listening to them sing and swaying to the music. When she felt like it, she got up and danced again. There was always more food and wine and song and stories when she wanted those, too.

She woke from a comfortable slumber and discovered she had been asleep on the shoulder of a mother who was nursing a small cub.

"Are you well, little friend?" she asked. The circle of sky above them was a clear, deep blue. A feather of cloud was edged with a streak of light. The bonfire had shrunk to waist high. A dozen or more bearkin still circled it. Lakanta was among them, as was Captain Teryn. Tildi stretched.

"Is it morning already?"

"Morning and morning again since we began our dance," the female said, shifting her hold on her baby. "I think this is the first you have slept. No dreams?"

"Only good ones," Tildi said. "I feel wonderful."

"I take joy in that," the female said. The baby, its fur wiry brown plush, reached out and touched Tildi on the knee. Its little round eyes regarded her with trust and affection.

Tildi felt a rush of love for all living things. She had never felt so comfortable and protected. Then she sat up, alarmed. The dancers had been circling the fire for hours. They could have churned the forest rune up into anything while she slept! She peered through the dancers' legs, looking for anything amiss.

"All is well," the mother said gently. "Whatever you fear, it has not come to pass."

She was right. The hard-packed earth had been disturbed, true, but no more than one would expect from having a hundred gigantic creatures with thick claws on their back feet. The rune looked exactly as it had been when she stopped paying attention to it.

"I . . . think I must be restoring it in the back of my mind," she said.

"I thank you for that," the mother said. "You are a good wizard."

"Not yet," Tildi said with a blush. "I have a long way to go yet."

"Then I wish you joy of your journey. I hope you have found peace here."

"Oh, I have," Tildi assured her. "I love it here." She reached out to pat the baby. It grabbed her hand in both of its small paws and mouthed it. She laughed.

In the soft, bluish light, Tildi saw Serafina and Magpie dancing alone together next to the fire, and a small measure of her happiness seemed to
drain. They were embracing warmly, out of step with the music, but in step
with each other. Like the guards, threads of their runes began to intertwine
together. Tildi had an urge to interrupt them, to stop it.

Hold hard, she said severely to herself. Was she truly upset on Lady Inbecca's part, or was she jealous? Why and wherefore did she have a right to
interfere in the happiness of others? The princess had decided to stay behind with her aunt's knights, or so Prince Eremi had told her. The engagement must have been broken off. Inbecca had selected the Scholardom over
her beloved. He was free to bestow his affections where he chose, and
wasn't Serafina a worthy person to be given them? *I was meant to cast away the
sorrows of the past,* she chided herself. *So were they. They need each other, if not
forever, then for now. I will need them both for what we must do. If they joy in each
other, then they won't be lonely any longer. A master wizardess, though young, was the
equal of a third-born prince.*

The female looked at her sagely. "You need to dance some more," she said.

Tildi got to her feet, ashamed of herself. She paced slowly, looking for a
chance to catch up with the double ring of dancers and get into the pattern.
She let her arms rise and fall with others, but could not seem to find the
tempo of their movement. She no longer felt as if she was part of the collec-
tive peace that the ritual had created. Once again, she was out of place and
out of step. Her sense of belonging was fading.

The bearkin seemed to pick up on her distress. The second ring widened
out, and the paws of the dancers parted to take her hands in them.

Tildi took in a huge breath. Their enveloping touch restored to her the
feeling of being in harmony with the world around her. All of them were part
of the same music. A poem that she had read in school had talked about the
"music of the spheres." The phrase had intrigued her at the time, but her
schoolmaster was dismissive that she would ever be able to understand such
a complex notion. She was living it now. Her childish mind had pictured the
twinkling of harp strings or the jangle of bells, but the true music was so
deep she felt it rather than heard it. Her mind had learned to distinguish
complex beats within the humming, pounding, and thumping. It all worked
together, as all the odd parts of a clock did, producing one giant pulse. Tildi
let herself be carried along by it. She had her own small part in the music, a
very faint pulse. She became aware of the sounds that distinguished her
friends, as individual as the runes on their chests. Magpie's was more
thoughtful than she would have guessed. Lakanta's was not the liveliest; to
her surprise it was the reserved Captain Teryn whose tempo felt like a
happy dance step. All things had their own pulse, whether simple or complex, even the Great Book.

But when Tildi concentrated upon the book, she felt her feet faltering. The book, which floated sedately behind her like a benevolent cloud, had its own pulse, but it did not fit comfortably within the complex dance. Its tempo was not even or comfortable to listen to. True, the contents of its pages changed all the time, but, she wondered, since it contained all of nature, wouldn't it fit in with the rest?

The answer appeared to be no. Though she tried to fight against it, the book's influence became more insistent, until she could not keep up at all. She put a wrong foot down on the dancing ground, and Neva stepped on it. Tildi let out a cry of pain.

At once, the elderly bearkin realized her error and pulled up short. The line of dancers behind was caught off guard and tripped over one another. Tildi dodged to avoid having the big creatures land on her, and fell over her own feet. Instead of their crushing weight, she felt the warmth of power. She looked up to see the mass of fur arrested a few inches away, as if against a glass window.

The thrumming died away to a low hum. The huge bonfire died away to embers as though snuffed by a gigantic thumb and forefinger. The bearkin helped one another up and dusted each other off. Serafina rushed to Tildi's side. Jorjevo lumbered behind her.

"Are you injured?" she asked, feeling Tildi's ankle.

"I don't think so. I apologize for ruining the dance," Tildi said.

"Only for a moment," Jorjevo said mildly. "No fear; it renews itself even now." The humming rose again, and the bearkin resumed their stately gavotte. It went perfectly once Tildi had left. She grimaced.

"It's the book," Tildi said. "It upsets everything. I don't think it can help itself."

"I perceived that," Serafina said. "It is what it is, Tildi. It's not in harmony with the world because it is out of place. It jars, because it is trying to reconcile a dual existence. It is a physical thing, so it is in the world, but because it contains all the world within it, it also exists outside reality. The changes is wreaks are gradual, subtle, but inexorable."

"It will eventually change everything it is near," Jorjevo said gently. "It has undoubtedly changed you."

"I don't mind that," Tildi said. "The book is dear to me. I have kept other things as they are." She appealed to Serafina. "I can do it."

"But it amplifies your feelings, too," the wizardess pointed out. "It defends you. It made a creature out of your rage. It distorted solid matter near you because you were having a nightmare. You didn't control it. You cannot."

"Even a strong and experienced wizard would find this wonder too much to handle," Jorjevo said. "We don't blame you, but it should not be out and about in the world."

"It should never have been made," Danevo said.

"I agree," Serafina said. "We have been here too long. We must leave very soon."

"I don't want to go yet!" Tildi exclaimed.

"You must take it to where it can do no harm."

"I will," Tildi said, feeling the support she had felt dissipate like morning fog. "I am. I promise. Just let me rest here awhile longer."

"I am sorry," Jorjevo said, his kind eyes very sad. "We have done our best to heal you and set you in balance. While that healing is strongest, you should begin your travel. Tomorrow."

Tildi slumped. Not even the soothing feeling the book offered her assuaged the sense of abandonment she felt.

"It is cold out there," she said, "and not just because it's autumn."

"You must brave the cold, smallfolk," Jorjevo said, though not unkindly. "Your task can be undertaken by no other. Would you waste the rescue that brought you away from those who would stop the book in its tracks, by ending your journey here yourself? You must go."

"No," Tildi begged. "Please, don't send me away from here. It has been so long since I was happy." The book snuggled up to her, and she pushed at it. The voices inside it sounded distressed. She started to cry.

Jorjevo captured her in a massive hug and pulled her to him. She vanished into the depths of his fur. She snuggled in, never wanting to come out. If she never again saw the sun, it would be fine.

Still, she could not escape the rumbling voice that permeated her whole body.

"Would you waste the sacrifices of all who have been with you? If you do not go, the peril of the book remaining aboveground will cause chaos. We have held it back, for a time, but what becomes of the world when we go into our winter sleep? The spell will weaken. The book will break free of our control. Change will come. Will you never become weary of repairing the damage it leaves in its wake?"

"I'm tired now," Tildi murmured into the enveloping fur. "I thought I had found peace here."

"You have, but it was to give you strength to go on with your task, not to stay here as if nothing else would happen. What about your friends? Will you expect them to remain with you? Again, they are as welcome as you, but they have their lives to return to. This is a moment out of time, no more."

She realized what he said was true. She pushed herself free and looked him straight in the eye.

"I know," she said miserably. "I wish none of it had happened. I wish I could be back home before all this came to pass."

Jorjevo's huge hand patted her shoulder as though she were an infant.

"Now, now, do not let the sorrow build up again. You danced yourself free. You can start afresh, from now."

"Control yourself, apprentice," Serafina said severely.

A rumbling noise from Jorjevo sounded like a gentle admonition to the wizardess, but Tildi obeyed. She did need to pull herself together. She straightened her back. Jorjevo put her carefully on the ground.

"I have two surprises for you, Tildi," he said. "Here is the first." He reached between the feet of the dancers and picked something out of the barren firepit. He put it into her outstretched hands.

Tildi gazed in astonishment at a much-folded white cloth on which lay a hand-carved flute, a belt knife, and a small parchment scroll. "My brothers' tokens!" she exclaimed. "But I thought the fire consumed them!"

"The dancing fire takes away only the unhappiness," he said. "I told you you would lose nothing you treasured. Your cap, it seems, was more sorrow than substance, so it was indeed consumed. The others should find their items among the ashes, if they care to retrieve them." He glanced up at Serafina, who dipped her eyes gratefully.

Tildi put Pierin's knife back on her belt and tucked the other things into her pouch. "Thank you!" she said. "What is the second surprise?"

"We have had a message from Komorosh," Danevo said. "You must go to the port town of Lenacru on the west bank of the Arown. Olen will be waiting for you. He is on board a ship. He advises you to take the sky path. It will be the fastest way."

"Master Olen?" Tildi asked, torn between excitement and sadness.

"May I read this message from Master Olen?" Serafina asked, holding out a hand.

Danevo smiled. "Of course you may. But it is not in a scroll or a piece of parchment. Listen. I will try and help you to hear that part of the earth's heartbeat in which Komorosh embedded his message."

He took Serafina's shoulders between his hands. "Close your eyes. Listen deeply. The heaviest sound is that of our beloved Alada's heart. The next deepest sounds are those of the largest masses of land and the most active bodies of water." He beat a tempo on her arm with the tip of one pad. "Listen for this rhythm. Can you hear it? It seems to be irregular, but it has its own complex pattern."

"I . . . I can feel it," Serafina said. "What is it?"

"It is the town in which Komorosh makes his home when he is not with us. Many people have added their own sounds to it, as you can tell, but the deliberate beat is Komorosh. He is always in harmony with us, no matter how far away he is."

"How do I understand what it says?"

"Give it time. It will make sense to you."

She smiled. "I see the ship," she said. "I am amazed at this marvel. I will have to study it further when this task is done."

"You are welcome back among us at any time," Danevo said. "As are you, little one. We love you already. We look forward to seeing you again."

Tildi was sad but resigned. "I hope to return to Silvertree, but I will come and visit you when Master Olen permits me."

Jorjevo set his huge hand on her head. "Go in peace, Tildi Summerbee. Return to us whenever you choose. It will be most interesting to discuss ancestors with you again. Find your family tree if you can. I would not be surprised to find we have relatives in common."

"I would love that," Tildi said, her good humor returning. She gave him a cheeky grin. "How I would adore to introduce you all to Mayor Jurney as our long-lost cousins!"

The kotyrs bounded upward through the earth like salmon leaping in a stream. They sought not sunlight, but the rune at the heart of their beings. They sensed the thraiks that circled far above them. In their primitive, angry brains, they wanted to leap at those winged beasts and hold fast to them, but an overriding command told them the thraiks were the hunters who would catch what they, the hounds, located. Once they reached the surface, they spread out, covering as much of the land as they could.

The glint of their skins drew stares from other living beings. A fisherman, his bare feet wet from hauling in his nets, noticed the pretty things racing toward the surf and tried to capture one of them with his hands. His friends and neighbors, riverfolk all, laughed at him. The kotyr, shocked that anything should touch it against its will, turned faster than a hornet and plunged its fangs into his wrist. The fisherman cried out and, as his companions watched in horror, sank to his knees. His wrist swelled and turned purple. Before his shocked wife could run to his aid, he fell down dead. By that time, the kotyr had forgotten about him. All it cared for was finding the source of the rune it bore.

Chapter Sixteen

Once day had dawned on the first morning of their captivity, Inbecca found she had awoken into a different world. The Patha who came to awaken her was no longer a silver-gray wolfkin in a loose green tunic, but a human woman with long silver hair braided down her back. Green became her. It picked up emerald lights in her eyes, which were almost as yellow as they had been in her wolf phase. Inbecca was amused to note that Eremi's eyes were almost the same color, and he had no werewolf in his ancestry at all. She knew his family history back to the first kings of Orontae. Patha had overseen Inbecca's breakfast and morning ablutions, then brought her out to be secured underneath a venerable hornbark tree where she would be shielded from the direct rays of the sun. Though the year was growing old, sunny days were still hot. She doubted whether her fellow knights were grateful for the consideration. Certainly her aunt, still assigned the tree next to Inbecca's, was not.

The other werewolves, who had been similarly transformed, went about the tasks of their day as if nothing had changed, for they lived all their lives with the moon-borne alteration. It was only strangers who found anything to remark upon in the shift from body type to body type. Eremi had once told her werewolves were natural sailors, because they had an instinct for moons and tides that no human could match. Inbecca couldn't stop herself looking at each person who passed by, trying to guess if she knew which one had been which wolfling. The big, good-looking man with thick black hair who closely resembled Patha had to be Grolius. She guessed he must be Patha's son. As for the rest, Inbecca didn't yet know. She fancied she had a good deal of time to learn each, though.

Though in between visits by Alada's two moons, the Pearl and the Agate, they were human in form, the elders were able to transform into wolflings at will. The first time Inbecca saw it happen, on that second day, she knew it was rude, but she could not help but stare. A young man, about Inbecca's age or a little younger, sought to move the tongue of a cart laden with boxes into the yoke between two oxen. She thought privately that he didn't look strong enough to accomplish the task. Her fears nearly came true as suddenly the cart shifted and rolled forward a yard. Inbecca let out a cry of warning. The young man didn't lose his grip on the tongue. His face turned red with strain, and Inbecca thought he might drop the metal phlange. Suddenly hair began to sprout from his arms and face. The bones of his forearms lengthened, as did his jaw. Inbecca thought it looked agonizing. The spine bent under the weight of the cart curved, then straightened, as if the young man had found a reservoir of strength within himself. His ears, which had been small and hidden within his light sandy hair, grew into tall triangles lined with fur. A brushy tail appeared at the rear of his spine, and swished intently from side to side. He bared his teeth with effort, let out a wordless grunt, and pushed hard. The cart tongue slid forward and clicked onto the hook attached to the underside of the yoke across the oxen's shoulders. He let go, and rubbed his hands, now much longer and covered with sandy hairs, together. He noticed that Inbecca was watching, and winked a yellow eye at her. She blushed.

Her fellow knights who sat nearby were also agog, some of them aghast.

Inbecca guessed that it reminded them of the death of poor Bertin, though the young knight had contorted himself without the knowledge to make the transformation safe. She knew it was different; the Makers had thought through how one species could become another without harming itself. It was masterful magic, but to the Scholardom, Inbecca thought with despair, it must just be further evidence of the unworthiness of werewolves to continued existence. In contrast, she was fascinated. Whenever she noticed the change beginning, she tried to look, but not stare. The werewolves did not mind. In fact, they became aggressive if any human looked as though they disapproved of what was to them the natural state of things.

Patha was a good organizer, Inbecca thought, watching her oversee the camp. It looked to her like any outdoor domicile, with the added task of goods to be sorted and packed. The werewolves must have visited Orontae and Levrenn, at the very least. Inbecca recognized the realm's stamps on the packages. The large, rounded bales were undoubtedly textiles, possibly the fine fleeces that her people raised. Smaller boxes, dwarf-made, were being tallied by a middle-aged female with brown hair streaked with white. Lakanta could have identified the various dwarfhollows for her, but she, too, was gone.

Patha was taking full advantage of the time she and her people must sit idle. Over the last few days, groups of werewolves had arrived and departed. Those leaving took bundles of goods stamped from the southern continent. The returning parties led oxen-drawn wagons full of boxes, bales, and barrels. Often, the topmost layer contained fresh fruit and vegetables and bags of flour. Meat the werewolves had no trouble hunting for themselves. At least two deer and a handful of fowl or small animals were needed to feed the party, swelled as it was by the arrival of dozens of humans. Unlike the Scholardom, most of Patha's people took some part in food preparation. Their cooks would have been an asset to any court. All of them were competent, and some were inspired. She spotted two middle-aged women beginning preparations on a folding table across the fire circle from her, and was pleased to note that the one on the right had a particularly light hand with pastry. Blackberries were in season, and baskets of berries had been gathered by the many children. Hand pies were in the offing, a treat Inbecca enjoyed, one easily eaten by those with restricted movement. The werewolves had been kind, in spite of their task as jailors.

She glanced at her aunt. Sharhava had said very little since the night of the attack. She was vulnerable as never before. Tildi was right to fear the horror of the thraiks. Sharhava's attempt to take the Great Book from Tildi had left her with a legacy she had not foreseen, nor accepted the warnings that the smallfolk girl had given. It was one of which the Scholardom must not have been aware, though the wizardess and the others seemed to know. The thraiks did indeed seek out and attempt to carry out anyone who had made contact with the book. If the curse could be undone, the Scholardom did not know how. Inbecca had seen her imperious aunt scan the skies with a look of fear in her eyes. Who knew when the greasy-skinned monsters might reappear and try again to carry the abbess away?

The other knights were as solicitous as they could be at a distance, but Inbecca was more worried than they. Her aunt might conceal her personal fears from her knights, but Inbecca knew her. Sharhava feared being helpless. She craved authority that was denied her as the second daughter of Levrenn's dowager queen. Her position as abbess gave her a force that would follow her commands and protect her in case her fearsome will was not enough. Now that she had touched the book she was vulnerable to the thraiks. No measure of discipline or stern glances could drive them away. With the book gone she lacked the power to fend them off. It was a blow to her pride that she had had to accept help from people whom she scorned. She watched the skies at twilight, the thraiks' preferred time to hunt. The creatures saw her as their lawful prey, and she was right to fear them. Inbecca was grateful that the werewolves' protective amulets worked. A few of the knights understood, too, and showed their hosts open respect. Sharhava did not, but neither did she revile them as she had before.

Four children, ranging in size from little to large, ran across the encampment, shrieking with laughter. The first one came to an abrupt halt almost at Inbecca's feet, and the others piled onto her. They rolled together upon the ground like dogs, play-gnawing on one another's arms and necks. They were in their human forms, but they growled in the rough wolf-language. Inbecca couldn't help but smile at them as the littlest boy pretended he was injured and yelped in pain. The others all stopped fighting to see what was wrong, and he sprang out of their reach, sticking out his tongue. The rest of them gave chase, and the melee removed itself to another part of the camp. Inbecca laughed with delight. A masculine chuckle came from a few feet away. Inbecca looked across Sharhava to see Auric, the oldest knight, with a grin on his face.

"I'd never seen the children before," Inbecca said. "Traders come to our court in packs, but always the adults."

"They fear humans will be hostile to them," Auric said. "The children stay in the camps. I've studied them over the years. Know the enemy, 'tis said." He shook his head, and Inbecca knew he didn't mean the werewolves, or at least they were enemies no longer. Inbecca was glad. Some of the knights had come around to his understanding. Not all, by any means. They were constrained by their abbess's words to behave cordially. Sharhava herself, when she was forced to speak to one of them, followed her own orders, though Inbecca saw that it took bone-deep effort. Yet some were of Auric's mind. They were becoming enlightened.

She caught more than one knight watching the werewolves going about their business. Once the midday meal had been served and the dishes and leftovers dealt with, a group consisting mostly of women each brought a big bag to the center of the clearing. They dumped them out onto a spread canvas, and Inbecca realized she was looking at the camp's mending. The elder women sat on the rounded stones, but the younger ones sat with their legs drawn up to one side like does. They gossiped and laughed like Inbecca's ladies-in-waiting did sitting around the big tapestry frame in her room, while doing fine embroidery together in the queen's chamber, or while fletching arrows or cleaning their horses' tack in the stables. Inbecca felt suddenly homesick.

Inbecca glanced at her aunt, where she sat tied to her tree. Her face was stony, but her eyes looked at everything. Emotions played across her face, then faded into an expression of pain. Inbecca thought her mind must also be going back to that other place. Sharhava had seen it as her greatest triumph in her many years as abbess.

"Aunt," she asked gently, "are you all right?"

"The magic is gone," Sharhava croaked hoarsely. She turned to Inbecca, and her eyes burned. "I cannot follow the order's rules any longer. The book is gone. We had the treasure. It was ours! That is the worst thing that could ever have befallen me. We must have it back. We have to have it back!"

The despair in her voice tore at Inbecca's heart. She regarded Sharhava with sympathy.

"It's no longer ours, Aunt. It is far away."

"I cannot bear it! Our trust was to protect it." Sharhava wrenched at her bonds. "We must follow those misfits and retrieve it. These people trust you, Lar Inbecca. Compel them to let us go! The book must be in our hands. We will protect it. We are the only ones who can. It is our mandate."

Privately Inbecca thought the Scholardom had been doing less to protect the Great Book than rejoice in having its power, but saying so would only reapply the whip already belaboring Sharhava's back.

"The Scholardom did protect it, for a while," she said soothingly. "Now it is in the hands of others. They will see it safely back to its resting place. Be satisfied with that."

"No!" Sharhava said. The plaint came out as a wail. "It was entrusted to us! We have failed." To Inbecca's horror, her impervious, unbreakable, unshakable aunt began to cry. Her chest heaved a few times as though trying to contain her sorrow, but she could not. Tears dripped down her cheeks, made haggard by sleepless nights. She raised her right hand to wipe away the bitter drops, but the sight of her burned hand in its ragged bandages brought forth fresh sobs.

"Oh, Aunt, please," Inbecca said helplessly, pulling against her own bonds. She longed to put her arms around Sharhava and comfort her, as if she were a child. "Please. What can I do? Please don't cry."

"What is troubling her?" A man stopped to squat beside Sharhava. Inbecca recognized him as the healer Dunnusk only by the medallion he wore about his neck. "Does your hand pain you?" Very gently, he took Sharhava's hand in both of his and unwrapped the bandages. She did not protest or pull away. He let out a sharp breath at the sight of the blackened, shriveled fingers. "What a terrible wound! I can treat that burn, my lady. Your hand still may not regain all its function, though. I am not the healer my grandfather was, but I can help."

Frantically, Sharhava pushed him away with her good hand. The man scrambled backward, but reached out once again to her. The abbess cradled the blackened limb to her chest, keeping it out of his reach.

"No, don't touch it! Don't touch . . . I am the only other living being who has touched the Great Book. I . . . touched it." Her eyes were filled with the wonder of that memory, but she still looked downcast. "I hoped it would understand my devotion. It *burned* me. It mortified my flesh. Look at my hand! I have served the book faithfully all my life, and it injured me. But it exists. I will bear this pain with joy, knowing that my beliefs have been proved true."

Inbecca was touched to the heart. She had never really believed the depths of her aunt's feelings. She had thought of her instead as being in love with her power as the head of her order, but Sharhava took her faith deeply to heart. She reached out to her aunt, but the bonds caused her arms to jerk to a halt in midair. Dunnusk came to Inbecca's aid and slashed the ropes holding her. She scrambled to kneel at Sharhava's feet and put a hand on her knee.

"The Great Book is just a thing, Aunt, truly. A thing of great power, perhaps, but a thing. It couldn't really know anything. It would not understand your devotion. That comes from your heart."

Sharhava shook her head fiercely. "The girl said it talked to her. She heard voices in it. I wanted it . . . I wanted it to speak to me, too." Her sea-blue eyes were despairing. "Inbecca, if you could only know how we all longed for that day when the Great Book would be truly with us. And now it is gone, out of our reach, forever. All we wished to do is serve."

"It didn't sound like that, to be truthful, Aunt," Inbecca said, shocked.

Sharhava's proud shoulders slumped. "I know. The power was too heady. It was more than I could resist. I lost all my good sense. When in your life have you ever seen me lose control that greatly?"

"Never," Inbecca said, and was glad to be able to say it honestly. "You have always held firm before this."

Sharhava held her head high, but tears began to spill from her eyes again.

Inbecca put her arms around her, and found to her amazement that her aunt, who had always seemed a huge and towering figure, was no bigger than she was. Sharhava's spine stayed erect for a moment, then she rested her head on Inbecca's shoulder.

"You will be a good queen," she said. "Give mercy to your enemies."

"You are not my enemy. I love you, Aunt."

"I have not shown mercy," Sharhava said. Inbecca looked down at her. "Those creatures," and Inbecca did not need to ask which ones she meant. "I did what I thought was best. Then I went too far. Your betrothed was right. I didn't believe him at the time. I could not. You must know I have seen the horrors every night since then. Every dream I have is about them, but the damage is done. I cannot undo it, but I will regret it all of my life. I would not admit that before. Pride. Pride should have no place in service to the book. These people here"—she stretched out the black-clawed hand— "these *are* people."

It had cost her something to make that admission. Inbecca's heart went out to her. "Yes, they are. You haven't ever really known any werewolves before, have you?"

"No. I have been in the order since I was many years younger than you. We held ourselves apart from any but true humans. You know what we believe. It is *wrong*. We must go back to the first precepts of the order. The book is to be protected. That is all. The secondary laws, laid down by the first abbots, were different. They passed along to us their certainty that we must also turn back the changes."

"They meant well," Inbecca said. "And at the time, who knows if it would not have been better to reverse the transformations made by the Shining Ones? But in the context of years it cannot be right."

"No. It is too late," Sharhava said miserably. "It is centuries too late. I see that. These, these *people* have all taken on a life of their own. I have come to realize it. It goes against my training, but for decency's sake we must learn to let time pass, as Father Time orders in the faith of my childhood. We scholars have remained in the past. That's not only against Time but Nature. These people live in the same world as we do."

Inbecca was deeply touched. She said nothing, but squeezed her aunt's arm.

The werewolf doctor was sympathetic. "I know it is hard for you to give up your beliefs, Abbess, but it is better for you. Your heart cannot hold hate and remain healthy. It is good for you to let go. Allow me to care for your pain." He took her hand gently in his, and held the amulet above it. He closed his eyes and murmured softly to himself. To Inbecca's relief, the shrunken flesh filled in somewhat, but the skin gradually changed from black to scarlet. She knew she looked shocked, and the healer gave her a weary smile. "Blood supplements the spirit within it once again. In time it should regain its normal color. It has been terribly damaged, but it will serve her now." He set the hand down on her knee and patted it. The fingers trembled as Sharhava squeezed the fingers slowly toward the palm. Inbecca let her shoulders relax. It was the most movement she had seen in the injured hand since the injury had occurred. "I hope that is all that pains you."

"Thank you for your skill, Doctor," Sharhava said sadly, looking at her hand, "but you cannot give me the one thing I need."

Dunnusk's brows lowered over his yellow eyes. "I wouldn't give you that big book again, no matter what."

"Not for myself," Sharhava said, her eyes meeting his with equal fervor. "The girl will need us. The enemy, the true enemy, is still there, watching, he who is master of those . . . those *monsters*. One elf woman, one wizard, two soldiers, will not be enough to stand against a host of thraiks. Who knows what other fiends he has at his command? You must let us go. We have to catch up with them. This time I swear we will protect the book. I will make no demands as to its disposition. I am not fit to make that decision, but our order was created to protect it, and we should fulfill that precept. We *must* go. Can you help me? Will you help me?"

Dunnusk stroked his chin. "*That* is a worthy goal. I will see what I can do." He rose and strode away.

Sharhava was filled with impatience all the while Dunnusk was gone. The fingers of her restored hand fidgeted upon her knee. Inbecca, her arm around her aunt's shoulder, could feel energy thrill through her as though she had been struck by lightning. She had a new purpose, and her fount of energy longed to be free to pursue it. Auric looked a question at Inbecca behind the abbess's back. Inbecca gave him a noncommittal look of concern. She did not want to reveal her aunt's request lest the werewolves refuse it. No sense in giving the other knights hope that would cause trouble for their hosts. If Sharhava had truly had a change of heart, they could do so much good. But would Tildi trust them? If she was in the smallfolk's place, she wouldn't.

The sun had tilted from overhead to an acute angle before Dunnusk came trotting back with Patha in his wake. The silver-haired chieftess looked stern. She wasted no time on niceties.

"Why should I give you freedom before it is time?" she snarled. "The entire purpose of your confinement is to prevent what you say you want to do. I have heard all the stories of your treachery. You have contrived at the death of one entire race and threatened the lives of another. What has changed that will make me believe that you do not want to pursue that cursed book for your own purposes? Who is to say that if it falls once again into your hands you will not come back here and harm us as well?"

Sharhava met her gaze straightforwardly. "Do you know the purpose of my order?"

"Yes, to denigrate and destroy all things that speak that are not humans," Patha said, her yellow eyes ablaze. "We in the south have heard of you for many centuries. Our children are made to obey with threats of the humans in blue-and-white coming to take them away."

Sharhava's face turned as red as her healing hand. "We deserve that. But that was not our original mandate. The Scholardom was formed to find and protect the Great Book from harm. It has more power than any other object ever made by humankind. No matter what you have heard, we helped Tildi Summerbee come this far. If not for us, she might have been set upon anywhere between Oron Castle and the riverside."

Patha said dryly, "Fewer beings might have suffered, had she not traveled in your company."

"I do not dispute that. I have regretted my actions ever since that day. But it was you and your people who showed me our long-held beliefs have no place in my order, not today. Not so long after the fact. You saved me. I will never forget that. We have strayed from our purpose. I would make amends. We will put ourselves into Tildi Summerbee's service."

"She will send you away."

Sharhava bowed her head. "So be it. It may be we cannot catch them now. She and her teacher are wizards. They can fly. They could be all the way to Sheatovra by now."

Patha's eyes glinted, and she jerked her head as though she had come to a decision. "They are not."

Sharhava's head flew up in startlement. "How could you know that?"

Patha made a rueful face. "I know where they are going, and how. If your aims are sincere, Abbess, I will break my promise to Irithe and give you aid. She Who Gives Life knows that I do not wish that book to fall into the hands of anyone else. Do you swear that is your goal?"

Sharhava held out her hands, red and white, palm up. "I swear by all I have ever known and all I hope to be. My knights and I will defend the book with our lives. I hope that I might die without seeing another sunrise if I lie."

Patha's mouth drew up on one side in a vulpine smile. "Then I will see to it that you may fulfill your goal." She stood up and let out a sharp yip. Every werewolf in the camp turned at once to look at her. Patha growled out a series of orders in their harsh guttural language. All over the camp, the tallest and strongest bore down upon the knights and slashed the bonds that held them to the trees. Patha herself cut the ropes on Sharhava's arms and helped her to her feet.

"Now," Patha said. She beckoned to the eldest of her people, Grolius,

Dunnusk, and three others. The six of them leaped together, changing in midair into their wolf shapes. They bunched together, their long noses brushing one another, as Patha literally barked her orders to them. Grolius and the others who had not been privy to the conference began to yelp protests.

The knights hurried to Sharhava and clustered around her, clamoring for information. Auric hushed them.

"She'll tell you in good time! Hold your peace!" the old knight declared.

The others outshouted him, peppering the abbess with questions.

Their voices were drowned out as Patha and the others lifted their noses to the sky and began to howl.

The plaintive cries split the air, like an approaching windstorm strong enough to tear down a fortress. The high tones cut right into Inbecca's brain. She covered her ears and hunched her shoulders. Goose bumps broke out all over her skin, and she found that she was panting in terror. She well understood how the bloodcurdling noise struck fear into ordinary men who had no assurance of the werewolves' motives.

Did she? she wondered.

The howls filled the entire clearing, gathering in strength, riding the harmonics until they formed a single pillar of sound that cast the humans to the ground like ninepins. Then, as if the sound was a solid living being with wings, it lifted high into the air and resounded down the valley.

When she feared she could tolerate the terrifying noise no longer, the werewolves fell silent. Inbecca picked herself off the ground and listened as the wailing, sustaining a life of its own, receded into the distance, seeming to go both north and south at the same time. Soon, it died away. Inbecca's heart slowed to its ordinary pace. She went to put her arm around her aunt and squeezed her good hand.

"Now, we wait," Sharhava said.

They did not have to wait for long. The sky did not remain silent. To Inbecca's surprise, she heard a response. Faint howls sounded in the distance, a lone werewolf calling out from somewhere to the north. A second, nearer voice picked it up and passed it along. Patha and the other elders cocked their ears toward the sound. The knights murmured among themselves.

"What are they saying?" Vreia asked. She no longer looked terrified, but fascinated, as did most of the others. Only a few, like Mey, still harbored fear.

"I don't know," Inbecca replied. She should have known more languages than a little dwarf and elf. Eremi always told her she was too provincial. She agreed with him now. When she returned home, if she returned home, she would find a teacher of languages.

Patha stepped toward Sharhava, changing back to human shape as she came.

"Your opportunity is within your grasp. Do not waste it."

"I will not waste it if I should ever have it in my power again," Sharhava promised. Inbecca was not satisfied with the way her aunt phrased her vow, but Patha was. The chieftess nodded.

"Good, then. Prepare. You will be departing from here soon."

Chapter Seventeen

hee!" Rin cried, her hooves rising and falling in rhythm as she ran upward toward the sky. Tildi clung to her back. Her hair streamed backward, whipping into her eyes and mouth. "This is freedom at last, little one!"

"Keep steady!" Serafina cautioned her, bringing the black-nosed mare up behind the centaur's striped haunches. "Tildi could fall off!"

"Not a chance!" Rin said. "We are one in flight, are we not?"

"I hope so!" Tildi said, holding on to the rough mane. No matter what power flowed through her, no matter how far she had traveled from her home, she was still terrified of heights. She risked a glance down. The tree-tops were receding to the size of broccoli clusters. If they were that small, then the bearkin were tinier yet, and in comparison she was a fingernail paring. Her stomach lurched at the thought. She squeezed her eyes closed.

"Tildi! Be back with us!" Serafina commanded over the rushing wind. "Help me. Study the map. It will take your mind off the heights."

Tildi obediently took the flapping chart and surveyed the section that showed the part of the river that had become visible as a shining pathway to their right. The book obediently opened up to the runes that described the landscape. Tildi saw the ancient name of the province, which she could just barely read, and compared it to the modern chart. The book was far more accurate. Her heart was in her throat, but as they flew up into the thin clouds, she tried to convince herself the landscape below was no more than another piece of parchment.

"Whee-hee-ah!" Rin caroled, spreading her arms out with joy. Leaning over the mane of his horse as though he were in a cross-country race, the prince-troubadour came bobbing up beside them.

"This is marvelous!" he shouted.

"I don't think your mare agrees," Tildi called back. Tessera rolled her eyes so Tildi could see the whites.

"She'll get over it," Magpie said, patting the piebald's neck. "She just needs to know she can trust a road she can't see—oh, I envy you wizards, being able to fly like this whenever you wish!"

"We must be careful of thraiks and other perils of the air," Serafina said sternly. "We have a long way to go, and we are vulnerable." Teryn and Morag appeared to agree with her. Under their helmets, their faces were a study in caution. They rode at fore and flank of the group, constantly changing position to give the greatest coverage. Tildi didn't envy them. It was difficult enough for two soldiers to protect a party while on the ground. In three dimensions, the hardship grew fourfold.

"Storm clouds," Lakanta said cheerfully. "I don't mind which way we go, as long as it isn't back toward those gloomsayers, with apologies to you, Prince. Hard to believe they and the bearkin can exist in the same world, isn't it? I feel free as a bird, and I'm not a whit ashamed to say it."

Free as a bird, Tildi thought to herself. In spite of the stomachful of butterflies, she did feel free of the fetters that had held her back for weeks. What was ahead intrigued her more than frightened her. For a moment, she chided herself—what respectable smallfolk looked forward to possible danger and hardship? But at the moment, not even the threat of thraiks could hold back her joy.

"You look as if you could sing," Magpie said, grinning at her.

"Can you read runes now?" Tildi asked him boldly.

"No, faces. I wish you could see the way you glow. The bearkin seem to have set you free of the unjust strictures your upbringing set upon you."

Tildi felt her cheeks grow hot. Seemliness withdrew even farther from her. She was behaving like a mannerless hoyden, wasn't she? No one in the Quarters would ever talk to her again, even if they could get past her doing magic and consorting with wizards. They would cast her into shame and crow about the downfall of a girl who had forgotten how decent people behaved.

But what did the opinions of those cockerels matter? Olen was waiting for her! The thought cheered her up.

A faint, plaintive sound broke out below, too far away for her to guess from where it came. The howl made her think of her enemy whom they had left among the werewolves. But Sharhava was imprisoned far upriver, no longer free to follow her. The abbess was no danger to her. An answering cry, fainter, came from the thick forest ahead and to the right. *But how could it be werewolves here?* she wondered. Some natural wolf must be calling for his mate, who answered him from many miles away. It was a wonder how far they could hear each other. The thought before she had left home on this adventure would have chilled her to the bone, but how well she knew now that there were worse things in the world than wolves, or things in the shape of wolves.

Magpie looked over her shoulder at the book. "What a wonder!" he exclaimed. "It's better than any chart I have ever seen, whether made by wizard or cartographer."

"This is the whole world," Tildi said complacently. She had come to terms with his friendship with Serafina. They supported each other, and how could that be bad? Tildi had become more aware than ever of people's emotional state. It took an effort not to cry when someone else was sad.

I have become like the book. I reflect reality around me, she mused. It was an interesting lesson that the bearkin had taught her. She felt more clear-minded, and ready for what lessons she had from Serafina while they flew.

Birds circled them, wondering at the ground-people invading their domain. In spite of her discomfort, Tildi laughed at their open curiosity. It was as large as hers.

"They aren't very intelligent," Serafina said, showing her the part of the rune that defined their thoughts. "They still want to know. They fill the cup of learning to the brim as best they can. It isn't a big cup, but it suits them."

Serafina's intelligence occupied a much larger and important part of her thoughts. She must have guessed Tildi's thoughts, and made a sharp gesture with her hand. Tildi stopped her snooping.

Serafina showed more confidence in her leadership. Besides supervising Tildi's lessons, she took grave counsel with Magpie and Lakanta, the other seasoned travelers of the party. They agreed to follow the river instead of the roads, but at a distance, to attract the attention of the fewest wayfarers. They descended only to rest the horses and to lunch when the sun was at its highest. Rin told them that running on air was far less tiring to legs than any road. The runes confirmed it. The horses returned to the sky with more enthusiasm than they had left it. Even Tessera came to enjoy her invisible road.

The moon named the Agate rode the sky, casting faint light on the landscape, but more than enough to see by high above the clouds.

"We should set down," Captain Teryn said, peering uneasily at the last vestiges of orange light that decorated the western horizon. "The river is still visible, but I would feel more confident continuing in full daylight."

"We will bed down after moonset," Serafina declared. "Until the horses tire, I see no reason to halt."

"As you wish, my lady," Magpie said.

"I could run all night," Rin said. "Another hour or so will be fine."

"Melune is all right," Lakanta said. "With a sack of oats to look forward to, she will go on as long as you please, same as me."

As usual, Teryn merely saluted. Her suggestion made, she followed the orders of the company's leader. She gestured to Morag to ride right flank, and she took the left.

Tildi was growing sleepy. With Rin's permission, she leaned forward and rested her cheek against the centaur's thick braids. She cradled the book across her lap, open to the leaf that showed the length of the river. All was secure. One more night over the forest, and they would be with Olen. She could hardly wait to tell him all her adventures, that which he had not seen already in his crystals and glasses.

In her drowse, she felt a familiar urgency. She sat up and looked around. The thin moonlight dyed her friends' faces blue. The sense of worry didn't belong to any of her companions. She looked up and gasped. Silhouettes floated above them, arrowing back and forth across the star-washed sky. The rune imposed upon each was unmistakable. She stiffened in fear.

"What is it?" Serafina asked. Her eyes followed Tildi. "Thraiks! There must be a dozen of them."

"Thraiks!" Teryn exclaimed. The two guards went on alert and spurred their horses to ride the air above Tildi's head. "Descend swiftly, honorable. We will protect you."

"Too many," Lakanta said. "We should have gone down before. This is their hunting time."

"Go, Princess," Magpie said, drawing his sword. "I'll ride beside you. Tildi, keep your head down. Go."

"No!" Serafina ordered, holding out her staff. "Don't move."

"What?" Teryn demanded. She reined back her horse, which reared nervously. "They're above us. Look! They are coming down."

Serafina set her jaw.

"They cannot see us. They can sense the book, but they do not know where it is. The wards protect us. Watch. They can come nowhere within those boundaries." She indicated the faint rune that surrounded them like a crystal sphere. Tildi was so used to it being there, she had almost forgotten its presence. "Bring the horses together. We will be as still as we can."

"Will the warding keep them back?" Magpie asked.

"It should," Serafina said, no longer looking confident. "Don't speak. They can still hear."

"Then we are not safe!" Rin exclaimed.

The sound of their voices had excited the creatures. Swiftly, they all turned in midair and dove toward Rin. The sight of the rune glowing in their dark eyes and the gleam of their teeth made Tildi's heart pound until she feared it would leap out of her chest. The centaur held her place, though she quivered like a rabbit. The thraiks slowed suddenly, their nostrils quivering, then turned away again to make another pass. Serafina held her hand up before Tildi could say anything. She shook her head.

Magpie moved Tessera silently to Serafina's side. "How smart are they?" he asked. "Are they hounds or hunters? Will they figure out what we are?"

"I . . . I don't know," Serafina said uneasily.

"They can see us," Lakanta said. "They can tell we're not birds."

"Is your warding a shell or a stone?" Magpie pressed. "Can they blunder through it? It won't kill them, will it? As Sharhava set it?"

Serafina looked stricken. "No, it will not."

"Then they can pass through."

"We are in peril," Rin said, drawing the whip from her hip. "They are many, but we have the Great Book. We can tear them apart!"

"Hush!" Serafina held the reins of her mare, whose eyes showed whites all around the iris. She whispered to Tildi. "Aid me! We must drive them back." When Tildi didn't move, she shook her arm. "Tildi! Be with me! Control yourself."

"I cannot!"

"Be still, apprentice! Aid me now. If we cannot thwart them, we will destroy them. That is wrong. They are only creatures. They are not evil."

"Kill them," Rin said, her voice rising shrilly. "Kill them all!"

"I am a healer," Serafina said. "No, we must not. It is unnecessary."

"You don't know what they can do," Tildi said. "My whole family died because of them."

A huge thraik was only a few yards away from her, seeking backward and forward, sniffing. Its eyes were blind to the rune, true, but she saw the image in her mind of the thraik that had tried to kill her in the field beside her home in the Quarters. Instead of pupils, it had glowing runes in its eyes, making it terrible and fearsome.

"Tildi, pay attention!" Serafina held her staff on high, drawing pale silver lines upon the sky. *"Ano cnetegh morai!"* A great sign took shape upon the night sky, small and thin at first, but growing rapidly.

Tildi stilled her nerves. She felt for the knife at her belt. Serafina finished the first sign and turned her mare to begin the second. She would have to hasten to catch up. The rune was a difficult one, but she had a good deal of practice at scribing over the past weeks. The voices coming from the book distracted her. Tildi concentrated hard to ignore them. Her hand shook. The monsters kept looking in her direction. How could they not see her? But Serafina must be right. The thraiks swooped back and forth, like plowmen covering a field, sniffing and listening to what their eyes told them was not there. Melune danced uneasily, unhappy with standing on nothingness. Lakanta leaned over and threw her cloak over the stout pony's eyes, all more silently than Tildi would have credited she could do. Protecting them was up to her.

A wall of translucent bronze sprang into being between them and the thraiks before them. Tildi hastened to complete her first rune. The fine lines

jumbled together densely, small enough for the winged monsters to fly around.
She had to close her eyes again and force them to move outward. Suddenly
the rune was like the bars of a cage, ten times taller than the creatures. As
Tildi forced her thought into it, the lines thickened, then spread out like
honey, until a second barrier, deeper in color, formed behind Serafina's. The
influence of the book made Tildi's stronger than the more experienced wizardess. She had only two more to do, but she must hurry. The thraiks, losing
their scent on the one side, began to sally around until they found it again.
The second was easier, though she had to whisper to Serafina to ask for the
incantation. Her fear waned as she followed her master's confident motions.
By the time they completed the third side of the triangle, she was only a
stroke or two behind Serafina. Once the three sides were joined, they stretched
upward and downward to close the bubble around the party. Tildi thought it
looked like the points of a prism. The bronze sheen of the protective magic
picked up light from the Agate and glowed warmly, as if to reassure Tildi
that it was working.

"Well done," Serafina said, examining the double walls of the spell with a
critical eye. "They cannot touch us."

"Can't they hear our voices?" Magpie asked.

"It does not matter," Serafina said. "Watch."

"Why?" Magpie asked, avid as a child over matters of magic. Tildi saw
the gleam of his yellow-green eyes. "What does it do?"

"It will drive them away. That is all we require."

Would the warding be enough to keep them back? Tildi thought it might
have been the hardest thing she ever did, holding still while the fearsome
green-black monsters sniffed around only yards away from her. Their long,
sharp teeth showed in their open mouths as they scented. She clutched the
book to her as a talisman.

Go away! she thought. *Leave! Now! Please.*

"How much longer?" she asked breathlessly.

"Until they are gone," Serafina said. "Be calm. Do not let your emotions
affect the spell."

Tildi blanched. Being close to the book had caused everything she did to
be amplified. She would not let her ancient enemy undo all the good the
bearkin had done her. She thought of Jorjevo and his warm brown eyes,
imagining him instead of the muddy orbs of the thraik. Her memory of his
resonant voice made her feel a little better.

Unable to ignore them, she stared at the unseeing eyes. The book's rune
looked as though it was part of them, taking the place of the pupil, as though
they had been born for no other purpose than to pursue it.

Poor things, Tildi thought unexpectedly, then blanched at the notion.
These were not poor things, but monsters! Yet she could read a good deal of

their emotions in their own runes, those on their chests. Those proved what Serafina had said, that they were animals: intelligent, but animals nonetheless. The huge one circling before her and coming close over and over was curious, growing hungry and bored, and afraid.

Why would a thraik be afraid of anything? she wondered. Then she realized that her friends and relatives had brought down at least one of the monsters in the field beside the farmhouse at Daybreak Bank. They could die while searching for the Great Book. *Then why do it?* Tildi saw in each of them the trace of another's will. Their fate was not their own. They were under orders to search. He who had sent them would be angry if they came back without their prize. The presence behind them was somewhat familiar to her. She had sensed it before. Nemeth had been afraid of the same being. He believed it to be either Father Time or one of the Makers. He was mad, but she did not doubt his terror. These suffered the same dread. She still feared them, but she knew them to be real creatures. She almost felt sorry for them.

Rin could not contain her nerves. Her skin twitched and her eyes darted to follow the thraiks' movements.

"I cannot bear this," she said. "If they do not go soon, I will kill them!"

"No, don't," Serafina said. "I swear they will go. I swear it. Trust me."

"We are outnumbered," Magpie said.

"Don't touch your swords," Serafina said. She spoke soothingly, as if the thraiks could understand her words. "We are harmless. We do not have what they want. How often have you heard of them attacking anyone who has not touched a fragment or a copy of the book?"

Tildi saw Lakanta's face stricken by fleeting grief. "Never," the trader said stoutly. "Hold on, my friend," she told Rin. "They're nothing but big butterflies."

Rin's face twisted, but she held firm for the sake of her friend. "Ugly ones."

"It will not be for long," Serafina promised. "Hold steady, Princess. It begins."

Slowly, Serafina's spell took effect. Tildi watched as the thraiks seemed to forget what they were doing. They broke formation and sailed around beyond the surface of the bubble. A couple of the larger ones sniffed the area thoroughly, then began to squabble between themselves. The smaller ones kept their distance from the shrieking and growling, as though waiting for orders. The biggest thraik hissed fiercely at his rival, for the other could be nothing else, as if bringing the argument to a halt. He clapped his wings hard against his side. The movement propelled him high above the herd. The sky gashed open, making the stars behind it wink out, and the thraik sailed into it. The others looked at the rival. It seemed to shrug, and followed the first. The group disappeared into the blackness one by one. The company watched the stars reappear. No one seemed to breathe for a moment. Serafina broke the silence.

"I apologize to you all," she said. "We should have set down before."

"It's all right," Lakanta said, pounding her chest with the flat of her hand. "I needed to reassure myself that my heart would beat that fast."

"That was an elegant solution, my lady," Magpie said, his voice heavy with relief.

Serafina pursed her lips in a smile as she turned her mare to lead the way down to the nearest clearing. Tildi followed, but not without a final glimpse at the face of the moon. No thraik, and the new warding was intact. She intended that it would remain around them until they were safely in Olen's hands. Still, she was glad Serafina had chosen to show mercy to the thraiks, a thought that was as strange as it was right in her mind.

Chapter Eighteen

n the third day galloping through the skies, Tildi saw the Arown's rune shimmering in the distance long before they came upon the river itself. It was as she had seen it months before, broad and shining, visible through the runes of cloud, tree, and headland that were between her and it. She consulted the map for the town they sought, Lenacru. In the book it appeared as a cluster of the symbols for *ship*, with the words for *house* and *shop* repeated often but in tinier letters, as though they were far less important to the townsfolk than the vessels that provided them with a livelihood.

"How close?" Serafina called to her.

"An hour or a little more," Tildi said, measuring the map with her fingertips.

"Not long," Rin said. "I can smell the water."

"The last bit is always the longest," Lakanta said. "I can't wait to get there! I know a good inn in town where we can get a decent meal and superior beer."

"We have to find Olen," Tildi said. "He is waiting for us."

"He'll find *us*," Lakanta assured her. "He knows we're coming, doesn't he? Well, then, he'll have worked out where we will be."

By the time they met the Arown, the town of Lenacru was in view, occupying a semicircular recess in the cliff walls on the west bank of the river that faced a corresponding bend in the river that passed on either side of a long spit of land. Lenacru was thereby protected from the strongest current, providing a natural harbor. Nearest to the water were broad, gray-roofed buildings of immense size.

"Warehouses," Lakanta pointed out. "The traders and fishermen live behind them."

She pointed. Tildi squinted at the gray-walled, wooden houses in rows on narrow streets. As they came closer, she began to see that the streets themselves were crowded with carts and beasts laden with bales. Sounds began to reach them: the cry of gulls, the murmur of voices, and the creak of axles. How different from the bearkin's lodge, full of song and the trill of birds.

The sun had passed slightly west of its apex by the time they trotted to a halt on the wooden sidewalk that ran perpendicular to the wharves and piers. Tildi was suddenly struck by the fivefold increase in noise, and the hundredfold increase in smells. A wave of rotten fish odor engulfed her, and she screwed up her face in disgust.

"Ah!" Lakanta said. "Makes me feel quite at home."

"So it is true that dwarves like their fish stinking," Rin said. A rheumy-eyed carter eyed her as he passed, hunched over the reins, and she returned the scrutiny fearlessly.

"Indeed we do," the trader said with a grin. "I don't share my kin's taste, I must say. I like mine best in a waterside tavern with a side of sea chanteys."

"And sauced with a brawl or two," Magpie added eagerly. "The Mermaid's Tail?"

"The very same," Lakanta said. "It's just up the road past the warehouse with the red doors, over there." She pointed.

"We can't go," Tildi said worriedly, hugging the book to her. "What about Master Olen? Where is he?" She swept her eye over the many ships along the riverwalk. Many, tethered to bollards with stout cables, bobbed up and down against bundles of cloth-wrapped wood to protect their sides from the piers, but some rode at anchor out in the strand. On none of the decks did she see a man with long white hair and beard and curling black eyebrows, nor could she distinguish his rune among the crowds of people who streamed past them on both sides. If she had not been on Rin's tall back she would have been lost among their knees. The onrush of runes dazzled her.

"Trust the bearkin and Master Olen," Serafina said. She still did not have her confidence back. "If they received word that he will be here, then he will be here. Come, let's find a vantage point to watch the harbor. No one will pay us heed if we stay out of the way. I don't want to draw attention to the book."

"I beg your indulgence, Mistress Serafina," Magpie said with a laugh, "but a man with tricolored hair on a tricolored horse, riding escort upon a dwarf woman upon a shaggy pony, a slender, elegant, dark-haired woman in a green cloak and wizard's robes, two soldiers, somewhat the worse for the road, and in their midst, the object of their protection, a tiny, wide-eyed smallfolk girl wearing boys' clothes and with hair cut shockingly to her shoulders, sitting on the back of a glorious, ebony-skinned centaur with snapping green eyes and a black-and-white-striped pelt and tail and a scarlet silk blouse, is going to excite comment. A small thing like a book bobbing on the air by itself will attract little attention by comparison."

Lakanta laughed but Serafina blushed. "You are right, of course, highness. I . . . have not been out in the world that much," the young wizardess said.

Magpie put his hand on hers where it rested on the saddlebow. "I am sorry. I don't mean to tease."

"I say we leave this spot and go for beer," Lakanta insisted. "I am eager to hear the news since we were last in a town. Master Olen's a powerful wizard. He'll find us. He'd probably appreciate a draught himself."

"Go if you wish," the wizardess said, her eyes scanning the waterfront as Tildi's had done. "I will wait here with Tildi." She put out a hand to the smallfolk. "You may sit behind me on the saddle, if you wish. It would be cleaner than standing on those bollards." Tildi was grateful that her master understood her anxiety.

"What?" Rin asked, her dark green eyes snapping with amusement. She twisted her flexible torso to confront Serafina directly. "Do you think I will abandon my friend for the sake of a glass of brewed grains? I will remain here with her."

"Thank you," Tildi said. She felt safer between the centaur and her teacher than she would have with only one protector.

"I will stay, too," Magpie said. "It would be unwise to divide the party if Olen scoops you up and wants to depart at once. I wish to see the end of this enterprise, come what may."

"Oh, very well," Lakanta said reluctantly. "I see when I am outnumbered. But the bearkin aren't wizards. Who is to know if they got the message garbled or not? We don't know how long we must wait. And how are you going to explain *that* to these folk?"

She pointed at the runes that decorated everyone and everything within sight. Tildi realized suddenly that people had noticed the golden letters and were exclaiming over them. She was horrified.

"We have to warn them not to . . . not to . . . ." In her mind, the humans began to mutate into monsters, wailing that it was evil sorcery, and it was all her fault. "We have to leave at once, master."

Teryn nodded to Morag. The two soldiers quietly divided and guided their horses to either end of the party. The captain unobtrusively put her hand under a fold of her cloak and placed it on the hilt of her sword.

"Don't fear," Serafina said, suddenly calm. "This is not an unworldly place. Do you see?"

Tildi fidgeted, but she drew her attention to a group of men that Serafina indicated. They saw the runes on their chests. A couple of the younger ones reacted with alarm, but the elders among them shook their heads with confidence. One graybeard held out a wooden disk on a string about his neck. He was hard of hearing, she realized. His voice was pitched so loudly that they could hear him halfway down the boardwalk, but what convinced Tildi was that the symbol for ears in his rune was shrunken abnormally though the ears on his head were of normal size.

"Will that amulet save him from a mishap?" Tildi asked. Serafina glanced at it with an expert eye.

"No. The word upon it tells me it is designed to protect against a deliberate spell. The charm upon it supersedes cast magic, of course, but at least you can see they know enough not to meddle with their runes. A few unwise ones might try, but they will soon discover it's a bad idea—I hope before they reach the state of that pitiful knight who perished."

"Shouldn't we leave this town?" Tildi asked nervously. She had not been around so many big people since she left Olen's house. She had forgotten how overwhelming crowds could be. The carts barreling down upon them made her jump, though Rin stared down the drivers, making them veer hard to avoid her. "Should we wait elsewhere?"

"We cannot. We do not know from where Olen will come, or if he is here already. We must be patient," Serafina added, growing impatient. "We shall have to do our best to repair any damage that comes. Stop asking questions! Olen will come when he comes. I do not see the ship of the message. It must not have come yet. We will wait."

And with that Tildi was forced to content herself.

"Ignore them," Lakanta said firmly. "You're a bit of novelty, that's all. You'll give them something to talk about while they're unloading bales of wool. Just think, you'll be the talk of the town for months to come. His Highness is right: one at a time we might be overlooked, but as a group we're a circus show. Enjoy it. You can stare at them as much as they stare at you. Pretend you've paid a penny to see them."

Tildi chuckled nervously, but the trader's advice was good. She studied her surroundings to make herself feel less awkward. Lenacru was very different than the other human towns she had been in. She had never been to any of the fishing villages in the Quarters, so she had no means to compare them. At a distance, though, she could pretend the human fishermen were smallfolk, and therefore not so terrifying.

"There, that's better," Serafina said.

A man passing by let out a long, lascivious whistle. Shocked, Serafina turned to look, and he winked meaningfully at her. Her cold expression made him give her a more careful glance. He noticed the staff in her hand, and quickened his pace. When he reached the crowd of men, they laughed at him.

"Winking at wizards!" the oldster cackled in his loud voice.

Rin snorted. "I would kill him for his rudeness, were I you."

"He appreciates an attractive woman," Magpie said gallantly. "And he's paid for his cheek. His friends will give him no peace about flirting with you."

"What did he think he was doing?"

Magpie was kindly, but his eyes twinkled. "Well, at that moment he saw a girl about twenty years old. That you were bearing a staff he did not notice. Perhaps you can array yourself around with sigils and clouds of light? I would advise it. The men over there are grumbling about the runes, and are looking for someone to blame . . . I suggest you try to look as unapproachable as possible, as quickly as you can."

"She is a wizard. How much more formidable need she look?" Rin asked.

"It has always amazed me," Magpie said, "how much credence people put in what they can see, in contrast to what they know to be true."

Serafina's cheeks were aglow with shame. Tildi glanced up at her master. For a moment, she felt protective of the young wizardess. To ease her discomfort, she sought to distract her.

"Master, there. I have noticed something."

"What?"

"There's a hole in that ship," she said.

"Where?" Serafina asked.

"In the hull, just above the waterline. There." She pointed to a spot in the rune, which consisted of many strong lines wound into an egg balanced on its side. At the left edge, the strong lines were interrupted, and the rune for *water*, with characteristics that met those of the Arown herself, intertwined with it.

"What of it?"

"Should we tell someone? They'd fix it if they knew."

"What's the trouble with it?" Lakanta asked curiously.

"That is the word for decay," Serafina said. "The boards in that spot have rotted through. They might not notice the leak until those collapse inward. If we knew the ship owner, we could inform him."

"What a wonder to be able to see through walls. Can't you simply fix it?" Magpie asked. Tildi looked at him uneasily. "You can see the sound wood around it to use for an example."

"Could I?" Tildi asked Serafina.

The wizardess studied the bobbing rune, a line between her thin brows.

"Very well. It might be a good exercise. Well spotted. I don't believe it could cause any harm, no matter what you do. It would be a kindness to the ship's owner. Go ahead. I will watch to make sure nothing untoward happens. In any case, it will be a very judicious change in a very small part of the rune. If you do not think you can control it, do not proceed. Do you understand me?"

"I do, master." Tildi steadied herself on Rin's back and drew her knife. She trusted the sharp point more than her fingertip. She immediately regretted volunteering to try. It wasn't remaking a man or a road, but any alteration made Tildi nervous.

Magpie's suggestion had been a good one. She studied the part of the rune that stood for sound wood. There were several different kinds making up the ship: oak, hornbark, ash, pliable willow.

The rune was perfectly clear, but too small to make fine alterations. She closed her eyes and pictured it growing in size until it was as big as the ship itself. She heard exclamations from the men on the quay. She opened her eyes. The defect showed up much more distinctly. Tildi could see that the piece had once been oak, polished and varnished like the rest of the hull, but a gouge in it, perhaps from rubbing against other vessels, had caused it to begin to leak.

"Oak," she said aloud. "Pine resin. Paint."

The thin line wavered as she touched it with the knife tip. She could feel the reality of the ship as if she had touched it with her hand. It took but a moment to fix the rotten place, even to shore it up, until it showed as bold as the other lines of the hull, then sealed it with the proper varnish and even the color of paint of the surrounding hull. The ship rocked suddenly. Tildi jumped back, startled. A man's face glared at her from between the tines of the rune.

"Here, here, ye're magicking my ship! Ye wizards, ye! Think'e can meddle with that what doesn't belong ye! Cursing a man's livelihood!"

"We weren't . . ." Tildi protested.

The man spat and shook his finger at her. "Course ye was! Think I cannot read what ye say on yer own lips? And look at all they lines all over here you're tanglin' about. I could ignore 'em, until you see fit to sink her under me!"

"There was a hole in it!" Lakanta exclaimed. "She repaired it. If you want her to change the wood back to pulp and termites, just say so. I'm sure she'll be happy to oblige, you old fool!"

"If you please, good captain," Magpie said smoothly, pressing in between Tildi and the angry sailor. "This is the great wizardess Serafina's latest apprentice. I am sure that you understand how much work goes into learning to be a proper magician. One has to practice everywhere and everywhen. Now, you heard her speak the incantation. It may have sounded like normal speech, but I assure you it is ancient language that has taken her years to learn. She has taken the wood of your ship and made it sound."

"Aye?" the captain asked, beginning to eye Tildi with less hostility. By now, they were surrounded by the crowd of idlers.

"What, just by twiddling about with these fooly words that's on everything, ye can plug a hole?" the old man asked, his protruberent eyes bulging toward Tildi. "What else can ye do with 'em? Can ye make it so's I hear proper again? Hey? I'd pay ye for such wizarding. I got money. I'll bet she don't gi' ye much in the way o' pay. What about it?"

The need he felt suffused his whole being. Tildi almost said yes. The others pressed in, their longing just as poignant. She could help them all. It would take less effort than keeping the quay from changing under their feet. They surrounded her with eager faces, all hoping. Tildi opened her mouth, ready to promise help, then a thought imposed itself upon her with the force of a blow.

If you say yes to one, they will ask for more. And more.

"How about it, girl?" the old man asked. "Eh? Go on, it's a good bargain, isn't it? Well? Answer me!"

A clap of thunder made the men jump.

"How dare you address my apprentice directly?" Serafina demanded, magnificent in her dignity. The young wizardess sat upright on her mare's back, the staff held aloft. The green jewel on the top glowed. "Do you think that magic is to be bought?"

The old man was too old and too stubborn to take the hint. "And why not, lovely lady? Don't ye have to live, like the rest of us?"

"I have money, too!" a thickset man exclaimed. "Got the rheum. It does me lungs in terrible. All it takes is a wave of yer hand, don't it? You can do it. How about it, now?"

They began to press in upon Tildi, clamoring at her, shouting out their wants. They smelled of sweat, onions, fish, and fear. They were afraid of her magic, but desperate for her help. The look on their faces was like that of poor Morag, when he begged her to change him back to a normal man. But she couldn't, for the same reason she couldn't help these men.

"I don't know enough," she said. "I can't do it." Her small voice was swallowed up by their booming demands. "No! I can't! I don't know how!" She felt hemmed in. The voices were becoming agitated, and not just those of the crowd. The Great Book rose higher, and the pages began to turn from one spindle to another.

The old man's white eyebrows rose at the sight of the bobbing scroll. "What's that, yer book of wizardry? Show us the spell to fix ships! It'd be worth a gold coin to ye."

"You helped him," the thickset man persisted. "Why not the rest of us?"

"We can do no more today," Serafina announced. "Stand back!"

"Don't touch it!" Tildi shrieked as the old man reached for the book. The voices sounded angry, offended. They would strike him down! "It will kill you!"

"Aye? The words won't kill but the book does? Is this a trick?" the thickset man asked. "It's a ruse. Get the book, and we'll do the chantin' for ourselves!"

"Let us alone!" Rin said, rearing on her hind hooves, "or I'll ride the whole herd of you down! My friend has said no. Take the one kindness, or may the Father of Winds never give you good fortune again!"

But the rivermen had focused upon the one certain piece of magic that they could see.

"No!" Tildi shouted. She grabbed the book and jumped into the air, making it solid beneath her feet until she was more than two man-heights above the quay. The excited men jumped up onto the deck of the ship, clambered up stanchions and ropes to try and touch it.

Suddenly Tildi and the book were surrounded by a bubble of golden light. It repelled the riverfolk, who continued to beat against it like moths at a lantern.

"Stand away from her!" Serafina sat on her mare, magnificent above them like a queen, the magic reflecting in her eyes. "I said stand away from her. You do not know your peril!"

"All right, all right, lady dear!" the deaf old man trumpeted. He stood back from the edge of the bubble. "My, oh, my, ye didn't have to shove a wall in our faces!"

"I'd say she did," Magpie told him humorously.

Serafina looked severely up at Tildi. "Come down at once. You do not need to behave like a jester. You are receiving the education of a wizard. Pray show some dignity."

Tildi was abashed. She stepped down hastily and took her place on Rin's back, the scroll resting serenely in her arms. "I am very sorry, master."

"Be there nothing that can get you to strike a bargain?" the heavyset man asked hopefully. "We vow to keep our distance from ye."

"I have said we can do no more," Serafina informed him with an austere expression. "Would you challenge a member of the Council of Wizards? It will go hard with you if the town of Lenacru ever has need of a great working, and you had offended one of us."

"And say thank you," Lakanta said, turning to the sea captain. "It isn't as if the wizardess deigns to perform wonders just anywhere. You've been greatly favored, and you ought to know it."

The captain spat again. "Hmph! Well, I've never thought to say blessings to the magical folks, but thanks. Saved me from drowning, near like. Is she sound in the rest o' her timber?"

It sounded like a test. Tildi glanced nervously at Serafina, but she straightened her back to answer.

"It is. I can't say if it's all put together in the right order—I've never been on a boat in my life—but it won't leak."

The captain grinned. "Good for you, lassie. Mother's blessings on ye. Come on, ye oafs. They told you not to touch, and don't touch!"

"But what about them wizard-words on us?" the crowd wanted to know.

Serafina smiled. "They will fade as soon as we are gone. You have my word, as a member of the College of Wizards."

That was good enough for most of them, but the deaf old man wasn't convinced. "If it's not a spell, then it doesn't belong."

"That is true. Please be patient."

"There's no more to see here," Magpie said. "Go on, then." He reached into his pouch and brought out a handful of small coins. "Go on, then. Have a drink on me."

A cheer went up. The old man fixed his bulging eyes on the prince, then snatched the money out of his hand. "It's not what we want, but we'll settle for the kindness. Thanks to ye."

The group departed, chivvying the old man ahead of it, in search of the nearest pub. The captain of the ship made one leap and landed on the pier, his three sailors following him.

"That," Serafina said dryly as the last man disappeared up the grimy street, "is a good example of why we are so reluctant to do any magic at all. It is not just that a change can have repercussions beyond that which we know, but we must take into account human nature. We always want more. Yes, and I am human, too."

"I am sorry, master," Tildi said ruefully. To think that she had offered to repair the ship to distract Serafina from her thoughts!

"Don't be. You wished to do a kindness and practice your skills. Both are worthy aims. Next time keep your mind on your surroundings as well as your goal. This will show you yet another good reason to get the Great Book back where it belongs."

"We cannot get this thing underground too soon," Magpie said.

Tildi nodded, stroking the book in her lap. More than ever, she hated to let it go, but she knew that he was right. All of them were right. At least her effort had succeeded. Serafina sounded as if she had recovered all her authority, and more besides.

"Well!" Lakanta said with a huge outrush of breath. "And how many times are we going to have to fend off a crowd of favor-seekers in this town?"

"Not one more," Serafina said, turning her eyes to the river. She pointed out over the water. "The ship has arrived. Olen is here."

Chapter Nineteen

n a rose-tinted tide, a huge merchant ship glided toward the city. Her rails were cunningly carved to show running horses and leaping fish that seemed to be moving as the ship bobbed on the water. Her hull was freshly painted in white. The prow had been decorated with a most colorful design of waves and sea creatures. The gilded figurehead, which Tildi could not see well in the dimming light, seemed to have the head of a dog. The sails were edged with a wide stripe of gold, and she bore three flags: one with the twin stars of Sheatovra, and two others Tildi did not know. Tildi couldn't see Olen on the deck, but she knew he must be there. Many runes told her the ship was carrying a great many people, but his she knew better than almost anyone else's. She stood up on Rin's back and began to wave with both hands.

"Master! Over here! Over here!"

No familiar figure with long white hair stepped to the rail, but others did. Howls broke out from the ship and echoed across the water. Behind Tildi, a shutter smacked open, and answering howls came from behind her.

"What is that?" she demanded.

"Master Wizard Olen's caught himself a ride on a trading vessel from Sheatovra," Lakanta said. "The crew's mostly werewolves."

"What?"

Lakanta raised an eyebrow. "Stands to reason, if you think about it, which I have never imagined you needed to, but it's my trade and profession. Don't worry about it. Even if they're the same family as the ones who separated us from the knights, if they have taken on Master Olen's commission, they'll treat us well."

Serafina led them to the open dock to which the longshoremen from the warehouse streamed after answering the call. They looked like normal humans. Barefoot, with whipcord muscles shifting beneath their stained and worn tunics, they ran to catch the cables thrown out to them by the men and women on board and hauled at them to bring the white-hulled boat in against the pier. Floating barrels wrapped in rope echoed hollowly as the hull rammed into them. The longshoremen made the cables fast with expert flips of the wrist. One of them, a brown-skinned man in his thirties, grinned at Tildi's eagerness. He signed to the others to help bring the gangplank out from the side of the ship. Tildi jumped off Rin's back to be the first to race aboard. The book in her arms hampered her only a little.

"Master!" she cried.

To her delight, the old wizard was waiting for her at the top of the gang-plank. He looked exactly as she had seen him last. His curling gray eyebrows nearly met over his long nose. They shielded his brilliant green eyes from the warm light of the setting sun. He wore his heavy cloak, the ends of which whipped in the wind. His long hair was neatly braided down his back to prevent it from following suit. His long face creased in a warm smile as he saw Tildi.

"Greetings, my child!" he said. "Still energetic as always, I see. Welcome aboard the *Corona*."

Seeing him made Tildi feel as if she had come home again at last. She threw her arms around his knees and hugged him. The book took to the air to avoid falling on the deck. "Master Olen, I am so glad to see you!"

Olen seemed bemused. "My goodness, thank you for that. It is not necessary, though it is enjoyable." His long fingers stroked her hair. "You have accomplished much since we last met. You are looking well for all your adventures. Looking forward to hearing all of them, if you don't mind."

"I'd love to tell you all of them!" Tildi exclaimed.

"Well, then, first: show me your treasure. Lives have been lost and kingdoms ruined over it. Let us see if it is worth the price paid thus far."

Tildi felt as proud as the winner of a tournament to present the book to him. She beckoned it back to rest in her arms and held it out to him.

"Master Olen, this is the Great Book."

The wizard's eyes twinkled. "What else could it be? Hmm hm hm," he said, chuckling. "Well done, my child, well done. May I?" He lifted a hand.

"Of course," Tildi said. Olen waved a hand.

"*Jirdeg!*" he said.

The book did not move. Olen looked bemused.

"How very interesting. Will you set it in the air, my dear?"

Tildi let it go. The scroll flew into the air. Olen held out his hands, but it did not move toward him. Tildi found it strange that there was any spell that Master Olen could not do, but the book refused to obey him. It hung where Tildi had left it.

"Well, my dear, you must feel honored," Olen said. "We shall take advantage of your talent. Show me."

Olen never touched the fine parchment, but the spindles parted to show the current page Tildi had been perusing, that which described the town of Lenacru, and spun to display the next in sequence. Olen looked as pleased as a child receiving a birthday gift.

"A marvel," he said. "A genuine marvel. But I must not bury myself in its beauties now. I have other people to greet."

Swiftly, she raised her hand and closed it. The book snapped into a tight roll once again and descended into Tildi's waiting grasp.

By then, the rest of the company was making its way more sedately up the walkway, leading their steeds, Serafina at their head. Tildi tilted her head back and whispered to the wizard.

"Master Olen, why didn't you come for me once I obtained the book? It . . . things might have gone differently."

Olen put his long fingers gently on Tildi's head. "Why, I knew that you would reach me, either through your own resourcefulness, which I have found to be surprisingly admirable, or by means of the young lady approaching, or that young man, whom I have found to be a great aid in tight circumstances. I am sorry to say that nothing could have undone what was done. Edynn knew that it was almost certain she would not return from this journey. By my art I was sure of your success, but just to make certain, I employed a friend of yours. I knew you would trust her when no one else would do."

"Yes," Tildi said. "Irithe told me not to tell all my secrets."

"And so you should not," Olen agreed. "I could not leave my post, Tildi. Others were relying on me, and I must continue my researches, the fruit of which you will see in time. And I ventured here, where I knew you must come at last, to escort you the rest of the way. How good it is to see you again, my dear," he said, offering a helping hand to Serafina. Two sailors took charge of her mare and led it away.

"Haroun!" Lakanta shouted. She stuffed Melune's reins into the hand of another mariner and shot past Tildi and the wizards. She seized the most well dressed of the barefoot crew in a powerful embrace and dragged his head down to scrub his hair with her knuckles. "Haroun Betiss! Look at you, you cub!" He returned the hug, and for a moment it looked as though the two of them were going to engage in a mock wrestling match. Clearly, they were good and old friends.

Olen drew Serafina close and tucked her hand into the crook of his arm. "Serafina, I share your sorrow. My acquaintance with your mother went back centuries, and our friendship not that much younger. Forgive me." The green eyes were solemn. "I recall many happy times, which I look forward to sharing with you in time. I honor Edynn's memory. I could not countenance a world without her, and now I must."

"Master Olen, you honor me," Serafina said, her voice low. "You have put my grief into words. That is exactly how I feel. I did not think I would survive it, but I did. I knew it was coming."

"As did I," Olen said, putting a kindly hand upon her arm. "But foreknowledge is not preparation. It wasn't a surprise, per se, but it was a shock. There will be time one day to heal, perhaps even on our voyage to the south. We have much to do before we can rest, and we must remain vigilant."

Serafina straightened her spine. Tildi almost smiled. Olen had a way of inspiring anyone with his words.

"We shall, master. Thank you. It is good to see you again."

Olen bowed and released her hand. "The joy is mine. Princess, welcome. I have a message of greetings for you from your brother. Your clan is well, and they are moving to their winter home."

Rin bowed at the waist to him. "I have been concerned, but there was no way to get news on our journey. I was concerned with my friends' well-being. Thank you for the tidings."

"The honor is mine. Ah, Lakanta, greetings," he called. "I hope it has been an educational journey thus far?"

"Yes, indeed," Lakanta said, freeing herself from the embrace of the captain. She gave the slender man a hearty slap on the small of his back that sent him stumbling. Beaming, she went to Olen and shook his hand heartily. Her blue eyes shone with glee.

"What a wonder it is to see Haroun again! I haven't seen him since he was a pup, hanging about his mother's skirts, trying to take in all the details of a good bargain. And now he has his own trading string. Captain of three ships! And some fine skills of his own."

"Captain Betiss has been good enough to trade with my house," Olen said. "Silvertree quite likes him, though perhaps not all of his friends. One young ruffian spent a good three days in one of the cellar roots until she saw fit to release him. Hmm hmm hmm." Olen chuckled to himself. "I believe he lost the last ship to the south and had to hire a skiff in Tillerton to take him home."

A fierce glint in the otherwise mild-looking man's eyes made Tildi take a step back behind Olen's knees. "He is a werewolf, too?"

"Of course," Olen said. "The whole crew is. They are excellent sailors as well as merchants. Who else knows so much about the moons of Alada and their tides? I would count absolutely upon their instincts to sail us safely to our destination."

"If you say so, Master Olen," Tildi said doubtfully, which made him chuckle again.

"It is not I, but your companion who gives him his character. I trust your judgment," he added to Lakanta.

"And well you should," the trader said, looking pleased with herself.

Magpie waited on the swaying bridge for his turn to greet the old wizard. The green eyes glinted at him.

"I knew you had received my message, highness," Olen said. "Well done. I know you have been a great help to my small friend here."

Magpie smiled at Tildi. "It was my pleasure," he said. "It isn't every day one is called upon to save a world. In this case, it was my own country. Bad as it is, I do like to think that I prevented the damage from being worse. I would have gone, no matter what it cost me. And,"—he sighed—"it did cost me. But I would have paid the price willingly."

"Ah, yes. That." Olen's mustache lifted a little at the corners. "We will see what the future holds. In the meantime, be welcome."

"Thank you, Master Olen," Magpie said. He paused. "Perhaps, later, if you don't mind, I would ask a favor."

"I think I can guess what it is," Olen said with a knowing smile. "I have brought my crystals. We will see how your ladylove fares. Although I can tell you already: she does well by her wits."

Magpie sighed. Then Inbecca was safe. "You have relieved my mind already, sir."

"My pleasure." Olen smiled next at Teryn. "Captain, I may not be the one to thank you for your service. That honor belongs to your lord."

"I see," Teryn said stiffly. Magpie could tell that she felt disappointed, even dishonored by the omission.

"My lord Halcot," Olen called softly.

One of the tall men standing in the bow turned about. Bright hair surmounted by a thin gold crown with a brilliant blue sapphire in the center capped a suntanned and red-cheeked visage. Deepset, bright blue eyes peered out from under corn-colored brows. A short beard, cut to an elegant point, emphasized the strong chin. He wore a tunic of bright red with a white flying horse outlined in gold upon the breast over practical trousers and seaman's boots.

Captain Teryn startled, then bowed deeply. Morag followed suit a trifle more slowly. Smiling broadly, Halcot stalked over to them.

"Well, then, well met. Captain, Olen has kept me apprised on what he could of your progress. I am glad to see that you and Morag have not failed in your duty to me."

"We have striven to serve," the captain said, straightening up and jutting forth her chin. "It has not been an onerous duty. Mistress Summerbee has given no trouble."

"But circumstances have," Olen said. "Well done for reaching us so efficiently."

"You deserve my thanks and praise," Halcot told them. "I have brought the rest of your company. Take your place at their head as you deserve." He gestured toward the stern of the vessel. About twenty men and women in Rabantae's livery stood there. As Teryn stared, they raised mops, paintbrushes, and hammers into the air and cheered wildly.

"Hail to our captain!" cried a man. "Hurray!"

"Hurray!" the others chorused, hoisting their tools on high. Magpie realized with a grin that they had been put to work on the voyage by the enterprising young ship captain.

"Hail to our sergeant!"

"Hurray!"

"Thank you, Your Highness," Teryn said, holding herself more proudly. Her cheeks flushed with pleasure. She saluted again, and marched toward the cheering company. They rushed to salute her and clap Morag on the back. The guards were proud of them. Magpie was glad.

The second tall man made his way more slowly to Olen's side, a deeply disapproving expression on his face. Descending suddenly from vicarious triumph, Magpie felt as winded as if he had been thrown off his horse. His father, here? He sank to one knee. When no words were said, he peered upward through his hair, which had been tossed untidily by the onshore breezes. His father glared down at him.

Soliandur of Orontae always looked, said a minstrel who had once stopped over one cold autumn night and was not asked to stay after dinner, as though he had not slept well in years. His long oval face, so very different from any of his sons', was the color of walnuts, and shaded darker in half-moons underneath his eyes and at the corner of his pinched mouth. His hair was the same shade as Magpie's, though shot through with startling white streaks. More white, Magpie noted with shame, than had been there when he had last seen his father. His fault. No one needed to say it; he knew it.

"So you live," the king of Orontae said, surveying his third son. "I thought you were dead."

"Would you have preferred it?" Magpie asked, unable to help himself. His father was silent for a long while. "I see," he said sadly. "Nothing has changed."

"It's not like that at all," Halcot said, closing the distance between them with a long stride. "My brother king was deeply concerned for your safety." He looked from one to the other, a bemused expression on his open face. "Well, *I'm* pleased to see you. When you disappeared from the hall . . . well, you caused a good deal of talk."

"My brother!" Soliandur exclaimed. His face went very red.

Halcot clapped his brother king on the shoulder. "We need not talk about it. That's water under the bridge and long down the river. It's what caused us to agree to commission the ship when Master Olen sent us word it would be needed. But where is your ladylove, lad? She went after you with purpose in her eye."

"She . . . chose to stay with her aunt," Magpie said.

His father gaped at him. "Boy, you have brought endless disgrace upon my house and the house of your ancestors yet again! I weathered the storm of humiliation that fell upon us when you left that night, from each and every noble who serves the Tiger of Levrenn. The master wizard here has been at pains to assure me that you left for good reasons—but how dare you return without Princess Inbecca *this* time?"

Magpie could stand it no longer. He raised his voice to overpower his father's.

"She *chose* to stay with her aunt!" he bellowed. Everyone on deck turned to look at them. Seeing the shock on his father's face, he dropped his eyes. "I did not abandon her. It was not my choice. I would have brought her. I would prefer to have her away from the Scholardom. They do her no good."

"You could have borne her away," Soliandur said. Magpie gawked like a street urchin.

"Father, you've known Inbecca since she was a baby. Do you really believe that I could bring her where she did not wish to go?"

Halcot hid a smile behind his hand. "From what I have seen of the young lady over the years, brother, I believe that the lad speaks no more than the truth. I would not call her willful, but rather strong of purpose."

Soliandur frowned, unsatisfied. "But what *is* her purpose?"

Magpie was reluctant to say. How would he explain a convenient bank of fog and an ambush, a hurried conference, followed by a midnight ride to meet a pack of bearkin who listened to the pulses of the earth?

"It is complicated," he offered, knowing that his words sounded weak and inadequate.

Soliandur glared. "'Complicated'? How could it be more complicated than interrupting the joining of two dynasties, before every important guest in the northern continent? Your mother usually has an explanation for your behavior, but even she was hard-pressed to find an excuse. Your antics over the years have caused me much embarrassment and worry, but this was greater than the sum of everything else."

Magpie hung his head. "I am sorry, sir. I thought I had made my meaning known to my lord Halcot, but there was no time to explain further. If you had only seen what I saw in Oron Castle. Sir, I believe that as bad as things turned out, we kept it from being far worse. I had to be there. For the sake of your kingdom, sir, and for every living being in it. Including, I do have to say, myself."

"Well, then," Soliandur said. Magpie couldn't tell if he was mollified or not. The king turned to shout. "Cortin!"

A page came running up, holding a package wrapped in oiled leather. Magpie recognized the shape and raised his eyes to his father's. Soliandur looked a trifle embarrassed, but his voice held all its usual bluster.

"Thought you might like to have this with you. You left it behind when you went."

Magpie unwrapped his precious jitar and tried the strings. They only needed a bit of tightening. The wood was intact and looked as if it had been newly polished. He raised his eyes to his father's. "I cannot tell you what this means to me, sir."

"Perhaps. Perhaps not," Soliandur said. He cleared his throat uncomfortably. "Once you were gone I was treated to hours-long tirades on your virtues. As if I wasn't aware of them myself. Still, I hear my brother here nearly stabbed you to the heart before the betrothal ceremony. I'm sure you deserved it."

"I rather fear I did, sir," Magpie said sheepishly.

"No doubt you did."

"Thank you, sir."

Soliandur glanced away, but not before Magpie had seen in them something that had not been there for years: love. "It's nothing. Your mother is worried about you!"

Magpie felt his heart swell. "I will send her a message, sir."

"See that you do." Soliandur backed off, as though unable to bear another moment of raw emotion. "By the stars, I could use a drink. Is there anything fit for purpose aboard this vessel?" He stalked away. Magpie turned to Halcot.

"I know I have you to thank, my lord. For bringing him. For this." He stroked his precious jitar, glad of the feel of the smooth wood, and the hum of the light song the wind played in its strings. He felt as though a missing dimension had been restored to him. No, two dimensions. When he took a deep breath, it was as though his heart expanded with his lungs.

"Not me," Halcot said. "It was all his idea. Once he learned you lived he couldn't wait to see you. He holds back, son. He's afraid of falling over the precipice if he says one kindly word too many or one more compliment, but the love is still there. Admit I was surprised. I'm used to his outbursts; known them of old. But you'd have been gratified if you'd seen him when word came back that the Oros Valley had been destroyed, and you not seen or heard from."

Magpie held himself stiffly. "I am sorry to have caused so much worry."

Halcot waved away the apology. "I think the concern was good. It unlocked a door in your father's heart that has been closed for years. But what good are regrets? You and your companions have done a worthy thing! Now that the Great Book has come this far, we will ensure that it will go the rest of the way back to its place. Master Olen is being unnecessarily mysterious about where in Sheatovra we are going, but he will have to tell someone sooner or later. Perhaps you can help persuade him to loosen his tongue. Now, I wish to pay my compliments to the young lady who has made it possible. Come with me." He slapped Magpie on the back.

Tildi, of course, was tongue-tied to be addressed with respect by a king, but Halcot had the gift of diplomacy. Magpie left him drawing her out about her experiences on the road, and went to see to his horse.

At the rear of the vessel a ramp had been fixed to allow horses to descend to the middle deck, an enclosure that also held livestock. The first horse Magpie spotted was Olen's beautiful mount, Sihine. The shimmering silver-white animal bowed its head to him. Feeling honored to be recognized, Magpie bowed back. Sihine gave him a curious look that echoed that of its master, and went back to its feed.

Tessera had been stabled beside his father's favorite riding horse, a pale gray gelding named Honpera, who had never shared his father's animus for his third son. They nickered at one another. Honpera was a savvy one. He stretched his nose in the direction of the feed box. Magpie found a bag of treats hanging on a nail above it. Honpera had a sweet tooth. He offered a handful of the sticky biscuits to both horses.

As he returned abovedeck, he could hear Soliandur's voice rising peevishly over the thuds and bumps of crew loading cargo. When he emerged, he could see the kings and wizards all gathered about Captain Haroun.

"What do you mean, we do not take sail? We'll lose the wind before too long," Soliandur said peevishly.

The werewolf captain was unmoved by the dignitaries confronting him. "Pray listen, honored ones," he said, his thin face respectful. His accent was typical of the south, thick with slurred consonants and sudden gutturals.

Magpie tilted an ear, but it scarcely required keen hearing to discern what Captain Betiss referred to. The sound of howling came again, not from the warehouse where the longshoremen had awaited the ship, but from farther away. It was echoed on the pier by the workers, and picked up by the sailors themselves. Halcot frowned.

"Too much echo. Can't pick up what they're saying."

"They say," Betiss said patiently, "that we cannot set sail yet."

Little Tildi stood by Olen's knee. Every time a fresh howl went up, she quaked. Magpie hurried to insinuate himself into the conversation.

"Is there nothing we can do, Captain?" he asked. "Is it a matter of a fee or a visit to a dignitary that is missing?"

Haroun smiled, showing his sharp teeth. "No, honored one. I see you are experienced in the ways of the watermen. It is nothing like that. We must wait, that is all. The eclipse has not come yet."

"An eclipse?" Magpie asked keenly. "I had no idea one was foretold."

"No, master," the werewolf said, his expression one of pity for someone too stupid to understand his meaning. "*The* eclipse."

"It is all right, highness," Olen said, his even tones meant to soothe Soliandur. He was the only one of the group who was not put out by the setback. "I foresaw this. It is right. We will wait."

"But the runes," Tildi said, her small face set. Magpie guessed that she had been putting forth her argument while he was out of earshot. "The town is in danger while we are here."

Olen shook his head. "Lenacru must put up with us for a while longer, I fear."

"Can you turn them off? Can you block the magic from touching them?" She held the scroll up to him.

"The power of the Great Book is far beyond me, Tildi."

"She has been maintaining the runes of what is around us, to prevent mishaps," Serafina said, and explained the process.

"I see," Olen said thoughtfully. "Most admirable. So you see it as your responsibility, Tildi? And you have been a good teacher, Serafina, to show her how to fix a problem rapidly and without thinking too deeply. A skill useful to any wizard—or any soldier—and make no mistake: this is a war in which we are engaged."

Serafina dimpled, and her pale face took on a becoming rose color. "Thank you, Master Olen." Magpie gave her an encouraging grin. She looked grateful and embarrassed at the same time.

Olen turned back to Tildi. "You have borne too much of this burden yourself, though it was a good experience for you to learn. We two will take it in turns to share it with you now. I welcome my chance to learn more about this marvelous artifact while there is time—I hope that there is time. The enemy has yet to move against us directly. He will not wait for much longer. I have seen a gleaming silver weapon, but the shape of it has not been made clear yet."

Tildi looked down at the book, which spun in her hands. Magpie leaned over her shoulder, but he saw nothing he could recognize, silver or not.

"There is much to do while we do wait, but not all at once," Olen said. "You must wash and eat and tell me all your adventures. I know much, but because you were hidden from me, I could see only portents, then the impressions that remained upon the land and air after you had passed. You can be seen, as you know, but it is good to know that the protections that Edynn laid upon you and which you maintained after her death withstood even an old friend like me. That means that an enemy, with no claims upon your thoughts, cannot penetrate with any knowledge. He has missed many times, but he is intelligent and growing impatient."

He led them all into the main cabin behind the wheel. The room, as tidy and well made as any Magpie had ever seen on a sailing vessel, had been arranged as a drawing room. Three bunks lay in alcoves beneath deep windows that overlooked the starboard, port, and stern of the vessel. Some of the barefoot sailors followed them in and arranged folding wooden seats in a circle facing a trio of grand chairs lapped with tapestry and cushions. Olen stood before the center chair and waited for the two kings to be seated in the other two. A scribe wearing the livery of Olen's servants in his home, the living wonder Silvertree, spread out his tools on a small desk that jutted out from one of the bulkheads, and took up a sharpened quill. The wizard gestured to the others.

"Pray make yourselves comfortable. I call this second Council of Elders, and offer my congratulations and greetings to the company, formerly under the guidance of the Master Wizard Edynn and now under her daughter, the equally esteemed Master Wizard Serafina. In the names of the lords of the noble countries of Orontae, Rabantae, and the nation wherein my own home lies, Melenatae, I bid you all welcome."

Magpie chose the U-shaped seat at the farthest point of the circle from his father. The jitar in his hands provided something for him to clutch. Soliandur paid him little attention. He sat drumming his fingertips on the arms of his chair, staring at nothing.

"Now," Olen said, sitting down and clapping his hands upon his knees. "Tell me all."

Chapter Twenty

veryone spoke at once. Lakanta clapped her hand over her mouth and laughed.

"It's Tildi's story," she said. "Let her tell it. We'll all join in if she's missed something."

Serafina inclined her head. "Agreed."

Tildi blushed. The book in her arms almost seemed to nudge her. Her shoulders relaxed. "So much has happened. I'll try, but I am sure I have forgotten so much."

"I am sure it will all come along as soon as you try," Olen said. "Tell me the thing that comes first to your mind."

He always did have the means of bringing out her best. Tildi took a deep breath, and began to speak.

By the time she paused, her throat dry, her eyes sagging closed of their own accord, the sky visible through the square ports were dark except for the gleaming runes that named each and every thing on board the *Corona*, and a hint of pink lightening the inky blue in the eastern sky. Captain Teryn's contingent of guards had been assigned in turn to serve the company. They set up a trestle table, laid it with a white cloth and priceless gold and porcelain dishes encrusted with gems. Tildi hardly knew what she ate, though she remembered savory tastes and a touch of honey afterward. Small dishes of hearty food brought on board from cookshops along the quay were offered to her during the course of the evening. Wine and water were always at hand, offered by silent-footed guards in red-and-white livery.

Crewmen had been passing the open door, leaning in as they scrubbed the floor for the ninth time, or gave a touch of strong, pine-scented varnish to the framework, or loitered with a lantern as they made the rounds on watch. Olen didn't mind their listening in, so she didn't either. When she swallowed, a big man with deep lines bracketing molded red lips bowed solemnly to her and offered her a chased golden wine cup that looked in his hands no larger than a songbird's egg. She accepted with gratitude, and swallowed the sweet red nectar within. The wine spread its warmth through her body and stopped the shivering of her tired muscles that she had not even perceived until then.

Halcot nodded to himself. "What wisdom you showed, smallfolk, providing Prince Eremilandur with the means of restoring himself in the case of malign magic."

"Truthfully, Your Highness," Tildi said, "it was more of an accident than anything else."

"Coupled with my curiosity," Magpie said. "But I would not have been restored were it not for her three gifts."

"You have my thanks, young woman," Soliandur added. "Though I don't understand what it is you did." Tildi blushed.

"She rewrote me, Father," Magpie said. "As if I was a story that ended badly."

Soliandur gave him a sour look. "A pity she could not have given you more character."

Magpie bowed. "Your servant, sire. Tildi could not create what Nature had failed to provide."

"But I couldn't save that poor young man, the knight. He didn't write his rune down. He died." Tildi shuddered, recalling how Bertin had looked when his overtaxed body had succumbed. "I wish I had done it for all of them."

"Even the Scholardom, as cruelly as they treated you?" Olen asked, his curling brows high on his forehead.

"Yes," Tildi said decisively, after a moment's thought. "Even them. It was horrible. No one is evil enough to die in that fashion."

"Well, then, who shall say we must not all have the same protection?" Olen asked. He pointed his staff toward a cupboard built into the wall. "*Ano srdeg ia!*"

A gleaming square like a piece of solid sunshine flew out and landed before the wizard. It was a sheet of polished gold or bronze half the height of a man. Its own rune glimmered in its surface like a reflection. "You see your new adornments, written large upon your bodies. We shall take copies, like good scribes, of all of our origins. Should the worst happen, each of us can be returned to our original state. That is not to say, returned from death. If you cross that border, my friends, there is no turning back. The body might be revived, but your spirit will have returned to Father Time. All of our fellows upon this task will be inscribed hereupon, to give us a record to which we may refer in case of an attack by an ill-intentioned wizard. What say you all? Are we agreed, then?"

A few nervous murmurs, then Halcot sat up. "Of course we want protection from malign magic. We *are* guarding against a wizard, aren't we?"

"You are so easily persuaded by words," Soliandur said, frowning. He gestured angrily at the sigil that glowed like a second heraldic device upon his slate-blue robes. "They are but words, a wizard's trick—no offense to you, Master Olen."

"None taken, but you ought to believe in your son's own account of near disaster."

"But how can a gleam of light be dangerous?"

Halcot cleared his throat. "Brother, trust my word! Ah, but you have not seen the Great Book before. I was present at the first council meeting."

Soliandur pursed his lips. "My son represented me there, as you know. He returned with many stories such as one might hear around a feastday fire. I see a scroll that floats upon the air. That is little more than a ruse performed by prestidigitators to entertain me in my court."

Halcot raised an eyebrow at him. "Are you suggesting that I am so easily fooled by a trick?"

"I cannot say what you find credible or incredible. I cannot believe in it. If the book is so powerful and dangerous, why has it not been destroyed?"

"It must not be destroyed," Olen said. "Do you not realize that is how Orontae came to lose an entire river valley? That came from the ruin of a small piece of parchment from the book's pages. There is tremendous power in words."

"You would say that, Master Olen," Soliandur said, his dark eyes snapping. "Such rhetoric is why magic has more influence in this land than it deserves."

Magpie snorted. He thought his father had done with being unreasonably stubborn. He pointed toward the glimmering word that lay between them on the floor like an elegant hand-tied rug. "Father, if you want to test the power of the runes, run your foot through that one, then jump back. I am not certain what will happen."

"I will not jump," Soliandur said harshly. "A king does not flee shadows. Do not try to make me behave like a mountebank."

"Very well, then, Father, allow me."

Cautiously, Magpie scuffed his toe over the least little finger of the rune that he hoped only said *deck*. The subtleties of the ancient language were myriad. It would not do to destroy the ship that was to bear them to Sheatovra. The tendril of light detached and withered to nothingness. Soliandur looked down. Nothing seemed to have happened. A yell from one of the sailors made them all leap from their chairs and rush to the door.

In the pale light of sunrise, they saw a sailor, legs akimbo, straddling a gap in the deck, his body half changed between man and wolf. He clutched a pail of varnish to his chest with one arm. The kings looked toward his feet. A board in the deck had gone missing. The seaman spat.

"What in the void? Wizards! Curse them!" He must have felt eyes upon him, for he looked up. At the sight of two kings, a prince, a centaur princess, and two master wizards looking at him, he assumed full wolf shape and leaped away from his precarious post. "Respect, sirs and ladies, respect to you!"

His mates, who had been distracted from their own tasks at the sound of his yell, came to examine the hole and exclaim over it. They had a brief discussion, then one ran to get a new timber to lay in place, and another for hammer and nails to secure it.

"It is more subtle than I thought," Halcot said. "I'd never have guessed that each board has its own name in the word."

"It's straightforward," Magpie said, offering an apologetic grin to the sailors, now busy measuring the wood, "though I cannot read the language well. Master Olen will probably come and take me by the ear for meddling blindly."

"I think I can forgive you," Olen said mildly. "A demonstration was very much in order. Wasn't it, my lord Soliandur?"

The king of Orontae was solemn. "This gives me much to think about." He eyed his son closely. "A good deal to think about. The rune upon that gold sheet will heal one?"

"No, sir," Magpie said. "But it will give *Tildi* the model she needs to restore you."

Soliandur shook his head. "Such a lot to think about. How would one ever guess that the world would turn upon such ordinary things as a book and a smallfolk girl?"

"As you will, my lord," Olen said. "Let us rest for a time. We will reconvene later today, when the rest of our party is complete."

"Complete?" Halcot echoed. "With the arrival of Mistress Summerbee and her companions, we are complete."

"Not so, my lord," Olen said. "And I hope to add a further ally later on. That remains to be seen. Oh, indeed, yes." He waved a hand. The werewolves measuring the piece of wood jumped, and the missing plank reappeared just where it had been before.

Across the deck, Magpie heard a muttered curse from one of the seamen. "Wizards."

The kotyrs began to diverge from their initial instruction to head in the direction of the last known location of the Compendium. Knemet let them follow their noses. He had no idea if the bearers had continued toward the southwest, or if they had another goal altogether. So much of the continent still lay before them. The thousands of silver ribbon-shaped chimera spread out across the landscape, seeking the rune, the meaning of and the reason for their existence.

A kotyr in the southeastern ranges of Ivirenn detected a sign of the rune and nearly went mad with excitement racing toward it. In Knemet's mind, he saw the ground racing beneath him, the sky wheeling overhead. He had flown on pegasus-back that swiftly only once. One of Boma's special creations, the winged steed was too much for a non-horseman to handle. All the Makers had tried their luck on the pegasus's back, and returned to earth terrified or exhilarated. The wealthy merchant who had commissioned them took them away, laughing. Still, that moment of breathless excitement was never to be forgotten. Knemet had it then, without having to risk his neck on high. What was it that the kotyr had detected?

The competing visions in every part of his mind almost made him dizzy. Knemet let go of them so he could concentrate upon the one that offered promise. The kotyr raced over stony, unfruitful wastes, glided over knobbly roots and through grasslands upon which grazed herd animals who glanced up at him, then went back to their browsing. Knemet became aware that more of the kotyrs had picked up the same scent. Near. It was near! Had the book made it to the western banks of the Arown?

The kotyr overtopped a huge stone at the edge of a field. Knemet had one glimpse of the expanse of golden crops before it dived down into the earth. The sunlight disappeared. Knemet's mind's eye, unlike his body's, needed no time to adapt to the darkness. Tiny runes, each with its own mark of creation, became streaks as the kotyr tunneled toward its prize. What were the wizardesses doing underground with the Compendium? Knemet wondered. He did not attempt to redirect the lithe beasts. They knew what they were doing. They had only one objective in their lives.

More kotyrs joined the first, circling the rune with the satisfaction of hounds who had brought down their prey. Knemet spotted a curl of white parchment. The book was there! He made ready to summon the thraiks. Then, as the kotyrs circled around, he had a better view of the object.

The rune that drew them came from a small roll of parchment. It protruded from what remained of a rotted leather pouch. Clutching it in the pebbly bones of what had been a long, slender hand was a skeleton. By what was left of a dark green wool tunic and a heavy leather hood, it was that of a man, probably a scholar. Knemet was not a fanciful man, but the clothes looked like those of a well-to-do scholar. By the appearance of the remains, he had been dead a very long time. The other contents of the bag had been ruthlessly turned out and scattered beneath the body. The kotyr rooted through the murdered man's possessions a second time after his shameful and shallow burial, then raced away, unmoved, the victim still unfound by his grieving loved ones, themselves fifty years dead.

Such scrutiny gave Knemet little satisfaction. He saw through their eyes, first time in how long since he had seen the outside world. But it meant he would see through all subterfuge. The Compendium could not be hidden from the kotyrs. So far they had eluded him by means of the simplest spell possible. He was rusty. It didn't matter now. He would find the book and get it back.

Chapter Twenty-one

The book spun in air, its pages reeling from one spindle to the other, gleaming white in the noonday sun. Tildi barely felt that she was controlling it. It seemed as though it was delighted to display its gorgeous illuminations to an interested audience. Serafina stayed close to her to offer advice, but it was scarcely needed. She knew how to keep it hovering with a mere thought, and was able to stop it unfurling the moment she was asked. Magpie sat at a distance from the small circle, his fingers making tunes on the jitar strings to which the book appeared to dance. The kings watched from their carved seats with mild curiosity, but Olen was rapt. His curly eyebrows contorted into more shapes than Tildi could ever have credited.

"What the Shining Ones created was a work of art, Tildi," he said. "Well and truly I can see why one was never in danger of mistaking a copy for the real thing. For how could you ever see the sun, then believe in the light from a candlewick?" He shook his head. "It would require lifetimes of study just to peruse it, let alone begin to understand how those wizards of old were able to set such a spell in motion. To have everything in the world perfectly represented, so perfectly that the runes change with the changing of the object is a marvel. No one had ever succeeded before in capturing all of reality in a symbolic fashion as they had, and none since. At least, none of whom I have heard. I must be fair, of course, but I believe my sources are fairly comprehensive. Will you roll it back to the Necklace Mountains? I would like to see that image again. I believe they have changed significantly since the map I have at home was drawn."

Tildi urged the scroll to turn, taking up yards of the shimmering white parchment until it was open to the rune he wished to examine.

"What draftsmanship," Olen said. "Do you think that it began with one wizard who had a talent for calligraphy, or did the talent develop as they enlarged upon their idea for a comprehensive volume?"

"I couldn't say, master," Tildi said.

"Nor I," Serafina said. "I wish we could ask the Makers. I have so many questions."

"As have I," Olen said. "Even studying the copies I found myself wishing that their time was not so long gone. I can find images of them in my crystals and bowls, using ancient scrying spells, but I get so little that it frustrates me. Ah, but that is a scholar of magic for you. The more we know, the more we want to know!"

Tildi felt as though she had come home. Seeing Master Olen in the midst of the white wooden bulkheads reminded her of the happy days she had lived in Silvertree. He had returned to his familiar ways of discussing magic as though she were an old compadre of his instead of the rawest student he had ever taught. Serafina, too, felt the pull of his companionable manner. She started out a trifle suspicious that he would look down upon her, as one might be of a known authority in one's chosen subject, but Olen never threw one's shortcomings back at one. Serafina began to relax. Tildi saw her warm to him. What gave her the greatest confidence was his having her take responsibility for inscribing the crew's runes upon the sheet of gold.

The werewolves accepted the explanation that it would protect them against transformation with little concern. Most of them had found occasion to overhear Tildi's description of the battle in Oron Castle. She had no doubt that the story had spread to those not near enough to listen.

"We change with the moons, will we or won't we," Captain Betiss said with a shrug. "Such a notion might frighten you humans, but not us. So we change a little more than usual."

Tildi had sneaked a glance at Morag, who waited his turn with the rest of his company in the belly of the ship. She was glad no one had dragged him forward to tell his story. The Rabantavians all knew it, and if the werewolves accepted it casually, that was up to them.

"Will you at least permit us to offer you such protection as we would give to our own company?" Serafina asked.

Haroun Betiss showed a glint of the humor that Olen said he had. "If it makes you feel better. What do you want us to do?"

Most of the work fell to Tildi. Serafina had instructed each of the crew to come forward one at a time. Tildi's task was to copy the rune onto the imperishable metal. Serafina stood over her with an eagle's eye, correcting her anytime she made a mistake. Tildi made a few, but her practice at restoring the roads and forests along their long journey had made her a speedy and expert draftswoman. One after another, she sketched the complex sigils onto the gleaming surface beneath the names of the two kings and the rest of Tildi's companions, tweaking lines and scrollwork where it was needed. Olen oversaw the entire process, rendering each of the runes into metal as soon as both Serafina and Tildi were satisfied with it. A few, like Morag, stopped to stroke his or her finished name on the surface.

When they had finished, the metal square resembled an enlarged view of a leaf in the Great Book, though all of gold instead of just the words. Olen had sent it whisking away to safekeeping in the cupboard in his cabin. Of course, nothing could equal the actual object. Tildi reached up to touch the silken surface of the parchment, still whirling in the air like a ribbon of cloud.

Olen glanced at her with a wise expression. "You are going to find it difficult to give up, aren't you?"

Tildi bowed her head. Every time she thought of parting with the book, it wrenched at her heart. Sometimes she awoke at night to find herself staring at the sky, foreseeing a bleak future without the warm presence of the scroll, or the encouraging wisdom of the voices. "I'm sorry, master."

He placed his long hand on her shoulder. "Don't be. Older and more experienced hands than you would have difficulty letting go of such a wonder. I only hope it does not cost you more than you are willing to give."

Tildi straightened up. A Summerbee kept her bond, no matter what. "I will give what is needed."

Olen smiled. "You have hidden depths, my dear. I was fortunate in my choice of apprentices. Wasn't I, Mistress Serafina?"

Serafina gave Tildi a stern look. "I would expect no less, master. And I must say, she has been assiduous in her lessons, though her mind does wander on occasion."

"You have schooled her well in my absence," Olen said. "Your mother would be proud."

The young wizardess paused. "I hope so."

"You may depend upon it. I knew her many centuries. She had great hopes for you. You are fulfilling them."

"I don't know how I can ever aspire to be a second Edynn," Serafina said.

Olen smiled. "She wanted you to be the one Serafina. As this young lady will someday be *the* Tildi. If she continues her studies."

Both of them fixed their gazes on her. Tildi crouched, wondering how she could escape being the focus of two such masterful teachers. One at a time had been much easier to take!

A thin howl sounded from the top of the mast. Tildi looked up at the werewolf sitting in the small basket above the furled sails, his nose pointed to the sky. The captain came rushing up from belowdeck and cried out a question in their tongue. The lookout yipped, his yellow eyes glinting in his dark-furred face. The captain turned to bark, literally, his orders at his crew. The others looked joyful. The gangplank was laid down again. The people on the dock who had been hanging about since Tildi's wonder-working looked up at them hopefully, but a handful of the werewolf sailors stood guard upon the ramp.

"What is going on?" Rin called from her comfortable seat against the rail. The ship, though it rocked only gently, was difficult for hooved creatures to remain standing. The centaur had claimed the spot at the hindmost point of the upper deck and settled there on a nest of cushions to sun herself.

"Another ship," said Olen. "Our hosts are part of a merchant fleet from the south. This is what we have been waiting for."

"We don't need a second ship," Halcot said.

"Apparently, our needs are superseded by the company's requirements," Olen said cryptically, and Tildi knew he was refusing to tell what he knew. She wished she knew herself.

Magpie leaped into the rigging along with half the crew to watch the approach of the second vessel, which now appeared in the shipping lane to the north. It was painted white, and shaped much like the one on which they rode, but instead of golden trim, it had deep slate-blue. No question that it was a Sheatovran vessel, and a handsome one at that. She clove the water with confidence. Her crew, werewolves again, had gathered in most of her sails, but a few still belled out proudly in the sheets.

"Come up and see, Tildi," Magpie called to her. "They don't have many craft like this in the Quarters! It's a beautiful sight!"

She glanced at her two masters for permission. Serafina deferred to Olen.

"It is safe, child," Olen assured her. "Go ahead."

Tildi left the book hovering and went to the rigging at Magpie's feet. He held out a hand to her. Tildi eyed the distance doubtfully. Even if he helped her up, the space between the swinging ropes was made for the long legs of the crew, not short stumps like hers. Instead, she hardened the air and walked up to stand beside him by means of the air. There had never been such a useful spell for a smallfolk as the one that Master Olen had taught her. Magpie grinned widely. The crew gave her an appreciative yip and helped her to settle among them. The approaching ship was lovely, as in command of her surroundings as a swan on a pond. The smells of the river seemed stronger from her perch. She didn't find them unpleasant, merely unfamiliar.

"You can see much better from up here," she agreed. "Though I wouldn't like to sit up there." She pointed to the crow's nest.

"It's not a bad job, if you like swaying twice as far as anyone on deck every time the ship heels," Magpie said. "He has to sit out the whole watch up there, until the bell rings. Think what it's like in a storm," he added playfully.

Tildi let herself imagine heaving back and forth for hours on end, and clutched the ropes harder. The men around her laughed.

"Look at that," he said. "She's riding heavy with merchandise. It looks as if it was a good season for Captain Betiss's company." Tildi looked at the massed bundles wrapped in cloth in the stern. It was well laden. "Oh, I see why he said we had to wait for the eclipse. That's her name. *Eclipse*." He pointed to the name on the stern. She did not recognize the word. Doubtless it was in the werewolves' own tongue.

"Are all werewolves merchants?" she asked.

"Not all," Magpie replied. "Those that are range far, and they have many home crafts to trade. I have traveled among their villages in Sheatovra. They are proud of their craftspeople. Their metalwork is as famous as the smallfolks' embroidery and clothwork. Only a few like traveling into human-populated lands, you know. This company's done well this season. Everyone looks prosperous. They're very well dressed." He hesitated, and peered forward.

Tildi, too, noticed the people on deck as the ship drew nearer. Dozens of them crowded to the port rail to look at them. The sun blazing from above set the bright white clothes they wore alight like moonglow. What a contrast with the sailors aboard the *Corona*, who favored vegetable dyes and bare feet. No, their garments were not all white. A cloud passed before the sun, letting her see color in the garments that covered the arriving party from head to toe. There was blue in them, too. They were wearing the habits of the Scholardom. Tildi felt her heart pound. They had been betrayed.

"Master Olen!" she cried, swinging herself around. Instantly, the book flew to her side to comfort her. Olen's eyes were sympathetic under his gray brows.

"I know, child, I know."

Then, there came a joyful bellow from the man beside her. Swinging from the net like a monkey, Magpie waved his hand over his head.

"Inbecca!"

A tiny figure on the deck waved back. Cheeks red with delight, Magpie beamed at Tildi.

"She's here!" he cried.

"*She's* here," Tildi said. The chill of terror closed in around her again. She hugged the book to her chest.

You knew they were coming," Tildi said, as close to accusingly as she dared, as she and the others waited on deck for the newcomers to dock.

"Tildi!" Serafina exclaimed.

"No, let her have her say, Serafina," Olen said. "She is honest, and one of the things I have prized in her is her honesty."

The smallfolk girl stayed close behind Olen and Serafina as the second vessel was pulled to the wharf beside theirs. Her heart pounded against her ribs. Sharhava was visible among the crowd in the waist of the ship, but Tildi felt as if she would have known the abbess if she had been under a blanket. The lady Inbecca hovered close by, much closer than Sharhava's lieutenants. Tildi believed that some of the knights were missing, but that didn't matter. Her enemy was present, and she could focus upon nothing else.

The crew of the *Eclipse* swarmed down the gangplank the moment it was in place, and up onto the *Corona*. Captain Betiss met his counterpart, an older male with grizzled side whiskers and thin hair. The two of them embraced. Tildi guessed by their resemblance that the older man must be an uncle or a cousin. Not a father, since he deferred to the younger man. An older female dressed in green came to clap them both on the back and murmured to them, too low for anyone nearby to overhear. Tildi wondered if she had seen her during the rout in the fog, when she had worn her wolf shape. The yellow eyes glinted at Tildi with an air of familiarity. Tildi blushed and looked away.

"It is true, I had intimations that this could come to pass," Olen said. "It became much more of a certainty when the howling began, since Haroun was not going to let this ship depart. Still, a chance remained. I do not like to confirm suppositions without greater proof. It is much better not to build up hope—or despair—before it comes to pass."

"I never wanted to see her again!" Tildi said fiercely. "If you knew the things she said! What she did!"

"I do know, my child," Olen said. He knelt before her, so they were eye to eye. "I don't lie to you, you know. If I said I promise that things will not be as you assume they are, would you trust me?"

The green eyes were as limpid as a forest pool. Tildi hesitated, but she felt tears filling her own eyes. "I trust you. I just don't trust *her*."

"And who can blame you? But I am here, and Serafina is here, and my lord Halcot is so impressed by your fortitude and perseverance that he would do anything for you. If you asked him, I believe he would have his people throw the abbess Sharhava over the side and into the water, whatever her dignity. How about that? Could you meet her again on those terms?"

Tildi giggled through her tears. "I hope I am not that venal, master."

"Good!" Olen said. He straightened up. "Then let us face your greatest fear, shall we?"

Rin shouldered her way over. "Did you see her?" she exclaimed. "Your friend lied to you! They said they would keep them away from us!" Her nostrils flared as she confronted Olen. "You let them hold us until they could catch up with us? Tildi, come with me. We shall find another way southward. I will carry you to land's end and beyond." She held a hand down to the smallfolk girl.

"Peace," Olen said. "Princess, we were about to allow fate to take its natural course. Would you like to join us?"

"What?" the centaur demanded. The mass of white and blue appeared at the head of the gangplank. There was no escaping them now, unless Tildi jumped over the side herself and swam away from the ship. But Serafina had put a firm hand on her shoulder. Tildi looked up at her. Serafina's lips were pressed together, but she refused to move from her stance. "If you remain, I remain. I will guard you against them. I must warn you, Master Olen, they have learned how to use the runes against us."

"I consider myself warned. Here they are."

*I*nbecca remained at her aunt's side through the wait at the river's edge during an endlessly long day and night that followed the howled message and its reply. Patha had promised a ship, but Sharhava fretted it would not come or would not arrive in time. No amount of reassurance by her niece was sufficient to stay her endless pacing or wringing her half-healed hands. In the end, Inbecca let her tire herself out. It could do no harm. The werewolves had already informed her curtly that they would leave the abbess tied to a tree on the bank if she continued to harass them for news. It would come when it came, and not a moment before.

The *Eclipse*, captained by Patha's own brother, Temur, docked as promised, in the middle of the second day. Sharhava would not be soothed during the further delay, when the entire merchant company and most of the knights were conscripted to bring all the merchandise, wagons, and personal goods on board. Then the livestock and horses had to be settled belowdecks, fed and watered, and a meal hastily prepared on shore for the company and the order before they departed. Sharhava had picked at the excellent meal. Inbecca had felt guilty for enjoying the pastry of late apples brought in from southern Orontae, savory root vegetable stew and the juicy, grilled fish, caught in a trawl net by the sailors as they neared the docking point.

Inbecca herself could hardly believe that they were free, and traveling as the werewolves' companions instead of their prisoners. She, Sharhava, and Patha shared the captain's cabin. If it had not been for Sharhava's impatience, she and Patha might have enjoyed themselves. Patha was glad to be on her way home at last with the season's earnings and trade goods they were bringing from the north. She was in an expansive mood, almost friendly to the humans. Though always courteous and respectful to Inbecca herself, she had little patience for Sharhava. Inbecca did her best to keep her aunt out of the busy merchant's way during daylight. Meals were served casually, as they had been in camp, so they ate in the bows, perched amid a mass of unused nets and ropes.

Half of her hoped that they would not reach Tildi and the others in time. The other half felt wistful. She missed Eremi deeply, more than she thought she would. Though she had put her hastily taken vows ahead of him, she could not—and would not—set aside a lifetime's affection. She dared not think of love, not when the goal of securing the Great Book was so far from being achieved.

Loisan and the others were just as impatient as their mistress that they should reach the port of Lenacru in time, but they used their energy to more useful ends. The lieutenant volunteered the services of his brothers and sisters of the order to Patha and Temur to use as they saw fit. The captain accepted gravely, and put them to work at whatever task came to hand. Inbecca did not join them. She and Loisan reached a silent but tacit agreement that her time would be better spent keeping Sharhava out of the way.

Temur, for his part, laid on all sail and set his crew to rowing whenever the winds died down. Inbecca admired his skill. She loved the water. It was a shame her duties left her so little time for pleasure boating. Whenever the royal house took to the river, it was usually for a journey of state to visit brother or sister rulers or to attend festivals such as the Last Harvest and Year Birth. She slept well, lulled by the rocking of the ship. Sharhava had been muttering in her sleep, no doubt the result of troubled dreams. The creaking of the boards below and the snapping of the sails above them almost drowned them out.

"Should reach them today," Temur said, coming to stand over the two women as they made their breakfast. "My son sent word last night he has his passengers. All's well, then. You can stop worrying."

Sharhava glanced up from her bowl of cooked grains and grilled meats. "If you tell me the hour we will reach them without fail, then I will stop."

His patience exhausted at last, Temur lifted his long nose and let off one sharp yelp. After a brief pause, he was answered by the tenor yodel of a young male in the wheelhouse. "Noon, lady. Sun reaches its highest, we'll reach the *Corona*. I'll bet my cargo on it. If that doesn't ease your fuss, then nothing will." He stalked away.

Nothing made Sharhava's energy rise more than the appearance of disrespect. Her humility and concern abated, leaving her indignant. She glared at the captain's back.

"How dare he?" she demanded.

Inbecca hid a smile. "Forgive him, Aunt. He has many cares. He cannot make the ship move faster than it does."

"If we could only fly," Sharhava said. "But, no, the power is no longer ours." Inbecca searched her face for any signs of resentment at the loss. Certainly some of the knights had never gotten over it. She often caught them looking at their chests in hope of seeing their runes in place.

"Where are we?" Inbecca asked a crewman who had just tied off a line, as the ship rounded a bend.

"On the Arown," he replied shortly, too busy to be pestered by one he saw as unnecessary and unprofitable cargo. She continued to regard him with a mild expression. He relented, shaking his head as though to clear it of her gaze. He went up to the wheelhouse and returned with a glass ball just larger than his palm. He held it out to her. She looked into it and gasped. Within was a tiny image of the ship, slate-colored trim and all, lying upon a ribbon of blue that twisted this way and that. The werewolves used far more magic in their day-to-day lives than Inbecca saw used in a month in Levrenn. No doubt they were more comfortable with it, living as they did with their natural tendency toward transformation. "About four hours from Lenacru, lady. Weather's fine. Wind holding, we reach there for midday meal, no trouble." As soon as she had had another good look, he returned the navigation glass to the wheelhouse and went back to his chores.

Four hours to learn whether Sharhava was serious about her change of heart. Four hours to see if Eremi was waiting for her. She didn't know if she could bear to do nothing for all that time.

"Excuse me, Aunt," she said, taking the neglected breakfast dish from the abbess's lap. "Please call me if you want me." She took the bowls down to the galley and handed them to the sour-faced cook, then she went in search of the captain. Someone must have a task that an inexperienced land-lubber could do.

With the sun beating down upon her hood, Inbecca spent the next few hours shelling kidney-shaped green-speckled beans into a pail and throwing the pods over the side for the fish.

The crew in the bows sent up a yowl of joy as they rounded a bend. Inbecca looked up. Sharp tips like quill points rose up from the water. Within a moment or so, they grew into spindles, with sails wound around them instead of wool. Houses and shacks appeared between the dark green pine trees on the bluffs. By the time Inbecca stood up for a look, they had come in sight of a broad cup along the riverside. Ships and boats of all sizes filled it, bobbing placidly at anchor or moored along an array of piers that jutted out into the water. Shore birds dipped and wheeled, screaming a challenge to the newcomer, whose whiteness was as dazzling as their own. A town, goodly sized, buildings painted mostly in shades of gray, rose up from water's edge to hilltop. Inbecca scanned the water, wondering if she could guess which was the ship they were looking for. In a moment, she had her answer: *Eclipse* had a twin. A shining white ship edged in gold bobbed gently at quayside. Inbecca felt her heart begin to quiver. He was there, she knew it. Her happiness was quelled when a shadow fell on her. She looked up. Her aunt's haggard face was silhouetted against the sun.

"Come," Sharhava said. "We are arriving. We must make ready . . . I would welcome your support." Inbecca stood at once, and the unshelled beans slid from her lap onto the deck.

"Of course, Aunt," she said.

She waited at Sharhava's side at the rail as the town slid nearer. Braithen, Loisan, and Brouse hovered close but did not address them. Inbecca knew all the morning's tasks and devotions had been attended to. For all her difficulty with their aims, Inbecca admired their military precision in attending to detail. It left Sharhava with more time to think about what was to come. Inbecca worried on her behalf, but the abbess watched their approach with no expression on her face.

Sharhava would never ask for support in front of her subordinates. That left Inbecca free to gaze at the bobbing white ship.

From it, a cry broke out, and a flurry of movement ensued. Dozens of men and women, in human and wolf shape, scrambled into the rigging to get a better look at them.

In their midst, Inbecca caught sight of a tiny form sitting among the hooting and yelping crew. Unless one of the werewolf children wore thick boots, it must be Tildi Summerbee. Patha had kept her promise. They had caught up with the Great Book. A male with long dark hair bent his head to address Tildi, then looked out toward the *Eclipse*. Inbecca could see the streaks of white and red on the left side of his head. He looked out toward her, eyes as yellow in the noon sun as the werewolves'. Inbecca felt her heart race joyfully. He spotted her, Nature knew how, among the identical habits of the Scholardom, and waved his whole arm to get her attention. She fluttered her hand back at him, feeling as if she could burst with happiness.

Sharhava, at her side, did not look so sanguine. She stood stiffly beside Inbecca as the ship slowed and docked. The only movement she made was to grasp Inbecca's wrist tightly when the gangplank was thrown down and all the crew swarmed off it and onto the neighboring ship. There were howls of delight as the merchants greeted one another. The children leaped into the arms of the relatives they had not seen in months. Families embraced one another, and began to chatter happily. Inbecca could see the faces of Serafina, Lakanta, and Rin as well as Tildi, and knew they would not receive such a warm welcome.

"Abbess, it is time," Loisan said, his big face full of concern.

Sharhava nodded sharply. "Yes. It is time, and long past. Let us go."

Chapter Twenty-two

f Rin was incensed at the reappearance of the Scholardom, Lakanta was in full flame. She marched toward the gangplank and stationed herself at the head of it, before the first of the arriving knights could set foot on deck. Abbess Sharhava and Lady Inbecca, at the head of the line, stopped short, taken aback by the sight of the small trader woman, her face red and braids askew.

"Haroun Betiss," Lakanta bellowed. The tone of her voice made Tildi quail. "Do not dare let a single one of these people on board this ship, or I will curse you and every one of your family never to earn another copper in the rest of your days!" She broke into the snarling and guttural language and carried on with her tirade.

Haroun made his way toward her across the crowded deck, followed by the newcomers, protesting in a mewling voice like a puppy. Lakanta stretched up and took hold of his ear and dragged him down to her eye level. He dropped to his knee.

"Don't give me an excuse like that! What in the name of the Mother were you thinking? And you!" She turned on the older male. "Have you been fooled by words? Did they bribe you? How much money could possibly have persuaded you to break a promise and set free the killers of people like ourselves?"

The older male protested. "Do not say such things! I would never break my given word."

"Wouldn't you?" Lakanta asked, stabbing behind her with a thumb. "Then, what are they doing here?"

The woman gave a short howl to interrupt her. Lakanta, still holding firmly to Haroun's ear, turned. In her indignation and fury, the dwarf woman seemed larger and more formidable than all three Sheatovrans.

"Halt, stone sister." The woman held up a hand and offered a series of yips and wails. Lakanta started to interrupt her, then halted, mouth open.

"What is she saying?" Tildi whispered to Master Olen, whose mouth had turned up at the corner.

"Hush, my dear, I'm listening."

The gray-haired woman offered a musical arpeggio that scaled up and down in a minor key, though it sounded far from mournful to Tildi. The explanation went on for some time.

Lakanta listened, then laughed heartily. "Is that true, then? By Father

Time himself," and her voice trailed off into an ululation that ended in a high bark. The senior female replied shortly. Lakanta's blue eyes gleamed like the werewolves.' "Well, moon sister, I'll have to take your word for it. As you say, seeing's believing." She let go of Haroun and put her hands on her hips. The young captain sprang out of reach and rubbed his aching ear.

Lakanta eyed Sharhava up and down. "It'd better be true, then, or there's going to be a wetting, and I am ready to dispense it."

Olen had listened throughout with an answering glint in his green eyes. "Come here by our side, then, Lakanta. You'll have the vantage to see and hear whatever it is that my lady Sharhava has to say."

The werewolves stilled their happy badinage and parted to form an aisle. The exchange in their tongue had evidently let the crew of the *Corona* know for what purpose the knights had come. Lakanta marched as proudly as a queen and took up a stance with folded arms at Rin's side.

The stern woman at the head of the Scholardom had cheeks of fire. Beside her, Lady Inbecca had gone pale, but both of them held themselves proudly. Tildi had another moment of shock, when she saw Sharhava's right hand, which had been burned to a black claw the last time she had seen it, restored to flesh, though it was an angry pink. Much, clearly, had changed.

What is it?" Soliandur's peevish voice came from behind her. Olen turned and gestured grandly to the two kings.

"Come, my lords, and greet the new arrivals."

"Who is it?" the lord of Rabantae demanded. Halcot pressed forward, Soliandur close behind. Magpie moved to make way for them. "Who holds the ship? Great heavens, Lady Sharhava. Is it you? You look like you've aged a century."

"I thank you for your courtesy," Sharhava said haughtily. "I did not expect to see either of you here."

Soliandur looked a trifle discomfited. "Master Olen informed me that my son would be here at this time in this place. I was concerned for his well-being—as it seemed you were, when you left my hall in such a hurry."

"It was a matter of the greatest importance, my brother," Sharhava said.

"So my lord Halcot has told me," Soliandur said dryly. "If this is the end of the world I never want it said that I didn't do my part to help save it."

"How comforting that you do not come to your duty too late," Sharhava said. "I am sure that your concern will be of interest to my sister and goodbrother."

"It will be my honor to send a message to them. I am glad to see my prospective gooddaughter is looking well."

"No thanks to your irresponsible son!"

Halcot clapped them both heartily on the back. "I am glad to see that the miles and months have not changed your affection for each other." They both glared at him.

Olen cleared his throat gently. "You mention duty, my lady," he said.

Sharhava recovered herself magnificently. Tildi trembled as the formidable woman turned away from the two kings and gazed down upon her. She backed up until she bumped into Olen and Serafina. Then, to her deep and memorable shock, Sharhava dropped to her knee before her. The sea-blue eyes bored deeply into hers.

"Mistress Summerbee," Sharhava began, "you have no reason to trust me, but I will ask for that faith. I apologize for the distress I and my knights have caused you. I and my people lost sight of our order's original aim. I've found it again. I was wrong in my thinking. Recent events"—and she glanced at the senior werewolf female—"have made me reexamine our beliefs. I may deplore the circumstances that brought you and those like you into existence, but it is not up to me to question your being now that you are here. I hope you will forgive us—me—and permit us to accompany you on the rest of your journey. Our mission, as of old, is to protect the Great Book. We ask only to guard you and your burden where you bear it, to where you choose."

For all the words roiling up inside her, for all the anger she bore and the fear that had haunted her since the moment Tildi had seen Sharhava on board the neighboring ship, she could not think of a single thing to say. She stared at the abbess.

"So you no longer wish to destroy our likes, do you?" Rin asked, her nostrils flaring and eyes disks of jade fire.

"No, Princess," Sharhava said calmly. "I have come to agree with those of wiser perspective. Do not chide me. I will not take abuse. I offer my apologies for past transgressions. Take them or leave them."

"You don't sound that repentant," Lakanta sniffed.

"She is, my friend," Inbecca said. "Please be satisfied with it. You don't know what this costs her."

Lakanta blew out between her lips. "Do I care what it costs her? I'm only glad she came up with the right answer before she decided to turn my people into rocks, or whatever they had in store," the trader said. Sharhava pursed her lips tightly, but she bowed her head. Lakanta raised her chin triumphantly.

"The timing was fortunate," Magpie agreed. "Come, let's make peace." He put out his own hand. Very slowly, Tildi followed suit. Sharhava clasped it in both of hers without hesitation. She looked down, a little surprised and, could Tildi believe it, disappointed?

"I expected the fire," the abbess said.

"No longer," Serafina said. "The danger has abated, but only in Tildi. The book is still as perilous as ever."

"I am glad of it," Sharhava said. "I am not the only one who will ever be tempted by it." She seemed reluctant to let go, but she released Tildi's hand.

"The other chapters of the order will be displeased with you," Halcot pointed out. "Whatever your timely revelation, the rest are still practicing as they have been. They will consider your actions anathema, won't they?"

"So be it," Sharhava said. "I will explain myself to them one day, in my own good time. They will accept my reasons. I am their abbess. They follow me and my interpretation of the rules of the order. I do not do what is popular. I have tried to do what is right, though I have not done right, as history finds me. We have gone astray from our mandate. I wish dearly to make amends for it. My knights feel the same."

"It's a trick," said Lakanta, speaking aloud the thought that gnawed at the back of Tildi's mind. "Don't trust her."

What should she do? The abbess kept staring at her hungrily. All over again, Tildi felt the fears and dreads she had suffered among the Scholardom. How had Sharhava managed to get the werewolves to break the promise they had made to Irithe?

She felt a hand clasp her shoulder. Serafina. The young wizardess held tightly, and through the grip Tildi felt a light quiver, like a rhythm, that permeated her bones. The quiver spread until it filled her entire body, then slowed very gradually to a walking tempo, a pulse. She looked up at her teacher, who smiled at her. Yes, she needed to regain her balance as the bearkin had taught her. She closed her eyes and let the soothing beat slow her racing heart.

With Sharhava's gaze no longer troubling her, she let herself listen to the abbess's own pulse. It was jumpy and thready. *She* was frightened. Of Tildi?

"May I have your answer, Mistress Summerbee?" Sharhava asked, sounding almost humble. "I would like to know if we have made this journey in vain. If you do not wish us to serve you, then we will go. Captain Temur will not follow. We will find passage back to Levrenn, and not trouble you further."

"I would not turn down such an honor guard, Mistress Summerbee," Soliandur said softly, "though it is your choice."

"I am satisfied with the one we have had," Tildi said, turning to smile at Teryn and Morag. "They have been enough for us. They have been so brave, Your Highness."

Halcot harrumphed, but he looked pleased.

"We could not defend you against them, honored one," Teryn pointed out. "Give credit where credit is due: they are a force that little can withstand. Their organization and training . . . well, it's formidable. I'd take the offer."

"Do not deny us a chance to serve the Great Book," Sharhava said. "It is what our order was formed to do, after all. Forgive us."

"I . . . it's not my place to give someone like you forgiveness," Tildi said, feeling very uncomfortable. Sharhava looked dismayed. She hastened to explain. "You're highborn. I mean, if things were different, you wouldn't even speak to someone like me, would you?"

Sharhava's mouth twisted wryly. "Most likely you are right. My pride would have prevented me from conversing with a mere farm woman, and I would be more the fool, wouldn't I? I cannot do what you are doing. I can only offer to aid you."

"As do we all," Loisan said. The other knights murmured agreement. Tildi felt overwhelmed and very small.

"Then, all I can say is thank you," she said. The book seemed to bob with pleasure at her side.

"Even they . . . ?" Olen prompted.

"Oh, yes," Tildi said. She looked up at Olen. "I meant what I said." She turned back to Sharhava. "Master Olen has inscribed all our runes on a sheet of metal in case . . . in case . . ."

Sharhava's lips tightened. "I understand."

"So, we have to do the same with all of you. It would have helped, you know, but I never thought Bertin would . . ."

Sharhava looked at first as though she had been slapped, then reached out to take Tildi's hand again. "Since my eyes were opened I have met the most remarkable people," she said, "all better than I could have imagined, and better than I am myself."

"A*no srdeg imva!*" Olen commanded.

Tildi enjoyed the bespelling more the second time. Master Olen, in his wisdom, had provided the means. At his command a second sheet of gold metal came flying out of the cupboard in the main cabin and presented itself before him. Patha refused to have her name beside the knights'.

"Even if it means some of us will be on the back of this piece of metal," she said, her fierce golden gaze meeting Olen's mild green one.

"Oh, I think there is room," he said. "The first board is only two-thirds full. There is plenty of space for you." Tildi gave him a suspicious glance, which he met with a twinkle. She should have known he did everything to a purpose. "I shall bring it out." And he did. Patha looked satisfied.

How very different it was from the steadily worsening weeks she had spent in the Scholardom's company before. The knights were humbled and honored to be included.

"You did tell the boy, mistress," Auric said, his kindly gaze bent upon her as she copied his rune onto the metal. "We should have done this weeks back, I believe. Many of us thought it after that time. You did try to help him. I hope your conscience is clear on that."

"It is," Tildi said. "I'm only sad about his death. Thank you."

"Thank you, gracious lass." Auric bent and placed his hand on his heart.

Once the names had all been inscribed, Olen took his place on the high aft deck to address the throng. The kings stood to either side of him. Tildi felt dazzled by the illustriousness of the company, but reminded herself how serious an expedition they were mounting.

"My lords of Orontae and Rabantae join me in making you welcome in our company. Only a few of you were present at the council in which this task was undertaken. I will reiterate for those who have become part of our mission. Tildi?"

Tildi gave a whisper of thought to the voices, and the Great Book soared into the air over their heads. The knights murmured to themselves. It sounded like one of the litanies she had heard in their camp. The werewolves exclaimed upon the book's beauty, and a few speculated on its probable worth to collectors. Tildi's face must have reflected her shock, for Lakanta leaned over and poked her in the side. The dwarf woman looked amused.

"Don't be surprised; they *are* merchants. I've valued it myself." Tildi giggled.

Olen cleared his throat to silence them. "Behold the Great Book. I am very pleased to be able to see it in the flesh, so to speak. It is a marvelous object, and a dangerous one. All of you have seen by now the runes set upon your bodies. These are reflections of your reality reduced to a symbol. They are present all of the time, visible to wizards and others with the second sight, but the presence of the book among you renders them visible to all— and vulnerable, as some among you can attest. To change the rune is to change reality. An appealing power, you believe?" Olen looked around at his audience. "Not so. That change can be permanent and devastating. Because of this effect, the book is a danger to you—to all of you. It will continue to be a danger as long as it is about in the world. Our duty is to remove it to the place where it was safely kept for thousands of years, and secure it once again. It is not so simple a task as it sounds. The book is being stalked by at least one foe, the one who controls the creatures called thraiks. He, or they, want it enough to kill for it. It is worth killing for."

The werewolves yipped to one another.

"We have taken what steps we can to protect you, but be ready for attack. I have foreseen several possible outcomes to our mission. I can only thank you all for being willing to undertake this journey with us.

"Now that everyone has arrived, we must make ready to leave here. I see by my art that we have little time before we will be separated. I hope to complete the party before that moment, but my vision branches out into too many possibilities.

"As there are too many for one ship to carry, the *Corona* and *Eclipse* will sail together. I am reliably informed," Olen added with a smile, "that they had always intended to do so. The third ship in their party will meet us above Tillerton, to make the crossing to the south. With such a strong company, I hope that we will be able to withstand any further incursions that may be made by our unseen opponent. We will be protected by steel, but also by spells. Mistress Serafina, would you be so good as to increase the wards to encompass the second ship and her complement?"

Serafina colored lightly. "As you please, master. Tildi, you may assist me. *Crotegh mai ni eng!*"

Hastily, Tildi drew her knife and followed Serafina's lead.

Olen watched for a moment and murmured to himself, "Must see about getting you a wand."

*I*nbecca stood with Sharhava at a distance from the wizards, watching them work their wonder on the sheet of metal. Her aunt was so relieved that Tildi had allowed them to offer their service that she found it difficult to rise from her knees. Loisan and Auric had helped her up and found her a seat. Sharhava stared incessantly at the smallfolk girl and the whirling scroll, the object of her affection, not to say obsession.

She could still hardly believe that King Halcot of Rabantae and King Soliandur were there. She blushed when she looked their way. The last time she had seen either man, she had not been in a good mood. Her rash behavior had been an awkward thing she could ignore while on the chase to find Tildi and in the long weeks on the road since, but there before her were two of the most important witnesses. She put her chin up. She had to live with the consequences, no matter how much shame it brought her.

A warm hand caught hers, and a warm scent made her startle. Eremi stood beside her. He smiled.

"You were so deep in thought."

"Were you surprised to see your father?" she asked.

Eremi's bright eyes glinted like peridots. "I thought I would turn to stone," he said, a note of wonder in his voice. "But he came. He brought me my jitar."

"He did?" Inbecca asked, her voice rising to a squeak. Both of them knew how difficult it was for Eremi's father to make a kindly gesture toward his third son. "Is it . . . I apologize for asking . . . is it playable?"

Eremi laughed out loud. "It's even been polished. It looks like new. It's there, in the stern." He pointed aft. "I'll show it to you. How are you?"

Inbecca glanced at her aunt, who still concentrated upon the book. "I am well."

"He was angry that I left you behind." Eremi didn't have to tell her which "he."

She turned to face him fully. "It was my choice."

"Your pardon, as always, but my word is the last one he will ever admit he trusts."

"I'll tell him myself. Come with me." She turned to Sharhava who, after one loathing glance at Eremi, had gone back to her own thoughts. "Abbess, may I have leave to greet His Highness of Orontae?"

"Very well," Sharhava said without looking at them. "Do not be long."

The two men were conversing in the cool shade of the cabin when Inbecca bore down upon them, Eremi in tow. She hated to interrupt them. Eremi had told her how uncomfortable the détente between Orontae and Rabantae had been since the end of the war over timber rights. In years past they had been more like brothers or cousins.

Some time between the unhappy end to the betrothal ceremony and that moment, the two kings had gotten over their enmity. The way they addressed each other with the ease of old friendship warmed Inbecca's heart. She knew Eremi rejoiced in it, too. The war had been a foolish mistake and cost both sides more than either wanted to admit. Halcot, who had been forced to admit fault, had given more to achieve peace, but Soliandur had had to sacrifice his notorious pride. Halcot said something she did not catch, and the solemn Orontavian chuckled. It was a sound Inbecca had heard perhaps a half-dozen times in her life.

The two men became aware of their visitors. When they noticed Inbecca, they rose from their seats and inclined their heads. She bowed more deeply, as befit the daughter of a queen regnant to brother kings.

"How kind of you to honor us," Halcot said, smiling. "We are glad to see you well. It will be my pleasure to send a message to your mother that you have arrived. Though she would welcome a message from you."

"I thank you, Highness," Inbecca replied. "I will write to her. She deserves a full explanation of my long absence. I am ready to give it to her."

"We have heard most of it from the others," Halcot said gravely. "I trust you did not suffer from your brief . . . detention."

"Not at all, my lord. I found it most educational. I haven't had a chance to get to know many of the moonfolk from Sheatovra. I intend to spend more time with them when they visit Levrenn in the summers in future years. I have missed meeting the most interesting people."

"And there is my worthless son, standing in your shadow," Soliandur said.

Eremi held his ground. "I am here, sir." Halcot snorted.

"If you believe him to be so worthless, brother, I will adopt him. He has spent enough time in my castle over the last few years."

"More time than he has spent at home," Eremi's father said, but without rancor. "His mother wants to see more of him. If his princess will come as well."

Behind her, Eremi squirmed.

"I would be delighted to attend Her Highness," Inbecca said evenly, "but I have duties to perform before that day might come." She took a deep breath to help her force out the awkward words. "I have taken vows."

"We witnessed them," Soliandur said. "But the first as well as the second."

Inbecca well understood what he did not say. He felt it was a personal rejection, and no doubt Inbecca would have felt the same. She must find an explanation that he would accept. She turned to the other prince.

"My lord Halcot, you were at Master Olen's council some months ago, weren't you?"

"Yes, indeed I was."

"If your queen had gone off in pursuit of such a dangerous item, and you wanted to join the hunt, how would you have gone about it?"

"What I did, I suppose," Halcot said. "I have responsibilities to my kingdom. I sent my guards as escort to those whom I trusted to secure it."

"But had you no kingdom and no force of guards . . . ? Or at least, you were not yet on the throne?"

One golden brow rose on the broad, ruddy forehead. "I see what you mean, though. Yes, I would have liked to have gone myself. If it was that important to my lady and I feared for her safety, I would go. You allied yourself with a force that would not otherwise accept you so that you would not be traveling alone. I see it."

"But why break your first vows when they were but hours old?" Soliandur burst out, his dark face scarlet over the cheekbones. "How does swearing fealty to the Scholardom equate with chasing down my son because you love him? Knights are not permitted to have personal ties."

Inbecca bowed her head. "I acted in haste, my lord, and for that I owe you and your family a deep apology. I did not think my actions through. I was angry, as what bride would not be, having her groom abscond without an explanation? I had waited years for that moment, as I am sure you did, sir. I hope all will come right in the end, but until that time, I have duties to the abbess."

"Well," Soliandur said hoarsely. "That night changed many things. I, too, have been persuaded to the import of this journey. I will travel with my brother king. We will fight side by side with you and the Scholardom against the minions of the enemy in whom I did not really believe until I heard that young smallfolk lady's account."

"That will be of immeasurable help," Inbecca said, leaning forward and touching him on the hand. She smiled at him.

"I can't see how one overage, out-of-practice swordsman may do any good," Soliandur said, but she could tell he was beguiled. The shadows around his eyes lifted a little. "But for your mother's sake, who has always been a good friend to my realm, and for her daughter's, who for a time lent grace to our court, I will give whatever I have."

"Now, brother," Halcot said a little hoarsely, "you were always a deadly hand with a sword. I mind when we stood together against the pirates from the south of Balierenn."

Soliandur sighed, and his dark eyes looked weary. "Time was, but I had hoped never to have more dealings with war."

"This is a different kind of war," Inbecca said.

"If it is the only way to persuade you to resume your engagement to my unworthy son, I am well prepared to go to Alada's ends."

"I cannot think to discuss that matter until this one is settled, my lord," Inbecca said. "We will all be glad of your aid."

"Then, you shall have it. I have given my word, and you will see that it is good."

"I thank you, sir." Inbecca wished she could reassure him further, but Sharhava had greater need of her than any of those men did at that time. "I must go. My aunt expects me."

"Your servant, lady," Soliandur said, nodding curtly.

She could tell he was not satisfied. His pride would not be assuaged without absolute reassurance, and she wouldn't give it. She bowed to him and to Halcot, and withdrew, feeling very awkward.

The conversation that had been going on when they had arrived continued.

"Well, *why* can't we use that book to go to where it must be bestowed, and bury it right away?"

"I am your fellow soldier," Halcot said. "Olen is our general. You must ask him. But it's a good question. You should ask him. There must be some reason it would not work, or they'd do it. Magic is a chancy thing, you know. Don't interfere with it myself."

"I've never much cared for magic. At least you have a court wizard who knows how it is made. My fool caused this whole catastrophe to be set in motion. No, don't you go, boy," Soliandur ordered as Eremi prepared to follow her. "You can answer some of these questions."

Behind her, Eremi let out a low groan. Head high, Inbecca pretended she was not listening. She strode back toward Sharhava's seat.

Chapter Twenty-three

he sun was already halfway down the western sky by the time all cargo had been brought on board and the ships were made ready to go. The kings sent their riders off to the north, bearing messages and welcome news to the three kingdoms. A few hardy traders waving goods of all types tried for one last sale to Patha and Temur, but were shooed, protesting, back to the dock.

Though Sharhava had protested, the Scholardom was forced to return to the *Eclipse*. There simply was not enough room on the *Corona*. Privately, Tildi was glad that they could not travel close together. She didn't really trust the knights, no matter how many protestations they made that they had changed. One of the young men especially worried her: Lar Mey. His rune told her that he was more ambivalent about the Scholardom's new mission than the others.

Tildi still mistrusted the new and amenable Sharhava, but the core of resolve that had always been at the human's heart had become a sturdier stroke, and the swirling insanity had settled. Pain still plagued her, and likely always would. For that, Tildi was sorry. She was glad to have the troubled woman at a distance.

With the Scholardom out of reach, Tildi could again enjoy being in Olen's company. She was overawed by the presence of the two kings, but Olen managed to make it feel as if they were all his honored guests. At dinner he kept the conversation moving from one to another, asking questions and eliciting stories that kept the mood as merry as the meal.

"Lakanta, I would welcome all of the news from Jorjevo. You said that four new cubs had been born to them since the council? Komorosh is too stingy with information."

"Twin cubs, one pair of them," the trader said cheerfully. "A rarity for any people, but the bearkin have twins or triplets less than the rest of us. They are called Yarro and Yemiro."

"Brother heroes of ages past," Olen explained to the others. "I have a copy of their history somewhere in my boxes in Silvertree's storerooms. I will send them a scroll with the story on it to read to them by the fire. It makes good telling."

"Tell it, then," Rin said, toying with her wineglass. "A good dinner demands a good tale."

Olen sat back at his ease. "As you please, Princess. I recall that in that time, giant lizards walked the land. Some say they even flew! The valley city of Randeri was one that they invaded time and again . . ." Tildi felt her head begin to nod.

"Was it a human city?" Tildi asked, unable to stop herself from interrupting.

"It was. This was in ages before the Shining Ones," Olen replied. "To continue: the beasts killed cattle, and woe betide any poor farmer who sought to protect his herds . . ." Tildi felt her head begin to nod.

"Come, Tildi," Olen's voice said, interrupting her drowse. She glanced up at him with a start. "We are not moving fast enough. We must see if we can do something about that."

"What about the end of the story?" Halcot called. He looked puzzled, as did the others.

"Perhaps later, my lord," Olen said.

"Hurry, Tildi, wake up," Serafina urged her.

Tildi shook herself fully awake and sprang to her feet. The book bobbed up beside her like a friendly ghost. She followed them to the wheelhouse, where Haroun plied the wheel. He glanced at them, then back at the small glass on a standard beside him. By the light of the two lanterns burning on the wall behind Haroun, Tildi could see the shape of the vessel in miniature inside the glass, riding a ribbon of blue. Even these were tinged by the aegis of the book. All parts of the navigation crystal had tiny runes upon them.

"We need speed," Olen said to the captain.

"We are going six knots." Haroun took the crystal out of its bracket and held it out for him to see. Olen shook his head.

"Six knots is too slow. I want to reach the south coast as soon as possible. I am seeing an attack on these ships. I wish to avoid it."

That got Haroun's attention. "Sir, the winds blow inland at night. We can only go easy, and I fear we might collide with other ships in the dark if we go too swift."

"You cannot fail to see anything at all that is invested with runes by the Great Book. If I may, Captain, I'll use a little weather to blow the sails."

"Against the prevailing breeze?" Haroun asked. "It will kick up the waves a lot, master."

"Nevertheless, I believe it to be necessary. Will you trust me?"

"Certainly, if you will guarantee the safety of my ship."

Olen smiled, his eyes shadowed in the lantern light. "I believe I can do that, although it may be a thrilling ride. Are you ready to try?"

Haroun showed a grin full of sharp white teeth. "Why not? I've ridden out storms you wouldn't believe."

"I'd love to hear the tales sometime," Olen said. "Perhaps later. Will you stand ready, Captain? Tildi, come with me to the stern. And will you join us,

Serafina? I'd be grateful for your knowledge as well. It is a matter of weather magic adapted to a new purpose."

"I have no experience with weather magic," the girl said, a little embarrassed.

Olen beamed. "Good. Then you will give me a fresh perspective. We all learn from one another."

"What are you planning, Master Olen?" King Soliandur asked, coming out of the cabin. "Do you intend to make us fly?"

"Your suggestion of this afternoon made me think, my lord," Olen said, making his way to the rear rail of the ship. Tildi followed him and looked down at the water churning over the mighty rudder. Lanterns colored red for port and white for starboard hung on the rear of the ship. "Now I propose to make use of it. Do you care to observe?"

"Why not?" Soliandur said. "I wouldn't mind a chance to see genuine wizardry."

"We will do our best to please. Tildi, if you would not mind setting the book aside for a time."

With a thought of apology to it, Tildi sent the book down the hatch and into the small cabin set aside for her and Serafina by Haroun. She could see its rune right through the deck. It settled onto something, she hoped a bed. She turned to Master Olen.

"Very good, we are ready."

"What did you see, master?" Serafina asked. "When Captain Teryn handed you the pitcher of wine, you stopped speaking."

Olen pressed his lips together. "Possibilities, my dear. The trouble with my art is that I foresee true events more often than not, but they are not so considerate as to offer me the date of their occurrence, nor the true shape. These ships are vulnerable. I have seen a force clad in silver armor that will beset us with poison knives. I have no choice but to act upon my visions, instead of waiting for confirmation. In any case, it will serve us to move more swiftly."

"How do you propose to make them less vulnerable?" Serafina asked.

"By adding one more to our complement, I hope. The sooner the better, for we are ill-prepared for the onslaught that may beset us."

"Who?"

"I don't know."

"Should you not alert our allies?" Serafina asked, glancing over his shoulder at Halcot and Soliandur, both of whom had joined the ranks of the curious. "Should they not be made ready in case the onslaught is imminent?"

Olen gestured toward Captain Teryn, who sat bolt upright, her keen eyes scanning the ship. "They are ready. They have always been ready. The question is, are we?"

"But the kings," Tildi asked, "what about them?"

Olen sighed. "I am afraid that Soliandur has been disappointed by prophecy in the past. A half-formed vision will not please him. If I am able to make more sense out of it with more intense study, I will inform him what we face. It is not as easy as looking at a picture, Tildi. When we have time to give you instruction in scrying, you will see how nebulous such warnings can be. My lord of Orontae did not appreciate the gift his wizard possessed."

"Oh," Tildi said. She realized she *had* thought that such visions were like pictures. She and Teldo had never gone as far as the study of prediction.

"Let us begin," Olen said. "Captain, at the speeds I hope we will travel, it won't be so easy to call to the other vessel."

"We will be able to signal back and forth to them," Haroun assured him.

"That will be sufficient," Tildi said. "Won't it?"

Olen chuckled, as if he could read her thoughts. "Yes, it should. If we are moving too swiftly for friends, we will also be more difficult for foes to overtake as well."

"Thraiks can fly very fast."

"They cannot see through the warding, as well you know," Serafina reminded her sharply.

"Come, let us not bicker," Olen said. "We have work to do."

The night sky seemed darker than the water below, but only because the runes depicting stars seemed less numerous than the myriad tiny creatures that each merited their own silver-gilt sigil. Olen scanned the sky.

"This is going to be a matter of catching that which is coming toward us and diverting it to push us forward," Olen said. "There, do you see?"

He pointed to long narrow runes that streamed overhead. They divided, slipped over one another, then collided and became one again. Tildi watched them in fascination.

"What are they?"

"Winds. Breezes. We are going to capture them and make them fill our sails."

"How?" Serafina asked.

Olen smiled. "It's almost like clipping fleeces," he said. "If we took all the winds from the sky we would create a hurricane. We will skim the lowest-flying breezes, mold them, and set them in place behind us. Tildi has already had some experience in capturing winds, have you not?"

"Yes, Master Olen," Tildi said.

"We have an advantage in working at night in that we can see the runes to the exclusion of most of the rest."

"But where will we put them?" Serafina asked.

"Why, we will use warding," Olen said. "You have considerable experience in creating walls. These will be more like great sacks, to continue our shearing metaphor. Let us construct those first, so they will be waiting when we gather up the wind. They will need to be strong. Follow my lead, and place one within the other. *Fornlau chnetegh voshad!*" He pointed his staff to the rear and above the stern of the *Corona*.

A new rune sprang into being and began to spread out. Instead of the roughly rectangular gate that Tildi had seen made before, this one was round. Olen opened his hands as if to plaster the rune across the sky. It grew larger and larger until part of it seemed to dip below the roiled surface of the Arown. Olen nodded, as if satisfied, then beckoned with both hands. The edges of the shimmering wall turned and rolled toward him. Tildi was delighted. It did look like a big sack!

"Tildi, you next."

Hoping that she had seen everything that he had done, Tildi held out her belt knife and repeated the incantation.

"*Fornlau chnetegh voshad,*" she said.

A tiny dot appeared within the mouth of the bag.

"Tildi, put some force into it," Olen said. "That is a most unconvincing ward, no matter what you would use it for."

Stung, she urged the disk to grow. As it touched the inside of Olen's molded spell, it began to turn and change shape, lining the glowing bubble with an inner skin brighter than the outer. The edge of her wards were not as neat as Olen's. Tildi glanced at him guiltily. He beamed at her.

"Wonderful!" he exclaimed. "I had not yet seen how your magic prospers under the aegis of the book, but it has made you capable of prodigious spells. We will make great use of that in days to come, wait and see." With a wave of his hand, the uneven wards met and married with the outer shell. Bound together, the sphere glowed like the light of a lantern in the fog.

"Very pretty," King Halcot called, "but it isn't doing anything!"

"Not yet, my lord," Olen said. "Now, Serafina, will you assist me in creating such a ward for our sister ship?"

Serafina seemed to feel, rightly in Tildi's view, that it was a test, and a public one at that. The apples of her golden cheeks darkened as she stood with Olen at the high stern rail. The wonder-working on the *Corona* had not gone unnoticed aboard the *Eclipse*. Crew and visitors alike crowded the rail. Most of them pointed and commented to one another. However, when the werewolves noticed the wizards pointing at them, they set up a howl of protest. Captain Temur came running up the ladder from his cabin. Tildi couldn't understand the series of yelps that passed between him and Haroun, but it was clearly a demand for an explanation. Haroun gave a musical yodel ending in a downturn of tone that sounded like a positive conclusion. Temur seemed satisfied with it. He repeated the ululation to his people, who settled down to watch. He clapped his helmsman on the shoulder, and waited at his side, looking curious and excited.

"Well, that is settled," Olen said. He swept his staff across the sky. The wards took shape. The second time he did it, Tildi noticed how the rune itself changed as it billowed outward. Serafina watched, too. She bit her lower lip between her teeth. When Olen turned to her, she raised her staff. Her movements were jerky and unpracticed in comparison with his. She recreated the sign in the air well enough, but when the time came to make it expand outward, she glanced back at the glowing shape hovering in the air behind their own ship. She changed a line or two so they matched better, but it was not perfect yet.

"Don't forget the crosspiece at the top," Tildi advised, watching her with a critical eye.

"I am supposed to be teaching you!" Serafina said crossly, embarrassed at having been caught copying, as though she was borrowing answers from an examination.

"Ah, but, you see?" Olen asked. "Even one more practice session can create great differences in technique."

Serafina was not placated. She slashed her hand across, and the missing line took its place. The spells melded seamlessly. Following Olen's instructions, the two young women reached out to the swirling lines over their heads. It was rather like clipping gigantic sheep, Tildi thought. She felt the powerful waves under her hands like muscles under smooth skin. With her hands in the air it looked as though she were winding the wind like a ball of yarn. Only when zephyrs kicked away from the mass did she recall that it was a living force.

"Mold them and set them in place," Olen instructed. As the wizardess and apprentice pushed the glowing, twisting runes into the confines of the bags, he closed them. "Well done!"

"I confess, master, that Tildi's is neater than mine," Serafina said, albeit mulishly. "I apologize."

"Now, don't be too hard on yourself. It's a specialist subject," Olen said pleasantly, seeking to diffuse the argument. "I go to my fellow wizards for further education, when they are expert in something that interests me. I will definitely send Tildi to Volek for instruction in weather magic."

He called out to the sailors at the wheelhouse. "When I let go of this, Captain, it will send us flying. Are you ready?"

Haroun grinned toothily. "Ready and willing, master!" he said. The others echoed him in their rough voices.

"Then, we will let fly! Slowly first, then increasing until we have the full force behind us. We can make them stronger in the daylight, but we must make speed all the while. Ready, now? Go!"

Olen dropped his hand. Tildi held tight to the rail. She and Serafina opened the necks of the spells. The pent-up winds gusted out of their insubstantial containers. The sails billowed forward and snapped taut. The ships jumped forward, twin dolphins leaping on the black breast of the river. Tildi had to bend her knees to keep from being thrown off her feet. Serafina grabbed unceremoniously for the nearest spar and held on.

Howl of delight came from the captain and his crew.

"Oh, what a joy!" Haroun yelped. "Where were you when we were trying to make time this spring, master?"

Master Olen! That ship is full of water! And that little one beside it."

"You can let it out, if you choose," Olen said. "Is there anyone on board any vessel? Tip them up gently, so whatever tools and nets are within do not spill out, and empty the water. Can you?"

"I will try," Tildi vowed.

Serafina guided her to correct the keel of a few of the boats, but Olen stopped her when she tried to right them all.

"I appreciate that you want to help everyone you can see," he said dryly, "but it is part of the peril we must all share. They will be much happier having to bail out their vessels than finding them changed into sea monsters, or whatever it is this rogue Maker wants of the book."

"A Maker," Serafina echoed, intrigued. "So, poor, mad Nemeth was right. Are you sure? Do you know who he is?"

"I believe I do, but we are going where we can get confirmation. I want to speak with the Guardian, the only other Shining One I know to be abroad in the continent of Niombra."

Tildi goggled. "A Shining One? A living one? Where is he?"

"Down on the coast," Olen said. "At this rate, no more than two days' sail, I hope. He is the reason I wish to make haste. With his help, we might withstand the attack I have foreseen."

"The Guardian?" Serafina asked. "Do you mean the statue that stands at the mouth of the Arown?"

"I do."

"But it's not a person."

"I believe it is," Olen said. "Not only a person, a human, but one of the Shining Ones."

"If he's real, what's he doing there?"

"Guarding, I imagine," Olen replied. "We will ask him if we can."

"How do you know? Why does no one else know of him?"

"Because I have been looking for him, and no one else has," Olen said. "I do not spend all my time teaching apprentice wizards, my dear."

Angry shouts came from off the port side of the ship.

"Hey, there! Slow down! You're fouling our nets!"

Tildi ran to the side just in time to see a cluster of small fishing boats, lit by small lanterns hanging from single poles in the sterns. The smock-clad humans on board were shaking their fists at the passing ships. They were too slow to get out of the way.

"Ah, well," Olen said. "Sometimes one must simply take action." He raised his staff. A brilliant green light burst upward from it. It arced high, then fell down toward the fishermen. They screamed as the luminous sphere exploded silently over them, raining down green light. Tildi didn't see what had happened, but the screaming stopped. She could still hear hoarse shouts as the boats dropped far behind them.

"Master Olen, what are you doing?" Halcot asked, coming up behind them. He looked somewhat shocked.

Olen threw a hand in the direction of the angry fishermen.

"I put a charm of generosity on them, and a spell of attraction on their nets for tomorrow," he said. "It's the least I can do to make up for tonight's spoiled catch. But who knows what those catches may be if we fail to keep the book out of the Maker's hands? Now, ladies and gentlemen, I left my story unfinished. Would you care to hear the ending?"

King Soliandur led the way back to the cabin and called for wine all around. The servants in slate-blue livery sprang to his bidding, filling cups and handing them to the guests as they returned to their seats.

"By the stars, master, I have never seen the like!" he said. "It would be a different world if ships could travel as swiftly as this. Why do wizards never lend their skills in that fashion? Commerce would prosper. I for one would make it worthwhile to the man who could do that—or woman," he added, courteously, to Tildi, just inside the door.

"Wizardry is not a common or simply-won skill, Your Highness," Olen said. "You were fortunate to see two extraordinary talents this evening; three if you include me. I would not have captured the wind in this fashion if I did not feel it to be of vital importance to the world, not just to one merchant or one kingdom."

Soliandur frowned. "That is what he always said—Nemeth. Not that he was capable of more than a waking dream."

"I would not denigrate his talent, highness," Olen said gently. "True sight is not an easy gift. Think of it: not only would he know the truth of what lay before him, but he would also know ahead of time when he would or would not be believed when he spoke. How many of us would continue to speak out, when only disappointment awaited?"

"Hmph. You sound like my son. Where is he, by the way?"

Tildi refused the cup of wine offered to her by the dark-skinned servant and slipped out into the night. She knew where Magpie had gone. When the Scholardom had debarked for the other vessel, he had gone with it.

She made her way to the rail. At *Corona*'s side, the *Eclipse* plied her way on the heaving waves as easily as a horse might canter over a meadow. It had taken little time for the ship's complement to become comfortable with the increased speed. They had gone back to eating, laughing, and telling stories. Even some of the knights were taking part in the festivities.

Two who did not sat alone together on the steps leading to the upper deck. Tildi didn't need a lantern to distinguish their runes: Magpie and In-becca. They did not touch, but their runes were twined together. Still, she could see distance between them. They were held apart by an element in Inbecca's. She heaved a sigh of pleasure that they were together.

Watching them, alone at the rail was Serafina. Tildi made her way to stand beside her teacher. She felt sorry for Serafina, who had to witness the joy of their reunion, with a hearty embrace and a shy, tentative kiss, but this was the way Tildi thought things ought to be; though, she realized with dawning maturity, it was not her choice to make one way or the other. There was still a distance between the lovers, one that could not be denied. The unhappy Sharhava's rune did not seem to hold sway over the girl. Rather it was an element of Inbecca's personality, strength of will, that held back the complete joining that the two clearly wished. The lady was still wearing the habit of the order. Time would only tell what would be the right outcome.

Serafina wore a wistful look. Tildi glanced at her and was ashamed of herself. She wished she had not been so fierce in her disapproval of any dalliance her teacher had enjoyed. It was not her business, either. "I am sorry, master."

The wizardess gave her a quick, sad smile. "It was not meant to be. We were lonely together. I did not misplace my trust, I assure you. It is not his fault that I allowed myself to hope; she was always in his mind. It shows me, though, that my mother was right, as she always was. I have to learn to open my heart. Not yet, but someday." They looked again at the couple on the steps.

Satisfied that it was the way things were meant to be, they left the side of the ship and rejoined the company.

Chapter Twenty-four

inding the wind spells was not difficult, only time-consuming. Olen had stood the night's watch, yet he seemed as fresh as if he had slept and breakfasted at his leisure. Tildi, who had taken over for him at dawn, saw the sun reach its midmorning station and felt as if the day had been going on for a week. The morning air had been crisp with frost, reminding her that winter was pursuing them from the north. She had found it hard to get out of bed, and even harder not to think of returning to the cozy bunk. Tildi could correct any problems that arose, usually with a single line added or removed from the twisting, billowing runes, but the fragile nature of the spells made it difficult for her to leave them. The increased speed of the ship also made it imperative to be certain that the hull of the ship was not damaged by the water over which they raced. The rune was larger and far more complex than the fishing vessel she'd repaired in Lenacru. Not only the waves endangered the ship's coherence: the horses were brought a few at a time up the ramp from below to take exercise around the large main deck. Rin had joined them, happy to get a chance to stretch her legs.

Tildi had a further spell to maintain. Olen wished to see more of the Great Book.

"As much as humanly possible, until we need to put it aside," he said emphatically. Since she loved the old wizard as dearly as she did the book, she was all too happy to let the scroll hover near him, turning it to the next page at his instruction. But her duties did not end there. She had to take her turn to maintain the integrity of the ship so the runes that were disturbed by the rush of the Arown beneath the hull did not cause it to break apart or change into another material. Serafina also insisted that her daily lessons go on until their attention was claimed elsewhere.

Serafina often took her place beside her to learn from Olen as well. For anyone else to set aside her authority and become once again a humble student would be a challenge to dignity, but Serafina proved she was more devoted to her craft than her pride. Tildi respected her deeply.

She tried not to waste a single moment of their time, as she had at Silvertree. She thought of the great tree fondly, and had to ask after her welfare.

Olen smiled, his thick mustache lifting over the corners of his mouth. "She is well, thank you. Oh, I forgot. She sent you a gift." From a pouch at his belt he brought forth a curling leaf, transparent and green, and still smelling fresh. "She does not shed her leaves while they are green, except for you, it would seem. Once you make your wand from the twig she gave you, you'll change that twig's fundamental nature, and that will be your own. But the leaf will always have Silvertree's rune for you."

"I will treasure it," she said, holding it to her breast. The fragrance made her remember those happy days all over again. "I will keep it with the things that belonged to my brothers."

"Well, it's not as though you will never see *Silvertree* again," Olen said, drawing her attention away from her sorrows. "She would like to have you return. Anytime you would like. Your room is yours, as long as you would like to have it. It is your home. At the moment you have none."

Tildi felt a yearning to return to that cozy room, but pushed it aside with an effort. "Please, Master Olen, don't talk to me of home. I can't even think of it right now. I won't be able to finish my mission if I know I have a safe place to go to."

"The trouble with a fallback is that one tends to fall back upon it," Olen agreed gravely. "Sometimes, my child, you are wiser than I. I should have more faith in you. You have no need of a reward to move forward. That puts you ahead of any number of heroes and kings I could name."

Tildi looked guiltily at the two royal gentlemen seated together on U-shaped chairs at the stern, enjoying the thin yellow sunshine.

"They cannot hear us, child," Olen said. "In any case, it would not apply to them. For all their failings, both have always sought to do well by their people at the cost of their own happiness."

"She does need a wand, Master Olen," Serafina said firmly. "If she has the materials, perhaps the moment is at hand."

"You are quite right, Master Serafina," Olen said, giving her her proper title. "Tildi, do you have the twig here?"

"With my things, master," Tildi said, feeling her heart race with excitement. Olen smiled kindly upon her.

"Go get it. This will be a good lesson for you, and a useful reminder in technique for the two of us."

Serafina gave her a gracious nod of approval. Tildi beamed.

She dashed down the steps from the high stern, past the kings in their grand seats. The parade of horses was still circling the wide deck. With a bare thought, she solidified the air under her feet and leaped over the back of a black mare, who threw her head wildly. Rin, two behind the black horse, grinned up at her and tossed her long, waving hair.

"Sorry!" Tildi called back to the startled groom leading the mare as she pelted down the steps to the lower deck. At last she would have her own wand! She yanked open the cupboard where her knapsack was stored and dug through it, looking for the cloth-wrapped twig, the gift from Silvertree.

*T*he school of kotyrs galloping along the high bluffs of Ivirenn made no sound when they saw the rune far to the east, but turned toward it as one. A sheer drop of over sixty feet lay at their feet, but it did not frighten them. An arch of silver droplets, they dove off the cliff and plunged into the Arown. They saw their goal, and that was all that mattered to them. Their sharp noses sensed the true rune. Their long bodies wriggled through the water as swiftly as the current.

Knemet, woken from his restless meditation by the sudden change in vision, was excited, a sensation long lost from him. He sprang up from his chair and threw his arms to the sky. This time, he felt that the kotyrs had found their true mark. The image was tiny, but they did not make mistakes. He did not create them to make mistakes. He focused upon what was within their sight. A ship, midstream, sails puffed out against the wind. Its hull clove the water like a blade. It moved more rapidly than the other craft on the water, much more rapidly. Wizards were at work here. He flew toward it in his mind's eye. The kotyrs saw what the thraiks never could: this ship was protected by warding to defeat magical sight. But anyone within sight would have noticed this vessel, could not have taken their eyes off it. It was decorated all over by golden runes, the runes of creation that he and his colleagues had set free by creating the Compendium. The book must be on board. He urged the lead kotyr to surface and focused upon the ship. At his command it leaped into the air. Could he see the scroll through its wide eyes?

He recognized her from Nemeth's visions: long dark hair, golden skin like an elf's, slender as a sapling. She was younger than he had thought. The man was unknown to him, but he bore the marks of wisdom and wit, silver hair and bright, curious green eyes. Knemet saw some of the others from the seer's visions as well, the other two wizardesses: the magnificent centaur woman with flashing green eyes, and the sturdy dwarf woman with her thick gold braids. Apart from them was the smallfolk, a tiny, scared creature sitting on the deck. Their kind did not have magic. Good. One fewer opponent to concern himself with.

Over the wizards' heads flew the object of his quest. The Compendium, half open, dancing in the air like a pennant. His heart pounded in his chest. At last!

He called out. "I see it, my children!" The thraiks kicked off from their eyries above him and flew around impatiently in circles. "Go! I will guide your hand. Go now! Bring it to me intact! Do not destroy it before I can."

The air above him tore open, and they vanished into it.

Eels," called Captain Betiss, pointing off the starboard rail. "We'll have a roast of them for dinner. Cast nets!"

The crew howled their assent and raced to obey his orders. The merchant captain bowed to Olen and the kings who approached him with crossed arms and legs akimbo, watching the leaping silver shapes.

"If such a meal would please your honors," he said. "I apologize for not asking."

"Sir, a guest is glad for whatever his host chooses to regale him with," Olen said, his eyes twinkling from under his curling brows. "Do you not agree, my lords?"

"Course I do," Halcot said bluffly. "Means I've eaten some rotten food on my travels, but never gone hungry. Not in your halls, brother," he said, slapping Soliandur on the back.

"I am gratified to hear it, brother," the Orontavian king said dryly. "My cooks do well for us. I have no complaints of them."

Olen turned to Tildi, who hastily stood up at the approach of the two kings.

"Tildi, has your family eaten eels? Do you have a suggestion as to their preparation?"

Tildi felt herself blush. "I used to stew them most of the time," she said. "My brothers liked it that way."

Haroun was eager to please his illustrious visitors. "We will stew our catch if you choose."

"No, please," Tildi said, embarrassed to be deferred to by two kings and two wizards. "Whatever you would like."

"Roasted it is, then," Olen said. "We must return to our spell."

Haroun shouted more orders, and three sailors threw out a bundle that spread out into a huge net. It slapped onto the water's surface and was dragged underneath by the current.

Tildi glanced over the stern of the ship at the tame cloud that blew into their sails. The werewolf crew had come to terms with having their own wind source, and were even enjoying tacking a bit to the right and left to test the ship's maneuverability at that speed. Even the horses had ceased to fear the deck rocking beneath their feet. Olen had taken over the responsibility for the ships' runes, leaving her to concentrate upon the making of her wand.

At Serafina's instruction, she had rubbed the twig smooth with oil. She didn't want to peel it and lose the beautiful silver bark that reminded her so much of her master's home, but the young wizardess assured her it would not affect the finished implement.

"As long as the shape is there, suited for pointing, you can ornament it as you choose, or not." Serafina smiled and removed her own wand from the pouch at her belt. The white willow wood had been etched with a delicate pattern like withies, tiny leaves fanned over the surface like lace.

Tildi admired it, but couldn't make up her mind whether to carve hers or leave it plain. The longer she dithered, the more impatient she became. She was so eager to have it done that she had just about decided upon leaving it as it was.

Good enough for a plain-thinking smallfolk, she thought practically.

"I won't carve it," she told Serafina at last.

"Very well then," the wizardess said. "Let it go to hover in the air. It should rest upon the merest whisper of power. Good. Hold your hands just away from either end and concentrate upon it." She nodded approval as

Tildi placed her hands in the air. "You will have the tool you make, so keep your thoughts clear and pure, so that spells that flow through the wand are not obstructed in any way. Flawed wands can burst with the effort of trying to force magic through them."

The notion alarmed Tildi so much she had to force herself to stop worrying about it so she could empty her mind. The book seemed excited about her work. It dipped close as though it was looking over her shoulder. Tildi smiled at it as she would at a friend. The voices sounded encouraging, but there was a note of warning in them. Indeed they might warn her; Olen said that to create a wand was to put a part of one into another object so that it would understand her will and aid her when she used it to work magic. But how much?

She closed her eyes and thought about putting herself into the slender stick.

"Oh, no, no, no," Olen said, his voice full of horror. He sprang up and waved his staff to attract Haroun's attention. "Silver armor—poison! Captain! Captain, cut loose those nets!"

How hospitable, Knemet thought, seeing the seines draped alongside the ship's hull. They were providing a ladder for his hounds. He aimed them for the great scroll itself. He could almost weep at the sight of his long-lost treasure. They would pinpoint it for the poor, magic-blinded thraiks.

Like silver arrows fired in a barrage, they poured up over the side of the ship and made for the Compendium. Knemet saw the faces of the moonfolk. Like all of their kind, they responded swiftly to stimulus. His sight of them had risen only half a man height before they all began to change to their wolf shapes.

"Make for the Compendium," he ordered the kotyrs. "Surround it so there is no mistake. The thraiks are coming."

The kotyrs slithered between the legs of the horses on deck. The sensitive animals screamed their terror and bucked furiously, kicking and biting at the grooms who strove to calm them. Knemet was glad of the distraction; half the crew would be unable to hurry to the aid of the Compendium before his servants reached it.

"To me, Rabantae!" shouted a tall man with golden hair and beard. He raised his sword above his head, then ran to the aid of the smallfolk girl.

Human guards in red-and-white livery came from every corner of the ship and hurried toward the stern. Some of them had been exercising horses and had to hand over their frightened charges to other humans. With their captain at the head, they forced their way toward the Compendium. To protect it, Knemet supposed. He sneered. What were twenty men? He had hundreds of kotyrs, and thousands more on the way.

The centaur maiden, her jewel-like eyes flashing in her dark face, seemed to discern the kotyrs' intention—little surprise for one of her breed. She wound her way among her equine kin, dodging thrashing hooves and snapping jaws, seeking to follow. That would not do.

"Bite the horses! Not all of them. That one, the chestnut, and that white one."

The kotyr in which his vision dwelt at that moment obeyed his will with relish. It snapped its narrow jaws around the ankle bones and bounded on-ward. Knemet sought the eyes of one of his creatures farther back, and saw the two horses foam suddenly at the mouth. Their caretakers exclaimed hoarsely and tried to separate their moaning charges from the others. Their fear infected the others, who began to scream and try to break away from their handlers. The hysteria impeded the soldiers, who were forced to re-treat away from the suffering animals.

"Poison!" cried the senior wizard. "Avoid their bite!"

The dwarf wizardess avoided the thrashing horses by clambering up on the rail and running along it as if she were a squirrel. Knemet sent three ko-tyrs squirming toward her. A bite would put her out of the way. The fewer defenders with whom he had to engage, the better. She was warned, though. She grabbed up a stout pin from a rack and advanced upon them fearlessly. He ordered the kotyrs to attack her. One sprang, but her aim was good. She smacked it in midair and sent it flying into the waters of the Arown. The other two soon followed their fellow over the side. They swam after the ship, keening their frustration. Knemet commanded others to attack the dwarf woman, but had little interest in her. She did not have the book, and that was all he cared for.

He scanned the stern where he had seen the book from the water. It was no longer flying free. Where was it? He let his mind drift from kotyr to kotyr, looking for the precious scroll. Did the human wizardess have it? No, it was in the hands of the smallfolk. The girl clutched it to her like a baby. All to the good. He was curious that it did not burn her, as it did anyone who had not been involved in its making, but never mind. She could not keep it from his minions. The golden-skinned wizardess spread out her hands, and a thin dome like half a bubble formed over the girl. Knemet smiled grimly. Not enough. Not against his forces.

The sky tore open in a black gash, shocking against the clear blue. The dozen or so thraiks flitted through it and circled. The lord thraik let out a questing cry.

"Thraiks!" came the cry from a hundred throats.

"Get it!" he ordered, his words echoed upward to the hunters in the shrill voices of his silver hounds. "You can see the kotyrs! Go to where they are! The smallfolk girl has it."

The thraiks were uneasy diving for a target they could not see. The book's rune was still concealed from them by the wardings. Knemet repeated his order. The thraiks had no choice but to obey. They dove for the girl. She stared up at them, large brown eyes pinned open with terror. She did not move. *All to the good*, Knemet thought.

The wizard, glowing even in the kotyrs' vision like the noonday sun overhead, was at her side in moments. He fell to one knee, his arms raised. Suddenly the thraiks bounced away from the girl. Knemet cursed. The man had erected a near-impenetrable ward in half a second. The winged beasts rose, keening their displeasure. Arrows whistled toward the thraiks. Two missiles struck their marks, but the rest arced harmlessly below them and plunged into the river. The thraiks descended again, kicking fruitlessly at the warding. The girl cowered low over the precious Compendium.

Three of the guards reached the girl's side. Together with their lord, they began to stab and slash at the kotyrs. The captain, a stern woman with blue eyes, gutted one with a sweep of her blade and flung the still wriggling body at the others. Knemet growled, forcing more to leap at her, but her thick mailed gloves and sturdy leather armor turned aside their bites. Her soldiers swept them off her and stamped them into the deck with stout boots.

The wizard stood up, forming a rune between his hands. He flung it at Knemet—no, at his kotyrs. They staggered backward, but only a few feet. A deep breath, and they surged forward again. The wizard looked surprised. Knemet was pleased. He had given his creation a good deal of resistance to magic. Was it enough to force their way through the warding? He commanded them to keep on with the attack.

All at once, defenders from all over the ship were rushing to aid the wizard and the girl. The werewolves threw their netsful of kotyrs over the side and sought to catch more. They howled in pain as the snakelike creatures evaded the traps and sprang at their would-be captors. The human wizardess made her way to those who were wounded, and wove runes of healing over them.

Shouting came from the second ship. The thraiks sailed wide of the first vessel, keening their confusion. At his order, they dove again, making for the girl and the book in her arms. It would take time, but with the help of the kotyrs they could beat their way through the spell. Knemet was prepared to be patient.

The second ship hove near to the first. A huge wave leaped up between them, cascading water over the horses in the belly of the ship. The gray-haired wizard made a gesture. Over a bridge consisting of a single glowing rune, humans in blue-and-white leaped from rail to rail, swords or war hammers in hand. They ran to surround the smallfolk girl.

Some of the blue-and-white-clad soldiers, still on the second vessel, had stepped into bows and snapped the strings into place. At the word of their female commander, they nocked a second flight of arrows and loosed. Knemet ordered the thraiks to get out of range. The thraiks were only too glad to obey. They clapped their great wings and sailed high. Only one arrow found its mark, in the leg of one of the smaller and younger flyers that had been too slow. It shrieked in pain and gnawed at the shaft. Knemet ignored it. He must have the book.

He commanded the kotyrs forward. Frustrated at being made to withdraw from their designated prey, they attacked anyone within reach. The wizards were too well warded, but the many warriors were vulnerable.

At his word, the kotyrs leaped at their throats.

Chapter Twenty-five

aster Olen, help us over!" shouted Magpie. Tildi saw the elder wizard throw a hand in the direction of the stern of each ship. The bags of wind collapsed, and the ships juddered to an amble as the sails sagged.

The *Eclipse* maneuvered close, its wolf-faced captain anxious at the wheel. Olen raised his staff, and a long, narrow rune bridged the rails between *Eclipse* and *Corona*. The Scholardom was already crowding the side. A few had bows up, firing at the thraiks. The evil, winged monsters hovered just out of range, howling defiance. Tildi was terrified of them, but she was more frightened still of the snakelike creatures that filled the deck.

"What are they?" she cried.

"I don't know," Olen said. "I have never seen their like, and I have looked at thousands of species over hundreds of years. Their bite is poisonous. That's a rare trait. They aren't eels, and they certainly aren't snakes. I am afraid we are dealing with an entirely new species." To Tildi's amazement, he sounded curious rather than alarmed or frightened.

A writhing cluster surrounded them, flinging themselves at the warding over and over. The pale gray wall of force knocked them away like a backhand blow, but there were always more to try again. Tildi cringed every time they did it. The Rabantavian guard streamed up the ship's ladder and formed around them. The silver-skinned creatures slithered to avoid them, but the guards drove them back with kicks and sword point. It did not keep them back. The warriors did their best to scoop them up and fling them overboard without getting bitten.

Serafina hurried among them to heal those who had already sampled the intruders' poison. Olen had called for her to join them within the spell's protective bubble, but she shook her head firmly. Tildi admired her bravery. The sight of the thraiks made her shiver uncontrollably.

"Are you injured?" Captain Teryn shouted to Tildi.

"I am all right!" Tildi reassured her, trying to bring her terrors under control. She worried about the two kings. Surely they should be inside the wards with her. She looked around for Halcot and Soliandur. They stood with their backs to the protective spell wall. Slate-blue and scarlet-red halberds, black and golden manes, they moved like longtime brothers in arms, defending one another—and her. Tildi knew from Magpie's quiet stories that they had been enemies only a few years ago. Had it been this mission that brought them together as allies? Olen noticed them as well, and opened his hand. The walls of the ward opened farther, encompassing the two men. The silver eels shrieked as they threw themselves against the magical barrier. King Halcot's jaw fell.

"What just happened?" he demanded.

"This is a minor annoyance, my lords," Olen said. "I see no reason to risk the crowned heads of two nations."

"Minor annoyance!" Soliandur echoed, his dark eyes glaring. "There are thraiks out there!"

"Who do not seem to be attacking anyone else, did you notice? All they want is Tildi and her treasure."

"Guard the Great Book!" Tildi heard Sharhava's voice high and clear over all others.

"You see?" Olen said. "She has discerned their one aim."

The blue-and-white habits joined the red and white tunics in the circle around her. Tildi feared for their safety. There seemed to be an endless stream of the snake-things. The creatures' screaming tore at her nerves. Their huge eyes fixed upon her like starving dogs. She knew they would do anything to get at her.

Her eyes just as hungry, Sharhava forced her way through them and peered in through the gray wall. "We will keep you safe, Mistress Summerbee. Do not fear."

"I won't," Tildi promised. Before the words left her lips, Sharhava had turned away to concentrate upon her defense.

"We should be out there with her," Halcot said. "She is the sister of queens. My armor is better than theirs."

"And mine!" added Soliandur.

Olen shook his head. "They may not have your armor, but they have the advantage of having practiced using the book's magic, my lords. See."

"Repel!" Sharhava shouted. At her side, Loisan barked her orders in a louder voice. The knights responded by holding out their shield-hands. The silver creatures, captured in mid-leap, flew backward several feet, landing on the deck. They sprang up, hissing, and redoubled their effort, only to be met by the swords and hammers of the Scholardom.

"By the stars," Halcot hissed. "And they are ordinary folks, not wizards? I underestimated the Scholardom."

"As did we all," Olen said.

Morag, only an arm's reach from Tildi, had his teeth gritted. He had had to switch his sword to his left hand. The right was swollen and red. A flurry of green robes, and Serafina alighted behind him.

"Do not jump, my friend," she said. "I will heal you."

The craggy-faced sergeant gave a curt nod. Serafina reached around to touch his right hand and murmured to herself. Tildi could not see more, but the guard's back straightened and his blows doubled in speed. The wizardess moved on to other victims. Some were reduced to weeping on the deck with the pain. Tildi's heart went out to them. She feared for them more than she did for her own well-being.

"Can we not protect them all, Master Olen?"

"At the moment, Tildi, you and what you hold are more important than anyone out there. Anyone. They knew their lives might be the price of this journey." His face was grave. Tildi felt unworthy and wished she could give up her place to the man on his knees not five feet from her.

"There is my son!" Soliandur exclaimed. Tildi glanced to her right. The troubadour prince fought bareheaded in the midst of a group of Scholardom warriors. The small figure of Lady Inbecca was at his left hand. Grim-faced, she dragged her sword overhead and brought it down hard. A loud shriek told those inside the wards that she had made a kill. Several leaped up at her, but Magpie drove himself between them and her. Together they cudgeled and elbowed the beasts away from their faces. "Let me out of here, Master Wizard!"

"My lord, I cannot keep opening and closing the wards! They are our best defense."

The dark eyes in their shadowed sockets flared as if the embers within them had been blown upon. "I have not come this far to see him or his dear lady die of poison. Either let me out or bring him in here."

"We must solve this problem in its entirety, my lord," Olen said, not moving to open the wards. At that moment, hundreds of the silver creatures smacked audibly into the protective spell. It let out a loud crackle, like the stem of a glass snapping. Tildi saw lines of the rune that formed it weakening. To her horror, the deck beneath them was changing, too, with none of them to keep an eye on rebuilding it. The fine, stout boards were thinning and turning black, as though they were charring. She cudgeled her terrified brain for the way the *Corona*'s rune had been before and reached out toward the floor.

"Tildi, no," Olen snapped. "Only my spells must go through this ward, else it weaken. It is already fading against the onslaught."

Tildi stopped, but not because of his admonition. She jumped up at the glimpse of movement beneath her feet. Was the deck falling apart already?

"Master!" she screamed.

Olen looked down. The kings followed his eyes and swore. Below them writhed dozens of the silver-skinned creatures. They had come up through the floor and twisted this way and that like maggots found under a rock.

A louder scream came from above, echoed by hoarse shouts from the fighters around them. Tildi was rocked off her feet by a heavy blow. A shadow had suddenly blocked the skies. She tried to stand up, but a second strike upset the three men, who were cast down with her. The thraiks had returned, and were trying to pound their way through the wards from above.

Teryn and Loisan barked orders, and the guardian force divided to deal with the second menace. The largest swordsmen pressed in to slash at the feet and wings of the thraiks. Bowmen leaped away to find high points to aim without endangering their fellows. Werewolves, with crazed yellow eyes, jumped high, seeking to drag the winged monsters down. Tildi could see nothing but frenzied movement all around her. The screaming seemed to rend her nerves. The eel-things stared at her. Their wide, glinting, avid eyes terrified Tildi. Her heart tried to pound its way out of her chest.

"We're holed!" came a cry. Some of the werewolves pulled themselves away from the melee and disappeared from Tildi's sight. Her conscience battered at her.

"Master, I should be able to fix the ship!"

"No, Tildi. We will solve this dilemma before we sink, or it will no longer matter. Let Haroun cope."

A pair of dark eyes suddenly claimed her attention from the side of the bubble. Serafina had forced her way over.

"Master Olen!" she cried. "How can the thraiks be attacking her, master? The warding is the same we have been using for months. How can they see her?"

The elder wizard's eyebrows rose, and his eyes widened.

"They cannot," Olen said. "They never could. The silver creatures are guiding them! I understand! Fool that I am, I understand at last! Thank you, my dear."

Magpie plunged his blade down and came up with one of the ribbonlike creatures impaled upon it. Its moonlike eyes fixed on him, and the small, sharp jaws snapped, though it hadn't a chance to reach him with its teeth. He grinned ferally and brandished it at his father before flinging it away. The king of Orontae regarded him warmly, but turned to glare at Olen.

"What is it, Master Olen? I have never seen its like."

"I do not know, my lord!" Olen said. "Tildi, show me these creatures."

Tildi, glad for anything to focus upon, opened the book and mentally pleaded with it to show her the right page. As ever, it obliged, spinning in air, until she saw the rune for the ship. She spread out her hands, and it seemed to enlarge between them. She could pick out each of the people on board. At the center was the book, with the thraiks and the strange beasts surrounding it, only a dozen of the former but hundreds or thousands of the latter, and more crowding in all the time. Though she and Olen and the kings were closest to it, they were of less importance to whatever intelligence drove the book. She held out the book to Master Olen, and pointed to the shining image. The wizard crouched beside her, careful not to touch the parchment.

"Why can you not drive them away, the way you did the Madcloud?" Tildi asked.

"I cannot," Olen said. "The Madcloud was but one entity. To surround it as we did was much less difficult. I am being thwarted. There is an intelligence driving them—their creator!"

"Can you see him?" Tildi asked, scanning the page as if she would find a pair of malicious eyes glaring back at her.

"No, I can't, curse it. He blocks me again and again. I must find the vulnerability within the beasts, somehow . . ." Olen studied the rune. "This image I have never seen before. So well crafted. I regret this mightily, Tildi, but I have no choice. *Achochta!*"

The image on the book changed slightly. Instead of a host of eel-creatures, she saw one large one. Tildi realized Olen had asked to see the single sigil that represented the species, the master rune.

She felt a rush of air around her.

"Master, the wards are gone!"

"Our enemy makes his own move," Olen exclaimed.

The silver creatures, as though summoned, surged upward, twining around their legs. Tildi lifted up a yard from the deck, but they clung to her, straining toward the book, wriggling out along both her arms. She screamed. The kings seized the creatures and threw them to the deck, following with blows of their swords. More and more tried to jump toward her. They screamed, and the thraiks answered. Two of the winged devils ceased their circling, and dove toward them.

Olen looked up. "There's no time to waste!" He seized the knife from his belt and pricked his finger. A drop of blood appeared upon it. He drew that finger in a spiral across the head of the beast. The tip of his finger burned black from contact with the white parchment, but the eel-creatures began to jackknife and writhe on the deck. They shrieked angrily.

The thraiks stopped in midstoop and retreated high into the sky, keening their confusion. Olen, his hand shaking with pain, began to redraw the wards. He stopped, wiped them from the air, and began to start over.

"What did you do, Master Olen?" Soliandur asked.

"These creatures guide the thraiks, my lords!" Olen said. "I have struck them blind."

"That will hurt you like a stab wound, master," Halcot said, eyeing the burned finger with sympathy. He turned to shout. "Healer! Come here, swiftly!"

Serafina heard him, and began to pick her way across the slippery and blood-soaked deck. With the creatures at least partially disarmed, the guards were taking out their anger and frustration, spitting as many of them as they could. The silver animals shrieked and struck out—blindly. Tildi shuddered at the slaughter.

The lack of wards had its own effect, though. The thraiks were no longer blind to the rune themselves. The lord thraik turned his mud-colored gaze upon Tildi. He cried out an order, and all twelve gathered like archers pulling back their strings. They closed their wings and descended toward her, their eyes glittering with the rune of the book she held in her lap.

"They shall not have you so easily," Olen said, his face sweating with the strain. "*Voshte!*" He brought his hands together in a thunderclap over his head. The winds stopped as if Tildi had shut a door. The thraiks wheeled above them, shrieking with fury.

Knemet shrieked out his own fury.

He had been watching for his moment. He shouted his orders.

The kotyrs were undeterred that the crew threw them into the river. They could swim as well as any of their fish forebears. They could also burrow, using the means of other ancestors. At his command, they had twisted their way through a timber in the hull that had thinned and darkened like the rest of the ship and flowed upward, twining along beams and up ladders. Passage by so many prized the board into splinters. Water flooded in behind them, but what of that? *They* wouldn't drown. They made for the Compendium. Its rune glowed through the solid but less real deck. The kotyrs followed the beacon, as many of them getting as close to it as they could. The thraiks hovered high, ready.

A bark of command from the lord thraik set the winged beasts into motion. Down, down they plummeted. Every face on the ship was upturned with terror. They still could not believe their doom was upon them.

Suddenly his vision went black. Knemet clawed at his eyes. The pain was enough to bring him back to his stone chamber. His own eyesight had not been destroyed, but that of the kotyrs had been!

"Who will interfere with my creation? Who dares?" Knemet summoned the rune that he had used to create the kotyrs and examined it. A line was there that had not been before. His perfect design! He tried to change the rune back, but he could not remove that line. He tried again and again. Either the wizard with whom he dueled at this great distance was fast and prescient, or he had changed the rune in the Compendium itself. No! They had not only been struck blind, but all the parts of the mind and eyes that controlled sight had been destroyed. It had been made real, too real to undo easily.

He was losing time. He could still hear through the kotyrs' ears the wailing of the thraiks, who shouted that they had lost their prey. With the kotyrs struck blind, he could no longer guide the thraiks by sight.

"You know the rune; go to it!" Knemet shouted at them.

The lord thraik bellowed out a protest. They could not see the rune any longer.

He cursed. That other wizard was his enemy for now and for all time remaining. "You know the smell of the book. You were close enough to take it! I should not have to guide you! Go to where it was! The wizardesses have it! Take it and return! Return to me."

Chapter Twenty-six

he walls of the protective spell seemed different: thinner and more brittle, and almost blue in hue. Olen knelt beside Tildi, his hands trembling as if with a fever. He noticed her look of concern, and his mustache lifted at the left corner in a wry smile.

"Our opponent has made intelligent strikes, Tildi. He is trying to frustrate me even as I frustrate him. Look how cleverly he waited until his silver snakes were ready before he brought down the wardings. Magic is not without its price. I am weary, but I will not stop until we are out of danger. Neither will Serafina."

"Let me help, master," Tildi said.

"You must not," Olen said firmly. "All your strength must be intact in case he beats through our defenses. You must be ready to defend the book against all his tricks." He grimaced and closed his eyes for a moment. "He has found me." Tildi saw tendrils surround Olen's rune. They changed rapidly, and Tildi tried to guess what was happening. "Guard yourself," he ordered.

Outside the small shell, the complement of both ships dispatched or kicked aside the now helpless eel-creatures. The huge, round eyes gaped, fixed on nothing. That looked almost more terrifying to Tildi than when they were focused upon her.

The thraiks had been called into play now, seeing or unseeing. Tearing the air with their cries, they descended, their green-black wings blocking the light. Red blood splashed off the spell's dome as their claws found purchase in the flesh of victims. A man in Halcot's livery fell against Tildi's shelter, half his throat torn away. Tildi screamed. Olen extended the protection over the man and stretched both hands over his body. Sadly, the wizard shook his head. The man's eyes were already dulling in death. Tildi wept for him, knowing his rune in the book was changing.

Tildi saw a shadow she knew rear above them and crack a whip. The lash stung one of the thraiks in the leg and brought forth a wail.

"That is for you and your foul master!" Rin shrilled. The whip sang again.

The thraik struck back with its terrifying claws. Rin avoided their grasp, but a werewolf beside her was not so lucky. The flying monster grabbed the brown-furred female and lifted it to its jaws to bite her head off. The female fought back, tearing at the beast with her own teeth. A score of her relations leaped up, dragging the thraik down. They clawed and bit it until it let go its prey. Bleeding from countless small wounds, it thrust them away and reached for another victim, Romini, one of the Scholardom, and hastily lifted him too high for any of the others to reach. Many rushed to follow its path, shouting encouragement to the knight, but the thraik toyed with them, making them chase it up and back over the length of the ship. Tildi could see the malicious gleam in its eyes. Suddenly it dropped him onto the heads of the crowd. He landed on the stairs and sat up, clutching his ribs. Three of the knights hurried to aid him. The rest of the thraiks wreaked similar mischief, wounding where they could and causing confusion.

Two of the thraiks hung in the air high above the fight, too high for arrows to strike.

"What are they waiting for?" Tildi asked wildly.

"Never fear," Olen said. "They cannot touch you. They cannot see you."

Serafina had also noticed the two thraiks. "*Idir!*" she cried, pointing at the nearer thraik.

Its wings stopped hovering, and it fell like a stone into the river. The wizardess pointed at the lord thraik. "*Idir!*"

Halcot's scarlet face almost matched his tunic. "Master Wizard, destroy them all!"

Olen looked perturbed, as if the king had roused him from deep thought. "What would you have me do, highness? A windstorm? A clap of thunder? We are as vulnerable to such a working as they would be while they are among us. The ship is already damaged. It could sink if I drew down a force of nature like that. Mistress Serafina is doing an admirable job of picking them off one at a time."

"I want them all gone!"

"As soon as opportunity arises, my lord. I do not want to further endanger the lives of those who trust us."

Suddenly the thraik seemed to lose patience with the game. It flicked its wings and arched high into the air, turning over and over. It let out a lazy, derisive squawk. As many of the others that could still fly suddenly disengaged from the fray. They spread out across the heavens, then flew outward. The defenders backed to protect Tildi. They did not know which way to look.

"Ah, at last," Olen said. He stood up and moved outside the guardian spell. "Brace yourself, Tildi." He stretched out his arms and pointed the head of his staff straight upward.

As swift as the wind itself, the thraiks closed in on the ship, claws and teeth bared.

"Archers, loose!" cried Sharhava.

Arrows flew outward like the spokes of a giant wheel. It was too easy for the thraiks to avoid them. The defenders crouched against the coming attack.

"Ah," Olen said. "At last. *Fornlau cnetech voshad!*"

He brought his staff down upon the deck. The wood splintered underneath its foot, but Tildi felt something like a tide rush outward from that small, round point. In seconds, the ship was surrounded by an enormous rose-tinted bubble.

The thraiks could not stop in time. They crashed into the surface. It flung them outward again. At least one seemed to have been knocked insensible by the impact. It hung limply on the air for a moment, its dark, translucent wings billowing upward, then dropped into the water. The werewolf crew howled and laughed. The human defenders shouted for victory.

The lord thraik recovered its wits before the rest. It let out a terrible scream.

The eel-creatures that remained alive responded, their voices piercing Tildi's delicate hearing like knives.

The lord thraik screamed again. Its followers flew inward toward the bubble. Pools of black rent the sky as they vanished into them. The darkness fled, leaving only pink-tinted sunshine around them.

"Well, thank the Father," Halcot began.

His gratitude was premature. Blackness blossomed within the confines of the spell itself. The thraiks struck them all like a tornado coming from all directions. The defenders were thrown in all directions, cannoning into one another. Olen shouted and threw a hand, not at the thraiks, but at King Halcot. The defenders struggled to regain their footing and strike at the assailants. The thraiks were no longer there to strike. They had lifted into the air, two victims in their grasp. One held Rin around the striped barrel of her body. The other clutched Lakanta to him like a child's doll.

"No!" Tildi shrieked.

Olen lifted his staff. Light lanced from it. The thraiks seemed to be dragged downward, then kicked free with force. The glow faded. Olen's face twisted with strain.

The centaur and dwarf were not willing prisoners. Rin kicked out with all four hooves. She threw the lash of her whip around the neck of the monster holding her. Lakanta belabored the face and skull of her captor with her wooden pin.

"Let me go, you bat-winged menace!" She jammed the pin into its eye. "Do something!" she shouted over her shoulder.

"Help them!" cried Magpie. He grabbed Serafina's hand and ran down the few steps to the herd of terrified horses. He pulled the piebald mare out of the group. "Help me!" he pleaded. Serafina understood. Magpie swung onto Tessera's back and pulled her head back by her mane. She obeyed, and galloped into the air, on solid footing provided by Serafina's magic.

Captain Teryn grinned ferally. "Morag!" she shouted, waving her sword in the air. The two guards ran for their mounts as well.

The thraiks saw Magpie coming. They opened their jaws at him as though they laughed at him. Too swift to catch, they skimmed away in a band, flitting their tails derisively. Behind him, Olen shouted out a command. Three of the thraiks dropped out of the air, dead or senseless, but the two carrying the friends were shielded by the bodies of other monsters. Olen threw another bolt, this one of hot yellow flame. The enchanter's fire caught only the wing tip of a thraik, but it spread over the sails and ribs as if they were made of tissue paper. The thraik wailed as it was consumed by fire. Pointing a hand, Olen drew a rune ahead of them. Tildi stared at it, urgently, waiting for the thraik to fly into it and get stuck, like moths in a spiderweb.

Only yards above the deck, the sky opened on darkness, just short of Olen's trap. The thraiks sped through. It closed and vanished. Olen's next blast of power sailed past and dissipated. The three riders reached the spot, but nothing was left except empty air.

For a short time, there was only silence. Tildi stared at the place where her friends had vanished, not able to believe it. Suddenly she felt suffocated inside the small shelter. It had protected her, and left everyone else in danger. She fought loose of the spell and stood up. Tears pricked her eyes. When she blinked to clear them, more poured down her cheeks. Her chest tightened as if bonds of iron closed around her heart. The voices in the book sounded almost tender and soothing. She pushed it out of her arms to hover beside her. It was to blame for her friends' deaths. If not for it, they would be safe and alive.

A low moan came from somewhere in the crowd of defenders on the deck. A male werewolf lying on his back amid the bloody ruin waved a feeble hand for help. Another werewolf, a healer by his businesslike gait, loped over and lifted his head into his lap. The sound set Tildi free. She fetched in a breath, and it went out as a gasping sob. Her knees refused to support her. She sat down on the top step of the stairs and wept.

Serafina, too, seemed stunned by the horror. She stood rigid at the side of the main deck, her eyes closed, hand clasping her staff so tightly her fingers were squeezed bloodless.

"My ship, Master Wizard, my ship!" cried Haroun, bounding over the wounded and the dead. He still wore his wolf shape. His fur was as black as his hair in his human form. He pulled at Olen's arm.

"How can you be so heartless?" demanded Lady Inbecca, pushing forward. A streak of blood ran along her cheek, and her habit was spattered with more. Her sea-blue eyes were cold with anger. "Two people have just been carried off for slaughter by the thraiks!"

Haroun turned his bright golden eyes on her. "Because, knight, we will all sink and die if Master Olen does not spare us. Look!" He waved a long paw. The *Corona*'s masts were at an acute angle to those of her sister ship that now rode by her side.

Olen seemed to wake from his shock. "You are quite right, Captain. I apologize. Tildi, would you care to . . . ?" He glanced at her. She set her jaw stubbornly as tears continued to drip down her cheeks. She was unashamed to show her grief. He nodded. "Ah, I see. You feel that I have failed you. You can blame me no more than I blame myself, my child. Allow me." He spread out his arms. The color of the deck under their feet turned from ash to golden, and the small cracks and gouges closed up. The whole vessel groaned as the timbers in the damaged hull regained their integrity. "You must still bail, Haroun, but she is sound once again."

"I thank you, master." The captain bounded away, crying orders.

"Lar Inbecca! Attend me, if you please!" Sharhava snapped. "I apologize for her outburst, Master Olen."

Olen bowed slightly. "I do not take offense, Abbess Sharhava. I wouldn't be so patient with me, either. It would seem I needed to have greater foresight than I had." He sighed. "And greater strength. I am getting old, I fear."

The indignant young woman gave Olen one final look of disdain and went to stand silently at the abbess's side. Olen shook his head sadly. He leaned upon his staff. Tildi realized she was wrong to think he did not mourn. The skin over his cheekbones looked tightly drawn, as if he had aged a hundred years. His green eyes looked as dull as dead leaves.

"Master Wizard," Sharhava said, "when all this is cared for, I want you to teach me and my people the flight spell. If they return, and they undoubtedly will, we must take the fight to them, not let them attack us where we stand. The advantage has been theirs. I will lose no more knights to that menace."

"You are right, Abbess," Olen said. "I will be happy to instruct you, though Mistress Serafina has the more practical experience. In any case, you shall learn."

Sharhava nodded sharply, and withdrew, taking her followers with her.

There were not so many dead as Tildi had feared. Five werewolves had been killed, more by the eel-creatures' poison than by thraiks. Three humans, one from Teryn's company and two of the knights, had died. Each one was carefully laid out. Their faces were washed of blood, their wounds and gashes hidden by clean clothing brought up from the hold, then each was wrapped lovingly in white shrouds. To Tildi's surprise, a ring of both werewolves and knights of the Scholardom gathered to grieve over them, regardless of species. Sharhava offered ritual prayers in the ancient human language, humbly asking the Mother and the Father to receive the dead. Tildi was almost convinced of Sharhava's sincerity of reform. When she had done, the werewolf female known as Patha led the group in a howl. The sad, liquid voices in which werewolves cried for their dead sounded more like true grief than any dirge sung by bereaved smallfolk in the Quarters. Tildi hung her head and wished Rin and Lakanta with the Mother and Father.

King Halcot wiped the blade of his sword carefully on a cloth he took from his belt, then carefully sheathed it at his side. He looked as stricken as Tildi felt. "Valiant. Both. I will go to their homes and proclaim their bravery. Prince Lowan will receive me. Best you let me off in Balierenn, Master Olen. I will carry the ill news from there. My soldiers will stay with you. I will not need them."

"The princess of the Windmanes fought like an army," Soliandur said. "The, er, trader also. I would hate to have an army of her people stand against me."

"I regret their passing," Sharhava said. "If they had been humans, their names would be in the annals of the Scholardom." She grimaced. "They will be so inscribed. They protected the Great Book to the very ends of their lives. They were better guardians of it than we were."

"Their deaths will not be forgotten," Magpie said. He and the others had ridden back to the deck and left their horses with the stunned grooms. The horses were calmed and led below. Those in the herd that had sustained injuries from the eel-creatures or thraiks were tended. He wished that a rubdown and a bag of sweet feed would soothe his shock and sorrow as easily. He glanced toward Inbecca. She seemed to be all right. She had fought like the tigress she was. She sorrowed for the lost ones, though her outrage at Olen was that of a bystander, not a friend or companion. It was for Tildi his concern was greatest. The smallfolk girl's usually pink-cheeked face was pale, except for her nose, which was red from crying. Her eyes bore a haunted look that he fancied he shared. Too well did he understand why she was upset with Olen. He had made a choice to use his magic to defend her and what she carried. It was a decision only a king or a leader could make, to sacrifice others for the greatest good. Seldom had he ever been so grateful that the duties of kingship were not his. Magpie was able to contemplate his own grief. He had genuinely admired the centaur princess and the cheeky dwarf trader, and enjoyed their company. He knelt before Tildi and took her hand. "I will write them a song that will live five thousand years."

"That would be fitting," Soliandur said solemnly. "I would look forward to hearing such a tribute sung by you." Magpie was a little surprised, but warily pleased in spite of his sorrow. He risked a glance up over his shoulder at his father. The moment had passed with its usual swiftness, and the king pursed his lips impatiently. He wiped his sword on a cloth handed him by his groom and sheathed it as he walked away. Magpie tried not to feel let down. He sat on the steps and let Tildi lean upon him. The book lay propped on her lap, devoid of its usual dancing energy.

"They are so alive in my mind I can hardly believe them to be dead," he said.

Serafina's crisp voice broke over his.

"They *are* alive."

All of them turned toward her. She remained erect near the rail, her eyes closed.

Olen said, hurrying down the stairs, "They are? Tell me, my dear."

"I can hear them," the young wizardess said wonderingly. "I . . . I hear their rhythm. Their songs."

"Are you certain?"

She looked fully at him, her dark eyes wide. "Master Olen, I am certain. I studied hard while we were among the bearkin. I learned to distinguish the . . . the songs of each of my companions."

Olen's green eyes brightened to jewels. "Where are they?"

Serafina shook her head very slowly. "I do not know. If the bearkin were here, they could tell you, but I cannot. The skill is too new to me. I can only hear them, braided within the rhythm of the rest of nature as I can yours or Tildi's."

"Bless that skill, then," Olen said, smiling. "I never doubted you were your mother's daughter. Well done, my dear."

Serafina looked proud for a moment, then confusion came over her face. "But why steal away Lakanta or Rin? They do not have the Great Book."

"His spies who could penetrate our spells could no longer see Tildi or the book. The thraik leader showed more intelligence and cunning than I believed they had. They made a grab at random, and they think they have gotten what they wanted. Had either Rin or Lakanta ever touched the scroll, Tildi?"

Tildi thought hard, trying to remember over the many weeks of their journey. "Lakanta might have when she pulled me from the fire after I took it away from Nemeth," she said. "I don't know about Rin. I don't think so."

"Many times, I am afraid," Serafina admitted. Tildi looked at her in surprise and dismay. Serafina touched her arm. "You don't know, Tildi, because she asked me not to say, but when you were riding on her back, you touched her with it now and again when you drifted off to sleep or were inattentive. I healed the burns for her. She was proud to bear the pain for your sake. She said it was much worse for you."

Tildi's heart wrenched. "I am so sorry!"

"It doesn't matter now. We know that our friends are alive."

"But where?" Olen asked. He sat down beside Tildi on the steps. Teryn sent her guards running for chairs, but he gestured to her that they should be set forth for the kings and the abbess. "Tildi, let us consult the Great Book. Now that we have assurance that they live, we should be able to locate their runes. The direction in which the thraiks disappeared is not an indication that their lair lies hence, of course. At least we know that we will find them, as long as Mistress Serafina can hear them."

Tildi felt the horror and grief that had paralyzed her begin to leave her limbs. She reached for the scroll, which leaped toward her like a favorite pet. She spread it out upon the air and concentrated upon finding her friends. *What a task!* she thought as the pages began to unfurl themselves. They could be anywhere in the wide world. *But at least they were in the world*, she thought, and the notion comforted her.

"Why not you, then?" Magpie asked Sharhava. "Why were you not carried away as well? You certainly had your hands upon the book."

"Eremi!" Inbecca exclaimed.

"Lar Inbecca, it is a fair question." Sharhava laid her right hand upon the small amulet that Tildi now noticed lay upon her breast and that of each of the Scholardom. "I was spared because of a gift from our new allies. I had no idea of the others, or else I would have suggested they be given the same protection."

"Or I," said Halcot. "But you were not there at our first council, Abbess. I handled a scrap of parchment that burned my hands to the bone. I was lucky not to be carried off."

"Yes," Serafina said, regarding him with concern. "They could have taken you once the first wards fell. You were vulnerable. Why not you?"

"No," Olen corrected her gently. "It was not luck. I knew he had touched the copy. You were the one who healed him, I recall. I put wards upon him as soon as the thraiks burst through the protective spell. I did not know about the others. I regret that."

"It would seem that I need one of these amulets, my friend," Halcot said to Captain Temur.

The werewolf's eyes glinted. "It would be my honor."

"But what about your allies?" Sharhava asked. "You say they live. They will be the prisoners of the master of the thraiks."

"Indeed they will," Olen said, and amusement tweaked the corners of his eyes. "He will have his hands full with those two."

The abbess looked outraged. "Aren't you concerned about their well-being?"

He turned his gaze full upon her. "Of course I am, but I would be much more worried if one of your knights fell into his grasp. You know too much of the history of the book and its powers, and you might comply with his orders just because you know the legend of the Makers rather than the facts that would unroll themselves before you. Rin does not give a toss for the legends. In fact, I think she would like to give more to him than that, on behalf of every centaur, unicorn, and pegasus in the world—all the horsekin."

Tildi didn't know whether to be offended or scared by his cavalier expression.

"We must free them," she insisted.

"Of course we will, my dear," Olen said mildly.

"Yes," Serafina said thoughtfully, and she laid a hand on her chin in an unconscious echo of Olen's gesture. "I have a feeling that we will be given every opportunity to do so, and we must take none that are offered."

"What? Not save them if we can?" Magpie demanded.

"Oh, no, I didn't say that, did I?"

Olen smiled. "You sound more like your mother every day." For a moment Serafina looked mulish, then she laughed.

"Thank you."

"How is it that this Shining One lives in the world without anyone knowing of him all these years?" Soliandur asked. One of his footmen brought wine for him. He gestured to have it served to the abbess before him or his brother king. On silent feet, the werewolves moved around them, putting the ship to rights. Tildi scented a whiff of firewood and the smells of cooking. The lunch that was to have been made of the eel-monsters was being prepared with a much less perilous main ingredient. She was surprised to note that she felt ravenous.

"We may never know that," Olen said. "But we have gleaned other information. We now know that the Maker is not all knowing or all powerful, because he can be fooled. I believe that he has been seeking the Great Book a long, long time. Your brothers, Tildi, had touched the true copy of this book, so the thraiks fetched them away thinking that they had the book."

"And my parents?" Tildi asked, pale.

"Almost certainly. They bought the scrap for you, not knowing its significance. Considering your own surprising immunity to the book's effects upon living flesh, they probably possessed it as well."

Serafina considered the question. "It is possible that that is true. The book has only been free since Nemeth broke into its fastness. Before that, he might have sought for it. Your parents had handled the scrap. I can imagine them turning it over. And so had the peddler who brought it to them, Lakanta's husband."

"This Maker has had his creatures seek out everyone who has ever had contact with even a single rune?" Halcot asked.

"We are still not certain that it is a Maker who is looking for the book, master," Serafina pointed out.

"Very well, Mistress Serafina, I will cede your logic. But a powerful person, nonetheless, who controls the thraiks. Where the thraiks have gone, they have taken our colleagues. I hope they can remain alive."

"It is a game now," Olen said. "A serious one, but a contest of strategy and will, between us and our unknown enemy. Our mission has changed. Now it is more imperative than ever that we reach the mouth of the Arown as quickly as possible. We need our last ally more than ever before. Perhaps the urgency of saving our friends will move him to action. Time knows I have tried often enough before this."

"An ally?" Halcot asked.

"Yes."

"Who is he?"

"His name is Calester," Olen said.

Chapter Twenty-seven

The screaming lasted as long as the rushing of the air. Lakanta took her hands away from her ears and opened her eyes.

"Oof!" she cried. She lay on her back for a time, working her arms and legs, clenching her hands, to make certain everything still worked. It did, thank the stone. But where was she? She felt out with a hand, and brought a handful of what lay upon the ground back to her nose. Foul straw, so old it almost dissolved in her palm. It smelled of rot and droppings. She wiped her hand on the side of her voluminous skirts. "Pew! No one's done any cleaning in the last century or so, indeed they have not."

"Is that you, Lakanta?"

"Rin!" The dwarf woman sat bolt upright. Pain shot through her back, and she winced. She felt along carefully, but the ache was only bruises, not broken bones. "Are you intact? That was a surprise. No wonder Tildi had nightmares about those monsters. I had seen many a one in the sky, but never touched one like that. They are ugly enough to scare my hair white. Not that it's not going that way to start with, what with customers being so slow to pay, and the road getting worse, no matter what all the town councils say . . . !"

"Yes, it is I," the centaur's resonant voice cut through her plaints. Lakanta heard rustling, followed by the clack of shod hooves on stone as Rin, unseen but close by, regained her feet. Lakanta felt her way along the uneven floor until she came to a narrow column like a young tree, but warm. "There you are," Rin said.

"Ah, yes, but where are *we*?" the trader asked. "Those monsters took us into a tear in the sky. Now I know what it was Tildi meant. I really had hoped never to see it for myself, but there you are."

"Here I am," Rin agreed. "Here we are. The truth is much more chilling than any campfire story. I felt as if my lungs were being pressed out of my body when we flew into the blackness. And as soon as I could draw breath, they dropped me on this floor. We are not still within the spell," she mused, her voice echoing. Lakanta imagined that she turned her head to survey their prison in search of light. "The runes are gone. We must be far away. The wind over the ship was sharp and crisp. This place is hot and dank. It smells."

"Wait a moment, I am forgetting my wits! They should be tied around my neck in a bag, I declare." Lakanta felt at her waist. Her belt pouch was still there, firmly attached to her stout leather belt. "Here, let me see if I can make a light. It would be handy to have young Tildi here. She's a game hand with fire."

"Demon fire," Rin said. "Fire should not be green."

"It's less green than it was," Lakanta said absently as she felt through the capacious leather sack for her striker box. Steel and flint felt differently to fingers that were not aided by eyes. The steel felt coarse, as though it had been combed with tiny wires. The flint was smooth, with sharp facets. In another compartment of the small box lay tinder: birds' nests, bits of lint from the yard goods she carried, fluff from milkweeds, whatever was to hand. She set the tinder on a pile of the noxious straw and struck the flint and steel together.

The first hot, yellow spark was echoed in dozens of paired reflections all around them.

"Bless me, Mother and Father!" Lakanta cried. She almost dropped the firestones.

"We are not alone," Rin said dryly. "Are any of you friends?"

Not a sound. Lakanta snorted. Shadows in the night were not going to deprive her of a comforting fire! She lit the tinder, and held a fistful of the dank grass over it until it started to burn. Though it smoked fiercely enough to make her cough, red flames ran up the stalks. Lakanta gathered up the largest pile she could without moving from the spot she stood in, and set it alight.

"Brook reeds," she said with a professional eye. "Won't last long."

"I hope we will not be here long," Rin said.

"Ah!"

The eyes, for the twin lights had to be eyes, had moved much closer, close enough to touch. A thick snout brushed up against Lakanta and pressed its way up and down her skirts, snuffling. It was not a rat, or she hoped not. Rats should not be the size of small pigs.

"Shoo!" she said, swatting it back.

The thing responded with a growl.

"What are they?" Rin demanded. "I have never seen their like in our lands."

"Nor have I," the trader said. "What I can see of them, anyhow, and I cannot say I like what I see."

The small detail her dwindling light afforded them gave Lakanta the chills. The creatures had thick fur, beady eyes, and lopsided, triangular ears. She tried to push her way through them. They showed their teeth. Lakanta recoiled. She had no taste for bitten fingers. "There's too many of them between me and the wall."

"Up on my back!" Rin commanded. She gripped Lakanta's hand with hers and swung her upward. The trader grabbed for the thick mane and hung on as the centaur bucked and kicked, trying to drive back the silent beasts. They leaped for her, mouths closing on whatever limbs they could reach. One caught her ankle between its teeth. Lakanta hissed at the pain. She struck at the coarse muzzles with her steel block as the dark beasts tried to pull her off her perch, tearing at her skirts and the ends of her sleeves.

"That'll do for you!" she exclaimed, bringing the block down on one's head, hard enough to break the bone under the tough skin. The creature still made no noise, but it slithered down off her lap and onto the floor. She heard the snap of Rin's whip and the *smack!* as it struck one or another of the enemy.

A faraway clanking of metal on metal caused the beasts to let go. The small fire dwindled and went out. They were left alone in darkness with the taste of rancid smoke in their lungs.

"Are you all right?" Rin asked. She sounded out of breath.

"A few bites," Lakanta gasped out, leaning her head on the springy hair along the centaur's back. "They'll heal. But who is coming?"

Light flooded her eyes. She could almost hear the crack of her pupils as they contracted. She held up a hand to protect them. Figures were approaching, at least three. She couldn't see their shapes properly, but something about the way they moved disturbed her greatly.

"What are they?" she asked.

"I have never seen anything like these, either," Rin said.

"I know most of the beings that walk in the caverns beneath the earth, to a certain depth, anyhow. Those stubby things are new—that's it, new! Someone is making new people. Like the eels. Those had no history, like Master Olen said."

Rin twitched nervously. "Tildi's foe. We knew he ruled the thraiks. He has others to do his bidding, monsters he has made. Do not let them near us!" She cracked her whip. The first of the gray-green people halted for a moment, then continued. Rin struck out at it with the lash. Its head parted where it hit. It did not stop moving. "Monster!" she cried, backing away. She struck again and again. The whip drew lines across the being's broad chest, but it never halted, nor did its fellows. The two friends found themselves surrounded by a host of nearly identical creatures standing shoulder to shoulder, ring within ring. The centaur could no longer leap out without landing upon more of them. She began to dance in panic, her hooves clattering on the stone. "Where is your face? It has no face!"

"Easy, easy now," Lakanta said, patting her on the shoulder. She felt as if she were talking to her pony. "If they meant to hurt us they would have. Look at them with their green pelts, like the ugliest hedge ever clipped."

"Are they plants?" Rin asked, interested in spite of her fear. Her eyes showed white all around the jade-green irises.

"Bet they started out that way," Lakanta said calmly. "Or a moss, if you look at the texture. I've squeezed water out of enough of it to know. I've never been threatened by any moss in my life, and I don't expect to be so now. Wizarding and gardening don't match well, in my opinion. They want us to go somewhere." The rings of moss-men had elongated in the direction of the bright light, and she felt some of them nudge Rin from behind. "I've no doubt they can pick us up and carry us. Wherever we are going, I'd rather go there on my feet or, rather, on yours."

"It seems we have no choice," Rin said. She wound the whip into a coil and held it, ready to strike as they were urged in the direction of the light.

Knemet stood up from his cold stone seat as the liches escorted the newcomers into the great chamber. A centaur! He had not seen a centaur in hundreds of years, not since they had claimed the land of Balierenn as their domain. He did not need to see her rune to know how terrified she was. The horsefolk had always been skittish. They hated enclosed spaces. The dwarf upon her back was a hearty-looking female, still pretending defiance even though she, too, showed signs of dread.

The mark of the Compendium was upon them. Not a copy this time. They had touched the actual object. Avidly, he watched them approach, anticipating that hoped-for moment of laying his hands upon it at last. The wizardesses must cede it to him, and without demur. He was not in the mood for bargaining.

He stopped suddenly, and studied them further. They had been in contact with the book, and recently, but they were not wizardesses. Nor did they have the Compendium with them. No trace of magic did they display, except for a knickknack or so on the person of the dwarf woman. Had he been fooled again?

"Where is it?" he demanded.

The dwarf woman looked at him in astonishment. "Who are you to ask us anything? Where are we? You don't think that we will tolerate being stolen away at your whim, do you? We demand you send us back at once! And not in the care of those . . . those things!" She waved her hand at the ceiling, where the thraiks circled like buzzards over a dead animal. "They are too rough. We expect better treatment."

Knemet stretched out a hand. He grasped the blond female in a web of magic and wrenched her sideways, flinging her off the centaur's back and across the room. She sprang up from the floor and started toward him, the light of battle in her eyes. He brought her to a halt with a mere flicker of power. She strained against it, angry rather than frightened.

"Do not pretend you don't know of what I speak," he snarled. "I am too weary for games! Tell me where is the Compendium!"

This time they both looked genuinely astonished. "What is the Compendium?" the centaur asked.

"A book. My book. I have tracked your triumvirate of wizardry across the face of the world, and I will not wait another moment!"

The dwarf reschooled her features into a shrewd expression. "Well, you'll have to, as we have no idea what you mean. What do you want this book for? I am a merchant. I travel in my trade, all over Niombra, and I have connections on all four other continents and the archipelagoes. Perhaps I can help you find it. What does it look like?"

Knemet glared at her. "Don't be disingenuous," he said. "I have seen you before in my visions. I can read your very soul. You know. My thraiks could not bring it to me. You shall."

"I don't trade something for nothing," she said boldly, putting out her chin. "When you tell me what it is you are looking for, and tell me what price you will pay, and possibly add in a commission and perhaps a gift because you're being such a pushy customer, then perhaps we have a beginning point to our negotiation."

Knemet could hardly contain himself. There was such a difference between these and any other captives that the thraiks had brought him. They were intelligent and aware. Not only that, they had seen the book itself. They had handled it. The scent was fresh upon them.

"I do not negotiate. The Compendium belongs to me."

"Then you're careless with your possessions, Master Rainbow-Eyes," the dwarf woman said. "No one gets something for nothing. What do you offer?"

"If you do not aid me, you will never leave this place!"

Instead of being terrified into babbling out everything they knew, the pair held themselves aloof, though Knemet could see them quail inside.

"I don't mind," the trader said with a nonchalant shrug. "My people have lived beneath the hills for . . . how long is it since you made us out of stone, eh? I've always had questions. I don't suppose you'd care to answer any?"

"I . . . I, too, have questions," the centaur said, holding up her head proudly. "Were we meant to be subject races or free?"

"That's a good one," the dwarf said cheerfully. "I'd rather like to know, though it matters little after so long. We've hardly made it a practice to interact with humans. I do, but I don't mind people."

"You seek to cloud my mind with your prattle," Knemet said. He hated them as he had hated no others for millennia. "You were not alone. I saw you among your companions. They will want you back safely. I will trade for you. I will accept only one price. I must have the Compendium! I need it back! You cannot deny it from me forever!"

The dwarf woman gave him a pitying look. "There must be a thousand books of magic in the world. Why do you need this one so badly?"

Knemet's temper flared. "You wretched fool, I want it back so I can destroy it!"

Both women gasped.

"But why?" the trader asked. "If you prize it so highly, why? How could you even think of destroying it?"

"You know of what I speak," Knemet said with grim triumph. "It is in the forefront of your mind. You have no secrets from me."

The trader crossed her arms across her round chest. "I won't tell you a thing."

Knemet gripped his hand, and the spell constraining her tightened farther. She let out an involuntary squeak. He moved closer to her. She was only a few inches shorter than he was. He tipped up her chin. She flinched at his touch, but she could not avoid it. Once she met his eyes, she was trapped.

Such a different mind from Nemeth's, and from the trace of the other wizard he had sensed briefly just after Nemeth's death. He was not the judge of character that Deelin had been, but he could find thoughts that were uppermost. All he had to do was read them in her rune. He saw it all: her mental strength tempered by grief; her intelligence, sense of humor, and deep, enveloping warmth that could flare up to a terrible fire when needed. *For what?* he wondered, seeking more deeply.

"Where does your loyalty lie?" he asked, and unwillingly, her mind turned to those she would protect against all threat. Fear, awe, and love surrounded one tendril that extended to surround a ghost shape. Knemet concentrated upon it. A female figure. A child. No, it was the smallfolk girl he had seen through the eyes of his kotyrs, the one he had last seen among those guarding the Compendium.

"Who is she?" he demanded. "What purpose has she in your company?"

"None," the dwarf gritted.

"You cannot conceal the truth. Tell me."

Her blue eyes went as blank as stones. "You know all, Master Mushroom-Face. You cipher it out yourself."

Fear alone would not wring answers from these two. They were warriors, unlike the pathetic specimens of humanity he had faced before. He flung out a hand, and the wall beside her exploded into fragments. One of them grazed her cheek, drawing a thin line of blood. She was a true stone-child; that sharp rock would have laid open the face of any other race.

"I could do the same to you," he said.

"Then why don't you?" she asked. "You'll get the same answers from me either way."

He knew she was telling the truth. The thought of torture sickened him, but he would not balk at using it if he believed it would work. He had not the talent for reading thoughts or the ability to scry, as a few minor magicians he had once known. She must tell him. He had the knowledge to cause her to confess. He hated to ruin such an admirable specimen of dwarfdom by making her compliant, but his need was great.

The trick had nearly been played upon him, once. His fellow Shining Ones had nearly succeeded in applying the skill to him. Once he had seen the rune gleaming above him, he had never forgotten it, not one single detail. He drew it then in lines of gold, causing it to hover in the air between him and his subject. She eyed it suspiciously.

"It won't work," she said. "No matter what you do to me."

"Don't change her!" the centaur shrieked. "Don't do it."

"What?" Knemet asked in surprise, turning to her. "You have seen this manner of transformations done? Who is practicing this skill?"

The centaur, seeing that she had said too much, pressed her lips together.

Knemet could see in her thoughts that she was fearful of the rune. He meant to give them no choice.

"It does not matter whom I use it on," he said. "If you are worried for your friend, then you shall tell me what I want to know."

"You *are* a monster!" the dwarf woman shouted, her pink cheeks darkening to red. "Come back here. Don't touch Rin. She's a princess, much too good for the likes of you to touch."

Knemet would not answer them. He merely shifted his hand. The rune glided toward Princess Rin. He followed it at a safe distance, waiting for it to do its work before he came close. Her eyes widened until white showed all around her irises, a throwback to her equine heritage. She was a better choice than the dwarf. Horsefolk could be trained more readily.

Rin struggled, pressing herself to avoid contact until the very last second, but the rune touched and melded with her own sign. He watched the metamorphosis. Though there was no physical alteration, she was different. The fire of her personality was banked, and he controlled the damper. He approached and took her dark hand in his pale ones. She twitched and shivered in fear.

"You wish to aid me," he said in a soothing voice. "Where is the Compendium? It belongs to me. You believe in justice; I can see it in you. You are strong and honest. Help me to regain my property. Who guards it? Where are they?"

He locked her gaze with his. In the back of her mind she was screaming, but she had no choice but to comply.

"Ship," she gritted out between her clenched teeth.

"Where? Is it still in the Arown, or has it set out to sea?"

But the centaur could not stop. One word, one syllable at a time, Knemet gleaned the names and numbers of the guardians. Werewolves and soldiers. Those he could dismiss. He had heard of the Scholardom. They had nothing to do with the Shining Ones who had deprived him of the Compendium, but they must have been influenced by them. They had skill at magic, but it was dependent upon proximity to the Compendium. Two kings and two wizards and one apprentice. He had seen them all through the eyes of his kotyrs. The elder wizard was a wily one, but no match for him—or as he had been in his prime. The female was young and inexperienced. He had seen her reactions when the thraiks had attacked. She was skilled but too slow. The smallfolk girl, now, there was an interesting creature. She could do magic, an enormous departure from the origins of her people. None of the created folk but the bearkin had inherited magical abilities. She held the book, had actually wrested it from Nemeth, and maintained an uncanny connection with it. She had done the transformations, restoring the body of a minstrel in their company. A powerful magician, for all she was only an apprentice. She was the one he must guard against.

"They value you?" Knemet pressed. Blood burst from the centaur princess's nose and the corners of her eyes. She tried so hard not to respond to him that she was tearing herself apart inside. Her heart was pounding hard. "Will they come for you? Will they trade for your lives?"

"Not if they know what you want to do!" the dwarf shouted at his back. "I won't let them. You will have to keep us locked up until the end of time!"

The end of time. The phrase evoked a long, dark, empty corridor in Knemet's mind. He could not bear to look at the two women any longer.

He flicked a hand at the liches, who moved to surround the dazed pair.

"Lock them away," he ordered. "Make sure they do not escape." The gray-green beings inclined their blank heads toward him.

"Don't say any more," the dwarf called to her. "Rin, he wants to destroy the Great Book! Stop!"

He released his spell and let the women be herded out of the room. The centaur whinnied in fear. He heard her hooves clatter and slide on the stone floor. A shout and a curse came from the dwarf woman. He took dark pleasure in their discomfiture. They had not wanted to aid him. It sounded mad to anyone who had not suffered as he had. Ten thousand years of life was too much.

The book was so near! The end of his suffering had been within his creatures' grasp. He owed death to the ones who had thwarted him. He looked up at the ceiling, where the thraiks circled and wheeled, too terrified to come down. He shook his fist at them.

"You failed me! You failed me again! How could you be so careless! A promising new species, wasted because of your foolishness!"

They wailed their apologies to him, begging him to forgive them. They didn't deserve forgiveness. They were useless. He had to try again, but with what tool?

Chapter Twenty-eight

ildi's hair streamed and whipped over her collar as she stood in the bow of the *Corona*, watching the monolithic sculpture approach. Her cheeks were red and stiff with cold, but she did not move. For the first time she missed the cocoon of warmth in which the book had held her for the first months of her caretaking. It was important that she not let it rise again, for it was a symbol of the imbalance the book created between itself and the reality it described; her anger could set it free. She had kept her eyes on the far horizon, waiting for the narrow finger of rock to rise out of the surface of the water. They had been sailing for four days. As soon as the ship had been cleaned and the wounded restored with the aid of the metal plate they had made, Olen had revived the wind spell that propelled the two ships southward, then gone below, where he had slept for a night and a day. Tildi and Serafina were left to mind the bags of wind that had kept them riding at that rapid pace night and day with only short intervals for rest and to gather food. Sailors in vessels that they passed followed their speedy progress with curiosity, fear, or open envy. Tildi paid them little heed. All she could think of was getting to the Guardian so they could find Rin and Lakanta before it was too late. The thraiks' master would have discovered at once they did not have the Great Book. How long could they live in the face of his disappointment? What perils would they face? No matter what, now, he had made her his enemy. What small powers she had she would bring to bear upon him. She had sorrowed before, but now she was angry.

At least now they knew where her friends were: in the south of Ivirenn, in the hills above the human-inhabited port city of Tillerton. She and Olen had pored over the page that the book had revealed to them. There was no doubt about it. Their runes were there, in the middle of a boiling of thraiks. There was no sign of a wizard among them, nor any combination of strokes that would denote a man of power and vast age. Still, Rin and Lakanta were there. Tildi had to check innumerable times to make certain she was not mistaken. Both runes showed they were frightened, but that reassured Olen and the others. The dead could not fear. Tildi was so relieved that she had burst into tears all over again. Her friends were within forty miles of the Quarters.

She had searched the portion of the huge rune that described all of Ivirenn closely. Could she have found her brothers, even if they were alive, even if she knew what their runes looked like? After so long, she had no hope for them or her parents.

A stream of bulky shadows passed over her head, but Tildi did not flinch or even look up. Not to say that a herd of flying horses did not provoke interest, but the sight had lost its novelty. The company of guards from Rabantae and the entire Scholardom rode in formation, breaking off into smaller groups that galloped silently upward and downward, taking defensive positions all around the pair of ships. Their leaders shouted orders. Voices and the clanking of harness and the sound of weapons being drawn were the only noises they made. It was eerie, like watching an army of ghosts.

Once the ships were under way again after the battle, Serafina had not hesitated in giving the Scholardom instruction in riding the skies. They were capable of creating the spell to create secure footing for their own steeds.

They tackled the skill as they did everything else, with determination and perseverance. It took longer for their horses to get used to galloping through the air than it did for the knights themselves to become at home and, shortly, masters of their new domain. They created a series of maneuvers that so impressed Captain Teryn that she asked to have her people drill with them. As they had no means to control the book's power, Serafina offered to cast the spell for them.

Sharhava was a much more skillful rider and general than Tildi ever dreamed. She gained the respect from Teryn and her company that she had not had before. They practiced whenever they were not eating or resting. They were preparing for the battle they knew must come soon. It seemed appropriate for the Rabantavians, with the symbol of the winged pegasus upon their breasts, to fly through the air. King Halcot himself had not been able to resist it. With some difficulty he had persuaded his fellow king to take to the air alongside him. Soliandur had not been keen to try in the beginning, but once he had experienced it, he was the first one up during drills, and the last one down. His son followed him every moment, flying just behind and below to catch him if he fell, but Soliandur was as good a horseman as Sharhava. The monarch's usually mournful face lifted and became youthful. He and Halcot led mock battles against the well-disciplined force of the Scholardom that left the watchers on the ships breathless with excitement.

There seemed no doubt that they faced one of the ancient Shining Ones. The werewolf traders were fully convinced, as were the Scholardom and Teryn's company of guards. When the two kings proved still skeptical, Olen had shown them one of the eel-creatures that lay dead upon the deck.

"It is neither male nor female, my lords," he had explained. "Such a thing was made, not born, and made for a purpose. Can you doubt that it was to lead the thraiks to the treasure that we guard?"

Halcot, who had been party to the earliest councils, had been already half persuaded. It was the lord of Orontae who was yet to come to terms with the threat of an immortal enemy, a legend from long ago. As Prince Eremi had said, his father was a hard man to convince of anything in which he did not believe. Yet no matter what his personal beliefs were, he joined in the common defense of the Great Book—and its guardian.

The company kept a close watch upon Tildi, whether she was sleeping, eating, studying, or bathing. She had reached a point where she could feel the others' eyes on her as though they were touching her. She had always been a modest and private person, and she hated that they were always looking at her. No matter where she went, at least one guard in blue-and-white and one in red-and-white followed her. There was no peace or privacy on the ship except there in the bows, tucked into a small corner beyond the forward hatch where only she could fit. She had taken to going there when she could not stand it any longer. Though she didn't complain to anyone, Serafina had noticed. The wizardess had ordered everyone, including Olen, to let her alone there with her thoughts. They had respected the stricture, until now.

Olen appeared beside her, his green eyes avid with curiosity. They were close enough that the back of the statue's hooded head loomed high above them. He settled onto the hatch cover beside her.

"Do you see it, Tildi?" he asked. "He is there."

The figure of stone puzzled her. "It's there, master, but it's not alive."

"Ah, but it is. All of my research says so."

Patiently, Tildi brought the Great Book and opened it to the page on which had been inscribed several individual features of this part of the world. Painstakingly wrought in gold was the rune. It showed a statue hundreds of feet high, standing on a pedestal of rock. It was beautifully made in the image of a man with a long, narrow face; keen, hooded eyes, and a sharp chin. One long arm reached out to sea in a palm-out gesture of warning. The hooded cloak that covered him from crown to heels had been wonderfully carved so that it looked like vast folds of cloth. It only lacked one detail. "There's nothing alive in it." No being, human or otherwise, lay within it or under it, or anywhere near it for miles. She didn't want to say he was mistaken. He was so seldom wrong, but her confidence had been shaken when he had been taken by surprise by the eel-creatures. She merely showed him the rune.

Disconcertingly, Olen seemed to read her thoughts. "I do not know how to reconcile what I know with what you can see, my dear. Only experimentation will take us further. Nevertheless, we must find Calester. We need his help. I, too, am worried about our friends."

Captain Temur held tightly to the wheel as Olen and Serafina let the winds spill from the bubbles behind the ships. Gradually, the *Corona* and the *Eclipse* glided to a near halt. The wizards controlled the release so that there was no harsh transition to the speed of the natural current of the Arown.

Tildi had never been farther than the southernmost Quarter, but her brothers had traded goods in the human-owned towns and villages along the south coast. "My eldest brother, Gosto, often told stories of the Guardian. It is said it has been there since Father Time set it in place, at the beginning of the world."

"It is not quite that old," Olen said with a smile.

As they neared it, it seemed to fill up the sky.

"I don't see where we can dock, Master Wizard," Haroun shouted, coming up beside them. "Our chart shows the riverbed here is treacherous. We usually stay within the channels." He pointed to colorfully painted wooden floats tethered in the stream.

"Don't trouble yourselves," Olen said. "Find a safe harbor. I shall be making my visit by air."

Tildi was delighted when one of the werewolf crewmen brought Sihine up from the hold. The silver mare was Olen's own steed. Tildi had ridden with Olen to perform her first great task, to turn the Madcloud away from Overhill. It felt as if it had been a lifetime before that she had last seen the lovely mare, but Sihine put her velvet-soft nose down into Tildi's palm and whickered, looking for a treat. Olen reached into the pouch at his belt and brought out a sugar crystal. He handed it to her and let her feed it to the mare.

"Come with me," he said. "You have had so much experience traveling in this fashion, you should no longer be afraid of heights."

"I still am," Tildi said, a little shamefacedly.

"You are wise," Olen said kindly. "It is I who am reckless."

Serafina had already led her white mare up to the edge of the deck. Teryn followed her, leading her sturdy gelding. She saluted Tildi, but addressed Olen.

"I should accompany you. My guards are prepared to join us. My lord has given us permission." She gestured toward the belly of the ship, where Morag had the others waiting.

Loisan, Sharhava's lieutenant, came bustling up the steps with his horse in its full tack behind him. Its hooves clattered on the deck. His craggy face was red with strain.

"Master, we are the book's guardians! We should be the ones to protect Mistress Summerbee."

"There should be no need for rivalry, Captain and Lieutenant," Olen replied, nodding to each. "You may come along, of course. There is room in the sky for all." He helped Tildi up to sit sideways just before him on the saddlebow. The book floated into her lap. Sihine gathered her great haunches and leaped upward. Tildi clutched the big scroll. The voices inside were excited. They were airborne.

The Scholardom launched itself and spread out into a hemispherical formation around the two wizards. Teryn and Morag flanked Olen and Serafina. The rest of the Rabantavians streamed out behind their leaders. Tildi was annoyed with all of them. Why must the two groups fight over precedence? She felt, not for the first time, that they were thinking less about her and more about their own glory.

Olen brought the horse close to one of those huge eyes. "Calester!" he shouted. "Calester, I am Olen! I need your help. One of your colleagues has abducted two of my companions!"

"He doesn't hear you," Serafina said, listening closely. "I hear nothing within."

Olen rapped upon the left eyeball with his knuckles. "Calester!" He paused to listen. There was no sound but the crashing of the waves on the island and the roar of the wind. He turned Sihine with a rein on the neck. They flew around to one of the ears that showed just beyond the edge of the hood. Tildi peered into the opening. It seemed to go a long, long way in, dwindling from a hole larger than her body to one she could have covered with a palm.

"Could be you were wrong about this, master?" Loisan asked, trotting forward. "We have records that date back to when the Great Book was made. It makes no mention of the Makers transforming themselves into statues."

"There are things that the annals do not record, my friend," Olen said. "This happened long after the war between the Shining Ones, I know not for what purpose. I have spent many centuries divining where this Shining One might be, and this is he. I have tried to communicate with him before, but he has always ignored me. Once I made the discovery, I have spent years trying to make contact with the man within this monolith. Not worth his trouble, I suppose. I had nothing to interest him. I have never located any of the others. This is our time of deepest need. I believe that if we can get his attention, we can gain his aid. And we sorely need it. Our combined power will not be enough to wrest our friends from the master of the thraiks."

"We will wake him, sir," Loisan assured him. He flew back toward Sharhava, who listened with a grave face to his news. While Olen studied the ear with great concentration, the Scholardom flew forward in an arrow formation, and spread out. On Sharhava's signal, the knights pointed their right hands toward the chest. Tildi saw a vast rune form on it, just where the heart would be if it had one. It sank into the image. Tildi fancied she could hear a rumbling coming from inside the ear. Just as quickly, it died away, leaving only the cry of gulls and the sounds of the sea.

The knights tried many times with different sigils, no doubt gleaned from the mysteries their order had gathered for centuries, to awaken the giant. She did not understand most of what they did, but each attempt ended in failure.

"We are not real enough for him," Olen murmured at last.

"What is real?" Tildi asked curiously.

"Something he made," Olen said, bringing the horse around to the eye once again. "Tildi, show him the book. Show him the page that shows where our friends are imprisoned."

Tildi felt more than nervous leaning out over thin air to hold the book out to the huge eyeball. Did she imagine it, or did it move a tiny bit? She looked down. The right hand was held out almost at the level at which they hovered, offering a warning to invaders from the south, but the left was upturned, held back nearly to the figure's waist. Had that empty palm ever held anything? Was it meant to hold something?

"Showing it won't help, master," Tildi said. "He isn't looking."

Olen glanced downward to see what she was looking at, and a broad smile lifted the corners of his mustache. "You are quite right, Tildi. We must let him touch the book."

"No, master," Serafina said warningly. "You do not know what response you might set off."

"It is possible that it will be nothing," Olen said. "It is worth a try."

"It is too risky!"

"All magic is risk-taking," Tildi said. Olen's hand squeezed her shoulder. He had said that to her the first time she had gone with him to undertake her first major magical working. She didn't feel much braver than she had that day, but the image of Rin and Lakanta being dragged through that hole in the sky kept coming into her mind and making her tremble with fear and anger. Someone had to wake up the stone giant, and it looked as though the only person who could do it was her.

Serafina pursed her lips. Edynn had undoubtedly told her much the same thing, for she nodded. She looked at Olen.

"There is no sense in sending Tildi unprepared. We should place wards around her."

"Not if it will prevent the book from touching the flesh, as it were," Olen said. "That would negate our efforts. But a guard on Tildi herself would make the most sense, if you would."

Serafina did not look satisfied, but she pointed a finger at the smallfolk girl. "*Voshte*," she said softly. Tildi felt as if she had put on another cloak that also covered her face. She could scarcely feel the saddle under her rump. She nodded.

"Very well, then," Olen said. He laid the reins on Sihine's neck.

The mare trotted downward in a spiral as easily as if she were on a gentle, grass-covered slope. A bare touch of Olen's knees brought her to a stop before the enormous hand.

"Go ahead, Tildi. If you are right, let this be your doing." He gestured toward the vast, gray stone palm, no smaller than Olen's study in Silvertree.

Keenly aware of the still monumental drop beneath her feet, Tildi boosted herself off the saddle with the book under her arm. She stepped out onto the edge of the thumb. She stepped over the crags and crevices that on a smallfolk's hand would be shallower than the thickness of a hair. When she reached the middle, she looked back at Olen. He gave her an encouraging nod and a gesture.

By then the entire party of guards had gathered at the edge of the hand.

"What are you doing?" Sharhava demanded of Olen. "You place her and the book in danger!"

"Not really," Olen said. "I am placing her, I hope, in the best of hands. Hm hm hm." He chuckled to himself. "Go ahead, my dear."

Tildi was reluctant to let go of the book. This, after all, might be one of its original masters. It might forsake her. But she thought of her friends. They were worth the sacrifice of any treasure, however precious. With an act of will, she set it down in the center of the palm.

The moment that the book touched the stone, Tildi saw thready tendrils of gold spread out from the scroll and wind their way into the surface. A glow of light started from the center of the palm and rushed outward, along the massive arm and out into the body, like the edge of a bit of paper catching fire. Rumbling, or perhaps the opposite of rumbling, for it was seen rather than heard or felt, began deep within the statue.

"Come back, Mistress Summerbee!" the abbess shouted, holding out her hand to Tildi. A crack appeared in the stone folds of the robe just above the base of the arm on which she stood. She solidified the air and stepped up off the stone. Or thought she did. Her foot went straight through the rune she had made and set down again upon the palm. She realized that she couldn't move from her place.

"Master Olen!" she cried.

Olen had seen her distress. He pointed his staff at the palm beneath her feet. "*Othatku!*" he shouted.

More runes sprang into being. Tildi pulled at each foot, trying to free it.

Above her, the statue seemed to be breaking free from the depths of the ages. As Olen had said, it was a living, giant creature. It was not so much that it was made of stone, but the accretion of years—ten millennia—had layered dust upon it until it was solid and the being within it slept. Beneath the cracking shell, the ancient visage was at once fearsome and yet beautiful.

To her horror, the statue began to collapse in on itself. Olen seemed to soar away above her. She realized, as he turned Sihine's head to follow, that she was dropping away from him, dragged down by the grip on her feet. An angry wind whistled in her ears. She was falling with the wreckage of the statue, unable to free herself. Debris fell around her. She cringed, but nothing touched her, a tribute to Serafina's protective spell. How far was the ground? Would she be killed on impact in spite of the magic?

"Tildi!" Magpie shouted, his clear voice cutting through the rumbling, which was now audible.

"Help me!" she called back. The soldiers and knights yelled to one another, trying to find her in the dust that filled the air. She coughed and batted at the obscuring cloud. Shadows of enormous boulders made her flinch.

Before she knew it, she felt a hard blow to the soles of her feet. The giant stones struck the ground with thunderous booms. She staggered sideways, but something held on to her arm and jerked her upright again. A hooded man loomed over her in the haze. She knew him as if she had spotted him in a crowd. He had the same face as the statue, but instead of stone gray, his face was the color of warm oak wood, almost as dark as Magpie's. She looked down. Toils of golden light held her as tightly as ropes.

He brandished the book at her. His eyes, deep-set and light in color, blazed at her. Tildi gazed at him in confusion.

"Thief! How came you by this? Do you serve Knemet? Answer!"

"That's the name!" Olen exclaimed, pleased with himself, as he alighted beside them. Sihine pawed unhappily at the knee-deep dust into which her hooves sank. The wizard swung out of the saddle. "I knew it must be he or Ayrcolida."

Riders surrounded the tall, hooded man. "Release her!" Captain Teryn ordered, pointing her sword at him. The Scholardom ringed them, bows drawn. "She has done no wrong! Release her now or face us."

The tall man suddenly became aware of the others. He turned to survey them and waved a long hand. A blue-tinted bubble enclosed him and Tildi. The dust that filled the air settled swiftly, leaving all standing knee-deep in dunes and heaps in the midst of a broad hollow that had been where one of the statue's giant feet had been. They were surrounded by the deep pine forest that cut off all sight of the water. The soft grains shifted at any movement. Tildi dug at the thick debris, fearing that she would be buried. The tall man realized her distress and flicked a hand. She found herself dragged upward until she hung suspended eye to eye with him.

"Speak of this book. I demand an explanation!"

"I didn't steal it," Tildi said.

"She is not a thief, good sir," Olen said, moving forward. He passed easily through the spell that enclosed Tildi and the stranger and closed it behind him.

The hooded man turned to eye Olen and peered at the rune upon his chest. "A wizard, eh?"

"Yes, sir, like yourself. An admirer of yours and your work. I am Olen."

"I am Calester," the stranger said slowly, as though trying out the long-disused name on his tongue.

Olen looked enormously pleased. "I assumed so. I have tried many times to make contact with you by means of my art, but you have never responded to me. I see that I lacked the proper stimulus. I am glad that I have succeeded at last. Our need is great."

Calester peered at him. "I see no guile in you. If you are not thieves and you are not in the employ of my enemy, why does she have the Compendium? And who are these people?"

"Sir, we are on the same side in this battle," Olen said, "but this is a very uncomfortable place to give you what will be a very long explanation. May we invite you to join us on board the ship on which we travel? It is anchored to the north of this island."

For the first time, Calester looked around. The ground around them was littered with chunks of rock the size of cottages. They had landed in piles and heaps, splintering the wind-weathered trees. He smiled. It lifted the long lines of his face into a pleasant, even appealing visage. "I have been here on this island so long, it almost seems wrong to abandon it. But you are right. There is little in the way of hospitality I can offer you. I accept your invitation."

Olen upturned a hand. "May I then ask you to release my apprentice?"

Calester raised an eyebrow, but the bonds surrounding Tildi released at once. She caught herself with her own magic just before she dropped into a heap of dust. "Apprentice, eh? They take them younger and younger every day, now. Stars and moons, but I have missed a great deal. I look forward to hearing your tales, good people. I trust I have not found myself in a future where there is no wine?"

Olen laughed. "Not at all, sir. I think you will find things much as you left them." He came over to take the other's arm. "Now, how long ago did you set yourself to stand here, and why?"

Chapter Twenty-nine

I liked being a giant, sir," Calester said, tipping his wineglass in Magpie's direction. The Maker sat at the head of the semicircle of chairs hastily arranged in the captain's cabin. The Great Book lay across his lap. "It gave me perspective and a chance to think. Too much time, perhaps. I set myself there at the mouth of the Arown to catch the Compendium, should it ever return to Niombra, and I missed it by months, you say?"

"Yes, Master Calester," Magpie said, not wanting to relate the precise circumstances. "Several months at least. I believe I was close behind its thief as it went northward, but I lost all trace of it thereafter."

"And a fair amount of harm it has done in that time."

His father sat across from him, stony-faced Soliander was angry with him again and unimpressed by the newcomer. "Foolish enterprises, putting yourself and others into unnecessary danger," he fumed. "You allowed the lady Inbecca to fall into peril, and what about Mistress Summerbee?" Magpie's ears were still burning. As usual, his father's admonition was unfair. He had kept very close to Inbecca all the time they were airborne, and made sure she was in no peril from the flying shards of rock. As for Tildi, she had had two wizards looking after her. How much safer could she have been? He had underestimated Calester's reaction to being awakened, but so had they all.

Beside Soliandur, Halcot could do nothing but stare in awe at the visitor. The ease with which the newcomer handled the perilous scroll alone had convinced him of what Olen had said upon introducing him, that this was one of the famed Shining Ones. Sharhava, on the other hand, was united in skepticism with Soliandur. Her green-blue eyes were flinty as they bored into him. Patha, Temur, and Haroun, in seats of honor among the company as representatives of their people, also stared at the newcomer. "That time is over," Calester said, patting the book. "The Compendium shall go back to its place, as soon as may be. I hoped that it would remain buried until Father Time calls an end to eternity. This time it shall be. I am in your debt, good friends. Captain Betiss, I request your assistance. What be your price to convey me southward to Sheatovra as soon as possible?"

"Well, sir, southward was our intent," Haroun said, clearing his throat. "Right up until a few days ago, that is."

"A few days? Why should that make a difference?"

Tildi sat in her small chair between Serafina and Olen, not far away. Magpie felt sorry for her. She could hardly take her eyes off the Great Book. How likely was it she would ever have it in her keeping again, when it had returned to one of the ones who had made it?

As if any proof of ownership was needed, Calester handled the scroll with gentle fingers. It responded to him as it had to Tildi, the crisp, pure parchment almost caressing his fingers as he turned the spindle to look at the pages. It affected him no more than it had Tildi; less, perhaps, because it was his own creation.

Halcot cleared his throat. "Because two of our valiant friends, sir, who had been instrumental in preventing the Compendium, as you call it, from falling into the wrong hands, have been carried off at the orders of your ancient colleague, or so we believe."

Calester turned up his hand. "Ah, no, then I could not think to delay. If Knemet is indeed in pursuit of the Compendium, we must hurry to get it far away from him. The sooner that it is once again out of the world, the better. What are two lives against the safety of the world?"

"Those two lives are precious to us," Olen said gently.

The long lines of Calester's face were as obdurate as if they were still carved in stone.

"I am sorry for your grief, then. If it is Knemet who seeks it, then all the better to thwart him by taking away the prize. If it is not, it would be better if the book did not fall into the grasp of someone who does not truly understand its power. They were lost in a good cause. I hope that gives you some measure of comfort, my friends."

"They are not lost!" Tildi burst out. "They are alive. They were carried off by thraiks."

"Thraiks?" the Maker echoed, looking at her curiously. "What do you know of thraiks?"

Tildi's face got hot. "Far too much for my lifetime," she snapped. "Anyone who has touched the book or a copy of it has been carried off by thraiks. All of my family, and almost me."

Calester studied her closely. "You are a smallfolk, aren't you? I did not pay close heed to you when you woke me from my doze. My goodness, look at you! A smallfolk, and so well formed."

"There's no need to be insulting," Tildi said, feeling her cheeks redden.

"Please forgive me," he said, reaching out to her with one long hand. Tildi kept both of hers folded in her lap. Calester withdrew his and rested his long fingers upon the curve of the Great Book. "It has been so long since I had seen one of your kind. When smallfolk were created, they were much more crudely shaped." He tilted his head to one side to study her further. "They were our first attempt to combine traits of humans with plant life—mostly human, of course."

"Trees?" Olen inquired.

"Smaller woody plants," Calester confirmed. "Nancols, they were called. Rare, but just what we needed. Pliable, capable of growing delicate limbs and deeply rooted for toughness. You are much more human-looking than the earliest progenitors, lass. Did your ancestors choose to marry those who were more human, or did they just develop?"

"I don't know," Tildi said, trying not to feel as if she were undressing in public. "My people don't like the idea that they haven't existed since the beginning of time."

"They do not want to go all the way back to the family . . . tree," Olen said wryly.

Calester threw back his head and laughed. "Mother Nature," he exclaimed. "Oh, I wish I had stayed out and about longer to study, but change is so slow in coming over the years. I had set myself up to wake every century or so, but I fell out of the habit. I see I have missed much. You are a success beyond anything we thought possible. There's an elegance to you, now: a smoothness of line, as if everything knit together over time. Do all your folk resemble you?"

"My friend," Olen said, holding up a hand to forestall the outburst anyone could see Tildi was building within her, "as you say, the book should be laid to rest as soon as possible. Let us not hare away into other matters, no matter how fascinating they are. I would know more, so much more about you and your colleagues. You have become legend to us. I have thousands of questions to ask you, but I, too, must stay my curiosity. It is a matter of grave importance to us not to allow our friends to languish. How long can hope survive?"

"I see," Calester said, his expression souring. "You would have me delay for no better reason than that?"

"No better reason . . . ?" Patha repeated, her golden eyes catching fire. "Loyalty is not a good reason? What reason then should we require from you for your purposes? It makes no difference to me if we take you to Sheatovra, or make you wait until spring when we return to the north. If I give the word, no werewolf trader will carry you now or at any time in the future, no matter how long you wait. How would you like to be set back upon your island?"

Calester looked surprised and a little hurt. "My lady, I thought that perhaps I could receive your cooperation. After all, without the efforts of me and my colleagues, your folk would not even exist!" He offered a wistful smile.

"And for that you wish our gratitude?" Patha snapped. "I would kill you if I could. Generations of my people have suffered from living two lives, subject to the whims of the moons."

Calester sighed. "It was not our intention, my lady. Joining human to wolf was not an easy enterprise. The only way to build stability into your first ancestors was to add the moons' magic. That magic proved to be changeable with the lunar phases, but we saw no other way at the time. I regret it if it has caused you woe."

"The fact that you meddled with Mother Nature's purpose caused woe to more than the werewolf folk," Sharhava said.

"I see that time has not been kind to our reputation," Calester said ruefully. "We went into our studies with the best of intentions, my lady."

"Intentions!"

Olen held up a hand and appealed to Abbess Sharhava. "What's done is done, as you yourself have remarked rather recently. No one will undo the work of millennia past. What matters is today."

"And today, good sir," Calester said, "I hope that you will understand the urgency of my mission. We must go south at once. Please set sail as soon as you can, Captain."

"You do not command this ship or this company," Patha said.

"What was your purpose when you took your place as the Guardian?"

Calester lowered his eyes modestly. "You will think it a conceit, but I wanted to protect my homeland from any possible incursions by my old colleague. After the battle, many centuries ago—do you know of it?" The others nodded.

"We know some tales," Olen said. "I would know all."

"And I will tell it all," Calester promised, "when peace and safety have once again been obtained. Briefly, then: two of our number had died during the course of our defense against Knemet, Reck and Deelin, dear friends of mine. Knemet was vanquished, but not dead. Once he had disappeared, we placed the Compendium out of reach, or so we believed. Our war had consumed decades—centuries. We were all deeply tired. We required rest, but we could not be at ease, since we knew not where Knemet had gone. We discussed the matter honestly, knowing that Knemet might return to take his revenge. I offered to be the one on vigil. We believed he could come back at any time. I took up the place where you found me. At first I was more active, but over the years I found I was able to accomplish deeper thinking if I stayed in one place. I created the form you saw over time. It gave me a matchless vantage to continue my watch, but in a passive manner, and I could not be disturbed, save for a threat.

"As you know, thousands of years have passed. Outlanders attacked this land in the earlier years. I used my influence to drive away intruders, but I never sensed enough of a threat to awaken me from my study. As the incursions grew less, I became more interested in my inner thoughts than what went on around me. Most recently, I was deeply pondering a matter of creative magic that took me over five centuries to consider, and in so doing, I allowed my attention to wander . . . but never mind," he said, disappointing Olen, who was watching him with avid eyes. "Knemet must be preparing to set himself up as a power once again. This poor mad wizard you spoke of must have fallen into Knemet's power to have found it and retrieved it."

"But he did not bring it to him," Magpie said, surprising himself by speaking. "He had other plans for it." Briefly, he explained the destruction Nemeth had inflicted upon the land in northern Orontae. Calester listened with fascination. He caused the book to spin to the damaged pages and exclaimed over them. The light eyes turned woeful.

"All our work! Oh, what a villain this Nemeth must have been, to see such a work of beauty and yet be able to harm it."

"He was a fool," Soliandur said in a hoarse voice.

"I could say the same things about you so-named Shining Ones and your penchant for fooling with Mother Nature's pure designs!" Sharhava snapped.

"But are we, my friends and I, not also creations of Mother Nature?" Calester asked, drawing his chin down.

"Perhaps!"

"Then how could the use of our talents be anything but as natural as a bird taking wing?"

Sharhava's eyes widened in outrage, and she sat tall, prepared to do philosophical battle. Calester seemed to welcome it. He sat back in his chair, his elbows on the arms, long fingers tented together. Magpie saw what could have been a historic moment beginning to deteriorate into hard feelings and acrimony. He stepped in between them and faced Calester, drawing his gaze. The wizard looked up, startled.

"You say that you are in our debt, good sir," Magpie said carefully. "You are most kind to say so. We require you to discharge that debt. We need your strength. It is perhaps no accident that you wore that stone guise for so long. You are as a giant compared with the rest of us. It will take your skills to find your ancient enemy and to obtain our friends' release."

"Are you one of our creations?" Calester asked with a wry twinkle in his eyes. "Are you part nightingale, young man, that your sweet voice charms one to do your will? You have a skill with words that goes beyond any bard I ever heard."

"He is no nightingale," Soliandur said hoarsely. "He is my son, a prince, descended from the first kings of Orontae."

Calester bowed. "And resembles his ancestors, my lord king. He does, I promise you. I but jested. He has a diplomat's skills. You could do worse for an heir."

Soliandur's dark face became purple. "He is not my heir! But he is my son, so I would prefer you treat him with respect."

"I shall. Forgive me if you do not believe that I do. I have been alone with my thoughts a remarkably long while, and before that in an academic community where much was said aloud that perhaps," Calester said with a small smile, "*perhaps* should not have been said. I will guard my tongue more carefully."

Magpie fixed his eyes upon him. "You may say whatever you like to me, if you will aid us."

Calester returned the gaze gravely. "You do not understand what you ask, highness. You must know that we promised him everlasting misery should any of us ever cross Knemet's path again. We settled for exile, but he deserves pain. I hate to be the one to inflict it. We were friends once."

Tildi could not help herself. She was all but twitching being out of reach of the book for the first time in months, and to listen to this self-satisfied wizard talk about their distant foe and thraiks as if they were no more trouble than a splinter in the thumb snapped the last thread of restraint holding her. She flung herself out of her seat and marched up to look him in the eye.

"How dare you? Rin and Lakanta saved my life many times. They've been good companions. I have never had such true friends. This is more serious than anything you can imagine. My friends are terrified. Who knows what tortures they have endured in the last few days? You treat our request as if it is a mere inconvenience. Don't you think we want to make the book safe as soon as possible? I have scarcely slept under a roof for months, performing the task that you should have. If you had intercepted the Great Book when it first came here, we wouldn't have fallen into danger over and over again. Edynn would not have died! I want to go *home*, sir. I want to go back to my lessons. We woke you up so you could help us. If you don't want to be of use, then I suggest you go back to sleep!"

The room had fallen silent. Tildi looked around. King Soliandur regarded her gravely. Halcot hid his mouth behind his hand. She suspected from the twinkle in his eyes that he was smiling. Magpie grinned openly. Sharhava looked outraged. Inbecca, beside and just behind her aunt, nodded her approval. Tildi blushed hotly, then stared at Calester.

"Well, madam apprentice," the Maker said sternly, "if you served me I would chide you for speaking out before your betters." Tildi opened her mouth. His expression softened, and the hooded eyes lightened. "I cannot fault you for your courage nor for your fidelity. Would that everyone should have such champions! Therefore, I cannot refuse you. You are right. The task should be mine. I ask humbly that you share it with me, though I am not worthy to walk by your side."

Tildi was mollified and a trifle embarrassed. "It would be my honor, Master Calester."

The Maker grinned. "Then we shall be honored together. Your friends shall not suffer longer than may be. Let us formulate our plans."

Magpie cleared his throat. "We are not certain that it is Knemet that we seek."

"I am sure," Calester said, "for I know where the others are. Tell me where he is."

"Ah," Olen said. "That we do not know, precisely. I believe him to be in southern Ivirenn. All of my arts have been unsuccessful in finding him, but it is logically where he must be. He has hedged himself around with so many protective spells that we cannot see him. Even the Great Book failed to show him. How is it that every living being on Alada is pictured within it, but not him? Unless he is not with his thraiks and our friends whom they took prisoner."

"Oh, he will be with them," Calester said with confidence and not a little scorn. "Never has there been such a mole of a man, who preferred to be hidden away in a study than to enjoy the greater gifts that Mother Nature gave to us all. He would seem to be the most unlikely of wizards to have created the thraiks, since they range far and wide, and he has never liked to do so. We could have done him no more terrible punishment than to banish him from Niombra. And, as you say, he has returned here, though not to our college. There was likely no secure place he could hide himself in that locale. Where do you *believe* him to be?"

"May we?" Olen asked. Calester made as if to offer the Great Book to him. Olen gestured to Tildi, who lifted her hands. The book flew toward her and opened like a pennant in the wind, billowing and tossing. Calester's eyes went wide.

"May I be tipped down a well! What are you, child? None of us has ever been able to make the Compendium do that!"

"You haven't?" Tildi asked. "But it's yours."

Calester was dumbfounded but delighted. He came to crouch beside Tildi, all trace of severity lost from his long countenance. He looked like a schoolboy who had been given a new toy. He spread out his hand. The big scroll remained hovering where it was. He shook his head in astonishment. "Our invention, perhaps, but yours in a way that was never ours. Why, we cannot make it rise from a table without lifting it by hand. It resists all magic."

"I don't know why it does that," Tildi admitted. "It just began one day."

"It responded to her will after a time of great fear and stress," Serafina added with a sideways look at the abbess. Sharhava's brows went down, but as Serafina did not add to her explanation, she said nothing.

"Whatever the cause, you have shown me a wonder," Calester said. "None of us were ever able to compel the book to do anything like that. You have my admiration, smallfolk wizardess. We will explore this ability of yours when we have the time. I must know how this was accomplished. Now, show me where Knemet is hiding."

The book responded obediently by rolling up so that only a section as wide as the span of her arms was showing, then it spun a length of a few yards.

"This is where we found our friends and all the thraiks," Tildi said.

"Ivirenn," Calester murmured. "Along the coast, near a large town or city. A safe harbor. Well populated. Not far away from us. I knew that of old as a village, when it was called Esterik."

"In ancient terms, Tiller," Olen said.

"What is this place?" Halcot asked.

"Tillerton," said Captain Betiss. "I do not need to be able to read the ancient words to know a large town on the south coast. We are making for it already." He barked an order, and one of his crew changed into his wolf shape and bounded away. In a few moments he returned with a rolled-up chart. Haroun spread it out upon the table. "There."

Calester paid them no mind. His attention was upon the parchment.

"How could I have missed him? The wretch, he probably passed by me during a time I was contemplating, and laughed at me." He shook his head.

"There are many ways onto the continent," Sharhava said, "especially when one is not constrained to land or sea travel."

"Ah, true. Thank you."

"And there are our friends," Olen said, creating a point of light that danced over the smooth parchment and spread into a tiny ring. Calester opened out his hand and the runes expanded. "Ah, yes. Still alive, thank the Mother."

"Show me," Calester said. "There are many people in this small space, and more than one each of centaur and dwarf."

"Tildi, will you draw one of their runes, so he may see whom we seek?" Serafina asked.

Through her long training, Tildi had no trouble producing a creditable copy of the images she had seen hovering before her, day after day. Calester followed every stroke she made with great interest.

"A centaur, and a comely one at that," Calester said, stroking his chin. "How all things have changed. I was vigilant for so long. I cannot believe that my attention slipped in the way it did. I didn't know the Compendium had come to the north."

"We all miss things," King Halcot said kindly.

Calester gave him a sharp look Tildi had last seen on the face of her schoolmaster. "You don't understand. We are not used to making mistakes."

"Not that you admit to," Sharhava said.

Calester studied her. Tildi knew he was reading her rune. "You are steadfast. I would have had much trouble with the likes of you when we Makers were together."

"Perhaps I would have been able to stop you," Sharhava said with a touch of her old hauteur.

"Perhaps you would. Then you would not have the delightful company you presently enjoy." Calester raised his eyebrow at her. Sharhava nodded.

"That would have been my loss."

"Ah," the Maker said, pointing to a spot on the page not far from Lakanta's sign. "He is there. He cannot hide from the Compendium. For how long has he remained dug into that hole?"

"Since I was a small child at least," Tildi said. "Ten years or more." She peered at the page. The place he indicated still looked as though it was blank.

"I cannot see him," Olen said. "There are many people, but none such as you describe."

"For that matter, we can't see you in the pages of the Compendium, as you call it," Magpie said.

"Ah, well, that is part of the nature of its construction," Calester explained. "We *are* the book. We put part of ourselves into it, so it is of our substance. We exist within the pages, not on the surface, as all other things are. But we can see one another. Let me try to bring out Knemet so you may see him." He began to scribe on the air. The lines, unlike the dark or silvered strokes that Tildi or Olen made, were a fiery red.

On the white surface of the page, a shimmering word appeared beneath his fingertips. Tildi could read the parts that indicated *man* and *magic*, as well as parts that indicated sharp intelligence, weariness, and deep anger.

"A formidable foe," Olen said.

"There are other red names here," Tildi said excitedly. Two more had appeared upon the page, moving around like fish in a bowl. "Where are they? Are they near Knemet? Can they help us find him?"

"As I told you," Calester said, "we Makers are seen only by one another. The ones you see no longer live in the world. There they are. Nuthen. Ayrcolida. Boma." He stroked each in turn.

"They are dead?" Inbecca asked sympathetically.

"They have rejoined their runes, my lady."

"They're *alive?*" Magpie asked.

"Aye, of course they are alive." Calester seemed insulted by the question.

"They are trapped inside the book?"

Calester looked shocked. "No! Not trapped. This was their choice."

"But would it not be a dull existence, to live inside a mere book?" Soliandur asked, curious in spite of himself.

"They have the world to study, Your Highness, and one another for company. They are happy. I told you two of my friends perished during our battle. One, Zecayre, passed away a few centuries later, his dearest wish after a long and fruitful life. Most of us preferred immortality so we could see and protect our work. It turned out to be a gift that was both sweet and sour. I cannot die or change. Nor can they. Nor can Knemet. My three friends whom you see grew weary. They wanted to retire from the world. It was the safest place for them to go. They do not exist in the world as you know it, so they do not appear on pages, except when I reveal them." He turned to Tildi. "You see why I do not want to march into Knemet's lair, little one? I do not want *my* friends to fall into his hands, either."

Olen was rapt with delight. "Living men and women inside the Compendium?"

"Indeed, yes. It was not so difficult a translation as we feared it might be. They exist as long as the book does."

"So the voices I have been hearing are real," Tildi said. She felt as if a great weight had been lifted from her. "The book was not affecting my mind."

"Not at all," Calester said, smiling at her. "They have been speaking to me just as you are. We have so much to say to one another after being apart for centuries."

"And what do they say about Master Knemet?" Halcot asked wryly.

Calester's face turned solemn. "You may guess. But, soonest attempted, soonest finished." He tapped the parchment over the single red rune. "This is his fastness."

"There are so many people of many races in this area," Magpie said with a glance at the page of the Compendium. "How is it that no one has seen hordes of thraiks moving to and fro?"

"He is too intelligent to allow his emissaries to be seen. As long as they are moving, they can vanish from fairly small spaces. Is there a castle or manor in the area, preferably one hidden by trees or within a valley?"

"No," Captain Temur said. "There is an old citadel that was once used by the lords of the shores to protect their people in case of pirates, but it is visible from the water's edge. It's all cliffs and escarpments along there. No estates of any size. Beyond the bluffs lies the rivers that surround the Quarters."

"He lives in the caves," Tildi said, as a memory came to her with sudden clarity.

Everyone turned to look at her.

"How do you know that?" Sharhava asked. "What caves?"

"The whole headland is riddled with tunnels," Tildi said. "My brothers used to take them down to Tillerton to trade. It is a much shorter trip than going over the hills."

"Aye, there are caves near the town," Temur agreed. "Above it as well. The original fortifications against pirates are in them. Tillerton was built outward from them. They use the old places for storage."

"That is the way I recall the place," Calester said. "It has grown much from those days."

"Yes, but tunnels?" Halcot asked. "We've traded with Tillerton for centuries, and I've never heard of them."

Tildi felt a little foolish explaining. "Smallfolk don't like many people to know about them, but everyone does. They're very low. Humans don't like them because they have to stoop over. They probably don't think of them, because they're always there. But outsiders rarely use them. The passageways worm through the stone, not straight like a road."

"Probably the result of natural wearing," Olen said. "The Quarters are blessed with an abundance of fresh water that flows from the Eye Lake at their center, and it must go somewhere."

"Tell me more," Halcot said. "How far do they go?"

"That's all I know. Some of them lead right back to my home Quarter. I've never been in them."

"Ah!" Magpie said. "Then wouldn't it be possible that there are tunnels to the west as well as the east?"

"Of course, that's what these signs mean," Olen said, following the complex rune around and around with his point of light. "There is at least one great chamber. Many branching tunnels. My heaven, but he has quite a kingdom, if you count all the passageways in which you can see thraiks. But none to the east," Olen added. "If as you say traders travel through them and use them as storehouses that would explain all the runes arranged so."

"Can we enter through the cave mouths?" Soliandur asked.

"Almost certainly," Haroun said. "I have been in those storehouses myself. So have we all. I never thought to seek their end." He nodded to the others who signaled their agreement. "You have given us all the information we need, Mistress Summerbee. Now we need to work out how to use it."

"Indeed, yes," Sharhava said thoughtfully. "And how do we put paid to a wizard who cannot die?"

Chapter Thirty

I do not like being used as bait," Rin growled, for the hundredth time or so. "How could that mushroom-colored creature thing use me to betray my friends? Me! A princess of the Windmanes!" She stamped a hoof on the stone floor of their cell. The sound echoed hollowly in the darkness.

"Seems to me he's used to getting his way," Lakanta said, feeling the piles of straw she had propped against the wall. Since they had been thrown into it by the moss-men, Lakanta had counted five days by the sounds of expansion and contraction of the stone as the sun rose and set far above them, warming and cooling the earth. By her reckoning they were quite far underground. "In nearly everything, or so it seems. And keep in mind he might be listening to us."

"I do not care!" Rin replied indignantly. "What more can he get from us that he did not get? Oh, why did I tell him?"

"There was nothing you could do," Lakanta said, also for the hundredth time or so. "My dear, we are not wizards or knights, and I doubt there are many of those who could withstand those strange eyes of his. No wonder the Orontae wizard went mad. We are just lucky that he has left us alive."

"He still wants us as hostages," Rin said. "We are trade goods. What a humiliation!"

"He is completely mad. He wants to end the world. If only there was something we could do to stop him." Lakanta shook her head. "I hate it when only one party in a transaction has all the advantages. If only we knew where we were. I wonder how far we are from where we were."

Restlessly, Rin thrust herself up and onto her feet. Lakanta did not have to see to know what she was doing. She heard the whisper-click of the centaur's hooves feeling their way over the unevenly hewn floor.

Bang! Bang! Bang!

"It won't do you any good," Lakanta said, pitching her voice over the sound of Rin kicking the door of their cell. "That door's good stone and it's more than two feet thick. It would take ten of my cousins with steel hammers and chisels a month to hammer through it. You're not even chipping it."

"I have to do something!" Rin said. Her voice had a sharp edge of panic in it. "Will he not at least give us some light? I hate being in darkness!"

Rin returned and settled down beside her. Lakanta felt the warmth of her body and appreciated it. "Thank you for your courtesy. You must be as uncomfortable as I."

"I've had worse accommodations," Lakanta said, forcing cheerfulness into her tone that she did not feel.

"At least we are being fed," Lakanta said. "I almost miss poor Morag's cooking."

Rin laughed, well diverted. Lakanta was relieved. She had achieved a moment's calm. It would not last. "Do you?"

"Almost, I said. Burned meat would be better than none at all."

A hand sought hers in the blackness and squeezed. "If I had to be shut away in a tiny stone box with only bread to eat, I am grateful to the eternal ones to have a friend like you to save my sanity."

"Don't say that," Lakanta said, squeezing back. "You'll ruin my reputation for heartless dealing."

"As if anyone could hear you talk for a moment and find you heartless," Rin said. Lakanta felt her heave herself to her feet again. "Ah! It's so quiet and hot in here! What I wouldn't give for light and clean air!"

Her hooves clattered across the floor, and she started kicking again. Lakanta shook her head. Rin was as obdurate as the stone she was attacking. She should be doing something, too, but what? The atmosphere in the place muddled her mind. The enormous ratlike creatures scratched around the doors, and who knew what else was out there?

"Stop a moment," Lakanta said, sitting upright and frowning. "I hear something."

"That is me kicking the door."

"And I see something. Green light. Just a tiny dot, as if it's very far away. Where in the mountain's name is it coming from?"

"Your eyes are so starved for sight they are playing you tricks," Rin said. "The only way to see light is once we are back on the surface and free. But first I will kick the life out of that . . . that creature. How dare he cage us up!"

"Please, my friend," Lakanta said. "No one would like to cast about threats more than I at the moment, but I hear scratching."

At last Rin allowed herself to calm down, and she came to where Lakanta's voice was. She listened.

"By the Mother's mane! I hear something. And I do see a bit of light."

Lakanta tapped the stone with a fingertip. "I know stone as sure as I know my own bones, and it sounds thin here." She raised a shoe and kicked at it with all her might. It fractured like a pie crust. Lakanta jumped back at the glare of green light that flooded from the hole. A face looked up at her.

"Hello," it said. "We are friendly. Who are you?"

"Well, now," Lakanta said, rocking back on her heels. "Rin, my dear, you are right. I am hallucinating. I am seeing Tildi with a beard."

Neither Serafina nor Olen had time for lessons; nor could Tildi have concentrated upon them if they had. She was all too clearly aware of the proximity of her homeland. She felt that the elders were looking down disapprovingly upon her from the high bluffs as the pair of ships sailed out of the mouth of the Arown and turned westward, making for Tillerton.

All enmity had been put aside in the name of the cause. The Scholardom had united with the werewolves for the sake of defense. Sharhava and Patha had formed an alliance that surprised everyone for everything except its intensity. Tildi saw something new in Sharhava's rune: she had formed a bond of friendship with the werewolf matriarch. Though she loved her niece, she had few tendrils that reached out to others. Tildi was glad to see it. Serafina maintained a spell bridge that allowed free passage between the two ships so anyone could come and go as he or she pleased. Tildi also noticed that Prince Eremi spent whatever time his father did not demand on the *Eclipse* training in company with the Scholardom. He and Inbecca knew how dangerous the coming days would be, making every moment together precious. Tildi often heard the sound of sweet music in the evenings as he played his precious jitar for Inbecca. Magpie stood at his father's side now, as Inbecca flanked the abbess on the opposite side of the ship's wheel. Every person in the company was on guard, as prepared as they could be for what might come. She hated to see any of them thrown into danger, but they had to get her friends back safely.

A howl came from the lookout's basket. Captain Betiss pointed with his chin at a dark spot in the cliff face in between a narrow pair of waterfalls that tumbled down into a pool and flowed down the shorelands to the sea. Reckoning by the book, they had sailed westward for a day. The cave mouth was on the coast in a wild area that was claimed neither by the humans, the smallfolk, nor the dwarves, who lived under vast tracts of the mountains farther to the west.

"There's one of your ways in to the tunnels, masters," he said. "This place was occupied once, long ago, but it's been abandoned just as long. You see the ramp cut into the stone below it? That's wide enough for two carts to pass abreast. Just like back in Tillerton."

"Plenty of room for a force to march upward," Halcot said, eyeing the cave.

"But not enough for them to stand upright, if Tildi is correct," Olen reminded him.

"We will put up with whatever discomfort necessary," Captain Teryn declared. Morag stood at her shoulder. Tildi noticed how closely he watched everything Calester did. Such scrutiny was not lost upon the Maker, who seemed to enjoy the scrutiny. He gave the sergeant a solemn nod and pointed to a spot on the page to which the Compendium was open.

"Put into the cove," Calester said. "This is near enough."

Captain Betiss set up another howl that split the cold sky. The werewolf crew sprang to their posts and spilled air out of the sails. They launched a small pilot boat that guided the ships through the narrow neck, avoiding the jagged pillars, so sharp that the dark blue sea was torn to white rags upon them. Seals and gulls on the rocks let out their own harsh cries as the ships passed.

"The bottom's deep in the middle here," Haroun said as the mate repeated his barked order to drop anchor. "We are lucky to have such fine weather, in spite of the lateness of the season. Too many rocks. We could tear out our bottom if we were blown out of the channel. It's a good thing my people don't have to row you to shore; one good thing about having wizards aboard."

"I see no thraiks," Magpie said, peering at the cliffs. "He must not let his pets run where they could be spotted. No doubt they exercise as far away from here as they can."

"He is in there," Calester said, looking down into the book and up again. "Not close by, but within that complex. Mistress Summerbee is right."

"How far from that point will we find this Knemet?" Soliandur asked.

The Maker frowned. "This is not a map, highness, it is a symbolic representation. If you were to measure the tunnels as they are indicated here, they would appear to grow or shrink. It could be a matter of hours or days."

The crew picked up local gossip along with supplies. The missing statue and huge chunks of rock on the island where the Guardian had stood was the talk of the seaport.

"They call it a bad omen," Captain Temur said, shaking his head with merriment in his eyes. "I would've told them we have the Guardian on board our vessel, but no one would have believed me."

In spite of his light words, he took his responsibilities seriously, as did his son. Everyone was making ready to invade the underground fastness.

"We must not come too close to Knemet before we are prepared," Olen said. "There is no hiding the effects of the book. Once he sees runes appear, he will know it is close."

"We are all prepared to fight," King Halcot added. "My guards are trained to a razor's edge."

"As are my knights," Sharhava added. "We can provide protection on land or in the air. We have been practicing protective wardings under the tutelage of Mistress Serafina. We are well provisioned, and our weapons are ready. When the confrontation comes, you may rely on us."

"You won't be coming," Calester said.

"What?" Sharhava demanded, her chin out. "You cannot dismiss us out of hand. You will need us! Who knows how many miles of tunnels we must search to find the missing? We can help."

"I cannot risk you," the Maker said. "Your skills are not enough to protect you from one of my kind, especially one so irresponsible and callous as Knemet. You would never persuade him to give up your friends, and you might become another prisoner I must rescue or bargain for. Master Olen and I have been discussing the matter. I must be the one to face Knemet, so I must go, of course. Master Olen is nearly as accomplished a wizard as we are, and will help rather than hinder the effort."

"Thank you for the compliment," Olen said dryly. Tildi didn't see a bit of rancor in his rune. Evidently he had taken the Maker's personality into account and did not take offense at what was an outrageous insult.

"I need the Compendium with me. Without it, my abilities are too closely matched to his. We know all of each other's tricks and ways of thinking. I require its advantage. Since it would encumber me I would like to ask Mistress Tildi to accompany me and help keep it out of Knemet's reach."

"I will come," Tildi said.

"Knemet will have the advantage of the book as well, once it is within reach," Olen said.

"But he is not expecting it," Calester said. "With the wardings in place, he will not know exactly where it is until I allow him to know. By the way, I see you have been using a variation on the protective spells I invented," he added, looking up with pleasure at the pale silver veils that enveloped the ships. "I appreciate the refinements you have added."

"Thank you," Olen said. "It is a most elegant rune. Mistress Serafina has maintained our wards during most of the journey. Her mother, the wizardess Edynn, was responsible for adapting this part of the spell for greater protection."

Calester bowed to her. "I see I am in the presence of a most puissant magical dynasty."

"Never mind the pleasantries," Serafina said with a touch of asperity. "See, the runes are climbing up the hills. They will touch the headlands soon. We do not have very much time until he knows we are here."

"I understand that, lady," Calester said. "That is why we must make our move at once."

Sharhava was outraged. "You can't take the book straight into his hands. It must stay here, safely out of reach, and Mistress Summerbee as well, where we can guard them. That is our job."

"I must take it," Calester said firmly. "He will see the runes when they touch him. The effect, as you well know, reaches out far in advance of our arrival. I must take the risk."

"Bad planning," Soliandur said firmly. "You may be a wizard, but not a general."

"Then what, my lord?"

"We have discussed this time and again over the last days! You need a diversion."

"I had already made that decision," Calester said. "A two-pronged attack will distract him."

"Two-pronged?" Halcot asked.

"Aye. A force here in the bay will distract most of his protectors so that it will be possible for a smaller group, led by me, to go inside the stronghold and search for the lost ones. I will agree to take guards with me if the rest of you remain here and keep the thraiks dancing for as long as needed. The moonfolk are a commanding force on board as your guards and knights are in the skies. We will send a signal to you when we have the others safe."

"That sounds acceptable," Soliandur said. "I would be pleased to go with you."

"And I," said Halcot. The two kings looked almost eager for the chance. Olen cleared his throat.

"No, my lords," he said ruefully. "I cannot think that it would be wise to denude the thrones of two countries of their kings if the situation goes awry. We have no advantage except surprise. Once we are within Knemet's realm, his rules take precedence. We do not know what we face. None of us can identify some of the runes we see in those tunnels. He has given rise to one new species of which we know; there will surely be others, possibly more dangerous than the eel-creatures."

"We accept the chance of danger," Halcot said, his jaw set.

"But I cannot allow you to take it. I would rather take a few of your guards. I do not value their lives less, but it will not cause a catastrophe in the dynasty of Rabantae or Orontae if we do not return. I offer you an alternative task, one of equal importance to the survival of our company."

"And what may that be?" Soliandur asked, his hooded eyes glowering.

"Protecting Mistress Serafina. One of our number must remain here to maintain the spells to allow your steeds to take to the air and to provide the necessary magical protection."

Tildi looked up at Serafina. By the set of her jaw, the young wizardess had just barely agreed to be left behind, but she understood the necessity.

"It sounds like you wizards have everything already worked out," Halcot said sourly. "We poor folk who lack magic are only pawns in your chess game."

"Not at all," Olen said, regarding the golden-bearded man with some sympathy. "None of these decisions are lightly undertaken, my lord."

"Very well," Halcot said with ill grace. "May I and my captain choose those who will go with you?"

"And I?" Sharhava asked, equally miffed.

"Of course," Calester said, bowing to them. "We trust your judgment."

Halcot nodded to Teryn, who saluted and marched back to her company. Sharhava had a quick word in a low voice with Loisan. He nodded and walked over to the rail where the Scholardom stood waiting impatiently for news. He returned with three knights in tow, each well armed and carrying a full pack. Tildi recognized Lars Mey, Pedros, and Vreia, the three shortest in stature of all the Scholardom except for Princess Inbecca. Teryn brought back Morag and a lithe, dark-skinned woman she introduced as Demballe.

"Very well, that many and no more. I do not want to have to protect an army." Calester caught the look of disapproval on Tildi's face and smiled down at her. "You do not like the way I lead, little one?"

Once she would have been embarrassed to be singled out for her opinion. Tildi straightened her shoulders, lifted her chin, and looked the tall human straight in the eye.

"You could at least leave people their pride," she said.

"You are the one who told me that the matter was urgent. Could you do better? You have never fought a war."

Tildi was not going to let him talk down to her, not when she knew she was right. "But I have run a farm. If I needed to have a second team of threshers in a distant field, I must trust them to take the task and do it as well as they can, without my eyes upon it. For that, I must show them the meaning of their part of the harvest. If I only snap out instructions, they will feel I don't trust them to understand."

Calester looked indignant. "I *am* trusting them."

Olen chuckled. "I believe Tildi thinks that counsel should be taken with all parties involved, Master Calester, and I can't disagree with her. Perhaps we have been high-handed, my lords. I believe the conclusions we would have reached would differ little. We must go as silently and swiftly as possible, therefore a large party would be a detriment. The force that remains here must be strong and well organized. Do you not agree?"

Soliandur snorted. "Is it any wonder I mistrust wizards? Everything is done in secret in the dark, and the rest of us mortals must deal with the aftermath."

"I will not deny that is often true, my lord, though it sometimes takes a good deal longer to explain our workings than simply to show them."

"You say we are going to create a diversion out here?" Captain Betiss asked.

"That is correct," Calester replied. "We cannot conceal the book, so we must overwhelm Knemet with its presence. We will slip ashore silently, but that will reveal the ships to him. In fact, I mean to divide my old colleague's attention. It may even bring him out himself, though I have my doubts as well as my hopes. He always was a snail in his shell."

"And how are we going to do that?" Magpie asked.

"Like this," Calester said. He pointed his hand at the main deck of the *Corona*. A small spot the size of a coin appeared on the boards just forward of the main mast. Lines began to spread outward from it in a complicated pattern. Tildi peered at it. She thought of all the ancient symbols she had learned, but this one was unfamiliar as yet.

"What are you doing?" Haroun asked, alarmed. "What have you done to my ship?"

"Creating the diversion," Calester said with a charming smile. He turned to his chosen companions. "It won't hurt the ship itself, Captain, I promise you."

"And that will tell the other wizard we are here?"

The Maker clapped his hand on the werewolf's wiry shoulder. "I guarantee it. Make haste to be ready, my friends. It won't be long."

Tildi ran for her cloak.

Chapter Thirty-one

akanta could not fill her eyes enough with the sight of the four smallfolk men who huddled with her and Rin on the floor of their cell around a tiny green fire. They were pale and thinner than they ought to be, but that mattered little to the fact that there they were. If in her mind she cut the long shaggy brown hair, shaved the beards of three of them (the fourth had barely a whisker to his name as of yet), and put them in whole clothes instead of dirty rags, she could picture a respectable family of smallfolk farmers. She had to keep looking at the first one, with his oval face and large brown eyes.

"I almost think I could name you each," she said wonderingly. "You're Teldo, without a doubt, because you look enough like Tildi to be her twin. She always said you were closest to her. The good-looking one has to be Pierin. Tildi told us many a story of you." Pierin, possessed of the darkest, curliest hair and a well-molded chin and cheekbones, nodded and grinned. His brothers laughed and nudged him. "As for the other two, one looks older and one looks younger, so you're Gosto, and you're Marco." The beardless boy gawked as she pointed at him. "I'd love to hear you play a tune someday. Tildi says you have real talent."

Gosto, the one with thin, almost straight hair clinging to his very round head, grasped her hand. "You cannot think what a gift you have given us, mistress. I am so grateful to you I can never repay the debt. You really do know Tildi. Since we were locked up in here, we have questioned whether she was captured, too. That human"—he put a thumb over his shoulder in the direction of the corridor—"wouldn't say, no matter how often we asked. All he wanted to know was about a Compendium, as though we knew what he was talking about. He kept raving about it. When he was finally satisfied, he had us thrown down here. We can't agree on how long it's been. The ugly ones feed us, but he's never called for us again. As far as we know, he has never called for anyone he has thrown down here. I am sure he's forgotten about us. We've been left to our own devices. If we hadn't been together, we probably would have died of despair."

"And cold," Pierin added. "Thanks to Teldo we had fire, at least, even if it's a strange color. If we ever see daylight again, I swear I will never make fun of Teldo and his magic again as long as life is in me."

Gosto, true to Tildi's assessment of him as the practical leader of the family, got right back to the point. "Are you saying that it is because of that little parchment our parents bought for Teldo all those years ago that the thraiks carried us here, that piece of paper that hurt to touch?"

"I am," Lakanta said. "It was a copy of this Compendium, or a page of it, at least. That terrible man is called a Shining One, one of the wizards who helped make it. It's a book of all reality."

Teldo opened his mouth. "But that's impossible. The Shining Ones have been dead for centuries."

"He's been telling us tales of them while we have been locked up here," Marco added.

"Not impossible, or the six of us wouldn't be sitting in a dungeon together," Lakanta said. "He wants it more than he wants air to breathe or water to drink. He's killed and kidnapped to try and get it."

"But what does it do?" Teldo asked. Lakanta saw the keenness that marked his sister.

"It describes everything in the world," Rin said. "And somehow, the words in the book are tied to the real object. Change the word, and the thing changes. Destroy the word, and . . ."

"A quarter of Orontae vanished with the piece of parchment it was painted upon," Lakanta finished. "Two months ago, now. No, a bit longer." The smallfolks' eyes were huge, dark pools of amazement.

"The world's changed a dozen times since we were locked up here," Gosto said, and whistled.

"And to think we had a leaf of that very book in our home," Pierin said.

"A copy, thank the Father and Mother," Teldo corrected him. He turned back to Lakanta. "Are you saying that the thraiks could smell it on us somehow?"

"Yes," Lakanta replied. She took a deep breath, knowing that what she was about to say would sting. "On anyone it touched. And on your parents, most likely." She regretted the stricken look on their faces. "You have not been able to find if they are here?"

"No. We have given up hope for that," Gosto said sadly. "When we were first locked up, we called and shouted to anyone who could hear us. There were other prisoners. We know of at least a dozen. We hear them mostly when they first arrive, but after a time . . . I think they just give up and die. I fear . . . it has been ten years, mistress. I don't know that we could have survived such a long imprisonment."

"Do . . . do you know if there is a dwarf here? My husband went missing two years ago. He is the one who sold the leaf of the book to your parents. His name was Adelobert."

"The trader?" Gosto asked in astonishment. "Old Glad-to-see-you was your husband? The dwarf with the big blond beard and three braids down his back?"

"I don't think we ever knew it," Pierin said, abashed. "We always called him trader or friend. He *was* our friend, mistress. We were glad to see him, too. Always."

"He gave us good bargains, as well. He remembered I like music," Marco said.

"I don't think there's anyone in a hundred miles around Daybreak Bank that didn't know that," Teldo teased his youngest brother. "But Adelobert— I am glad to know his name—did keep these things in mind when he made his visits. That's no doubt why he brought the leaf to my mother all those years ago, since he knew we had a mind to higher learning. He was a good man, mistress. We shall miss him."

It was as close as he would ever have to a memorial gathering. Lakanta felt deeply grateful to Tildi's brothers. "Kindness runs in families," she said. "I'd have known you were related to Tildi even if I couldn't see you."

"Is Tildi well?" Teldo asked.

Lakanta put aside her own sorrow. She had always known Adelobert must be dead. The fresh grief she felt at having it confirmed she suppressed firmly when she surveyed the anxious faces. "Is she well?" she echoed, finding a little of her old spirit inside. "She's the companion of wizards and kings! She's as brave as lions. She's faced down werewolves and danced with the bearkin. The Great Book itself is her very own plaything. A prince has written a song about her. You'd be so proud of her, it would make your chests pop. Unless you're the kind of smallfolk fools who believe that a girl shouldn't strive for anything past cooking a good dinner and mending socks."

"Not at all, mistress," Gosto said. "Our sister's the equal of any of us, and better than most of those who look down on her. We've all winked at her learning magic alongside Teldo. I just thought she didn't have much of an aptitude for it. Seems I was wrong, and I take joy in knowing better."

Teldo grinned. "And to think the last time we studied together she could just barely make a spark of fire, and that not all the time."

"Oh, she's moved far beyond just flame spells," Lakanta said, waving a hand. "She can conjure things without even thinking about them. By the motherlode, she will fly to the moons and back when she learns you're all alive. She's been grieving for you all this time."

"But how did you come to meet her? Dwarves and centaurs rarely come to the Quarters."

"We met her in Overhill," Lakanta said.

"Overhill?" Gosto echoed. "What in muck was she doing there? A respectable girl should be safe at home."

"The way that we understand it," Rin said gently, "she took Teldo's letter offering an apprenticeship to the wizard Olen and went there."

"But why did she leave home?"

"She couldn't stay," Lakanta said. "Any more you'll have to ask her yourself. By the stone that spawned me, you shall see her again to ask."

"We have to escape," Gosto said, "and from what you say, we must do it before she and your friends figure out where we are. I have no wish to have that madman get his hands on the book she guards. Are her protectors strong enough to keep her safe?"

"They'd give their lives for her," Lakanta said firmly. "I'd have said that would be enough."

"We have many tales we can tell you about all of them," Rin said, "and I have no doubt we will have more than enough time, but how did you manage to break through the walls?"

The Summerbee brothers looked at one another. "It started with a loose rock in the side of our cell," Gosto said. "There's precious little fresh air down here. Marco felt a bit of a breeze and went looking for the source. It took all of us to work it loose. We were hoping it led to the outside, but it didn't."

"It was the wall of the dungeon next to us," Pierin said. "When we began to pick away at it, hoping to get more air, a voice spoke to us. A human man was locked in there, only a foot or so away, and we never heard him. We started talking about getting out of here. We scratched at our side with our rock, and he scratched at his. We were so close to breaking through to meet each other. One day we heard screaming, then nothing. When we did make a hole big enough to look in, there was no one there. I think the ugly ones caught him and gave him to the charnives."

"Charnives?" Lakanta echoed, and the name summoned up horror stories of her childhood. "But they're myths. Those things out there can't be charnives."

Rin stamped a hoof. "What are charnives?"

"A legend. They're the beasts that sneak up on people traveling underground and drag away the one at the back, never making a sound."

"Those black-furred beasts?" Rin asked. "Why can't they be?"

"Well, I lived underground half my life, and I never knew anyone who was carried off by them. But tales came back with traveling folk."

"We heard of them taking victims in the tunnels between us and the trading port south of our homeland," Marco said. "Maybe they were invented by these Makers of Teldo's, and that's why they are here. He brought them as his hunters, to keep his prisoners from escaping."

"And it's worked, too," Pierin added. "If anything's kept us in here, it's them. There's swarms of them, and they can run down anyone who gets out. That's why we're going through the walls of the cells instead, breaking rock and using Teldo's fire to melt through where it's thin. We're safe from the hunter-beasts in here. We have broken into four cells already. You're the fifth, and the first one where we've found anyone else." He didn't say "alive," but both Lakanta and Rin understood it.

"Charnives," Lakanta mused, shaking her head. Another legend come to life, as if the Great Book wasn't enough.

"We figured to get as far uphill as we can before we get out into the corridors and make our run," Marco said. "It's slow going."

"I have been trying to kick down the door," Rin said.

"We heard you for the last several days," Gosto replied with a grin.

"Never mind bothering with the door; it's bespelled," Teldo said. "But the wall holding it up isn't."

"Really, now?" Lakanta asked. Her spirits lifted. With such a talent at hand, she could see her way clear to a future that existed. "I can tell you where the stone is sound or weak. That's my people's greatest gift. Let's see what we can do together."

"Aye," Rin said. "Six of us stand a better chance of getting away than any of us alone."

Gosto gave a good-natured snort. "We'll see if we can live up to our sister's reputation. I'd hate to let the family name down."

Soliandur and Magpie led their horses up from belowdecks into the midst of the preparations. Magpie had been in a military camp before, but never on a warship. The atmosphere was much the same, flavored as it was with a sense of urgency, fear, and anticipation. Everyone hurried about him on his or her own business, seeking to be as ready as they might be. Three of the women sat on the deck among armloads of leather barding, mending straps, and hammering in bronze and steel plates to replace missing or damaged pieces. A gray-haired male sat at a grinding wheel. Sparks flew as he set new edges on swords and knives. A werewolf blacksmith, his limbs narrow but as tough as the steel he worked, melted the links shut in the repairs he made to chainmail shirts. Soldiers and scholars alike saw to their own gear, making certain that the arrows in their quivers were straight and well fletched, dents in helmets were hammered out, and boots were sound and whole. Cooks served up huge bowls of hearty fish stew and chunks of bread that steamed in the cold air. People sat wherever they could to eat their rations. Knight, guard, and trader alike, they toasted one another in draughts of beer, and passed a joke or a friendly word as if they were the final gifts they might give. Who knew which of them might be hurt or killed in the days to come?

With a tilt of his head, the king directed his son to follow him to the sheltered spot beneath the wheelhouse, where Serafina stood. Magpie saw that she was looking at the rune. He wondered what it was for. Calester ignored any questions he didn't like, and Master Olen had been too busy to indulge Magpie's curiosity. A pity he didn't have time to ply Tildi. She had more luck with Calester than the rest of them, since she could do something he couldn't, and she might be able to wheedle more information out of him.

"We are at your service, mistress," Soliandur said.

"I am honored, Your Highness," Serafina replied.

"What can an army of two do, Father?" Magpie asked. "I obey your command."

"An army of three," Soliandur said with a gleam in his eyes as he peered over his son's shoulder. "Yes, I thought it. Here comes Halcot. Told you off, did she not?"

"She did," Halcot said, looking sheepish. He brought his mare up beside his brother king's and made a great business out of tightening a stirrup strap. He glanced up at Magpie. "I asked my captain if I could fly in their company. She said no. I was fool enough to argue, and she told me in words that even a child could understand what my proper place is."

"I can't imagine her being disrespectful, sir!"

"She was more respectful than I deserved. She reminded me my guards' duty is to protect me and my house. I'll be in her way if I try to go with them. This is not a war; it is a diversion. All we seek to do here is to keep this wizard's forces busy until our friends have attained their goal. If it becomes impossible to continue, we are to abandon ship. Then my guards will see to the safety of my person. In the meantime I am not to endanger it unnecessarily. If My Highness wishes, she will assign guards to me for the duration." Soliandur laughed. Halcot joined in, though he sounded pained. "Captain Teryn is right and I am wrong, lad. I cannot force her to divide her attention away from the battle at hand. Therefore, let us devolve upon our original plan."

"What plan?" Magpie asked, intrigued and concerned at the same time.

His father answered instead. "My brother king and I have discussed the division of duties. Captain Teryn and Abbess Sharhava will defend the ships by air. Mistress Patha is in command of the merchant crew, our land forces. We three have the most important task. We will protect this young lady from direct attack. If necessary, we will sweep her to a place of safety." He offered a nod to Serafina, who nodded back gravely.

"What about Inbecca?" Magpie asked anxiously.

"I have spoken to the abbess," Soliandur said, careful not to see the exchange between the two.

"And gotten an earful, I imagine," Halcot said with a twinkle in his eyes.

Soliandur scowled and swung up into his saddle. "Never mind that! She will keep the lady as safe as she can, but she deserves to share the task of her fellows. To demand she stay below and out of sight is to deny her rank and her courage. She is a future queen. I would be as insulted if anyone tried to require me to remain out of this battle." A defiant glare at his son, who admitted to himself that he wanted to do just that. "Now, mount up. Be a credit to your ancestors."

"Very well, Father," Magpie said, concealing a grin.

The stranger came down the steps from the ship's wheel with Olen, Tildi, Captain Betiss, and the five guards behind them like goslings following a very self-important goose. Calester had the Great Book tucked under his arm. Magpie could not help but notice that Tildi's eyes kept darting to it. Poor thing, he thought. Serafina's eyes fixed upon the enormous scroll and widened. Magpie followed her gaze, then looked at the rune in the center of the deck.

"It's the book," he said.

"My lords," Calester said, "I hope it will be a matter of hours rather than days before our return. We face grave danger, as do you. I bid you good fortune."

"Good hunting," Halcot said.

Calester met his eyes with a smile. "We seek two kinds of quarry today. As you know, sometimes one must use bait to lure out one's prey." He reached into the air and spread out his long fingers. Magpie felt as much as saw the pale gray curtains that surrounded the ship dissolve into nothingness. The thin sunshine beat down upon the big rune, which seemed to glow. "That should be enough. Farewell."

"Wait, Master Calester," Serafina cried. "The wards—why did you do that?"

One moment the "hunting party" was there, and the next it was streaking away from them toward the cliffs swifter than a fish could swim. Magpie ran to the side to see the tiny figures of Olen, Tildi, and Calester alighting on the narrow foreshore with the dazed guards staggering unsteadily behind them.

"Mother Wolf, what has he done?" Haroun wailed.

Serafina's face twisted with strain. "I cannot close the spell again. He said it was his design. He must have done something that prevents me from recasting it."

"Find something else," the captain begged her. "Save my ship."

"He said he would create a diversion," Halcot said grimly. "And it looks like he has. See there!"

He pointed upward, as scores upon scores of thin-winged monsters began to appear out of black scars in the cold blue sky. In a single moment, all the werewolves changed shape to their lycanthropic forms. The children who had been playing on deck ran toward the ships' ladders to hide belowdecks. All others drew weapons and braced themselves. "To horse, my brother!"

"To horse," Soliandur echoed. "And you ask why I do not trust wizards?"

Chapter Thirty-two

Jubilant, Knemet watched the last thraik circle the ceiling and vanish. All around him, runes lit up the gloomy confines of his chamber like fireflies, lending the room such beauty as he had not seen in centuries. The book was near, so near he could almost feel its silken pages under his fingers. He could see it in his mind's eye. How much stronger it seemed than he remembered. It had been so long since he had had it in his grasp. He tried to fix his thoughts upon it and see its surroundings. Did the strange smallfolk girl still have it in her care? He did not see her.

How curious that the wizards had removed the spell shielding it from his sight. The book would soon be in his hands.

He called for the liches. The stocky, gray-green figures stalked into his chamber and massed silently, awaiting his command.

"Fetch me the last two subjects," he said. "I want them here."

The faceless heads nodded on the thick, spongelike necks and stumped away.

He closed his eyes and watched the flashes of activity that were close to the unshielded scroll. The lord thraik was wise to the weapons the invaders carried. He kept most of the flight high above the futile arrows that flashed in the feeble winter sun and fell, having missed their target. A pass, by one of the quick youngsters that Knemet had altered for the greatest speed, up-set the werewolf crew, who bounded toward it. It swooped, claws out, down toward the book, then let out a shriek of protest. It clapped its wings hard and ascended again. The gray-pelted lycanthropes sprang up to grab at it. They fell to the deck, unsuccessful.

Knemet was puzzled. The thraik had come so close to taking the book from the midst of its defenders. Why had it not taken it? He wished he could see more than shadows. He could make his way out of his labyrinth and guide his thraiks in person to their goal. The bearers were so close.

No! Knemet smashed a hand against the wall. The thraiks would get it for him. It would be brought to him. He did not need to set foot outside in the world that had rejected him.

"Get it, my children," he hissed. "Do not fail me."

*T*ildi tiptoed as lightly as she could through the dank corridors holding the book tightly in her arms behind the hunched figure of Sergeant Morag.

You did not have to come, she reminded herself. *But I did,* she thought more firmly. Rin and Lakanta had never hesitated to come to her aid even when danger threatened. Lakanta had literally crawled through fire for her, and she would never forget that.

The tall humans around her were uncomfortable having to walk crouched over. The guards carried knives or maces in their hands, for there was no room to wield a sword, should they come face-to-face with danger. Even Olen carried his staff under his arm. The sole exception was Calester, who had donned a spell like a garment that made him as small as she was. Olen found the technique fascinating, yet chose not to have it applied to him or the others.

"I will want to know everything about this as well, my friend," he had said to Calester when they first entered the caves, "but like all my questions about your talents, my thirst for knowledge will have to wait until we are all safely away from this place."

"The floor slopes down ahead," Morag whispered back to the other guards. Within a few steps, Tildi found herself stumping along a slope. Water flowed in thin streams on either side of her boots. Her feet were getting damp inside them. She feared she could lose her footing on the slick stone.

"Will those flying monsters come through here?" murmured Lar Pedros, his blue eyes wide and wary.

"Thraiks don't need an open path," Olen reminded him in a low tone that did not carry beyond their ears. "These quarters are too constricted for them. That is not to say that there will not be other defenders. Knemet has defied discovery for a long time. That cannot be by accident."

"Aye," Calester said, his voice squeezed to higher registers by the confines of his spell. "Unless the thraiks farm the land and fish for Knemet's supper, then someone or something else fetches and carries for him. I almost dread to see what it is."

The passageways wound through the native rock like woodworm in chestnut timbers, with plenty of dips and bends that Tildi had to be careful not to walk into.

She was glad to have Olen nearby. How dearly she had missed him over the last many months. He had such a way of lessening terrors by finding the good in them, as he did then.

"Good heavens, Tildi," he said. "And you have had this incredible opportunity these last months to see runes independently of their objects? What a chance to increase your vocabulary of ancient signs, and to study linguistic structure. The subtleties between similar examples of runes is absolutely fascinating. See that spider just above your left shoulder? That is a common forest spider grown to immense proportions in this underground environment." Tildi glanced up and nearly jumped out of her skin at the shimmering rune. Just before it landed upon her she shifted hastily to the right, and it fell on Calester instead. He paid it no attention.

"Let me see our progress," the Maker said, tapping the book in her arms. A soft blue light arose above her, lighting the translucent parchment. She let the book unroll, knowing it would open to the correct page. No map existed of the caves; that the werewolves had discovered on making inquiries in Tillerton. The closest to a chart they had was the ever-changing image.

"We are deep into the hillside now," Olen said, letting his flicker of red light play upon the exposed leaf. "Knemet seems to be very close, but he could be several hundred feet above or below us. Where are our friends? Ah." He twirled the tip of his forefinger in a small circle, and the light went to play upon the pair of runes, not very far away from them or Knemet. Tildi was relieved to see that they appeared much as they had when she had last looked for them. Neither of her friends had been injured or killed.

"How can we reach them?" Sergeant Morag asked.

"Easily, my practical-minded friend," Calester replied. "This passageway will take us up and around like a spiral staircase. It should deliver us to where they are waiting."

"It doesn't look like it to me," Tildi said, peering over the edge of the page.

"Well, it will," Calester said, deliberately closing the scroll before she could see for certain. He tucked it under his own arm. "Don't argue. There can be only one leader, and I am he. Do you agree, or not?"

Olen's eyebrows rose when she glanced at him. "I agree," she said. She wanted to say more, but Olen shook his head. Why was he allowing Calester to behave so imperiously? Olen was a more natural leader for the party, with the respect of all the parties involved. Calester was a newcomer, one prone to alienating others with his peremptory attitude. "But . . . ?"

"But, what? Do not delay us further. It will be neither easy nor safe to reach your friends. Do you wish to endanger us by beginning a discussion that will end the same way as it began?"

A distant sound interrupted him.

"Master, what is that?" Lar Vreia asked.

They all stopped to listen. Tildi heard roaring and the hollow bang of stone upon stone.

"I fancy it is one of Knemet's other creations," Olen said. "Hope that it does not come this way."

Calester beckoned to them with the blue light radiating from his hand, and pointed to a passageway that opened off to the left from their path. "Hurry," he said. "Something is happening here. I hope it distracts Knemet enough for our purposes."

"What do you mean?" Tildi asked, hurrying to catch up with him. "We want to avoid him."

The Maker glanced down at her, his eye sockets rendered hollow by his witchlight. "Of course we do. But if we must face him, I cannot wait to show that ruffian that I have the book once again, and all hopes of him obtaining it are dashed. We were rivals of old."

"But he is as strong as you, isn't he?" Tildi asked.

Calester was dismissive of the question. "He is as experienced as I, yes, but he is alone, and I am not. I have all of you. Your skills will help to tip the balance against him. It would be sweet revenge, if we should face him."

Morag led the way into the new corridor.

Tildi dropped back so she was beside Olen, who made the best speed he could walking with his shoulders bent. "Master, all we came to do was to bring back Lakanta and Rin. Did he tell you what he is planning? He can't march us into Knemet's study."

Olen hesitated for a moment. "Tildi, what will happen will happen. I promise you that my first interest is in your welfare, come what may. Will you trust me?"

"I trust you," Tildi said as she slipped into the new passage ahead of him, "but I don't believe that I trust *him*."

"Something is different here," Morag said. "I feel a current in the air."

"Of course it is different," Calester said, holding up his beacon. It began to glow brightly until the walls and everything between them were all bathed in ghostly blue. A whisper of wings and a faint shriek came from the bats disturbed by their voices and the intrusion of light. "The ceiling is higher here."

Tildi glanced behind her. The low doorway through which they had just come seemed like a mouse hole compared with where she now stood. This passage, a mere slit between two immense walls of rock, reminded her of a narrow mountain pass. The guards cautiously levered themselves upright and massaged their back muscles.

Olen straightened up and placed the foot of his staff on the floor between his feet. "We have reached the edge of his realm."

Calester's thin mouth stretched in a humorless smile. The rune wrapped about his body melted away, and he grew to twice Tildi's height. "Yes. We are not far away now. Let us hurry while we can move upright."

Lakanta held a burning wisp of straw against the head-deep gash that the six of them had already broken into the wall behind the hinge of their cell door. She marked the stone with a big X that seemed to waver in the greenish firelight.

"There. That bit'll fracture if you heat it up, then strike it above and below."

Teldo produced a fresh handful of fire and launched it at the spot she indicated. The wall glowed red where it touched. The other three Summerbee brothers hammered upon it with chunks of stone, heedless of the leaping smithereens that burned holes in their beards, hair, and clothing.

"Let me," Rin said. The brothers backed away to make room for her. She turned and kicked out with her hind feet again and again. With every blow, chips rained to the floor.

"No more from that vein, Princess," Gosto said, risking his nose by peering past her hooves. "Let's go again. You're a gift from the Father, mistress. We've done in an afternoon what it took the four of us a month to accomplish."

Lakanta shouldered past them and began to feel at the wall again. How odd after all the years she had been on the road to be using the skills she had learned at the knee of her father, a master stonecutter. "I guess that what they say about early learning is true: it stays in your mind no matter what else you pile upon it," she said. "Here and here, Teldo. Then, just move down a bit. This part's formed around an old stalagmite. It's so rotten that I could kick through it myself, without Rin's help."

Teldo cupped a new gout of fire in his hands. Lakanta could tell he was tiring. Magic seemed to use up a lot more strength than manual labor. It had never been an issue with Tildi or Serafina, for however bad the food was they had while on the road, there was always enough of it. She resolved that when the moss-men "ugly ones" dropped off their sorry rations she would give Teldo half of hers.

"There," he said, flinging the green flame at the wall.

Marco let out a gasp. "Teldo, what did you do to us?"

"To you?" Teldo asked. "Nothing at all. Just to the wall." He turned to his younger brother and let out a gasp of wonder. Lakanta saw what he saw and let out a jubilant yelp. Runes blossomed like glorious golden lilies all over the place, including on the chest of each Summerbee brother, and on her and Rin as well. The centaur met her eyes with a broad smile.

"What in the name of Mother Nature is that?" Gosto asked.

"It's rescue," Lakanta said, unable to keep herself from grinning like an idiot. "Keep working. That means they've come for us. They're out there somewhere."

The snuffling and warbling grew louder, as if the appearance of the runes troubled the charnives as well.

"Tildi?" Teldo asked, his gaunt face taking on more life than she'd ever seen in it.

"Without a doubt," Rin said, greatly relieved. "We knew they would not forget about us."

"But that's terrible," Pierin exclaimed. "Didn't you tell us that the wizard wants that book of hers? You're the goods he means to trade for them, aren't you?"

"Aye," Rin said, her eyes showing white around the green irises. "I can't face him again. I would rather face the beasts."

"Well, now," Lakanta said firmly, "then we won't be here for him to trade. Come along, then. We've got more to do."

A sound attracted her attention. Gosto flattened himself on the filthy floor and listened at the crack at the bottom of the door.

"The charnives are stirring. That means the ugly ones are coming. Why now? We were only fed a while ago."

"He's noticed the runes," Lakanta said, and she didn't have to explain who he was. "How could he not? Unless it's too late and he's taken some of our friends prisoner. He could be sending them down here."

"Tildi!" the brothers exclaimed.

"We must get out of here at once," Rin said. "If they are in trouble, we will help them."

"We're not even close to breaking through," Gosto said.

Lakanta felt an idea tug at her ear.

"So we'll have to get them to open the door for us," she said.

"How?"

"Make them think we're already gone."

Marco looked puzzled. "How do we do that? Shout out that we have escaped?"

"No, lad," Lakanta said. "But we will give them a reason to open this door and find us gone."

She murmured her idea to them. Rin let out a whinny of a laugh, and the lads grinned at her in approval. They hurried to gather all the straw from the floors of the now connected cells and laid it in a heap by the door.

"Now, be ready to move swiftly," Lakanta said. "If hiding in the shadows doesn't fool them, then we'll charge over them and walk on the ceilings if need be. Now, give your best shout. We want to make sure they hear us, if they have any ears in those moss heads of theirs."

"Fire!" the brothers bellowed in unison.

Teldo Summerbee obliged.

It did Lakanta's light-starved eyes good to see the shooting star of green flame arc overhand into the pile of fetid straw. It flared up, shooting fire in all directions, including out the break in the wall. She heard frantic movement. The hunters yelped. They must have fled, for their voices receded swiftly. Lakanta hurried to flatten herself against the inner wall of the adjoining cell and close her eyes.

After what seemed an eon, the heavy door opened, its hinges creaking ponderously. She could not hear the ugly ones' footsteps over the crackling fire. She did not dare look. If the ugly ones used any initiative at all, they would come through the opening in the wall and find them. Would the flames drive back men made of moss? She waited, listening. Was that the sound of her own breathing, or the fire, or the ugly ones coming to take her back to that terrible Maker?

A hand tapped her on the arm. She jumped in alarm and her eyes flew open.

"Come," Teldo whispered, a dancing green flame balanced on his palm. "I think they've left the door unlatched."

Rin was the first to wriggle through the wall. She raced to the enormous stone portal and leaned all her weight against it. It shifted, rasping on the stone floor. Rin's hooves scrabbled as she lost footing, and the others ran to help her. Lakanta reflected on how strong the ugly ones must be to maneuver the doors so effortlessly.

"They are gone!" she exclaimed, peering out into the corridor. "Come, let's find a way out of this terrible place. Make haste!"

The four Summerbee brothers picked up armfuls of rocks and followed her. Lakanta, the last to leave, took a wary look around as the light from Teldo's fire receded. She had never before been afraid to be underground in all her life, but she was afraid of this place, and she did not like it.

"Fretting never got anything useful done," she said, and resolutely marched out behind the others.

Chapter Thirty-three

rive the devils back!" Captain Teryn shouted, signing to her company to divide into two groups. The first flew to port of the *Corona*'s mainmast, the second to starboard, pursuing the pack of eight or so thraiks away from the belly of the *Corona*. One of the winged monsters lay dying on the deck, its wings sliced into pieces by the last clash with the Rabantavian guard, its dark blood steaming in the cold air. Little human or horse blood had been drawn yet, but more was inevitable. Magpie had never known there were so many thraiks, and they all seemed to be here at once, wheeling and gliding high above them. Their shrieks curdled his blood. Only the blue fire of the Scholardom kept the greatest number from descending en masse and attacking.

Teryn's guards, supported by the wizardess's magic and not bound by proximity to the runes, followed the thraiks out over the harbor. The winged monsters bounded in and out of strokes of blackness, staying low over the toothy rocks. Abruptly, they spread out and angled back, trying to throw off their pursuers and get to the decoy, but the Rabantavians stayed upon them like hounds to the hunt. The two squads, led by Teryn and her second sergeant, a hearty, gray-haired man named Belaft, flanked them, ready to engage the demons if they should turn to fight. The humans shouted words of encouragement to one another, a counterpoint to the ear-tearing cries of the thraiks. From the deck of the *Eclipse*, Knights of the Book rose up, ready to intercept the foe before it could reach its target.

One thing the defenders had had to add to Calester's decoy rune was a book of some kind. The thraiks' eyesight was keen. They were drawn to the spot, as the Guardian had known they would be, but became confused and rose up, shrieking, when they did not see a book. The Scholardom feared they would soon see through the ruse. Captain Betiss had volunteered an ancient book of maps. It lay on top of the target. With a visible goal, the thraiks would never leave until they had attained it. That both relieved and chilled the defenders.

If there was one good thing that had come out of this terrible time, it was the rekindling of an ancient friendship. His father and King Halcot had taken to the skies as brothers in arms. The war between them, the shame of financial ruin and public humiliation caused by Magpie's abrupt departure from a royal betrothal feast, were all forgotten in the heart-pounding excitement of battle against a common foe. In their company, Magpie felt as if he were once again a boy in his father's train on a state visit. They talked over his head, making oblique references to old jokes the two had shared long before Magpie or his brothers were born. Once in a while Soliandur even smiled at him, willing him to get the jest. Magpie felt a moment of longing for the lost years in between, but he treasured the gesture. He dared not hope it would last beyond the quest.

"Ware!" bellowed one of the knights, wheeling his steed through the rigging in pursuit of one thraik that had broken away from the pack. It turned its head on its long neck and hissed at him. He spurred his horse to catch up. It closed its wings and dove toward the rune. On its present course it would be almost upon Serafina. Was it smart enough to realize she was important to the humans' defense? Magpie spurred Tessera to a gallop, sword flat on the mare's neck.

Before he could reach it, two shadows passed between him and the pale sun.

"Rabantae!" Halcot bellowed, kicking his mount to greater speed.

"Orontae!"

The two kings swooped directly up into the thraik's path. It pulled up and back, screaming its frustration. The knight behind it caught up and slashed at its right wing. Halcot jerked back in his saddle. The thraik's claw missed him. Halcot riposted. His sword tip grazed the slimy, green-black skin and drew blood. The injured thraik went into a frenzy, striking out in every direction. Soliandur was more daring. He urged his horse higher. As it passed the creature, he leaned out of his saddle and struck it point-first under the wing with his sword. The thraik's reaction nearly pulled the blade out of his hand. It twisted its head to bite his arm. Soliandur refused to let go of the hilt.

"Father!" Magpie shouted. He kicked Tessera, turning her to race to his father's side.

Halcot was nearer. He urged his horse upward, placing himself between the snapping teeth and his brother king. He rammed the creature in the neck with the top of his helmeted head. It withdrew, choking.

"Thanks, friend," Soliandur called, wheeling his horse around for another sally. Halcot grinned, patting his head as if to reassure himself that it was still there. By now several of the Scholardom had arrived to take on the thraik.

"My lords, below!" Lar Loisan called. The two kings looked about to realize they were above the level of the lookout's basket. Sharhava's lieutenant's craggy face was full of disapproval. "Leave this to us, if you please!"

Sheepishly, Magpie brought Tessera down to her previous circuit. Soliandur and Halcot flew outward and down, avoiding the ongoing battle. The thraik screamed and struggled in the midst of the well-drilled crowd of defenders, who were determined this one would not escape. The deck below was full of werewolves, eager to tear yet another thraik to ribbons. The other warriors broke into smaller groups to pursue the rest, always aware of the horde of winged demons like a cloud of midges above them. Magpie was aware that the thraiks could afford to lose more than three-quarters of their force before the humans matched them in numbers.

The thraiks had added new tactics, varying their attacks in an effort to mislead their foe. Instead of a dart and dive maneuver to capture whoever bore the Compendium's mark, they sought to distract the defenders and draw them as far away as they could, then vanish, leaving the guards wondering until they chose to reappear and strike. He watched the tactic now. At a signal from the largest and fiercest of the winged demons, a force of fifteen or so fled from Teryn's soldiers. Any moment, they would disappear. Yes, there they went.

"Ware!"

Magpie braced himself and brought Tessera to hover directly over Serafina. The sky split open a few feet from the mast, and thraiks came tumbling out of it like potatoes from a sack, all intent upon the rune on the deck. They never reached it. The matriarch Patha, standing on the wheelhouse, let out a cry that could have been heard for a hundred miles. Her kin, all in wolf form, leaped to grab for the winged beasts. The tallest and broadest male bounded to the rail and threw himself onto the back of the nearest thraik. It bucked and twisted as he raked its neck, but it could not dislodge him until he had drawn blood. It flew off toward the mountains with him still clinging to its back. His kin wasted no time mourning him. They sought to make their own mark on the demons. Battle was truly joined as the thraiks turned to retaliate.

Sergeant Belaft, Teryn's second officer, brought the second squad around. The warhorses balked at charging the thraiks. Magpie could tell they didn't like their smell or the abrupt way they moved, but they obeyed their riders.

The beasts were so strong that it took three to six warriors to hold on to the wing of a single thraik. All the humans could do was wear them down, and hope for luck and skill to give them room to strike at a vital spot. Flailing wings and flashing claws took their toll on humans and horses alike. A guard in Teryn's company let out a yell. His sword fell from his hand. Bright blood stained his livery, and his arm hung useless. Teryn waved him away, toward the healers who waited on board the *Eclipse*.

The thraiks angled around, moving closer to the center of the ship, wanting to get at that precious rune. At a cry from the lord thraik above, four of them disappeared into blackness. A rider in white and red spurred after them, and nearly made it to the gash before it closed. He rode through the spot and reined his horse in a half circle.

"What in the timeless void do you think you're doing?" Teryn barked as he returned to his company.

The same question must have occurred to the guard, because his swarthy face was gray with shock.

"Get back in line!" Belaft shouted. "More help there to the right! Up, guards, up!"

The thraiks screamed and struggled. One was weakening. Magpie could tell it was using all its strength to stay aloft. Two more of them vanished, leaving the injured one and a small one alone among the warriors.

"Ware!" Teryn shouted, looking around for the others.

They were not long in reappearing. Suddenly the defenders were surrounded by the six and a dozen more. The warriors were beset both ahead and behind by the winged monsters. Teryn wheeled her horse on its hind hooves, striking again and again at two thraiks. Belaft's force finished off the wounded beast, which dropped heavily among the werewolf crew. They swarmed over it, slashing at it to make certain it was dead. The last one vanished from sight.

Bursts of blue light dazzled his eyes. He shielded them, squinting. Four shadows arrowed in from above: the next wave. Flame hit one thraik square in the back. It shrieked an earsplitting cry and bit at its own back. The blue fire caught on its jaws and spread out over the thin wings. The thraik threw itself into the sea. Magpie saw the brilliant light descend swiftly until it was extinguished. He wondered if the thraik was dead or if it could vanish underwater.

"To me, knights!" Sharhava cried, charging down from above, sword high over her head. Two troops of six knights followed her as they pursued the winged beasts. The largest thraik spun in midair to face her not far above the mast of the *Corona*. Its snakelike head angled down, then struck upward, aiming for her horse's throat. Sharhava threw her sword in the air and caught it hilt downward. She stabbed the back of the creature's neck. Magpie let out a crow of admiration. The beast jerked its head back and up, and struck out with its claws. Sharhava faced it fearlessly, parrying the talons with one canny stroke after another. It brought up a back foot to rake at the horse's chest. The horse screamed, but it was not injured. Its barding turned the blow. It kicked out with iron-shod hooves. Flesh and ichor flew from a wound in the creature's ribs. It was the thraik's turn to scream.

By then, the rest of her troop was at her side. Lar Braithen and Lar

Thyre, coming in low, jabbed and struck at the thraik's legs. It twisted around, snapping its whiplike tail. The tail hit Thyre square in the chest, knocking him out of his saddle. The werewolves below him braced themselves and caught his body before it slammed into the deck. Once he caught his breath he thanked them, then put his fingers in his mouth and whistled. His horse, realizing it was riderless, galloped in a downward spiral to return to him.

Magpie gripped the hilt of his sword, aching to throw himself into the fray. Even his erstwhile ladylove fought on the front lines, while he was relegated to a defending role. Inbecca, sword-trained as all children of royal houses were, rode in a troop under the command of Lar Brouse. Magpie shielded his eyes against the sun to look for her. He caught sight of Brouse's generous silhouette leading a group back from the west, and scanned the party for Inbecca. She sat tall and proud. Three or four of the knights were wiping their swords on cloths. How many thraiks, he wondered, had they slain? She caught his eye and nodded, a small smile on her lips. One, at least, and she'd had a hand in it. He felt a swell of pride for her. He must ask her later for the whole story. It might make a song.

"To me!" Sharhava shouted again. Brouse raised a hand over his head. His company rode in to flank the thraiks facing the abbess. She withdrew slightly to rest her right hand. It was still scarlet in hue, though the color faded daily. She had yet to tell the story of how it came to be healed, only that it had been done by a werewolf physician, something that still filled Magpie with wonder. None of the knights, not even Inbecca, would reveal all the details of her change of heart.

Blackness bloomed almost under his nose. Tessera bucked and cried out. Magpie pulled her upward just in time. Three thraiks came pouring through.

"Ware!" he shouted.

The attack above had been another ruse. These were meant to try again for the "book." Tessera, a proven warhorse, recovered her wits in a moment and galloped to intercept the leading flyer, a slender thraik with very long paws. Encouraging shouts from above told him that the other warriors were coming to aid him.

"Father, ward Serafina!" he called over his shoulder.

The king of Orontae needed no instruction. He and Halcot cantered side by side to take up a guardian position above the wizardess. She could not be better protected.

The thraiks led him out over the tossing waves. Magpie's long hair whipped him in the eyes and the cheeks. The leader aimed its ugly face backward to shriek defiance at him. He grinned. They were going to disappear again. They thought they were fooling the poor humans, when the joke was on them. Keep them busy, that was all he need do. He waited, as if for a jug-gler at a feast to perform the trick. One, two, three!

Blackness tore open the sky, and the thraiks vanished into it, just a few feet from the rocky shore. He pulled Tessera in a wide circle and looked up at the endless number of beasts. Was that frustration etched upon their runes? He put a thumb under his chin and flicked it at them in a gesture of derision. He and his fellows could keep the thraiks occupied a good long time, while their strength held out. Serafina could restore anyone to strength with the guidance of the engraved runes. He was almost enjoying flouting the unknown wizard.

He looked back toward the east, where darkness was already gathering on the horizon.

And a strange darkness it was. Magpie tried to put his finger on what was wrong with that end of the cove. With the setting of the sun the tide was go-ing out; that was normal. The winds changed so the clouds scudded in the direction of the prevailing winds; that, too, was normal.

The runes!

He had lived with the golden sigils for so long that the absence of them on every surface was a shock to him. Yet the rocky pillars at the edge of the cove were plain, as was the sea beyond them. He knew then that Tildi must have moved so far away that the book's influence no longer held good. He looked up at the knights. Did they notice? Would the thraiks understand what it meant?

The void crept toward the ships a few paces at a time. He spurred Tessera back toward the ships. Five or six separate battles went on in the air above them. Where was Sharhava?

It was difficult to distinguish one blue-clad knight from another in the growing twilight. He realized then that he had never troubled to learn their runes. It had not seemed a priority before. He wished then he had taken the trouble.

It did not matter. They were all in danger.

Thraiks twisted and danced in the sky like a basket of snakes, all strug-gling to get at the object they so craved. Knights and guards, inside the sin-uous, moving framework, strove to drive them outward and away.

The shadow was running toward them faster now. Yes, running. He hoped that it boded no ill for Tildi and the others, but it certainly changed the equation for those who fought out there in the open. A group of knights burst free of the cage of thraiks, driving the creatures outward with sparks of blue light and swords that caught the dying brightness from the sun. They careened out over the harbor, nearly touching the blankness. Was Inbecca among them?

Magpie urged Tessera from a canter to a gallop. He must stop anyone from flying into the void.

Between his knees, the mare began to pant.

"Are you tiring, my dear?" he asked, patting her on the neck. She turned one large, brown eye in his direction. In it he saw love and devotion, but also determination. Tessera would not let him down.

The thraiks were growing increasingly desperate in their bid to gain possession of the book. They sought to get past the troop of knights, whom they outnumbered but seemingly could not outwit. As long as the defenders held the advantage, they could keep the thraiks at bay. The void continued to grow.

"Now!" Vreia cried. She rose in her stirrups and brought the point of her sword down through the top of the creature's head. Its face froze in startlement, and it plunged toward the sea. Vreia just had time to pull her blade free. She wiped it on her saddlecloth and moved to aid one of her companions.

"The book is moving," Magpie said. He pointed out toward the rocks, but the void had grown well past them. Vreia's eyes, weary until then, widened.

"We must find the abbess," she said. She cast about, then pointed to a rune bobbing in the dusky sky. "There she is, highness. Go. Tell her. She will know what to do."

"I will," he said. He angled off toward the faint image, trying to fix it in his mind. How was it that he had never learned one from another? The knights had learned their lesson after the tragic death of Lar Bertin. He'd held himself aloof from joining in their studies, and it might have been good for him. Now that it was nearly dark, he could no longer see Inbecca.

Sharhava saw him long before he reached her and came to meet him.

"There is urgency in you," she said. "Tell me your need."

"The runes are vanishing," he said.

Sharhava raised her eyes past him and surveyed the tossing waters. Already half the bay was bare of the golden images. Her mouth set in a straight line.

"We must continue as best we can. See if the wizardess can spare you. I can release none of my knights to stand vigil."

"I will," Magpie promised. "The lady Inbecca . . . ?"

Sharhava looked at him sternly. Her neat habit was torn at the sleeves and across the breast, and wisps of her hair had escaped from beneath her chainmail coif. "Is going about her duties, as you should be. No time for nonsense. We will do what we can. Go!"

Without hesitation, she flew back into the battle, and Magpie made his way through to the *Corona*. Lamps had been lit and hung against the wall before the captain's cabin and in the rigging. There, Serafina knelt on the deck beside a knight whose belly was a mass of swollen red. It took but one glance to realize that the mass was the man's insides. Magpie swallowed hard. A werewolf and another human crouched beside the man. They, too, had been horribly wounded, but they were whispering encouragement to the victim, whose eyes showed white all around his irises. He jerked and twitched with the pain. A werewolf healer held a cup to the man's lips. He managed to swallow a little, but the rest of the dark liquid rolled out of the corners of his mouth. It looked like blood.

The young wizardess held her hands over his belly. She looked over her shoulder toward the wall where the metal rolls had been placed. Magpie watched in wonder as the man's rune, which was on the third row, fourth from the left, glowed into being over him. It lowered onto the sign that was there. The brilliance increased as the old rune faded, leaving only the restored one in its place. Magpie, who freely admitted himself no scholar of the ancient language, had no trouble seeing the difference. He blinked as the magic caused the man's skin to crawl back into place like a blanket being drawn over a bed. In a moment, he could sit up. His eyes no longer strained in agony. He looked down at his stomach, once again well muscled and rather hairy, and nodded deeply to Serafina.

"Better find a new mail shirt," he said. "My thanks, lady." He struggled up and helped the werewolf to lie down in his place. Magpie leaped forward to assist them. Serafina repeated the spell.

Halcot swung down from above. His horse's hooves touched lightly onto the deck and trotted to a halt.

"Time for your rest, lad?" he asked. "Mother and Father know I need one. I'm not as young as I was."

"No, sir," Magpie said. "I have news."

"You look grim," Halcot said. He came to grip the young man by the shoulder. "What is wrong?"

"What news?" Serafina asked, glancing up at him for a moment.

Magpie explained what he had seen. Serafina closed her eyes briefly, and nodded. "I can still hear our friends. They are all well, but you are correct: they have gone out of our reach. Unless they stop, the influence of the book will be pulled out from over us in a short time. That may draw the thraiks away."

"It may not," Magpie said. "If they have been fooled by the false rune for so many hours, won't they still seek it?"

"I would fear for our friends' safety if the thraiks suddenly lose interest in us," Halcot said, looking up at the dancing shadows beyond the lamps. "Those creatures must not return to their lair, lest it inform our enemy that what he seeks is not out here. How many more can you sustain in the skies if the runes should fail?"

Lines of strain creased the corners of the girl's eyes, but she set her jaw. "I will do what I have to. They will learn of our weakness soon enough. Let us hope it is enough time for our friends to return to us."

Chapter Thirty-four

 nemet glared at the cluster of liches.

"Gone? What do you mean, the subjects are gone? Where could they go?"

If the gray-green creatures had had any personality, they would have hung their heads in shame. As it was, they stood still, faceless, impassive, their message delivered. The prisoners were gone.

"Impossible!" Knemet flung himself away from them and paced to the curved wall. He pounded his fist upon it.

It was no use raging at the liches. The women *must* be wizardesses. How had he been so deceived? Was there a way that had evolved since his exile to conceal magical talent? On the eve of recovering the book and ending his long torture, had he missed power greater than his own?

He felt a stirring of magic nearby, strong magic. The familiar touch alarmed him. He had not sensed it since the last upheaval of the world sent him scurrying for shelter.

Knemet turned, and his eyes widened with alarm.

"You!" he snarled.

Light flooded the chamber, and the floor broke into shards under his feet.

Tildi had only a moment to see the face of the human they confronted before the room was blotted out in a flash and a roar like lightning. However she had pictured the man who had killed her family, it was not as a small, frail-looking human with thin hair. His eyes, though, were like nothing she had ever seen, not even during the last few months, when her life had been turned upside down and she had seen wonder after wonder that surpassed every fairy tale she had ever heard. His eyes were rainbows, brilliant and beautiful and dangerous. What else she saw in them surprised her: astonishment, anger, and hope.

From the knife-thin, narrow chamber, Calester had led them at a rapid pace. Tildi had sensed that they were walking steadily uphill. The last passageway had been squared off, by magic or stoneworkers, and smelled of smoke, dung, and spoiled vegetation—lived-in scents, she would have said. At the top of that passage, he changed size again and led them under a low lintel that was a tight fit even for Tildi. The guards had to hand their packs and weapons through before crawling on hands and knees. Olen, last to pass through, took the doorway in his stride, only ducking a little. Tildi had to blink. Had he enlarged it by magic? He gave her an encouraging smile and laid his finger to his lips.

Beyond it, Calester rose to human proportions again. The room in which they had emerged was large and high, almost the shape of a beehive. The floor of the chamber ran with damp, and gleaming white moss decorated the walls. The walls were riddled with openings, including four that seemed to lead into other corridors.

Tildi had felt rather than heard something approaching. She looked around and let out a gasp. Dozens of man-shaped creatures, no taller than a dwarf, moved silently to surround them. Tildi was horrified to see that they had no faces. Morag and the other guards drew their swords and interposed themselves between the man-things and their charges.

"Hold," Calester said. "You can't hurt them. Don't waste your strength."

"What are they?" Tildi asked.

"Liches. Simple minds, dedicated to serving us. They are strong and nearly indestructible. If I needed confirmation that a Maker lives here, this is it. They can guide us to him."

"I mistrust these," Olen said. "If Knemet made them, they will betray us."

"They have no will of their own," Calester said. "They will obey me just as readily." He turned to them and spoke in the tongue used by the people who lived in the Compendium. They obeyed without surprise. As one, the liches turned and stumped toward an opening that was a foot or two above the wet stone floor. Water dripped down the wall over a lip of moss that had formed there. The liches used it as a ledge to help themselves climb up. The guards boosted themselves after the plant-men and held out a hand to the wizards. Calester waved them away imperiously and pushed ahead to be the first to follow his guides. Tildi didn't like the idea of touching the moss and solidified the air so she could walk on it. Olen smiled at her as he stepped up beside her.

"Are you frightened?" he asked in a low voice.

"Angry, I think," Tildi said, though the feeling in her belly could have been either one.

"Good. But do not lose sight of the purpose of our journey, as I believe Calester has." She glanced up at him, a little startled. He smiled and put a hand on her back. "Hurry. We must catch up."

The liches moved so quietly that Tildi was only certain where they were by the runes bobbing along ahead. Calester had extinguished his guide light. The floor was fairly level, so Tildi felt as if she were walking endlessly in place. Her thighs began to grow numb from carrying her. A drop of water began to gather on the tip of her nose and splashed off onto her collar. She had just brushed it away for the third time when Calester whispered.

"Halt." Tildi could see attention and curiosity in his rune, as though he was listening. "An opportunity, a rare opportunity."

"What?" she couldn't help but ask. "Have you found them?"

"Sh! Follow!"

The passage took a sharp turn to the left. Doorways appeared on both sides of the corridor, huge, wooden doors with metal straps. Tildi listened as they went by but heard nothing behind them. The smell of smoke was even stronger than it had been below. More liches came behind them and surged forward until she could not tell which group was which. Calester seemed well pleased.

Light bloomed ahead, a small patch of whiteness that drew her forward. The gray heads of the liches emerged from the dark, taking on being, then Calester's tall form, the three knights, and, most comfortingly, Olen beside her. She felt as if she really existed again for the first time since the narrow chasm.

Calester took a few paces back and pressed the book into Tildi's arms.

"Take this," he said. "I don't want all my advantages to be lost at one time. Stay well back. This is my time."

Tildi opened the book, scanning the page by the faint light. They were not near their friends. What was that man doing? Olen's hand dropped upon her shoulder, and she looked up at him.

"Guard yourself," he whispered. "Remember where you stand."

The light came from ahead. Tildi got the impression of a large room, much larger than the chamber of doorways. Throwing his hood back, Calester strode forward, outdistancing all of them but the liches. They passed inside, but he remained just in the shadow beyond the fall of the light.

Tildi could not see over the heads of the others, but she could hear a man's voice shouting. He was angry that someone was missing. Her heart squeezed in her chest. Had he discovered that they were not on the ship as he suspected?

Olen's hand urged her forward. For the first time she saw who was speaking: a small human. He swung around. His skin and thin hair were gray-white like the moss on the walls, but his eyes were rainbows. He saw Calester. He was surprised, but Tildi thought he looked glad to see him. Then the tall Maker swept up a hand. The floor exploded in a burst of stone shards and the small wizard plunged through it. Calester stood looking grimly pleased. Runes appeared and danced above his head.

"Look out," shouted Demballe.

Calester glanced up. A part of the wall detached itself and fell toward him. He flicked a hand at the slab. It shattered around him like ice. He shook a finger toward the hole in the floor.

"Oh, Knemet, what a pathetic retort. After so many centuries I would have expected more from you."

Pieces of broken rock hurtled upward like a fountain, cascading in every direction. The guards threw themselves before Tildi and Olen, seeking to protect them.

Olen pointed his staff. *"Voshte!"* he commanded. The shards struck an invisible wall and pattered to the floor. Calester clapped his hands together. Fire fountained upward from the pit. The crack in the floor zigzagged toward them, and the halves tilted up. Lar Mey tripped and started to slide toward the dark gap. Demballe cried out and sought to reach out to him. Tildi reached out to Mey, thinking the words of the solid-air spell as hard as she could. The knight scrabbled with all four limbs as he was lifted up from the uneven floor. Swiftly, he regained his wits as well as his footing. Olen gave Tildi a look of approval and gestured toward the others.

Just as she was about to oblige, a terrible weight seemed to land upon her shoulders. Tildi fell to the floor, the Great Book beneath her.

"I see you have brought me a gift, Calester, my old friend."

Tildi looked up. The rainbow eyes were glaring down upon her. Knemet, too, stood upon thin air. Tildi realized the wards that had concealed her and the others since they left the ship had disappeared. Calester must have taken them away. The gray-skinned wizard pointed to the book.

"That is my property, twig-girl. It was rightfully mine. Give it to me now."

"No!" Tildi said, wrapping herself around it.

Calester was there between them before the other wizard could draw breath. "Knemet, you fool, it is no longer yours. It serves me and my companions."

"The one who holds it is the one who controls it," the small man said, his beautiful eyes burning with an inner fire. Tildi dragged herself and the book as far from him as she could go. "I require it. I crave the touch of it. Only the touch." He reached out to Tildi. Her body lifted from the floor and began to float toward him. Terrified, she clutched the book to her chest.

Calester made a gesture with two fingers as if he were cutting a thread. Tildi floated gently down again until she was sitting on a chunk of shattered stone. Olen stood beside her, staff at the ready to defend her.

"What a clever man you are," Calester taunted. "If she was not holding it you could not compel it to you. Tildi, put it down. Put it down."

With the greatest of reluctance, she set the scroll on the floor beside her and glanced warily at Knemet. The two wizards glared at one another. Knemet swept the other with a summing eye.

"I would not have known you after all this time if not for your arrogance," Knemet said. "You are much thinner. And taller."

Calester considered the statement. "I refined myself to my liking. As, I see, did you."

The other nodded. "I have. I have found the optimum shape to continue in my studies, and the ideal home." Knemet gestured around him with a hand. "Until you destroyed it, it was the perfect place for me to remain for the rest of my days. I shall have to remake it. Perhaps you will help me. You were my closest friend and ally for centuries. I would welcome your assistance."

Don't trust him! Tildi felt with the whole of her body that he lied. The voices inside the Great Book were agitated. She tried to calm them. No telling what kind of trouble it would cause if the book was to fall out of balance here. With so much magic in the air the mountain could explode.

If the book had been out of harmony, Knemet was worse. He vibrated like an out-of-tune harp string, grating on the eardrums in a discord that rang on and on. It was painful. He didn't *belong*.

"What is that, twig-girl?" Knemet asked, looking down at her suddenly. The rainbows suddenly flooded her vision. She could hear his voice both in her ears and in her mind. "I lie? I don't belong? You are right. That is why you are here, to rid me of my pain."

Tildi was horrified that he could read her thoughts. Knemet shook his head. "I was there when your kind was engendered. You are my Nature's Child. Why should you not be as an open book to me?"

"No," Tildi said weakly, fighting the draw of those eyes. She closed her own. "My kind has nothing to do with you!"

"But you knew you were created by one of us. I can see it in your face. You know the truth of your origins. Why the shock to learn which of us it was? Come, bring the Compendium to me. It is mine. Isn't that why Calester brought you here? As a messenger to return my property? To cure me?"

"I feel the pain," Tildi croaked, overwhelmed by it. "It isn't physical. You need healing. We have a healer, back on our ship. The bearkin could help you. They cured me."

"Not that kind of healing. Mine can only come from that." He lunged for the Great Book.

"Together, now!" Morag barked. The guards leaped to catch Knemet by the arms. Knemet snarled. Runes burst into being.

Morag went flying backward, crashing into the carved-stone seat that was the room's only furniture. Demballe crashed into the doorpost and sank to the floor, looking dazed. Knemet stood untouched. Morag lifted himself to hands and feet and crawled toward the wizard, his usually muddy eyes glaring blue in his craggy face.

Lar Vreia signed to her companions. In each of their hands bloomed the blue fire that the Scholardom had made their own weapon. The six points spread until they formed a ring around Knemet. It blazed up into a cylinder of fire that closed in on him like a cocoon. Inside it, Knemet screamed. Tildi winced at the tearing sound, pitying him.

Olen stamped the foot of his staff on the uneven floor. Knemet froze for a moment like a figure in ice. With a grim smile lifting the corners of his mustache, Olen sought to build upon the spell's strength. Knemet began to move. His hands twitched. Olen's face twisted. He threw up his hands, and the runes he had been building burst outward, vanishing in golden light. The knights went sprawling. The blue fire faded. Knemet came to life again. His face was blistered. The rainbow eyes glared at Olen. As she watched, the shining patches on his face faded to red, then to the pale mushroom hue of his ordinary skin.

"I have seen you before," he said. "How dare you blind my kotyrs?"

"How else was I to stop them telling you all of what they saw?" Olen asked reasonably. "I did not want them to."

The small wizard's voice climbed an octave. "You ruined an entire species! My beautiful creation!"

"I do not see how you can be angry, when you caused the death of my apprentice's entire family. You claim that you created her kind as well."

The colorful eyes were startled. He looked from Olen to Tildi and back again. "That is only a few of the smallfolk. There are many others left. You cannot claim that the matter is equivalent."

"They matter to me!" Tildi said.

"I am afraid I must take her part," Olen said. "Intelligent individuals are as important as the whole of the species. I did not see much in the way of independent intelligence in the—kotyrs, did you call them? You left us little choice of action."

"I see," Knemet said. The evenness of his voice told Tildi that he was only keeping his temper in check. He still vibrated with pain. "I shall not underestimate you again. *Parthray!*"

The word seemed to linger on the air, ringing in Tildi's ears. A rune she did not recognize wrapped around her body. Her skin burned and froze at the same time as she struggled against the magical bonds. The voices in the book in her arms cried out. She understood part of their words, and cudgeled her memory for the lessons Serafina had given her on the ancient language. *Back—turn back—turn it back!* In her mind she made a ball of the rune he had thrown at her, and flung it back in his direction. Knemet flung up his hands to ward off the spell. It tied itself around his limbs like a length of creeper vine. He took a step backward and sprawled. Cursing, he banished the bonds and rose to his feet.

Olen, too, was moving again. He raked the air, and the runes dropped away from the guards. Demballe sprang toward Knemet and wrapped her arms around his knees. Morag moved in from behind, throttling the wizard with his huge hands.

In his momentary distraction Tildi was free to move. She felt Knemet's ache as if it were her own. She wanted to escape from it. She would go mad if it didn't stop. Tildi grabbed up the book and fled toward the doorway. Clawlike spikes of power pierced her arms, dragging her backward through the air. She cried out.

"Come back here, girl!" Knemet bellowed.

The pain fled as swiftly as it had come. She fell, but an arm in a gray cloak caught her. She looked up into Olen's brilliant eyes. Knemet upturned a hand, the fingers beckoning. Olen, too, lifted a hand. The pull on Tildi stopped at once. The rainbow-eyed man snarled at Olen and pointed a finger at him, moving it in the air like a stylus. Tildi was horrified as Olen's face stretched out so that his lips were pulled back from his teeth like a death's head. The skin of his hands thinned until they were skeletal. Olen closed his eyes, films of skin over bulging orbs. His face returned to normal for a moment, then his features bulged like a bag of potatoes. His limbs swelled. Though Tildi could tell he fought the spell-making, he was unable to hold her. She fell to the floor, the book on top of her.

Furiously, she overwrote the new whorls and crosses that he had added with her own firm memory of what Olen's sign should look like. Knemet grinned at her.

"So you are a wizard, little one. A remarkable accomplishment for one of your kind. I am proud. What do you say to this, then?"

Tildi gasped, but no sound came from her throat. Her vision blurred, as though she were looking through a piece of glass.

"Knemet, stop that. You are torturing her," Calester said. The shorter wizard turned to confront the tall one.

"You are torturing *me*! Did you only bring the Compendium here to taunt me, Calester?" Knemet asked.

"Certainly not," Calester said. "I have brought it to use as a tool. You have two prisoners whom we want returned to us."

"Is that all? Why are you involved in such a petty exchange?" Knemet asked.

"Why? Because you captured the two women in mistake for the book itself, didn't you?"

"It was not a mistake," Knemet said. "They have been instrumental in keeping the Compendium from me. Was that your doing?"

Calester shook his head. "They were taking action against you long before I was brought into the matter. Indeed, I must confess I have never met them."

"Then what do you care for their fate? You should have been concerned with me, your old friend and ally." The rainbow eyes met the blue ones and bored into them. Calester blinked and laughed. He turned a hand. A whirlwind of bitter cold surrounded Knemet. Tildi recoiled from the chill blast. The small man drew his palms together and thrust them toward Calester. The winds gathered themselves between his hands and flew outward in a torrent of needle-sharp ice crystals. Calester caught them in his palms. Water dripped to the floor and steamed around his feet. Knemet glared at him.

"We were indeed friends and allies," Calester said, countering Knemet's moves more swiftly than Tildi could follow. "Souls together in our quest to discover what we could and to make better that which could be improved. But we became greedy and careless. Didn't you grow tired?"

"I did. That is why I am so glad to see you. You can put an end to my agony."

"Willingly," Calester said. "But how?"

"Give me the Compendium!"

"Why?"

"So I may end this unwanted existence!"

Calester looked at him curiously. He dodged to one side to avoid a black, spiky rune that Tildi could not read and did not want to. It vanished into the wall in a puff of black dust. "You would destroy all that we held dear for your own sake?"

"What choice have I? I see that you are in the same quandary as I! Nothing will remove you from this world. Why are you still alive?"

Calester seemed surprised and amused. "I? I wanted to see our creations come to their full maturity. We but set them in motion. They were a fascinating study."

"*Were*, brother," Knemet breathed. Tildi felt the book moving in her hands and yelped. The Maker had been attempting to force her to send it to him. "I can tell you lost interest in the greater world yourself. Where have you been all these long years?"

"I confess it," Calester said evenly. "Once you were gone, or so we thought, I took many centuries to contemplate our work. I set myself on guard to prevent the Compendium returning to the north."

"But you missed it, didn't you?" Knemet gloated. "You were as weary of this world as I. You just refuse to admit it."

"I am not," Calester said. "Indeed, there is more here in which to rejoice than there was when we . . ."

". . . Lived?" Knemet finished for him. "Yes, that is right. I have felt dead for centuries. I only want to be dead in truth."

"But you cannot!"

"I can!"

A rune as large as a man appeared between them. Tildi knew it at once. It was the book. If he could not have the object itself, he would change it at a distance. Knemet reached into its heart with both hands and twisted the intricate marks. Tildi heard the voices moan.

Almost without thinking, she drew Pierin's knife and rewrote the broken strokes. Knemet gave her a fierce look and wrenched the rune outward. Just as fervently, she remade it again. Like the hero in tales of swordplay she had heard around the fire at Meetings, she watched the wizard's uncanny eyes to see what part of the name he tried to unmake next. She must not let him destroy a single serif. All her practice on the road helped her to avoid making even a single mistake in its intricately complex rune. She kept it firmly in mind, knowing it was still all right by the rhythm that came from it.

"Good girl, Tildi," Olen said, his green eyes intent. His hands were moving, too.

Knemet laughed. "You have learned one trick, little one. It is a good one, but what will save *you*?" His right hand drew another rune upon the air in burning silver. Tildi recognized her own. Her hands became paddles. She gasped as air refused to pass through her nose or mouth. The hot air dragged into her starving lungs through slits in her neck. Olen's magic swept around her like a cooling breeze, restoring her energy. Knemet redoubled his efforts. The burning rune expanded as the wizard sought to subdue them both at once. Olen staggered as his legs thinned to spindles and the protective veil vanished. Tildi felt as if her skin were being torn off, but she kept her mind on the book. A part of it had been scorched, nearly destroyed. She let out a cry of alarm and worked to restore the damaged part. Olen restored himself and her, letting her keep her mind on her work, but Knemet scorned her efforts. He clicked his tongue. The tables were turned now. He was watching to see what she did, and undoing it right behind her.

"There, what do you think you are doing? What have you wiped out there?" Calester demanded. He threw a rune at Knemet that knocked him across the room.

"I want an end to this existence," Knemet snarled, undeterred, rising above the ground. The huge rune kept on unmaking itself, with Tildi frantically working to keep it intact. "I will have to destroy it all to take myself out of this world. We were foolish! Tying ourselves into the very fabric of being!"

"What is done is done," Calester said. "You must learn to live with what we wrought."

"I no longer wish to," Knemet said. "I shall not! I want peace!"

"We cannot kill him," Olen said, stroking his beard. "Because of his immortality he can be released in no other way than the destruction of us all. A knotty problem."

"Master, how can you contemplate that as if it were no more difficult than what to have for dinner?" Tildi asked, outraged.

"My dear, what good does it do to flood the facts with emotion? It gets us nowhere . . . ah, don't do that, Master Knemet."

A burst of red flame appeared inches from Tildi's nose. She felt her skin blister as a white-hot fire met it. She jumped. The rainbow eyes glittered. He was trying to distract her. Olen scribbled a couple of fine spirals in the air and the ache in her nose stopped. Tildi found the damage he had done in the meantime and brought it back to normal. The voices chattered and jabbered in her mind.

"Stop it!" she snapped. "You are distracting me!"

Calester appeared between his enemy and the book's rune.

"Knemet, your fight is with me. These others do not matter."

The pale-skinned wizard glared. "You are right. I must efface you from existence as well—all of you!"

He clenched his hands and drew them outward. The enormous rune stretched and stretched until tears began to form in the center, in the one small part that matched the sign for the room inside the mountain where they stood. Tildi worked frantically, trying to restore the damage. Reality was being pulled out of shape. Calester opened his arms and pressed inward. The rune shuddered, and so did the world around them. Tildi strained against air that was too thin to breathe, to see by light that seeped away like water in a leaky bucket.

Remember where you stand, Olen had told her. Could she recall the room the way it had been? With her lungs bursting, Tildi redrew the rune in her mind and sought to force it to be real.

"Curse you!" Knemet's voice howled. Tildi kept the image true in her mind and held on to it as everything else went dark.

Chapter Thirty-five

veryone's eyes were upon the approaching edge of the runes as full night descended. The thraiks seemed to sense unease among the humans, for they increased the frequency and fierceness of their attacks. Where eight had sprung out of scars in the sky, sixteen or twenty came. Teryn's guards, empowered by Serafina, concentrated her forces on the southeast side of the ship. The Scholardom was conscious of the limit of its power, ceasing pursuit if the thraiks went too far in the direction of the harbor mouth.

The winged monsters knew something had changed. They leered at their enemy, sticking out their tongues between their sharp yellow teeth, daring them to go beyond what they perceived as new boundaries. The Scholardom still had magic, though. Many of the thraiks that dipped close to the edge of safe distance found themselves the target of blue fire. They died or disappeared screaming as their bodies were consumed by the flames.

Near midnight, the Agate rose. Magpie had landed to give Tessera a rest and a meal. The sailors seemed energized to have the additional light of the lesser of Alada's two moons shining over them.

"It's part of our curse," Patha said, helping him to tie a nosebag on the piebald's muzzle, "but we draw strength from the Agate and the Pearl."

"I wish we had such a bond," Magpie said.

The werewolf matriarch shook her head sternly. She patted Tessera's neck. "Be grateful. They are intemperate masters. When they both ride the skies at the same time we have no control over our state." She glanced upward and gawked. "By the light, look at that!"

Magpie followed her eye. The number of shadows circling overhead had increased.

"Where did they all come from?" Patha asked. "I thought that we had killed or driven off half of the monsters."

"Impossible!" Halcot exclaimed, circling a few feet overhead. "There must be twice as many as before. We cannot withstand this force."

"We will because we must," Soliandur said. "Skill, brother, skill and strategy. They have been beaten before. Keep them busy. I will wager that they will flee when the mind driving them is gone. I hope that Master Olen can defeat this Knemet."

"Don't you mean Calester, Father?" Magpie asked, the need for rest making his muscles ache all along his back and arms.

Soliandur glared at him. "Don't presume to correct me. I do not have much respect for one like him. He knows nothing of life. He was only driven out of his comfortable study because he and his companions learned the consequences of indulging every magical whim they had. We are at their mercy now. I trust Master Olen's common sense. And that girl's courage."

But the truth was that the number of warriors fit for battle decreased every hour. No matter how many wounded Serafina and the healers brought back to health, the survivors were growing demoralized at the deaths of their friends and the endless stream of thraiks. "Help! Help here!" Captain Teryn called, flying in from the level of the lookout's basket. Magpie urged Tessera upward to meet her. Across the saddle lay a man's body. Magpie could tell by the way his limbs flopped loosely that it was almost certainly too late for him. When they reached the deck and dragged him down for Serafina to examine, Magpie saw that the man's throat was laid open. Gouges left the windpipe visible. The man was not breathing, but Teryn stonily maintained optimism.

"Can you help him?" she asked hoarsely.

Serafina regarded the man's rune. It was changing before Magpie's eyes. He had seen that change before. The wizardess shook her head.

"He has gone back to the Mother," she said. "I am very sorry."

Teryn shook her head. She said nothing as she returned to her saddle and rose above the deck. The king swung his steed around, and his gaze caught Teryn's. They exchanged sharp nods of respect. This was no longer merely an essay to rescue two lost friends. It was a war for the safety of the world. He must find out the names of all those who had died. The song would be painful to write, but those names must not be lost to the void.

"Ware!"

"Son, guard the wizard!" Soliandur's voice grated from somewhere above. Magpie had but a moment to glance over his shoulder. Dozens, no, hundreds of thraiks arrowed toward him, the runes in their eyes glowing like brands. Feeling like a reed caught in the rapids, he spurred the whinnying mare down in front of Serafina. He leaped out of the saddle and threw himself across the wizardess's body. The thraiks shot overhead only yards above them. Tessera danced and screamed as she was buffeted by their wings.

He had never seen so many thraiks this close to the ship. They must have decided that numbers would win the battle at last. Magpie braced himself over Serafina and her patients.

The flock passed him like a hurricane and were gone into the dark skies. He doubted that was all their intention, and he was right. Five of the younger and swifter beasts broke away from the mass and swirled low, making for the decoy scroll. Soliandur hovered overhead, facing the enemy. He struck at wildly thrashing wings or legs, whatever came close to threatening Serafina or his son. Halcot floated nearly back to back with him. The thraiks gave the two kings a wide berth, and dove as one for the rune in the center of the deck.

Patha howled fiercely. Claws out, she leaped down from the top of the wheelhouse onto the nearest flyer. A dozen of her kin followed suit. Their fur was nearly scorched off their backs as a troop of knights followed in the wake of the enormous throng, heaving gouts of blue fire at the thraiks.

A handful of the dancing flames caught in the rigging.

"Fools!" Patha shrieked.

"Sorry!" shouted the scholar-knight, before he, too, was gone. Swearing, Haroun and some of his crew swarmed up the ropes with buckets and anti-fire charms slung over their shoulders. Magpie rose carefully to his hands and knees.

"Did I hurt you?" he asked Serafina. He helped her to stand. The wounded, two men and one woman, crouched against the cabin wall.

"Not at all, but I fear for your mare," the wizardess said. "Go calm her. I am all right here. I have much to do." As if to confirm her words, she drew a complicated rune on the air and sent it flying toward Teryn and her guards.

Magpie caught Tessera by her bridle and pulled her head to his chest. "Come, come, my dear. Are you going to let those creatures bother you? They're not as smart or as brave as you."

The mare rolled her eyes and whimpered into his tunic. He patted her nose, feeling her breathing slow. She was a true warhorse.

"Don't waste time, boy!" Soliandur shouted. He glanced back at the triumphant cry as the werewolves brought down one of the young thraiks. They hauled the body to the rail and heaved it overboard. It disappeared into the waves with a loud splash. The other four looked panic-stricken, but kept looping about, trying to find an angle past the defenders. Their hides were running with ichor from slashes and bites.

Magpie leaped onto the mare's back and brought her aloft. He hoped the wizards would return soon. A cold wind whipped up, stinging his face, and he saw that the runeless edge had crept to the edge of the wheelhouse. He joined his father. The two of them braced themselves as the main flock of thraiks came around for a second pass. He struck at the creatures, keeping the flow away from Serafina. She had just helped a man to stand up. His chest was covered with blood, but he was whole and well again. He grabbed up his sword and ran into the ship's belly to aid in its defense.

A second troop of knights had joined the first, harrying the flock. In the midst of it he recognized Inbecca. She was too intent upon her prey, a muscular, long-bodied thraik, to see him. She leaned low over the neck of her borrowed mount, sword flat over the saddlebow, ready to strike if she got the opportunity. The beast was a swift one. It led her a wild chase up around the mast and over to the *Eclipse*. Her fellows saw the void and turned back, letting their quarries escape. Inbecca paid no attention, but stayed on the creature's tail.

"Inbecca!" he shouted. "Inbecca, come back!"

Soliandur turned at his son's outburst. His dark eyes widened with alarm. "Lady Inbecca!" he shouted. "Boy, go after her!"

Serafina smacked the end of her staff down on the deck. Gray light went up around her and her patients. "Go!" she cried. "I will be all right."

Magpie was already spurring into the night. The thraik knew what it was doing. The void had nearly reached all the way to the decoy rune. She drew her hand back. It filled with fire, its blueness lighting her eyes. She threw the ball of flame. It scarred the black night. The thraik dodged it, and fleered at her over its shoulder. The fire arced like a holiday skyrocket and dropped into the water. Her face set, Inbecca drew her hand back again. No fire. She looked back. Magpie saw the fear in her eyes. The rune on her body went out like a candle flame extinguished. Her horse reached for purchase for its hooves and found none. His stomach gave a sickening lurch as the poor creature let out a cry. It plunged toward the rocks, Inbecca clinging to the saddle.

He spurred Tessera for all the speed she could give him. The mare seemed to sense that this was no ordinary run, and opened her stride as never before. No time to get below the horse and try to save them both. He rode straight for the fluttering habit and grabbed a handful of cloth as he passed overhead.

Inbecca's weight pulled them all down a little, but Magpie changed holds and hauled the young woman up, first by an arm, then by her belt, until she was lying across the saddlebow. He heard the terrible scream stop abruptly, coupled with another, more sickening sound. He spared a short glance over his shoulder at the pathetic body shattered on the rocks, the waves already licking at it like the flames on a funeral pyre. The thraik let out a cry of triumph and alit upon the body. It bent to tear the still warm throat with its yellow teeth.

"Inbecca, can you speak?" he asked.

She flailed against his hold and tried to pull herself upright. "Eremi, thank you," she said. "My horse?"

Magpie shook his head. He helped her to sit up against his chest and brought her back to the *Corona.* The two kings met her on the deck to assist her down from the saddlebow.

"I thank you, Your Highnesses," she said. Her voice sounded shaky.

"Sit down, my lady," Soliandur said, helping her inside the captain's cabin. "Eremilandur, fetch her wine."

"No, sir, I must return to my troop." Inbecca tried to stand, but her knees wouldn't hold her. Magpie hurried to put his shoulder under her arm and brought her to a chair. She settled into it, but looked perturbed at requiring it. "Thank you," she said. "I lost sight of the danger. I am not accustomed to magical battle. I will do better. The poor horse. It died for trusting me."

"Do not chide yourself, lady. None of us would have done better."

"My fellow knights all did better," she said. Magpie could not miss the bitterness in her voice. He poured wine from the sideboard and knelt beside her while she drank it. Serafina came into the cabin, her staff in hand. Patha followed her.

"Is your lady wounded?" she asked Magpie.

"Not in body," he replied. "Shaken, as any of us would be." Patha came to her other side and checked her eyes.

"You are brave, my lady. You will be all right."

Serafina held her hand over the cup of wine. A thin rune formed upon the surface and dissolved into the liquid. "This will steady you."

"I thank you, wizard," Inbecca said graciously. She took a sip.

"Where is my niece?" Sharhava's voice came from outside.

Chapter Thirty-six

harhava strode in with Lar Colruba at her heels. When she saw Inbecca, she checked her pace and came to look down upon Inbecca like a hawk on a branch.

"Are you well, my niece?" she asked.

Inbecca gave her a curious look, then the schooled set of her features returned. "I am well, Aunt."

"I am relieved." She turned to Serafina. "We are losing this battle. The Great Book has gone out of our reach. Without its magic we can no longer sustain the magic needed to keep ourselves in the sky. Look about you!"

They did. Magpie was horrified to realize that the ship was devoid of runes for the first time since they had set sail on her.

"Is the battle lost?" Patha asked grimly.

"It should not be, not with this lady's help," Sharhava said.

"I understand that," the wizardess said gravely. "I will do my best to maintain spells for all of you as well as the guards, but I don't have the experience or the strength of Master Olen."

"Never mind that man," Sharhava said. "You have all the skills you will need. We prefer to be self-sufficient."

"How?" the wizardess asked. "All I can do is give you a road upon which you can ride. I cannot give you powers of your own."

Sharhava looked grim. "We will make do without the demon fire, although that has been a more useful weapon than our blades."

"What, then? I can do little more than I have."

"You can do far more than that," Sharhava said. "I have been watching you all day and night. What you are doing is precisely what we require. I want you to change me and my knights so that we can carry the battle into the beasts' own domain."

"What?" Soliandur demanded.

"I must not do that," Serafina said, shocked.

"Do you call yourself a master wizardess? Of course you must. This is not a time for hesitation. We have no choice. We must take drastic measures.

They will kill all of us. They are decimating the horses. The animals are not fit to take on these monsters. We are! Give us the means to fight without them." She met Patha's eyes. The werewolf matriarch nodded slowly. "I have seen how change can be good as well as evil. This would be for the best reasons possible."

"You want me to make you into werewolves?" Serafina asked. "I do not know if I can."

Sharhava exploded with impatience. "What good would that do? Give us wings at least, girl! Hurry. We will not live to see the dawn if our defense is halved."

"Wings? Change you into thraiks?" Serafina's eyes were wide with horror. "That would be an abomination in truth. I cannot do that."

Sharhava gripped the girl's arm. "Yes, you can. To my cost I know what the runes can do. The book is not here, so you must be the one to do it, or I would do it myself."

"You cannot! You do not have the training. What about poor Lar Bertin . . . ?"

"I would rather die trying than give up to those creatures. Give us the means to protect the ships, or they won't be here when the others return."

If they return, Magpie thought, but didn't say so aloud.

The sound of something heavy falling onto the deck above their heads made everyone jump and look up.

"King Halcot's guards are getting the worst of this battle because we can no longer aid them," Sharhava said, pointing upward. "Don't you see? Don't hesitate. Do it. You can read their runes. I can't see them any longer, but I know the word for wings. Theirs are powerful and long. Give us the same. Steal from this wizard's own design to confound him. Start with me! I will send my brothers and sisters back to you."

"I . . . I cannot! I need to study. I can't take a chance on harming you."

"You must! Your mother was a war-wizardess at one time. Take pride in your heritage, curse you! Wizards have always let others take the blame for their inaction. I will not allow you to stand still." Sharhava's face was as red as Serafina's was pale. Magpie could see that Serafina longed to debate the issue further, but Sharhava was right: there was no time. If they were to stave off the winged monsters for much longer, they needed enough defenders to maintain the balance.

"Should I not go first, Abbess?" Colruba asked. "In case there is any problem? I would rather have it happen to me than to you."

Sharhava put an almost tender hand on the young knight's shoulder and smiled down at her. "I will let my knights take no risk I will not take myself. Come, wizardess. Now, where may I find a pen?"

Patha took two long strides to the wall and unlocked the cupboard that was built into the wall above the captain's desk. She returned with a brass pen and inkwell. Sharhava dipped the pen and seized Magpie's hand.

"Be useful for a change, boy," she said. She began to inscribe fine lines upon his palm. He felt foolish being used as a piece of parchment, but the pleading look in Inbecca's eyes made him swallow his protest. When she was finished, she held it out to the wizardess.

"Simple and elegant. You can follow it easily."

"I object to this, Abbess," Serafina said.

"I know. Disagree with me later. Action, now." She turned her back.

Serafina clutched her hands together. She closed her eyes for a moment. Gradually, her face relaxed. When she opened her eyes, Magpie fancied just for a moment he saw Edynn look out of their dark depths. She pointed the head of her staff to each of the directions until everyone in the room was surrounded by a thin gray veil, warding against interruption or corruption of the work she was about to undertake. She studied the design on Magpie's palm and nodded to herself.

The young wizardess tweaked a stroke here, a whorl there, then sent it gliding until it touched Sharhava's back. The shimmering lines suffused her, changing her. Sharhava's face twisted in pain. Inbecca gasped as the habit at her aunt's back split. Wings almost identical to the thraiks' but of the color of Sharhava's pale flesh sprang forth and unfurled fine, translucent sails. The spines looked like long delicate arms, terminating in a pointed finger with a sharp nail on the end. Sharhava's face took on a strained expression as she tried to flap them. The resultant backwash lifted her off the deck. Her face lit up.

"Abbess, it is a marvel!" Colruba exclaimed.

"In many ways," Patha said.

Sharhava let herself settle. She drew one of the fine sails around to examine it.

"Well done, Mistress Serafina," she said. When she smiled, Magpie saw that her corner teeth had sharpened. Perhaps the trait was tied to the batlike wings. "Now I am prepared to take these monsters in the sky. No time to practice. I'll have to go as I am. Now, remember what I said! I shall have each of my people come to you for the same."

Inbecca rose from her seat and placed the wine cup on the floor.

"I shall go next, Aunt."

Sharhava looked shocked, then drew herself up to her full height, augmented by the arch of the wings. "Not you, Inbecca."

Inbecca set her chin and turned to the wizardess, who looked from one to the other. "Don't pay her any attention, Mistress Serafina. Change me, too. I will serve with my fellow knights."

"You will not, Lar Inbecca. You may take my horse. I will not need him until . . . later."

"But I am one of you," Inbecca said. "I took the vows."

Soliandur stepped forward to intercede. "You are and you are not," he said very gently. "There are some dangers we fellow kings will allow you to take, but that is not one I want to explain to your mother. Will you ride with me and my son? We would be honored."

"She will," Sharhava said. "I order it. Will you obey, Lar Inbecca, or will you set a poor example for my other knight?"

Inbecca's mouth was open with indignation. She glared at her aunt, who was so changed in body but not at all in spirit. Colruba regarded her with pleasant, guileless respect.

"I will obey the orders of my abbess," Inbecca said at last. Sharhava gave her a regal smile.

"Good. I have left my troops uncaptained for too long. Let us go. Lar Colruba, come when you are prepared."

"I will, Abbess."

Sharhava nodded sharply and strode from the cabin, a grinning Patha at her side. Magpie and Inbecca hurried in their wake.

Though without the runes the ship seemed darker than before, every eye turned immediately toward them. A few of the humans gasped openly at Sharhava's transformation. Halcot, who had remained aloft when the others descended, stopped his horse in midair and gaped.

"What in the Mother's name have you done to yourself?"

Sharhava regarded him austerely. "I have done what I must to carry the fight back to these creatures, my lord." She opened the pale wings, and the werewolves let out howls of glee. "Wish me good luck."

"The best of luck goes to those who have done what they can to earn it, as you have, my lady," Halcot said, sweeping her a salute with his sword. "Fortune favor you."

Sharhava inclined her head. "I thank you." She drew her sword. The massive wings flapped, and she soared into the dark sky toward the nearest troop of knights. The thraiks scattered in alarm at her coming, freeing the Scholardom to gather around her. Magpie squinted past the lanterns. He could see her pale hands gesturing, then pointing down toward the deck.

Lar Colruba emerged from the cabin similarly changed, and spread her wings to join her abbess.

"What freedom," she cried as the cold gusts of wind lifted her skyward. "By the Book, what have we missed?"

Magpie noticed Patha smiling as she watched the knights in their new shape pursuing thraiks into the runeless zone. "What is in your mind, my lady?"

"I was thinking I will never have better revenge than this," the werewolf female said, her jaw dropping in a wide, toothy grin. "To have my enemies turning beyond friends into kinship—the Father of Time could not have planned it better."

A few at a time, the Scholardom arrived to undergo their own alteration. Some were willing, others curious. The rest were apprehensive, and a few openly offended. Lar Romini stood with his arms crossed and an expression of fury on his face.

"This is anathema," he said. "We will be struck down."

"Easy, brother," Lar Brouse said, patting his friend on the back. "I will accept this is necessary for the moment. The abbess would not require this if it were not."

"I can accept that our mission has been changed, but how can she ask us to destroy the sanctity of our bodies?"

Brouse bowed his head. "We are but servants of the Great Book, my friend. If this will keep it safe, what does it matter what becomes of us?"

"Well, you see what, right here!" Romini blurted. He pointed.

Lar Auric emerged from the cabin, pale wings clinging to his back like a cape. He was so tall the top joint banged on the lintel. Swearing, he ducked down to clear the wooden post. He went by his comrades, shaking his head. "New ideas," he said scornfully. Once free of the obstruction, he stretched his wings and took off to join the abbess.

Brouse and Romini watched him go.

"We can be restored again later, can't we?" Brouse asked with an expression of unease on his broad face.

"That is why the runes were taken," Magpie said solemnly, though he longed to tease the bulky almoner. "Yet you might wish to remain in that shape permanently. You might enjoy having wings."

"I would rather have the shape Mother Nature gave me, Highness," Brouse said stuffily, "but it is the abbess's orders." He marched into the cabin as if he were going to his execution. Romini watched him go and shook his head.

Sharhava's knights spread out across the dark sky and dove into the fray as nimbly as if they were fighting duels with novice swordsmen. They took to flight as swiftly and naturally as they had to riding horses on thin air. Magpie had to admit that he both respected and envied them. More of the knights than Colruba had found joy in catching the winds underneath the sails of their wings. All around the ships was dark. Only a few lengths away, the sea still danced with runes, maddeningly out of reach of the defenders. The thraiks now understood the humans were reluctant to follow them into the blackness, and made full use of it. Once the winged humans had arisen, the thraiks had nowhere to escape, save through the tears in the sky.

When Serafina had remade the last of the knights, she returned to the bloodstained patch of deck to watch over the wounded and mourn the dead.

Halcot landed to give his mount a chance to rest. Magpie, his father, and In-becca went aloft in his place.

On her second borrowed steed, Inbecca rode close to Magpie as they kept their circuit low above the wheelhouse but high enough that no one else could easily hear them.

"Are you well?" he asked her.

"I am ashamed," she replied, turning her head so she could not see his face. "I did not want any special treatment."

"Don't be ashamed," Magpie said flippantly. "We may not survive this battle, so no one will ever hear of your shame."

She reached out and pushed his shoulder in response to his tease. "True. Then if we are going to die, I am glad I am fighting side by side with you."

He felt a rush of warmth, pride, and courage. "I would face anything to be with you."

She smiled, a little sadly. "It's as it should have been," she said.

"Let us hope appearance of winged humans will turn the tide in favor of the defenders," Magpie said.

Chapter Thirty-seven

akanta walked at the head of the file through the eerie night of the cavern. The faint sensation of a breeze was all she had to go on. No matter how many runes there were around them, they still didn't tell her which way was out. They decided that it was better not to rely upon Teldo's handful of fire for a light source in case someone else turned up in the passageway. Bad enough that her boots and Rin's hooves rang on the stone floor.

After so many months on short rations, she knew the Summerbee brothers were tiring. They supported each other over the slippery ground and whispered for her to wait when one of them fell. She was determined that she was going to bring them back alive to Tildi. The girl had been so kind to her. Not that they weren't good men, too. Lakanta felt it to be a sacred duty to reunite her friend with her brothers. If she couldn't have her own family restored, at least she could bring joy to another. It would be a tribute to Adelobert.

"I scent the sea," Rin said, tossing her head. Lakanta glanced back over her shoulder toward the end of the file. The centaur's eyes gleamed against the dark of her face. "I smell salt. It is blowing into my face."

"But we are walking uphill," Gosto said. "If we were beneath sea level these caverns would be full of water instead of running with them. Perhaps we should follow the flow down. It must go somewhere."

"It could go to an underground lake that has never seen daylight," Lakanta said. "I know many such in my kinfolks' mountains. I want the source of that breeze. Winds do not whistle beneath the earth."

"All right," Pierin said gamely, but she heard the sheer exhaustion in his voice. "Let us go on. As long as it doesn't take us into that madman's hall again."

The moss-men had not been seen since they had left the cell. They could have been following, but it would have to be at a great distance. Rin would have spotted their runes in the dark. They didn't strike her as subtle creatures. Anything with a lick of sense would have searched the room and found the hole in the wall.

The green light flickered and went out, leaving Lakanta momentarily blind. Her eyes recovered swiftly. The world was filled with a tracery of gold. She sought about for the nearest of the moving runes near her.

"Teldo, are you all right?"

His voice sounded breathless. "Just lost my concentration for a moment. I'll be fine." A flicker of green appeared and spread until the hand-sized ball of flame had resumed. In its light, Lakanta surveyed his hollow eyes. He saw her concern and smiled. "Hope we find that open air soon. I wonder what time of day it is outside."

"Time to go home," Gosto said jovially. "Come on, lads, let's put on some speed. We're holding these ladies back."

Lakanta started up the slope again. Was it her imagination, or did the air smell more foul than it had a few paces back? She sniffed. Probably the remains of some other poor fellow that the thraiks had carried off.

The shining walls of the corridor narrowed ahead, and the faint rush of cool air felt stronger. If it weren't for the Summerbee brothers, she would have stumped up the slope at a good pace.

Another swirl of air stirred the skirts near her knees. Was there a cross-corridor beyond the bottleneck? With her stone sense, she would have felt it. Dear mother of the earth, it had been too long since she had spent so much time belowground.

The low breeze came again, this time behind her. She glanced down. A low, dark shape paced her on the right. She dodged to the left. Her knee struck something warm. She looked down into glowing red eyes. Black lips drew back to show rows of gleaming fangs. Lakanta gasped. Rin let out a scream and reared on her hind legs, striking out at the beasts.

"What are they?" she shrieked.

"Charnives!" Gosto bellowed. "Run for your lives!"

"Help me!" The youngest boy fell to the floor and was dragged away into the darkness.

"Marco!" Teldo shouted, running to catch him. The fire in his palm roared higher. He threw a gout at the nearest face. It turned tail and fled into the darkness. The Summerbee lads followed the forlorn cries of their brother.

Lakanta kicked at the creatures, about the size of foxes or medium-sized dogs. A host of them grabbed the hem of her skirts and tried to drag her down. Others leaped to catch her arms or hands in their teeth. With difficulty, she fended them away. One bit down on her left wrist, worrying it. She gasped with pain but kept her head. She snatched the club from her belt and dealt the beast a whack on the skull. It collapsed where it stood. Lakanta jerked her wrist free, hissing at the pain of the four seeping fang marks. Some of the others stopped attacking her and tore into the body of their fellow.

"Not too particular what you eat, are you?" she said grimly, smacking blindly at heads or spines of the remainder. The ones she wounded never made a sound when she struck them. They recoiled or died as silently as they attacked. It was oddly terrifying to face a foe that she could only see or smell, never hear. A weight struck her in the back. She fell to her knees. Hot breath on her neck was the only warning before the sharp teeth closed on the nape of her neck. She staggered forward, clawing at the charnive's rough pelt.

"For the Windmanes!" Rin cried. Lakanta heard the crack of a whip. The weight dropped abruptly. The hot breath stopped. Lakanta turned to see her friend trampling at least three charnives into the ground. More leaped at her legs and belly. Lakanta steadied herself on the wall and forced her way past the thrashing bodies to her friend's side. Two of the charnives attacking Rin turned to leap at Lakanta. She flailed at them with the club, not caring what she struck. One took a nip out of her right arm. She battered it in the face until it reared and fled. She hung against the wall, swiping at the second charnive. A hot stream ran from the wound down the back of her neck. She knew it was blood, but there wasn't time to stanch or bandage the wound.

"Are you all right?" the centaur asked.

"I'll do," Lakanta said, swallowing hard. "Might not have in a moment. My thanks."

"We must get to Tildi's brothers," Rin said. She reared high and came down hard. The skull of a charnive crunched beneath her hooves. Its surviving kin shouldered her away to attack the raw flesh. Lakanta cringed at the sound of teeth grinding bones between them.

"I see flame," Lakanta said, pointing to the faint glow of green downslope.

"On my back," Rin said. A hand touched Lakanta's shoulder. She clasped it, and was swept upward. She landed on the warm, curved withers. "Hold on!"

Lakanta clung on as best she could. She felt the powerful muscles under the lightly furred pelt gather and extend. Rin leaped over the massing runes limned on the half-seen shapes. A few bounded after her, but she outdistanced them easily. They seemed less interested in the two of them, now that they had plenty of their own dead to eat.

"Thank the Stallion that the mad wizard feeds his guard dogs as poorly as he does his prisoners," Rin said.

"Aye," Lakanta said grimly. "Though there had better be four brothers left alive, or I'll kill the man myself."

They spotted the faint green light less than a hundred yards downslope, past a dozen dead charnives. Lakanta squinted past Rin's shoulder. Teldo stood over Marco's body, flame flickering on both palms. Twenty or more charnives surrounded them, braced and waiting. Lakanta could tell only the magical fire kept them from leaping on the smallfolk and devouring them to the bone. Teldo was growing weak. The flames flickered low. The one in his right hand went out, and the beasts on that side rose to spring. Gosto and Pierin pelted them with the rocks they had gathered from the ruins of their cell.

Rin charged into the midst of the circle, kicking and snapping her whip. Lakanta, heedless of her own wounds, slipped off her friend's back and knelt beside Marco. His wide brown eyes were open. She helped him to sit up.

"I'm alive," the boy said with a brave smile that won Lakanta's heart. "Just bruised, is all."

"Behind you!" Gosto shouted, and flung a rock over her head. Lakanta heard scuffling on the stone floor. Another one fled. "That's all of mine, boys."

Pierin fished two stones out of the remains of his shirt and passed them to his brother. "Make these count, then!"

Rin danced and reared, her eyes shining green with the reflected light. Another charnive fell, and was pounced upon by the three beasts nearest it. Teldo spun around suddenly and launched the fire in his hands at the hunters behind him. The green fire adhered to the fur of the two it struck. One let out a gasp, the only sound Lakanta had ever heard one make. The flames spread, singing its filthy fur. It raced in a circle, trying to escape from its own immolation. It crashed into the other burning charnive, rebounded, then sprang at it as if blaming it for its pain. Taking advantage of the confusion, Rin and the Summerbees struck at the hunters. Pierin cried out as one of them sank its teeth into his right arm. He cracked it on the head with a rock.

"Burn it!" he shouted.

Teldo drew back his hands and stared at the palms. "That's all," he said simply. "I've no more in me."

"I've enough strength," Lakanta said, rising to her feet. She brandished the club at the glowing eyes. "Come and try your luck."

Several of them charged her at once. She braced herself, then swung hard at the first beast. The two who were on fire ran away, leaving her staring at moving runes, hoping she was not going to strike a smallfolk by mistake. Lakanta hit out at anything that came near her. The satisfying thud of the club on bone told her she had scored a solid hit on the pate of one of the charnives. Ignoring the nips and bites as she stooped, she pounded the fallen beast until she was sure it was dead, then backed away to let the others eat it.

"Look out, that's me!" Pierin's voice said as she bumped into someone.

"Sorry," Lakanta said.

"Not you, Teldo," he said. "Teldo, what's wrong?"

Lakanta glanced back. Two runes leaned together. It was clear something was wrong. "Rin!" she cried.

"Here!" A large rune hovered before her eyes. She felt out blindly until she touched her friend's side.

"We've got to get away now. Can you outrun them?" Lakanta asked. A nose touched her leg. She struck at the spot with her club before teeth closed on her flesh. It retreated a little.

A snort ruffled Lakanta's hair. "Can I? Can a Windmane outrun hounds? Of course I can!"

"Well, Teldo and Marco can't walk."

"Up on my back, friends," Rin said. "You shall have a privilege few enjoy. I can carry you all."

"Time and Nature smile on you, Princess," Gosto said. Lakanta found his sturdy rune at her right hand. With his help, they fended off the charnives long enough to help Marco into Rin's arms. Teldo followed next. Pierin's rune virtually jumped to the perch, though it was high above his head. Gosto was the last. His fingers touched Lakanta's head and felt downward for her hand.

"Come up," he said.

"There isn't room for me, too," Lakanta said. In her mind's eye, she knew that four smallfolk were as much as the centaur could manage. "Run! I'll follow, I swear it!"

"I go, my friend," Rin said. "But I am not leaving these caves without you at my side."

"I'll catch up," Lakanta promised.

The centaur's hooves clattered away. Lakanta was left alone in the dark. At least Tildi's brothers were safe.

Hot breath surged upon her from three different directions. She smashed out at the nearest source. If she had to die, then this was fitting, where her husband had breathed his last. She would sleep well near his resting place.

"Come on, then!" she said. "See if you like mountain blood!"

A surge of heat came from just near her right wrist. She jerked up her arm and brought it down hard. The beast anticipated her move, for her club whistled through empty air. Something rammed into the back of her knees. She staggered forward. Her outstretched hands felt a wet nose and wire-sharp hairs. The charnive snapped its head up and bit at her. Lakanta grunted as a fang caught in the skin of her left hand. She dragged it free, tearing the flesh. Eyes filled with tears, she struck out at the circling runes. When she connected with a body, she belabored it as hard as she could. The charnives retreated to the edge of the corridor. At least a dozen remained. Though she could no longer see their eyes, she could feel them upon her. She was outnumbered. All they needed to do was harry her until her strength was gone. She was determined to make them wait as long as she could.

A rune rushed toward her. Pain lanced up her leg as teeth fixed into her ankle. Lakanta almost dropped her club in shock. She fumbled with it, getting a good grip, then brought it down hard. She connected with something soft, like a neck or a belly. The charnive closed its teeth tighter. She grasped the stick like a butter churn and thudded it down on the beast. The thudding sound told her she had struck the skull. She pounded it over and over, turning when she had to fend off attacks from the side, until the hot mouth sagged open. She kicked the limp creature toward its fellows.

"Is that all you can do?" she asked, her voice ringing with challenge in the hot corridor.

The beasts seemed to confer silently, then gathered, their runes a mass. Lakanta felt behind her until she had her back against the wall. This was the last rally, then. They must bring her down. The first one leaped. She hit out at the shining lines of the rune. She heard a crunch. She must have smashed the creature's jaw. It dropped. The others surged toward her. Lakanta could hardly separate one tangle of golden lines from another. Teeth and blunt claws grabbed for her flesh from every direction. She struck and punched and kicked with all her might. *This child of the mountains will not surrender quietly*, she vowed.

The mountain seemed to agree with her. The silence was broken by an enormous *BOOM*. The charnives halted their attack for a moment. The noise came again, filling the corridor, flooding Lakanta's ears and making her rib cage vibrate.

The charnives' runes seemed to vibrate, too. The unexpected sound made them nervous. She was nervous, too, but she refused to show it.

"Yes, I did that," she told them, pushing away from the wall. "I'm a great wizardess, or hadn't you heard, eh?" She stalked toward them, swinging the club. "Do you want more of it? I can do it all day!"

The thunderous sound shook the mountain again and again. The char-nives sought about in terror. They were used to the silence that camouflaged them. They didn't like noise. Well, she would add to it.

"Go away!" she shouted. "Go find yourself a hole to hide in! Get away, or I and my kind will find you and hunt you down!"

The threats didn't move them, but the noise certainly added to their fear. They backed farther and farther away from her. They withdrew with every shout, every bellow, every wild yell.

A few more feet, Lakanta begged, *a few more yards and I can run.*

At last, the runes pulled back out of sight. Lakanta didn't wait to see if they were coming back. She started limping uphill, in the direction Rin had gone. *Oh, let me be faster than they are!*

"Rin! Wait up! Wait for me!"

She set out running uphill after the faint, fast-retreating sound of hoof-beats.

Above you!" cried a deep voice. Magpie ducked low over Tessera's neck. A long-tailed, winged shadow passed overhead, followed by three smaller winged, pale shapes. With a hard flap of his nearly translucent sails, Lar Braithen surged forward, his left hand stretched out. He caught the thraik by the tail just ten yards off the starboard rail. The beast reversed in midair, try-ing to snap loose the knight clinging to it. By then the other two had caught up. They flitted in underneath its wings and stabbed for its heart. It twisted and spiraled upward. It could not lose them. The knights were its equal in nimbleness. Braithen let go of his handhold and flapped upward, coming be-tween its powerful legs, and plunged his sword into its belly. The thraik shrieked, but it was done for. It dropped into the sea. Magpie and the others watching cheered. The knights spared them a moment to acknowledge the acclaim, and angled back after the next nearest thraik.

The defenders were holding on, but it could not last. The fear the thraiks had shown at the appearance of the strange new fliers had driven them back for a time. Without having to consider the welfare of their horses, the knights showed themselves to be an unstoppable force. The lord thraik re-sponded by sending in larger and larger groups. He had more than ten times their number. It was only a matter of hours before the humans, changed and otherwise, had run out of resources to hold them back.

The most vital resource of them all was showing signs of exhaustion. Pride had kept Serafina upright through the whole long night. When she stood up to assist the latest fighter whom she had restored to health, Magpie saw her sway on her feet.

"I must go down to her," he told Inbecca. "Come with me."

Inbecca's eye was not dimmed by a night of battle. "Has she not rested this entire time?"

"Not for a moment, that I could see," he replied. He gave a wave to his father, who kept one eye upon his putative daughter-in-law and one upon the nearest battle between guards and thraiks. Soliandur gave him a worried frown. Magpie shook his head, hoping he would understand that nothing was wrong with Inbecca.

Three horses in stained and torn Rabantae livery clattered to the deck ahead of them. Teryn dismounted and hurried to help a woman who was leaning over her mount's mane. Magpie turned Tessera toward the stern deck of the *Corona*, out of the way, and hopped out of the saddle. The piebald mare twitched and shook. He patted her on the neck and beckoned to the werewolf groom who was caring for the Scholardom's horses to give her feed. Inbecca carefully landed her aunt's horse and dismounted behind him.

"I am all right," Serafina protested to Captain Teryn. "Help her to lie down. I will restore her."

The guard captain crossed her arms. Wisps of her hair that had escaped from her coif flew around her face. "You need healing more than she does. It's a gouge in her face. It's painful but not life-threatening. She can wait until morning if necessary."

"That is not . . . that is not necessary," Serafina said. Her voice shook.

"It can wait." Magpie put a hand on her shoulder. She glanced up to see his face and nearly collapsed against his shoulder. Inbecca, beside him, did not display a whit of jealousy. She took Serafina's arm and led her to a chair inside the cabin. The room was filled with the bodies of the dead, their faces wrapped in sailcloth or their own cloaks. *So many,* he thought. *I did not realize we had lost so many.* By the shocked look on Inbecca's face, the reality had not struck her until then, either.

Serafina sat down as though she would never rise again. Her normally straight shoulders slumped in her cloak.

"I apologize for showing weakness," she said. "Give me a moment to rest. I will be ready to go on."

Magpie looked at Inbecca. Her sea-blue eyes searched his.

"There must be a way to stop this battle," Inbecca said. "We cannot last until the wizards return."

Magpie turned to Teryn. "Let the ruse go, Captain," he said. "Speak to the abbess and your lord if you must, but it is time to end the charade. Either Olen and the others have succeeded and rescued our friends, or they have not."

"What are you saying?" the captain asked.

Halcot's steed trotted to a halt just outside the door. He swung off and strode in. Soliandur was only a pace behind him.

"What is wrong here?" Magpie's father demanded. "Is something wrong with Mistress Serafina?"

"She is tired, sir," Inbecca said, putting a gentle hand upon his arm. "As are we all. Your son has a suggestion. I believe we should listen to him."

His father glared at him. "Well?"

Magpie took a deep breath. He was a king's third son, not a general, not a wizard, not even a royal consort, but he gave his words all the authority he could muster. "I am saying it is best not to lose any more lives. Let the thraiks have the decoy. What good will it do them? It isn't really the Great Book. We know that. Either we have given Olen enough time, or there is no hope. We never thought we would face so many thousands."

Soliandur glared. "Is this cowardice talking, boy?" he asked.

Magpie braced himself against his father's disapproval. "No, sir, it's practicality. Can we not trust three wizards to get themselves out of trouble? We were meant to be a diversion, not the action itself."

Halcot gave a blunt nod.

"I agree. Good thought, lad."

"As do I," Soliandur said, after a moment. "We became caught up in the battle. Wizards pushed us into this—though not you, my lady," he added, with a nod to Serafina. "Common sense says we should stop it if we can. Will it work?"

"I don't know, sir," Magpie said frankly, "but it's the only thing I can think of."

"Give it a try," Halcot said. He turned to Teryn. "Captain, it is so ordered. Stand down. Lose no more of my brave soldiers."

"Yes, my lord," Teryn said. Magpie thought he saw relief on her face. She saluted and marched out. Halcot slapped his gloves into his palm.

"I'll go find the abbess and explain it to her."

"No," Inbecca said. "She is my aunt. I will tell her."

Soliandur fixed his gaze upon his son. "Go with her."

"I shall, Father."

He followed Inbecca outside. Salt-laden wind slapped them in the face.

"Weather is coming on," he said, squinting at the sky. A few silver-gray clouds were smeared across the stars. "We should move farther out to sea."

"Ware!"

A huge thraik zipped over their heads almost as soon as they had taken off. Its humanlike face was contorted with hatred for the beings in its wake. Five of the knights flew in its wake like white arrows winging after a raven. Magpie still felt a chill at the weird wings that flapped upon their backs. Inbecca snapped him back to the task at hand.

"There she is!" she said, pointing upward. Magpie spotted a troop of the Scholardom flying back and forth in the face of a huge crowd of hissing thraiks. She pulled the reins up, and the borrowed horse galloped willingly toward the fray.

"Aunt!" Inbecca shouted as they came within a dozen yards. "Aunt, can you hear me?"

"Not now, Lar Inbecca!" Sharhava stopped in midair, and the beast she was harrying fled into the darkness to the south of the ships. Her distorted face turned toward them. Inbecca's own face twisted at the sight of the fanged teeth and the knobbly cheekbones. For a moment Magpie thought she might cry.

Inbecca stood up in her stirrups. "A decision has been reached, Aunt. We must let them take the decoy. Do you hear me?"

"Let them take it?" Sharhava echoed. She wrinkled her forehead. "Never!"

"It's not . . . it's not real," Inbecca said, not wanting to say too much lest the thraiks understand her. "You know that! Let them have it, Aunt. Enough people have suffered."

Sharhava vacillated for just a moment. "That is true. Very well, then. I concur. But we must not make it seem too easy. The lord thraik is intelligent. Leave it to me! Tell them that!"

"I will, Aunt." Inbecca reined the horse away, heading back down to the deck.

The Scholardom responded to Loisan's cry to assemble. The winged humans sailed together high above the ships. Magpie watched them with fascination as they spread out again.

Teryn had given her company the order to stand down. The remaining guards took their steeds to the *Eclipse*, out of harm's way.

The weather added to the confusion. The wind blew hard enough to cause the ships to rock hard at anchor.

"This is growing foul," Haroun shouted up to them as they circled low, between the rigging and the masts. "I see lightning!"

Magpie glimpsed a jagged streak in the distant sky that burned a yellow image upon his eyes. Thunder rolled across the sea. The storm would be upon them shortly. "The thraiks must succeed before then."

One pass. Two passes. Five. Gradually, Sharhava was pulling her knights away, sending them off into the distance, leaving fewer and fewer defenders on high. Their vulnerability left Magpie chilled, but he knew it was necessary.

The first drops of rain hit him like the sting of a whip. More lightning gashed the sky. Careful not to look directly at it lest it blind him, Magpie saw his shadow burst in stark blackness on the cabin wall. The shadow of a thraik was behind him. He looked over his shoulder at the largest beast he had ever seen.

"Eremi!" Inbecca screamed.

Tessera whinnied with fear. Magpie kicked his heels hard into her side and pulled her upward and around, heading directly into the face of the lord thraik. Tessera bucked under him, frightened of the creature's glowing eyes.

"Forward, dear one, forward now! It'll be over soon, I swear it. It will be all right . . ."

The beast came toward him with its tongue flicking out of its horrible fanged mouth. He brandished his sword, prepared to slash the monster's throat. Their lives would cost it dearly.

Suddenly the thraik ducked beneath him, so close to Tessera's hooves that the backwash of wind sent them tumbling head over heels. The mare screamed. Magpie held on with both arms and legs as the mare struggled to right herself. Rain lashed them, drowning him in midair. His foot slipped out of the saddle, and his sword hilt twisted in his hand.

The lord thraik closed its wings and dropped. It landed upon the deck only yards ahead of King Halcot and King Soliandur. It seized the scroll of maps in its claws, then bounded upward. Triumph was written upon its ugly face as red and yellow lightning burst in the sky over their heads. It screamed, and its subjects echoed the cry.

Magpie whispered to Tessera, trying to calm her. They were upright again. The mare turned white-rimmed eyes to him.

"Let's go down, my dear," he said.

Inbecca was at his side, her soaking wet, too large habit flapping around her, on her borrowed horse. "Are you all right?"

"I am," he shouted back. They reached the deck of the ship just as the bulk of the storm rolled in upon them like an avalanche.

"Has the wizard brought this down upon us?" Haroun yelled over the howl of the winds. "Lightning is not red!"

"It's not his doing! We've seen this before," Magpie replied, dragging Tessera toward the ramp that led belowdecks. Rain began to lash the rigging. By the light of the lanterns he could see it was a sickly green in hue. The clouds twisted and bulged like a living creature. "It's called the Madcloud! It's wizard weather!"

"We need to get out of it," the werewolf captain said. "The *Corona*'d be torn apart on the rocks if we don't."

"We must not leave this place," Serafina said, running after them. "Master Olen expects to find us here."

The captain turned wild yellow eyes upon her. "My lady, if we don't go, all he will find is flotsam and jetsam!" He let out a sharp whistle and a howl that cut through the wail of the wind. The crew answered from every corner.

"We'll need to row," Patha said. "Every hand that can move an oar, we'll need."

"One good thing about this weather," Halcot said, his beard streaming with rain. "All the thraiks are gone. Look!" Above them, the winged beasts vanished into the blackness. Magpie wished he could step through reality, too. The Scholardom fought against the wild winds. He and Inbecca handed their way across the deck to help them down one by one.

"These wings aren't so good in bad weather," Loisan said with gruff humor as they pulled him aboard. "Have to remember that for the next time."

"There's my aunt!" Inbecca cried, running to intercept a body plummeting toward them.

Sharhava, her hood blown off her head, leaned into the maelstrom, her wings nearly closed against her sides. Patha leaped into the air and wrapped her arms around the abbess, bringing her down onto the deck with a thump. They struggled to their feet, leaning on one another, wolf woman and winged warrior. Sharhava looked as triumphant as the lord thraik had been.

"We did well," she said, embracing Patha. "It was worth the change."

Haroun and his crew herded everyone toward the cabin. "If we live through this, it will be worth it."

Chapter Thirty-eight

istress Summerbee," a voice whispered urgently. "Listen to me. You must wake."

Tildi fought her way back to consciousness. Precious air flooded her lungs. She opened her eyes with a gasp and felt around for the book. It lay beside her. She looked up at the anxious face of Lar Mey, who knelt beside her. She had succeeded in rebuilding the big chamber, down to the wizard-lights that clung to the walls. Weapons drawn, Morag and Demballe stood on guard with their backs to her. The other two knights flanked Master Olen. He stood outside a cocoon of brilliant gold in which the two Makers stood with the Compendium's rune between them. The book itself stretched and shrank, twisted and bent like a snake with a bellyache in response to the damage being inflicted upon its true name.

"Why did you come here, Calester?" Knemet asked. "You knew that destruction must result if we met again. I welcome it! You do not. It was foolish of you."

"I came for the sake of friendship," Calester said.

"What? Ours? You were one of the ones who betrayed me."

"No." Calester's long cheeks creased in a smile. He glanced out at Olen and the knights. "Theirs. They convinced me to come here to find their loved ones. I agreed, because it would give me a chance to shut you away from the world once and for all time."

"What?" demanded Lar Mey, from outside the glowing ward. "You lied to us! You said you would help us save Mistress Summerbee's companions!"

They ignored him. Knemet sneered at Calester.

"That is your solution? You would shut me away to suffer eternity in this drab world?"

"Not in the world," Calester said. "You do not deserve access to the world. You do too much harm. I think it will have to be a tomb. If you comply peacefully I will help you to sleep away the eternity you do not wish to face. You are too dangerous to leave free."

"That is not enough!"

The golden bubble expanded outward. Its force threw Tildi and the others against the walls of the chamber.

Knemet reached through the spell and seized the Compendium by a spindle. Tildi fought against the magical force holding her in place. He must not have it!

"Mine!" he cried, holding it high above his head. "Peace at last."

Tildi concentrated all her will upon the book. It had been her dearest and closest companion for many months. He wanted to destroy it. He must not have it.

Obediently, it flew out of Knemet's fingers and up toward the conical ceiling. The pale wizard looked stunned.

"How have you gained power over the Compendium?" he asked Calester. "How, when none of us could make it move a hairbreadth?"

Calester gave him a superior smile. "I told you that it didn't belong to you." He rose into the air toward the book. Knemet kicked away from the ground and sped toward it. Calester looked back at him and flung out a hand. Runes grew into walls, fire, a rain of blobs that adhered to the small Maker's skin and spread outward, threatening to suffocate him. Knemet threw off each of the attacks without trouble and angled past the taller wizard. He clapped his hands in Calester's surprised face. The Guardian was stunned by a burst louder than thunder. Knemet kicked upward past his old colleague and reached for the scroll.

He would not have it. Tildi caused it to fly downward, away from him. Knemet pursued it with all the fervor of a hawk chasing prey. It penetrated the golden wall again and into her waiting arms. Knemet flew toward it, and bounced off a thin wall of gray. Knemet glared at Olen and back at Tildi.

"It was not his talent after all, but yours, twig-girl," he said, wiping out the golden cocoon with an angry gesture. The guards dropped to the ground.

Tildi just kept herself upright with the aid of her spell. Knemet's eyes seemed to whirl with curiosity. "That is why your companions said the Compendium is special to you. It is a marvel I wish I had time to examine. No matter. Prepare to die with it, then." White-hot fire grew between his hands. When Tildi could no longer bear to look at it, Knemet turned unexpectedly and flung it at Olen.

The gray-cloaked wizard put up his hands to protect himself. The fire burst upon a hastily made shield and consumed it. Olen shouted spells to counter the fire, but he vanished within a pillar of flame. Tildi cried out in horror. Knemet turned back to her.

Calester recovered his wits. He brought his fists together with a mighty clap. Blue light surrounded Knemet, and he froze. Calester descended, his hands out, applying rune after rune to the initial layer. Knemet fought him, throwing off one spell after another, but he could not keep up with Calester.

"You are weaker than you were," Calester said. "Do you yield? You will be at peace."

"Yield to you?" Knemet snarled. "You always robbed me of my heart's desires, Calester."

"I never did. What did I ever steal that you truly desired?"

"What about Boma?" Knemet asked. Calester looked genuinely astonished.

"We were colleagues. Her heart turned away from you when you began to destroy indiscriminately."

Now Knemet looked baffled. "I did not! They were making weak things! She couldn't see that what they did would not prosper. They caused suffering, and they couldn't see. She couldn't see it."

"She had her weaknesses, brother. So did we all. But we did not seek to thwart one another, nor to do harm. You did. I tried to tell you that."

Knemet set his jaw. Gouts of pure power flew at Calester, counterspells against his magic. "You abandoned me. You all abandoned me. She betrayed me. She turned to you."

Calester avoided the spells, diverting them to fly upward and away from any of the others in the room. "Not in the way you think. You terrified her. You seemed to have no boundaries left."

"That is what we were *doing*, escaping all boundaries to see where magic could lead us. We were greater than creation itself, greater than Time and Nature!"

"In the end, we were not," Calester said sadly. "Time especially became too much for all of us. Even I took a respite from the world. It is then when the Compendium passed by me."

"You drove me out," Knemet snarled. "You, my greatest friend. She, my dear one. She betrayed me for you."

Calester looked stricken. "She never did, and in your heart you know that. She just could not stand to be by you any longer. You meant the destruction of all things that she knew. That has not changed. You still mean to destroy, and for the most selfish purpose of all—you want to be at peace."

Knemet's face was grayer than ever, and the rainbow eyes were dimmed. "I would not destroy myself if I had anything to live for. She would have given me that reason!"

With an effort, he flung his hands outward. Runes danced upon the air. Liches swarmed into the chamber and surrounded Calester. The tall Maker fell to one knee as moss-men tumbled in on him. He blanketed them with runes of his own, but nothing seemed to affect the faceless creatures. They were as strong as an avalanche. In a moment, he was buried beneath a writhing blanket. The guards ran to help him. They pulled liches away, but they surged back. Lar Mey was knocked off his feet by their strength and their sheer numbers. Morag, his eyes glowing blue, kicked them away, seeking to free the trapped wizard.

Knemet turned toward Tildi. She backed away, filled with loathing for him. "You are without defenders, child. I applaud your valiance. You cannot keep it from me any longer."

One of the voices cried out to her. Calester had called her Boma. Was that the one whom Knemet was mourning? What would he do if she spoke to him now? Could she cause him to stop his mad rush toward destruction, or would it not matter at all?

She looked at the Great Book. It was dearer to her than her own life's blood. She was willing to die to keep it from Knemet, but she feared for the others. They would never leave the chamber alive unless she took a terrible chance. The voice, ringing insistently in her mind, might be the only way to stop him. She held up the book and commanded it to fly.

"No!" Calester cried. The guards had just helped him to stand. He reached out to Tildi, but it was too late.

The huge scroll smacked into Knemet's arms. Instinctively, they folded around the round body of white parchment. His fingers caressed it. His pinched face relaxed, and his eyes closed.

"Boma," he said, his voice full of wonder.

"Yes," Calester said. "She is there. Girl, how could you do that? Take it back, hurry!"

Tildi looked at Knemet. His face wore a genuine smile for the first time since she had seen him. "Not yet, master."

"*Cnetegh!*" Olen's voice bellowed, and the flames that had surrounded him died away. He regarded the scene before him and beamed at Tildi. The sleeves of his robe were scorched. His long beard and curling eyebrows had been singed by the flames, but he was otherwise unharmed. "Well done, apprentice."

"How can someone be in the Compendium?" Knemet asked in disbelief. He turned to Calester. "What are they doing inside it?"

"Why was I a statue for so long?" Calester countered. He gave Tildi a startled glance, but turned back to Knemet. "I wearied of life. We all did. A few of our number allowed themselves to die. They had not done what you and I had to prolong their existence, so it was possible. The others chose to spend their eternities together. It was a new kind of magic that we invented together. I was not yet bored or lonely enough to be one of them, and I am not yet. But you are. You can join them. You can be at peace."

"An elegant solution," Olen said approvingly.

"No, he has killed too many!" Lar Mey shouted. "Find a way to kill him without endangering the book!"

"It cannot be done," Olen said. "You saw that neither magic nor weapons can harm him."

"What about my parents and my brothers?" Tildi asked. "What about all the others he had brought here to die? Will he not be punished at all?"

Morag glared. "He wanted to destroy the book, and all it controls! Our world was to perish, to satisfy his whim."

"It is so he could perish," Calester said simply. "He wants to leave the world. He shall."

"There must be consequences," Lar Mey said. "We know our friends to be alive, but what about the others?"

"He killed them," Demballe said angrily.

"I don't believe so," said Olen thoughtfully. "He seems to lose interest. More likely older prisoners died of neglect and starvation."

"Never starvation," Calester protested. "We *always* fed our subjects. Cruelty was never tolerated, not even by him."

"But what is more cruel than stealing a family away?" Tildi asked.

Calester spread out his hands. "What would be a worse punishment than to condemn him to live on forever? How else? I cannot change what he is. That part of reality cannot be rewritten."

"I can't forget what he has done," Tildi said.

"No, but it seemed that he has forgotten us," Olen said.

Knemet was not listening to the argument going on about him. He seemed enraptured by the voices. Tildi could not hear them, but she imagined the woman's voice having a conversation with the shrunken wizard. No, an argument. Knemet lifted his voice sharply to retort in the ancient language to something he heard. He cut off in midsentence to listen. His face flushed angrily, giving him color for once. He broke out in an extended protest, clearly defending himself. He halted to listen again. The next time he spoke, his tone softened. The others watched, reluctant to interrupt. At last, Knemet lowered the enormous scroll. He turned his rainbow eyes to the taller Maker.

"I beg you for this, brother."

Calester nodded.

"Then you shall have it."

Thraiks appeared in the chamber, chittering with terror. Tildi had never seen fear in the fierce creatures. Knemet looked up at them in annoyance.

"Don't interrupt me, children. I am speaking with a colleague."

They did not seem to be able to help themselves. One let out a wail of pain and fear. It held out its wing. The sails were torn and burned. Tildi pitied it, heard the panic in its song. Knemet frowned.

"The storm rages? Red lightning? Not that again!"

"What does he say?" Demballe asked. "What about lightning?"

Olen turned to her. "The book is unshielded. The Madcloud is here. We must turn it. Open the book, Tildi."

Hastily, Tildi unwound the scroll and peered into it.

Olen shook his head. He pointed toward a cluster of signs that were intertwined though they had nothing else in common. Tildi recognized the troubled turmoil of the Madcloud's rune. "Our friends are in danger. The ships cannot move easily. They will be torn to pieces."

"Stop it!" Tildi begged Knemet. She showed him the twitching, writhing image on the page. "We can send it away, but it will keep coming back."

"We know it as the Madcloud," Olen explained. "It is a weather phenomenon that is attracted to great magical power, like the Compendium, but also what we have done here today. It is horrendously destructive, and has troubled Alada greatly. It has been known to level entire villages. It will make short work of two ships."

Knemet frowned at them. "I know it well. It is indeed a terrible misuse of power. I hate it. I wish it would vanish as well. My thraiks fear it, as you see."

"You made it, didn't you?" Tildi asked, puzzled.

"Is that what he told you?" Knemet asked, pointing at Calester, who suddenly wanted to look everywhere but at them. "*He* did, not I."

Calester looked abashed. "I was not always mature of judgment," he admitted. "I learned better, but the storm went away, and I forgot about it. I have not seen it since."

Tildi was agog. She had been right all along about Calester. He was highhanded and arrogant.

Olen smiled. "There is no reason to allow such destruction to continue. Our friends are in danger."

"Undo it!" Knemet said.

"I shall, my colleagues." Somewhat humbled, Calester placed his hand over the rune in the book. Beads of sweat broke out upon his forehead. Tildi peered at the runes on the page. She saw the storm in her mind as she had when she and Olen faced it in the hills above the city of Overhill. It was a frightening mass of tossing, greasy, gray clouds from which shot multicolored lightning. She pitied those who were caught in it. "I . . . I cannot."

"What do you mean, you cannot?" Knemet snapped at him. "It was your toy. You set it loose! Now, bridle it before it begins to rain lightning down on my home! *Fool.* The irony pleases me that you came here with the intention of defeating me, yet you end by requiring my aid to put down some of your own mischief."

He clapped his palm down on Calester's hand and closed his eyes.

Tildi watched the troubled rune glow and begin to unwrap itself. Calester's face started to ease, then tightened again as the Madcloud wrenched itself away from their control. It appeared as though it was trying to save itself from destruction. Olen added his hand to the others' and gestured to Tildi to do the same. She recoiled at the thought of touching Knemet's hand, and made very sure that Olen's flesh stood between him and her.

The moment she touched Olen, it was as though she could feel the wizards' minds open to her. There wasn't time to wonder at the vista of possibility that it opened to her. The three intelligences struggled against the rogue power, each trying to catch one turn of a very long and muscular snake. She joined them, feeling as though she were hanging on to the creature's tail.

The Madcloud responded to three wizards and an apprentice as it did to all other forms of magic: it attacked them. Tildi gritted her teeth as the terrible force took hold of her and whirled her mind until she thought she would be sick with dizziness. It screamed at them, begging for an end to its pain.

Like Knemet, Tildi thought, and blanched at herself for feeling pity.

"Dissolve that bond," Knemet ordered her, as if he did not sense what she was thinking. A twisted vine that was a stroke of the rune reared up near her. She envisioned nothingness, and caused it to descend upon the bulging line. It vanished, and the Madcloud paused in its frenzy. She saw other fragments disappearing or changing, and knew that the two Makers were working together upon the problem, as they might have done ten thousand years before.

"There, Tildi, another," Olen instructed, distracting her from the thought. A red light illuminated a curlicue deep within the throbbing mass of lines. "Remove that. It is what keeps it seeking out power."

As she moved to blot it out, it surged toward her own rune, seeking to envelop it entirely.

No! she thought at it. She harkened back again to the day they had driven the storm back. She drew it before the advancing cloud of spiky lines. The

Madcloud touched it and tried to retreat. She caused the wall of gray to expand outward and wrap itself around the rune. Golden clouds of power
struck it. The Madcloud shrank, twisting as though in agony. It shifted from
one side of the enveloping spell to the other, seeking escape. The wizards
excised one part after another, until the rune subsided, and lay upon the
page like any other. It had loosed its hold upon the ships and the rocks, and
moved away from the mountains.

"Just an ordinary storm," Knemet said.

"Now it will just rain itself out," Olen said, sounding pleased. Tildi
opened her eyes and backed away, putting her hands behind her back.

The thraiks vanished. In a moment, one came to hover over their heads.
It dropped a scroll at Knemet's feet and let out a cry.

"What is that?" the small wizard asked, picking it up and unrolling it partway. "Maps?" He looked up at the thraik.

"A ruse," Olen said. "To divide your attention long enough to accomplish
our goals. All our goals. It is not their fault."

"Ah," Knemet said, giving him a very shrewd look. He thrust the scroll
aside. "You are a worthy opponent, as I surmised. Now, I would wait no
longer. The twig-girl wants me out of the world as soon as possible."

Tildi felt embarrassed to be singled out, but she could not deny her feelings. She put her chin up with stubborn pride. He was a murderer. One good
deed didn't undo a lifetime of evil acts.

"So do I, brother," Calester said. "You won't find it peaceful when you
cannot escape our colleagues' wrath."

The rainbow eyes gleamed. "It is better than the half existence I have
now. First, I must set my children free." He beckoned toward the ceiling.
The thraiks swooped and flitted nervously, but one, the largest that Tildi
had ever seen, came down and hovered eye to eye with Knemet. The wizard
touched the monstrous creature's nose as though it were a beloved dog.
Knemet pointed his forefinger at the thraik's eyes, and the golden rune at
their center winked out, leaving the orbs a plain, muddy brown. The thraik
blinked, puzzled, then retreated toward the ceiling. When it neared the others, the rune vanished from their eyes, too. They chased one another around
the high dome, and a great blackness overspread the runes along one wall.
The thraiks scudded through it and disappeared. Knemet bowed his head.
"It is done. They will no longer seek the Compendium. Let me go now."

"Will you hold the book for me?" Calester asked Tildi.

"Willingly," she said.

He instructed her to open it to his full arms' width. He extended one
hand toward the page and the other toward Knemet. He murmured in a low
voice. The words echoed gently, taking on substance. Tildi felt as though
the air were thickening like jelly. The rune etched in red upon the open leaf

of the Compendium grew until it was man-sized. It expanded toward Knemet, meeting the identical image in the center of his body. When they touched, Knemet cried out wordlessly. His body began to waver and tremble. Then, to Tildi's horror, it seemed to break apart. No, she realized, it was taking on the shape of his own rune. The red glow brightened until it hurt to look upon. It collapsed in upon itself slowly, retreating toward the page.

In a moment, the rune had shrunk to the size of her fingertip. The brilliant glow faded, leaving a beautifully drawn sigil in red, illuminated with gold and purple. Tildi put her thumb down on top of it.

The other red runes crowded in from the sides of the page and converged upon the newcomer. The voices burst out in her inner ear. A new one was among them now. The first three were haranguing it, and the newcomer defended itself vigorously. Peace and punishment had begun. Tildi looked up at Olen and Calester.

The Maker smiled.

"Now, my friends, we must take all of them home."

Chapter Thirty-nine

Carrying lights from the chamber's sconces as torches, the guards marched proudly flanking Calester, who bore the Compendium like a trophy. Olen and Tildi walked side by side behind him. He had virtually forgotten they were there. Tildi knew he was listening to the discussion that must be going on within the confines of the Great Book.

With both wizard and thraiks gone, the big, empty room echoed their footsteps like a haunted house. Tildi was not satisfied. In her eyes Knemet had gotten away with all of the terrible things he had done. Even the book seemed less precious with him inside it. He soiled it. No matter that it had been his creation in the first place! And she . . . she was one of his creations, too. Smallfolk and thraiks were brethren. It was too horrible to contemplate. If the Elders would cavil at knowing they were created by humans and not natural beings, they would go out of their minds knowing what else their Maker had done. They would never contemplate asking the thraiks to come for feastday meals. The absurdity forced an inadvertent laugh from her belly, which turned into a sob.

"What is the matter, Tildi?" Olen asked, his voice gentle.

She looked up at him, her eyes filled with tears. Even he had betrayed her. Olen, the one she had trusted beyond all others, had led her into danger.

"You knew that this was going to happen, didn't you?"

Olen bowed his head. "I foresaw that Calester would not be able to re-sist challenging Knemet. It was a necessary risk. If we met—as we did—we would need Calester's help. And he would need yours—as he did. I decided to let the events unfold as they would. I am sorry for you, my dear. You know now how alone one would be as a wizard. The only time we feel true com-munion is as you saw, and that is filled with peril, magically and physically and emotionally. We had no choice, none of us. I am sorry if it was unwitting on your part, but the action you took, deliberately, without my prompting, saved everything."

Tildi felt better. "I was so frightened when I thought you were burning to death."

"It was a little closer to such an end than I have ever suffered," Olen ad-mitted. "We are all a little bruised and scorched," he added, picking up the blackened ends of his beard, "but it was the best possible outcome. The threat to Alada is ended, and the Compendium will go back where it be-longs. You did so well. I am proud of you."

"But how did you know that it would come out all right?"

He put his hand upon her shoulder. "I did not *know*, my dear. Foresight is inexact, as I have told you many times before, but I also saw the outcome as a success. I believe it to have been worth the risk, don't you?"

"I don't know," Tildi confessed.

"Well, you should be optimistic. All our goals will be met."

"We haven't found Rin and Lakanta yet," Tildi said sadly.

Olen smiled, the corners of his singed mustache lifting. "Ah, but they have found us. Listen."

"I tell you, it is them! That man is as short as I am. He's not there," Lakanta's voice announced. "Hurry! I see light."

Tildi felt her heart lift.

"Lakanta!" she cried. "Over here! We're over here!" She waved one arm in the air though she couldn't see anything but runes past the dim blue glow of the wizard-lights.

"By the Mane, it is!" An excited clatter of hooves rang on the stone floor.

A familiar rune appeared in the dark passage that resolved into a more fa-miliar face. Rin galloped toward her, arms outstretched. Tildi felt as though her heart would burst with joy as the centaur scooped her up and hugged her.

"Hold up, hold up!" Lakanta shouted joyfully. She hurried up on her much shorter legs. "Oh, you darling, we knew it was you when we saw all the runes! We are grateful, but you put yourself in so much danger coming for us."

"We couldn't have left you," Tildi said. "Oh, and wait until you meet the man who helped us." She glanced toward Calester, who gave the newcomers an absent nod. "How did you get free?"

"We burned our way out," Rin said.

"Burned? But everything here is made of stone!"

"We will tell you all." Lakanta took her arm anxiously. "What happened to that wizard, the one with the weird eyes? He wanted to destroy the book, Tildi!"

"He's not going to bother us again," Tildi said firmly. "He is locked up forever and ever, in the very book he wanted. Do you remember the voices I thought I heard? There are people living inside the book itself! And they don't like him very much. At least, I believe they don't."

Rin snorted with laughter. "Hah! A fitting end. Master Olen, I greet you."

Olen bowed. "My greetings to you, Princess. I am relieved to see you well."

"Well enough," Rin said. "When I have had ten good meals and a bath and five days' run in the sunshine, after this place. Tildi, we have a surprise for you!"

Lakanta's eyes were sparkling. "Indeed we do! It's the best thing in the world. I hope you like it. Well, it's only half the surprise we were hoping to have—perhaps a third of it. . . ."

"Isnt that just like a trader, can't keep a story to a measurable length, no more than she could keep a yard the same length twice in a row?" asked a familiar voice. Tildi spun on her heel. Gosto held out his arms to her.

Tildi couldn't believe her eyes. Her four brothers swarmed around Rin's legs and made straight for her. She didn't know which one to embrace first. They were all thin, pale from long imprisonment underground, filthy, long-haired and bearded, but healthy, well—and alive. She could hardly breathe for the joy of it all.

"How?" she asked at last, when she had hugged each one at least ten times. "How did you survive for all these months?"

Gosto grinned sheepishly. "Teldo's magic. The magic we all made fun of. That fire kept us alive, along with hope and grit."

"And music," said Marco. "I sang songs."

"We told each other stories," Pierin added. "Some of them true. Some not so true, but it kept us going."

"In other words," Teldo said, smiling into her eyes with that familiar, beloved look, "we had each other. And now we have you again. These ladies here tell us you've become quite a personage. Do we have to pay a groat to talk to you now?"

Tildi was torn between laughing and crying, threw her arms around him in a fierce hug that squeezed the air out of him. Just for good measure, she embraced all her brothers one more time.

Gosto stood back to admire her, then frowned. "Tildi, you are not wearing your cap! It looks . . . indecent."

"I don't wear my cap any longer," she said. She refused to let the joy she had at having her family back be damped down by the old ways. "I don't have it. Women outside the Quarters don't wear them unless they want to. And I don't want to." She tossed her head defiantly. "I'll wear a hat when the weather's bad, that's all."

The brothers exchanged a brief look as they summed up the statement. "Well, it's a different world, I suppose," Gosto said thoughtfully. "Oh, little sister, I thought we would never see you again!" He threw his arms around her. Tildi rested her head against his shoulder. He accepted the change. He would not force her to go back to the old customs against her will.

She noticed Lakanta's wistful eyes on her. "But what about your husband?" she asked.

Lakanta shook her head sadly. "It was too much to hope," she said. "Well, then, I only saw him a small part of the year. It will be like he's hardly missing. I won't know he's gone. He . . ." She stopped, and tears overflowed and ran down her cheeks. "Curse the man. He was never where I wanted him to be when I wanted him, so why would he now? No. I only hope he has a chance to rest in peace. Life on the road's a hard one. He's well off away from it."

"There, my dear friend," Rin said, kneeling to take the trader into her arms. Lakanta sobbed for a moment, then pulled herself together.

"Ah, well, what's done is done."

"And our parents?" Tildi asked.

"We have not found them," Gosto said. "We knocked on the door of every cell, but there are few occupied by the living. I am sure that they must be dead. It has been such a long time, and they did not have hope to live upon. We will try to find which of these cells contain their bones and take them home for a decent burial in Daybreak Bank."

Tildi bowed her head for a moment. Just for a moment, she had hopes that they would be somewhere safe, but it had been too long.

"Ahem." Olen cleared his throat.

"Oh, yes," Tildi said, abashed. "This is Master Olen. Master Olen has been my teacher. He lives in the most wonderful place." As if she was presenting the most precious treasures in the entire world, she said, "Master, these are my brothers. This is Gosto, Pierin, Marco, and Teldo."

The Summerbee brothers nodded politely as they were introduced. Olen raised a shaggy eyebrow.

"Teldo, eh?"

"Yes," Tildi said proudly. She took Teldo's hand between hers and squeezed it fondly. "Our mother always said we were like twins separated by a year."

Olen bowed to them, hand on heart. "My pleasure. I am happy to know the family that Tildi treasures so greatly. May I present Master Calester?" The Guardian did not look up. Tildi frowned. Ah, well, he was not important. She was surrounded by those who were dearest to her in the world. Only Serafina was missing, and Prince Eremi, if she could be so bold. She clasped her hands in delight.

"Oh, this is the best day of my life!"

Teldo grinned at her. "I've heard about a magic book you have. May I see it?"

Tildi couldn't wait to display the treasure. "Master Calester, may my brother see the Compendium?" Calester did not look up. Impatiently, Tildi stretched out with a thought, and the book lifted straight out of the Guardian's hands. He looked up, startled.

"What is it?" Teldo asked avidly, reaching for the large white scroll.

"Wait, young man, don't touch it!" Calester exclaimed.

"My friend," Olen said, holding him back, "he is perhaps the one other person on all Alada who might be able to touch it."

"What, more smallfolk wizards?" Calester asked. He studied them all with curiosity in his deep-set eyes.

"Perhaps," Olen said mysteriously. "Go ahead, Teldo Summerbee."

"Ow!" Gosto said. "Curse it, it burned me!" Tildi looked at his fingers, but they were just a little pink at the ends, instead of burned black, like the abbess Sharhava. "What about you three?"

"No, thanks," Pierin said. Wide-eyed, Marco just shook his head.

Teldo put his hand on the parchment. Tildi held her breath, but it only turned pink. He clenched his fingers a little as if his skin pricked, but he didn't draw back.

"Why, it's just like the bit of a book that Mother bought for us," he said in wonder. Tildi felt in her belt pouch and produced the scrap.

"In truth, *this* is a bit like the book. It's a copy." Proudly she touched the Compendium. "*This* is the real thing."

All the brothers stared in admiration as she turned it from one page to another, showing them the moving and changing runes. She found even more delight in it than she had before, in spite of the deep, croaky voice that had joined the original three inside the pages. Firmly, she ignored Knemet, and displayed the wonders of his creation to her brothers.

Teldo whistled. "It's a wonder. What will you do with it now?"

"We must take it away and bury it," Olen said.

Teldo shrugged. "Seems a waste to do that. I would think there was so much we could learn from it. Why can't you keep it?"

Tildi took a deep breath, realized it was too big a story to tell him all in one sitting, and let it out again.

"We just can't," she said. "You'll have to trust me on that."

May we depart now?" Lakanta asked. "There's nothing in this terrible place I wish to see again. I want a glass of beer and ten days of sunlight before I ever want to go into shadow again."

Olen put his hand on her shoulder.

"Gladly. Sergeant Morag, if you will lead us?"

Tildi had never seen the craggy sergeant so erect and proud as he stepped out down the corridor. Demballe, at his side, held a wizard-light to guide their feet.

Tildi felt she could never fill her eyes enough with the sight of her friends and her brothers. She kept looking from one to another, as if she feared they would disappear if she kept her gaze off them.

"How did you reach us so swiftly?" Rin asked as they walked. "It seems as though not that many days have passed, although it felt like an eternity."

"We are half a day's sail west of Tillerton," Olen said. "It seems that Knemet's lair was close to where Nemeth came ashore. Both he and Calester missed the arrival of the Compendium."

"There's no need to mention that again," the Guardian said, a trifle miffed.

"Tillerton!" Gosto exclaimed. "Do you mean we were a few days' walk from home, and we never knew?"

"That must be why there were charnives here," Marco said. "I never heard of them haunting tunnels anywhere else."

"That's right," Gosto said. "Tildi, you ought to hear how your friends faced off two score of them all by themselves."

"I look forward to it," Tildi said, "if you tell it before you go on shore."

"I want to go home right away," Pierin said. "Heaven only knows what Lisel will say when she sees me like this." He flipped the ends of his beard with his fingers.

"She thinks you're dead," Tildi said, her face flushing scarlet. "They all think you are dead, after the thraiks carried you away. That's why I'm here." She shook her head. "It's too much to tell you now."

Gosto patted her on the back. "We will want to hear all your adventures, Tildi. Later seems time enough. The wonder is that we are alive to hear them."

Lakanta guided them to the remaining cells in which they had heard voices. Sadly, only two other people remained alive of those the thraiks had stolen. Tildi's brothers refused to allow her into the cells where the dead were found. To Olen's delight, they located a scholar from the wizards' college named Vibun, who had kept himself sane by working out magical conundrums in his head, and a ragged man who threw himself at Tildi's feet, crying out about "mir'cles."

When at last they emerged from the cave mouth, the sky was pink with the light of a winter dawn. The ships were not in sight.

"There they are!"

Tildi heard Sharhava's voice, and looked around for her. No one was waiting on the stony beach.

Suddenly shadows began to drop from the sky. She cringed, fearing the thraiks had returned, but Olen smiled up at the sky. She followed his gaze.

Coming toward them were some of the strangest figures she had ever seen. They had the wings of thraiks, but instead of black they were pink or brown or golden. Their bodies were clothed in flapping lengths of bleached cloth. It took Tildi a moment to realize those were habits of the Knights of the Book. They hovered off the edge of the stone ledge, cheering. The first of the figures landed on before her.

"Welcome back," said the abbess Sharhava. It *was* she, but not as Tildi remembered her. Her face was misshapen, and her teeth, especially the pointed ones at the corners, were larger and longer. Her fingers seemed longer and more knobbly, with curved talons in place of fingernails.

"It seems that there are those with greater tales to tell than we have," Olen said, eyeing her curiously.

Sharhava frowned at him, resenting the familiarity. "Never mind that. I see you have succeeded in your quest."

"In more than you know, dear lady," Calester said. He patted the Compendium proprietorially. "It was a great success."

More normal figures hovered into view: men and women on horseback who galloped toward them in midair. Prince Eremi was at the head of the pack.

"You are alive!" he cried. "Serafina promised you were all right, but seeing is believing." He scanned the group, beaming. "It is good to see you all back again."

Lakanta took a great breath and let out a gust of white clouds. "It is good to be here. You'll have a whole feast's worth of songs from what we have to tell you."

"And we," Magpie said, grinning. "But who are these others?"

"My brothers," Tildi said proudly. The minstrel-prince's eyes widened in wonder.

"Then this is a day of rejoicing," he said. Inbecca caught up with him, astride a different horse than Tildi recalled her riding before.

"Abbess, what is the meaning of this?" Lar Vreia asked at last, horror on her face.

"It was necessary in the defense of the Great Book," Sharhava said imperiously. "That is all you need to understand."

"It was amazing!" Lar Colruba exclaimed. Her plump face was alight with joy. "It has been most exciting to fly free. Blessings upon the sacred writings that made it possible!"

Tildi was struck by the faces of the knights who had accompanied her through the caverns. Two of them wrinkled their brows in concern, but seemed to decide that what their abbess decreed was so. Not Lar Mey, he who disapproved of anyone who was not human. He looked from one of his fellow knights to another, unable to form a word.

"And what are you staring at, brother?" Sharhava demanded.

The knight goggled at his brethren breathlessly, then collapsed in a heap at their feet.

Serafina greeted them all on their return to the ships with more effusiveness than Tildi had ever seen her display. It seemed that the time they had been away had changed everyone they had left behind in ways it would take time to understand. The werewolf crew was torn between wanting to hear all the stories and needing to guide their vessels out of the rocky waters. Olen decreed that anyone who had a tale to tell would be given full hearing. He and Prince Eremi worked it out between them to record all for the archives of the three kingdoms who had had a part in the rescue of the prisoners and the defeat of the Shining One known as Knemet.

Morag and the others who had been wounded in the caverns were restored to wholeness by means of the runes inscribed upon the metal sheets. To the great relief of those who had guarded Tildi, and not a few of those who had been transformed, the Scholardom returned to full humanity. Morag looked wistfully at the runes etched in metal. Tildi's heart went out to him. There was no healing for him there.

Services were held for all the dead, then the bodies were given to the sea. Tildi mourned for those she had known. She gave thanks to Mother Nature and Father Time for their valiant service, but she also had a private prayer of gratitude. Though there had been death, life had been given back. She did not take that for granted.

Tildi spent every moment she could with her brothers. She saw to it that they were the first to be given use of the wooden tub in the captain's quarters, even ahead of the kings and her fellow wizards, with copious hot water furnished by means of her talent. Teldo admired openly and without jealousy the growth in her skills.

"You'll have to give me lessons now," he teased her.

"Anything," she promised him. It was so good to have her brothers back—from the very dead, or so it had seemed! She was happier than she could ever recall being. With their well-being in mind, she persuaded the werewolves to give her some of their children's clothes to replace her brothers' ragged garments, and she gave all four boys haircuts, as she had been accustomed to doing in the kitchen at Daybreak Bank. In a way it felt as if she had never been away from them, but in others, nothing could be farther from normal. Even as the ships brought them closer to the Quarters, she felt she had never been more distant from her old life. She hated to lose touch with her brothers again, even for a few weeks for the journey to Sheatovra, but she knew that she would never return with them.

In Tillerton, they left off Vibun and the man from Walnut Tree.

"I will see him home on the way back to the college," the scholar promised cheerfully. "We will have plenty to talk about. I am interested in his definition of miracles."

"We can let you off here as well," Haroun offered. "You're only a few days' walk. We will trade for supplies to get you there. It would be my privilege. You will want to get home and set your affairs right."

"We may never go into those tunnels again," Gosto said with a rueful grin. "I've had my fill of them. But if you don't mind, Captain, we'd like to see our sister's journey through with her. I don't see as another few weeks will make any difference. We'll send messages with anyone going toward the Quarters to start the process of getting our property restored to us. Better if we're not there, to let them debate all the sides of having people return from the dead. If you knew what smallfolk were like, a year might not be time enough."

"That, too, would be my honor," Haroun said with a grin. "I think I can find room for you on board."

Tildi beamed.

Chapter Forty

ith the passage of each day, she knew the Compendium would soon be out of her hands and out of her sight forever. She wondered how she could possibly let it go.

Calester allowed her to have custody of the book as long as she wished during those days, to allow her to prepare for the separation. It was kindly meant, and Tildi appreciated it. She kept it hovering by her while she served her brothers or ate her meals. The voices had calmed down from their initial fierce arguments. Were they enjoying that mental concord that she had experienced when she and the other wizards had unwound the Madcloud? They had so much knowledge. It was a terrible waste to put this beautiful thing, this endless resource, out of reach. She knew she would miss it greatly.

She was aware that others watched her from a distance, concerned about what was in her thoughts, particularly Serafina, whose dark eyes were often fixed upon her. Tildi knew she was listening to the turmoil in her heart, but she couldn't bring herself to discuss it with anyone. She didn't know what she would do, nor would she until the moment came.

At the edge of a plain so ancient and isolated it was nameless, Calester called the procession to a halt.

"There it is," he said. "I thought I would never see it again in all eternity."

Tildi glanced up over Rin's head at the grand mountain peak before her, set alone in the heart of the valley against a brilliant blue sky. The mountain was so perfect in shape, it looked like the way the surface leaped up after a drop fell into a glass of water. Snow decorated the top third, but the rest was covered with brilliant green vegetation.

"Like the Mother just put it there," Pierin said. He and Gosto rode pillion behind Captain Teryn and Sergeant Morag. Teldo and Marco shared saddles with a couple of the guards.

"Is the sanctuary up there?" Serafina asked.

"No, we felt that would be unsafe. The Compendium had been laid to rest beneath the mountain's root."

He urged his horse forward. A guard of honor, consisting of a dozen each of Halcot's guards and scholar-knights, followed him, but it was scarcely needed. The plain was deserted except for plants and animals. Tiny, dark brown monkeys with faces like men but covered with hair hung from branches and screamed at them as they went by. Rainbow-colored birds flashed past over the path that opened up before the Maker as if it had been waiting for him. Tildi took in all the scenery with wide eyes and an open mouth. For all the beauty of Niombra, Sheatovra offered sights that were unlike anywhere else, or so Magpie told her. The werewolves, in their moontouched form, trotted alongside the riders. In this place, they fit in as much as the gorgeous birds and exotic creatures. Tildi realized that smallfolk and humans alike were strange in that landscape.

"Of all five continents, this is the most beautiful," Magpie said, leaning over to speak to her. His jitar was strapped to his back. As the Compendium was to her, his instrument was never far from his hand or his thoughts. "I have often traveled here to meet the people, but also to gain inspiration for my work." He glanced at his father, who pretended not to hear his son speaking as if he were truly a common troubadour.

"It is wonderful," Inbecca said, looking around with shining eyes as she spurred her horse up next to Magpie. "I wish I had been as free as you."

"Duty comes first," Sharhava said imperiously. "Lar Inbecca, back in line, please!"

"Yes, Abbess." Dropping her chin mulishly, the young woman pulled back her steed. It was yet another borrowed mount; unfortunately there had been several riderless horses to choose from after the fight against the thraiks. Tildi was grateful that the winged monsters had not been seen since they vanished from Knemet's chamber.

"By the Void, look at that," Olen said as they neared the foot of the mountain. Beneath the canopy of spread fronds and green crowns of trees, the ground was torn up as though a terrible battle had been fought there. Scorch marks as wide as a house stretched hundreds of yards up the slope. Trees that still stood on either side were bent away from the empty patches, their hunched sides blackened as though from a powerful fire. Enormous rocks, entire chunks of the mountainside, were thrown up like a child's building blocks.

"Such devastation," Halcot said. "Who did this?"

"Nemeth," Olen said.

"What? My inept court magician couldn't light a candle."

"With the help of the Compendium he could," Olen pointed out. "With the copied pages that you gave him, he had enough power to destroy—and to kill."

He pointed to blackened heaps half grown over with jungle vegetation that Tildi had not noticed before. She realized that they were bodies. When Rin drew nearer, they could see that they were the huge skeletons of winged beasts, but ones as unlike thraiks as Tildi could imagine. Even without flesh, there was something noble about the faces of the creatures.

"They were our guardians," Calester said. "They had the bodies but also the hearts of lions, borne skyward by eagle's wings. Their minds were as fine and wise as any philosopher's. I regret that I must mourn them." He bowed his head and closed his eyes.

"Did you make them?" Serafina asked gently.

Calester turned to her. "Yes, but we could not give them the character that they brought with them. They had been soldiers and scholars. Brave, intelligent, and self-sacrificing, they guarded the Compendium for a hundred centuries. Who would have guessed that one man could defeat them and undo all that we did?"

"Nemeth was desperate," Olen said. "He was desperate and angry and hungry with curiosity. The thought of the book drew him so strongly he was willing to kill for it."

"It is my family and people he nearly destroyed, Master Wizard," Soliandur said dryly. "You can be less admiring of him."

"I must admire one who managed to undo the wills of six Makers," Olen said. "And, you must admit, my lord, you are not blameless in the episode. Because of you, a mouse transformed himself into a serpent."

The king glared, but Halcot put a hand on his shoulder. "What's done cannot be undone, my brother. Our creators know that once time passes, what happened in that moment is set forever." The ruefulness of his expression was not lost upon his brother king.

"Ah, well," Soliandur said with a glance at Halcot. "If you can forgive, then I must. He cannot come back, and I shall not make the same mistake again."

"Nor I," Calester said. "This time when I close the path it will be for good. I cannot leave the possibility of access to an ill-meaning wizard. The world is too vulnerable as it is."

"How will we do this, then?" Olen asked keenly. "I see a road that leads onward past this spot."

"Where?" Tildi asked. "I don't see anything but more trees and plants."

Serafina smiled at her. "If you can't see, then listen. Some of the trees are illusory. You will hear no song from them. In fact, it might be wise to follow this path with one's eyes closed, and go where there is inner silence." Tildi concentrated. Serafina was right. The trees did make their own sound, everywhere but a narrow section to the southeast. That part seemed empty, like a hollow log.

Calester beamed upon her as if he had invented her, too. "Well thought out, Mistress Serafina," he said. "Though the way is not unguarded, even without its protectors. We designed this place never to be approached alone. I will require you to open the path for me, and keep it open until my return, or I shall be trapped within the mountain until the end of time. No matter what you think of me, little one," he added, to Tildi, "does that seem fair?"

She felt her cheeks burned. "No, master, it does not."

"But if no one can approach it alone," Magpie asked, "how did Nemeth do it?"

Calester looked startled. "I do not know. Had he allies?"

"None that I know of," Magpie said. He glanced at his father. Soliandur's eyes burned with shame.

Olen sighed. "I fear the secret died with him. What do you require of us?"

Calester tactfully ignored the expressions that passed between father and son. He gestured in the direction of the emptiness. "Think of the passage inward as a long tube of cloth that lies flat until it is needed. It must be raised and held open. One wizard can do it. Who shall it be?" He looked from Tildi to Olen to Serafina.

"I would like to see the book settled in its place," Tildi said. Her voice rang brittle on the clear air. "May I go with you instead?"

Calester eyed her. "I had planned to go alone, but as you have borne the Compendium all this time, the request is not without merit. Master Olen?"

"I will maintain the way," her teacher said. "With these fine people to guard me, I should have nothing to fear from mundane interruptions."

"Then I shall come with Tildi," Serafina said in a firm voice. Calester snorted.

"Three, then, but no more!" he said, holding up a hand to forestall protests.

Magpie sat back in his saddle. Tildi could see he had been about to ask. She smiled apologetically at him.

"When you come back, tell me all of what it was like," he said to her. "I can't end my song without it."

"I will," Tildi said, but in her heart the words did not have the force of a promise. She gave him a wan smile. He looked concerned, but she turned away hastily. She stepped down from Rin's back. The book floated after her.

"Don't go doing anything foolish," Gosto said.

"I won't!" Tildi said impatiently. She stalked over to stand beside the Guardian. Serafina rested a hand on Tildi's shoulder. Tildi shook her off, feeling as though everyone was looking at her. She hated the sensation, more than she ever had. Well, it would be over soon, one way or another.

Olen turned back the sleeves of his long robe and held up his hands. He closed his eyes and reached out. "I feel the edges of the spell," he said. "They are heavy but malleable, like . . . curtains made of lead."

Calester nodded approval. "You have it, my friend. That is our doorway. Can you manipulate it?"

"Oh, yes." Olen opened his eyes. "I wish you all good fortune, my friends. Tildi, there were promises made. Do you remember them?"

She looked up at him, startled, as if he were reading her thoughts. "I remember them, master."

His green eyes fixed upon hers. "Good. I will see you upon your return." He raised his hands slowly, as though he were balancing something flat upon his palms. "Hurry, then. I will not fail you."

Calester led the way. He ducked as he passed Master Olen and gestured to the others to do the same. Serafina reached up, and her hand flattened upon something that Tildi could not see.

Lead curtains was an odd idea, but Tildi could understand what Olen meant. Though they walked in green-dappled sunshine for more than a mile, she was aware of the feeling of being closed in. The air in the passageway smelled like a closet that had been closed for a long time. Not musty, but cold and abandoned. The book floated beside her serenely, glowing in the brilliant sun like a beacon of ivory. The voices sounded excited. She wished she could share their joy. The pathway wound through exquisite countryside, spiraling in toward the mountainside.

Calester, ahead of them, suddenly held out his palm. Blue light burst into being on his palm. Within two steps they had passed under the foot of the mountain, and all the sunlight was extinguished. The book still held its own light. Tildi kept a hand on it.

They walked through solid stone, where there was no passage but the magical corridor, and across secret caverns that had never seen sunlight. Stalactites hung from the ceiling in lacelike profusion. An occasional plunk of water resounded in the magical roadway, though no water ever touched them. Runes lit up the walls in the winding passage. They were not only the names of the objects themselves.

"What are these inscriptions, Master Calester?" Serafina asked, peering curiously at an elaborate sigil.

"Spells, instructions, and warnings that we left here when we sealed the book away the first time," Calester explained. "Look there." He pointed to some signs that did not look as perfectly scribed as the others. "Your book thief's work. He undid these words of power. He must have been a powerful seer to know which ones would allow him to pass. It is a pity I did not have the teaching of him. In our company his gift could have made him great."

And that was all the eulogy that poor Nemeth would ever have, Tildi thought. She wondered what words would be said over her one day. Unbidden, Serafina's hand touched her shoulder. Tildi forced gloomy thoughts away from her.

The darkness around them gradually grew grayer. Calester let his beacon of light drop. He followed the curve of the corridor around to the left.

"Come, Tildi," he said. "This is the final place. The entire mountain is above us now."

Tildi trotted to catch up with him, and had to throw up her hand to shield her eyes. Calester led them into a flattened dome, a broad, low, smooth-sided chamber like a hollow lens. Runes decorated the narrow rim, but the room was entirely empty except for a pillar of light at the center. Tildi approached it warily.

"You may touch it," Calester said. "It is wizard-crystal. As you see, it was purposely made to contain the book. I continue to marvel at the way the Compendium was removed, without doing damage to the pillar. Somewhere Nemeth must have found a record of our spells, or he simply intuited them."

Tildi put her hand on the smooth surface. She felt the prickling of great power coming awake. Light coruscated from the center and surrounded the Compendium with rainbows. The book danced, and the voices cried out for joy.

"No!" Tildi exclaimed. Her voice echoed in the hollow chamber.

"I am afraid yes," Calester said, not without sympathy. "It knows the object it is meant to protect. You must let it go now, Tildi. I will allow you a moment to say your farewells."

Tildi snatched the book out of the air and clutched it to her. At that moment she knew she would not be able to let it go. She felt its smoothness, its texture, its cool surface.

"You cannot take it from me," she said defiantly. "It is part of me now. It is the only thing that makes me happy."

"Tildi!" Serafina said warningly. "You have always known you must give it up."

Tildi felt her eyes flood with tears. "I know, but now that I must do it, it's too hard!"

"I will get Olen," Serafina said. "If I can't talk sense into you, he can."

"No," Calester said, his deep-set eyes glowing blue like sapphires. "She has to make the choice. You have been touched by it, Tildi. It will always be a part of you, but you know what destruction it can cause."

"I know," Tildi said. She put her chin up. She had been thinking hard for days, and she knew that she had the only solution. "I will stay here with it. Put me inside it."

"You can't do that," Serafina said. "Your entire life is ahead of you."

"But look at Knemet! He was separated from it, and it drove him mad."

Calester shook his head. "It was not the lack of the book that changed him. It was loneliness, and lack of purpose. But you may stay if you wish. You will be left alone here forever with the book. Is that what you want? Think of your family. You rescued them, but you will never see them again." He took a step toward her, his hand outstretched, palm up. Sensing a trick, Tildi backed away. Calester stopped. "They are just a few miles away from you. What would they think if their sister entombed herself, when you had just been reunited?"

The voices invited her to join them. Knemet, the newest, sounded joyful and content, his translucent red rune on the back of the parchment now intertwined with Boma's, even offered his welcome in words that she could understand. They were happy. She could be happy with them, if she wished. But Tildi had no love to spend her eternity with.

"You would be lonely, with no purpose, for all the rest of time," Serafina said, as though she could hear that insecure thought in her mind. "You would be with the book just to be with it. You haven't even finished your education as a wizard. Let go, Tildi. Come back. There is so much for you out in the world." She, too, extended a hand to Tildi.

Tildi burst into tears. She fished Gosto's cloth from her pouch and buried her face in it. The voices echoed in her mind, inviting, persuading. She felt a reluctance growing within her. They were strong, but they were strangers.

Her brothers were waiting. Master Olen had all but made her promise to come back. Silvertree was waiting. She hoped to get a new twig from her to replace the one destroyed by the kotyrs. That might never happen now.

"You said you would describe this place to Prince Eremilandur," Serafina reminded her. "How will he know what is here if you do not tell him? *I* won't."

"You won't?" Tildi asked, astonished.

Serafina set her narrow jaw. "No. He asked *you*. I won't say a word."

"Well?" Calester asked. "I can wait forever, but Master Olen cannot. The spell will begin to weary him. You would not trap Mistress Serafina in here while you dally."

"I am not dallying!" Tildi said, provoked beyond her endurance by the irritating Maker. He grinned, and she realized he had done it deliberately. The words were the most difficult ones she had ever forced past her lips. "Very well." She put her hands on the bobbing scroll. After enjoying its touch for a moment, she pushed it toward Calester. "Take it."

"You will let it go?" Serafina asked. Tildi looked at her and realized how concerned she had been that Tildi really meant to stay. "You will come forth again?"

Tildi went to embrace the young wizardess, realizing how dear she was to her. "Yes. You are right. I can't leave the world just yet."

"But the Compendium must," Calester said impatiently. "Hurry, now. The longer we wait, the more regrets you will have. Since you have been of so much help, I will allow you the singular honor of placing it in the crystal." Serafina gave her a fierce hug, then released her.

"Thank you," Tildi said, her eyes shining with more than tears. "Show me what to do."

Calester knelt beside her and put his hand on hers. "There is a way into the pillar of crystal, but it does not exist in the world. It is only inside the Compendium. Find it."

With her free hand, she gestured at the book, which spun obediently to a page. She gestured to it to draw near, so she could look at the runes depicted on it. There were the symbols for *chamber* and *round*, and the runes for the three of them in between them. The pillar stood at the opposite corner of the page from them, as if it existed in a different realm than they did. Tildi opened her hand to expand that symbol so she could see it better. The symmetry of the word was as perfect as the object itself, and decorated with rainbow illuminations. Tildi searched it, looking for anything that said *door*, or *opening*. She stared at it again and again, until she realized that tendrils from the sides appeared to stretch outward to infinity. "It isn't closed at all."

"Not inside the Compendium. You must concentrate upon what you see there, at the same time that you send the book into the pillar."

"She has to put the book into a rune that exists only inside itself?" Serafina asked.

Calester pursed his lips humorously. "It wasn't meant to be a riddle any fool could work out," he said. "Come, now. Concentrate. Keep it in your mind. The Compendium contains all of reality, therefore what you see before you is real. Believe it."

Tildi closed her eyes. In her mind she saw the image of the pillar as it appeared on the page. The rune for the book was before her. With Calester guiding her hands, she pushed the two of them toward each other. The book was within the crystal pillar that was within the book. She held her breath until she felt something snap just like the lid of a box. Serafina let out a gasp. Tildi's eyes flew open.

The Compendium hung before her, sealed inside the crystal. Tildi pressed her hands upon it, but it was solid. The book was out of her reach now, forever. She felt as though she might cry. It looked so perfect there, perfect and not quite real any longer.

"It is done," Calester said. "Thank you for your assistance."

As soon as the crystal was sealed, all the runes except those that had been written by the ancient Shining Ones winked out. Tildi looked a question at Calester.

"The pillar dampens its influence," he explained. "Otherwise it would continue to make mischief in here. You can still see runes in everything because you are an apprentice wizard, but no one else can."

Tildi flattened her hands on the case and stared at the scroll. Its companionable presence was gone. Only the image remained. "I feel as if a piece of me has been cut off. I will miss it so much."

"Remember the Law of Contagion," Serafina said.

"The Compendium will still be a part of you," Calester said. "You just won't be able to touch it. You have the leaf, don't you?" Tildi fished in her pouch for the pathetic scrap of parchment that had started her on her journey. It was only the second time looking at it in months. She sighed, looking at the glorious scroll. She had never and would never again see anything as beautiful as that. The poor, ragged leaf hardly compared. "There, you shall have a link to it forever."

Tildi smiled. "It's not the same, but it's enough. It's all that someone like me ought to have, truly." She bid it one final farewell. One last glance over her shoulder at the perfect parchment scroll, suspended in glistening crystal, and she turned away. Even the voices were muted by the pillar's substance, but she fancied she could hear them saying goodbye, even Knemet.

But as they walked out of the lens-shaped chamber, Tildi realized that she could still feel the book. She had a special bond to it, and always would.

"Come, sister," Calester said, smiling benevolently upon her.

Tildi hesitated at the word. He bent down to touch the top of her head. "Oh, you deserve the title, my dear smallfolk. Not only have your people developed beyond our greatest dreams for them, but you and your family have proved to me that they can be great in the world as well. Your future will be as glorious as you care to make it."

"Well!" Tildi said, ever harkening back to her practical roots. "We'll see if it ever needs to be glorious. I will settle for being able to learn again, without having to risk so much."

"Magic is always a risk," Calester said, redrawing the runes on the walls of the round chamber, "as I believe your friend told you. He is a wise man. I look forward to many days in his company."

"As do I," Tildi said. She took one more backward glance at the book, held forever in midair, as if waiting for someone to open it and read its beautifully drawn pages. But that would never happen again. She touched the tightly rolled fragment in her pouch. All that would come hereafter was a pale imitation. Better to embrace real life.

Chapter Forty-one

shout went up as they came toward the end of the path. Olen stood as they had left him, arms raised, keeping the spell-gate open, but he was chatting over his shoulder with Teldo. As Tildi stumped down the long passage in Calester's wake, she could hear a bit of what they were saying.

"Of course I am proud of her accomplishments," Teldo said. "I always knew she could do as much as I. Never thought she could do so much more. It's nice to have a hero in the family."

"I'd never say as much to her face," Olen said, slewing his eyes in her direction to show that he knew she was listening. "It might give her a big head."

"Aye," said Teldo, his brown eyes alight with mischief, "so it might."

Tildi opened her mouth in outrage, then closed it. They were teasing her. She had almost forgotten what that felt like.

"Hurry, then!" Olen called. "The gate is closing. I could hold it open longer, but I shouldn't. You want it as strong as possible."

"The ages demand it," Calester said. He vanished from just in front of Tildi, and reappeared the next instant at Olen's side. "Well, come on, child, don't hold us all up!"

Abashed, Tildi ran through the gate, feeling walls she could not see looming nearer and nearer. Serafina walked sedately at the back of the file. As soon as she passed, Olen lowered his arms. A wind rushed into their faces as though a heavy curtain fell. "There. It is done?"

"It is well done," Calester said.

Olen smiled down upon Tildi. "I am glad that you have returned to us."

Tildi took a deep breath and let it out. "I am glad, too."

"The way must be closed for all time, now," Calester said. He took a small wand from his belt and began to scribe upon the air. Line built upon silver line, growing in complexity, but not before Tildi recognized the base word as *wall*. With every stroke the Compendium was placed farther and farther from her hands.

"May I assist?" Olen said.

Calester gave him a friendly glance. "I would be glad of your help."

Together the two wizards wove lines into the rune until it was a woven knot as dense as chainmail. Calester gave it one final tap, and the rune spread across the face of the mountain like a curtain. It sank into the surface and vanished. Tildi could still feel its presence, tingling just below the ground. The book was safe for then and all time.

"Do you still have regrets?" Serafina asked softly.

Tildi looked up at her. Her mind was easy now. "No. No regrets. It was an adventure and a privilege. I am ready to be done with both."

"In regard to privilege, Master Calester," Sharhava said, pushing forward.

Calester turned. "You will require new guardians for this site."

"Indeed I will," the Maker said amiably. "I shall create them, using characteristics that are most desirable from across the animal kingdom. You will find the process most interesting."

"You will make them out of nothing? Is that how you did it in the past?"

Calester smiled. "Not then, not after the wars. We had many volunteers. Many who wished to keep the Compendium safe from my brother who is now inside it. I have not that force behind me. But no matter. I can create what I need."

"You need not form such creatures from nothing. We offer ourselves for that duty," Sharhava said. "You know the purpose of our order."

"You committed to guard the Compendium, and make use of it for your own reasons," Calester said. "I have heard."

Sharhava's face turned red, but she pressed on. "The aim became perverted over the course of years, but I assure you that we have come back to our original mandate. We want to take the place of those guardians that were killed. You may change us as you see fit. You will find us as intelligent and brave as anyone who stood forward in the past."

Magpie felt his mouth drop open. He had never expected it. The Scholardom had behaved differently since they had returned aboard the *Eclipse*, but he would never have expected such a request. Calester regarded them with some skepticism, but Sharhava was completely sincere.

Most of the Scholardom stepped forward, expectant looks on their faces. Loisan nodded at the assembled knights. "We are all in agreement—well, nearly all of us. We wish you to transform us so that we may guard the book for all time. It is our task and our honor. And truth to tell, some of us would like to be winged again. That was a marvelous experience." The knights at his back nodded enthusiastic agreement.

"You are resolved to this?" Calester asked, regarding them with respect and, Tildi was sure, a little awe. "Once the runes are laid, it is permanent. You see me as I am, and my poor brother as he was. His only choice was translation into the Compendium. You will be changeless throughout history."

Sharhava straightened her shoulders. "I would be proud to undertake the challenge. My whole life has been spent preparing to protect the Great Book. It is here; what else have I to look forward to?"

"Don't shoulder this burden if all that awaits you is finding a new path," Olen said, but his green eyes were alight.

She smiled at him wryly. "You know me well, Master Olen, or you would not have shut me and my knights out of your first council. When I am resolved, I keep my bond. I am resolved."

"Forever is long," Calester said.

"So is faith," Sharhava said. "If you please, those of us who would become the permanent guardians of the Great Book await your pleasure."

"And I," Inbecca said, pushing forward. "I am a sworn knight. I will be part of this as well."

"No, Inbecca!" Magpie said, horrified.

She turned to face him. "I made you a promise, Eremi, but my second vow supersedes it. If the abbess leads, I must follow. I have no other place than here, in her service, and in service to the Great Book." Her sea-blue eyes swam with tears. "Perhaps you will visit me sometime. You said you do come to Sheatovra. I hope I will still recognize you."

Magpie locked her in his arms. "You can't take her, Sharhava. This is wrong."

"I gave my word," Inbecca said. She pushed free and went to stand by her aunt.

"No, child," Sharhava said. "You took your vows in anger. Though you kept faith with me most admirably, you are not part of this company. Go. You have a task before you that more befits your talents: to see if you can mold this young ne'er-do-well into a fit consort for a queen."

Soliandur stood forward and cleared his throat gently. "I would consider it an honor to my house, Your Highness, if you would give my son a second chance. You might find him to be . . . amusing. He does write songs well."

Inbecca looked from one to the other, her face pinched with emotion and uncertainty. Magpie was sure she did not want to stay until the world's end as a half lion, half eagle, but her word had always been as powerful a bond as her aunt's.

"Inbecca, stay with me." Magpie smiled at her. Sharhava let out a "tut!" She plucked up Inbecca's hand and tucked it into Magpie's palm.

"Go. I absolve you of your vows. Think of me sometimes."

Inbecca embraced her aunt. "I will. Please know that you taught me much."

Sharhava smiled down at her. "And I learned from you, Inbecca. Now, don't delay this any longer. The Great Book must be guarded. You others," she said, addressing those in livery who did not stand with Loisan, "I absolve you, too, of your vows. May you find peace on some other path." The knights, Lar Mey among them, looked ashamed of themselves, though Magpie could understand their reluctance. "If you please, Master Calester. But if I may ask a boon of your magic, can you leave us the power of speech?"

"You shall have all your faculties," the Maker said with a quirk to the side of his mouth.

"And Master Olen," Sharhava said. "May I ask a favor of you as well?"

"Of course, my lady," Olen replied.

"Leave the plaque with our runes upon it here in the valley, so that those who come may know who we were in years past."

Olen bowed deeply. "It shall be done."

Calester regarded the knights with grave respect. He removed the small wand from his belt and drew it upward like a conductor about to address his orchestra. The knights held themselves proudly erect as Calester wove new runes before them, murmuring to himself all the while. Tildi could see the word for wings intertwined with many she did not know. Beside her, Serafina and Master Olen followed each stroke with smiles of anticipation on their faces. When Calester finished scribing, they nodded their heads as though they had just witnessed a masterful performance by an artist or musician. The rune hung in the air, glistening. It was not like any spell she had seen before. There was a sense of permanence to it, as though it had been wrought from steel instead of silver. She almost wanted to touch it to see what it felt like, but common sense kept her hands twined before her. Calester gave one more glance at the assembled Scholardom.

"One last chance before it is done," he said.

"Finish it!" Sharhava said impatiently.

Calester smiled broadly. "I shall. *Arvteg!*"

The steel rune opened out, forming a broad disk many yards across. It flattened on the air. Calester gestured at it, sending it to hover over the heads of the knights. Sharhava and the others looked up, just as blinding golden light lanced down upon them. Tildi's eyes squeezed to slits against the glare. Within the glow, she saw forms bulging and shifting like storm clouds. She heard cries and moans from the knights that made her quail with pity, but the sounds turned to exclamations of joy, even laughter. The rune sank over the bodies like a blanket, and dislimned into nothingness.

Those that stood before Tildi and the others were creatures the likes of which she had only ever seen in a book of legends. They had the bodies of lions, with shaggy bodies, black manes, and sharp, curving claws, but broad black wings. Their faces were still human in cast, except for mouths full of pointed teeth.

"Magnificent," Olen said.

"Thank you," said one of the beasts. It flashed sea-blue eyes at them, and Tildi realized it was Sharhava. "We go to take up our duties, then. Master Calester, you shall not find us remiss. The Compendium will never again be set free upon Alada."

Calester bowed deeply to her. "I depend upon you."

"I shall visit you when I am home for the season," Patha said, coming forward to embrace the shaggy neck. The sable wings spread out and surrounded her like a pair of arms.

"I shall look forward to it," Sharhava said in her new gruff voice. "Bring me the news. I will be curious to hear what is happening in the world."

Patha's yellow eyes glinted. "I will, my sister. "Good hunting."

"Farewell!" Sharhava said. She sprang into the sky. The Scholardom followed her with a cry as if the freedom of the winds was what they had been waiting for all their lives. As they had in the battle against the thraiks, the Scholardom spread out across the sky and began to circle the mountain on their broad wings. No threat would be able to approach it ever again.

Inbecca watched them go with regret on her pretty face. Tildi noticed one other expression of rue among those watching, Sergeant Morag. She realized she had never kept her promise to him.

She went to tug the Maker on the sleeve. "Master Calester," she said. "Could you manage just one more transformation?"

"Eh?" Calester said. Tildi led him to the sergeant, who stood at rigid attention, refusing to look either of them in the eye. "My proud escort? I wondered what had befallen him. Tell me, brave warrior. How came you to enjoy this . . . unique physiognomy?"

"A magical accident during the war," Morag blurted out.

"How is it that you never asked before?"

"He did," Tildi said. "I wanted to help him, but I don't know how. The Compendium only showed him as he is now, not as he was."

"Ah," Calester said. "Perhaps you know it is possible to reach back into the memory of an object that you owned. We wizards have a spell that can seek the past by means of the present."

Morag marched to the train of pack animals and brought from it the collection of humble pots and pans in which he had cooked their meals for months. He offered them to Calester. The Maker shook his head.

"Not these humble things. They bear a trace of you, but it is as you are now."

"My sword?" Morag asked.

Teryn stepped forward and cleared her throat. "That, too, is new, Master Wizard. His was lost at the ford when he was wounded."

"I need something that is closer to you," Calester said. His eyes lit upon Captain Teryn. "Or someone. You are the friend of his heart, are you not?"

"Master Wizard, do not embarrass us in front of my guards!" Teryn snapped.

Calester bowed. "I apologize. But you are two handsome people. Would you not have accepted him if he had asked you?"

"I . . . but, he never did."

He couldn't, Tildi thought, watching the shame and longing on the craggy sergeant's face.

"Will you help him?" Olen asked her. "Will you be the book of his past?"

She looked from one wizard to the other. "I . . . I will."

"Good," Calester said. He took Teryn's hand and looked into it as if it were a page in a book. He glanced up at Serafina and Tildi. "Is one of you quick to scribe? For if I am successful, I will see this rune only for a moment. It must be accurate, or we will kill this noble soldier instead of remaking him."

"I will do it," Tildi said. She hurried to Calester's side.

"Let your mind go back to those happier times," the Maker told her. "Relax."

Teryn fidgeted, unable to do just that. Tildi could see how awkward she felt as the center of attention. Calester held her wrist firmly. Suddenly silver lines appeared on the skin of her palm. Tildi hastily began to draw the rune in midair, exactly as she saw it. She must not be wrong.

She had barely added the final flourish to the name when the image on Teryn's hand winked out. Tildi studied the sign. She could see how closely it resembled Morag's present rune. Had she gotten it right?

"Well done. Now, will you apply it to this good man?" Calester asked.

"Why not you?" Tildi asked.

The Maker shook his head. "Ah, this is not my time. It would be like a bonfire where a careful glassmaker's lamp is what is needed. You are more than worthy, and he trusts you."

"Very well," she said. She looked up at Morag. He was as nervous as she. "I don't know if you can trust me."

"I trust you," Morag said. "Any outcome will be better than I am now, even death."

Tildi winced. She looked at the scribed rune from several directions.

"It isn't going to change just sitting there," Teldo said. "Either it's right or it's not. Think of the fire spell. You've done it many times, haven't you?"

Tildi nodded. She held her hands around the rune as if steadying it, then let it float forward until it touched the rune she could see on his chest. The silver rune overcame the pale image, overspread it and changed it, lengthening that stroke, bending that spiral. She looked up at Morag.

The sergeant covered his face with his hands. The fingers that had been clublike and twisted straightened and squared until they looked as capable as a carpenter's tools. Morag lowered his hands to stare at them. Tildi, and everyone else, stared at his face.

He would never be called handsome, but the mild brown eyes, pale-lidded, looked out from under straight brows. The nose between them was a triangular beak. His jaw and cheekbones were prominent but proportionate.

"He looks younger than he did," Serafina said, eyeing him critically.

"The rune of his health is the rune of his younger days," Calester said. "He will age, but normally. He will make you a fit consort, Captain."

Teryn blushed. "He could look for a younger woman, now that he is healthy again."

Morag's face turned scarlet, too. He bent his head, as if he was still trying to conceal his face.

"But, I want no one else, if you will have me. You stood by me when anyone else would have taken away my pride and seen me retired from the guard, pushed me away. If maybe you still care for me."

Teryn's face, unaccustomed to tenderness, nevertheless softened. "I always have. I would like nothing better."

"But he cannot marry a superior officer," Halcot said peevishly. Teryn looked at him in dismay. The king smiled at her. "Therefore, he must also be made a captain. He has been heroic enough throughout his long and distinguished service. I decree that you, Captain Teryn, will be the leader of the palace guard, and Captain Morag will be leader of the town guard. So neither of you answers to the other. Not while on duty, in any case."

"And they ought to live happily ever after," Magpie said, in delight. "As all the best stories end."

Very shyly, Teryn put out her hand. Morag took it. The Rabantavian guard burst into cheers.

"Now, let us return to the north," Halcot said. He took Magpie's and Inbecca's hands in both of his. "I would be proud to hold a wedding feast for this young couple."

"A wedding feast?" Magpie acted surprised. "I would say yes, my lord, but I don't know if Inbecca has forgiven me."

Inbecca looked outraged and raised a hand as if she might slap him. He grinned at her. She took him by the ears and brought his face down so she could kiss him. "How could you think I would want anybody but you? My lords, we should renew our betrothal before you."

"You are not really answerable to kings for your promises," Halcot said. "Only to the Creators and each other. You could renew them before the community at my castle in Rabantae."

"The honor is mine," Magpie's father said sourly, all but shouldering his fellow king out of the way. "He is my son."

"But my home is closer," Halcot said. "Let it be, brother. There's nothing to stop you holding another fête later on, and this time the revelry will end as we expect it."

"It had better," Soliandur said with a warning look at his son.

Magpie knelt before him. "I promise, sir. All will be as you hope, and more. After all, there are no more crises to pull me away, are there?"

Soliandur snorted. "Hmph. Well, I don't expect a miracle." He extended his hands to Inbecca. "Welcome, daughter. I hope you will accept our poor hospitality."

"There is nothing I would like more, goodfather," Inbecca said, a smile dimpling her cheeks. "I know my mother looks forward to visiting you. And to have you in our household. This alliance has been a long time in coming." She looked up at Magpie. "A little too long."

"A bit longer than anyone expected," Halcot said. "But I am patient. I won't be satisfied until I am the godfather of this couple's first child."

"First things first," Soliandur said. "He must wash those foolish stripes from his hair. They are disgraceful."

"I consider them a compliment to my mother's throne, goodfather," Inbecca said, with a grin. "I'd like him to keep them."

"As you wish, my daughter, it's you who must look at them."

"There is one thing I would like to ask you, Master Calester," Magpie said, doing his best to cover his embarrassment. "The question came up at our first council meeting, and none of us has the history to answer it. You and your brethren made most of the races we know from humans, but are humans a naturally evolved species themselves or are they a joke by the elves? That is what they told us."

"Ah," Calester said. "Come over here, my friend, and I'll tell you the truth of it." He pulled Magpie to one side and whispered briefly in his ear. Magpie listened with dawning amusement. He had to enjoy the look on the faces of his companions. "Now, I must trust you not to reveal what I have said to another living soul. Do you promise?" The deep-set eyes bored into his.

"Very well, sir, I promise."

"What did he say?" Inbecca demanded at once.

"I . . . I can't say."

"Eremi!"

Magpie backed away from her with his hands up, laughing. Inbecca pursued him about the clearing. Tildi laughed to see them happy and together at last.

"And what about you, my friend?" Olen asked Calester.

"I have been in one place too long. I wish to see this beautiful world. I am sure much has changed in my days of immobility. My companions who said that they would remain to see that nothing went wrong seem to have taken their leave, in one fashion or another. Those who are still alive I hope I will see along my way. I wish to travel over the face of Alada, at my leisure, to enjoy that which we built. In truth I never thought that I would be in one spot so long. I fancied that I would stay for a while and turn back the threat, then resume my studies. Little would I guess that I would miss the threat when it came! For that, friend Olen, I thank you." Olen bowed. Calester returned it. "You brought me back to my senses and reminded me of my responsibilities. I will use my talents to replenish, restore, and renew that which has been neglected." He caught Tildi's expression. "Yes, my child, like those poor creatures, the orind, that you left behind in the north."

"You will help them?" Tildi asked.

"Oh, yes. They are not very intelligent, but resourceful and noble."

Tildi felt infinitely satisfied. All was well. The book was back where it belonged, her friends were safe, and her family—her brothers!—were alive and well. Once they were back in Silvertree she could resume her studies. She could hardly wait to get back and tell the household staff all her adventures. She went to Olen, who laid his hand on her head.

"Well done, Tildi. I am proud of you."

"I am so glad it is over, Master Olen," she said, "I am longing to return home to Silvertree. I have kept my promise, as you bid me."

Olen's face grew sad. "And I must keep mine, my dear. As much as I want to keep both of you, the place in my household belongs to your brother Teldo. You may make your home there, of course."

"No, Master Olen, don't do it," Teldo said, grabbing the hem of his sleeve.

Olen looked down at him with friendly exasperation. "He won't say so, Tildi, but he does want the apprenticeship. As I offered it, I am obliged. I am afraid that I cannot continue as *your* master. I cannot tell you how profoundly sorry I am. My word was given to him. Not to you."

Tildi felt as if someone had pulled her insides out and replaced them with ice. "You knew."

Olen's bright green eyes were kindly. "I did. Not at first, but it was revealed to me, as many things are. I hoped you would tell me yourself. I must admit I was disappointed that you didn't. When you discovered him alive I expected you to say something. You did not. I couldn't intrude upon your joy at that time, but I am sorry that it didn't occur to you to speak thereafter. If you had told me the truth about your circumstances I might have been able to make certain arrangements to find you a place. You did not."

Tildi was shocked to her core, but she could not escape the consequences of her own failure to speak. She swallowed hard. A Summerbee never shirked responsibility. "I understand. I did tell you a lie when I came to Silvertree. I was never really meant to be your apprentice. It was Teldo you were corresponding with, not me. I just used the opportunity to escape from the Quarters. I couldn't stay in such a situation as I had been left in that day. My whole family was dead, or so I believed. I had nothing left but that last letter. I had to try. I came so close so many times to telling you the truth, but I never did. For that I am sorry. I never wanted you to lose faith in me."

Olen nodded. "You took a risk. But I accepted you, and you did well under my tutelage. I have enjoyed so much having you as a pupil, but the place belongs to Teldo. His work earned it for him. You would not rob him of it? If he had not lived, I would have been proud to keep you on, no matter how you came to me. You may live with us, of course, if you prefer not to return to the Quarters. I will give you every opportunity to continue your education on your own."

Tildi clasped his big, bony hand in both of hers. "I apologize with all my heart, master. Teldo will be a much better pupil than I was."

Olen's mustache twitched upward a little at the corners of his mouth and glanced up at the mountainside, now circled by the beings that had been knights. "I can scarcely imagine a pupil who will accomplish more than you have, child. I will miss being your teacher. You will always be welcome as a guest. Silvertree would be angry with me if you never came back to visit. She will want to give you a new wand to replace the one burned upon the ship."

Tildi tried to smile, but her heart had fallen to somewhere near her shoes. Visits would scarcely feel like enough, and when she had to leave, where would she go?

"No, Master Olen," Teldo protested. "Keep her on, please. Gosto still needs me on the farm. I will wait until another opportunity offers itself."

"And how do you know it would?" Olen asked, drawing down his shaggy brows. "Asking comes once in a lifetime. The opportunity is yours. If I did not think you had the potential, I would not have given you the place."

"It's yours, Teldo," Tildi said, her heart torn in two. "I only took it because I thought . . . I thought you wouldn't need it any longer." She made herself smile, though she was truly willing to relinquish her place to her favorite brother. "I am glad that you can start again. You will be very happy in Silvertree. There's so much to learn. He's much smarter than I am, Master Olen."

"No, I'm not," Teldo said. He put his arm around her waist and held his cheek against hers. "Two peas in a pod, that's what Mother always said about us. There's not a thing to choose from between us."

"It's true," Lakanta said, surveying the pair of them. "You're as alike as twins. Except for those thin cheeks of yours, lad, and they'll fill out again once we've all had a few more cracking good meals. I know I could use a few more."

"Then it's settled," Tildi said. "Teldo will have his rightful place."

"Never mind, Tildi," Gosto said, dropping an arm around her and giving her a tight hug. "Come home with us. The stories will make great telling. The folks in Morningside Quarter won't know what to believe. We'll be a family again."

"That's what you need, Tildi," Pierin said. He and Marco joined the circle and embraced their sister warmly.

Tildi thought desolately of the restricted life she would lead, the hard work, and the endless disapproval of her friends and neighbors. She felt tears prick at her eyes. Never again to return to Silvertree? Never to sit with Olen in his dusty attic and listen to stories? Ah, but what must be must be. She wiped her eyes with the cloth she had carried across two continents. She cleared her throat. "After all that's happened, how can I go back to the Quarters? Magic still isn't respectable, you know."

"We'll make it so," Gosto promised. "With two wizards in the family, we'll make the others pay respect as they ought."

Tildi couldn't restrain a giggle through her tears. "They won't like it. I can just see the look on Mayor Jurney's face."

"I haven't ever found anything that he does like," Gosto replied. "He'd turn down gold and say it wasn't shiny enough." Tildi giggled again.

"Come to Melenatae," King Halcot offered. "I would give you a place of honor in my court." Behind him, Teryn and Morag encouraged her with their eyes.

"We would be delighted to have you at our court in Levrenn," Inbecca said, kneeling to take Tildi's hand. "I'd be proud to have you as my court wizard."

"And I," Soliandur said. "You could teach my sons a thing or two about courage."

"You can stay with me if you like," the Guardian said. "I will teach you well. I am finding it pleasant to stretch my legs upon the earth once more. Perhaps you can teach me some manners in the meanwhile."

Tildi looked up at him. She was too unhappy to smile.

"Wait a moment," Serafina said. At her imperious tone everyone turned to look at her. "I have not yet released Tildi as my apprentice."

"Eh, what, my dear?" Olen asked.

Serafina's face was set in her fiercest and most stubborn scowl. She felt in her belt pouch and produced a tight roll of parchment. "You transferred Tildi's apprenticeship to my mother, Edynn. Upon her . . . departure, she put Tildi in my care. I have not yet given her back to you. And I do not care to."

Olen's shaggy eyebrows rose high on his forehead. "You claim her as your apprentice?"

"I only state what is true," Serafina said. She looked down at Tildi. "I realize I am very new to my own mastery, Tildi, but I will teach you everything I know—everything my mother taught me. You've been a good companion. I . . . I did not give you a fair chance at first. Forgive me. But come with me. You'll be a friend as well as an apprentice. We can reach for greatness together, though I'll have a long run before I can catch up with your achievements. Will you?"

Tildi caught herself goggling. She embraced Serafina around the knees. "With all my heart. My! I can hardly believe it!"

"If you cannot believe you have confirmed your place after all you have done, I don't know what I can do to convince you," Serafina said brusquely. "I have one other gift for you. Rin will be going back to her own people, so you will lack a steed. I can't have you running after me on those small legs of yours." She clapped her hands and nickered. Both of the white mares threw up their heads, but only the one with the green tack trotted toward them. "This mare belonged to my mother, as you know. She would have been pleased to have you take her as yours."

Tildi's eyes went huge. The white mare leaned down and nuzzled the top of her head with its soft lips. "But she's so big!"

"That should not matter," Serafina said. "I saw you walk up the air to get to Rin's back often and often again while we were on the road."

Tildi looked at the mare in delight. "I don't really deserve Edynn's horse."

"You do. Or you will. Take her." Serafina thrust the reins into her hand. "You will have to name her. A wizard's horse should have a name that means something special between the beast and its owner."

"You are a wizard among wizards now, child." Olen smiled.

"But I hardly know anything," Tildi protested. She stroked the mare's silky nose. It nickered softly.

Olen's mustache drew upward. "That is the mark of a true wizard, to know what you don't know. Your name will be inscribed among those of the great. Trust me on that. And I hope you will invite me to your learned councils when you hold any." His green eyes twinkled, and she knew he was teasing. "Let us make our progress to the north, then. Gosto, as the spokesman for your family, I invite you all to Silvertree for the first of what I foresee as many celebrations. Will you come?"

"Well, it's been a long time since we've been home," Gosto began slowly, fingering his beard. Then his eyes slewed to Tildi.

"I can't believe you're turning down a chance for a fine feast!" she exclaimed.

He burst out laughing, and the others joined him. "Wouldn't miss it for the world, and thank you greatly, Master Olen. It'll give us all stories in plenty to tell in the Quarters when we go back. Sure you won't come home with us, sister? Do you mean never to come back?"

"Perhaps someday," Tildi said thoughtfully. "I'll come back to visit when I have stories of my own to tell."

"Stories!" Teldo exclaimed with a laugh. He gave her a hug, and she felt as though she had come home again at last. "You've written the Book!"

Magpie went to the bow of his saddle for his jitar. He bowed before the smallfolk girl.

"I promised you, Tildi, that when you finished your quest I would sing you another song."

"I'm honored, Your Highness," Tildi said.

"It is I who am honored," Magpie replied. He struck a chord.

Tildi listened with delight as he sang.

> "My tale of Tildi comes to an end,
>   Her courage and heart have made all her friend,
>   Her company larger than it were,
>   Increased by those who believed in her.
>   Werewolves and knights have set aside
>   Their ancient hates and let peace abide.
>   Wizards everywhere you turn,
>   And lo! Those who were lost return.
>   Brother kings find peace simpler than it seemed,
>   A bride's consoled and a groom's redeemed,
>   Two soldiers whose lives were held apart
>   Found they shared but one true heart.
>   The Great Book at last is put aside
>   In the crystal room where it will abide
>   Under the mountain's verdant slope
>   Forever and a day, we hope.
>   Such large successes for one so small:
>   Friendships forever have been made
>   An old path ends, but a new one's laid.
>   Hail, Tildi! Hero of us all!"